SUNSET SEALS

The Series
Books 1–4

SHARON HAMILTON

SHARON HAMILTON'S BOOK LIST

SEAL BROTHERHOOD BOOKS

SEAL BROTHERHOOD SERIES
Accidental SEAL Book 1
Fallen SEAL Legacy Book 2
SEAL Under Covers Book 3
SEAL The Deal Book 4
Cruisin' For A SEAL Book 5
SEAL My Destiny Book 6
SEAL of My Heart Book 7
Fredo's Dream Book 8
SEAL My Love Book 9
SEAL Encounter Prequel to Book 1
SEAL Endeavor Prequel to Book 2
Ultimate SEAL Collection Vol. 1 Books 1-4 /2 Prequels
Ultimate SEAL Collection Vol. 2 Books 5-7

SEAL BROTHERHOOD LEGACY SERIES
Watery Grave Book 1
Honor The Fallen Book 2
Grave Injustice Book 3
Deal With The Devil Book 4

BAD BOYS OF SEAL TEAM 3 SERIES
SEAL's Promise Book 1
SEAL My Home Book 2
SEAL's Code Book 3
Big Bad Boys Bundle Books 1-3

BAND OF BACHELORS SERIES
Lucas Book 1
Alex Book 2
Jake Book 3
Jake 2 Book 4
Big Band of Bachelors Bundle

SLEEPER SEALS SERIES
Bachelor SEAL

STAND ALONE BOOKS & SERIES
SEAL's Goal: The Beautiful Game
Nashville SEAL: Jameson
True Blue SEALS Zak
Paradise: In Search of Love
Love Me Tender, Love You Hard

NOVELLAS
SEAL You In My Dreams Magnolias and Moonshine

PARANORMALS

GOLDEN VAMPIRES OF TUSCANY SERIES
Honeymoon Bite Book 1
Mortal Bite Book 2
Christmas Bite Book 3
Midnight Bite Book 4

THE GUARDIANS
Heavenly Lover Book 1
Underworld Lover Book 2
Underworld Queen Book 3
Redemption Book 4

FALL FROM GRACE SERIES
Gideon: Heavenly Fall

NOVELLAS
SEAL Of Time Trident Legacy

All of Sharon's books are available on Audible, narrated by the
talented J.D. Hart.

ABOUT THE BUNDLE

SEALed At Sunset

SEALs Don't Poach on another Team Guy's girl.

Navy SEAL Andrew Carr needs a lot of mindless beach time as he comes home from his first deployment. He visits a friend he met in BUD/S at a small Florida coastal town. But what he finds is something he cannot have: another SEAL brother's girl.

Aimee Greer is running from the stress in her life, and knows the beach, and the arms of her hot new boyfriend should do the trick. But when Andrew Carr comes to visit, she's not prepared for the explosive chemistry that develops between them.

When Carr is forced to defend her from her past, she realizes she has found the one she's been searching for her whole life.

Second Chance SEAL

Navy SEAL Damon Hamblin's life is in turmoil after he's served with divorce papers during his last deployment. He crashes into a sleepy Florida Gulf Coast town to drown his sorrows and just fade into the background, where no one knows him and he can drink, surf and lay out on the beach until his insides heal. The last thing he wants is to rebound into another relationship.

Martel Long came to Sunset Beach five years ago to visit a friend, and never left. She's tried to forget the man who broke her heart back home, and had been doing a good job of it, until she comes face to face with him at a Bachelorette party for her best friend at a local beach bar.

As sparks fly and old wounds are torn open, the sands at Sunset Beach help to heal a beautiful love story that could have been, and will be again.

Treasure Island SEAL

Navy SEAL Ned Silver is lured to the Florida gulf coast by the friend of his fathers, a former Navy diver now turned treasure hunter. Between deployments, S.O. Silver is addicted to adventure, and searching for pirate booty is right up his alley. What he hasn't counted on is that his net has also captured a local mermaid.

Madison Montgomery has done freelance underwater modeling and film work, but she's also an experienced scuba diver. Between jobs, she tends a salty beach bar catering to whatever the sea blows in. She's unprepared when her heart is hooked on the muscled beach bum she's hired to work with on a treasure dive.

As their underwater love affair smolders like a hyperbaric welding torch, the pair will have to discover who is captain and who is captured.

Escape To Sunset

Navy SEAL Jason Kealoha comes to Sunset Beach to release the ashes of his SEAL brother, who was killed in an attack in Nigeria. A Pacific Islander by lineage, Jason is unfamiliar with the Gulf Coast shores his buddy grew up playing in as a child. He befriends a beauty one night at sunset, as she roams the surf, skipping shells, lost in her own world.

Kiley Worthington is on the run from a sex trafficking cartel she stumbled upon as an investigative reporter in Portland. She decides hiding out in her sleepy beach hometown in Florida makes sense until she can figure out where she can spend the rest of her life in safety. The one-night stand was nice, but the last thing she needs is a huge tatted overly-protective guy who won't leave her alone. His attitude is all hardboiled, but his lips are warm and seductive. If she's not careful, she may never escape.

But Jason turns out to be the right kind of wrong for Kiley, as her enemies find her. In Jason's arms she finds a true sanctuary, as well as a safe place to hide forever.

AUTHOR'S NOTE

I always dedicate my SEAL Brotherhood books to the brave men and women who defend our shores and keep us safe. Without their sacrifice, and that of their families—because a warrior's fight always includes his or her family—I wouldn't have the freedom and opportunity to make a living writing these stories. They sometimes pay the ultimate price so we can debate, argue, go have coffee with friends, raise our children and see them have children of their own.

One of my favorite tributes to warriors resides on many memorials, including one I saw honoring the fallen of WWII on an island in the Pacific:

> "When you go home
> Tell them of us, and say
> For your tomorrow,
> We gave our today."

These are my stories created out of my own imagination. Anything that is inaccurately portrayed is either my mistake, or done intentionally to disguise something I might have overheard over a beer or in the corner of one of the hangouts along the Coronado Strand.

I support two main charities. Navy SEAL/UDT Museum operates in Ft. Pierce, Florida. Please learn about this wonderful museum, all run by active and former SEALs and their friends and families, and who rely on public support, not that of the U.S. Government. www.navysealmuseum.org

IF YOU GOT ANY CLOSER, YOU WOULD HAVE TO ENLIST

I also support Wounded Warriors, who tirelessly bring together the warrior as well as the family members who are just learning to deal with their soldier's condition and have nowhere to turn. It is a long path to becoming well, but I've seen first-hand what this organization does for its warriors and the families who love them. Please give what your heart tells you is right. If you cannot give, volunteer at one of the many service centers all over the United States. Get involved. Do something meaningful for someone who gave so much of themselves, to families who have paid the price for your freedom. You'll find a family there unlike any other on the planet. www.woundedwarriorproject.org

TABLE OF CONTENTS

SEALED AT SUNSET

Sunset SEALs Book 1

SHARON HAMILTON

CHAPTER 1

APAIR OF green Nikes haunted Special Operator Andy Carr. He was used to dreaming about girls to take his mind off anything he wanted to forget, but this was new. It didn't make any sense to dream about running shoes. Yet, night after night, he saw those shoes lying by the side of the road, attached to skinny brown legs wrapped in the brightly-colored skirt of one of the local girls who brought them things from the village.

She was one of the ones he couldn't save.

Maybe that was why he remembered the shoes and not the girl. It was self-preservation, and he refused to dwell on it. Time for that later when he was ready to talk to someone about it. Not now.

Like crowning out of a deep blue wave, he arched up out of his mattress so fast he almost hit his head on the ceiling. The motel room was tiny, and the ceiling was shallow but much taller than the bunker they'd been holed up in on their last deployment to West Africa.

He was home, and as usual, he wanted to feel normal, and only a woman could do that. He'd gotten home two days ago, after nearly twenty hours of being jumbled and jostled in a transport plane. He let that sink in before he acknowledged he'd had another one of those dreams. It would drive half the male population insane to do that more than once in a lifetime.

He could still smell the smoke and hear the sounds of the village people, even the children playing with wooden sticks, Coke bottles and toys they fashioned from the detritus of war. Somehow the kids always played. Even after some of the worst attacks he'd ever seen, after the cessation of battle, after the smoke cleared, the children would slowly creep out into the open and begin to play.

Life moves on.

The village people wanted peace, and he knew their SEAL Team 3 mission was to try to extricate several bad guys who extorted and preyed on them. These were hired guns, mercenaries without any allegiance to their land or culture, militiamen encroaching on the docile village life coming all the way across Africa or from neighboring Nigeria. They were nothing but bullies.

Although he wanted to save the villagers, he wasn't there to do that. He was there to pluck the bad guys from the salad bowl that was their war-torn country and get them out of the mix. And in that way, perhaps he'd save the village or help them save themselves, if that was possible.

Some of the older SEALs warned him to harden himself against some of the things he was going to see. It in no way properly prepared him. This was his first deployment, and he couldn't say whether he would be able to walk into the next mission more hardened or softer from the knowledge of what real war was all about. He'd seen the movies, and he'd been trained. He'd been counseled about how his emotions would rise up, how he would feel like taking a M4 carbine and slaughtering the bad guys instead of airlifting them to base or withholding critical medical assistance, just letting them bleed out. Why not?

But no, Andy was supposed to abide by the rules of his elite SEAL Team 3 unit.

They were not savages, after all, no matter how much anger or revenge boiled up inside.

Kyle Lansdowne, his LPO, told him that it was bum luck to have drawn this particular mission for his first. He hadn't cared. He'd been ready. He told himself that every day while he worked up to his deployment.

The day they got the call and were summoned to the Team 3 metal building at Coronado, he experienced fear. And he knew it was logical and normal to feel this way. But it didn't make it any easier.

Sitting now at the edge of the bed, he let his eyes accustom to the darkness at three A.M. It was turning out to be the most dangerous time for Andy. He'd had some rest after his fun little love dance with the green-eyed girl from the Oasis bar. She'd been willing, and he was hungry.

He knew the nightmare of the Nike shoes was going to wake him up again like it did every night. That's why, when she left close to eleven o'clock, he was grateful. The sweats on his body cooled the mixture of rage and fear that heated him from the inside out, making his mouth parched and his fingertips tingle. No reason for her to see any of that. It would scare her. He was supposed to protect innocents and do such a good job of it that they didn't even worry about the dark forces out there he was battling.

He heard the foghorns in the distance, that constant thrum he recognized as the ambiance in Coronado. Occasionally, he heard a seabird in the distance. He hoped that someday he would wake up to some soft willing arms or to the sight of a gentle backside he could study. He'd watch her come alive as the sun peeked through the window. New promise of a bright, lazy day. Someone he could spend all night with and still like her the next morning.

But for right now, all he had was the remembrance of the dream again, the shoes attached to those legs, lying lifeless by the side of the road.

He got up and splashed cold water on his face. He was grateful he couldn't see himself in the mirror. He knew he wouldn't like what his eyes reflected back to him and the message he would tell himself. It was one thing to run away from people. It was quite another to deny looking at a piece of himself.

He'd do it eventually, of course. He knew he could make it work. But he needed some time. And he needed some distraction.

Cory Phillips, his medic friend from BUD/S and Specialty School, had been picked up by an East Coast team and had deployed six months earlier with his group from Little Creek. He was a Florida native and had encouraged Andy to go with him to Team 4, even though Andy was from a little farming town in central California. He'd never spent any time on the other side of the U.S.

His friend had injured his arm in a training exercise and was healing from a full elbow reconstruction. The Navy gave him three months to get healthy before they'd decide to take him back. So of course, Cory made a beeline to the Gulf Coast, back to his old stomping grounds.

Cory'd bragged that the beaches in California weren't anything like Florida's picture-perfect, deep white sugar sand beaches and blue waters slicing the horizon. Cory told him about all the fishing and surfing they'd do. He told him they could stuff themselves on the fish they could catch off the many piers and on the shore. Live on the water if they wanted.

But when his buddy came home from the Middle East, even before his accident, he sounded different. Now that Andy had a deployment, he knew. Cory was probably also haunted by something, though probably not green running shoes…

The text message he got from him last week, complete with a picture of the beautiful nearly abandoned sugary beach on the Gulf, was damn tempting. And it didn't reflect any of the dangerous pauses and gaps in their conversation he had with Cory a couple of months ago. That had scared him.

Luckily, he had to cut the call short, because they were leading a small party into the bush. He'd been glad to be with his brothers on the mission that day because he didn't want to think about what he heard in Cory's voice. Those kinds of questions and concerns were never to be spoken over the phone. They had to be done in person.

The picture and the text message indicated he'd met a girl. He told Andy all he was going to do was savor the waves and the sun, chill at the tiki bars, and enjoy his new girlfriend, Aimee.

Andy thought maybe he'd give him a call and see if the invitation was real. It underscored what he told himself several days in a row—that the distraction would be good for him. Besides, he'd never seen Florida. And, okay, maybe he wanted to be able to prove Cory wrong. There was no way in the world Florida beaches could rival any of California's. He'd bought his ticket and was leaving for the Gulf Coast today before he had time to change his mind.

He knew sleep was impossible, so he took a shower and dressed. Stuffing clothes into a small duffel bag with the Bone Frog logo on it, he packed up his instant shakes and some energy bars he liked and headed for the airport. On the way, he would search for an all-night diner to grab some breakfast. With any luck, he'd be able to sleep on the plane. A couple Bloody Mary's would help in that department.

After an uneventful flight, Andy picked up his rental car at the Tampa airport and followed directions west toward St. Pete's, on his way to Sunset Beach.

Growing up in the San Joaquin Valley, he remembered being about ten years old when his dad first drove him to the coast where he played in the surf. It was an instant love affair, and he still could smell the salt, hear the birds, and feel the relief after clearing his ears of the sandy water from a spill bodysurfing. He respected the powerful forces of the ocean, and his dad warned him about the undertow occurrence and sometimes jellyfish he'd have to avoid stepping on.

That day with his dad, just the two of them, changed his life forever. He knew there was something about being in the water that would always be a part of his life.

His dad still operated a small farm, and both he and his mother worked long hours. Vacations were infrequent, and it was another five years before he saw the beautiful Pacific Ocean again.

But when he reported to Coronado after his Basic Training and Corps School in Michigan, he'd felt like he'd come home. That year, as they completed their further SQT, they spent time in Alaska and Mexico and had some big desert runs in Nevada. Then they'd return home to Coronado. He vowed never to live in a farming community inland away from the water again. He found swimming easy, the lifestyle in the San Diego area to his liking. The weather was temperate and sunshine nearly every day. And even in the wintertime, it felt like early spring in the valley.

Today, as he drove his rental car over the long bridge that led to the coastal towns of St. Petersburg, Redington Shores, Madeira Beach, Treasure Island, Indian Rocks Beach, and Sunset Beach, he was struck by all the water. Green tangled foliage made its way down to the water's edge. Coastal waterways linked together subdivisions of homes that fanned out everywhere on the water, almost making them look like terraforms on Mars. Huge homes rose up out of the foliage like crystals. He'd never seen so many private boats of all sizes and shapes. Unlike Southern California, he found more boats than swimming pools as he drove down the expressway ending in a dead end at Gulf Boulevard.

He turned right.

He instantly loved the beach vibe. The bright blue sky seemed bigger here. The weather was warmer. Large marshmallow clouds swept across the horizon as he glimpsed blue coastal waters between motels, condos, and restaurants. Enclaves of smaller homes and cottages were interspersed between the commercial buildings and occasional high-rises.

The cat-and-mouse game of hide-and-seek with the Gulf waters felt like he was chasing a pretty girl with big blue eyes who was playing coy and hard to get. He nearly rear-ended the car in front of him while craning his neck, peering between two large homes on stilts, built right on the ocean.

His phone GPS told him he was about five miles away. His telephone rang.

"Hey, asshole, where are you?" Cory sounded like he was extremely inebriated.

"I'm here. Just hold your knickers a bit. I think I'm about five-no, four—miles away."

"Okay okay Andy. I'm putting the steaks on now. They should be ready when you get here."

"You need anything? Do you want me to stop and get some beer or something?"

"No. Got it all. Even have apple pie thanks to Aimee. And I got enough whipped cream and vanilla ice cream to slather all over everything. So you just get your butt over here. We'll stuff ourselves, have a chat, and then I'm going to take you out to watch the sunset."

"Sounds like a plan."

The traffic slowed to a snail's pace under the late afternoon sun. In ten minutes, Andy's GPS indicated Cory's location was on the left. He waited for traffic to go by and then turned down the small alleyway bordering several brightly colored cottages arranged with a common yard. A two-story apartment complex sat farther down the alleyway. On the left side was a massive three-story home with a roaring fire pit in the front yard overlooking the beach.

Andy noticed a parking space designated for the address Cory had given him and pulled in. Before he could get his suitcase out of the car, he heard Cory yell, "Andy! Over here."

A gravel driveway, made with crushed white stones and shells, crunched under his feet as he hoisted the duffel over his shoulder and walked several paces to his waiting friend. Cory wore a red apron with a bright orange lobster screened on the front. Underneath the lobster where the words *'Don't kiss the cook. He bites.'*

And he was nearly falling down drunk.

With a beer in one hand connected to a forearm encrusted in a bright purple cast extending from just above his wrist to within two inches above his elbow and a large stainless steel spatula held in the other hand, Cory stumbled in place. Andy saw that his assessment of his BUD/S buddy was accurate. Cory could hardly stand up. He swayed from side to side, and after a brief hug, Andy was careful to make sure his buddy was firmly planted on his feet before he released him.

"Looking good, my man," Andy lied.

"So what do you think?" asked Cory.

"Pretty fucking nice, you asshole. But I still think you're lying through your teeth about the beach. I like the weather, though. So far pretty nice."

"Just you wait."

Andy was invited into the single-story, concrete block modest home bordering the Gulf. A large picture window in the living room revealed a spectacular view of the beach and the blue water beyond. Andy noted that there was only one couple walking hand-in-hand along the surf line. He was dismayed that the rest of the beach was completely empty.

Cory appeared next to him. "Pretty nice, isn't it?"

"This definitely does not suck." Andy put his arm around Cory's shoulder, stabilizing him. "You burning the steaks?"

"Oh, hell yeah. I get distracted by this view every day," Cory said as he pointed with the spatula. He finished his beer, picked up a dinner plate from the kitchen counter, and motioned for Andy to join him on the patio in the front yard.

Andy counted three huge steaks loaded on the plate, precariously balanced on the cast. "So where is she?" Andy had to ask.

"Aimee went to go pick up a friend. Thought you might like to have some female company tonight." Cory wiggled his eyebrows up and down.

Andy felt his cheeks warm. "Well I guess I can tolerate that. So tell me about her."

"I'll let you introduce yourself. She's standing right behind you."

Andy hadn't heard the two girls arrive. As he turned, he saw two shapely mid-twenties beach ladies in cutoff jeans and oversized T-shirts. The blonde wore a ponytail sprouting out the back of her baseball cap. The brunette smiled at him with deep lavender eyes.

She extended her hand.

"Hi. I'm Aimee. Cory has told me a lot of fun things about you. It's nice to finally meet the legend."

Andy glared at his friend. "Fun things? What kind of fun things?" he asked.

Cory just shrugged and disappeared into the kitchen, mumbling something Andy couldn't understand. He turned back to Cory's girl, aware that it was a very bad sign that he couldn't take his eyes off her. He suddenly wished he was a legend or could miraculously disappear like a superhero. Or he could have a redo of the introduction. He stepped forward.

He felt the earth move as he took her hand and shook. He also smiled at the pretty blonde standing next to her, who was attractively shy.

"Nice to meet you both," he said, his voice cracking like a prepubescent teen. "Maybe you don't know it, but Cory's one of the biggest liars I've ever met."

They all laughed, even as Cory protested.

"Anyhow, he's a really good friend and a super guy." He tried to direct his conversation to the blonde but kept coming back to Aimee. He shrugged. "I guess I don't have to tell you that."

In spite of himself, he blushed. Cursing internally, he purposefully bit his lip to remove the fantasies his brain was torturing him with. Those lavender eyes were peering straight down into his soul.

The blonde, who had introduced herself as Shelley, mercifully helped him out.

"Aimee says you're also a SEAL. Is that right?" Her cute up-turned nose and inquisitive blue eyes were a welcomed relief. He searched for something about her he could find distraction in. He decided he liked the shape of her ears, and the wispy strands of hair around her forehead. Her pink cap read, 'St. Pete.' He also loved her faint Southern accent.

"I am. Went through initial training with Cory. That's how we met. But I'm stationed in Coronado, on the West Coast."

"I love San Diego," she said, her eyes widening. "I wanted to go to school there but wound up at Florida State. That made my mamma happy."

She followed it up with a smile, and Andy was enchanted.

"You *sound* like a Florida girl," he whispered.

He took a step back because he was beginning to feel like he'd never been around women before. Cory was giving him a goofy grin behind the two ladies as he placed the steaks on the table.

"Let's eat before these get cold," he slurred.

Aimee pulled a salad from the refrigerator and asked him if he wanted wine or beer.

"Um, wine, please," he said as Cory pointed to a chair next to him.

"Wine, it is then. Shelley?"

"Please."

Aimee disappeared into the kitchen one more time, rounding the counter with a bottle of red wine and three glasses. She handed Andy a wine opener.

"Care to do the honors?" she asked. Her lavender smile gave him a sizzle down his spine.

"I'm terrible at that," he muttered, watching her put the bottle on the table next to the three wineglasses.

"Really?" she mocked. "A California boy who doesn't open wine? How do they let you live there?"

He glanced at Cory, who was engrossed in carving up one of the steaks for the ladies. Andy watched him carefully, ready to grab the knife from him before he cut an artery. Cory finally mastered the cut and plopped a half on each of the two other plates and gave himself and Andy the remaining two full-sized steaks.

"Yeah, Andy. How do you manage that?" Cory mumbled.

Before he could stop himself, he answered, "I buy wine in boxes or cans."

While Cory's jaw dropped, Aimee pulled the cork out of the bottle with a loud pop, which made Shelley jump. It slipped from her fingers, and as she bent to pick it up at Andy's feet, he gasped.

She wore green Nike running shoes.

CHAPTER 2

AIMEE AND SHELLEY rinsed off the dishes and put away the remnants of dinner while Cory grabbed another beer, handed one to Andy, and agreed to meet the girls out at the beach to watch the sunset.

"He's cute, Aimee. Does he have a girlfriend, or do you know?" Shelley was drying the large plates, placing them back in the cabinet.

"I honestly don't know." Aimee had been wondering the very same thing. "You know how Cory is." She brushed her hair from her face with the back of her hand, clutching a bottle brush in her fingers.

"Oh, I get you."

Aimee continued. "He doesn't volunteer much about his friends, or anything for that matter."

Shelley sighed. "I always forget that about guys." She walked to the living room window as Aimee watched her study the pair of SEALs.

"They're all like that, Shelley. It gets worse when they're together."

"My mom tried to fix me up with somebody from Little Creek. It was one of her biggest mistakes. I mean, we had absolutely nothing in common." Shelley wrapped her arms about her upper torso, swaying. "But oh my God, he was built," she added rolling her eyes.

Aimee hung up the towel and joined her. "I don't even know if I do or don't have anything in common with Cory," she said. "We just have fun. We laugh a lot. He's always the center of attention at any party, or bar. When we're not driving around or having a tickle fight or walking on the beach or other things," she said, closing her eyes, "his favorite thing is watching movies and eating popcorn." She felt a pang of sadness as she whispered, "And I like him better when he's not had too much to drink."

"Can you imagine what they carry around with them, though?" Shelley tipped her head to the side until the two friends touched foreheads. "And were you really looking for *forever*?"

Shelley had a knack for getting right to the point. She'd managed to bring up something Aimee had purged from her mind. "Very astute." She sighed. "I think right now, it's perfect. I don't want to have to work hard at anything. It's been a long year. Mom's at peace, and now I'm free. I don't want to make any plans. I just want to enjoy the beach and the sun."

She watched the two men splash each other in the surf and generally adopt pre-teen behavior. Being here was healthy. This was good for her. She could see Andy was good for Cory, too.

"Are you ready?" Shelley whispered.

"Let me grab a jacket and some waters. Unless you want wine?"

"No, thanks. Water's great."

The sun had just begun to touch the blue horizon. Within minutes, it began to melt like an orange popsicle. Cory wrapped his uncasted arm around her waist when they approached. She felt coolness from his soaked shirt but didn't complain. The smell of the saltwater on his skin was soothing.

No one said a word for several minutes as they stood in hushed reverence.

At last, Cory spoke.

"Well, Andy, my friend, this never ever gets old. I can remember wondering when I was a kid if there was some way I could grab and harness that sun. It looked to me like a great big golden cookie. I was sure it tasted heavenly."

"Butterscotch. That's what it looks like to me," Andy commented.

"So how long before you grab a flight back to San Diego?" Cory asked.

"I got two weeks starting tomorrow."

This was longer than Aimee thought.

"I think that's perfect. But you can stay longer, if you want to, right?" asked Cory.

Andy showed his wide smile and sparkling eyes. "All depends on how you feed me, brother."

"No worries there. And Aimee here will keep us stuffed with berry pies," Cory added, kissing her on the cheek.

The two couples sat down about five feet from the surf. Aimee sipped her water, leaning into Cory's muscled frame. He stretched his purple arm around her shoulder and gave her a careful squeeze.

"Happy?" Cory asked.

"What's not to love here?" She felt him tighten his grip on her shoulder then lean in and place another gentle kiss on her lips. She melted under his tenderness and felt her toes tingle.

"You?" Aimee asked, while watching the golden sunset splashing over all their faces.

"I got everything I need. I got my girl, I got my best friend, and I got my beer." He leaned forward and addressed Shelley, who was sitting on the other side of Andy. "I got Shelley here, too. Can't forget Shelley."

Shelley nodded and then smiled, her beautiful white teeth glowing in the sunset.

"I got my beer," Cory continued, holding up a nearly empty bottle. "I got this beautiful white beach. *We've*," he corrected himself, "we've got this beautiful beach practically to ourselves."

Andy had been fixated on the setting sun. He inhaled. "I think that's just about the prettiest thing I've ever seen. I don't like to admit I'm wrong, but I got to say I think you're right Cory. This *is* Paradise."

"Yep." Cory clinked bottles and finished off his beer.

The four of them sat in silence, watching until the sun's dying fireball extinguished into the water. Overhead, the blue sky began to darken, turning shades of deep peach and purple.

"Look, Cory. The sky is about the color of your cast." Aimee pointed out.

Cory pulled her closer. "Did I ever tell you about that beautiful girl I saw in the yellow bikini one day who had the most awesome lavender eyes?"

Aimee was embarrassed, looking down between her knees as he fondled strands of her hair between his fingers. Finally, she looked back up at him. "Yes, but I love hearing it over and over again."

"Ahh, Cory, I never took you for a romantic," giggled Shelley.

"I can play nice." His eyelids lowered as he drew Aimee closer and whispered, "I can play *real* nice."

His kiss was deep, his tongue exploring. She was moved by his tender display of affection. He was often so private about those things. After, she put her head on his shoulder, and he wrapped his arm around her, this time bumping the back of her head with his cast.

"Oops. Sorry." His eyes were playful and she knew his desire was growing.

"Okay!" Andy stood up abruptly. With his hands in his pockets, he shrugged. "Shelley, let's you and I go back to the house. Otherwise, I'm gonna watch something I will have a hard time getting out of my mind."

"I understand completely," she said and took his hand.

"Oh hell. Let's all go inside." Cory stuck his bottle in the sand, sprung to his feet, and gave her a left hand up. He picked up his empty bottle and proceeded toward the direction of the house.

Andy bent forward, addressing both of them. "Tomorrow morning, I'd like to take a run down this beach at sunrise. Is it very crowded?"

Cory shook his head no. Aimee added, "Never crowded at all in the morning. We get more people here at sunset, but tonight, I don't know where everybody is." She smiled at Andy and continued, "I do it all the time, just about every morning, unless I'm here."

Aimee was grateful he wouldn't be able to see her embarrassment. They walked several steps farther, approaching the weathered wooden bridge that lead over the sand dunes en route to Cory's backyard.

"I did not know that, sweetheart," Cory whispered. Then to Andy he continued. "She lives just down the beach about—what would you say, hon?—a half mile."

"I think it's easily half a mile," she answered. "It's perfect. Paradise."

The four of them made it to the backyard two by two. Cory asked Andy to help him put firewood in his poor man's fire pit, which was a large dented barrel cut in half. She'd spent several warm fall nights there roasting marshmallows and watching the stars while lounging in two bright yellow Adirondack chairs.

"I'll go get some pillows," she said.

Shelley followed her inside. Aimee pulled the patchwork quilt off Cory's bed, and picked up four beach-themed pillows from the front room couches.

Outside, she handed pillows to everyone and then slapped her forehead. "Oh darn, Cory. I forgot to get the marshmallows."

"No worries. We got pie. How about you bring that out?" Cory answered.

Andy dumped his arm full of wood next to the fire pit, arranged new wood onto glowing coals, then looked up at her. "Way better than marshmallows. It's my most important food group," he added.

Aimee danced back into the kitchen, cut the pie into quarters, and then halved the quarters again. She carried out the apple pie and cutting spatula, along with four small plates.

"Okay, so who wants a quarter and who wants an eighth?" She held her spatula up expectantly. Cory and Andy shared a glance between them and both shrugged.

"Honey," Andy said with a grin, "I'll take the biggest piece you'll give me."

BEFORE CORY FINISHED his pie, he brought out his favorite bourbon. Aimee declined, but Shelley had a pinch and then another two. While the men finished their huge pieces, the rest of the bottle was consumed. Shelley began to yawn. Andy brought more wood and spread the coals evenly one more time.

Aimee watched the snapping fire splashes levitate into the night's sky. No one said a word.

It didn't take long before Cory fell asleep, snoring loudly.

"Andy, can you help me get Cory into the bedroom?" Aimee asked.

Before she could stand, Andy scooped Cory in his arms and effortlessly carried him into the house. As she followed behind, he dropped him on the bed. She removed his shoes but left his socks on. She folded the sheets and comforter over on him.

"So Cory is done. I'm going to take Shelley home," Aimee told him.

Andy tilted his head, peering down at her. "Do you want me to?"

"No. I think what I'll do is take her home and then I'll let the two of you turn in for the night, okay?"

"You up for a run in the morning?" he asked her.

Her pulse quickened. "I thought you'd never ask." She liked the way it felt to smile at him. "You think you can make it at six-thirty?"

"You meet me here?"

"I'll come down the beach from the north, and if you're out you can join me. If I don't see you I'm gonna let you sleep."

"You got it, Coach," he said.

Shelley took Andy's hand and shook it. "It was really nice to meet you, Andy. Maybe we'll see each other again."

"I'll make a point of it, Shelley," he answered. Then he turned to Aimee. "You're sure I can't help take Shelley home?"

"Thanks a bunch. But I really need to get back to my own place. And Cory is out for the count, so I'm not needed here. Otherwise, I'd hang around a bit. But you've got two weeks, and I'm out of a job, so I'm pretty sure we'll be doing this again."

He extended his hand, and she found herself enjoying his gentle but extremely firm handshake.

The two girls drove in silence for the first few minutes. Shelley sighed then adjusted her seat back.

Aimee wished they had spent more time together, the four of them. She guessed Shelley felt the same.

"I can tell you like him. You don't have to hide it from me, Shelley."

Shelley shook her head. "Man, they don't make guys like that very much anymore, do they?"

Aimee agreed completely.

"You could have let him take me home, you know. I mean, it wouldn't have been the end of the world. You could have still gone home to your own place," she said, glaring at Aimee.

"So you're pissed at me, then?"

"Something like that."

"So why didn't you say something?" Aimee could see Shelley was struggling.

"Well, I am a year older than you are, Aimee. I really don't need protection, especially from that guy. Just think about it from my side."

Aimee felt like a chump. "I'm really sorry, Shelley. I hadn't even considered that. Next time, tell me, okay?"

"Thought about it. I'm not desperate. I didn't want to look that eager."

"So I think you played it perfectly, then. And I'll be sure to let him take you home the next time."

"Just as well. My place is a mess tonight. But dayam. Did you see those arms? And the way he shakes your hand? We don't have enough of that around here." Shelley wrapped her arms around herself and humphed, lazily glancing out the windshield.

"Maybe you should move up to Virginia. Or I'll make sure Cory invites some of his other friends from Little Creek down here. How about that?"

"Wouldn't that be nice? Are they mostly like that, Aimee? The one my mom hooked me up with was an animal. I don't need any of that. I want a gentleman."

"Shelley, you're only twenty-eight. There's plenty of time."

"I'd like to find someone before I need a wheelchair and have to go trolling in senior complexes."

"See there, you're in the right place," Aimee giggled. "I'm going to remind you when you find The One. Don't worry about it. It will happen, trust me."

"You and Cory?"

"Already asked and answered. Not saying anything more."

"Sorry."

After several more minutes, Aimee turned into Shelley's neighborhood. Shelley was beginning to gather her things.

"I can't understand how a guy that nice and that good-looking doesn't have a girlfriend. It just makes no sense whatsoever."

Aimee slowed down. "Oh geez, Shelley. Now I have to go on a fishing expedition?"

"Just find out what you can, and then don't worry about it. I'm a big girl."

"Will do." Aimee asked if Shelley would like to spend the night at her place, but her friend declined. "I should have asked you before we got all the way over here."

"He has that effect on you too?"

"Absolutely not." But Aimee wasn't convinced that was the truth.

"I have to be at work at eight o'clock, and it's just easier if I leave from home. I don't wanna show up at school in my cutoffs."

Aimee nodded. She let Shelley off in the parking lot to her apartment complex and waited until she was inside the lobby, the door closed. They shared a wave, and then Aimee was on her way to her own place.

FIRST THING SHE did when she arrived home was pour a tall glass of ice water and take it outside, sitting in her two-person swinging loveseat. She began rocking back-and-forth, enjoying the squeak of the springs, the sounds of the surf, and the appearance of stars peeking through a light fog coming off the Gulf.

She stopped long enough to take two large gulps of the cold water, kicked off her shoes, and pulled a blanket around her shoulders.

SHE WASN'T REALLY tired, but if she was going to get up at six o'clock for a run, she needed a good rest. She wondered if her parents ever sat on Sunset Beach like she was right now.

It has been a great adventure to come here. It was fun getting lost every day, learning about the area, finding her perfect little beach cottage to rent. Everywhere she went, she wondered if her mom and dad had been there. Did they stroll down the same beach or eat at the same seafood dive? She almost felt as if they were still here, watching her every move.

The swing's steady heartbeat, punctuated by the rushing sounds of water and the hiss of the white spray left behind and soaking into the sand, made her feel hopeful. It was like she had come home, finally, to a place she could relax.

She could barely make out the shadow of a lone bicyclist riding down the beach in a fat tire contraption under the moonlight. She considered searching for a bicycle with balloon tires so she could do the same.

Moonlight shimmered on the water as a seagull called. She was at peace on this night, as if an old painful chapter had been completed, and a new one was about to begin.

She wasn't going to try to control it, direct or evaluate it, or even study it for too long. She was just going to let it calm the anger and pain in her soul, wash over her like the surf, claim her, and then drag her out to sea forever.

CHAPTER 3

ANDY WAITED AT the surf's edge. The sun was barely up, but it still felt wonderful on his back, compared to those wet-n-sandys they used to do at Coronado at midnight during BUD/S. There was no breeze coming off the Gulf. A fine mist was lifting, emerging from the spray and the waves beyond.

He turned to his right and saw a pickup truck smaller than a postage stamp in the distance. There were single runners, pairs of runners, and a group of older women in sweats chatting away doing a light jog as a group. They all waved and greeted him with warm smiles.

Finally, a slim woman's figure emerged from the mist. When he saw the green shoes, he knew it was Aimee. He rose to greet her.

So she wouldn't have to stop, he blended in and ran at her side. "Good morning. You were right. It's nice this time of day. A little dark, but nice nonetheless."

Her cheeks were flushed, and her light caramel colored hair stuck in dark ringlets about her face. She wore a lavender-colored zip-up fleece top nearly the same color as her eyes.

"Morning, stranger. Glad you made it. How's your head?" she answered.

"I'm fine. Really *fine*. I drank a whole bunch of water last night before I turned in. That always helps. Except for the fact that I had to get up like ten times to go pee, I slept like a baby."

She chuckled at that. "Welcome to my world. I'm the same way."

They ran in silence for several minutes. Walkers, beachcombers and two young men with metal detectors, passed them along the way. Other beach runners waved as they moved in the opposite direction.

"Can't believe how friendly everyone is," he said.

"I noticed the same when I first moved here. You meet all kinds of people on the beach too at sunset. I think here everyone's used to people coming from all over the world. Snowbirds come down from the north. It really gets crowded after Christmas. But it's just a couple of hours from the theme parks, and for some reason, there are a lot of people from Russia and the Balkan countries who visit. There's quite a community here. I have no idea why that is."

"Interesting."

Two silver-haired older men leisurely rode their fat tire bicycles toward them. As they got closer, Andy heard the gentle whir of a motor.

"Now that's smart. I like that a lot."

Aimee smiled. "There are rental places all over the place. You can also rent golf carts. Those with the fat tires are made for beach riding. They don't allow any vehicles on the beach, except the garbage crew. I'm surprised they haven't been stopped. But pedal power, that's the bomb."

She took a long drag on her water bottle and then replaced it in the pocket sewed into the back of her lavender jersey.

"You try to run every day?" he asked.

"I *try*. But I don't stress about it. Sleep is kind of delicious too. But I honestly think running keeps me from getting sick. And I feel so much better afterwards."

"I get you there. Nothing better than a good workout." He decided not to mention that he and Cory had planned on doing a couple of five-mile swims in the warm Gulf of Mexico during his vacation.

She checked her watch. Her eyebrows shot up. "Do you wanna run another ten minutes or so?"

"I'm easy." Andy cursed himself for saying so. But it was the truth, after all.

"I had to struggle at first to get into the running. I didn't start until graduate school. And I was so incredibly slow. But I learned to be patient. And now I love it."

Andy studied the variety of housing that overlooked the beach. They had easily passed through several different sleepy beach towns. Two- and three-story condos or apartments dotted the coastline here and there. Occasionally, there would be a vacant lot or two, and several small shacks were being torn down and converted into huge concrete modern multi-million dollar homes. It was a mix of afford-able and unassuming old Florida, and pretentious living in a house that matched the grandeur of the view.

As the sun rose higher in the sky, the heat began to climb. His shirt was drenched, and his running shorts had bunched up, giving him a nice wedgie he didn't want to pick. It should not matter to him about that, but it did.

Aimee slowed down and walked in long strides, looking down at her feet as she did so. He matched her deep inhale and exhales to start their cooldown.

"Wow!" she said. "I liked that. Thanks for the company."

"That was fun. Now what do we do?" he asked.

"If you like, there's a great breakfast place across Gulf Boulevard. They specialize in seafood omelets and homemade biscuits. If you join me, I'll pay. You can even have my potatoes."

Those lavender eyes were going to kill him. She was a true classic beauty. No makeup in sight, just a fresh, healthy face. He found a twinge of envy directed at Cory and immediately stuffed it down. One thing was as true now as it always has been on the Teams. If she dated another brother, that meant she was hands off. He adjusted his attitude, checking himself just to be sure he had his bearings. He knew from BUD/S that Cory could be a hothead sometimes, and he got situations wrong occasionally. Andy had busted up more than one skirmish during their training. In class, if anyone was going to get into trouble, it would be Cory. Andy vowed to make sure his friend didn't start to wonder about his loyalty.

But damn, she was honestly hard not to look at and so very pleasant to be around.

He justified that, since Cory was probably not gonna rise anytime soon, he could sneak some good dark coffee, biscuits, and a seafood omelet. No problem with that, he told himself.

And he could enjoy the view, as well as the view of the ocean.

"You're on, Aimee. Just point me in the direction of those biscuits. California makes them like hockey pucks."

Her green Nikes scampered over the sand dunes. She had better traction, and he actually had to work to keep up with her.

They found themselves in a narrow alleyway lined in pavers between two large buildings. Palm trees planted long ago were threatening to crack the foundations of both buildings, but because they'd gotten so tall, the fronds gave a gentle cover. It was like walking on a paved jungle path.

Finally, he found himself at the edge of a familiar street.

Gulf Boulevard. It snaked through over ten little beach towns on the peninsula.

Aimee turned right, and they stood in front of a tiny vintage-decorated mom and pop restaurant.

"They only serve breakfast and lunch. It's not fancy, but you'd have to travel fifty miles to find another place that has a better breakfast," Aimee told him.

"I'll take your word for it," he said as he opened the front door for her.

They were seated up front at the painted window. Someone had drawn fish, shells, mermaids and lobster in bright colors. All of the images hovered in a circle around the name of the place:

Connie's.

Andy switched seats, since they placed him next to Aimee. That would leave his back to the window, which was something he never did.

"I got a thing about being able to see the entrance and the exit." He shrugged and continued. "It's a habit now."

"Sometimes it's so noisy you can't hear unless you're sitting right next to the person. But we're early, so all's good."

Andy accepted a small tumbler of fresh-squeezed orange juice and a pot of French press coffee for two. He opened the sticky plastic menu and was dazzled by the fact that their omelet list was single spaced, covering both pages. He scanned to the bottom.

"Eighty-four?"

Aimee smiled. "You know the funny thing is I think I've eaten here about fifteen times. I always scan the menu, but I always order the same thing."

"So what's your favorite?" he asked.

"Number thirty-five. Crab, shrimp, mozzarella cheese, black olives and sour cream, with a slice of avocado on the side."

She had an honest face, delivering her line without a smile, totally confident. He wanted to ask her a lot of things, but he decided it was safest to let her talk without his prompting.

Buttermilk biscuits were to die for. He slathered his with butter and orange marmalade. Aimee broke her biscuit in half and ate the bottom, softer side without anything extra.

"Cory showed me this place," she began. "He said his parents used to take him here when he was in a high chair."

Andy scanned the room, noting the framed pictures covering the wall up front. Various celebrities had left autographs behind. He recognized several baseball players, a couple of football players, and a row of Little League teams that Connie must've sponsored. Several country stars posing with their guitars had also eaten here.

"Looks like all the best and the brightest come here," he said. "Now, if the omelet tastes as good as this place smells, I'm gonna be okay."

Andy ordered the same thing. Aimee instructed the waitress to leave all her potatoes on his plate.

"Thanks. I'll just waddle home, Aimee."

She chuckled.

Several local watercolor artists displayed inexpensively framed pictures which were scattered everywhere. Andy picked up a flyer in a plastic stand on their table and learned about a local gallery where several of these artists displayed their work. On the backside of the brochure was a map and a picture of a calendar, each month featuring a different brightly-colored beach cottage and all by a different artist.

"We have a lot of retired here," said Aimee. "There's a book club that meets in one of the rooms off City Hall, if you can believe such a thing. The local vet shares a building with the post office. And the post office shares a counter with the local DMV."

Andy was beginning to get the full flavor of the community. He put the flyer back in the stand when their omelets arrived.

A pile nearly an inch thick of fresh crab meat covered the top of the omelet. "I've died and gone to heaven, Aimee. Seriously," he said as he picked up his knife and fork.

It only took him ten minutes to finish the whole thing. He was suddenly self-conscious as he looked across the table, noting Aimee had barely eaten anything. He felt like a pig.

"God, you think I hadn't eaten in a week. Sometimes workouts do that."

"I'm the opposite," she said. "I'll take this back for Cory so it won't go to waste."

Andy watched her delicately pick up the crab and nibble on small pieces of the biscuit. She was well-mannered, eating properly with her left arm resting over her napkin on her lap. In between bites she dabbed her lips. She had everything but the hat and the gloves.

She frowned. "I feel weird you just sitting there watching me eat."

"I'm sorry. Didn't mean to offend."

"Am I sloppy, or dropping food?" she asked as she wrinkled her nose and checked out her shirt in front.

"No, not at all. I like watching, as a matter fact. I was just thinking that perhaps you lost your appetite observing me shovel it in."

She giggled. Pushing her plate to the center of the table, she leaned back in her chair, poured a fresh cup of coffee, added cream, and savored a long sip.

"Cory says you grew up in California. That's where I'm from too." Aimee sipped her coffee again.

"Yeah. I grew up in the central valley in a little town you've probably never heard of."

"Try me," she challenged.

"Clovis."

She rolled her eyes and then, after looking up to the right, began to nod. "Near Fresno, right?"

"Good job!"

"Well, you did say the central valley. And I was trying to think of all the little towns I've been to. I played club volleyball in high school. We had tournaments all over California and I think I've probably spent several hot and sweaty Julys playing in some junior high school gym with no air conditioning."

"An athlete, is that it?" he couldn't help but ask.

"I tried to play in college, to offset some of my fees, but I pretty much warmed the bench. We had a couple of Ukrainian girls that were over six-three, and that limited my playing time. I gave it up sophomore year."

Andy had watched the girls play volleyball down in San Diego and noted she had the perfect slim, agile body type. With her running, he figured she could probably jump and spike as well.

"Nonsense," he said. "We have a couple of Samoan and Hawaiian teams that are always playing against each other. One we call the Smurfs. They're one of the most competitive and toughest customers to beat. They just never let the ball drop. If you play like that, all you have to do is wait for the other team to make an error, because eventually, they will."

"Oh, I've played against girls like that in high school. Yeah, they're deadly."

"One of the tournaments at Coronado, the Smurfs beat one of our SEAL Teams. That really stung."

She smiled, rimming her finger around the top of her orange juice glass.

"So what part of California?" he continued.

"Davis, near Sacramento."

"UC. College town."

"Except I really grew up in a little town a few miles west of Davis. Woodlake."

"You got me there, Aimee. I've never heard of it."

"Don't feel bad. Our downtown is two blocks in each direction. No movie theater. About ten greasy spoons, a really good steakhouse, a bakery, two ice cream parlors and about fifteen drugstores."

He must've dropped his jaw because Aimee laughed.

"Don't ask me how come, Andy."

He didn't know how to read that.

"Well, in Woodlake, the drug stores have a lot of other stuff too since we don't have any chains. They sell hair dryers, shoes, even groceries. Oh, I almost forgot. We do have a funeral parlor and, I think, about six churches."

"So you lived there your whole life?"

"My dad was a doctor and had a part-time practice. But he was a biology professor at Davis. Teaching was his real love."

"Was? As in he passed away?" Andy was hesitant to delve further.

She was not looking at him but rather stared at her coffee. Very slowly, she nodded.

"Drunk driver. He was killed instantly, but my mom lingered for over a year."

He wanted to say something but wasn't on solid footing. He tried anyway. "You've had a run of bad luck, Aimee. Just meeting you for the first time here, I would have never known all this. I'd say you're a real survivor."

She gave him a brief smile. "I wish I could say that was everything, but what sustained me was that I had a wonderful childhood. Sort of a perfect life with my mom and dad and my big brother. The first time I saw Cory, he reminded me so much of Logan."

"Family's important. At least you have that."

"Not really."

Andy braced himself for a backlash to his inappropriate choice of words. He wasn't going to do anything but listen. He would not engage, because she wasn't asking for it. There was no self-pity. He saw a strong, resilient woman who didn't need to be rescued. If he wasn't careful, he'd get sucker-punched.

But her story had already touched him deeply. It made him want to call his own parents, who were thankfully still alive and active.

She turned her head, staring out the window at passing cars. Andy could swear he began to see tears form.

"That happened about eighteen months ago. But before that, when I was still in school, Logan started to get into trouble in his teens, so we drifted apart. I really missed my older brother. He always protected me."

Andy waited. It was Aimee's story to tell but only if she wanted to. He wasn't going to pry.

"Cory knows all about it so I might as well tell you too."

"Don't feel like you have to."

She studied his face, her eyes sweeping to the top of his head and then quickly glancing at his lips, before she smiled and poured on the steady lavender gaze that made his pulse quicken. Whatever test she had placed him under, he hoped he passed. He repeated himself.

"I sincerely mean that, Aimee. We don't have to go there."

She folded her hands together in front of her on the table. Their waitress brought another pot of French press, and she leaned slightly forward to watch the bubbles and coffee grounds moving slowly inside the glass beaker.

"My brother got into drugs and alcohol. He dropped out of high school and went on the road with a band one summer. He got arrested." She licked her lips and frowned, staring at her fingers. "My dad sent him to his first rehab when he was sixteen. And then again when he was about eighteen. And then again and again. He'd leave sometimes on his own for a week or two and then come back. He stole from my folks. He'd come home from rehab and steal my babysitting money. It was heartbreaking."

"I can't imagine how bad that must have made you feel. All of you," Andy whispered.

"I think they used their entire savings trying to get him straightened out. Logan just couldn't do it. They say it's hard when they start young. Arrests their development. I believe them."

"I'm truly sorry."

"Thank you. It gets a little easier the more I tell the story. One day, Logan left and never came back. That was about seven years ago. So when I finished college and started graduate school, my folks felt like they were done waiting for him to return. They'd tried everything. Police, private investigators, checking with the rehab places he'd visited. He was just gone. I didn't understand what it meant at the time, but I used to watch my mom search through the big picture window in our living room, just hoping he'd come walking down the street clean and sober."

"They left?"

"They moved to a little town outside of Nashville a few years ago. My dad retired early from the UC system. He got a part-time teaching job at Vanderbilt and set up a small practice being an on-call physician for several larger groups. He made house calls. Everybody loved him."

"I'll bet. Sounds like it was a calling for him."

"It really was. I was so happy they had those five years. I think they were the happiest I'd ever seen them."

Andy was feeling the blood pooling in his knees and ankles. He needed to move and get a good stretch in, so he asked.

"Can we maybe walk back? I'm getting kind of stiff, and I need to move around a bit."

"Sure." She reached for the bill, and Andy swiped it from under her fingers.

"Mine," he said.

"But I said it was on *me*."

Her pouty face mocked anger. She threw her arms around her upper torso and stuck out her lower lip.

Andy held the slip high in the air, twirling it slightly to get the waitress's attention. "You gotta be quick. Besides, you told me yourself that you don't have a job. I do." he said as he tapped his thumb to the middle of his chest.

She started to protest again, and he stopped her by raising his palm.

"It won't do any good, Aimee. This is non-negotiable."

Andy wanted to hear the rest of the story but feared he should've stopped her, and now she was embarrassed with the reveal. If she wasn't Cory's girl, he would do something stupid like touch her shoulder or hold her hand, or something to reassure her that, with him, she was safe.

However, Aimee *was* Cory's girl, and so he kept his distance, walking behind her through the palm tree path, and onto the white beach again, where he could breathe. All the heaviness of their discussion floated away.

The morning was still on the chilly side, so no one had set up beach chairs or blankets. Everyone they passed was either walking or running, singly or in groups.

Her pace was quick, which was exactly what he hoped for. Then he remembered the omelet.

"Did you get the—"

Aimee held up the white styrofoam box in a plastic bag with Chinese characters all over it in red. "Cory's breakfast." She checked her watch again. "If he's up."

The same two silver-haired older guys had removed their jackets and rode their fat tire bikes in flip-flops and their swim trunks. He hadn't noticed until now that one of them had a short ponytail.

"I just love those things." Aimee said.

"Well, let's try to get you one. Let's rent three and go for a ride."

"That would be so much fun."

Her lighthearted comment convinced Andy she was done with the sad tale. He started examining the crushed shells beneath his feet as they walked in tandem. A pair of brown pelicans flew overhead, heading out into the water, joining another pair. They took turns circling and then plunging into the water to fill their bellies with fish.

A small fishing boat trolled through the waters past the row of red buoys, a couple of lines dragging behind. The boat was being followed by a flock of about thirty seagulls, who fought over what must have been pieces of fish that had gotten chummed in the boat's propeller.

Aimee's phone rang. Andy recognized Cory's voice immediately.

"Wow, you're up about two hours before I thought you would. Are you hungry?" she said into the phone.

"Sorry, Aimee. I guess I wasn't much fun last night."

"I needed the rest. Andy carried you to the bed, and I took Shelley home. Anyway, I went for a run on the beach and picked up some old crusty barnacle here. We just had breakfast at Connie's, so I brought you the rest of my crab special."

She finished the call, tucking the phone in her zippered breast pocket.

"He okay?" Andy wanted to know.

"He sounds pretty damned good. It looks like today will be one of his good days." She looked up to him with a brave smile.

That look told him all he needed to know. She'd come to Sunset Beach to heal. Cory was someone she could take care of. He was consuming her entire world and helping her to forget.

Or at least trying to.

CHAPTER 4

A IMEE FOUND CORY sitting on one of his bright yellow chairs. He was sunning himself, his legs outstretched, flip-flop encrusted feet resting on the lip of the fire pit. He wore black wraparound sunglasses and was shirtless. Only thing missing was the tanning lotion.

His upper torso was packed, sculpted, and hairless. In fact, he was the most perfect-looking guy she'd ever dated. For all his casual and somewhat irreverent personality traits, staying in top physical condition was no joke to Cory.

"Hey there, sailor," she said as they opened the gate and entered the patio.

He sat upright, removing his glasses, and then scrambled to his feet when he saw Andy.

"So now you've seen Connie's, and how does it rate?" he asked.

"I don't think I've ever had a crab omelet like that before. It was an outstanding recommendation," Andy answered.

Cory paused slightly, studying Andy's face. Then he focused on Aimee, stepping forward to present her with a tender kiss. While she went up on her tiptoes and wrapped her arm around his neck, Cory was gingerly extricating the bag from her fingers. "Thanks babe," he whispered in his sexy, private, *'for her ears only'* type of voice that gave her a tingle down her spine. She wondered what she'd done to deserve such attention.

But she loved it.

His fresh, clean-shaven cheek and tender kiss had her melting dangerously. She broke free, trying to respond as if it was bedroom talk, rubbing his left butt cheek when she whispered, "I'll go get your fork. Be right back."

As she stepped into the doorway, his words followed behind her. "I'll be right here," he called, mimicking her voice and continuing to play along.

Inside the house, she grabbed a fork and napkin. As she passed the open door to the bedroom, she discovered Cory had even made the bed. Andy's room, in contrast, was completely torn apart with the coverlet and even the sheets halfway ripped off the mattress. She smiled to herself. He was either a thrasher, or he'd had company last night.

Once outside, Cory dug into the food, devouring it in mere seconds.

"I was going to offer to heat it up, but I can see that is completely unnecessary."

He gave her a cheesy grin and completed his meal.

"Was there some sort of alien abduction here today?" she asked.

Cory's eyes danced. Andy looked completely confused.

"Whatever do you mean?" He set the paper plate on the grill in front of him, begging for her explanation.

"You straightened the bedroom. You even made the bed, Cory."

Andy leaned back in his chair and chuckled. "I didn't," he mumbled.

Cory chuckled while he brushed biscuit and egg pieces from his trunks. "I like to surprise you now and then." His grin came late, but it was still a grin.

"I like surprises very much," she purred back.

"Yes, I know that."

Andy sighed. "Just tell me now, Cory. Should I get a room

somewhere? I feel like I'm getting in the middle of something."

Cory lazily leaned over in his direction. "Usually, the girl is in the middle, sport."

"Cory!" she screamed. She was genuinely shocked at his behavior.

"It was just a joke, and I didn't mean to disrespect you, sweetheart."

Andy's puzzled expression hung in the air like an old jacket. Carefully, he leaned back, crossed his legs, and waited for anything else to happen.

She changed the subject. "Do you want some orange juice or something else to drink?"

Cory smirked and picked up an opened longneck beer bottle. "I got it," he said, holding it up.

Aimee was slightly surprised but had seen this before.

Andy interrupted, nervousness making his voice wobble. "We came up with a great idea, if you're into it, Cory. How about renting some of those fat tire bicycles so we could ride up and down the beach?" he asked.

"I'm good with that plan," he answered. "Aimee has been wanting to try one of those motorized bikes ever since she saw them. Right?"

"I think it's a great idea," said Aimee. She looked down at her running outfit. "I'm gonna go take a shower and change, if you don't mind?" She'd directed her question to Andy. "We only have one bathroom, sorry."

That brought a frown to Cory's face, and then he spoke up. "Well, instead of waiting maybe he could join you." He widened his eyes and presented both of them with a Joker grin.

"You asshole," muttered Andy. "I had to carry your fat ass to the bedroom last night. That's what kind of a fucking host you are. We did you a favor and let you sleep."

"And I thank you for that, Andy."

"Maybe I should go find a spot to hang out for a couple of days, and then we can start all over again. Act like adults."

"No, don't do that," both Aimee and Cory said in unison.

"Go take your shower, honey," Cory instructed. She rose and headed for the house. Behind her, she heard Andy address her wayward boyfriend. She turned to watch the fireworks.

"Now, about tomorrow…" Andy pointed his forefinger at Cory's face. "I'm gonna pour ice water on you and get your butt up and on the beach for our morning run. And that's going to be oh-six-thirty, Casanova. You got it?"

"Yes sir. Whatever you say, sport." Cory had lost the scary grin but sat to full attention.

Aimee wasn't quite comfortable with the swearing back-and-forth between the two friends, but she got loud and clear the message, veiled as it was, that Cory wasn't happy about the run or being left out at breakfast. She retreated to the bedroom.

As she stripped and stepped into the shower she couldn't recall picking up jealousy in Cory's nature before. But then, she'd not seen him around other SEALs very often. Maybe that was how they played, a little rough, joking as if demonstrating a lack of respect. Every minute she'd spent with him, she learned little subtle things, like how Cory liked to live slightly on the edge. He could make fun of the most ridiculous situation. Nothing, except his commitment to his Brotherhood or his manhood, was sacred. Although they enjoyed each other, she came second.

She dried her hair and dressed in stretchy jeans and a halter top so she could get full sun on her back but protect her legs from the bicycle mechanism. She applied light pink lip gloss and blotted her lips. When she dropped the tissue into the wastebasket, she noticed something.

A golden plastic pill bottle lay on its side, partially obscured by other paper garbage. She bent down to pick it up. Cory had told her he was done with the painkillers. But, unless he flushed the contents of this bottle to dispose of the unused pills, this was evidence that he'd been lying to her.

Her surprise discovery worried her. Clutching the bottle in her hand, she joined Cory and Andy on the patio.

"It's all yours." she said, pointing to the sliding glass door.

Andy jumped to his feet and disappeared inside. Cory had put his sunglasses back on and continued to soak up the sun. She picked up his plate, his now-empty beer bottle, and leaned over to speak to him.

"Hey, honey, I'm going to take this inside. But can you first explain to me what this is?" She held the bottle between her thumb and other fingers.

Cory slowly removed his glasses and sat forward. She handed it to him. He slowly studied the label, turning it like he was seeing it for the first time.

"I had one left. I took it early this morning, because my elbow is just killing me."

He didn't look at her.

"But you still had alcohol in your system from last night. And look at you now. You're drinking a beer with your breakfast," she reminded him, her concern growing.

He nodded. "I know. I'm careful. It was just one pill."

"You know I've had some experience, some history with this, and it freaks me out. Being careful isn't the point. It's a little reckless, Cory. You know better."

Cory stood, tossing the bottle onto the chair, and enclosed her in those strong arms of his. "I'm sorry, sweetheart. It was dumb. You're completely right. It ends here."

Still standing, he leaned back at the hips to study her face, placing his palms at the sides. "I know you mean well, but you don't have to worry about me. I'm *fine*." He pulled her to his chest, gently rocking the two of them from side to side. "But thanks for looking out for me just the same."

His kiss and gentleness brushed aside her niggling worry.

Andy appeared, dressed and ready to go. "You want to drive the Jeep?" he asked, holding up the keys.

"Absolutely." She took in the trash and grabbed a jacket she'd left in the closet.

On the way out to Andy's rental, she saw Cory dump the bottle discreetly in the gray garbage can at the curb.

AIMEE SPED DOWN the beach on a bright red fat tire bicycle, screaming at the top of her lungs. She tried to stay out front of Cory and Andy but didn't take as many chances as they did, as they wound around beachgoers and other obstacles.

The motor was pegged to five miles an hour which, while not very fast on the road, seemed like jet speed on the beach. The boys were reckless, swerving to avoid people, umbrellas, beach chairs, and a small group of teenagers, who chased them every time they zipped by.

On a couple of occasions when they got too close to some beachgoer and weren't sure they'd clear, Andy or Cory would just dump the bike, sacrificing themselves.

Aimee wasn't able to ride without the assist, so she maintained just enough tension to make it a good workout, without imploding her quads.

Several hours later, her ribs hurt; she had laughed so hard. The sunlight on her face and then on her back as they traveled up and down the beach felt wonderful. They maintained a five mile loop until her legs began to burn.

She stopped and Cory told her to continue to a large wooden

bench a few yards north. Once she arrived, she noticed a beach access bridge with a large bench big enough for all three of them planted in the sand. The bikes were carefully laid on their sides as they caught their breath and talked to several groups of kids or curious onlookers who traveled the bridge for the day's adventure.

Cory volunteered to take the access toward Gulf Boulevard on an ice cream mission. Andy agreed to accompany him while Aimee stayed behind to guard the bicycles.

She sat still and just observed, letting her mind relax. There was something about Sunset Beach that settled her insides. The white noise from the turning waves, calling of sea birds, and the squeal of little children transported her back to her childhood and much happier days.

Mounted on the wall in her kitchen was a wooden plaque she bought in one of the local beach decor shops. It read, *The beach fixes everything*.

Sitting alone in the afternoon sun, she completely agreed.

The panoramic view in front of her was at least ten miles wide in both directions, where beachgoers looked hardly bigger than a grain of sand.

Maybe it was the salty air or the gentle wind in her face. She felt healthy, alive, freed from the pain of watching her mother lose her battle and her will for life. Everything important was in front of her, as if the past had been wiped away.

The bright orange sun was falling and would mate with the horizon in an hour. She could feel the rays warm her heart. All she came here for was distraction. Instead, what she got was her life back. She began to unthaw.

In a silent homage to the goddess of the sun and a God she knew loved her despite her flaws, she said a prayer. She was grateful, and like a mermaid who had emerged from the ocean for a life on land, she was firmly walking on two feet toward a bright future.

Her thoughts were rudely interrupted by the sight of the scoop of chocolate chip cookie dough on a waffle cone nearly the quarter the size of her head. Rivulets of vanilla ice cream had already traveled down the outside of the cone and over the fingers of her handsome Navy SEAL.

Cory was now kneeling in front of her presenting the cone.

"Holy cow, Cory. This is huge!" she said.

Andy appeared next to him. He handed her several paper towels and gave the rest to Cory. He had a ring of chocolate around his mouth and a small spot at the tip of his nose.

"I tasted yours, Aimee," Andy said. "Feel free, I mean, if you can't finish it, I'd be happy to oblige."

"If you value your life, you'll stay out of my ice cream, Andy." She was rewarded with a bright, wide smile and a wink.

"Cory's warned me about you. And based on what I saw you doing with that bicycle, I can see you are a competitor."

"Oh, but she is so wicked when she plays cards," said Cory. He put his hand up to his mouth, forming a megaphone, and whispered, "She cheats."

"I do not!"

But Cory wasn't paying any attention to her. He was prattling on about all the card and Monopoly games she'd won.

"Not fair! I call foul!" she said. "I'm a fighter because I don't like to lose."

Both men howled, Andy falling to the ground as if he'd been stabbed. He nearly lost his double scoop.

Minutes later, she handed the rest of her cone to Andy, who accepted it gleefully. She washed her hands in the drinking fountain beside the bench, drying them on her jeans.

The sky was turning a deeper shade of blue. It had been forecasted for rain, so large billowy clouds had sprung up while they rested.

As the sun dropped into the water, the clouds turned from white to various shades of purples, peaches and occasionally golden yellows.

Several groups of people had gathered on the beach to watch the sunset. Everyone was caught up in their own private thoughts, observing the death of one day and preparing for another behind it.

"Come on. Let's get home before it's too dark," Cory said. "And we have to get the bikes back to the shop before closing time at eight."

She walked between the two of them. It felt good to run this morning. Felt good to get to know Andy a little. The exercise on the bike was invigorating. She'd sleep well tonight.

"Anyone up for oysters?" Cory shouted. "We should go to JJ's. The drinks are half off until seven, and they make the best jambalaya in all of Florida!"

CHAPTER 5

T HE PARKING LOT was so full that the spillover also filled the church parking lot next door. Aimee trolled the row upon row of trucks, SUVs, golf carts, small camper RVs, and sedans. There were license plates from several eastern seaboard states, as well as several from Texas, Tennessee, and North Carolina.

"I think I see one over there next to the white truck," said Andy.

It was obvious that if they made it into the space, nobody would be able to open their doors to get out.

"I'm going to give myself more space," said Aimee. "I don't need another door ding. And there's got to be someplace along the street, as long as you guys don't mind walking a bit. Or I could drop you off and find a spot then meet you inside."

"Are you nuts?" Cory squinted his eyes and looked at her disapprovingly. Andy completely agreed.

"Yeah. You're stuck with us, Aimee," he told her.

Just as she was going to head out to find another spot, a huge four-door truck with tires nearly the size of a small airplane began to leave. The windows were blackened, and it had a custom paint job with a non-stock chrome grill and fancy custom lights that practically required sunglasses. But Andy still recognized it as a Ford.

Centered in the middle of all the crisscrossing chrome and extra lighting was a set of horns about twelve inches in length, mounted wisely upside down with the tips pointing to the ground for obvious reasons.

Across the blackened windshield in oversized scripted letters was the name, *Phyllis*.

All in white.

"Holy moly, Phyllis. How the hell do you get inside that cab, sweetheart?" Cory whistled and shook his head in disbelief.

The monster truck slowly wound through the aisles of haphazard and unmarked parking spaces. When Aimee turned off the ignition, Andy heard the blast of a special carburetor system, and the squeal of those oversize tires making a huge statement. A cloud of gray smoke trailed behind without any chance of catching up.

Inside, the place was packed. Long tables with benches were set up in the middle of the room. Tables for two rimmed the outside. He'd expected they'd have to wait, but they were shown to the end of a picnic table they were to share with a party of four, two couples.

Up front, he saw a raised dais, with microphones, drums, and equipment set up for a small band.

"We're going to have entertainment tonight?" Andy asked, his voice slightly elevated.

Cory craned to sneak a look up front and then turned back to their group. "We got the Flamingo Cowboys tonight. What the hell kind of band is that?"

Aimee shrugged her shoulders. "The only flamingos I've seen with cowboy hats are cartoons."

"Probably a local band," said Andy.

They ordered three bowls of jambalaya, and then Cory ordered a dozen barbecued oysters.

"And to drink?" the waitress asked.

Cory scanned a chalkboard she pointed to and picked a local IPA. "We'll have a pitcher."

"Three glasses then?"

Aimee pointed to a picture on the menu of an oversized margarita glass filled with pink icy liquid. A long pink and white striped straw had a pinkish orange paper flamingo attached to it.

"I'll have that."

"JJ Margarita special then. Just one?"

Cory and Andy looked at each other, and Andy spoke first. "Actually, make that two."

"Cory raised his forefinger, and asked for a sixteen ounce, instead of the pitcher.

Andy was having a hard time hearing anybody so he scanned the crowd. He didn't expect to see anyone he knew, but he'd been trained to assess any new environment. He noticed a rear door next to the kitchen entrance. Over his head, he saw at least six cameras attached to a ceiling grid that panned the crowd.

Narrow stairs lead to a short landing and a door beyond, indicating there was a small office or observation room above the kitchen. He figured it was where all the recording equipment and security detail was located, because he didn't see anyone of authority downstairs.

Cory had been searching as well. The two nodded.

The margaritas arrived, twice the size of what they looked like on the menu. Cory held his mug up, and they toasted.

"To Sunset Beach. To good friends and happy memories."

All three of them pulled on their drinks.

"Oh, I like this!" Aimee said. "Cory, you got to try mine."

Andy completely agreed. The drink was luscious and went down like fresh fruit juice.

Cory shook his head and waved her off.

"I think it's grapefruit and definitely pineapple, but I'm not sure," Andy said. "It has some Cointreau in it, too, and something else. Very smooth. I approve."

Aimee raised her glass, and all three of them toasted again.

"Out with the old and in with the new," she shouted.

"It isn't New Year's, Aimee," Cory spat back.

"It kind of feels that way to me, though. I'll just get a two-month start on it. Is that okay?"

"Whatever you want, sweetheart." Cory rubbed his thumb across her lips. "You can have Valentine's Day every day if you want it."

Andy watched Aimee blush and tried not to stare.

A table of young ladies were drinking just behind them. Andy knew immediately it was a bachelorette party. His internal radar flew into high alert. He turned when he caught two of the girls whispering and pointing in his direction.

Dammit.

Cory ordered another beer when they got their oysters and the stew. The hot sizzling barbecue and garlic butter was fantastic, and all dozen of the things were gone in a matter of seconds.

The jambalaya was to die for. It was spicy hot but not so much as to shatter his taste buds. It contained jumbo shrimp, crawdads, oysters, clams with their shells, and muscles, all in a brown okra gumbo. It went perfectly with the margarita. But he found himself closing his eyes when he drank, since the pink was distracting and didn't match what he tasted.

The band started playing, which made any kind of discussion impossible. He also knew that tomorrow on his morning run, his ears would be ringing.

Cory turned around on the bench so he could watch the band. A very tiny dance floor was located just in front of the stage. Cory grabbed Aimee's hand and pulled her through the sea of tables to join several other couples.

He watched Cory and Aimee move together. She was a good dancer, but Andy could tell Cory didn't know the first thing about leading. The combination Country and Latin beat was catchy, and before long, he noticed he'd been tapping his feet, as well as his fingers, on the tabletop.

The rest of the dance crowd were older couples, silver-haired snowbirds probably, drinking and dancing on a Wednesday night, which was likely something they never did at home. He liked the fact that the whole room of people had come from so many different places. Some were recent refugees to Florida, bailing from other high-priced areas of the country. Others were just here on vacation, escaping a blustery fall somewhere.

Aimee had told him she came for distraction. And that was probably true for all three of them.

The second set began, which was a slow dance. The older couples resumed their positions, probably used to dancing with each other for decades. But Cory and Aimee were clowning around, laughing, as Cory held her and then dipped her low to the ground and up again. They danced in a bear hug but as close as they could get. He watched her face as she leaned into Cory's shoulder and closed her beautiful lavender eyes in a daydream.

He felt a tap on his shoulder and looked up to find a very pretty, well-endowed redhead staring down at him.

"Care to dance?" she asked.

"Sure."

On their way to the dance floor, he heard clapping and laughter. Someone yelled out, "Go for Ginger!"

She stepped right up into him, her chest forming a pillow between them. He slipped his arm around her waist, directing her to an open space in the dance area, and she followed perfectly.

"Where are you from?" her orange lips asked in a soft Southern drawl.

"California. And you?"

"We are all from here. Well, almost all of us. But we all grew up here and have been friends since grammar school."

"Ah!" he said as he looked down on her. She smiled sweetly, a little shy, but she was comfortable around men, and he liked that.

She was easy to like and perhaps easy to talk to. As he gave a fleeting glance to the cleavage helped with some kind of a push-up bra, he thought probably she would be easy to fuck too.

But that wasn't really a serious thought. He could be the guy she was dared to ask, and he knew how to be a gentleman, so he would politely do his duty, help her look like a princess, and would return her to her friends.

He caught Aimee staring at him, and then she quickly glanced away. When Cory turned her around, he gave Andy a wide-eyed all-knowing smile.

"So how long are you going to be in Florida?" she asked.

"Two weeks. I have to get back to work."

"I see. Well, that means you'd be here this weekend. Would you come if I invited you to my best friend's wedding?"

He knew exactly what to say next. It was a standard answer whenever he got into situations he needed to exit cleanly. "I kind of have someone back home. I'm out here to visit my buddy." He nodded in Cory's direction.

She turned, looking at Cory and Aimee dancing. "I think he's local. Is he?"

Andy didn't want to speak for Cory, so he lied for him instead. "No, he's up in Virginia. He's just down here for some workman's comp time. Did you catch his purple cast?"

"Oh!"

Her eyes had drifted to Aimee. "Well then, I'm going to have to ask Gretchen if it's okay to invite all three of you. It's going to be a fun party. My friend is marrying Anson Moore III. You know, the Moore's who breed racehorses?"

"I'm afraid you know way more about that than I do." He paused and then tried to soften the turn down. "We have lots of plans to go fishing and do all kinds of things while we're here, so I'm afraid our days are pretty full. But thank you anyway."

She appeared to take it well. "All right." Her sweet voice washed over him, and he could feel himself get hard. He decided to just experience it, instead of trying to turn it off.

He was getting used to his arm around her waist, used to the way she blended her fingers with his, used to her subtle floral scent and the way her nipples felt brushing against his chest.

She was his for the taking. She'd be soft and loving. She'd make him feel good about himself. He'd enjoy watching her shatter beneath him. He knew he could satisfy her, and he wouldn't wake up the next day and feel dirty. But it wasn't what he was looking for.

It suddenly struck him how odd this was. The old Andy would never pass up the chance to spend a little fun time with a pretty girl.

Maybe I'm just getting old. Is this what I have to look forward to?

And then the music was over.

She held his hand, dragging him over to the table with her friends. Each time he tried to sneak a look at Cory, he was laughing. He knew there would be jokes at his expense tomorrow about getting ensnared, and fondled, even mildly felt up on his second day in Florida. He knew Cory would tell him that the girls here were beautiful. And they were.

As Ginger introduced him to the female side of the wedding party, he made a point of being courteous but not giving anyone too much attention over anybody else. He declined their invitation to join them for drinks.

"No, ladies," Ginger began. "He's here visiting his friend and his friend's girlfriend. Kaitlyn, honey, do I have your permission to invite them to the wedding?"

The bride wore a tiny white veil with miniature wedding rings, baby pacifiers, and several other flesh-colored charms he didn't recognize stitched into the veil. She looked ridiculous.

Kaitlyn, the bride, examined him as if he was a piece of meat at an auction house. She was cold as hell, but her eyes lit up when she said, "On one condition. I got to have one dance."

She opened her purse, leaned across the table and handed him an invitation to the wedding and reception. It was in two days. That's when he recognized the flesh-colored shapes sewn to her veil. They were penises.

"Obviously, you don't have to RSVP. The more the merrier," she said, the little penises bobbing with the movement of her head. Her smile was picture-perfect. Her eyes came alive when he took the invitation and stuck it in his jacket pocket.

"Thanks, Ladies" he said as he gave them an extremely shallow bow.

He got a bouquet of titters for his trouble. Cory gave him a standing ovation when he came back to his seat. Even Aimee was laughing at him.

"I can't help it if I'm irresistible."

"Damn straight. See what happens when you clean up and wear a jacket and a button down shirt?"

His pink margarita looked like a tired glass of Hawaiian punch. Even the straw was drooping, and the paper flamingo had fallen on the table. He looked over at Aimee's and noticed she had finished hers. Of course, that nice little glow at her cheeks would've told him that.

Their waitress told him he could get a refresher, on the house, so he asked to try a regular margarita with no salt on the rocks this time.

"So we got an invitation for this wedding on Saturday." He threw his thumb over his shoulder and explained, "The bride's the one with all the BS on her veil."

"Oh yes." Aimee giggled. "I see what you mean."

"Very tacky," he said.

"Shocking, even," Aimee added and then chuckled.

Cory leaned forward on his elbows. He had three empty beer glasses in front of him. "So what's the plan, Stan?"

Andy took the invitation from his jacket and showed it to Aimee and Cory. "They're all local. The bride's marrying some horse breeder."

"Oh a trophy wedding!" enthused Cory. "I love those. The old man must be ancient."

"I'm not sure." Andy tapped on the name.

"Anson Jonathan McKinsey Moore, the third?" Cory read. "Yeah, they're loaded. I think they're Pegasus Farms. He's a bigwig in local politics too. Owns a couple sports franchises—I don't know which ones." He leaned back in his chair, placing hands on top of his head and stretching to the side, and then moved his right arm up and down slowly, babying his brand new joint.

Aimee pushed the invitation back to him. "I don't think that's my kind of thing. But you guys could go."

"So let me get this straight, Aimee. You're encouraging Andy and me to go crash a wedding party with a bunch of oversexed bridesmaids and probably half the pretty girls in Florida, single and just dying to get laid by a Navy SEAL? Is that what you're saying?"

"No, of course not! I didn't see it that way. If I don't know anybody there it really wouldn't be any fun for me. I don't want to go just to say I attended some big wedding for the rich and famous. That's not really who I am."

"But why not?" he insisted.

"It would probably just be uncomfortable. I'd be so nervous I wouldn't enjoy it. That's all."

But Cory wasn't going to give up so quickly. "Let's see, they'll probably have a French chef, a Cuban chef, pastry chef, free booze, and a tribute band, that will be even better than the real guys. It says here it's at the Belle Meade Country Club in Sarasota. Now, the brief amount of time I was there—well, let me put it this way, before I got kicked out—it looked like a pretty cool place."

Andy couldn't help but chuckle. "And being totally practical, like Cory here?" He paused while Cory toasted him. "We'll need you to drive us home Aimee."

"There's Uber."

Andy tilted his head and then began shaking it no. "She doesn't wanna go, Cory." He placed his fingers at the top of the card preparing to rip it up when Cory stopped him.

"Give me that."

"Cory, what are you doing?" asked Aimee.

"I'm here to keep you two from making a huge mistake," barked Cory. "Trust me. I'd *pay* to go to one of those functions. And we got a free ticket in. I think you could even bring Shelley, if you wanted to, Andy. I'd bet she'd love it."

"Does that change your mind any?" Andy asked her.

"You really think this is a good idea? Do *either one* of you think this is a good idea?" Aimee said as she alternated searching both their faces.

Andy knew without looking at Cory what his answer was going to be.

In unison, they both said, "Yes!"

"I gotta go pee." Aimee stood and headed toward the kitchen with the bathrooms just beyond.

"You think we just screwed up, Cory?"

"No, she'll come around. And if she still is adamant about not going Saturday morning, I'll take her somewhere. You and Shelley should go. I think it will be a good way to check out how the better half lives in Florida. I guarantee you won't ever see anything like it again."

"I'm thinking maybe the three of us should go. Less things to manage." Andy read in Cory's expression that they were on two different pages. "No, no, no, Cory. I don't mean anything like that."

"Sure you did."

"It will give us all something to dream about. Something to aspire to. Something to tell our grandkids someday." He paused. "Remember what we said? To making happy memories? Now that's what I'm talking about. What were *you* thinking?"

Cory just groaned and rolled his eyes. Andy knew that by the time they made it home, he'd be in no shape to walk. In fact, Cory would probably be asleep as soon as he hit the backseat of the Jeep.

CHAPTER 6

ALL THE WAY back to her Sunset Beach home, Aimee thought about something that happened at the restaurant. She wrestled with the idea of telling Andy but decided against it.

They'd placed Cory in the back seat of the Jeep so he could stretch out over the bench. Andy insisted he hadn't consumed enough alcohol to be impaired, so he drove. That left the passenger side for Aimee.

She was in a very light-hearted mood tonight and was headed back to their table when she noticed two men arguing in the back-yard. The rear restaurant door was open, but a screen protected the inside diners from bugs. Both men were wearing white, indicating they worked in the kitchen.

One man began to shout at the taller one. He began pressing his forefinger into the other man's chest, making some kind of demand. He was rotund and shorter of the two, with black curly hair growing like weeds all over the top of his head. He even had a heavy mustache. The other man was extremely thin and much younger. He also towered over the angry man by more than six inches.

Several times, the force of the older man's chest tap became more like a small shove, causing the other one to step back. Finally, she saw the younger man hold up his hand and shout, "Don't you dare!"

The words echoed throughout the alleyway behind the restaurant and even made a neighboring dog start to bark.

Both men looked back to the screen door of the restaurant. Aimee froze in place and then noticed something familiar about the younger man. At first, it was his voice. Although he'd been pushed to anger, the basic timbre was very familiar.

She pressed close to the screen to get a clearer view and called out, "Logan?"

Both men ran in different directions. She heard a car start and another slam of a car door.

It can't be! Although she doubted the impossible, she still had to check it out.

She noiselessly unlatched the screen door, stepping out onto the paver tiles traversing the small yard. She stopped and listened again for any sound out of place and found none. Certainly there was no arguing.

She called out again, "Logan? Are you out there? It's Aimee. If you're there, let me talk to you. You don't have to be afraid."

No one answered. And although their white jackets could easily stand out in the moonlight, she couldn't find evidence of either man anywhere.

Suddenly, her knees began to shake, and her breath became ragged. The dark night felt evil, menacing, and she ran back to the safety of the warm establishment and her two SEAL protectors.

But the encounter with the two strangers had rattled her. She'd not been sleeping well lately, so tried to justify that it was a hallucination brought on by nerves, caused by a lack of sleep. And the more she played the strange visitation over and over again, as she watched the road and let the two-lane highway lull her back to normalcy, the more she began to doubt that it had happened at all.

It certainly wasn't Logan. It couldn't be. Logan would have appeared, come up, and talked to her. No matter what state he was in, he'd never just flee without talking to her.

IT WAS THE first time in the ensuing seven years that she'd actually seen someone that closely resembled him. There had been lots of false starts over the years, people who looked like him from behind. But when she examined their faces, they were complete strangers. She knew it upset everyone around her when these things happened. So, eventually, she made it a point not to search anymore. Her parents had moved on years ago. She adopted the same attitude.

Leaning back in the seat, she closed her eyes for a few minutes.

"You okay?" Andy asked her.

"I think I'm getting a migraine or something. My whole head hurts."

Andy pulled a water bottle from the pocket in the side of the driver door and handed it to her. "You need more water. Hydration will do the trick."

He was probably right. She thanked him and took a long swig.

She turned, pulling one knee up so she could sit sideways, and looked at his handsome face. Red and yellow lights reflected on his statuesque features. By contrast, her brother's face was very angular and sharp, and in the vision she'd seen tonight, if it was real, the features were even more so.

The last time she saw him, his eyes appeared to have sunk farther into his skull, revealing dark brown circles beneath. He still had the same prominent cheekbones, but below, his face was gaunt and the coloring was pasty white. Unlike the man she was looking at now, Logan seemed like he was near death.

"So tell me what's going on?" he asked. His deep voice was soothing and kind.

"I was just thinking about all the characters there at the restaurant. The girls who would have devoured you if you let them. The silver-haired couples. The wait staff, and the kitchen help."

"You should see it when I go overseas. Talk about a clash of cultures. Imagine if they were all speaking different languages."

She threw out a question she'd often thought about since high school. "Can you imagine if you wanted to orchestrate all these people coming together like they did tonight? If that was your job to choreograph that scene, how would you do it? When you think of it, it's a statistical miracle."

"Whoa! That's way beyond my bandwidth. You came up with that on your own?"

Aimee readjusted herself and smiled, facing front once again. "I could lie, and you'd think I was a genius. But I had a statistics professor in college who loved to throw that out to all his Freshmen. He said it was his proof that we were living in miracles every day."

"Or a grumpy farm boy like me might say it's proof of the randomness of life."

She couldn't suppress another smile. "Or you could say that."

"But man, what a place, right? Great food. Packed on a Wednesday night. That place is a goldmine."

Aimee was grateful for the conversation. "That's for sure."

"Except for the Flamingo Special. That one didn't grow on me like I thought it would."

"And I loved it," Aimee grinned. "They are so consistent, Andy. I never get tired of their jambalaya. Can you just imagine how much seafood they go through every evening?"

"And it was all fresh," he said. "I can see why you guys go back there so often."

"Creatures of habit."

"Purveyors of good taste," he corrected her.

She decided to let the differences stand where they fell and to change the subject.

"I guess we're going to be attending that wedding, then. I'm going to have to check my wardrobe because I don't think I have anything suitable to wear," she sighed.

"Well, after Cory told us about his little experience there, I don't think it's going to matter. We may only be in attendance for about five minutes, right?

Aimee nodded. "That was a new story for me. He must have thousands of them."

"He's got lots of stories all right. Some of them are even true."

She directed him to turn just after the dog park and the Pelican sanctuary. Although her house was a more expensive rental, though it was smaller than Cory's, she liked the neighborhood better.

"How long are you here for, or do you know?" he asked her.

"I'm on a two-month lease, but I can extend it up to a year if I want. Technically, it's just a month-to-month tenancy now."

"How come you don't move in with Cory? And don't answer that if it's too personal."

She leaned back into the comfortable lumbar support of the leather seat and smiled. "That's a good question, Andy. We've talked about it every once in a while, but it's sort of like I don't want to give up my house and he doesn't want to give up his. I couldn't tell you which one of us is the more stubborn, although he'll claim it's me."

"I can see the difference in the neighborhood already. Looks like they've torn down and rebuilt most of the smaller homes in this area. I think it's safer for a woman, living alone."

"And I have a handgun."

"Good to know," he said, nodding. "Bad for the bad guys."

"It belonged to my dad."

"You trained in how to use it, clean it, know the rules of engagement?"

"Not quite."

"You don't want to own a gun unless you're prepared to use it, Aimee. It will be far safer for you that way and for any innocent who happens to come across it. You should take it seriously."

She kept quiet. Finally, he added, "I don't mean to interfere, but you have to respect guns. Then it becomes a protective device and not something that could get you or someone else killed."

She didn't respond again.

"So I did it, didn't I?"

"You did. But I understand it was for my benefit. I'll add it to my list."

He touched her shoulder. "Thanks. Lecture over." Then he asked, "How did you find the place?"

"I couldn't believe I found it online. And it's quieter, too, than just about any other place I've looked at. The land slopes to the shore here, which makes it not quite as good for swimming, but it does block the traffic noise from Gulf Boulevard, and that's a huge plus." She pointed to the little bungalow on the beach. "Home sweet home."

Andy stopped the car and turned off the ignition. He accompanied her to her front door where she lingered.

"Are you going to be okay with Cory?"

"Just like I did the night before. He's a sack of potatoes."

She wanted to touch him but didn't want to be inappropriate. Taking the safe road, she extended her hand and they shook.

"It was fun. It was really, really fun, Andy. I can't remember when I've had such a day filled with so many activities. That morning run and breakfast was outstanding. Then we got the bikes. We ate ice cream and watched the sunset. Then danced at JJ's. It feels like a week has gone by. Normally, my life's a lot slower."

"Mine's a little different pace than that. When we're home, it's slow. But at work, things come up all the time. And you never know when it will just explode."

"Well, thank you, Andy. Now, do you want me to call Shelley and invite her for Saturday? Or do you want to do it?"

"Let me think about that for a little bit. Cory and I will talk it over unless you feel strongly about it."

"I just want to do whatever is more comfortable for you. I wonder if we should take two cars. That way, if someone wants to come home early, they can."

"Good point."

She suddenly realized that she was just making nervous conversation, like she didn't want him to leave. She gently placed that thought in the back of her mind, smiled, and said good night one more time.

Her house was a sanctuary of all the things she loved about living on the beach. She knew she was going to have to pay extra because she'd put so many holes in the wall with her must-have finds, mostly beach-themed plaques and pictures. A long turquoise fishing net stretched along one wall where she clipped favorite things to it with bright colored clothespins.

As was her nightly routine, she checked every window and every door to make sure they were locked. She had her father's handgun in the nightstand, loaded, but she doublechecked it anyway.

Andy would be proud.

The silvery water was calmer than it had been the night before.

SHE PEELED OFF her clothes, took a quick hot shower, and snuggled into a flannel nightgown. It wasn't quite cool enough now to wear the nightgown, but it made her feel safe.

Lying on her back, she mentally set her internal alarm clock for six a.m., took a deep breath, and let it out slowly. As she sunk into sleep, she began to hear music from the dance floor and the sounds of those silly laughing wedding party ladies. She remembered the look of Andy's smile bathed in the magical sunset. She remembered the taste of her ice cream and the way the sun surrendered at last to the blue horizon.

Then she saw the face of the young man she thought looked like Logan. But sleep was beginning to overtake her, and she didn't have the energy to explore further.

CHAPTER 7

ON THE MORNING of the wedding, Cory got a phone call from Little Creek that he had to take in private.

Andy watched his buddy walk out onto the patio and plop down in one of his favorite yellow Adirondack chairs. He didn't want to spy on Cory, but it didn't look like a conversation that originated from SEAL Team 4.

Last night, he and Cory had begun to talk about Cory's drinking. His cast was coming off next week, and he said he was looking forward to driving again. The problem for Andy was he hadn't seen Cory without a beer in his hand just about anytime from late morning to bedtime.

It also was something he knew Aimee was concerned about. But since Andy hadn't been there a week yet, he decided to put off all the suggestions and confrontations until just before he left.

Cory had also received something in the mail from Little Creek, which he ripped into shreds and threw it out in the trash without showing it to anyone.

All these things had begun to add up. And while Andy wasn't worried about the significance of any of these by themselves, the combination was more than he was comfortable with.

He read the local flea market rag after he noticed Cory had glanced over his shoulder a couple of times to see if he was being observed. Andy made sure he kept his eyes on the paper.

Finally, the call ended, and Cory came back inside.

"Hey, Cory, you want to try one of my meal replacement shakes?" Andy asked.

"Sure thing. Where do you get it?"

"A couple of former team guys put together a company, and they did a lot of nutritional research too. We actually take some of their stuff on deployments now."

He pulled out two plastic bottles from his duffel bag, and showed Cory the powdery mixture filled to nearly a third. After adding water, he shook them both vigorously and then handed one to Cory.

"Keep shaking for a bit. They're all natural, but they don't always dissolve right away. You know how it goes. No pain, no gain."

"Gotcha."

Cory started dancing around the room, exaggerating the meal prep.

"All right, showoff. I think you have it now, Cory."

They shared a smile and then opened the shake. Andy was used to taking it down all at one time, but Cory taste tested it and wasn't quite sure at first if he liked it.

"It won't hurt you. Lots of kick ass vitamins and it helps you hydrate. Stores for years. It's good stuff"

"Is this something my system has to get used to?"

Andy shook his head. "I don't know what you mean exactly."

"Is it going to give me the shits?" Cory spelled out.

"Nope. Good and healthy. Nothing like that."

"Okay, down the hatch," he said and then belched.

Cory picked up the two empties, depositing them both in the garbage under the sink. He slowly wandered back and collapsed in the loveseat in front of him.

"So I have some news, and I need to let you in on a few things that I'm kind of working on."

Andy was relieved that finally he might be getting some answers.

"That mean this phone call was good news?"

"Good and bad." He stared at the ceiling for a minute and then lowered his eyes, as he scrunched back into the seat. "Depending on what they find with my arm, and I'm pretty sure I'm going to be okay, I might be called up for an assignment."

The surprised Andy. "Where?"

"First, let me lay some groundwork. That trip to the sandbox was all screwed up, Andy. It was a huge botched job. People died who shouldn't have. And, I'll be honest with you, and I never want it to leave this room, some of that falls on me."

Andy knew this was serious. He adjusted his body and then leaned forward, resting his forearms on his knees. "You know, Cory, you shouldn't really blame yourself. Nothing ever works out exactly the way it's supposed to. Military stuff is messy even when the planning is nearly flawless. Stuff just happens."

"No shit. But I at least want to be honest with you. I mean we go over there as newbies, right? We try to follow the rules and follow instructions. But the bottom line is, even on the teams, you know we talk brotherhood and Rah Rah, everybody's together, and all that stuff. But if something goes wrong and the people in Washington or Norfolk start to look for answers or look for fault or blame, it's probably not gonna be the twenty-five-year guys they're going to blame."

"Yup. That's why we need to get a good LPO. My guy is great. I mean all of the guys on our platoon would die for this guy. And I've heard stories about all the people he saved, both civilian and military."

"I'm happy for you, Andy. But not all of them are like that. For some reason we had a whole cluster of newbies right out of the Academy. Anyway, I don't wanna make this too complicated, but the bottom line is there are a few people riding my ass. And it makes it even more important that I get this arm healed. But if I get injured again, they're probably going to quit me."

"For cause?"

"Not really, in my opinion. But you know shit rolls downhill, right?"

"Ha ha. And so that was your phone call?"

Cory burst out laughing. "Well, part of that was a little recreational thing."

"What does *that* mean?"

"I got a guy who sells me a little bit of weed now and then, to help me sleep. I found him through this girl that I met in the hospital actually. She's a nurse. I was trying to score something so I could go to sleep naturally. Weed does that for me. I'm still healing. I still have pain, and I have to get up. If I can't sleep well, I can't heal."

Andy couldn't believe what he was hearing. Cory had justified so many things, and he wondered if he still knew the difference between right and wrong. He thought about the expression 'dying of a thousand cuts,' and he wondered if the Navy had recommended he get some counseling.

"You should get a referral to somebody, Cory. I appreciate you telling me about all this stuff. But you need to talk to somebody else. It isn't healthy to not be sleeping, and as a matter of fact, you've been sleeping a lot, I think. So I don't quite understand. But if you need something to take before you go to bed, you should get it from the Navy. Let them manage it. Don't try to do it yourself, because it's dangerous."

"Now listen to you. Dangerous. We're fuckin' dangerous. That's what we do best." He scowled and crossed his legs. "But I even thought about that. Therein lies the problem. I don't want to give them anything that would make them want to toss me."

"Cory, have you even thought about this all being in your head, I mean maybe they're not really thinking that way. And asking for help, doesn't that show good leadership and courage? I'd hate to see you not get help just because you think it wouldn't look good on your file."

"Andy do you even watch the news? They're jacking guys all over the place for bullshit infractions right and left. Suicide rates are up. I mean, it's a mess. And to make matters worse, we're fighting a fucking war that we can't win."

"But that's not what we do, Cory. That's not our job. We're not supposed to ask those questions."

"Okay, Superman, I see where you're going with this."

"So let's just say you had a really crappy deployment and especially badly planned operation. Next one will be better." Andy could see he wasn't buying it.

"Oh, I get you. Power of positive thinking and all. Get me some Yoga tapes and start doing meditation."

"Cory, you're just an angry asshole. I'm talking about taking some definitive, positive steps to first find out if they really are looking for an excuse to get rid of you, and second, trust the system to give you sound medical advice. Quit managing it on your own based on what you imagine is happening. In fact, I'm wondering if that's really you or the drugs working."

"We're just going to have to disagree on that. Give me a chance to share some things with you. But dammit, you gotta shut up and let me talk."

Andy knew he'd make a lousy counselor, and Cory had just confirmed it. "I apologize. Tell me your plan."

"Before I left Little Creek to come down here, I put in for an extra training round at the burn center in San Antonio at the joint base. They told me it was a longshot, but since we had the long medical course, they said I might go to the top of the line. So I'm waiting for a slot."

Andy was thrilled.

"That's a good idea. Give yourself time to settle down. Heal up and in the meantime, get more training. Man, why didn't you tell me that in the first place? I wouldn't have given you the lecture."

"No, that's my fault. So at first they told me they wouldn't consider the spot until I was clear, which made no sense whatsoever. I don't have to just sit around the beach doing nothing until my fucking arm heals. As much as I love it here, you and I, we're men of action. Anyway, I got a call yesterday, and they told me that there would be a place for me."

"When would you go there?"

"They said it could be in a couple of weeks or another month. But one way or the other, I'm going."

Andy was puzzled by all of the little parts of Cory's story that somehow just didn't smell right. "So what's the problem then, man?"

"First, there's Aimee. And to be fair, she hasn't made any claim on me, Andy. She's been great. I'm a better man because of her. But I feel bad just getting up and leaving her, because I never told her about the letter or what I had applied for. I knew in the back of my head that this might happen, and I didn't tell her."

Andy was glad Cory was considerate of Aimee's feelings. "That's a good thing, Cory. If you love each other, you being gone for a few months isn't going to mess that up."

"Well, I was thinking I could ask her to marry me, and she could go with me to San Antonio."

Andy stared in disbelief. This wasn't at all what he was expecting to hear.

After several seconds of silence, Cory ventured a comment. "So I guess you don't think it's a good idea?" Cory jumped to his feet and started nervously pacing back-and-forth.

Andy wasn't sure what he should tell him. "I'm just shocked is all. Hey, if that's what you wanna do, go for it, go for all of it."

Cory drilled him a look but nearly seared his eyeballs. "I want to know what you're thinking, Andy. I want your *opinion*."

"I don't have an opinion. It's not one of those things that has anything to do with me. It's something you and Aimee should work out. Like I said before, whether she stays here, or she goes with you to San Antonio, those are all things you need to sit down and talk about. It doesn't matter one whit what I think. You gotta do what's right for you. And if this is the next step for you two, then I say go for it."

"That's what I thought you'd say. And I want to thank you for being honest. I got some details to work out, and of course, I don't have a spot until I see the paperwork, damn paperwork. But I know that with Aimee, it would be the kind of support I need to get through that course, and then she could help me decide where I'm going with the teams."

"Just. Be. Honest. That's my advice from start to finish, Cory. That also means taking a look at what we talked about earlier, getting some help, not doing the illicit stuff, cleaning your act up. She's a great gal. Very rare person, and I agree. I think she'd really be good for you."

Cory walked over to the picture window, placed his forearm against the glass, rested his forehead on the cast, and mumbled, "And I think I'd be really good for her too."

Andy hadn't seen any of this coming. Something made him nervous. He suddenly discovered what it was.

He felt an overwhelming need to protect her. That was beginning to be a problem.

How in the world can I be a best friend to my buddy when I know the woman he says he loves would be better off without him?

CHAPTER 8

AIMEE SPENT THE better part of the morning looking for one perfect dress. The ceremony was to take place at the Presbyterian Church in Sarasota, the old First Church, starting at four.

The plan was to attend the reception afterwards. She offered to drive so she could keep the boys, primarily Cory, out of trouble. Cory insisted they attend both. Because she'd never been to a huge formal society wedding before, she was glad she could be the only woman at the party with two dates.

Poetic justice.

The boys were to pick her up at her place around three.

She got up early, skipping a run, and got an appointment to have her hair cut and highlights added at a shop nearby. She also had an appointment to get her nails and toes done. At ten o'clock, when the mall opened, she planned to hit Neiman Marcus as well as a specialty high end bridal and formal shop nearby.

As far as jewelry, she had one set of pearls, which belonged to her mother. And that was going to have to do. She just needed to buy a dress with a scoop neckline, which would really showcase the beautiful pearls. Her father had spent nearly two months' salary to buy them for her, or so the story went. Her mother had cherished them and worn them all the time. Every time they went to the symphony in Davis, or she was invited to lunch somewhere, or they went to San Francisco for a play or opera or ballet, her mother wore the pearls. This would be the first time Aimee would wear them.

The Brides and Belle's shop was first on her list, since she'd read online it was where several of the society ladies had shopped in the past. It was just one dress and one pair of matching shoes she was investing in, so she felt like she could splurge.

No one knew that she had the proceeds of her parents' Tennessee home already in the bank, and she planned on keeping it that way as long as she could. When she was good and ready, she'd start looking to buy a little house like she was renting. But she wasn't ready just yet. She considered purchasing something she could later tear down and build something larger, but still modest. Right on the beach. That's where she knew she wanted to be. She could afford to be picky and take her time.

But for right now, the 1200 square-foot cottage suited her just fine.

She checked her watch and calculated she'd have about four hours to complete her shopping, and then she had to allow an hour to get home. She set her alarm for two o'clock, which would give her enough time to shower again and be ready for the boys to pick her up at three.

Just in case she couldn't find anything, Plan B was to wear the short sleeve cocktail dress with the pearls, even though it was black. But that was Plan B. She was going for something a little more exciting.

Once she walked through the front door, an attractive woman in her fifties introduced herself and asked her if she'd like a cappuccino. She was led to a small and very private sitting area with mirrors on three sides. It was furnished in red flowered wallpaper, which matched the red leather couch and ottoman. This "little" waiting room, as her helper described it, was larger than her dorm room at UC Davis.

Marlene brought her cappuccino in on a silver tray. "I slipped a couple biscuits in for you, since shopping sometimes causes us to miss lunch. I hope that was all right."

THE WOMAN SAT on the ottoman, crossed her legs, and placed a clipboard on her thigh, her pen poised, ready to take notes.

"So you said this is a big wedding? A society wedding?"

"Yes."

"Okay, and how much time do we have to get the dress ready?"

"The wedding's this afternoon."

Marlene looked like she'd just seen a naked man walk into the office. She quickly recovered, slid back onto the ottoman, and crossed her legs the other direction.

"Most of these dresses in the store are samples, which is what we order from. Many of them are just pinned so we can fit you perfectly. I can perhaps call and see if I can locate a certain dress if you find one here that you like. We also have some sale dresses. So I don't want to get your hopes up, dear. I'm not sure we'll be able to accommodate you today."

Aimee considered what she'd been told. "So then show me the dresses that you have in stock, if you have any. Once I see my choices, I can make a decision quite easily."

"What's your budget?"

She'd not thought about that. "If I like it, I'll buy it. I don't have a budget. I want something that will make me look fabulous. I want to blow my boyfriend's mind and make every other single girl at the party jealous." Aimee grinned.

"Color?"

"Something bright and dazzling. No white or off-white of course. That's reserved for the bride. Is that correct?"

"Indeed." Marlene made some notes on her clipboard, asked questions about her normal dress size, picked up a telephone, and requested the in-house seamstress join the two of them. "She will take exact measurements, so we can see if perhaps we can find a top that fits you perfectly. The skirt can be a different size if you need to. We have lots of flexibility that way."

Aimee thought that was a clever way to approach the problem.

"So what color is it that, when people see you wearing it, they tell you that you're stunning. Most people have one color that they just absolutely love wearing. What color is that for you, Aimee?"

"It would have to be red."

"Red, as in blood red, orange red, pinkish red?"

"Fire engine red. Five-alarm red. Bright, no gray tones."

"Is the wedding in a church or outdoors at a venue?"

"The wedding is at the old First Church in Sarasota. The reception is at the Sarasota country club. It's called something else, but apparently, it's a big beautiful one."

"That would probably be the Sarasota Silverado?"

"That's it. The Silverado."

"So can I ask you who the bride and groom are?"

"The groom's name, I think, is Moore, and I was told the family breeds horses. Racehorses?"

"I know exactly who will be at that wedding." She tilted her head and asked, "This will be quite an event. Are you friends of the bride or groom?"

"Bride. My boyfriend and I recently met her at JJs near St Pete Beach."

"Well, you're a very lucky lady. Don't be surprised if you wind up dancing with Tiger Woods or a famous NFL or baseball player. The Moores also own a hockey team, as well as two Mexican league professional soccer teams. They're lovely people."

MARLENE CHECKED HER watch and frowned. Picking up the phone again, she demanded to know why the seamstress had not checked in with her. While she was on hold, there was a gentle knock on the door.

Aimee opened it and looked down at an elderly seamstress, wearing a black apron with multiple pockets in the front. She wore three plastic tape measures strung around her neck like a stethoscope. She carried a small pad of paper and a pencil.

The woman spoke to Marlene in a Latino dialect. They exchanged information, and after, the diminutive lady nodded her head. She walked around Aimee, making notes, and then located a square stool that was hiding in the corner and placed it in the middle of the room. She motioned for Aimee to step up on it.

The seamstress's gnarled fingers suffered from arthritis, with her third and fourth fingers on her right hand the most advanced. She slipped one of the tape measures off her neck and began making calculations, jotting down various lengths. Her quiet, deliberate movements made quick work of everything, and she was done in less than ten minutes.

Tucking the pencil behind her ear, the woman explained her findings to Marlene. She gave a sweet smile to Aimee and then let herself out.

"Come, come. Finish your cappuccino, and then let's go see some dresses, shall we?"

As Marlene walked down the narrow space between overstuffed rows of beautiful gowns from sherbets to more vibrant colors, her fingers traced over the clear plastic zipper bags. Aimee soon realized that it could easily take her days to look at every beautiful dress.

"How in the world am I to decide?" Aimee asked.

"First, look at color. That's the easiest decision. And then we have to decide whether you want a floor-length gown or mid-calf or knee."

"You don't categorize them by style?"

Marlene had a huge laugh at that suggestion. "Every gown is different, and because of all the beading and intricate decorative work, that would be impossible. So let me show you what we have in red. That's a good place to start."

They carefully passed through a forest of light pink and yellow dresses, having to turn sideways to navigate the narrow channel. The majority of these were wedding gowns, but as they turned the corner, Aimee was ushered into a large classroom sized-space that was lined with racks of red cocktail dresses and gowns of varying lengths. In the center were several project tables, littered with plastic trays containing sequins, pearls, and ribbon. One woman was stitching pearls and rhinestones onto the white bodice top to a wedding dress.

Aimee turned her attention to the stuffed rows of gowns, pulling out ones that were the true red color she had in mind. Marlene examined her choices, and began relocating similarly colored dresses to a portable clothes rack so she could try them on.

In the space of an hour, Aimee found a dress exactly like what she pictured in her mind. As she stood on a pedestal in front of an arc of mirrors, the seamstress came back in and pinned the length for her. Within minutes, the hem was cut and the skirt on its way to being finished off. The seamstress made a note to adjust the waist by taking the fabric in nearly an inch.

Marlene handed her a strip of fabric that had been removed from the gown, and motioned for her to come up to the front of the store.

"What's this for?" Aimee asked.

"I'm going to have you pay for the dress now, and you can take that fabric to help you find your shoes. Your dress will be finished by the time you come back. If you can't find the right color, then buy something in bone or white. We can dye them to match, so keep that in mind if you find a comfortable pair you like."

"But I was thinking of some fancy sandals with heels, this being Florida. Something with rhinestones."

"Yes, you could do that. Make sure anything you buy has a one or two inch heel. Not only is that what your hem is measured for, it's easier to dance with a low heel than with a flat or a high heel. Just pick what you like and, remember, don't buy something too small or you'll have to sit out most of the dancing."

Aimee paid more for the gown than she'd ever paid for a dress before. But she was going to turn this into a Cinderella ball and hoped to capture the attention of her Prince Charming.

She located a comfortable pair of jeweled sandals that showed off her newly polished red toes, returned to the bridal shop, and tried the dress on one more time with sandals. Everything was perfect.

Marlene helped her load the dress into her car, gave her a chaste hug, and thanked her for her business. The entire shopping spree, including purchasing a new special bra, had taken her less than two hours. She was on her way back to Sunset Beach and had time to spare.

AIMEE WAS GLAD the men arrived early. She waited until she saw Andy's car before she put her dress on. Her nerves were firing on all rockets. She'd had to dab a towel to her underarms a dozen times in the last hour.

She examined herself in the bathroom mirror and approved. The bright red dress had a low-cut, form-fitting bodice that had necessitated her new undergarment, making her chest look twice her normal size. A multi-layered puffy sleeve draped at one shoulder, sloping down and off her other shoulder to leave it bare. The pearls were the perfect, simple complement to the elegant lines.

The skirt was slightly gathered. Layers of the lush red fabric pulled to the sides over her hips and attached at the back of her waistband in a faux bustle. She twirled, feeling the weight of the fabric perfect for the dance floor. It showed off all her best features and swayed with her body's movement. She had never felt more beautiful.

Aimee was glad her hairdresser convinced her to wear her hair down, showing off the new vanilla streaks and highlights she'd gotten this morning. She used more than her usual share of blush then added the bright lipstick and gloss. Since she was not used to seeing herself in makeup, the woman in the mirror almost looked like a strange guardian angel from one of her dreams.

Butterflies were not just fluttering inside her stomach, they were growling like bees, as she walked through her tiny living room and opened the door.

She'd never seen either of the SEALs in suits and ties, so the handsome gentlemen who were going to escort her to the wedding and party looked totally foreign. She could see they were having the same reaction to her. Nobody spoke. Cory's jaw was still gaping, his eyes wide.

Andy punched him in the arm so he closed his mouth and leaned forward to give Aimee a kiss.

She broke the ice. "Wow. Just wow. You guys are going to steal the show. Did you have to buy new suits?"

Cory nodded, rocking on his brand new black leather lace-ups.

"Shoes too?" she asked.

"Which are going to come off as soon as we can get away with it," muttered Andy. "I've already got a small blister just walking to and from the car." He fidgeted and then added, "But look at you, Aimee. I'm stunned. You're going to eclipse the bride! Don't you think, Cory?"

Cory was leaning against the doorway, his palm to his forehead, overcome. "You outdid yourself. We're going to be busy all night fighting off all the other guys, maybe even the groom, who I hear is a billionaire, so no games, okay?"

"Thank you." She could feel her cheeks heating up. "I'm totally speechless, at how handsome you two are." Aimee gasped.

"Ready?" Cory presented his elbow.

"Let me get my scarf." Aimee brought along an oversized red and white silk scarf her parents had brought to her from Hong Kong. With the bare shoulder, she wanted to be able to stay warm. If there was any wind, she'd need the cover.

They escorted her to the passenger side of the Jeep. Her skirt was a little restrictive getting in, even with the running bar, so Cory picked her up by the waist and hoisted her into the seat. Andy rounded the front and climbed into the driver's side.

She grabbed Cory's hand. "Where's your cast?"

"It didn't fit, so I cut it off."

"Cory!"

"I'm fine. It's only three days early. No biggie."

Andy was muttering in the driver seat, rolling his eyes. She started to ask him if he helped.

"Don't," he said, holding his palm up. "I caught him using a drill trying to get the thing off. He was lucky I walked in on him, or I think we'd all be waiting in the Emergency Room." And then he added, "And he'd still try to operate on himself if he could."

Aimee had told Andy she was more independent and stubborn than Cory, but now realized she'd been wrong.

The drive was easy and the traffic light. They parked, and then she hooked her arm in Cory's, and all three of them approached the church.

Several reporters were outside taking pictures of celebrities, and it wasn't long before they noticed the trio.

"Here comes our red carpet moment," Andy whispered.

Cory leaned in from the other side of Aimee, adding, "They'll never believe this in Coronado, will they?"

"I'm going to catch all kinds of hell for it," Andy shot back, whispering between his teeth, trying to give a winning smile to the photographer.

Aimee linked arms with Andy as well. "When the girls find you, it's going to be an Elvis moment, but I'm going to claim both of you, just so we're clear."

"I'm pulling for a cake fight over you, Andy. Hell, the bride might change her mind and grab you." Cory was just warming up with the jabs and pranks.

"In your dreams, Drillmaster. She'd take one look at my bank account and ask me if it was my beer money."

"It is. That's where it went," Cory answered as he turned and posed for a photo op. "Who cares if you're rich if you can't use your noodles."

Aimee gasped.

They paused to allow several long white limos to cross their path and park.

"See what you did?" whispered Andy. "On second thought, keep it up, ToolTime. Then I'll have the lady all to myself."

"Stop!" Aimee demanded. "You're making me crazy, and it's embarrassing. Can we just go inside and behave?"

Neither man said a word, but within seconds, they were both nearly doubling over in laughter.

"So much for manners. This is the bride's special day. Let's not ruin it," she scolded.

Cory leaned forward and whispered back, "I think Andy could make it even more special, right, Casanova? Or did you buy a crystal candy dish instead?"

Aimee dropped her arms and stormed off in front of them. She knew the comments they made about how the bustle on her backside bounced seductively were spoken just loud enough so she'd hear them.

She turned around briefly and glared at them.

The two SEALs stopped in their tracks. "You're right. She's even prettier when she's mad," said Andy.

Aimee whipped around and arrived at the church's foyer several seconds before they did. She was preparing to be escorted to the left side, but Cory intervened.

"No, no, no. Ain't happening, sport," he said as he removed Aimee's arm from the usher's clutches and unceremoniously pushed him aside.

The young usher's face turned bright red as he searched the church for an ally. Cory took off with Aimee in tow, searching for a seat.

Andy leaned over and whispered to the boy, "Better leave him be. He's a natural-born killer. An elite Navy SEAL. He wears ear necklaces and eats raw meat. I'd recommend not messing with him."

Cory started making dead cat noises, having difficulty holding in a laughing meltdown. Aimee could only imagine the expression that must have been on the young usher's face. At last, they found seats, Aimee between the two SEALs.

"Behave!" she whispered.

"Yes, ma'am." Cory said.

Andy didn't answer.

The smell of fresh flowers was intoxicating, and before long, Aimee noticed several members of the audience had begun to sneeze and cough. And then it hit Cory, who sneezed in a honk, like there was a horn lodged in his throat. People turned their heads.

"Now I know how you got kicked out." she murmured. "Can't you do *anything* without drawing attention?"

"Probably not, sweetheart. But at least I'm yours." He kissed the side of her cheek in an uncharacteristically sweet gesture.

It was a long, elegant ceremony. When they exited the church, the sky was turning bright orange, which meant there would be a gorgeous sunset at the beach. They followed the long line of cars, winding through neighborhoods with world-class tropical gardens and mansions nestled in the foliage large enough to look like hotels. Elegant gates guarded everything.

At the country club security gate, Andy handed in their invitation so they could be admitted. They parked under the shade of a cluster of palms.

They were ushered into a complex of enormous connecting white tents sporting brightly-colored flags. They were asked to sign the guest register, and Aimee did so, then handed the pen to Andy. Cassanova and ToolTime added theirs right below.

Bouquets of flowers, mostly shades of peach pastels and ivory roses, were hanging upside down so that people traveling under them would be showered with a heady aroma. Embedded in the flowers were LED lights that twinkled. It was truly a stunning display.

Cory immediately steered her to the bar like it was a grave emergency. Andy followed not far behind but got held up by the ladies of the bride's wedding party.

"You came!" Ginger said as she gave him a bear hug he wasn't ready for.

"Let's get him a drink," Cory whispered.

Aimee watched the ladies engage Andy in conversation. He looked smashing in his black suit. They peppered him with questions and were clearly vying for his attention. He was patient, taking the time to speak to each of them, even though she noticed he held his hands together and appeared a bit stiff. He caught her glance and smiled back, arching his eyebrows, to tell her he was uncomfortable with all the attention. Aimee had known men half as good-looking who were way more wrapped up in themselves.

Casanova. It was the perfect description.

"Come on, Hot Lips, let's rescue the old guy," Cory said as he handed her a glass of champagne. He held two long-necked beers in his other. Aimee followed. She noticed the relief in Andy's eyes at the sight of Cory coming to his aid. Cory jumped right in the middle of the circle to take some of the pressure off Andy. But Aimee realized, unlike Andy, Cory was completely comfortable and in his element.

She stood outside the ring of ladies surrounding the two SEALs, alone, enjoying the dance of mating rituals as old as the world.

CHAPTER 9

ANDY WATCHED CORY and Aimee on the dance floor. Of all the things he did for her, he was most appreciative of the fact that Cory made her laugh. He just made her happy.

Sometime during the weekend, Cory was going to let Aimee know about his plans to move to Texas. The burden felt heavy on Andy's soul, as if he was not keeping a promise. But he pushed it away, knowing that he sometimes had a penchant for overthinking and worrying about too many things.

When he looked at the staging of this affair—from the decorations to the money spent on throwing such a lavish party—it occurred to him that the bride's family was more interested in making a statement than celebrating the marriage of their daughter. Something about the whole scene was a little off, out of control, like a grandiose corporate event that must have cost a fortune and taken months in the planning. Another message, something else could have been done instead. Something personal.

Aimee danced with numerous other guests, while Cory talked to a table of people, telling stories or overtipping the bartender to make stronger drinks. Cory acted like it was his party, given in his honor. He talked too much about what they did as an elite unit. The alcohol made him boastful and proud, looking for praise that he never could get enough of.

Someone had to watch over *Aimee* in Cory's absence. Someone had to make sure that where they placed their hands on her body was appropriate, giving her the respect she so deserved.

One particular slow dance had him nearly jump to his feet and tear her out of the older man's clutches. The guy's palm wandered from her waist and down along her backside, which made Aimee jump.

But Andy waited, held himself back, because as they turned, he saw Aimee was smiling. He began to understand that she'd probably smile through everything in life. She was all alone, but she wasn't lonely. He knew that Cory was a flawed individual, but Aimee would always see the good in him. No matter what.

Several women had made advances toward him, letting him know that he could ask them to dance. He even offered a couple of times. He chatted with people who passed him as he stood against the wall and watched the arena like he used to evaluate battle scenes.

He remembered the lines of girls in high school who stood together talking all evening, trying to look like they were perfectly fine with being a wallflower. Some of them would stand there all night long and never be asked to dance. They'd probably go home and share it with their pillow. He could never do that. He wondered why they tried.

Maybe that's the difference between men and women. Maybe they try harder.

In Aimee's case, she was kind and did it because it was the right thing to do. And *because* it was the right thing to do, it made her feel happy.

But things changed as Andy sipped on his third beer. He took the blinders off his heart. That's when he realized something was growing there. And it went far beyond just wanting to protect another person. In a very short period of time, she had become more than just a sister, more than just his best friend's girl.

He wasn't going to go there this evening. That would be something he could consider when he was all alone, watching the waves or lying in his bed at night wondering, about...

Aimee caught him watching her. She murmured something to her partner and sauntered through various tables. Her head tilted to the side, not showing any embarrassment and not asking permission before wrapping herself in his gaze. He could see she'd figured it out. She knew he thought she was the most beautiful woman in the whole world. In her confidence and grace as she approached him she was telling him that she knew all those things, and more.

This is so dangerous.

"Do I have to ask you to dance, Andy?" she said when she reached him.

He stumbled with his answer when she took his hand and pulled him off the wall and toward the dance floor. He didn't want it to look like he was being dragged so he walked alongside her.

"I must've danced with ten different men tonight, but you never asked me once. Why is that?" she asked, her eyes focused on her trajectory.

"I-I was going to. Just didn't want to get in the way." The frog in his throat was extremely unfortunate.

Still holding his hand, she stood still, studying his face as if looking for something in his eyes. Luckily for Andy, he was an expert at masking what he didn't want others to see.

"Then I guess I have to ask *you*. Dance with me, Andy."

Her breath and her desire washed over him, making the request deeper than her words.

"I'd love to. I've wanted to all night long." It was just loud enough for only her ears.

She turned again, and he followed behind her just as the last song was ending.

"I have to warn you, Aimee, I'm not a very good dancer."

She turned. "Nonsense. I've been watching."

As they approached the dance floor, he searched the room for Cory and found him having an intense conversation with Ginger, the redheaded bridesmaid. For a fleeting second, Andy wished Cory would show up to rescue him from what he knew was going to be a very dangerous and indulgent few minutes.

He glanced in the corner again and saw Cory kiss the girl, and he was so disappointed. He hoped Aimee didn't see the transgression so boldly played.

And then a whole new set of emotions and feelings rose as he felt her step into his space, and lay a palm in the middle of his back, while he took Aimee in his arms for the slow dance that had just started.

It was one thing to sit with her on the beach, talk to her over the campfire, go for a morning run, or share a crab omelet. It was quite another to feel her body moving under his touch, responding to him, as he remained careful, respectful and she ever so slightly held him closer and tighter against him.

He could feel her breath against his chest and noticed a pleasant heat from her body warmed him all the way to his soul every place he touched her. She smelled like heaven itself. Her red lips matched the fabric of her flowing dress that enhanced her tiny waist. That whatever-you-call-it-thing on her butt was a challenge, telegraphing her stubbornness, her backbone for good, and her strength of character.

He was lacking that strength right now, stepping too close to the edge but unable to stop.

He looked down on the top of her head. It would've been so easy to just take a few strands of her hair that fell at the top on her shoulder and slip it behind her ear. He might let his finger trace over her neck and up to her lips just to see if she'd run away. He wanted to know, if he touched her there, would she shrink back?

It was so wrong to think about this. And it was also equally wrong to know full well that if he had to hurt someone, he would probably have to hurt her. Because it was absolutely unthinkable to fall for a SEAL brother's lady. That promise had been made long before he met Aimee.

But there was no question he was falling, perhaps to the point of not being trusted.

For right now, he danced with her. He let his thumb make a slight movement back and forth on her back between her shoulder blades. He could enjoy and accept her delicate warmth, as she inched closer still and arched her back in response. He answered her subtle response by pressing her tighter against him, feeling her heavy breathing and sinking in deeper, entwining and entangling themselves further.

She looked up at him and licked her lips, her eyes focused on him. The music stopped but he was hesitant to let her go, and she didn't try to leave. He knew she wasn't afraid to show him something that she could not say. Something that had to remain a secret.

He was risking too much, and the pain of knowing it was her risk as well made it all the more tragic. There was honor in that gaze she gave him. If he crossed that line, that honor would be lost.

He looked for Cory again and was unsuccessful. One of the bridesmaids descended upon them.

"Can I steal this hunk of a man?"

Once again, it pleased Aimee to see him desired. "I warn you, he'll sweep you off your feet, pull your heart out, and return it bloody," she said with a little laugh.

Now Andy's embarrassment started to bloom. The bridesmaid moved her hips from side to side, closed her eyes and pulled her hair on top of her head as she conjured her best feminine spirits. But of course, her potion was powerless against him. He pretended to answer her movements and give her a little of what she was expecting. But when he closed his eyes, his arms were around Aimee's naked waist as she shattered beneath him.

Oh God, I've descended into Hell.

Mercifully, the dance was over. He searched for their table but found no trace of either Aimee or Cory.

"Another?" she asked him. Her upper lip was moist with tiny beads of sweat.

"I'll take a raincheck. Gotta go check on something."

He worried, as he traveled outside into the gardens surrounding the tent city, that if Cory was doing something he shouldn't and Aimee might stumble upon him. He tore back inside, checking the dark corner he'd seen Cory in before and found it empty. He checked the bar near the wedding cake set up where a crowd had gathered to watch the bride and groom cut the five-tiered cake tastelessly decorated with horses.

Beyond the crowd, he spotted Aimee coming from the restroom, and he sighed in relief. She slipped by the gathering and returned to their table to join him. As she slid her chair up to the table, her leg brushed against his.

He placed his hand over hers and whispered, "I can't. I want to, but I can't. And I won't lie."

She focused on their hands lying flat against each other. She turned her palm up and then wove her fingers through his and squeezed before pulling away.

It felt like a kiss.

He didn't have to tell her she and Cory needed to talk. It would be wrong of him to let her know of his suspicions about her boyfriend, because that didn't have anything to do with how he felt for Aimee. Someone would think it was a crime of passion, and opportunity, yet it was so painful not to be able to explain all this to her. She turned her back to him and watched the dancers, showing him the perfect, soft skin he was hungry to explore.

Pretty girls were misbehaving on the dance floor, much to the delight of everyone who knew what it was like to be young, overflowing with passion and utterly dangerous. Andy continued to look for Cory.

He whispered in her ear. "Do you know where Cory is? I haven't seen him in awhile."

She turned her head slowly, her eyes drunk with lust. "Did you mean what you said?"

He wondered if she hadn't heard him properly. "Cory. I was asking you if you'd seen Cory."

"I saw him with some of the groomsmen." She smiled. "I'm guessing he's over in the cigar and brandy tent."

That made sense, and he was relieved.

"I should go check on him. He's had a lot to drink."

"Yes, I'm noticing the pattern too," she said coldly.

Andy stood. "I'll be right back."

She took his hand again. "Did you mean it?" she asked again.

"Every word," he whispered as he bent and kissed her on the cheek.

He asked directions to the brandy and cigar tent and headed in that direction. Something on his right caught his eye. He saw a white gazebo off in the distance and, after examining further, thought he saw movement there.

He toyed with the idea he should take the high road and check the tent first, but he played his hunch and made an arc to the other side of the structure so he'd be out of the path of the entrance.

It didn't take long before he could hear the sounds of two people. And they weren't talking. Between the gasps and moans, he could hear Cory's unmistakable whispers and the word *sweetheart* he'd heard so many times over the past week.

A concrete bench stood nearby, and he collapsed on it and hung his head, his elbows resting on his knees. His eyes teared up while he waited for the confrontation he knew was brewing.

He felt like he was back in Africa, helpless to tackle the wide range of situations and events that he had to be ready for at a moment's notice. Everything would be fine. They'd get their work done. Their presence needed to protect a village during a health vaccination program, or to make sure a duly elected official suddenly voted out of office would indeed vacate. Wars were fought over little things or things that started out small, at least. Most of the time, their Team just waited like he was doing right now. And then, someone would do something stupid, or maybe just make an honest mistake or act on faulty intelligence.

His stay at Sunset Beach was supposed to be lazy, filled with fishing and lying out in the sun. Get reacquainted with his buddy. Except that he hadn't realized his buddy returned from the Middle East a different guy than Andy remembered him to be. And that really scared him.

If he'd known all that, he would have turned down Cory's offer. He could have just chilled in Coronado with some of his other friends. Except then he wouldn't have met Aimee.

And that put a dangerous spin on everything. For his own sanity, he should leave right now and avoid the confrontations coming up. Except that would make him dishonorable, and he couldn't have that.

Somewhere in the distance, a sprinkler was going off. The yellow glow coming from the tents, mixed with the sounds of music and laughter, belied the fact that all was *not* as well as it seemed.

He heard shuffling of feet and a woman's soft giggle. Someone, probably Cory, asked for silence. Something was whispered, and then Andy heard the sound of woman's heels scampering down the stairs. He saw the redhead, pretty Ginger, with her skirts lifted, running across the lawn and disappearing inside the tent.

Andy stood, walking slowly to the base of the stairs, put his hands in his pants, and hung his head. He didn't want to do this.

"Shit, Andy. You scared the piss out of me!" said Cory.

"What the hell are you doing, man?"

"I don't understand," Cory answered, searching the grounds.

"She's back at the party. I think I'm the only one who knows. But of course you know, you asshole."

"Hey, wait a minute. Don't go all hero on me. It's not what you think"

"Really?" Andy hated the sight of him.

Cory climbed down the stairs and faced him. "Okay, it was a mistake. She's been after me all night. And this is something you *don't* know. Aimee… well, Aimee and I haven't fucked in about two weeks."

"What does that have to do with it? Do you think any of that could be your fault? You know, Cory, this and the whole story about you wanting to get married and shit, it's really gotten old. What happened to you, man? This is not the guy I knew."

Cory hung his head. "I know what you're thinking, and I want to make it right, Andy. I'm so sorry."

"You're apologizing to *me?*"

"Okay, okay, I got it. I fucked up. I think the pills, the booze, and the lack of affection has just messed with my head. I'll completely turn things around. You'll see."

"You're not listening to me, Cory. You're affecting everyone around you. Are you going to make me lie to Aimee? Do I have to do that for you? Do I have to watch you make nice to her, try to con her into your graces? You're lyin', man."

"It all happened after the deployment, Andy."

"Horse shit. Nobody gets out of here without making their share of mistakes. But, Cory, the thing is, you know you're making them and you keep doing it. You can't stop, can you?"

Cory brushed over blades of grass with his toe.

"You're right."

"You need to quit the pills, stop the alcohol, and go get counseling."

"Look, Andy, I'm stronger than that. Maybe, if you help me, we can do it together, brother. Would you help me?"

"Listen to yourself. It's embarrassing, Cory. I don't want to be any part of that, Cory. I don't want anyone thinking I condone that behavior. You need professional help. Maybe you need to go to a clinic. I think the Navy would pay for—"

"Shut up. I can't tell the Navy. They'll toss me."

"They *should* toss you. You could get yourself and someone else killed. You're spinning out of control. Making bad decisions. You're going to lose Aimee, you know."

"Not if she doesn't know."

"That's B.S. and you know it."

"Well, if you're not going to help, you butt out of my business. You get the fuck out of my house and get yourself back to San Diego. I want your word you won't meddle in my relationship. You know that's wrong."

Andy should have told him he'd already stepped over the line. It was a technical infraction, but it was just as if he and Aimee had slept together all the same. But Cory didn't deserve the truth, just like he didn't deserve Aimee.

One part of Cory's argument was sound. Andy was going to have to step away and let them work it out on their own. If Cory could really straighten up and be the man he once was, it wasn't his place to take that away from him, despite his feelings for Aimee. He doubted it could be done, but he had to give Cory the chance.

But if he broke her heart or harmed her in any way, Andy would have to insert himself, and get in his face, because she deserved protection. She deserved the truth. If she didn't get it from Cory, somehow, she'd get it from him.

He owed that to her.

"You go to Texas, Cory. You tell her about your pill problems and tell her you're going away partly to work on yourself. She'd probably wait for you, you lucky sonofabitch. But you gotta be honest with her." Andy delivered the ultimatum even though he was filled with doubt and more than a little sadness.

"Okay. And what about you?"

"This is in no way about me."

"But you won't say anything?'

"Not if you tell the truth, Cory. Not if you come clean. And you need to come clean about all of it—the girls—"

"Wait! That will end the relationship right there."

Andy's doubts just increased tenfold. He was in such a horrible situation. He was close to just blowing the whole thing up.

"Can you change, Cory?"

"With some help, yes, I think I can."

"Do you want to change? Even if it means you're tossed off the teams?"

Cory was looking for angles. Andy knew how his mind worked.

"It's a lot to take in. You're probably right. I need some help. I should give her a break, but on one condition."

"What's that?'

"You don't take my place. You let me handle it."

"You better come clean and get honest with her. No more B.S., Cory. I won't be a part of that. She deserves better. She deserves the truth. And it's your story to tell, not mine. So I'll stay out of it as long as you're working on getting honest and clean."

Andy wished that he'd not just promised this to Cory. He knew he would fail, but he had to give him the chance.

"Agreed. I'm turning over a new leaf, starting tonight." Cory held his arms out to the side. Andy gave him the embrace that was asked for.

"Good luck. I'll get a motel room for the night. I'll ride back with you guys so I can make sure you get home safe, and then I'm out of here."

"You're a good friend, Andy. A true brother."

"Yeah. Well, don't make me wish I didn't make that promise to you. I mean it, Cory. I'll be your worst nightmare."

CHAPTER 10

AIMEE KNEW IMMEDIATELY something was very wrong. Andy had been gone too long, but when she saw Cory step through the far tent opening with Andy close behind, they both of them quickly darted looks in her direction and then glanced away. She knew it was bad news.

The usual bevy of female attention surrounded Cory as he tried to make his way to her, but he seemed not to be interested. He pushed his way through the little crowd like a celebrity running from the media.

Many of the other guests were preparing to leave, and the reception took on the atmosphere of a changing of the guard. There were those who were nowhere near being partied out getting ready for some serious hell-raising. The other half appeared to be those who were ready to go home.

Just by the way Cory and Andy walked, she knew they were all three in the latter group. Neither man smiled. Neither man sought her attention from across the room. And when they got closer to the table, Cory averted his eyes. She sucked it up, hoping whatever had gone on outside in Andy's search wasn't too serious.

"There you are," she began. "I was beginning to think some of the bridesmaids had kidnapped you both. I'm glad I don't have to call the police." She played dumb and discovered they saw through the ruse.

Andy's expression was one of extreme internal pain. It was impossible to read him. Cory finally sat down and took her hand. She gulped in air and braced herself.

"Sweetheart, we have to leave. And…" He looked up at Andy first, and then blurted out the rest of his communication. "We need to talk."

"About what?" she demanded.

"Not here," he whispered, lowering his head so no one else could hear.

Her spine stiffened as she withdrew her hand, stood, picked up her purse, and threw the scarf around her shoulders. If Andy was going to shut her out and there was gonna be some kind of an argument or situation, she completely agreed with Cory. This was not the place she wanted it to happen. Clearly, her Cinderella evening was over.

"I'm going to go say goodbye to the bride and groom," she muttered, staring down at Cory's seated frame.

"Fine. You go ahead, and we'll meet you in the car." Cory added a brittle smile, which made Aimee feel worse. Andy continued avoiding eye contact and had his hands stuffed in his pockets. Finally, his face blank, he nodded agreement with Cory's statement.

She found the bride and groom in a cluster of family and friends, who were also giving their best wishes and saying goodbye.

When the bride saw her, she cut through the crowd and gave Aimee a big hug.

"I am so happy you came. Thank you for being part of our special day."

"It was absolutely enchanting. Please tell your parents for me I think it was the most beautiful wedding. And the reception? Well, it's just over the top. Completely over-the-top. Thank you for the invite. We had a good time."

They hugged one more time, Aimee said goodbye, and she nodded toward the group and then left. It was an awkward exit. The room suddenly felt oppressive, like a gauntlet or a walk of shame. She worried she'd burst out in tears before she reached the exit. The most ridiculous thing about it was that she had no idea what her tears were being shed for. She was just nervous, feeling things were about to spin out of control.

Finally, the cool evening air bathed over her face, and she took a deep breath, pausing to clear her head and face whatever was coming next.

The boys were leaning against the Jeep and, when they saw her, instantly sprang into action. Andy went around to the driver side, while Cory opened the front door for her. She struggled again to get up in the seat, and with Cory's assistance, she managed to do so without tearing her dress.

Cory pulled her seat belt around her and hooked it in place. Her nerves started to rattle when he didn't give her a kiss to her cheek or say anything at all. Andy gripped the steering wheel like it was a lifeline. She turned to say something to Cory, but found herself staring at the glass of the door's window. She heard Cory climb in behind her. Andy turned the key, and they took off.

Several minutes passed in silence. The longer things were quiet, the more fear began to constrict her breathing. She opened the window a crack to get some air. She was getting impatient.

"You want some heat or air?" Andy offered.

She saw some friendship there in his eyes before he expertly masked it.

"I'm okay. But I don't want to do this, sit here like this. Are we going to talk now or…"

"Not here." Cory's statement shook her.

"Maybe you could fix us some coffee at your place?" Andy said calmly. "That's what he means." He chanced a quick glance in his rear view mirror at Cory but then steadied his eyes on the road.

So this is how it is.

It wasn't fair, but she was going to have to wait nearly an hour before she knew anything at all. She mustered the courage to speak out again.

"I'm sorry, but this is just too weird. What happened? Can you prepare me for what you want to talk about?" she pleaded with Andy.

"Aimee, I really think it's better if the three of us sit down at your place. We have some things to iron out." Andy spoke these words without taking his eyes off the road.

"Fine." Aimee adjusted her seat and then straightened her skirts. She suddenly remembered that her mother used to do that all the time, especially if she was angry or annoyed.

She could do this, whatever it was.

AIMEE SUDDENLY AWOKE, startled that she fell asleep. The car had stopped, parked in her driveway. She didn't wait for Cory, struggling but successfully extricating herself from the passenger seat. Grabbing her purse and scarf, she led the delegation to her front door.

Her eyes began to water, and her fingers shook, making it difficult to find her key. At last, she located it and let herself in. The two men closed the door behind them.

Her feet were sore.

"I have to get these shoes off. Help yourself to anything in the refrigerator. I'll be right out."

Sitting on her bed, she removed the jeweled sandals and rubbed her toes, noticing she had several blisters. In her bare feet, she made it back to the kitchen to make some coffee.

Andy and Cory had been whispering but quickly parted when she appeared. Cory had removed his jacket, but Andy kept his on.

"Anything else other than coffee?" she asked.

Andy shook his head no.

"No, thanks, Aimee," said Cory.

She got three mugs down from the upper cabinet, poured half-and-half into two of them, and then poured coffee into all three. She gathered everything together, joining the men in her cozy living room, and placed the mugs on her coffee table.

"I made yours black, Cory."

"Perfect."

Andy reached forward and thanked her for his mug while Aimee sat back, crossed her legs and waited. The warm coffee tasted heavenly.

Cory and Andy shared a look, and then Cory began. He turned to face her.

"So, Aimee, I've got some things I need to tell you."

"I'm all ears, Cory." She didn't like the way it came out but didn't feel like apologizing.

"I've not been completely honest with you."

Aimee inhaled and waited for it, whatever it was. She already knew she wasn't going to like it. But her goal was to get through the evening without bursting into tears. She was hoping she was overreacting.

"Okay. Let's get this over with," Aimee whispered.

"Andy brought some things to my attention, and I thank him for that," Cory said tentatively.

Aimee sent a frozen glare at Andy, her impatience flooding her mood.

"Look, Cory. Let's just get this over with, whatever it is. Have I done something wrong? Have I misread something? Did I offend either of you?"

Both men were quick to answer no.

Cory continued. "I received word that I was accepted to a program, a burn specialty course in Texas. I had applied for this before you and I met. And I didn't tell you that I've been in negotiations with them over the past few days."

"Well, isn't that good news? More training is good, right?" She was seeking some ray of hope, first from Cory and then Andy, but got none.

She was confused why there was so much sadness and regret in Cory's communication.

"Yes. It is good news. I was worried about my position on the Teams. I think you knew that."

Aimee nodded.

"But there's more. I've been hiding some things from you, Aimee, and I've been thinking that I should get some help with my alcohol and drug use."

She was beginning to sense the problem ahead of her.

"So that one bottle I found wasn't the only one, then? What you're saying is you've been taking painkillers, is that it?"

"Yes. And some other things too. I've been having trouble sleeping. And I've not been—"

Aimee could see he was struggling with his words.

"Just say it, dammit." Aimee was starved for the facts of his situation.

"I've also been seeing other women."

"What?" She stood. She wanted to throw her mug of coffee at him. She backed up from the table, suddenly not wanting to be around either man. "You son of a bitch. When did this start?"

Cory remained seated, his body posture was completely deflated. Aimee could also tell that Andy wished he could be anywhere else but in this room.

"It isn't about *when* it started, Aimee. It never *stopped*. That's the truth of it. It's part of my addiction. They didn't mean anything, I swear. I just wanted to start telling you the truth. Telling everyone the truth of what I've become. I'd like to earn back your trust and love some day."

Aimee had heard her fill and wanted the words to stop. Her firewall came up to shield her, as it always did. Suddenly, there was no place to hide, no protection except behind that wall. What she'd thought was her world was in fact an illusion. She had to get to safer ground, and fast.

"I want you both out of this house immediately. I want you to go away and leave me alone. I don't want to see you guys—either of you."

She knew it was not what she'd intended to say, but she wanted the conversation to stop until she could hear it. Right now, it was too much to think about.

"Aimee," Andy interceded. "What Cory is trying to tell you is that he's sorry. And he's asking for your understanding and your help. He's going to need all of our help, if he gets clean. I know he loves you."

Andy's eyes were arched, his forehead lined with worry as she looked down on him seated before her. But it was not inside her to forgive anything right now. Her stomach was churned. Her brain was shouting, scolding her for being such a fool. Once more everything she thought was good about her world was gone. And the worst thing about it was she didn't know if it *ever* had been real. How could she trust her judgment going forward? What was important right now was not to show weakness for the sake of her own pride. She wouldn't let them have that satisfaction.

"Well, thank you for the information." She allowed herself to enjoy the ice water in her veins and drew courage from it, pacing back and forth in front of them. "It's impossible for me to understand how you could think any of this would be okay with me. I feel used, taken advantage of. And Andy, apparently you knew about all this, and didn't tell me, which means you were in on it all along."

"I didn't know all of it, Aimee, I swear."

"You're asking me to believe that?"

"I understand. I'd probably feel the same way. But there were two paths and only one leads to getting healthy. Keeping secrets is the unhealthy path."

She wanted to slap him for not being honest earlier, for not giving her warning. She'd bought into the old Boy's Club routine she'd heard about with the Teams because she thought she could trust them. She was angry that she'd allowed herself to feel attraction for him, for perhaps playing into their little scheme. Was Andy the substitute? Was that the plan between them? Was that why he came out to Florida? She was filled with conspiracy theories running fast and loose through her head.

So, it all came down to trust. She didn't even trust herself, her feelings, or her judgment now.

"Andy's right. This is all on me, Aimee," said Cory.

"That's all right," she interrupted. "I think I've heard enough. I'd like to be alone now." She adjusted her tone's volume down, softening her request. "Please."

Cory stood, approaching her with his arms open, ready to embrace her one last time. She moved to the side.

"Don't touch me. You have got some nerve!"

"Aimee, please believe me. I am so very sorry. I never meant to hurt you. I hope some day you'll believe me, honey. It's my fault. I let things get out of control and I hurt the one person I cared about the most. I lost my nerve, and I lost my way. I'm going to work hard to get my honor back. I'm hoping that going to Texas will help me do that. I need to get well. This is not fair to you. I'm sorry."

"You're damned right it's not fair. But I'm done with this." Aimee walked to her front door and opened it. "I'm completely done. I have nothing more I need to hear, and I don't want to tell you all the things I'm feeling right now, because you don't deserve it, you asshole."

Cory grabbed his jacket in anger and was out the front door in seconds. Andy lingered in the doorway for a minute.

"I'm sorry, Aimee, for my part in all this. I completely understand how you might feel I'm responsible for this, and I am but not in the way you're thinking. I want you to know that you didn't cause this. You deserve so much more."

He was going to continue, but Aimee stopped him. "No, Andy. Maybe it isn't your fault, but this is something you can't fix. I'm angry because I think you're the reason he's leveled with me. I should thank you for it, but right now I'm angry as hell. Please don't disrespect me by trying to take that away from me, okay? I don't need fixing."

"I understand, really I do. Call me if you want to talk."

"Are you nuts, Andy? Get out of my sight!"

With that, he turned and headed back to the Jeep. She watched them drive away then slammed the door, picked up the three partially consumed mugs on the coffee table, and placed them carefully in the kitchen sink, overruling the urge to smash them on the ground, or throw them at Andy's Jeep.

She was going to take a shower and go to bed but then remembered her little routine. These routines were going to be very important now until she could get to the space where she could fully accept what just happened. She was going to go through the motions of being alive, taking time for her runs, and enjoying the sunsets at the beach.

The beach heals everything.

She was counting on that big time.

Aimee did one more check of the windows and doors, making sure she was as safe as she could be. She checked her father's .38 in her bedside table, confirming that it was still loaded. She unzipped the side zipper on her skirt, unhooked the bodice of her top and carefully hung them on their special padded satin hanger in her closet. She'd loved wearing the dress, and that was real. She vowed that, someday, she would feel like wearing these beautiful things again.

She removed her under clothes and her pearls, turned on the shower, and stepped inside. After the warm spray hit her face, she allowed herself to finally cry.

The worst was over. Now she had to think about pulling her life back together, frame by frame. Memories of their happy times only solidified her resolve that what had been going on from her side was real.

And she was never going to let someone like Cory hurt her ever again.

CHAPTER 11

ANDY WAS DETERMINED to pack his bags and take off for a motel, flying home as soon as he could arrange it. At least, that was the plan he'd devised as he drove them both back to Cory's.

But he worried about leaving Cory alone and didn't trust that Cory would be safe. If his friend had been on one of his California Teams, he knew there were a couple of people he could call. But he didn't know anybody on Team 4 or any of the liaisons. He considered calling his LPO, Kyle Lansdowne, to get some advice. The one thing he was most concerned about was setting into motion something that would interfere with Cory's future.

Of course, Cory had done a pretty damn good job of screwing that up himself. Andy didn't like secrets and thought there was a possibility Cory could be a danger to himself. He would never forgive himself if that happened.

He followed Cory inside the house, hoping they could air out some of the bad blood he knew existed between them. Andy didn't want to leave with things raw and bloody between them. He also wondered how many of the promises he'd made Aimee that Cory really intended to keep. He had to find that out first.

Cory collapsed into the couch.

"So what do you think of your fucking good idea now, Andy?"

Cory's bitterness infused the room with tension. And he knew it was a dangerous sign. His conscience was telling him he needed to call the cops or take him somewhere.

"I'm not happy with how it went. You know that. But I understand how she feels. Cory, you know it was gonna happen anyway. I think if you get yourself..."

"I'm not listening to you anymore. I want to get my shit together and take off, get out of this fuckin' place."

"How about we'll talk about it tomorrow. But right now..."

Cory jumped to his feet and began to pace the room in front of him, then abruptly stopped. "Do you want to stay here? You go right ahead. I've got the place paid up for another few weeks. You should take it. You go live my life. Go take my girl, too, while you're at it."

"It's not like that, Cory. Don't you see that *you* caused this?"

"I know you're right," Cory walked up to stand a foot away from Andy's body. It was a dangerous and reckless move. "I just don't fucking wanna hear it anymore."

"Maybe I should stay here tonight and make sure you're settled. Or, I also could call somebody and let you be somebody else's problem. Get law enforcement involved? Not sure that would be a good idea, but if I have to, I will. But I don't know who to call. I'm fresh out of ideas. So you tell me, should I call the cops? Should I call your LPO? Is there somebody else I should call?"

He didn't back up but stood his ground, waiting for Cory to back down. He wanted to see if he could do it, to show him that he had some kind of control over his behavior. He added more ammunition.

"The way I see it, Cory, is that you're not thinking straight. You've gotten your head screwed up and you're not thinking like yourself anymore. I wouldn't trust any decision of yours right now, and most certainly not tonight."

Cory moved away slowly and turned, looking out the window to the water beyond.

Andy added. "It's stress, man. You had a shitty deployment, and that could happen any time to any of us. And it does. But you can think about all that tomorrow when you've gotten some rest."

Andy was rewarded with a sneer followed by a glance to the refrigerator, and he knew Cory considered getting a beer. He vowed to stop him if he had to.

Cory ripped off his jacket and threw it on the ground. "God dammit."

"You got to get out of your fucking head man. Whatever you're thinking, it's fantasyland. We'll get real tomorrow. Tonight you go straight to bed.

Cory sat on the couch and slumped over his knees. "Everybody I know is at Little Creek. I start calling up there and I won't have a career."

"Maybe you don't have one now. You gotta do what's right for you. And I'm worried about you. We do it one bite at a time. I'll stay over tonight to make sure you're in bed and safe."

Cory looked up at Andy, tears streaming from his eyes. "I don't have anybody."

Andy took a seat across from his best friend. He tried to think of anyone he'd run across who had found themselves in this position. He knew about a couple of guys who had gotten jacked for selling equipment and guns, trying to make a little extra money on the side. It was a horrible violation of everything they stood for. The Navy had taken swift justice on those men, including jail time. A few of the regulars who knew about it were also busted for not informing the Navy.

But this was different. And he knew he had an obligation to make sure that a damaged and wounded soldier somehow didn't get put back on a Team where he could cause himself or others harm from the mental distraction. But Andy was just out of resources.

And even if he could walk away, the Navy would not take kindly if he didn't report it. And that was the rub. Andy knew he was involved up to his eyeballs. If he could just get Cory into some kind of a program, maybe he could work things out.

"You need to hit the bed. We'll begin sorting some of this out tomorrow morning. But you go to bed, and get some rest. I don't want you to take or use anything tonight, you hear me?"

Cory nodded. "Yeah. That's probably best."

"I'm going to sleep out here. Do you have drugs in your room?"

"Yeah, I do."

"Do I have to go through your room and clean out your drawers? Do you have a weapon here?"

"I'll get my little stash and bring it out to you. I didn't bring my Sig."

Andy packed up his clothes and set the duffel next to the couch. He was amazed he had stopped thinking about how much his feet hurt. He sat down and removed his shoes, knowing what he was going to find.

He gingerly peeled his socks off and stared down at huge red blisters. He'd known it was a mistake. The whole evening was a mistake.

Trying to live someone else's life again.

Who were they kidding? They'd gone out, bought new suits and shoes, and tried to act the part of what? Some billionaire's kid? And for what? A few fancy hors d'oeuvres and some free booze? The whole idea suddenly felt ridiculous. It was a grown up costume party.

He was happiest at the beach—eating ice cream, screaming his lungs out in a race with big fat tires, and dodging all the other normal people in the world he had been tasked to protect. Not to take from or fawn all over rich people who didn't really care who he was. None of those girls who came after Cory cared anything about him. That was what was so sad. He was a piece of meat, a conquest. The price was too high.

He slipped off his suit pants and jacket, folded them neatly, and tucked them into his duffel bag. He placed his shoes underneath the rest of the contents, resting on the bottom. He was going to sleep in his red, white, and blue boxers.

Cory brought him a baggie filled with seven or eight pill bottles, a pipe of some kind, something black and tarry looking, and a small baggie filled with dried buds. Andy tossed the bag on the couch behind him.

"We're going to talk about this in the morning. I'm gonna sleep here, on the couch, just to make sure you stay settled for the night. You try to go get a beer and I'm gonna be in your face, Cory. I'm doing this because I care for you, man. We're brothers, and I would hope you'd do the same for me. But don't go jumping on our friendship, man. Don't test me, Cory, because I want what's good for you almost more than I want anything else. You're not gonna be able to stop me, so don't even try."

"I appreciate that. You're a good friend. You're my only friend, and we're brothers."

Cory turned to go into the bedroom, and Andy called out to him. "Cory, come here."

The two men briefly hugged, ending with quick pats on the back. Andy held him at arm's length gripping his right shoulder and shaking him. "I'm pulling for you, Cory. We'll get through this, somehow."

He watched Cory disappear into the bedroom. Andy waited until he saw the lights turn out, before grabbing a blanket and pillow from his bedroom, laying them out on the couch. He picked up the bag Cory had given him, and walked out onto the patio. He set aside the firepit grate, and pushed the old charcoal to the sides. He found some tin foil in the kitchen and lay it in a double layer on the floor of the pit.

He tossed the baggie on top, poured lighter fluid on it, and set it on fire, careful to step aside from the black, acrid smoke. The last thing he did was replace the grate on top and watched until the contents were reduced to ash. He heard a tiny ping and figured the glass pipe had exploded.

Inside, he hung by the large picture window and realized the moon was still shining, sending silvery shimmers to the calm ocean. He wondered if maybe Cory had called him as a cry for help. Maybe this was all supposed to happen this way. It wouldn't be the first time he'd missed an accurate assessment of the situation.

And it certainly wouldn't be the last.

Things had worked out much differently than he'd expected. He'd caught a couple glimpses of what he didn't want. He didn't want Cory's path. He didn't want that crowd he saw at the reception. He didn't want ever again to have to hurt the feelings of a woman who had only shown him respect and friendship, who was perhaps too trusting. Based on what he'd seen of the world, he thought he knew better. He couldn't fix the whole insane world. He could only do one thing at a time, and do that right.

He would stand for Cory for now. He'd let the beach and sand in Coronado take care of the rest.

As he lay back on the pillow and wrapped the coverlet over him, he thought about Aimee. He hoped she would be okay, and hoped she'd find a way to forgive. He was sad that his choices were so limited. If circumstances were different, Aimee would be just the kind of woman he could cherish.

Dwelling on that or what she thought of him was of no use, and was too self-serving. But it didn't stop him from feeling sad for what would never be.

CHAPTER 12

A IMEE WOKE UP early, her body ready for her normal six-thirty run on the beach. She dragged her legs over the edge of the bed and sat hunched over with her chin in her hands. She didn't feel like running. She felt like staying in her pajamas all day and watching sad romance movies and crying her eyes out.

"My whole life is a bad movie," she muttered.

Aimee stood and stretched, raising her fingers to the ceiling and then dropping down to touch her toes. She messed up her hair, rubbed her scalp, and then sifted it all back into place. She walked into the bathroom and was horrified with the woman she saw in the mirror.

Her eyes were nearly shut from puffiness, the results of the crying she did every time she woke up. Mascara had slipped down and created two dark wells underneath her eyes, streaked with tears. The black half-circles as well as faint traces of glittered eyeshadow were the only visible remnants from her Cinderella pumpkin ride last night.

She splashed water on her face, brushed her teeth, and brushed her hair, putting it back into a ponytail. She wore a baseball cap so she wouldn't have to show off her puffy eyes.

Then Aimee slipped off her pajama bottoms and her IRB tee shirt before she donned her sleek black running pants and lavender fleece top. She carefully put Neosporin on her blisters, and then covered them with anklet socks. She carefully slid into her green Nikes after making sure they were laced extremely loose.

Taking a water bottle from the refrigerator, she tucked it into her back pocket, opened her sliding glass door, and stepped out into the foggy morning. Carefully, she made her way through the sand dune and then down to the beach. She found it completely deserted. It was often like this on a Sunday morning. But this morning was unusually cold and uncharacteristically foggy, so she figured most of the tourists stayed away until the sun came out.

She'd have the beach mostly to herself. That was a good thing.

The ocean looked gray. The sunrise had left the sky purple, turning to yellow-orange in streaks that would soon disappear. She stretched briefly, set her watch for thirty minutes, and then headed down her usual course, finding the firm sand closest to the surf.

Images of last night danced through her head. She took it as a good sign she could still bear to think about her red dress, the smell of the flowers, and the lavish decorations. How it felt to slow dance next to someone warm who had powerful arms. She was happy for the young bride and hoped they were happy as a couple. She also trusted that the bride knew how lucky she was.

The bicycle twins passed her, their silver hair blowing in the breeze. She waved and gave them a warm smile, which they returned.

Later on, she found a group of women running together in a pod in the opposite direction. All of them wore pink, and one of the women had no hair. Aimee gave the group a thumbs-up, and she got seven or eight in return.

She passed a heavyset woman walking alone, snuggled in a ski jacket with a checkered scarf around her neck. She passed two men who sat on collapsible stools, fishing.

When her alarm went off, she saw the path that led down to Connie's restaurant. At some point, she'd go back there. But not yet.

She wasn't quite ready yet.

She headed for home.

She knew at some point she had passed Cory's house. Aimee was proud that she didn't even try to look for it or to see if anyone was awake. She was focused on the stretch of beach in front of her, the way her lungs filled with air, and the sparkle of the pristine, white crystal sand.

As the sky became more blue, she noticed the heat of the day starting. The fog was gone, and one by one, people came out from the houses and beach trails along the shore, to play, to walk, to just be there.

Aimee knew she was close to her house when she spotted the abandoned pink house five houses down from hers. She'd always wondered about that house. No one ever sat outside on the patio, or came out on the balcony on the second floor. The windows were boarded up. The paint peeled and part of the rain gutter on the side had come undone, hanging at an angle at the side, ready to fall down completely.

The house appeared abandoned.

On a whim, she ran up and over the dunes and then carefully trudged through the seagrass. Hopping over the shallow drainage canal, she walked up the nearly deteriorated wooden steps to the patio. A barbecue had been turned on its side, the contents spilled. Two rusty lawn chairs sat side-by-side in perfect view of the ocean. She walked along the side of the house to see if she could find any window not covered in plywood.

Aimee found a door open, leading to a storage room, which contained an old freezer. A dirty mop had been stuck inside, propping up the lid. Just past the freezer was a door which, remarkably, was open.

Stepping inside a large kitchen area, a small sliver of light coming from a hole in the plywood cover made the room barely visible.

All the appliances had been torn out, or removed and left broken in the dining room. The refrigerator door was left ajar. The huge L-shaped countertop was made of 1940's vintage pink and black tile, in somewhat decent condition except for the cracked and dark moldy grout lines.

She walked into the living room and discovered she could open the front door, which let in more light. That enabled her to walk the stairs up to the clutter of broken furniture and dirty old mattresses littering the three bedrooms there. Both bathrooms were also done in four inch green tiles, trimmed in black. Someone had removed a bathtub in one bathroom, and both toilets were missing as well.

As she came down the stairs, she imagined a home decorated in pastels, pictures of beach scenes on the wall. Pillows with mermaids, starfish, and sand dollars brightened the white furniture. She saw people mingling on the patio and smelled a barbeque fired up sending delicious aromas.

She took pictures of several of the rooms with her cell, and then closed the front door, making sure it was locked before exiting the doors through the storage area the way she'd let herself in. She decided to leave those doors as she found them—open.

Standing back on the beach, she was able to take one last picture, capturing both stories, and a portion of the yard in front.

What if I could turn this home into a showplace?

A project was definitely what she needed. And, if this house didn't work, perhaps it was time she started looking. Now there wasn't anything holding her back.

Walking back to her bungalow, she sat at the counter and reached for the pad of paper she kept there with a pen. Aimee made a list of all her questions, starting with who the owner was. From memory, she listed all the things that would have to be fixed, going room by room, looking over the pictures to make sure she didn't miss anything. Added to the list was finding contractors who she'd hire to do the work. She needed the name of a local Realtor to help her decide what it would be worth when she finished to see if it was even worth doing the project at all.

During her shower, she remembered the young man at JJ's who looked like her brother. That was another loose end she wanted to explore.

As she put moisturizer on her face and blow-dried her hair, the lady she saw in the mirror now didn't look anything like the wreck who had greeted her this morning. Even her eyes had started to lose their puffiness.

Her stomach began to call, so after getting dressed for a warm Florida fall day, she put on flip-flops, which would help with the blister healing and decided to go to JJ's for breakfast to see if she could find the kitchen helper she'd seen that night.

She called Shelley.

"Good timing. I was just going to cook some eggs. I'll meet you there in a half hour? Give me time to shower."

"Perfect."

AIMEE WAS FIRST to arrive and took a table in the corner by a large statue of a lobster holding a tray and wearing a tux. She'd seen tourists take their picture in front of it on many occasions.

Her server approached with the mug of coffee she'd ordered. "My friend will be here soon."

"Great, I'll come back then." The young server looked to be about high school age.

"Say, can I ask if the owner is here?"

"What's wrong?"

Aimee laughed. "Not to worry. Nothing's wrong. I just have a question about someone who works here."

"Who?"

"Well, do you know a Logan Greer? He'd be a little older than I am."

The server cocked her head and considered the question. "I don't think we have anyone named Logan here, but I only work the early breakfast on weekends. They have a full staff at night, especially when they have entertainment."

"Yes, this was on Wednesday, I think. There was a band here. It was packed. That's the night I saw him."

"Well, the owner doesn't usually come in on Sundays, but even then, I'm not sure he's as familiar with the staff. We have a restaurant manager. He hires us and the bartenders and some of the kitchen staff. And we have a bookkeeper who does the payroll. She comes in on Mondays, so you'd have to catch her tomorrow. That's the only day she works. I don't know when Roger will be in, but his hours are not set."

"Would you be willing to give me their phone numbers?" Aimee asked.

"You just have to call the restaurant. I don't even have a way to reach them outside of work. But calling the restaurant would be your best bet."

Aimee pulled out her clipboard and asked for the manager's name as well as the name of the bookkeeper. "Thanks so much."

Shelley walked through the door, and Aimee gave her a wave. "Here's my friend now."

"Hi there," Shelley said, giving her a big smile.

"Would you like some coffee?" the server asked.

"I'd love some."

The young girl went in search of coffee. Aimee was anxious to tell Shelley about the house she found.

"I was running on the beach this morning, and I found this house that's very close to my place. It looks like it's abandoned. I walked through it and I took some pictures. Let me show you."

She placed her cell phone on the table and scrolled through several of the pictures, watching Shelley's expression. At first her friend was excited, but as she viewed the photos, her expression grew sour. She pushed the cell phone back across the tabletop.

"What do you think?" Aimee asked.

"Honestly?"

"Yes!"

"I think you've lost your mind. This place is a dump. I mean, this is a contractor's dream. Do you have any experience doing any of that work? This isn't just paint and carpet and drapes, you know?"

"I *do* know. I've got a list of things I need to find out about, and of course I need to figure out what it would cost. But wouldn't it be great?"

"Well, Aimee, you're talking a lot of money here. And if you have to hire a contractor to do it all, I'm not sure it would work out. I mean, this looks like a money pit."

Aimee could see there would be no convincing Shelley that what she was going to entertain was a good idea. But that wasn't gonna stop her.

"What does Cory think?" Shelley asked.

Her comment made Aimee freeze in place. All of a sudden, her world got small. She temporarily forgot the pain of last night, and all her former confusion came screaming back. Along with all the pain and the tears.

"I haven't told him yet." She couldn't make eye contact.

"Well, I think Cory would know some people. He'd certainly know much better than I. But I suppose he'll have to go back to Virginia, so I don't know how all that timing will work for you."

Aimee decided not to tell Shelley about her situation. "I'm just toying with the idea. I thought it would be fun to look at places, maybe invest in a little place here."

"Sure, I think that's a great idea. Do you have the down payment?"

"I have some from my parents. I just wasn't sure I wanted to buy something here."

"Well, we're not that far from Little Creek, or at least closer than you'd be in California. I guess it depends on where you want to live, Aimee. Have you thought about that? Have you and Cory made any plans?"

That comment caught her off guard. "No, no plans. There is just something about this place that feels good to me, Shelley. It's not perfect. But there's something about the beach—this beach, in particular—that makes me feel like it's home."

Aimee was a little fragile inside, and when she felt tears beginning to well up, she quickly grabbed her coffee and took several long sips.

The server brought Shelley's coffee and a refill for Aimee. They ordered. Then came the awkward silence Aimee was dreading.

"Is Andy still around?" Shelley asked.

"I suppose so. Why?"

"I was hoping that by now he would call me." Shelley tilted her head and then looked up at Aimee. "Has he said anything? Anything about me?"

She didn't like lying to Shelley, but she had to.

"I'm sorry, but I really haven't had much communication with them. I've sort of left the two of them to be together. You know how it is."

"Yes, believe me, I do. But I just thought…"

"Sometimes I have a hard time understanding Cory."

Shelley nodded and drank her coffee. Aimee was glad that her friend didn't pry. She was positive that Shelley picked up that something strange was going on.

"If I see him again before he leaves, I'll tell him we spoke."

Shelley beamed. "Thank you."

CHAPTER 13

ANDY MADE COFFEE, trying to stay quiet enough to keep Cory sleeping. Pouring himself a cup, he drowned it in half-and-half, and then took the coverlet outside with him to sit on one of Aimee's chairs, watching the ocean.

The gray morning matched his insides, and even the coffee didn't do anything to change his mood. He wanted to go back to California as soon as he felt it was safe to do so. He was hoping Cory would be able to make contact with the people in San Antonio to get him set up.

He watched several beachcombers search for shells that had washed up during the night. The beach was nearly deserted. He sat back, closing his eyes and checking his insides.

Andy knew he should give his LPO a call. It was too early to do so for another few hours, but he decided, no matter what Cory's state of mind, that call would have to be made.

I should have left a message last night.

But last night, he'd been exhausted. He needed the rest just as much as Cory did. The lumpy couch was no substitute for a real bed.

As the sun rose behind him, he noticed more travelers on the beach. A dark form emerged from the distance and then crossed in front of the house. He would recognize those shoes anywhere. His heart skipped a beat as he did the only thing he could do, just watch as she came into view and then slipped back into the fog and out of his life.

It wasn't numbness but the costume, the mask he wore to hide emotions he needed to push back. It wasn't that he lacked caring. He cared too much and didn't have the capacity to do anything about it.

This wasn't the time for second-guessing.

HE MUST HAVE fallen asleep, because he heard the sliding glass door open behind him, as he jerked fully awake and discovered he had a stiff neck. It had gotten considerably warmer, and now the sky was bright blue. He figured he must have slept slumped in the chair for an hour or more.

Cory leaned over and picked up his spilled coffee. "You want a refill?" he asked as he held the mug up.

"Sure. Thanks, Cory."

Andy wondered now if the vision of Aimee running down the beach wasn't just a dream he'd had.

Cory was shirtless, wearing only polar bear flannel pajama bottoms. His hair was splayed all over his head, growing like tufted sea grass, and he yawned as he leaned over and gave Andy the warm mug.

"You look like shit."

Andy figured he deserved that.

"Look at you, ToolTime. Got your jammies on, I see."

Cory grinned, curling his arms and flexing his pectoral muscles. "We're the pair, aren't we?"

Andy sipped his coffee. It was bitter and too overheated.

"What the hell is that?" Cory was pointing to the tin foil and ashes in the fire pit.

"That's hopefully the last of your bad habits, Cory. I forgot to clean up." Andy removed the grate, peeled the tin foil up at the edges, and rolled the whole thing into a hamburger bun-shaped blob. He excused himself to the kitchen, and disposed of it in the garbage.

"You just put about six hundred dollars up in smoke."

"Better than in your lungs and bloodstream, Cory. Sit. Can we work out your next move?"

Cory pulled the other Adirondack chair closer and deposited himself. "I already made a call to San Antonio, but it's Sunday, and I'm not sure I'll hear back until tomorrow."

"Good. How do you feel?"

"I'm good. Feel like I've been eating garbage all night. My head hurts. I'm guessing it will really start hurting as the day goes on." He was tracing the top of the coffee mug with his forefinger. "And I even called a guy I know who's in a twelve-step program. A former Team Guy."

Andy was impressed. "That's a smart move."

"He's offered to take me to a meeting. What do you think?"

"That's the kind of friend you need right now, Cory. I don't have any experience with these programs, but a lot of guys get help there. Gals too. We aren't the only ones."

"He says there's a meeting tonight I can go to. Do you want to go with?"

"No thanks. I think that's something you two should do together."

"Okay, so if I do, will you be here when I get home? Or are you leaving?"

"I can stay. I didn't make any plans or change my flights home yet. Let's find out what's going on with San Antonio, and then I'll decide."

"Fair enough. Can I ask you another question?"

"Shoot."

"Have you ever heard about other guys like me? I mean, what did they do for help?"

"I'm guessing the answer to that is a resounding yes, but the old guys would be your best bet. I think your former Team Guy would be a great place to start. I'm not really qualified to answer. Only thing I'm here for is to make sure you stay willing to change. I don't have any special potion or advice. You're the one going to do the work, if you want it enough, Cory. If you were in California, I have a couple of guys I'd have you call. But not out here."

Cory had a craving for pancakes smothered in syrup, so he directed Andy to his favorite Samoan pancake house where they stocked up on carbs. When they returned home, Cory got the call from San Antonio. The Joint Base San Antonio-Fort Sam Houston Burn Center had facilities for him to stay right on the hospital grounds. They also had an outpatient drug and alcohol treatment clinic privately contracted by specialty physicians both inside and outside the military community. The services would be free to him as long as he was enrolled in the special training. Best of all was that there were counselors available nearly any time of the day or night.

Cory offered to fly out as soon as his paperwork came through, and they indicated that, if he flew out sooner, rather than wait the two to four weeks for the Navy to process it, he'd have a room and could begin class with the rest of the group who were due to start the following week.

And they said they'd take care of the final sign-off for his injury, as long as he didn't have any complications.

Andy loaned him the money to catch a plane the next day.

"You remember what I said about my bank account, Cory? I used all my savings on special equipment I purchased for the trip to Africa. I gotta have this back."

"I'll return every penny. Not sure I can do it right away, but I'll pay you back."

"Then I say go with my blessing. Make the most of your opportunity. It's going to get tough, but hang in there."

When Cory's friend arrived, Andy was introduced. The former

SEAL was a scary looking dude. He stood about three inches taller, nearly outweighing both Cory and Andy together. He looked more like a former NFL player. His arms were covered in colorful tats with scary dragons, snakes and fanged demons. It was obvious the man had pulled himself out of some kind of Hell. Andy was glad he'd decided not to go with them, but he knew Cory would be safe.

"I hope I'll be crashed. Looking forward to going to bed early to catch up on my sleep." To the big guy, Andy nodded, "Thanks."

"No problem, brother."

Andy watched them leave. Cory climbed into the passenger side of a black custom monster truck. The engine rattled all the windows of the house as Cory was chauffeured away in a cloud of smoke.

Remembering the truck at JJ's, Andy chuckled.

"Say hello to Phyllis."

He was still shaking his head, laughing, as he walked out on the sand, not wanting to miss the sunset. He worshiped dying sun like everyone else who had come out that night.

It was spectacular.

CHAPTER 14

AIMEE'S MONDAY MORNING run was easier than yesterday's. Convinced that routine and staying busy would help heal the wounds and disappointments of her heart, she showered, grabbed some yogurt for breakfast, and drove down to JJ's, hoping to see either the restaurant manager or the bookkeeper.

She had left a phone message for both of them.

The Monday morning crowd wasn't anything like Sunday, and she nearly had the restaurant to herself. She ordered coffee and a bowl of oatmeal and waited for the manager to come join her at the table.

Mr. Roger Valdez was a very trim man in his late forties, with a pencil thin mustache and dark black, curly hair. He spoke with an accent Aimee thought was either Cuban or South American.

"What can I do for you?" he said as he pulled up a chair across the table from her.

"Mr. Valdez, I was here last week on Wednesday night, and I saw two people in the parking lot. One of them resembled my brother, who has been missing for about seven years. I came to ask for your help, if you're able."

"This person was a guest?"

"No, I think he works here."

"We have a lot of turnover here, Miss Greer, is it?"

"Yes, but you can call me Aimee."

"Can I ask your brother's name, please?"

"Logan Greer."

Valdez sat back in his chair, folding his arms over his lap, tapping his four fingers on his left upper arm. "Like I said, we must go through probably three hundred, maybe four hundred people a year. The restaurant business is not very skilled, and we get college students who are in transit, people just passing through in all circumstances. A very transient crowd, I must say. It's difficult to find someone who will stay long-term. But I honestly do not remember his name."

"I understand your bookkeeper, Mrs. Jackson, works today?"

"Yes." He checked his watch. "She arrives, in about thirty minutes, if you can wait."

"Would it be possible for you to check your records?"

"Yes, we can do this. However, I have to wait for Mrs. Jackson first. She has all the files."

"The two men I saw in the parking lot were arguing. One was a rather short, heavyset man. The other one, possibly my brother, was tall and thin. They were having some kind of an argument, and when I called his name, both of them disappeared in opposite directions."

"So he didn't wait on you, or you didn't see him in the restaurant?"

"No, but they both wore white jackets. They looked like kitchen help. Perhaps cooks?"

Valdez crossed his legs and slapped his knee. "The kitchen staff. This is our biggest problem. I have an extremely volatile head cook, and many of our helpers find they can only tolerate him a little. I have tried very hard to explain things to Sergio, but this is his world. He is my only long-term employee, and the owner has made me promise that he will never be fired."

"Is he a bit heavy and not tall?"

"Yes, it sounds like him. I have seen him fire people before in the parking lot."

"So when does your cook arrive then?"

"Well, some of them are here now. And they are doing prep for dinner already. I think our Sergio doesn't like to get up with the sun. It will be noon. If you come back then, you'll be able to talk to Mrs. Jackson as well."

"Thank you for your time."

Aimee shook the manager's hand and wrote down notes on her tablet. She had about three hours to kill so decided to take a drive to the Tax Collector's office and do some research on the pink house.

Memories of Saturday night floated through her head, reminding her how she felt during the silence of the car on their way back to Aimee's house. This time, as she passed through several little beach towns along Gulf Boulevard, each one taking less than five minutes to drive through, she was in a different frame of mind. But she wondered if Andy had left for California. Or perhaps he took Cory to Texas on his way back.

She decided it would be a good idea to try writing down signs of houses that were for sale. She also needed a Realtor recommendation so she could familiarize herself with the market and prices.

Aimee passed multiple ice cream shops and two-story beach stores that sold everything from inflatable flamingos to boogie boards, bathing suits, and beach towels. She drove past the bicycle rental spot and one of her favorite ice cream shops that made the best Cuban sandwiches she'd ever tasted.

The Tax Collector's office shared a building with the Public Works Department. It was next door to City Hall, also in shared quarters.

Inside, a row of file cabinets lined one wall. On top of the last one was an oscillating fan, silently circulating air. A cheap radio played country music in the background. The office appeared to have two employees, both seated behind metal desks.

An attractive woman with black cat-eyes glasses, studded with rhinestones, looked up and asked, "Can I help you?"

"Yes, I'd like to find out the owner's name and address of a piece of property."

"You have the address?"

"Yes, right here." Aimee didn't want to shout the address across the room because she knew, with the town being so small, her chances of keeping her inquiry a secret were greatly diminished.

She held up her tablet to show the woman, who approached the counter, turned the tablet around, and then wrote the address on a slip of paper. "I'll be right back."

Aimee searched the walls, covered with local artist photographs, watercolors and oil paintings depicting various places around Sunset Beach. She noticed photographs of the dog park, a beach access bridge made of wood, the surf, and the sand dunes. She also saw a cluster of small oil paintings done in plein-air style, depicting small bungalows, brightly colored, and trimmed in equally bright contrasting colors. Examining one of the tags, she saw they were part of a local artist's collective, like the paintings at Connie's.

The attractive blonde woman had been combing through pages in a black three-ringed binder. She clicked it open, removed a small sheaf of papers and brought them up front.

"I'm afraid you'll have to show identification, and I will make you copies of these pages, but they are a dollar apiece."

"How many do you have?" Aimee asked, presenting her California driver's license.

The woman counted the pages scrolling at the upper right with thin fingers.

"I count thirteen."

Aimee opened her purse again and produced a credit card.

The woman shook her head. "I'm sorry, we only take cash."

Any produced a twenty dollar bill.

"I'm sorry, we don't have change."

From across the room the other woman spoke up. "Oh heaven's sake, Sylvia, I've got the change." She lay a ten and two fives on the counter. "That's the best I can do, sorry."

Aimee handed her the twenty. Then she gave the blonde woman fifteen. "Perhaps you can apply the change to your library fund," Aimee whispered.

Without answering, the blonde woman turned on her heel and brought the papers to a large copy machine and then returned with Aimee's copies.

Anxious to read the records, she sat.

The legal papers were confusing, but it appeared there was a living trust that had ownership, on behalf of a woman who lived in Sarasota. From the tax records, the trust had been created some twenty years ago by a man, whose address was listed as the property.

How could that be?

She knew that she might have to contact the attorney handling the trust and perhaps try to go search out this woman, Carmen Hernandez.

Checking her watch, Aimee realized it was time to return to JJs. She folded the paperwork, tucked it in her purse, and headed back south along the Boulevard.

This time, the restaurant was filled with people on lunch break. She looked for Mr. Valdez and waved to him once they made eye contact. He motioned for her to follow.

They climbed a narrow stairway leading to a tiny office cluttered with papers, boxes of more papers, and shelves stacked with papers. Aimee thought it looked like a hamster lived there, or at least someone averse to filing.

Hunched over her desk and buried in a handwritten ledger, was an attractive African-American woman, who wore her hair short, and dyed bright orange. Even her fingernails were painted orange.

When Mr. Valdez introduced her, Mrs. Jackson smiled, revealing even her lipstick was orange.

"You the nice lady who left me that sweet message?"

"Yes, ma'am."

"Well, Mr. Valdez says that this particular man was working here last Wednesday?"

"Yes, that's when I saw him. He was in the parking lot, and there was some kind of an argument going on."

Mrs. Jackson rolled her eyes and let her fingers flutter through the air. "That kind of thing happens all the time here. Mr. Sergio runs them out the back door almost as fast as we take them in."

"Yes, Mr. Valdez told me."

Valdez needed to get back to the floor. "Everything okay here?"

"Right as rain. I'll send her down in a couple of minutes." She closed her ledger. "So Mr. Valdez says your brother's been missing for more than seven years?"

"Yes. When my parents were alive, they tried multiple times to find him. He's originally from California." Aimee looked around the room for a chair to sit.

"Just take those boxes off that chair over there and put them on the floor. I'm sorry, I should've offered it to you." Her face showed concern. "Let me ask you this, do you have a picture of your brother?"

Aimee wasn't sure if she still had the family photograph she used to keep in her wallet all the time. "If I do," she continued to search the pockets of her billfold, "it was taken over ten years ago. Not sure you would recognize him now."

While Aimee continued to finger through cards, notes, receipts, and credit cards, Mrs. Jackson asked her, "So you haven't seen your brother in seven years, then? Has anybody seen him?" She'd pulled a manilla file out of her desk drawer, briefly opened it, but then covered it with her arms.

Aimee found the small picture, and carefully removed it where it had stuck to the back of her Social Security card. "Here we are. I was a sophomore in high school. He was a year ahead of me."

She handed the photograph to Mrs. Jackson.

"What a lovely family. You sure growed up nice. Your brother looks a lot like you." She leaned into the photograph and examined it more closely. "I'm thinking I've seen this boy. Of course, he's not a boy now."

Aimee's heart nearly leapt out of her chest. She had never hoped to find Logan, let alone find him here in Florida.

"So does he work here? Will he be coming in today?"

"I'm sorry, Aimee. I'm gonna have to refer you to the place where we get some of our helpers. I'm not supposed to give you much information, you know. It's the law. But I feel for you."

"What do you mean organization?"

Mrs. Jackson bit her lower lip, her eyes down cast.

"Please. I need to find him."

"Were you aware he's got problems?"

"Yes. That started not long after this picture was taken. He had a drug problem. Long history of drug problems."

"Okay, then. Well as far as coming to work today, I can tell you that's not happening. Apparently, if he's this boy, this man, I'm pretty sure he's the one that Sergio fired." She gave Aimee a long look before she said, "He came from a halfway house. It's a drug diversion program for drug offenses. Our owner likes to help those who can't help themselves, and we get a steady stream of these kids, men and ladies, and, well, many of them work out and go on to do other things. Over half of them don't make it. And I'm sorry to say, if he is your brother, he's one of the ones who didn't."

"Can you tell me where this halfway house is?"

"First of all, he doesn't use the name Logan Greer. I would probably get in a whole lotta trouble if I told you what name he used. But I can give you the name of the halfway house. Maybe he's still there."

Aimee hugged Mrs. Jackson, and she danced down the stairs, clutching the address of the Sunshine Palms rehab facility. She wasn't sure exactly what she was going to find, but now she knew that she might be able to connect with the remnants of her family.

She wasn't doing it for Logan or even for herself. She was doing it for her mom and dad.

CHAPTER 15

ANDY AND CORY left for the Tampa airport when it was still dark outside. He had a seven-thirty flight with one layover.

"If she asks, will you tell Aimee I made it? I'm going to Texas?"

"Of course I will. But she made it pretty clear how she wanted that to go."

"I'm just gonna keep it simple, Andy. This is going to be a really challenging course from what I've heard. But it should give me some good creds. I'm going to be a student-fiend, just focus on the work."

"And getting healthy."

"Absolutely. Put everything else out of my mind."

"I think that's wise. Take it a little chunk at a time, Cory. With nobody looking over your shoulder, don't go telling yourself you can have just one beer or some dumb shit. No creative thinking, okay?"

"Right. Some of the stories I heard last night, they started exactly like I've been doing. Some of these guys lost their houses, their families. A few of them even live under the freeway, and they still go to meetings."

"I think you should feel grateful. You let it slide one time, and then it starts all over again. You got to go back to zero."

"Well, I'm ready."

Andy pulled into short-term parking which got a reaction out of Cory. "You don't have to do that. Just drop me off at the curb."

"Nope. I'm making sure you're on that plane."

The airport was only half-open. Many of the airline kiosks were closed and the TSA lines were nonexistent. Cory checked one large suitcase and was handed his tickets. He threw his computer bag over his shoulder, and the two men hugged.

They parted at the entrance to the First Class line. Cory showed his military ID, and was shuttled to the front.

Andy lost track of him once he got through screening.

Andy muttered a little prayer for his safety. "Godspeed, Cory. Take the chance you're given. Don't fuck it up."

CORY HAD CONVINCED Andy to stay a little bit longer in the house. At first, all he wanted to do was go home and get someplace where it was familiar. He missed having bonfires on the beach with the guys, the workouts, and having beers at the Scupper.

The ride home was going to take more time, since it was a Monday and the traffic was heavy. He stopped to buy some breakfast and then continued back, headed at last toward the beaches.

Just like the first time he walked in, the picture window in the living room took his breath away. It had turned out to be a nice fall day after all, but rain was forecasted for tomorrow. He could see the huge gray clouds forming on the horizon.

He moved his duffel bag to the bed in the spare bedroom, then sat out on the patio and watched the water and the carnival of people walking by.

He decided to give Kyle Lansdowne, his LPO, a call.

"Hey, Andy, have you been good?"

"Not too good, thanks."

"I'm glad. You deserve a little R&R." After a brief silence, Kyle asked him why he was calling.

"I kind of ran into a situation here with Cory, and I wanted to run it by you."

"That's a shame. You two are close. Did you guys have a falling out?"

"Yes and no. It's complicated. I just wanted to make sure I handled it correctly."

"Okay, I'll see if I can help."

"Cory got himself jacked up on painkillers for his elbow fix, and to make matters worse, he was doing quite a bit of drinking. I didn't worry about it at first, because I didn't realize he was still using the pain pills. But he was drinking all day and would start right after breakfast. I got worried when I found out he was doing the pills too. That's when I had to draw the line."

"Ouch. Not good. What do you want from me?"

"I trust your judgment, Kyle. I just wanna know I did the right thing."

"Well, that depends, of course, on what you did."

Andy was annoyed with himself. It was a lot harder to talk to Kyle than he had anticipated.

"We had a pretty bad argument, and I pretty much got in his face and told him he needed to clean himself up, get some help or, I threatened to call the cops, which of course would get the Navy involved."

"I'll bet he didn't like that one bit."

Andy could hear Kyle's children in the background.

"Excuse me, Andy, I have to go break something up."

"Go right ahead." He listened while Kyle raised his voice, and after a quick discussion, several kids chattering at once, someone got a swift spank. Silence followed.

"I'm back. Christy's working today, so I'm watching the kids, and we have Danny's here too."

"No problem. Sounds like it got resolved."

"It did. It most definitely did."

"Anyway, I felt like a traitor, but I was worried he was going to do something dumb."

"Okay, so what happened?"

"I told him he should go check himself into somewhere and get some treatment. That's when he told me that he had applied to Burn School in San Antonio, and they accepted him."

"That's a good program. He was lucky to get in that one."

"Yeah, I thought so too. I really worried he'd blow the opportunity."

Andy watched as a little kid was riding on one of the fat tire bikes, and had the speed cranked up and was going too fast. Just as he predicted, the boy lost control when he got caught in the surf. The bike stopped, but he kept going, flipping end-over-end over the handlebars.

"I just saw a major wipeout with one of these beach bikes you can rent. The kid's going to be okay, though, it seems."

"You need to go check on him?"

"No, he had several adults chasing him to begin with.

"Got it."

"Anyway, I wasn't the only one he's been hiding things from. He had a really nice girl here, and she broke up with him, when she found out all the stuff he was doing. So, the long and short of it is, I shipped him off to San Antonio this morning. I paid for his ticket so he'd get there and have a room on the hospital campus. Apparently he can get some counseling and treatment there since he's enrolled in the school."

"Sounds like everything's going to sort itself out. I'd say you did good."

"I just want to know if I should have done more. Am I obligated to report this? I don't want the Navy breathing down my neck if they think I didn't bring it to someone's attention."

"You're doing that now, Andy. But I wouldn't worry about it. I mean, he's going to be in a hospital setting, a facility there where they can take care of him if he goes off the rails. They run a pretty tight ship. The Army doesn't take too kindly to SEALs messing up their program, so I think it would be dangerous to have someone intervene and give them advanced warning. Let them figure it out for themselves. He's going to be watched like a hawk. They'll bust him for anything, trust me."

Andy was relieved.

"Now, that's not to say he couldn't find somebody to get in trouble with, but if he's motivated, he should be okay. It's not like he's been doing this for a couple of years or anything, right?"

"Right."

"I wouldn't punish yourself or overthink it. I think you helped him dodge a bullet. That's good on you."

"Thanks, Kyle."

"Do you want me to give you some referrals, see if I can get some names over at the joint base?"

"That would be good. Just in case."

"Good. I'll dig around and text them to you tomorrow. So how much longer are you staying?"

"I'm supposed to come back in about a week. It's beautiful here. But it's way different than California."

"Oh yeah, that's nice over there on the Gulf."

"I was thinking… Cory paid up rent through the end of next month on this house here. I was wondering if I could extend my time here a few days longer. What do you think?"

"You had a tough one, especially for your first tour. I can authorize an extra week, even two, if you need it. If you stay in shape, all you'd be missing here is a little bit of work up. We don't have our next assignment yet. So stay and get some of that beach time that you missed before. It's hard on a guy when you have to watch out for somebody else. You're a good friend. He's lucky to have you. I've had guys who nearly get killed worrying about someone else on a mission, always watching for them to do something stupid. Just kick back and enjoy it for a little while, and then come home."

"Thanks, Kyle. I really appreciate that. I'll let you know a couple of days ahead of time."

"No problem. Don't expect a limo at the airport or anything."

Andy chuckled. "Can you believe it? I was going to send the Team some oranges and you can't ship them to California. Did you know that?"

"I do now. Get lots of rest, kid. And get some running in, and get to the gym. You know the drill."

"Yes, sir, I do."

"And, Andy, go get laid. That's an order."

CHAPTER 16

AIMEE HAD CALLED ahead to the Sunshine Palms, and she was told that non-patients—even family members—were not allowed to visit without prior medical authorization. She tried to get herself an appointment with one of the counselors, but she kept getting stalled.

In the morning she was going to keep to her normal routine. She'd take her hour-long run along the beach, and then she was going to attempt a visit in person. She'd see if she could worm her way inside.

She'd tossed and turned all night long, unable to sleep. Even the cup of hot chocolate and a little romance TV at midnight didn't help. She tried to read, and her eyes wouldn't focus.

Taking a shower usually relaxed her, so she used her lavender shower gel that always left a soothing, gentle scent on her skin. She changed her pajamas to a fresh nightgown and finally was able to fall asleep.

Six o'clock in the morning came very early. She slipped on her black running pants, and her lavender fleece top. Placing her hair in a ponytail, she decided not to wear her baseball cap. She grabbed a water from the refrigerator, placing it behind her waist in the pocket, and headed to the door. When her feet touched the outside, she realized she'd forgotten to put on her shoes!

Back in the bedroom, she applied first aid cream to her blisters, gingerly covered them with ankle socks, and once again slipped into her green Nikes.

There was no fog today. Just a beautiful rose, purple, and orange sky, reflections of a sunrise happening behind her to the east. She set her watch for thirty minutes, and started her run.

There were several more people out this early, since it was supposed to be an extremely warm day. She greeted the two bicycle twins, and the woman's group running to strike a blow for breast cancer, again.

"Good going, ladies!" she shouted.

"You too!" they said, along with several virtual air high-fives.

A pair of older men were working near the water's edge with metal detectors. A young couple sat on one of the benches next to a beach access trail. An older couple walked hand-in-hand.

In the distance, she saw the dark outline of someone sitting on the sand, watching the waves. As she approached, he turned his head in her direction, and she instantly recognized Andy.

She nearly stumbled, so surprised. Her left foot crossed over her right, and she lost her balance for a second. He was on his feet in a flash, but she'd already righted herself and didn't need assistance.

"What are you doing here?" she asked.

"I'm at Cory's for a few days more. I don't want to interfere with your run, but can I join you?"

Aimee felt her cheeks and neck turn blotchy red, like what always happened when she was nervous. Her swarm of buzzing butterflies set up a vibration in her chest that caused her breathing to hitch.

"Okay, let's go," she agreed.

Aimee resumed her somewhat faster pace, and he stayed right next to her, matching her stride in tandem. There were so many things running through her mind as she tried to focus on the crunch of shells beneath her feet, the sounds of the waves crashing on the beach, and the faint calling of birds. But she also couldn't help but hear his heavy breathing.

What she'd been most afraid of, came true. He knew what he was doing, she thought. *He knows if he doesn't say anything, I'll die of curiosity.* That was so unfair.

"You surprised me. I never expected to see you again, Andy."

"I saw you the day before yesterday on your run. I wasn't sure you'd speak to me."

Aimee paused. Then asked, "So when do you leave for California?"

"I haven't decided yet. Cory's gone to Texas and offered to let me stay in the house for a little bit. I'm supposed to box up his things and send them out to him in exchange."

"So, he's moved there, permanently?"

"It's a year-long training program, if he makes it through. Not everyone does."

Aimee developed a cramp in her side and stopped. She placed her hands on her knees and bent over, taking deep breaths.

Andy stopped as well. "Are you okay?"

She nodded. "Cramp."

Aimee pulled her water bottle out of the back of her fleece running jacket, unscrewed the top and drank several gulps. She handed the bottle to Andy.

His eyes were soft and friendly, the coldness of three days ago gone. It was so unfair how incredibly handsome he was. She watched him drink water, trying not to stare at the way his neck looked when he swallowed, and it made her thirsty too.

"Thanks," he said, handing the bottle back to her. She screwed the top back on and shoved it at her waist behind her, giving him a smirk, intentionally trying not to smile.

She looked at her watch. "Okay, looks like I have about ten minutes and then I'm supposed to turn around and go the other direction. I can go farther if you'd like." She resumed her pace.

"Can I buy you breakfast at Connie's?"

Aimee had practiced what she would say if Andy had tried to call her. But she hadn't been prepared for this.

"I don't know."

"You don't know if you're hungry or you don't know if you want to?" he asked, his voice smooth and level.

"I don't know."

"Are you still angry?"

"Shouldn't I be?"

"It's a choice, Aimee. It's up to you, but I'd still have breakfast with you, even if you are still angry."

She was losing the battle. He was so disarming, letting her completely run the conversation, sticking to her like glue as they continued down the beach. He wasn't going to stop.

"Okay, I give up."

"Just say when."

A few paces later, she pointed off to the left and then walked across the softer sand and up the steps to the beach access trail. They went single file between the buildings with the palm trees over their heads, just like before.

He turned the corner before she did, opening the door for her. She didn't make eye contact, but when they were seated at a table, he sat across from her. She couldn't avoid him any longer.

The plastic menu gave her some cover as she delved into every line, reading everything printed there, even though she knew what she was going to order, would always order.

Their waitress brought over coffee for both of them without asking.

Andy spoke before Aimee could open her mouth.

"We'll have two thirty-fives, with slices of avocado on the side. You can put the potatoes on my plate. One order of biscuits, please, no gravy."

She was shocked.

"Tell me, honestly. Don't you think I would remember all that, Aimee?"

His blue eyes were intense, almost dangerous. The question still hung in the air as she studied his face and then had to turn away.

He handed her the half-and-half, which she used and returned to him.

"I'd like to know how you're doing, something other than fine," he said.

Was he mocking her? Making fun of something she did?

"I've been staying busy. I've kept up the running and been busy with—" she didn't want to mention the house or that she was close to locating her brother—"I've gotten caught up in my reading."

He picked up the flaky biscuit, halved it with his knife, buttered both halves lavishly, and handed her the bottom side.

She pressed it carefully between her thumb and fingers and then took a big bite out of it, closing her eyes at the orgasmic taste and texture of the thing. When she opened her eyes, Andy had stopped eating and was staring back at her.

"How about you?"

"I took Cory to the airport yesterday early. Stopped by the grocery store. Oh, and I did some laundry and called my LPO back home.

"You think this will be a good thing for Cory to do?"

"He had good instincts on that one. It was his execution that was lacking."

A warm ripple of pain washed over her, and then was gone. "I try not to think about it," she whispered.

Their omelets arrived, and Aimee found her appetite had kicked into overdrive.

Andy held up the other biscuit and she shook her head no.

"He wanted to make sure you knew he'd gone there, made it."

Aimee picked away at the fresh crab piled on the top of her eggs. He was still watching her.

"Look, Andy, just what is this?"

"This is breakfast. Did I do something wrong?"

"You're looking at me too much."

He dropped his fork and sat back in his chair, finally releasing a short smile.

"What?" she asked.

"Can I ask you a question?"

"I'm not sure. You're being weird."

"I'm going to ask you anyway." He waited until she looked up at him.

"Go ahead."

"Are you intending to get back together with Cory?"

"Oh, that's an easy one. Absolutely not. I wish him all the luck, but with the talk about other women? I just go dead inside when I hear that. I don't wish him any ill will, but he's a stranger to me now."

"Then would you consider being my friend, perhaps a little more?"

Instantly she blushed. She nearly spit out her eggs.

"You tell me," she struggled to say. "Why should I consider this? Besides, you guys have this code that you don't—"

"I can't stop thinking about you, Aimee."

She scrambled to her feet, attempting to break for the door. He was there in an instant, held her by her forearms, and then gently folded her into his chest. She took two seconds of enjoyment, and then stiffened and pulled away.

"This is insane. You are insane. This is not happening."

"Are you done?" he asked, pointing to the table.

"Yes."

He threw down some money, put his arm around her shoulder, and led her outside.

"Look, Andy. I'm sorry. You ruined your breakfast. I feel bad about that."

He put his hands on her shoulders and steered her through the palm-studded path.

"I made a mistake, that's all. I should be the one who's sorry."

Aimee ached she was so uncomfortable. Why?

Neither one of them began running. They walked at a leisurely pace close to the water's edge, until they came to Cory's house. He was about to wave, or extend a hand for her to shake, when she suddenly realized something.

"Andy, I have some clothes there. Would you mind if I got them today?"

"Sure. No problem. Do you have a lot of things?"

"I honestly don't remember."

"I've got some boxes. We can see, and if it's too much to carry, I can drop them by your house later on, if you like."

"Could you drive me home this morning?"

"Sure, that works too."

The ghost of Cory loomed large once she was inside. She tiptoed, as if she was going to wake him, into the bedroom, and collected some underwear from a drawer, along with some jeans and a sweat-shirt. She found a couple pairs of socks, her toothbrush, some face wash, and a brush in the bathroom.

In the living room, she found two books. Everything she had fit into one box with room to spare.

Andy had made coffee, and he presented her with a mug, filled with cream. He clinked his mug against hers.

"Friends?"

"Friends," she repeated and gulped her coffee.

Aimee walked to the window to admire the view, as she always had in this little place. Andy sat on the back of the couch behind her.

She was on the edge of so much right now. Maybe she was going to find Logan. Maybe she'd find out about the pink house. Was she ready to let someone else in as well? Was she ready to share? And what if it didn't work out?

She'd done it before, and she was still standing. Her life was going to go on almost without missing a beat. Nothing was ever without risk. There were always unforeseen consequences. Cory hadn't been the man she thought he was. She knew that even before she learned about all his secrets.

But Andy, she'd liked him from the first day she met him. And right now, he was offering an invitation she knew she'd regret not taking.

Aimee took one last drink of her warm creamy coffee, set the mug down on the bookshelf next to the window, and walked over to him. She was so close that she felt the heat of his body. Their eyes locked as she removed the cup from his fingers, placing it next to hers on the bookshelf.

He continued to wait for her. She approached again, this time touching his face with her fingertips and running a forefinger across his lips. She looked into his eyes one last time, inhaled, and pressed her lips then her whole body against his.

Two powerful arms wrapped around her back, then slid lower to her buttocks, which he pressed into his groin. He gasped and pulled her up so her legs could wrap around his hips. With quick steps, he carried her into the guest bedroom.

Their undressing was slow with attention to every kiss, every bare spot that demanded to be touched, kissed, or tasted. She removed her snug running pants and stood before him naked.

He kneeled before her, parting her thighs and kissed her from her knees to the soft tissues of her sex. He sat down on the edge of the bed and pulled her to him, and then slowly, he moved backward onto the soft mattress, and with one arm wrapped tightly around her waist, brought her with him.

The sheets held his scent. He was careful to tuck her beneath him. She wrapped one leg up around his hip as he climbed her body, kissing her navel, and then working up to her neck, and lastly, her lips. She held his cock while they kissed, and then with long stroking motions, positioned him to take her. The length of him filled her, every inch. Her pulse quickened as he pulled out, and then lunged forward, deeper still, his lips sucking on her earlobe with the diamond stud in it.

His hips were fluid and gentle as he rocked her world, pleasuring her, changing angles, turning her over and taking her from behind. She followed his hands, her fingers entwined between his, to feel what he was feeling, touch and pinch where he touched and pinched. His hot tongue lit her on fire. She bit his earlobe and pulled at his hair when at last her climax was full upon her. He answered her pleasure with his own, holding her as tightly as she clutched him, stopping so she could feel the power of his pulse inside her. They remained entangled, limbs and sheets, until the spasms subsided.

She was right. There was no predicting where all this would lead.

All she knew was that she wanted more.

CHAPTER 17

ANDY COULD NOT believe that their connection was so complete, like they'd been lovers for years. He didn't want to stop. He could have stayed in bed all day. He knew she had things she'd planned on doing today, but they couldn't help but explore, fondle, kiss, and taste each other, savoring each delight and morsel, resting, and then starting all over again.

He lay in the noonday light and marveled at the shadows that played along the peach colors of her smooth spine, the gentle curve of it, the dimples above her butt cheeks, and the deep, dark places he could find when he slid his fingers down her belly. He'd never worshiped a woman so thoroughly. Every time he came inside her, he wanted to give her more.

She rolled over on her back, her forearm shielding the light from her eyes. He suckled on her right breast, bringing her nipple to a stiff peak, twisting it between his thumb and fingers until she arched up.

He pulled her limp body over his and felt her heart beating and the pleasure of her pubic bone grinding into his thigh, begging for him to plunder her again. She whimpered as he ran his fingers over her breasts, complaining that they ached. Her body wanted him even though her sex was swollen and bright pink. It drove him crazy that she was hairless in all those places he wanted full access to.

Flipping her over, he pulled her hips up and inserted a pillow beneath her tummy. His finger traced down her spine, over the cleft in her buttocks, down to where her swollen, glistening sex called to him. Her taste was exquisite. His tongue thrust deep, causing her to moan into her pillow, arch her back, and present her rear to him so perfectly.

Her taste had driven him crazy, making him rock hard. It wasn't fair she couldn't see what a beautiful sight it was to enter her from behind, spreading her fleshy cheeks as his hands kneaded them, his fingers bit into them as he rammed himself deep inside her.

Again, she moaned, and it made him harder and bigger still.

At last, he rode her, the pace quickening urgently, their thighs slapping against each other with every stroke. She pressed against him Her internal muscles milked his cock, clamped down on him tight. He felt her spasm. Her breaths gasped as she squeezed the sheets and screamed when her long, rolling orgasm washed over her, fully taking control.

He cooled the little warm beads of sweat on her spine by blowing on her. He brought her a cool washrag for her violated sex.

He whispered in her ear, "I wanted to let you sleep, Aimee, but I'm so sorry. I just couldn't."

She giggled. He pulled her hair from her face and smiled.

"Go ahead and get a little rest, but," he said as he kissed her soft behind, "no promises, okay?"

She moaned something, her eyelashes slowly moving up and down, and then she was asleep.

THEY AWOKE AGAIN in the early afternoon. Cory's shower was almost too small for the both of them, but they managed to soap each other off. He shampooed her hair, and she did his. As they were rinsed off, sluicing the soapy goodness down their bodies, he took her again, pressing her soft body against the cool shower tiles.

And, after another soaping off, they finally stepped out. The water had gone completely cold.

She changed into clothes she'd left behind. He opened some soup and made a green salad.

"So I have news about my brother."

"Really?" Andy was surprised.

"It was him who I saw at the restaurant, remember, JJ's? Remember, that night, I thought I saw him. I went back there yesterday and talked to the manager, and the bookkeeper. He came from a halfway house, and I've got the name and address."

"Do you want to go over there today?"

"That was the plan, originally." She blushed.

"I'm glad we did this."

"Me too," she said and kissed him.

She pulled the picture of her brother from her wallet and then showed him the address of the facility.

THE SUNSHINE PALMS appeared to be part of an old Florida office building at one time. It was tucked away in a forest of jungle foliage with a canopy of tall palm trees. The entrance of the center had an elegant lake, populated by a dozen pink flamingos.

It looked expensive.

"How did he manage to get in here?"

"I have no idea. Everything about my brother is a mystery to me."

At the reception area, a man in white uniform greeted them. Andy wasn't sure if he was security, or a health employee.

"Can I help you?"

"I'm looking for my brother. He disappeared from our home about seven years ago. I was recently told he was at this address."

"You have to be on the approved medical file list for next of kin. You have a name so I can check?"

"Logan Greer." Aimee added, "I have this family photograph, which shows him ten years ago." She passed the picture over the counter to him, along with her driver's license.

The receptionist typed in the computer then returned both the drivers' license and the photograph. "I'm sorry, ma'am, but we don't have anyone at this facility by that name. Could he go by any other name?"

"How about the counselors? Could we speak to one of them? I know he'd identify as someone else. We've tried to find him for so long, and as of last week, he took a job through his treatment here. Somebody must have seen him."

"In order to protect our patients, we don't let people inside unless it's recommended by a doctor."

Andy decided to step in. "Look, sir, she's just trying to find her brother. We'd like access to your staff and counselors, because he was sent from here to his job at JJ's, where he was last Wednesday. Can't we circulate the picture around and see someone?"

The attendant darted glances between the two of them.

"Why don't you have a seat in the lobby? I'll make a call and see what I can do. Just wait a few minutes over there," he said as he pointed to two red leather loveseats facing one another.

Aimee tried to listen to what was being said on the phone but without luck. He spoke to another party and then, ended the call with, "All right. I'll tell them. Thank you."

He approached. "If you'll follow me, I'm going to show you to the small conference room. Dr. Denby is going to see you."

"Thank you," whispered Aimee, suddenly heartened.

The conference room was anything but small. The conference table was made from the interior slice of a very large tree, the gnarly edges polished with clear coating. The tabletop itself varied in color from a golden amber in the center to darker and darker rings of brown radiating out, ending at the rough edges.

Aimee set her purse down, leaving the head of the table for someone else.

Andy sat next to her.

"Can I bring you some water?" the attendant asked.

"Please, two," answered Andy.

Dr. Denby was next to enter, carrying the two waters. Andy stood, shaking the doctor's hand. Aimee stayed seated and did the same.

"Thanks for this," she said, holding up the bottle.

He had pure white hair, worn long enough that it curled a bit at his collar. The top of his head was smooth and perfectly brushed, with every hair in place. His hands were marked with age spots and wrinkled, but his face was remarkably youthful.

"So what can I do for you two today? You have a missing relative you're trying to find?"

"Yes, my brother," Aimee said as she showed him the family picture. "That's him," she said as she pointed to Logan.

He squinted, angling the photo and then looking at the back side. He pushed it back to Aimee with his forefinger.

"What's this boy's name?" He got out his pen and produced a small spiral notebook from his white lab coat pocket.

"Logan Greer. This picture was taken about ten years ago. When we both were in high school."

He wrote Logan's name on the tablet, then the number ten, and underlined it.

"And how did you happen to come here?"

"I saw him last week at JJ's restaurant, you know, at Indian Rocks Beach?"

"You talked to him?"

"Not exactly. I saw him out in the parking lot. He was arguing with someone, and when I called out his name, he disappeared. I went back yesterday to ask about him and was told your center helps people with problems get jobs. She wouldn't give me any details, of course, but gave me this address. That's why we're here. I was told he'd been fired. I was wondering if he'd been placed somewhere else."

The doctor continued making notes and then added a period and set down his pen.

"I take it you are aware of his problem with drugs and alcohol?"

"Oh yes. My parents had him in rehab several times. It nearly bankrupted them."

"I hear that story a lot in these rooms. It's a very sad fact of life here."

"So can we see him?"

"Unfortunately, he's not here now. Even if he were, I'd have to get his permission. But in answer to your original question, I believe I helped with this boy's rehabilitation during his stay here. But he didn't tell us about having a sibling, or parents. And he didn't go by the name Logan Greer."

"What name did he use?" Andy asked.

The doctor looked toward the ceiling, trying to recall. "Ben Hawkins, I believe it was. Yes. Ben." He stared back down at the photo. "I'm afraid he didn't look like that, but I can see it is Ben."

"What do you mean?" Aimee asked.

"You have to understand, when we get homeless on an outreach fellowship, they often have advanced cases of mental disease, along with whatever other issues caused by their addictions. But years of abusing themselves makes them age, and of course, it wears on the body."

"So did he get transferred somewhere else?" Aimee asked.

"No, he was placed with that job, as I understand it, and a bed at a halfway house within walking distance to the restaurant, since they don't usually have a car. Apparently, he was caught stealing alcohol and was terminated. And then, he just walked away. Disappeared."

"That's exactly what he did to my parents."

"That's all so tragic. I have several parents' groups formed to discuss that very thing. It's heartbreaking."

Andy leaned forward to ask his question.

"What did you mean when you said *outreach fellowship*?"

"We are governed by a Board of Directors for a nonprofit foundation. Our charter stipulates that we reserve five beds at all times for the indigent or homeless, as long as they aren't a danger to the other patients. You would call them paying customers, I suppose."

"So how did he get here?" Andy asked.

"I'd have to get Ben's file, but most of them come from Emergency Rooms, an accidental overdose, or the police find them in parks. Sometimes an encampment is raided, and they distribute several of the homeless to various church groups, the Rescue Mission, and other clinics like ours. There are some state-run treatment centers, but most of them are filled up with criminal cases."

"So it was random, then?" Aimee asked.

"Yes. I don't know how they do it. Maybe someone thought he needed a break. I'd have to look at his record to tell you that."

"So where do you suggest she look next?" Andy asked.

Dr. Denby clasped his hands together on the shiny wooden conference table. "I don't think he can be found, because I don't think he wants to be."

Aimee felt like he'd slapped her across the face. She'd been so hopeful.

"I'll bet you're thinking I'm being quite harsh, but actually, I'm trying to help. The reality of the situation is that homelessness is a huge problem now, and we don't have enough facilities to deal with it. Many of them self-medicate. They try to monitor the underlying mental components of their disease, which in turn, deepens the cycle. They become more and more aloof and eventually get in harm's way or lose their connection to reality altogether. If you saw him on the street today, I'd recommend not engaging him or trying to help him. You'd be putting yourself in danger, in my opinion."

Aimee began to cry.

Dr. Denby placed his hand over Aimee's. "I'm so sorry, child. I wish I had better news for you. But you could devote all your time and all your money to trying to find and rehabilitate this boy, and he'd run back to the streets at the first opportunity. He may be alive, but he's not living."

"When he was released to the halfway house, was he well?"

Dr. Denby withdrew his hand from Aimee's. "Oh, we never get the well ones!" He chuckled. "Occasionally, someone gets out and breaks the cycle. Most of them fail. Although we talk about homelessness in one broad tent, it's not a one-size-fits-all type of problem. And we're not even scratching the surface. Every state, every municipality, treats it differently and with varying success. The worst thing we can do is what we are doing: Basically nothing."

Aimee didn't try to hide her tears any longer.

"This is the worst part of my job, bringing the reality of addiction to the very people who want to hang on to every hope. But like I said before, I think that's cruel."

Andy nodded, putting his arm around Aimee. "You have any other questions, sweetheart?"

All she could do was shake her head no.

Dr. Denby stood up, and Andy did the same. They shook hands again, and then the doctor placed his hand on Aimee's shoulder. "It's healthy that you care. That's the normal response. You suffer because you understand the truth. You feel pain because you're a good person, compassionate and generous, or else you'd never be here. Make sure you continue to bring that to the world, but I don't think you can fix this one, no matter how much you want to. Okay, Aimee?"

She nodded her head again and pulled herself up.

"Thank you, doctor," she mumbled.

Dr. Denby smiled for the first time. "I've flagged the file and will add your phone number, if you'll write it here." He pushed his notebook in front of her and set his pen down next to it. "If I hear anything at all, I'll be sure to call you. I can do that."

Aimee wrote her number down and handed back his pen. He walked to the doorway and held it open.

"Here's another tip that works well for some people." Both Aimee and Andy quickly looked up to his face. "Go some place you love being. Walk the beach, and remember him the way he was. Go have an ice cream as if you were sharing it with him." he said with a timid smile.

Aimee felt crippled. Her heart hurt. She was so sure she could find Logan. She'd anticipated sitting in his room, talking to him, catching up as if they'd been separated at college or long trips. He'd make her laugh. He'd play drums with pencils on every surface of her bedroom. Make her dolls talk. Peek out the window and tell her there was a dinosaur outside eating her mother's roses. The best parts of her childhood were with Logan.

How could she give up?

Andy took her hand while they walked to the Jeep.

"Sunshine Palms, what a depressing place. Why don't they just call it the Gates of Hell?"

Andy threw his arm around her, squeezed, and brought her in tight. "There's that pretty girl with the lavender eyes who's got me all tied up in knots."

"Are you suggesting?" She looked up at him, wiggling her eyebrows up and down.

"No worries, no rush. We've got time. I'm rather enjoying the getting acquainted part. Aren't you?"

She chuckled. "Roger that."

"Your chariot awaits," he said as he opened the door and hoisted her up into the passenger seat. "Where to?"

"I *don't* feel like ice cream," she said. "I want to think about something else." She wiped her cheeks with the backs of her hands. "I want to show you something near my house. Take me there, okay?"

"Anything, Aimee. Anything you want."

CHAPTER 18

ANDY HELD HER hand all the way up the coast until he turned down the alleyway toward the shore and the gravel driveway in front of Aimee's house. She'd been watching the little beach shops, eateries and Gator Golf stands as they whizzed by them. Her window was ajar, and the wind blew against her face, sending her light caramel hair in all directions.

Instead of going inside, she took his hand and led him down the Beach Access bridge and then turned south and walked in the soft sand in front of several houses. She stopped at a two-story rose-colored home with a huge balcony overlooking the ocean. All the windows were boarded up. She led him around the right side of the house, opening up a door and then through a windowless storage area and through another door to a kitchen of sorts.

The place was a total mess. Appliances looked like big, angular dead animals on the killing fields. A sliver of light enabled him to see a large wraparound counter and eating bar, tiled in vintage pink ceramic with black trim. She stepped carefully, avoiding broken glass and sharp metal pieces, leading him to a stairway with half the wooden spindles missing. She danced halfway up before Andy began.

Old furniture lay broken, and both bathrooms were missing toilets, vanity tops and shower heads. The master at the end had a sliding glass door, leading to the balcony. Aimee kicked a piece of plywood out, giving them a space to walk out on the deck.

"Careful, Aimee. I'm not sure this is solid." He was going to lead her away from the railing but examined the timbers below their feet.

"Look at that view!" she said, turning to face the now-dying sun. "I'll bet you get an extra two minutes of sunset with this balcony," she said.

People in clumps of two or three began to gather, everyone watching the same direction, as if getting nourishment from the sun's rays themselves.

"Pretty spectacular, I'll admit."

He watched her stand on her tip-toes, hanging on the railing for extra height.

"Careful, Aimee. I don't think that wood is very sturdy." He pulled her back. She turned, facing him, her eyes sparkling.

"What do you think, Andy. Should I buy it?"

"Buy it? You have a house."

"That I rent. What if I were to buy it?"

Andy noticed she hadn't said anything about him being part of that picture. "You want to live here full time?"

"Why not?"

He remained quiet and hoped that she'd self-correct a mistake he thought she made.

"Is it for sale?"

"I looked up the owner's name. It's left in a trust for the benefit of a lady who lives in Sarasota in one of those senior communities. I'm going to contact the attorney and see. Don't you love it?"

"It's broken. It needs a lot of work. Who—?"

She placed her palm over his mouth to stop him. Then she kissed him. "Would you help me?

"Well, you do remember that I live in California? Aimee, it would be hard to see each other very much if we were looking at two sunsets from different coasts. Right?"

"I thought about that. But you could help me find the contractors to do the work, maybe help me get organized. And I can stay here while you're on deployment."

The part that was missing was having her lined up with all the other parents, kids, wives, and girlfriends when their big transport came booming into town. Her being present at the bonfires and parties, walking with her through the shops in Coronado, having pizza and beers with some of his friends and their ladies at the Scupper. There was a whole life there, in San Diego, that he loved and didn't want to give up.

She was focusing on the last embers of the sun spilling into the ocean. In an instant, the sky and colors of everything began to gray and tone down.

She crossed in front of him. "Come on. We better get out of here before we can't see."

They silently traversed back until they were at the side of the house again. "I like the color, at least."

Her expression was smug, unreadable.

"Let's go to the Crab Shack, okay? I'm still going through withdrawals from this morning."

Even though it was early still for the dinner hour, the restaurant was nearly filled to capacity. There was a singer playing Margaritaville songs and taking requests. He tipped his hat at Aimee, but she didn't notice.

They sat up front, away from the music by her choice.

The waitress took Aimee's order of a strawberry margarita. Andy stuck to beer.

The way she sucked on her straw brought back some very sexy memories of this morning. She apparently knew it, because she let her tongue slip up the straw and back down again. Her eyes were dreamy, slightly out of focus. She stared right at him and licked her lips.

"I thought you wanted to eat tonight," he said.

"Promises, promises."

That little statement and the fact that her tongue completely coated her lips made his pants feel two sizes too small. She gave him a long, vacant look as she put the straw between her lips and sucked. Hard.

Andy had to look away.

The waitress arrived, and before she could mention the specials, Aimee ordered for both of them.

"He's going to have the breaded, barbeque oysters, a dozen, and we'll share a king crab legs special."

"Nothing healthy?" he asked. Andy had expected a salad they could share at least.

"This is healthy. Can't you feel it?" She grinned.

He knew how to change the subject. It wasn't that he didn't want to partake. He was starved for real food.

"So tell me about your plans for that pink house. Tell me how you're going to get a loan on that place in its present condition."

"I don't know what they want yet, but I plan to pay cash and do the remodel for cash as well. I can get a loan later, if I want."

"I was hoping you'd come with me to San Diego. Soon, Aimee. Or is this a little wrinkle, a change of plans. Or did I misunder-stand?" He felt his voice trail off, having trouble following where the conversation was going.

"You think I demonstrated any desire to take a detour this morning?"

"No, you certainly did not."

"Did I demonstrate a lack of enthusiasm?"

"Not one bit. I loved every moan, whimper, and....you fill in the blanks."

"Oh, trust me. I can," she purred.

"I'm rather counting on it. But seriously, honey, are we talking about a long-distance romance here, because I was rather sure I'd convinced you I wanted you with me twenty-four-seven."

"I want that too. But what if we had a special place at Sunset Beach to come? What if we owned it for years and years and years? What if we became like those older couples on the beach, and we watch the young ones, like we are right now, scampering home to do whatever? We could rent it out. Share our beach with other people and make a little money at it. We could share it with friends or give it as a gift for a week or two. Then our Sunset Beach would blow up and take over our whole lives. It would be bigger, better than just the private place where we met and…fill in the blanks."

"Fell in love."

"That's what I want, Andy. I want something that will never go away."

"You know what I do. That could still happen."

"But I'd have you here, always. You'd always be here with me, no matter what the age, where you were. This is for *us*."

The crab legs arrived and took up the entire table. A pint of melted butter was delivered in a Mason jar. Andy's oysters were tucked into the far corner, with barely room for his beer or her margarita.

"This is totally obscene!" he said.

"I'm going to be covered in butter," she said.

"One of my favorite flavors." He slid the first two oysters into his mouth and called them perfect. Aimee tried one as well.

She tilted her head. "An acquired taste but good."

She dove into the largest of the legs, pulling off the pre-cracked portions easily and dipping them into butter with her fingers. She fed him. He fed her another oyster.

When they were done, shells and small pools of butter were everywhere, covering the tabletop, even falling at their feet below. She finished her margarita.

She had her head in her palm, elbow resting on the table.

"I love your idea. I'm all on board. Let's make it happen, Aimee."

MONTHS LATER, WHEN they would think about this night, he would tell people that he knew the first time he saw her that he would make her his wife. That he never asked her and she never consented with words. They said their vows all night long, this time in her bed. It didn't matter how long they'd known each other, because their forever began with the first kiss and the number thirty-five omelet at Connie's.

It was all about the butter, the crab, and the beautiful Florida night air.

And the sunsets that would last for all eternity at Sunset Beach.

SECOND CHANCE SEAL

Sunset SEALs Book 2

SHARON HAMILTON

SECOND CHAPTER

CHAPTER 1

"**N**OW THIS IS what I'm talking about!" He poked his head outside, through the ten-inch opening in the sliding glass door and breathed in the cool early morning air.

Bright blue sky. Shockingly white sugar sand beach. Not a cloud anywhere. Waves lapping on the shore. Nobody there.

Special Operator Damon Hamlin of SEAL Team 3 knew this place would heal the black tarry puddle that was his soul.

"A few beers, some margaritas, some moonlight sex, some wasted days. That oughta do it. Maybe I won't go back," he whispered to himself.

A month ago, his soon-to-be-ex-wife, Charlene, had sent those papers straight to the forward camp they were holding up in Benin, West Africa. Of course, she didn't care that he was putting his life on the line, trying to find bad guys. She just wanted out.

I knew it was a mistake to leave after we had that big fight.

But he never thought she would actually go to the trouble of actually attempting to have their marriage dissolved without as much as a phone call first. No, the woman couldn't wait to shed off his carcass like a snake sheds his skin. More than likely, it was because she'd found herself another guy to perform unspeakable things to her body. That was Charlene, doing everything to excess. He'd liked it at first. Considered her a challenge. In the end, it was just drama, nothing but drama.

In the thick manila envelope was a cover letter by her female attorney. Very terse and efficient, the letter spelled out the instructions for ending what was a volatile marriage anyway. There wasn't an ounce of compassion or warmth in the words. And Charlene's only personal part in all the papers was that she signed it. A "wet" signature, they called it. That was all she could muster. Probably all that was required.

Wives who did this to active duty SEALs overseas on assignment were especially disliked on the Teams, and when word got round that Charlene had chosen to make their dissolution so public, he had got a lot of support. And that pissed him off too. Damon was *not* a wounded warrior. He had all his parts, even if he had a hole the size of California in his heart.

His BUD/S and nearly ten-year buddy from Team 3, Renny Walker, had slept in the bunk beneath him in their railroad car bunker home-away-from-home—the closest thing he'd ever gotten to an African safari.

"I've got to go to Florida to be at this wedding. When we get back home, why don't you tag along with me?" Renny had teased, his hairy blond legs protruding from below.

That got Damon thinking. What else did he have to live for? His job after he got home was always to get whole. That meant making sure he created some vivid memories that would wipe out any past Charlene history. Those were legendary fights and incredible make-up sex. He'd have to stuff all those things down just in case he was tempted to go soft and try to win her back. He didn't consider that to be a manly thing at all.

"I'm game. But I have no idea where to stay or...I've never been to Florida before. Don't they have crocs and hurricanes and shit like that, Renny?"

"Crocs are damned good eating when you can get them, and we haven't had a hurricane at that part of the coast in over fifty years.

But don't stress about a thing. We've rented five little bungalows all next to each other on the beach. You can stay with me. They're not huge but do have a bedroom and a decent-sized living room with a memory foam couch that is supposed to be comfortable. And, Demon Seed, it's right on the beach, in case I didn't say it before. *On the beach!*"

Renny had been right. This view, the smell of the water, the sounds of the wind and sea birds as well as the waves lapping on the shore was exactly what he needed. It would save him from having to drink several gallons of alcohol on his road to oblivion. His liver and kidneys would be thankful.

It was freakin' gorgeous here. He liked staring at the horizon, that place where the sky and the blue water mated. Uncomplicated. It didn't require any fuzzy logic, or any logic at all. It was an answer to prayer he hadn't had the courage to ask.

They'd gotten in so late last night that all he had seen were the stars in the sky and moonlight twinkling on the water. But he heard the waves all night long as he slept with the slider open.

Yup, Renny's descriptions of Sunset Beach were totally accurate.

He stepped into his trunks, slid on his flip-flops, pulled a T-shirt up from the tiled floor by the hide-a-bed where he'd tossed it last night, and made his way out, over the sand dunes and onto the white sugary beach. The glare and brightness gave him a headache, and he resolved to get a decent pair of sunglasses ASAP.

Black dots formed to the right and the left of him at the shoreline, which later morphed into people going or coming towards him. He let the early morning moisture kiss his face clean, which settled the headache he'd developed from all the drinks he and Renny imbibed on the plane ride from California.

Damon turned right for no good reason and marched over the white sand littered with ocean debris. Broken pieces of shells, water-worn twigs, and pieces of sea glass, and rocks crunched under the weight of his flip-flops as he walked. Two elderly gentlemen on fat tire motorized bicycles zoomed past him from behind.

"Morning, pilgrim," the one with the ponytail called out, his voice booming in a deep Southern drawl.

"Nice ride!" he answered back, admiring the expensive bikes. Their electric motors quietly did the work their legs didn't have to, and it made him want to get one for himself. The tires reminded him of the old Schwinn he had when he was a kid, even though his dad had bought him a girl's bike. The beast was way bigger than his little legs could pedal and stay seated. However, it saved injury to his balls, even though his classmates gave him all kinds of hell at school.

But they were wheels, and allowed him increased autonomy and mobility.

And a little trouble occasionally.

He heard his name called so he turned to see Renny standing in the backyard with a bright beach towel slung low around his waist.

"Hey, asshole, we're going out for breakfast with the groom and guys from the wedding party. Are you coming?" Renny shouted at him.

Damon's stomach was in dire need of something to settle it down. "Don't mind if I do," he answered. He attempted to run up the beach in his flip-flops but nearly tripped, so he removed them and ran barefoot the rest of the way.

The girl Renny had picked up last night stood behind him, also wrapped in a towel. She looked a lot younger this morning than she did in the bar last night. Her flawless tanned skin showed no evidence of her swimsuit line, either. Renny was more practiced in the art of dating since he'd been divorced for over five years. Legendary for picking real beauties, he preferred blondes. This one was stunning.

"Hi, Shannon," Damon mumbled in her direction, making her

blush.

She waved back at him with three fingers on her left hand, clutching Renny's shoulder with her right.

"So you want to ride with us then?" asked Renny.

"Can I shower first?"

"Yup. The bathroom is all yours."

THE GROOM AND best man along with two other of their friends had already seated themselves in the corner at a long table. Renny made the introductions.

"Hey, Greg, this is my Team brother—Damon—I told you about. I hope you don't mind that I asked him to tag along this morning."

The very tall groom with white-blonde hair, blue eyes, and a muscular frame, leaned across the table after he stood, gripping Damon's hand to the point of causing pain. Damon hated guys who did this. But he made sure he was able to pass a little pain back in his direction, in case Greg turned out to be a real prick.

"Welcome, Damon. Anybody who's with this asshole is a friend of mine."

They took their seats as several other members of the wedding party filed in. Soon the table was filled with platters of eggs, bacon, and pancakes the size of dinner plates. Damon stuffed himself nearly to the point of explosion. He decided this would be a fitting way to begin his days of excess.

"How do you know Greg?" he asked Renny after the other introductions were made.

"He and I worked construction one summer before I came to Coronado. He was headed to the Air Force to go for the Pararescue Swim Program until they discovered the poor bastard had a vision problem and was rejected. Can't be a pilot if you have bad eyes. We stayed in touch. I went off to BUD/S, and he got a pretty good job running a large construction crew, later owned his own business framing new homes. Somehow he wandered into a real estate office, and they talked him into sales. We were running around in our boxers, getting shot at, and killing those bugs the size of our little fingers—you remember those fuckers that smelled so bad?"

"Hard to forget those little Vienna Sausages."

"Yeah, well, he was wearing a suit and making more than Admiral Byrne times two. I think he'd already bought a home by the time we re-upped."

"Smart dude."

"Now he's marrying a rich girl. Dad was a big developer before he passed. We stayed friends, and he came out to San Diego once. Can't remember what you were doing then."

"I think I remember him. You brought him to one of the bonfires years ago right?"

"Yeah, I did. I didn't realize I shouldn't have. Kyle told me later on. He never liked Greg."

"I didn't like him either. 'Course I kind of thought he had an eye on Charlene."

"That's because Charlene had an eye on *him*. But don't feel bad. She was interested in *everybody*."

"Don't fuckin' tell me that. That's so disrespectful." It was spoiling Damon's appetite.

Renny grinned back at him, appearing not to take the comment to heart. He wrapped his arm around Damon's shoulder. "Best thing that ever happened to you. Did you get that tattoo?"

Damon had promised to remove Charlene's initials from his left bicep and replace it with a naked lady. "Didn't have time," he mumbled. Several of the groom's party were staring at them, so he shrugged off Renny's arm. "Get off me."

"Now you're acting like a teenager. That's how all newly divorced men act."

"Except it's not official."

"Impending divorce. Excuse me, Professor Demon Seed."

"Fuck you, Renny. I seemed to remember you having trouble adjusting to your single life back in the day. I'm just out of practice, man. And for the record, if you tell another lady I'm getting divorced I'm going to take you down or pour sand in your fuckin' bed. So lay off."

Renny was wiggling his eyebrows down to the other end of the table, connecting with some of Greg's friends. "Suit yourself, but don't be so touchy," he whispered out of the side of his mouth. "It wasn't your fault at all. All on her. A character flaw."

"So I'm discovering." Damon shoveled more pancakes and chased them down with a newly refilled mug of black coffee.

Several of the guys were telling stories about a recent fishing trip on the bay.

"So all these guys are from LA then, or Florida?"

"Some from LA, a couple guys from Sacramento, and Dieter over there is from Chicago, but he's German. The guy at the end of the table is Greg's brother, Brian. You want to keep your distance from that guy when he's drunk."

"Anybody military or served?" Damon wanted to know.

"Nah, I think it's just you and me, Damon. Greg was going to try out, but he dropped, due to his eyes again."

Damon began to feel comfortable with the group. Nearly all of them appeared to be about thirty years of age, the same age as he and Renny.

Greg leaned over and spoke directly to Damon. "I'm sort of on lockdown. Last year, one of Kaitlyn's friends had a groom they sent to Alaska during his bachelor party, and he missed the wedding."

"Holy crap. We had a Team guy that happened to. Do you remember who that was, Renny?"

"Yeah. Don't remember his name. Never did get married to her, as I recall." Renny shrugged, making a face to the groom.

Greg shook his head. "Well, they had the party without the ceremony, and the bride and groom had to get married at the courthouse when he got back. But Kaitlyn didn't want me to get any ideas."

"She sounds worried," chuckled Renny.

"Actually, it was her mother who made me promise every time I see her I won't let it happen." Greg gave a bright white grin to the two SEALs. "Like I said, I'm on lockdown. I love her, so I get to put up with this. I'm under strict orders. No strippers, no pole dancers, no naked orgies, and I have to come home on my own two feet, not carried."

"Shaken but not stirred," whistled Renny.

"Exactly."

Damon decided to mess with him a little bit. "So trannys and hookers are okay then?"

Greg and most of his party erupted in laughter. He mimicked using a firearm. "Bingo." And then he added, "He's all right, Renny. You hangin' out with us tonight? I like the way your mind works."

"Up to the kid here." Renny pointed his thumb at Damon.

"Sounds like fun. I got a few demons to exorcise. I might need some help with that," answered Damon.

"So I heard."

"Dammit, Renny. Who *haven't* you told?" he spat back to his buddy.

"That's it, sport. My lips will be sealed from now on," said Renny.

"Then it's settled." Greg gave him a high-five. "Warning, Kaitlyn and some of her girlfriends are pretty distracting. I'd say it's a good bet you'll find what you're looking for. And, if not, it will find you, for sure!"

DAMON WAS GLAD he'd packed one nice Aloha shirt and a long pair of jeans, even though it was warm. He wore his flip-flops. Renny drove them to the Crab Shack, which had a huge wraparound outdoor bar. Twinkle light-encrusted umbrellas decorated the tables. Instead of sawdust on the floor, like some of the haunts in San Diego, the patio was covered in crushed bleached white shells. He was getting used to the sound of the crunching beneath his feet.

A small band played island tunes. In the corner, several kids played horseshoes and darts. Renny cruised by the outside bar, picked up two long-necked beers made at a microbrewery in Florida, handed one to Damon, and sauntered across the patio to a large group of men and ladies. Damon recognized Greg right away. Renny discovered Shannon sitting with a couple of her girlfriends. She greeted him warmly.

Damon pulled on his beer and scanned the room. A few older couples hung to the outsides of the patio, but the center section was packed with men and women in their twenties and thirties. Some were dancing. Some, like in the group with Greg, were seated on picnic tables and stools, while some were eating dinner. The music was light and happy. The band had a steel drum, and the singer's tenor voice was fresh and upbeat. The heat of the day was wearing off, beginning to turn nippy. He abandoned Renny, who was preoccupied with Shannon anyway.

He stood at the fringes of a circle of men he recognized from his breakfast and tried to listen to their banter but found he couldn't hear. When the band stopped, he finally caught a few words. They were talking about going fishing and football, just as Renny had told him they would.

He noticed how pale his arms were in comparison to the other men he stood next to. He was going to have to fix that as soon as he could.

A group of four ladies made their way over toward Greg and the other men.

Damon felt like a teenager. Renny was right. He'd been married to Charlene for nearly four years, so he did feel rusty just going up to a lady and talking to her. Examining his hands, he noticed, to his horror, he'd left his wedding ring on, so he slipped it off and stored it in his front jeans pocket.

He was examining how the pale spot on his 4th finger was such a telltale sign, just as Greg put his arm around him and began introducing him to the four new ladies. Each one was more beautiful than the previous one. Greg tried to get the attention of the fourth lady, who was watching Renny and Shannon. When she turned at Greg's instruction, he recognized her immediately.

His mouth became parched, his tongue nearly stuck to the roof. He worked on his composure. When their eyes met, her smile and the twinkle in her eyes instantly vanished.

"And this little lady is Martel. She's one of my bride's best friends and a real Florida gal now, but she comes from Northern California too."

Damon couldn't move.

"I'm not sure she's ever met a genuine Navy SEAL, Damon. I was hoping you'd make her first time memorable," Greg whispered.

Martel began a step backward and looked to the floor.

"Whoa! Hold on there, little lady. He doesn't bite," the groom said. "Damon, say hello to Martel."

He knew exactly how her hand would feel as he shook it tentatively, which made him curse himself. He firmed up his handshake and vowed to act like an adult, for Chrissakes.

She'd filled out nicely in the nearly ten years since they'd last seen each other. Her dark hair hung long over her shoulders, even though he tried not to gawk. He knew she had a diamond stud in her belly button because he'd kissed that darned thing dozens of times. He inhaled, which was another stupid idea. Her familiar scent filled him with all the memories of their fledgling romance when she was so new to sex. After all these years, he still felt the guilt of taking her virginity from her just before he ran away to his enlistment. It was something he was forever ashamed of. He'd used her. And he'd never forget the look on her face when he did it.

Ever since, he'd tried to brush it aside and couldn't. It wasn't just the guilt, but something else he couldn't put his finger on. Something dangerous, just like those reminders of how he'd awakened her with soft kisses to her abdomen. And, he'd wondered just about every day whatever had happened to her. In his string of romances and one-night stands, she was the one girl, if he ever saw her again, he wanted to apologize to. It didn't age well, either. His thirty-year-old self now understood the depth of the violation he'd caused to this gentle soul who'd been so avid to please him. He'd been too dumb and stupid to understand it at the time.

She looked like an angel. Maybe not quite as wholesome as she did when she was not-yet-twenty, but an angel all the same.

She glanced up at him briefly and then lowered her eyes again, examining her toes.

Greg had been watching the two of them and their strange interaction. Damon knew the groom had a sharp radar. He wasn't helpful. "Damon here is—"

"Don't. Just don't, will you?" he barked at Greg, his voice sharp, stopping the groom from blabbing about his upcoming divorce. He made a mental note to have that private conversation with his new friend, even if it got him disinvited to the wedding.

"Okay, okay. Well, I'll leave you to get acquainted then," Greg said, chuckling and shaking his head as he left in search of the bar.

She wasn't going to look at him, but the awkwardness had to be filled. He sucked it up.

"Hi, Martel. Well, this is a surprise," his voice cracked, annoying him. He was an idiot to continue to hold her hand, so he dropped it quickly.

"No kidding. A SEAL, huh?" she said as she quickly studied his face and then cast her eyes downward again. "So you made it. I always thought you would." She continued to study her pink toes. He vaguely remembered her toes used to turn him on a bunch too.

Christ! Get a grip.

"Yeah, well, some guys do dumb things. I'm a sucker for getting blown up and jumping out of airplanes. It suited me after all." He shrugged. "Who knew?"

"Makes perfect sense," she said as she let her chocolate eyes fall on his face. He noted a bit of hardness there she was trying to mask.

Of course, why wouldn't she be mad, hurt or both?

He used to get lost in her chocolate brown eyes and was leaning toward her in spite of himself.

"I—I don't know what to say, Martel." The truth was, he had a lot to say, but he didn't want to say it. Then he noticed she had broken out in a sweat, little beads of perspiration hovering in the fine hairs above her upper lip. Her ample chest, alluringly helped by some undergarment that was completely invisible, developed reddish marks he knew to be from nerves. She was shaking like the first time he'd kissed her—her first real man kiss, not like the boys she was used to. He'd never told her he had been as scared as she was when he did it.

He cursed his insides, his courage failing him. This was not at all the way he expected to react when he saw her again.

"You look the same. Older, more muscles, Damon, but the same. Your face is harder." She stumbled on her next words. "I wasn't prepared for this." She squinted as if the sound of her own voice stung her.

"Yes. What are the odds?" He knew it was stupid. Completely stupid. He shook out his hands at his sides.

"Martel—"

What was he going to tell her? Was his fucking apology going to just spring out like his dick did sometimes? All he would do was violate her all over again. He hated that thought too.

"Damon, I'm not feeling very well. It was nice seeing you again."

She was lying, but she was brave. Her hand stuck out, and he did the gentlemanly thing. He accepted the shake.

"Yes, it was nice. You look great, Martel. You really do."

He knew it sounded like a consolation prize. He just couldn't get the right words. He hadn't had enough alcohol to get loosened up.

She glared at him and turned to go, after extracting her hand forcefully.

Brian, the groom's brother, approached before she uttered her final good-byes. He grabbed her elbow and spun her around to face him. Damon didn't like the way his hands were too familiar with her.

"Martel, remember, you promised me a dance?" he said.

"Oh, thanks, but I'm not feeling well and was just leaving."

"Nonsense! I'm not taking no for an answer," Brian insisted, winking at Damon.

Damon wasn't laughing, and neither was Martel.

Before she could protest, Brian had pulled her onto the dance floor, where his arms wrapped around her tiny waist like an octopus. With fucking suction cups. Brian drew her into his intimate space, her body pressed hard against his, as he moved her around the dance floor in full control and for his own pleasure, not hers.

All Damon was able to do was watch the two of them. Had he just missed his shot to defend her? To demonstrate he was a better man today than way back then?

He thought perhaps he had.

But no mission ever worked out exactly as they planned, something he'd learned during the years of training and the deployments to unstable parts of the world. He was more prepared now for the unexpected. He also understood he was being given the chance to right the wrong he'd done to her, if she'd let him.

She didn't look for him when the dance was completed but walked straight to the pretty lady in the hot pink dress he guessed was the bride. They hugged and kissed and then Martel slipped inside the building and was gone from sight.

He'd been lukewarm about attending the wedding. Seeing Martel again had never been part of the plan. But suddenly, he knew there wasn't anything in the world that could keep him away.

CHAPTER 2

MARTEL CLIMBED INTO her red Fiat, but before starting the engine, she laid her forehead against the padded steering wheel.

Why? Why now?

She'd spent the past five years proving to herself that moving clear across the country to Florida was the best way to forget him. She'd finally gotten to the stage where she didn't look for him in a crowd.

Why was it all coming back again?

He'd hurt her. He'd mishandled the trust she placed in him, dashing off to chase dragons and never once coming back to Sonoma County to even attempt to look her up. Not that she was waiting for him. She would never trust a man again like she'd trusted him. Never.

It left her certain she could not rely on her own instincts when it came to men. And here, tonight, as angry as she'd told herself she was vowing some kind of satisfying revenge for his despicable behavior, it was damned hard to pull away. But she had to. She'd never stoop that low or let him see the pain he'd caused. Admit the gallons of tears she'd shed before she learned to live with the fact that she'd never see him again. The emotional rollercoaster in the aftermath of his sudden leaving and the vacancy he left behind made her feel like he'd robbed her twice.

Yes, it was *all* his fault.

It was painful to recall the year she spent along the Oregon coast, staying with new friends until she could bring herself to get back in school. She got her teaching credential nearby in a small town close to Medford and considered settling in a little town near McMinnville where her mother had gone to school. The days were pleasant and the nights cold, but after having difficulty finding anything other than a preschool teacher or daycare worker, even with her Masters', she took fill-in teaching assignments, hoping to be hired for something larger than a twenty or thirty percent job-sharing situation. And then one day, she watched a TV program about the beaches and sunshine in Florida—a place as far away from that tough year in Oregon as she could travel.

The Gulf was to be her second chance. She told herself every day it was her lifeline. The old hurts of the past would just disappear with each swim in the bay, with every walk on the beach, and with the inhale of the calming sea breeze. She was restored, refreshed, her lungs filled with freedom and future, and she found that strong, successful, and confident woman she always knew she was.

But here Damon was, inserting himself into her life again. By accident. Not on purpose, which was the real problem with it all.

Her body was glad to see him even if her heart was sore and bleeding and her brain screaming *'Run! Run away now!'*

If she wasn't in Kaitlyn's wedding party, she'd do what her brain was trying to convince her was the only way to protect herself. But her fellow teacher and friend, who had helped nurse her back and been there while she cried herself dry, deserved more than her desertion. Kaitlyn was one of those women who showed empathy and compassion without knowing every detail of her life's drama. She was grateful for her kindness and patience. And for her discretion not to pry where she wasn't welcome. Some things just couldn't be said, maybe ever.

Martel was dreading the wedding and the reception now more than anything else she'd ever done. Maybe she could talk to Greg or whisper to Brian that she didn't want Damon there. Let the men in their circle of friends handle it for her. Or maybe it would be best to just tackle it head-on and tell him how uncomfortable she was around him.

Martel sighed, raising her head to watch couples walk from the restaurant hand in hand. Her beautiful dress and the makeup and hair appointments she was so looking forward to indulging herself in were just pieces of equipment to prepare herself for battle. If she collapsed, if she let him take away this too, she knew she'd regret it the rest of her life. And maybe she should just let him have what he so richly deserved—a boiling well-crafted piece of her mind. A sharp, pointy end of her opinion she could hurl like a spear. She could do it publicly, if she had to. As long as it didn't ruin Kaitlyn and Greg's wedding.

She drove home, following along the little two-lane freeway, the vein in the archipelago along the beach cities of Madeira Beach, Treasure Island, St. Pete's, and Sunset Beach until she reached her beach bungalow, her refuge. She threw her purse and keys on the kitchen table, kicked off her shoes, and walked through her tiny living room to the sliding glass door and the beach beyond. The white sand looked almost fluorescent in the moonlight. The moon was doing a fan dance with big puffy clouds hinting at some midnight rain like a Rubenesque model.

As long as the sun came up tomorrow, like in the musical score, everything would be okay. The beach had a way of healing the impossibly wounded.

It was too cool for a midnight walk on the beach, but she threw her grandmother's quilt around her shoulders, donned her pajamas and ran all the way to the surf, letting the frigid water spray up her legs and get the flannel wet.

With her hair blowing in her face, she kicked sand into the shallow tide with her toes, first the right and then the left. She felt pieces of shells beneath her feet and stooped, putting a handful in her pants pockets then throwing them two or three at a time into the spray. With darkness shrouding her, she lost her balance and fell to her knees just before the surf showed up to dutifully attempt to wash her back out to sea.

She screamed, but no one came to her aid. The constant, lapping waves made fun of her and didn't give up a soul. Checking to the right and then the left, she knew she was all alone with the powerful gulf. Gazing back toward her house, the fireplace lights welcomed her to the warmth of her bungalow's interior. She rose, soaking wet and full of sand.

Tomorrow was another day, and she vowed to make it stress-free. The wedding was two days after that. In the meantime, she was just going to concentrate on the primping, plumping, plucking, and tanning herself to perfection.

She was going to be the most perfect maid of honor who ever walked down a sandy wedding trail, intending not to pay even the tiniest bit of attention to a man who had his chance once and blew it.

Martel was going to make sure he paid for that mistake with unrelenting coolness a snowman would envy.

SHE WAS THE last to join Kaitlyn's wedding party mani and pedi. All eight of them sat in their motorized backslapping, butt-squeezing captain's chairs with the bubbly jets so fierce she couldn't hear the local gossip. The Vietnamese attendants shouted commands at each other while they worked.

"I'm having a Brazilian," Kaitlyn announced to her court. "Who's had one?"

Martel was the only one who didn't raise her hand.

"You're getting one too. It's on me!"

Whatever a Brazilian was, Martel was getting no clues from the faces of the other bridesmaids. "Just what exactly *is* a Brazilian?" she finally asked.

The titters were so thick they nearly stuck like spaghetti sauce on the walls of the little salon.

"They make you hairless. You get waxed, Martel, down there," one of the ladies pointed to her lap and then gushed a mischievous smile.

"That sounds like it would hurt," she answered the group.

The attendants were carrying on a conversation all their own, interspersed with laughter. She suspected the bridal party discussion translation was great entertainment for them.

"Oh no. Not really," said one of the ladies on her right. "They use special wax; even softer than the stuff they use on your lips and chin."

Martel felt her upper lip and chin to see if she could find any witchy hairs and didn't. "Never done that either. My part-Native American heritage comes in handy. I don't even have to shave my legs."

"Yeah, but just wait until they turn you smooth as a baby's bottom. It feels quite sexy, honest," Kaitlyn announced with a wink.

An hour later, her red fingers and toes looked spectacular. She was called to a small broom-closet type space Kaitlyn had just emerged from for her waxing experience.

"You take *eberything* off from the waist down. Put this on top," she said as she handed Martel a blue paper sheet. "I be right back."

She did as she was told. When the young girl returned, she spanked the massage table.

"Up. You sit here."

Martel hoisted herself up, modestly covering her bare private parts, and lay back, her head on a pillow provided. The attendant nearly tore the sheet from her clenched fingers, pressed the soles of Martel's bare feet together, and then pushed her knees down to the sides as far as she could stretch.

"You hold down. Press knees hard and out to the sides. Make a big smile."

A big what?

Having a strange woman standing over her, staring down at her fully exposed clitoris and lips of her sex, while she applied warm wax with a tongue depressor was embarrassing as hell. But this soon went flying out the window when a gauze strip was pressed over the warm wax and, after a few seconds, ripped away.

Martel sat straight up. "Oh. My. God." It was everything she could do not to scream.

"Only bad the first time. Each time better. You'll see."

At this point, Martel was positive this visit would be her last. The attendant gently pressed her head back to the pillow so they could finish. With each successive rip of the gauze, the pain grew, since much of the sensation was caused by the anticipation and not necessarily the sting itself. And then the humiliating task of having the girl pluck stragglers not picked up by the waxing was the cherry on top.

She was covered with an antiseptic of some kind then powdered with something medicated. Martel imagined her now pulsing private parts looked like a gaping pear-shaped beignet covered in powdered sugar.

"Well? Wasn't that divine?" Kaitlyn asked as she handed the attendant a credit card.

"You are the biggest liar," Martel said to the bride. "*All* of you are liars!" Martel scolded as she glanced into the faces of the laughing ladies.

The bride whispered in her ear, "Yeah, but you're going to be touching yourself all night long unless you get some help with it." Her eyes flashed. It was hard for Martel to remain angry for long.

"No pain, no gain," someone else commented.

Martel wanted to slap her.

CHAPTER 3

EVEN THOUGH DAMON was technically a sailor, ships had always made him seasick. He doubted he could ever go on a cruise. He used beers to hydrate between heaves. It didn't help that the six other guys who went out on the fishing charter were remarking all morning how quiet the ocean was.

Fuck them.

He was so miserable he nearly threw himself overboard just to get it over with.

They pulled up to the pier after their successful day, everyone carrying a bucket filled with fresh fish they were going to have a local bar prepare and serve for dinner. Damon was empty-handed.

"Hey, that's okay, dude," one of Greg's friends said. "My dad was an ironworker in New York when he was young. He told me those buildings used to sway back and forth and not many could handle it up forty stories. He had the kind of stomach to watch a bullfight and eat a tuna fish sandwich at the same time. But take him out on the ocean? Forget it. He would puke his guts out for days."

The visions and just the mere suggestion of eating fish and being sick again was too much for Damon to handle, and he dashed for the bar's restroom, heaving all over the dumb shit who was just coming out of the men's room.

As a result, he fell on the slippery floor and nearly concussed.

Disgusted with himself, he attempted to clean it up, after crawling to the kitchen and stealing a wet rag he found until a buxom barmaid quietly helped him. Her soft, scented chest and gentle demeanor made him almost propose to her on the spot. She placed her hands on his shoulders and sat him back against the hallway wall. She had a Tinkerbell tat on her left breast.

"You're in no condition to do this. Just take some deep breaths, close your eyes, and let me fix all this."

He couldn't speak, he was so grateful. Her little name tag bounced on her chest as she quickly worked.

"Julie. You're Julie," he muttered.

"That's right, sugar. All day and all night." She blushed.

He thought that was funny and started to laugh, until Greg and Renny appeared. The next thing he knew, he was posing for cell phone photos with the girl. He didn't even have the energy to protest.

"How the hell did you become a SEAL if you can't hold your cookies on a calm day?" Greg asked.

"You're a SEAL?" the barmaid whispered, reverence thick in her throaty voice.

He was getting snarkier by the minute and wanted to strike back at someone. Greg seemed like the best target.

"Because, asshole, I spend most of my fuckin' time jumping out of airplanes at night, getting shot at, or capturing bad guys who like to prey on women and children." He followed it up with the best glare he could muster, until he felt his eyes cross.

"Oh. My. God. Thank you for your service," Julie whispered, following it with a wet kiss and a little tongue action inside his ear. He felt somehow violated but couldn't remember why. The day was just going to continue into one big nightmare that would never end.

He'd learned long ago that when things were going from bad to worse, the best thing to do was just go with the flow. When he got back to the table, he took his shirt off and rinsed it in the pitcher of ice water they'd been served at the table, much to the horror of his drinking buddies, who separated like oil in water. Spreading the wet T out on the back of his chair, he sat bare-chested, showing off his new African tats, including the one with Charlene's initials. He drowned his sickness and his shame with the hoppy pale ale he was growing to love.

The men in the wedding party started introducing him to every female who walked past their table. Despite his protests, they told every one of them that he was in the process of getting divorced and was looking for a hot lay.

"Fuckers!" he finally said as he finished off the pitcher, letting excess beer run down his front. He sat back in the chair and nearly had a heart attack when his warm back hit the ice-cold T-shirt he'd rinsed.

"Arrgh!" he yelled. He didn't have to look up to see the heads turning all over the bar. The corners of his eyes caught everyone.

He wanted to go home.

"Should we call you an Uber?" Renny asked, stifling a grin.

He started to answer when he heard Julie interrupt behind him.

"I get off in about fifteen minutes. I can take him home, if you like" She leaned over, her face and lips too close for him to focus. "It would be my honor." Her timbre got very low and sounded a little stormy. Dangerous.

His insides were telling him it was a bad idea. His brain was telling him that his strength was that he could just accept life the way it had been dished to him. It also was the reason he probably would never be promoted. They would always want him as a valuable and creative part of the Team, but he'd never make a leader they would follow into battle.

He decided to embrace his faults.

"Thank you, Julie. I'll be right here, waiting for your chariot."

He knew all of this was going to get back to everyone else on

Team 3 when he returned to California, and he decided he didn't care anymore. He reminded himself of his lofty goals in coming out to Florida in the first place.

Expunge the memories of Charlene from his brain.

Like the conquering hero he wasn't tonight, he got a standing ovation by the entire audience at the Catfish Bar and Grille as Julie helped him out the front door, her arms around his waist as she whispered, "You're doing fine. Just a few more steps."

It was going to be all over Facebook tomorrow. Not his account, because they couldn't have an account due to what they did. But it would be plastered everywhere else, from Florida all the way to California.

He hoped Charlene saw it.

HE COULDN'T REMEMBER the house number of their cottage on the beach, so Julie suggested he sleep it off at her place. He was unable to protest much.

She lived in an ocean-front condo, about four floors up from the sand. It was an older building but had been remodeled, and, thank God, it had an elevator, or he'd be sleeping on the beach like a vagrant.

He headed for the door to the balcony overlooking the bay, but she quickly redirected him to the bathroom.

"You're not to get anywhere near that balcony until you sober up some."

He wasn't going to argue. She was cute and probably ten years younger than he was. Well, she had to be twenty-one at least to work there, so nine younger then. He loved basking in the attention she poured over him. There was a story there somewhere, he thought as he allowed himself to be dragged to the shower that was already running warm and steamy.

"You get those smelly clothes off, and I'll put them in the wash for you."

He was liking the opportunity to mess with her. "Then I'll be naked. I'm shy when I get naked."

She grinned, unbuttoning his jeans and expertly sliding her hand inside to massage his package. "Well then, we'll have to do something about that, won't we?"

Her eyes locked hard on him as she stripped his pants all the way to his ankles. His red, white, and blue starred boxers went too.

Under the spray of the shower, he began to sober up. He scanned everything that had happened over the past hour or more, and something made him tear up. Where was all this sadness coming from? His chest hurt.

He was really good at his job, and he loved being a SEAL. It was everything else in his life that was fucked up. He attracted women for all the wrong reasons. The women he was attracted to wouldn't have him. And the real gems, well, the ones worth loving, he didn't want to disappoint, so he just walked away. Yes, he was good as a SEAL. He was an outstanding Team Guy. But that was all he was. Everything else scared him into inaction.

The water turned ice cold, he'd been standing there so long thinking.

This is a bad sign, Damon. Thinking will get you killed. And on top of being sick, you're crying like a pussy.

Tonight, he was finding it hard to run away from things that just kept coming back again and again.

This must be what they call Karma.

He turned off the water and grabbed a pink flower-scented towel Julie had left for him on the toilet lid. He dried his hair and looked in the mirror.

Do I look harder? Who was it said that?

It was Martel, dancing under the twinkle lights, the band guitarist watching her every move as she carefully replaced Brian's hands into more appropriate locations. The guitarist smiled, and so did Damon.

He remembered those hands on his body, the big brown eyes staring up at him, terrified as he took her across the threshold into womanhood.

"Love you, sweetheart," he'd said.

"All for you, Damon. Take me. I want it to be you. Make me a woman."

He never got tired making love to her. He could go all night long, because it made him feel so good. He'd forgotten how wonderful she made him feel. Her little kisses and sighs, how her body tasted, and how she asked him to teach her...

He looked back into the mirror. God, he'd been a fool. She'd made him feel so good he didn't ever consider *her* feelings. He knew she expected more than he gave. He knew that's what he was going to do all along, and he just couldn't stop.

He intended to touch base after Basic. After he qualified. After his first work-up. Each time he thought about coming back to see her, and yes, apologize.

Until it was time to leave for Africa. That changed everything. That four-month deployment wound up being nearly an eighteen-month tour. Half the time he wasn't sure they'd make it out alive. He didn't want anyone waiting for him. He had to push out all distractions to stay alive.

So, to avoid breaking her heart, he broke it anyway.

He let the tears stream down his cheeks and drop onto his chest. He let himself see the raw pain that, even though he'd done his job, he wasn't a real man inside. Common, ordinary men could fall in love and take care of their women.

He could not.

He wasn't sure what he'd tell Julie but taking advantage of her wasn't something he wanted to do tonight.

He slipped into her sheets, pink with little dark pink and rose-colored flowers along the hemline and smelling like a Spring day in a flower shop. A light shone from the hallway, illuminating the picture of a young man in a Marine uniform on her bedside table. Beside it was a picture of Julie with her parents and this young Marine.

They appeared to be nice people. Their faces were decent, the photographer obviously posing people not used to having professional pictures done. They were uncomfortable with the process, he could tell, but making a memory to last for generations to come. Making a statement, "We were here. We were all together here."

These were the people he was sworn to protect. He looked into the eyes of her father. He couldn't take advantage of this man's little girl.

He'd never thought this way before.

IT WAS DARK when he awoke, hearing Julie's quiet sobs. He moved toward her in the bed and found her also naked.

"Hey, what's the matter?"

She jolted at first. "I'm sorry. Sometimes I have nightmares. I didn't mean to wake you."

She wrapped her legs around his hips, holding him like a scissors between her thighs. He brought his arm up around her shoulder and let her soft cheek feel the beating of his heart.

"It's okay. You're safe with me. No one's going to hurt you while I'm here, Julie."

At first, she inhaled sharply, then let it out, and then gulped in air again.

He placed his palms at the sides of her face, pulling her up so he could see her eyes and her glistening cheeks and rubbing her temples with his fingertips. "Shhh, it's okay. Honest."

"I'm so sorry. I just get sad sometimes," she whispered tentatively.

"I do too. I think about all the dumb stuff I've done, did tonight, and I don't—"

He stopped, pulling her down to his lips and gave her a gentle kiss. He rubbed his palm over her forehead, petting her silky dark hair. "You're beautiful, Julie. I imagine you make your father proud."

She sat up. He traced down her spine with his forefinger.

"You okay?"

"That's the third time you've asked me that." She sighed. She was fiddling with her fingers, looking down at her lap. "I need to come clean with you."

Damon's antennae shot up, and he suddenly worried he'd miscalculated everything. *Another exercise in being a jerk.* With one arm covering his forehead, he gently patted her back.

"Tell me, Julie. Just say it."

She rolled onto her belly beside him, her arms out in front, resting on her elbows. "I'm a virgin, and I thought—"

His heart raced. This was exactly what he didn't want to hear. Again, his head was screaming, *"Run!"*

He took several deep breaths and found the strength to ask her, "You thought what?"

She looked at him, even though most of her face was in shadow. "I thought that maybe if you were drunk enough, you'd agree to be my first. It would be my honor." She examined her hands again. "And I thought you'd be gentle with me."

He brushed the hair from her cheek with one hand. He let his forefinger rub gently across her lips.

"Listen very carefully, Julie. That should be something you save for someone you love very much. And when that happens, when you both love each other, then it will be gentle, and it will be the most beautiful thing in the world. Because that's the way it should be."

He saw he'd made her cry.

"I don't want to hurt you. Thank you for the offer. It truly means a lot to me that you ask. In my younger days, with a pretty girl like you—"

Even in the dark he could see her shy smile.

"I would have taken you up on it in a heartbeat. But you're too special, Julie. Making love is more than screwing or getting something out of the way. It's about opening up your whole world to another person, or at least it should be."

She brushed the tears from her cheeks and chuckled. "Well, I was willing to pretend, at least."

"For me? You'd do that for me?" he grinned.

She nodded. He smiled.

"You are special. That's the nicest thing anyone"—and then he remembered Martel—"well, almost anyone has ever offered me."

He gazed at her face, unable to read her eyes. He liked the man he was being right now.

"As much as I'm sure I'd enjoy it, I'd rather be truthful and honest, instead of pretending. I don't want to take the place of a gentleman someday who deserves the honor of your body with all the love and honesty I can see you have to give. It's a beautiful thing, Julie. You're an amazing, brave, and honorable woman. You deserve more."

She started to answer, hesitated and then sighed. "I wanted to thank you for your service. I lost my fiance overseas two years ago. I say good night to him every night."

"The Marine?"

"Yes. He was like you. He didn't want to do it until we were married."

"Well, I didn't—" He had to stop himself. "That's a beautiful story, Julie. You're keeping his honor. See? We both did the right thing…"

She laid her head against his chest again and several minutes later was snoring fast asleep. He enjoyed the feel of her unspoiled body against his own. Her glowing soul warmed him as they breathed in tandem. He couldn't believe what he'd just experienced. He wanted her respect more than he wanted to sleep with her. Her naivety made her vulnerable and he didn't want to take advantage. He didn't want to rob her of the fairytale. Besides, she could always tell her friends she'd slept with a SEAL. And it would be the truth.

Sweet, young Julie had taught him a huge lesson.

About himself.

CHAPTER 4

MARTEL HAD NEVER worn a powder blue cocktail dress before. She also never wore a pillbox hat with a small veil, covering just below her chin. She lost the battle with Kaitlyn, arguing that she wanted to wear her hair long. But it was Kaitlyn's wedding, and the bride had all the young women wear their hair up in French twists at the top of their heads. Martel was the only one who wore a hat and veil, as the maid of honor.

"You look like mother," she said to the mirror. A tiny wave of worry crossed her mind as she hoped she didn't look too matronly. The purpose of the facials, the painted toes and fingernails, the professional makeup artist, and the hairstylist were to make her look stunning.

Well, that's the bride's decision to make and hers alone.

Kaitlyn would be the star of the show, no question about that. Martel just didn't want to show up looking like her mother, like anyone's mother.

All the girls gathered in the pastor's study. Someone had brought champagne, and Martel grabbed a glass, downing it quickly. It did settle her nerves a bit. The bride sashayed next to her, looking sparkly and fresh. Her long blonde hair curled in soft ringlets, falling all over her shoulders and halfway down her back. It was how Martel had always thought she wanted to look as a bride.

"You look smashing, Martel." Kaitlyn's blue eyes were highlighted with light blue eyeshadow contrasting her pale pink lipstick.

"You don't think this hat and veil make me look too old, do you?" she asked Kaitlyn.

"No!"

Several of the other girls joined their circle, each dressed in a different pastel shade of the same style.

"You can take the hat off, if you don't like it."

Martel could see Kaitlyn was trying to please her but didn't really want her to mess with the costume.

"It's your day, Kaitlyn. I'd wear a bathing suit down the aisle if you asked me."

There was a collective "whoa" from the bridesmaids. More champagne was poured, glasses clinked, and they all started bantering like a bunch of chickens.

Pretty girls and idle gossip. They go hand in glove.

Kaitlyn's mother entered the room, and everyone ceased talking. It would be hard not to notice how thin she'd gotten just in the few months since the original wedding plans were started. The wig she wore over her bald head, due to the cancer treatments, was for a much younger woman. Martel could almost envision a bow of some kind on the side, more of a '60s style hairdo baked in.

She batted her hairless eyelids and smiled at her beautiful daughter, her cheekbones high, yet revealing gaunt and sunken flesh beneath.

"Sweetheart, I've dreamt about this day for many years. I'm so happy I lived long enough to see you married. I couldn't be happier with Greg as my new son. Thank you."

Kaitlyn was a bundle of tears, collapsing into her mother's arms. Her veil, with tiny star-shaped crystals sewn in, got temporarily entangled in her mother's wig, and threatened to push it askew. Mrs. Carrington was quick to stop the movement.

HER MOTHER LOVINGLY smiled at all the girls. In her right hand she carried a pink bag. To each of the bridesmaids she handed a small package wrapped in pink tissue. To Martel, she handed a tissue wrapped in blue.

"These are from me to all of you. Thank you for agreeing to be part of this special day. I know Kaitlyn and Greg are so delighted we could all share this together. I hope you enjoy these little trinkets and remember this special time and how happy you have made us."

As Martel and the other bridesmaids opened their packages, each found a gold heart on a delicate chain, the backside of the charm engraved with the date of the wedding. They helped each other put the necklaces on and, one by one, gave Mrs. Carrington a hug.

It was a sweet gesture, but so sad. Martel missed her mother's presence as she fondled the heart-shaped necklace around her neck and looked into the eyes of the woman who probably wouldn't make it to Kaitlyn and Greg's first anniversary.

"Thank you, Mrs. Carrington. Your daughter must be such a gift to you."

Then Martel's eyes filled with tears. She realized the moment she shared with Mrs. Carrington was something she would never be able to do in her own life. First of all, there was no man at her side like Kaitlyn had with Greg. And Martel's own mother had died shortly after she left for Oregon. She regretted not being able to attend the funeral. She'd told Kaitlyn Mrs. Long had died of a broken heart when her father left the family two years before. Damon had been a comfort to them both right after her dad left. Her mother was his biggest fan, until the end.

Mrs. Carrington knew she was stepping into a role Martel had artificially placed her in. "Your day will come. And in case it's not soon, your mother and I will hold hands and watch from above."

Martel heard the collective gasp as each of the women in the room tried to stifle an outburst of tears. Someone suggested more champagne.

WHY ARE WEDDINGS *so emotional?* Martel wondered. Maybe it was because younger people strive for their happy day, and maybe it was because older folks liked to fondly remember their youth. It was an artificial bringing together of families, made by choice and not accident.

As choices went, getting married probably was the easier one, Martel knew. She'd had her share of choices and had artificially plastered over all the objections and second guesses. Today, they came crashing down on her.

She ran to the bathroom.

What's going on with me?

She dabbed water on her face, trying to remove redness that collected in and around her eyes. A makeup bag was laid open on the counter and she applied concealer under her eyes before adding more silvery blue highlighter on her upper lid. She touched up her lips with the cherry red color she hoped might attract attention.

Well, she was not going to be in her twenties in a few months, as she celebrated her thirtieth birthday. Time to get real. Time to strategize the rest of her story, add some romance, and, yes, more than a little lust. She'd been brave, and worked hard for everything she achieved, covered up her sadness, and dealt with vacant places in parts of her heart. She'd gotten really good at that.

A gentle knock on the bathroom door was followed by Kaitlyn's whisper. "Are you alright, Martel?"

"Yes." She opened the door and smiled.

She had to tell Kaitlyn something even though her friend was too much a lady to pry.

"Just seeing your mother today, seeing how happy she is, it makes me miss my mom." She placed her hands on either side of

Kaitlyn's face. "You're so lucky. I hope every day for the rest of your life that you are as happy as you are today. That's my wish for you."

Of course, that brought on a flood of tears streaming down the bride's pretty face.

"It's going to happen, Martel. You watch. It will happen. Do you know how they say, *'the beach heals everything'*? I truly believe that with all my heart and soul. I'm so happy you came to Florida and we got to be friends. I hope you'll stay here forever and ever." She whispered, "And I'm gonna need you to babysit."

Martel dropped her hands and stepped backward. "Are you saying...?"

Kaitlyn nodded. "We got a little sloppy. I mean we were going to get married, right? But in all the planning and Greg's job—he's been so incredibly busy. We just got lax and voila! I think I'm about three months along."

"Does your mother know?"

"Don't say a word. We're going to tell her after the Honeymoon, if I can keep my mouth shut." She leaned forward, "I guess they call it a babymoon now."

Martel studied Kaitlyn's tummy. "You don't show at all."

"You haven't seen me naked. I have a baby bump, No question about it."

"I'm so happy for you."

Martel was the last one to leave the pastor's study and was whisked hurriedly to the back of the line to make her entrance after the bridesmaids. Her insides were jumbled. Her ears buzzed, and comments made by the other bridesmaids, the wedding planner, and everyone else around her were muted as if she was listened to them through water. She felt like she was sitting at the bottom of a pool looking up at the world and people performing on stage all around the edges.

Organ music got her attention. Brian, Greg's best man, presented his elbow. "Madame?"

She enjoyed hooking her arm in Brian's, tucking herself gently at his side, as they were given the go-ahead to march down the aisle.

The veil on her hat was scratchy, irritating her nose, and she worried the red lipstick would smear and leave marks all over her cheeks. But she smiled at the audience on both sides of the aisle and decided, even if her greatest fears came true and she looked like a painted clown, she wouldn't let them see her concern.

At the front of the church they separated, and she turned to stand at the left. She held her bouquet of tuberoses tightly to her waist, scanned the audience, and smiled.

The congregation rose as Kaitlyn and her uncle began the short journey to the front. She watched the bride's eyes laser-focused on Greg. She saw the determination of her friend as she crossed the threshold from single lady to a married woman, and future mother. How Martel envied the way Kaitlyn could depend on her man and that he was standing there in front of everyone, declaring his love for her with that action.

Martel found it hard to breathe all of a sudden but kept her gasps for air silent. She had so much in common with Kaitlyn, more than her friend would probably ever know. Her life was going to play out differently. She made peace with it, which settled her a bit.

These two made better choices. Well, even if they weren't better, this day was as the result of their choices. Their conscious effort to design a life together.

Kaitlyn smiled at her through the shimmering veil, handing Martel the exquisite bouquet she carried, a larger version of her own. As the bride turned to face Greg, the couple held hands. Martel was distracted by movement out of the right side of her eye.

Damon Hamlin's steady gaze was not focused on the bride and groom, which would have been much more appropriate. He'd been studying her. And he wasn't afraid to show it.

Martel made her choice. She did not smile but refocused her attention on the ceremony.

AFTERWARD, THE PICTURE taking went on for nearly an hour. They ended the photo session with a mock "worst wedding photo ever," and then the group peeled off and headed to the reception in separate cars.

Brian drove Martel and another couple to the beach that was going to be their party place. The sun had started to hang very low on the horizon, bathing the huge white canopy in warm orange light. The wedding cake and refreshments were set up in the Sunset Beach public gazebo, which was the only part of the reception that was rented. Tables and chairs dotted the beach in clusters. Two large boxes at the entrance were set up for people to remove their shoes. It was the bride and groom's express wishes, boldly printed on a poster above the boxes, that the entire wedding party "go barefoot" in celebration. Kaitlyn and Greg's shoes were the first pairs in the box.

They'd hired a mobile DJ to play dance tunes, most of them being 60s style surfing as well as popular Cuban songs and what Martel called "Margarita Music."

She was shown to her table and promptly removed her hat and veil. She was grateful she could finally breathe.

Several of Kaitlyn's students from their school were in attendance, lined up to give their teacher a hug and shake the hand of the man who had become her groom. She listened to mothers of the children gushing glowing words of praise on Kaitlyn. It was clear, even though Martel knew all about it, that she was a favorite teacher at the school. In fact, the two friends were usually voted most popular.

"Aren't they cute?" Kaitlyn whispered to her after several of her students passed through the reception line.

"Darling. Kate, they think you're a rock star."

"Actually, Greg's the rock star. He has a little group of devotees now. Isn't it great?" Kaitlyn angled her head and squinted. "You took off your hat."

"It was driving me crazy. The veil itched my nose. I thought I was going to sneeze all during the wedding. I'm never going to wear one of these again. Ever."

They both laughed.

She was introduced to several other friends of Greg's, relatives of Kaitlyn's, and other people who passed through the line without identifying how they got there.

She hadn't been paying much attention to who was "on deck," but all of a sudden, Damon was standing before her, extending his hand.

"I like your hair up. Because…" He leaned forward and whispered, "I think you're just as pretty as the bride."

She must have registered shock, because he let his eyes go big, and covered his mouth.

"Perhaps I shouldn't have said that."

"Nice to see you too, Damon." She tried to show him that she had no sense of humor, and the joke had fallen flat. She turned her head to the left and greeted the next person in line, forcing Damon to move to the side.

"Kaitlyn, thank you for letting me crash your party. I like your choice of venue," he said loud enough for Martel to hear.

"I know. It was Greg's idea. Isn't it wonderful?"

"The best." He addressed the groom. "Well, Greg, you got snagged, but I don't see you protesting."

"Good to see you, man. Julie fix all the places that were hurting? You put on quite a show at the Catfish." The groom punched Damon in the arm.

Julie?

Martel didn't pay attention to Damon's answer. The music had started. The line dispersed as the wedding party began mingling with the crowd. Martel left in search of something stronger than champagne.

IT WAS NEAR sunset when they cut the cake. With a swirling, lush orange and purple backdrop, they toasted the bride and groom and then watched the sun melt at the horizon.

She knew Damon had been watching her. She made a point of ignoring him as much as she could, but he caught her sneaking a glance in his direction that she tried to deflect.

Dancing was one of the things Martel loved to do ever since she was a little girl. She danced with Kaitlyn's uncle, and Greg, and several of the groomsmen, including Renny.

"I did not know that you and Damon were acquainted. I imagine you were just as shocked as he was to see you."

"Yes, he's the last person in the world I ever thought I'd see here. So you guys serve on the same SEAL team?"

"We do. He's been a good friend. I doubt I would've made it out of BUD/S without his help."

"Butts?"

Renny laughed. "BUD/S. Or Basic Underwater Demolition. It's the training we do before—well, *one* of the things we do before—we get pinned. It's that part you see on TV all the time. We have to stay up for six or seven days in a row. You've seen the films, right?"

"Oh yes. I know what you mean now. Tough journey for you both."

"Our class passed about twelve percent of the original class."

"Is that unusually low?"

"Actually, it's a bit higher than most."

"That must make you feel very proud. Have you wanted to join the military for a long time?"

Martel knew the decision had come quickly for Damon and wondered if it was the same for Renny.

"Yeah. My dad was a big fan, a former Navy man himself. He never made it to get his Trident. Sometimes I think I did it for him. Maybe when I retire I might give it to him."

"He must be very proud." Martel knew that Renny was on his best behavior. She wondered how much of her past Damon had discussed with him.

"When do you go back to San Diego?" She was mortified with her own question and wanted to take it back immediately.

"We got another week. Then it's back to that beach. We call it the Left Coast."

The music stopped, but they continued talking. She noticed Renny was scanning the crowd at the same time.

"Right back into the fray, I guess," she added.

"Not quite. We have a couple special training sessions in the desert coming up. And then hurry up and wait."

"Where do you go next?"

"Can't really say, Martel. Sorry."

"I shouldn't have asked." She shrugged. "It seems like it's so difficult to talk to people socially these days. Between politics and religion and job security and national secrets, everything is so complicated. Everybody's hiding something." Her mind drifted. She felt like she was fading into the horizon, the sun pulling her down into the water.

"Oh wow. Where did that come from?"

Martel shook her head and then shrugged. "I have no idea." She smiled up at Renny and saw a lot of Damon and his expression. His easy-going nature was attractive. She figured not much got under his skin. She imagined it was part of the selection process.

"Now that I know a couple of SEALs, I think I'll start paying more attention. Maybe next time, I can ask more appropriate questions. So, forgive me."

Martel knew that Damon would be curious about her behavior and would probably question his buddy. Feeling on display, she wanted to leave the party, get out of her formal clothes, and get her beach vibe on. Some of the guests were leaving, including several of the wedding party. Kaitlyn and Greg slow-danced as the waves lapped at their feet, getting her dress and his pants wet, lost in their own private world. They kissed, claiming their throne—the King and Queen of Romance tonight.

And they weren't afraid to show everybody how they felt about each other.

Martel was mesmerized watching them, especially knowing about Kaitlyn's secret.

"Martel Long, you've been avoiding me all afternoon." Damon's voice was smooth and dangerous.

She was glad he noticed her cold shoulder. Her plan was working!

She addressed him. "I've been enjoying the company. I'm surprised I haven't bumped into you on the dance floor. Do you still like to do that?"

Damon stood beside her, watching Greg and Kaitlyn. "Yeah. I used to do a lot of things I don't do anymore." He faced her. "I think I've grown up a little. I like to think it's an improvement."

His grin was disarming. She was counting the ways she could try to show him how little she cared for what was going on in his life. It was going to be an uphill battle.

She took a deep breath and tried to sound casual. "I like to think that we are the sum total of our decisions and choices in life. Thank goodness we learn from our mistakes."

They studied one another like it was some kind of competition. Her heart was racing, threatening to leap from her chest and go dive into the ocean. She couldn't stop shaking when his eyes traveled from her face all the way down to her toes with slow deliberation.

"You always liked painting your toes."

She didn't answer him, preferring to let him squirm a bit. It didn't take long for him to completely disarm her.

"Am I one of your mistakes?" His eyes lazily found her face again. His head was tilted slightly to the right, one hand covering his mouth and scratching the side of his cheek. There were the beginnings of a furrowed brow developing. He was nervously waiting for her answer.

"I can't answer that question." Martel watched two pelicans flying low, one of them crashing into the water with a splash.

"Is there any chance… what I mean to say, Martel, is that I'm sorry for some of that."

"Some?"

He stepped closer to her, and she immediately backed up.

"I owe you an apology."

She'd been ready with her answer for years. Martel was sure he wouldn't be. "Damon, you don't owe me anything."

That statement wasn't as satisfying as she'd hoped, but she needed to keep her backbone, demonstrate how she'd gotten on just fine without him all these years.

She was going to leave, but he grabbed her arm, urgently at first, and then released her.

"Let me put it to you a little more directly this way. Martel, I'm sorry." He held his hand over his heart.

She was alarmed that perhaps she had misread his intentions. She was feeling at the edge of some pretty skinny branches, holding steadfast, higher off the ground, about four floors higher than she should be. But the die had been cast. She'd promised herself.

"Like I said, Damon, you don't owe me anything."

"Are you sending me away?"

"I wasn't aware that you'd ever returned. You left, Damon. That was all a long time ago. I've moved on."

He stepped closer to her. This time, she didn't retreat.

"As you should have. I wasn't worthy of you."

"Really? Honestly, I didn't think you even thought about it at all. I figured I misunderstood everything between us."

"I should've done it differently. I'm so sorry."

The pounding of her heart was taking her breath away. She felt him take her fingers in his hand, draw them up to his mouth, and kiss them. He was going to call her to him by slipping his arm around the backside of her waist, but at the last minute, she dropped his hand and stepped to the side.

She made a big show of being brave. She stood straight and delivered her parting thought. "Another conversation for another day, Damon. I'm not ready yet. Not sure I'll ever be, if you want to know the truth."

She thought about her words all the way home. Scenes of their long, sweet lovemaking sessions warmed her, blotting up the pain and loss that was to follow so harshly afterwards. She licked her lips and missed the taste of his kisses. If she could have those kisses back without her having to work so hard to convince herself that he cared for her, maybe even loved her, she could welcome those into her life again, but she wasn't sure she could trust herself to accurately assess her danger or his feelings for her. That young, trusting woman she'd been no longer existed. There were rules—protocol that had to be followed—in order for there to be a relationship between them. Maybe it was unfair of her to require this, but he would have to go there in order for her to keep her self-respect intact.

If he knew what all those kisses had brought her, knew about the little girl she bore for him and then gave away, he would understand. But he hadn't earned that right yet. If he meant what he said, he was going to have to work it out the hard way.

Without her help.

BACK AT HER bungalow, she shed her clothes and unpinned her hair, combing it out. She stepped into the shower, soaping herself off and feeling the touch against her once innocent, now bare sex. One barrier had been broken, and she placed another protective one in its place as the warm water sluiced over her body. She wasn't yet convinced that there would be a second chance on the horizon, even though the sunset was beautiful.

Their daughter would be nearly ten now. She rubbed her belly, her fingers exploring the tiny stretch marks Martel had earned bringing their child into the world. These were her battle scars, not gold medals worn on a uniform.

But just as important.

CHAPTER 5

"**J**UST FUCKING CALL her. Honestly, Damon, sometimes I think you're more of a girl."

That pissed him off. He jumped to his feet, crumpling the little piece of paper Kaitlyn had written Martel's number on.

"You know one of these days you're going to say something, and I'm gonna pop you right between the eyes, and that'll be it. We'll both get tossed."

"No fucking way asshole." Renny stayed splayed over the couch, still in his pajama bottoms. "You made your bed, now lie in it. I'm here because I want you to stop being such a pussy. She digs you. I could tell. I always knew there was somebody you left behind. Remember? I used to accuse you of that all the time. You were so fucking tight-lipped about it."

"You don't understand," he muttered, gazing out the window at the beach calling him to run away again.

There were so many things that went right the last two days. And there were so many things that went wrong too.

"Don't understand? When I met her, I said to myself, '*Self, this sweet lady is the missing link. She took a little chunk of his heart and won't give it back.*' Am I right, or am I right?"

He didn't want to admit it, but maybe Renny had a point. He'd gone from one despicable mood to another in the space of forty-eight hours. He'd gone from the biggest jerk on the planet, to doing something he was proud of—proud of the way he treated Julie. And then at the wedding, when he saw Martel again, he thought perhaps this would be the time to do what he should've done years ago. Apologize. That was the manly thing to do.

Except it was so fucking hard.

Well, doing something hard was what they'd been trained to do. *Hard* was putting his body between the good guys and the bad guys. *Hard* was jumping out of an airplane and getting tangled up in your chute. Hard was pulling a buddy off the field, applying enough first aid so he wouldn't bleed out on the way back to medical. Hard was jumping up and running between buildings when he knew his job was drawing fire, so his Team guys could find the shooters and take them out.

But dealing with women? That wasn't really hard. It was impossible. Maybe being so terrible at one thing it made the other thing so successful. He shook his head. No, that wasn't it either. "I can't figure it out, Renny. I'm a fucking mess."

Renny rolled off the couch and joined him at the window, putting his arm around him. "You know when I got divorced, I just decided I wasn't gonna try anymore. Have you ever considered that maybe you're trying too hard?"

"What do you mean?"

"I mean, why can't you just call Martel, talk to her, make a date, have a good time, and give her a good time. That's what it's all about here, Damon. We're just here to relax and let off some steam, and let the girls—you know—have their fantasies, while we reap the harvest. That's what I call it, anyway."

"But I don't wanna live like that anymore."

He couldn't believe those words came out of his mouth. Apparently, Renny couldn't believe it either because he gave Damon that goofy expression that told him he was done talking nonsense. Their conversation was fully bagged, cooked, overcooked, and in the trash.

"I think you're right. You are a mess."

Renny headed to the bedroom and called out, "I'm going for a run. Are you up to it?"

Damon looked at the crumpled piece of paper just as Renny appeared in the doorway.

"Yeah. You're going to call her now. I think I'll give you a little bit of privacy."

In two long steps, his buddy was outside the sliding glass door, running over the sand dune, and headed straight for the beach.

Damon dialed her number.

"Hello?"

She sounded sleepy. "Hi, Martel." He heard her annoyed moan. "Don't hang up. Just hear me out a bit, okay?"

"Go for it."

"I've apologized to you I think three or four times, and…"

"I wasn't counting, Damon."

"Right. Right. I didn't mean that, I mean, I'm sincere when I tell you that I've had a chance to think about things. And I've grown up a lot since we parted."

"Since you left," she corrected.

"Yes. That's true."

"Glad we got that out-of-the-way. I heard you last night, Damon. I'm just not sure I believe you."

This was tougher than he'd anticipated. "Fair enough. Then would it be possible to perhaps buy you a coffee? Maybe we could talk a little bit."

"Talk?"

"Yes. Just talk. No date. Coffee."

He knew this was the safest option. An offer to buy her dinner might mean wine, alcohol, and who knows what that could lead to or what she might think it would lead to. So coffee was the right choice. He was hoping she was just curious enough to give him a chance to make amends.

He was right.

"Okay, but I have some errands to do this afternoon. Monday is a teaching day for me, and I've got some things to prepare for class. So I could meet you for coffee. But I can't take too long."

"Perfect."

THEY MET AT the Purple Haze ice cream and coffee bar. She wore a bright yellow big shirt that hung off one shoulder, black exercise form-fitting pants, psychedelic-colored running shoes, and no makeup.

She really didn't need any.

"Hey, thanks, Martel." He pulled a chair out for her, and she promptly sat on the other side. "What can I get you?"

"Just coffee. It's good here."

When he returned, she was leaning on the table, her chin in her palm. She cupped the mug with both hands and blew on it then took a timid sip.

"So you just went home from the reception?" he asked.

"I'm guessing you didn't."

"I hung out a bit with Renny and a couple of the guys. Everything broke up pretty early."

She shrugged and continued to sip her coffee.

He now wished he'd practiced something, because his brain had drained the moment he saw her in the parking lot. He scooted closer to the table, the metal legs on the chair scraping on the polished concrete slab floor. Then he cleared his voice.

He took a quick peek at her expression and caught the remnants of a smirk just before she erased it. It gave him a little courage.

"Last night at the reception probably wasn't the best time to talk to you, Martel. It's been a long time. I never expected to run into you here in Florida. My friends back home would call it dumb luck, not divine providence."

"Cute."

"Thanks, I worked on that a bit," he lied.

She was good at masking her feelings. That was a big change from before. In those days, her heart was transparent and her eyes said everything. Words were nearly unnecessary. But if he was going to do this right, he'd have to make do because he'd blown his chance at trust with her. And he didn't blame her one bit.

"I meant what I said about owing you an apology—" He held his palm up to her in case she was going to cut him off again. "You're probably thinking I'm scheming to get something from you, and I understand that. Maybe you will never believe me, and that's on me."

"You'd be correct."

"I understand. But I've had ten years to think about things. I should have tried to reach you. And the more time that went by, well, the worse I felt. I did hear about your mother, and I'm sorry."

"Your parents?"

"Yes, before they sold the winery, my mother sent me the clipping from the newspaper."

"Ah." She appeared distracted with something then sipped her coffee again.

"It said you were living in Oregon. I already knew about your dad, of course."

"Of course. I understand he never showed up for the funeral," she said.

"You didn't attend?"

"I was too ill."

"Oh. Anything serious?"

Martel delivered him a brittle smile. "I'm fine now, if that's what you're asking."

"Well, I liked your mom."

"She used to like you too."

"Yeah. *Used* to. I had that coming."

"Can we just get on with what you wanted to tell me, because I've got a lot of things to do?"

This irritated him. She was being very tough on him. But he was smart enough not to show it. "I'll be brief, then." He leaned forward. "What we had, well, to be honest, it *scared* me. I didn't know how to tell you."

"You honestly think this explains things? I can see this was a waste of time."

"I went off, joined the Navy—not because I *wanted* to be a SEAL but just to see if I could make it. I shouldn't have felt that way, but I didn't know how to tell you I still needed to explore that, to see if I was the kind of guy who could hack it. Become one."

He thought perhaps her eyes had moistened up but then decided he was wrong.

"You might have thought it was something you'd done. It was *my* immaturity. It really had nothing to do with you."

Her crossed legs were kicking reflexively, her shoe tapping on the leg of the table. She lowered her forehead a bit and spoke in a clipped, choppy tone. "You don't have to tell me that. I know full well it didn't have anything to do with me. None of it ever did."

She grabbed her keys and stood. That's when he realized he'd just done it again.

"If you say you're sorry one more time, I'll come over there and strangle you. I'll kick your balls and then I'll tie them around your neck. Don't come near me again, Damon. I am so done with you and your selfishness. You haven't learned a damned thing. It was never about me because it was always about you."

He didn't stop her. The black coffee she only partially sipped sat sadly on her side of the table, abandoned. Just like he'd done to her.

He was surprised she even had the courage to have coffee with him when he thought about it on the way back to the rental.

He closed the front door quietly and dropped his keys on the kitchen counter. He needed some of that sand and sunshine, because for all his personal pep talk, he felt pretty hollow inside.

Maybe nobody ever really changes.

He shed his first flip-flop on the sand dune. He took his second one off at the surf and tossed it into the gulf. He watched it bounce, float, sink, and then float again, rolling over. And then the sea brought it back to him.

This time, he cranked his arm way back and tossed it beyond the waves. A pelican was flying low, cruising the shallow water, and crashed down. He came up with the black rubber object he must have thought was a fish. Damon followed the trajectory of the pelican and saw the bird drop it in the dunes some distance from him and fly away.

He looked back at the ocean. He could throw things like that all day long, and that damned ocean would just return it every time. He was playing a surreal game of fetch with an inanimate object.

The ocean didn't react to the sight of the pelican carrying his flip-flop away. She just continued to roll, showing her soft lacy white underbelly, hissing at him, teasing him with the certainty that between the two of them, she was the more constant.

And she'd win every time.

CHAPTER 6

*W*HAT WAS SHE *expecting?*

She had predicted how he'd be. She knew it was going to be a waste of time, but she went anyway.

Why?

Still, it was nice that she gave him the chance. That part of it was good. She'd stood her ground, and he didn't make her shake like she used to. Seeing him so flawed didn't make their situation any better, but it helped her to understand that Damon was just doing the best he could. He didn't have the capacity to do anything else. It lessened some of the anger she felt towards him.

Choices, choices. Everything is about choices.

Her mood brightened, and her energy was back. All afternoon, she stocked up on food for the week She'd bought pens, pencils, and school supplies for her classroom from a big box store and finally stopped to buy herself some flowers from the little Latino lady around the corner from her house. She bought pink roses and scented tuberoses, to match the ones in her bouquet sitting in water in her kitchen.

She thought about Kaitlyn and Greg on their honeymoon in the Caribbean. That was one part of the world she had yet to explore and decided to check out some inexpensive vacation packages for Christmas break.

Now that she'd lost her traveling buddy, she would have to be on the lookout for another teacher friend to travel with.

Her telephone rang. It was Kaitlyn's mom, Mrs. Carrington.

"Well, hello there. You must be exhausted."

The older woman chuckled. "I think I surprised everyone. Kaitlyn's uncle and some of the cousins are passed out all over the house. They can't believe I'm still going strong. Of course, I didn't do any of the heavy lifting, and that's the secret."

"But you must have been the organizer," Martel added.

"Oh my, she hired this wedding planner who didn't know the first thing about running a business. She knew about weddings and was great with suggestions and creativity. But getting all the moving parts to work together? That talent was seriously lacking."

"It turned out beautifully. Such a lovely wedding."

"Thank you. I was pleased too."

"So, what's on your mind?" Martel asked.

"Oh, I can't help it. I was feeling a tad bit lonely, to be honest with you. I was hoping you wouldn't mind."

Mrs. Carrington did sound tired.

"I'm all ears. Do you have any last-minute details you weren't able to finish? I have school tomorrow, but if you need help with anything, I'd be happy to give you a hand later on, or perhaps after school tomorrow."

"No, Carl and the family did a great job with all that. The tables, chairs, linens, and dishes are back at the rental company.

"Based on your flowchart, no doubt."

She chuckled again. "How did you know?"

"Kaitlyn has told me how smart you are. And organized. Said you could have run a large company if you'd wanted to."

"I don't know about that. I was rather proud that I didn't blow up at the planner."

"There's a talent to that. My mother's father was a minister. He was one of those guys who had mastered the lost art of getting people, and volunteers at that, to work together. Every church he ran split into factions when he left."

"He sounds like a wonderful man."

"He was. I spent a lot of time around him. So what else is on your mind, Mrs. Carrington?"

"Heavens, call me Phyllis. I keep thinking you're speaking about my mother-in-law when you call me Mrs. Carrington."

"Phyllis, it is then." Martel waited.

"I take it Kaitlyn told you about their news?"

"Yes. She told me just before the ceremony. I'm happy for them, aren't you?"

"I'm happy if Kaitlyn's happy. I'm just glad her grandmother isn't alive to see it. She would never have understood."

Martel felt the hairs at the back of her neck stiffen. "She'll make a wonderful mother, Phyllis. She's in love with her husband, and I can see he's devoted to her. Bringing a little one into the world under those circumstances seems like exactly the right thing to do."

"You're probably right."

"Aren't you excited to be a grandmother?"

Phyllis paused.

"Phyllis?"

"I may not make it that far, Martel. May I share something personal with you?"

"I'd be honored."

"I'm being told to get my affairs in order. My doctor says to do it quickly because there's no telling how long I will feel healthy enough to do so. I'm really being very stubborn about it."

"Oh my gosh. I'm so sorry."

"Sorry. How I hate that word. I think they should just outlaw it, don't you?"

"I completely agree."

"There's this little girl Phyllis in me standing in the mirror with her hands on her hips frowning and saying 'no!' She's a very nasty little girl, denying my illness and my lack of a future. That little girl is giving me fits, Martel."

It wasn't what Martel had expected to hear. "So this means you haven't told Kaitlyn yet, is that right?"

"That's exactly right. I don't know if I want to. I don't know if I want to tell the family either."

Martel was alarmed. "But you should. You should be honest with them. Otherwise, don't you think it might make them angry? You'd be robbing them of the time they'd like to spend with you. You're taking that choice away from them. Do you really think that's fair?"

"I wish you weren't right, Martel. How did you get to be so wise?"

"I've made all the mistakes there are to make first. You're talking to someone who is deeply flawed and probably always will be."

"Well, I don't see it."

"Good. I've been working on my technique."

Both women laughed. Her eyes teared up all of a sudden.

"You know, I used to talk to my mother like this, all the time. I miss the connection I had with her. I could tell her anything, and she'd still love me. She wasn't always happy with it, but I always felt loved. Thank you for reminding me."

"Sounds like your mother and I could have been best friends. That was lovely, Martel. Thank you."

Martel felt something shift inside her chest. It had been so long since she'd cherished anything, felt like she truly loved someone and was loved in return. She let her tears fall without stopping to wipe her face. She made a bold decision.

"I have something I've not told anyone except my mother, Phyllis. With your permission, should I tell you?"

"Well, I'll answer you the same as you did. I'd be honored."

She took a deep breath. "I got pregnant at nineteen and gave my baby up for adoption. It's been one of the hardest things I've ever done. I think about her every day. I can't stop thinking about her."

"Oh, sweetheart. You're carrying that burden all alone?"

"That's the way it has to be. Now you know why I'm so happy for Kaitlyn and Greg. I never had that choice."

"You mean the father didn't want anything to do with the baby?"

"Or me."

"Oh honey. I have a gun. Can I kill this man?"

Martel laughed at the dark humor. "Not if I get him first."

"How old would she be, if I may ask?"

"Almost ten. I've had no contact with her or the parents who adopted her, and that was the choice my mother encouraged me to make before she died. She never got to meet my daughter before she passed."

"I can't imagine a man who would give up his responsibilities like that. That's just unforgivable."

"I never told him, Phyllis."

The silence on the end of the line made her nervous.

"Why?"

"He just left. He left without saying anything."

"That's unforgivable."

"I agree."

"Do you ever intend on seeing her?"

"I don't know if I can, based on how we handled the private adoption. But your secret is similar, don't you think? That's why I'm conflicted on whether or not I should tell him."

"You know this man?"

"I met him again a few days before the wedding. And he wants—" She wasn't sure how to finish the sentence.

"He wants to have a second chance?"

"I think so. Maybe. He's trying hard. I suspect that if he knew what I'd done, he wouldn't want anything to do with me. You see my dilemma?"

"I think you gave me the answer, Martel. You told me I should tell Kaitlyn about the seriousness of my health issues. What he did to you was unforgivable. So is not telling him, especially since you've now been given a chance to."

SHE THOUGHT ABOUT their conversation all afternoon and into the evening. Phyllis had told her she had to make up her mind what she wanted. The decisions she and her mother had made to send her to Oregon during her pregnancy and then to give the baby up for adoption could not be reversed. She was convinced that it was the best solution for her daughter.

But with respect to Damon, some of her animosity toward him had dissipated, now that he demonstrated his willingness to change. It would be a stretch to see them having a true second chance at love, but was there the space for her to let him try? She had to admit that she'd made choices without telling him, thereby robbing him of being part of those choices. It was too late for that now. But was it truly too late for a second chance with Damon?

Did her anger cloud those decisions? Could she have reached out and somehow found him, even after he'd left? Or did her pride affect the outcome she chose?

She decided the answer to those questions was yes.

That outcome years ago had also changed the life of their daughter. Good or bad, that fell squarely on her shoulders. And so was the choice before her now. If it was possible, should she turn away?

Her fingers were shaking when she picked up her cell and dialed that number he'd called from. He picked it up before there was a second ring.

"Damon, I've been thinking. Could I have a do-over?"

"You know the answer to that, Martel. You don't even have to ask."

"Just so we're clear, could we maybe just be friends, talk to each other? I don't want the whole thing. I just want to be friends *without* benefits."

"I'll take that. I'll take it any way you want."

"No strings. No expectations. No sex."

He cleared his throat. "Is that healthy?"

"Okay then, I'm hanging up, Damon."

"I get it. I really do. No sex. Just friends and see where it takes us."

"Exactly."

"How do you want to do this, Martel?"

"I'll fix dinner. Tomorrow night?"

"We'll watch the sunset, and then I'll leave."

"I can live with that."

"Okay then. And, Martel, thank you."

"Don't say that yet. You haven't tasted my cooking."

She texted him her address and hung up.

What have I just done?

CHAPTER 7

DAMON WAS UP early and took a run with Renny.

"I got to hand it to you, Demon Seed. You clearly have the touch."

"Don't say that. You'll jinx it."

"God forbid." Renny muffled a whistle when two lovelies bounced their way along the beach and right into their fantasies.

"I can't unsee that," Damon said.

"I wouldn't believe you if you said you could. Contrary to what the priest told me growing up, looking is not a sin."

"But you're single."

Renny stopped abruptly. "Whoa there, cowboy. You just wait a fuckin' minute. You're having dinner with your ex and a mighty fine ex at that. You picking out wedding bands and shopping for tuxes already?"

"I didn't say that. Besides, I've got this under control," Damon said as he ran away from Renny. It didn't take long for him to catch up.

"Just what the fuck are you doing? You're like that guy who keeps putting his dick in the electrical socket to see if it will plump up a bit."

"Trust me. I know what I'm doing. We're taking it slow."

"And that means you're single. You look. You're a red-blooded male. That's what we do. That's what we're supposed to do. It's an ancient rite. We get to be all full of testosterone and make them want to drop their drawers and have babies. It's human nature."

"Where did you get all this crazy shit, Renny? I'm learning a whole new side of you."

"You know, I seriously don't think you've been paying attention to me. Like ever. I told you there was something about her."

"Martel. Her name's Martel."

"The missing link."

"You're making me think of an anthropology class I had to take once."

"Now that's not a pretty picture. You like hairy girls, Damon?"

He laughed. It didn't matter what Renny told him this morning. Nothing was going to dampen his mood. She'd opened the door to him just a crack. It was all he needed. He felt like he was twenty years old again, so distracted by her beauty he walked into things all the time.

"As a matter of fact, she's part Native American, and she has very little hair."

"It could all be an act. Women get waxed. Men get clipped."

They both stopped running and looked at each other. "Ew," they said in unison.

They began running again. "At least you're thinking about it. That's a good sign. Just listen to your Uncle Renny, like you didn't do with Charlene. Remember I gave you all that advice?"

"Which advice would that be, Renny?"

"Remember when I told you she liked to spend money? Did you listen? No. Not until your credit cards piled up to over a hundred thousand dollars. Remember I told you when she maxed them out she'd be gone?"

"Yeah, but cutting up the credit cards doesn't work, Renny. They mail new ones."

"You close the accounts."

"And she gets new ones. New joint ones."

"I told you she was always looking in the mirror, checking herself out. She liked for people to like looking at her, and later on—"

Damon stopped again. "Just shut up, Renny."

"Just trying to be helpful."

They continued their jog.

"I'm not sure what kind of advice you're giving me on Martel."

"She's got good spirits, Damon. She's got you being nice to Julie. Her influence on you is to be a better man. She makes you stand up tall when she comes into the room. She makes you feel good."

"I can hardly wait for the advice."

"My advice is not to let her go. She has something you need. Something you didn't even know you needed. That thing that makes you excited to be alive, not wallowing in your mistakes. It's very simple, Damon. Charlene? Mistake! Martel? Go for it, and don't fuckin' let her go."

All the talk about body hair had Damon convinced he needed a haircut and a professional shave.

"I have just the right guy. Greg told me about him. The guy lost his hand in Desert Storm. He cuts hair with a hook."

"No way."

"Swear to God!"

"I'm not sure I'd want him around sharp blades, Renny."

"Oh, he does shaves. Greg said he's got a cute little Russian gal who does body waxing if you want that, though."

"Men get their bodies waxed?"

"Fuckin' A. My ex demanded it for the honeymoon."

"Did it make a difference?"

"Not to me. I guess she liked it. Cost around two hundred bucks too. And three days out, man, did I itch. Little stubble all over the place, you know, in your crotch, under your arms."

"Wait, you got your crotch and underarms waxed?"

"I did. And I can honestly say I will never do it again."

"Renny, why do I listen to you?"

"You don't, remember? That's what started all this conversation."

Sure enough, the one-armed barber did a perfect job with the haircut and shave. He also recommended a local tattoo parlor so Damon could have Charlene's initials altered.

He put on his one good tropical shirt, his freshly washed jeans, and Renny's flip-flops and headed out the door.

"How did you get a pelican to abscond with your flip-flops?"

"It's a very long story and I haven't got the time."

Renny came over and gave him a manly hug. "I'm rooting for you, painless. She says she just wants to be friends, just do that. Make her beg for it, man! You want her so wet and horny she'll be riding your gear shift lever and looking in the kitchen for the turkey baster. Be that guy she wants. That gentleman. I know it's hard, but try for it. I'll bet in one or two dates, you two will forget you were separated for ten years. You'll forget about Charlene, and Lydia, and that Candy chick, the dancer at Lonnie's?"

"Oh yeah. With the basketball tits."

"You've made, by and large, some good decisions, Damon. You just need to clean it up a bit. You get happy, she gets happy. You keep her happy, and you have a good life. You won't have to get waxed or buy her anything fancy or give her credit cards to keep her around. Hell, she might even do housework now and then!"

"Honestly, Renny, I don't think about Martel at all like that. She's different."

"There you go, sport. Good attitude! Just keep it tuned to that channel, and you're on your way!"

With that send-off, he stopped by for a nice bottle of wine and found a pear-shaped bottle of Francis Ford Coppola's "Sofia" wrapped in pink cellophane. It was a light pink rose blend. He stopped by Publix and bought some roses, hoping he made the right choice to bring her pink ones.

Best not to go overboard.

Martel was wearing a colorful kaftan over white skintight pants. She'd pinned her hair up, letting her bangs frame her pretty face. Pieces of her long strands fell down the back of her neck, some of them in curls.

She loved the rose and the matching roses. "My favorite," she said, placing them in water and setting them next to the bouquet from the wedding.

Her house was colorfully fixed up with beach signs and posters. An old surfboard was strapped to the corner by the front door, hooks nailed into it for a coat rack. Yellow lamps in the living room were shaped like seahorses.

Smoke billowed in the patio along the dunes where she was grilling zucchini, corn on the cob, and steaks.

"I don't normally cook this much food but didn't want you to go home hungry," she laughed as she plated the steaks, her other hand clasped around the wine glass.

He helped her bring things inside, and they sat down.

"Home cooking and with a tablecloth too," he said, admiring how she'd arranged everything.

"I'm glad you like it."

They toasted and then dug in.

Renny was right about how he wanted to be a better man around Martel. He noticed he did sit up straighter. He listened more and asked questions instead of talking about himself. He watched the way the little dangle earrings she wore caught the fire from the candles she'd set. The room became washed in the orange glow of a budding sunset outside.

He made note of it.

"Oh my gosh. I almost forgot. We can't miss the sunset!" she squealed, grabbing his hand and the bottle of rose. He let her tug him over the sand dunes onto the warm white sand and the hardened shore. Big white fluffy clouds had morphed into purple smokestacks reaching toward Heaven. Blushes and streaks of deep orange and yellow faded in and out around the sky as the sun touched the horizon.

He was standing next to her when she whispered, "My favorite part."

He'd been watching the side of her face and her hair that his fingers wanted to sift through and re-clasp in her clip. He completely agreed. She was his most favorite part, the part of his life before all the other stuff filled up with clutter and got complicated. She was the tip of the pizza, the center of the cream puff, the first lick of his favorite ice cream cone. She was the beautiful part of the song he played on repeat, that melody in the middle that made the rest of the theme tolerable. The change-up of key, the slight adjustment of pitch and tone that made the world magical and everything possible.

She caught him looking at her.

"You're not watching. You're going to miss it, Damon."

"I'm not missing a thing, Martel, trust me."

She gave him a sly, twinkling look while squinting one eye. "Remember what I said."

"I remember. I remember it all, Martel."

She turned and watched the sun. He slipped his arm around her waist and stood as close to her beating heart as he could, his face next to hers, and watched it with her. She was shaking. Her pulse had quickened, and her breathing deepened.

"Is it possible, Martel? Do we have a chance?"

"The truth?"

"We promised, remember?" He held his breath.

"I don't know yet, Damon. Until then, what I can give you is this sunset."

She pointed to the orange spot that was slowly erasing. He looked for the green flash, and thought he saw just a glimpse. It was fleeting. The orange was giving way to gray. The light blue was becoming indigo. Several early stars came out. People began walking back to the beach paths or into their backyards.

She drank out of the wine bottle and handed it to him.

He drank, spilling a little at the side of his mouth. She watched him, licking her lips, but did not kiss him. With his tongue, he captured the spill and studied her face. He could see from her breathing she was aroused, and it was a thing of beauty.

"Day's over, Damon. Our time is up."

Did she feel his heart groan, begging for her to give him some encouragement? If she could just do one or two little things, he'd do all the rest. He knew he could bring her happiness beyond her wildest dreams.

He took her hand, and this time, he led her over the sand dunes, through the patio and back inside the house.

"Thank you," he said as he brought her hand to his mouth and kissed it. "It was a perfect evening."

He could see the blush on her cheeks from the wine. Her plump lips glistened by candlelight. She faced him, pressing both palms to his and letting her fingers mate with his.

"Say something," he whispered. He held his breath and waited.

Her smile was gentle. "Someday. There's a lot to unpack, all the things that happened in those past ten years. The flight to get here was long, and I'm tired."

He was going to say something like "No need to unpack. We can sleep naked," but he didn't. Instead, he said, "Friends. I've missed you, my friend."

"Me too." Then she added, "Thank you for showing me this side of you, Damon. I hope there's more of that to come."

"There's a lot more of that. More than you'd know what to do with."

She snuggled into his embrace, and he began to feel the familiar magic happen all over again. He kissed her ear and did not follow up with the words his heart wanted to whisper.

I never stopped loving you.

It didn't scare him to feel it all over. She pulled away and dropped his hands.

"This was nice. Let's see what tomorrow brings."

"Fair enough." He walked over to the kitchen and picked up his keys. "Can I see you tomorrow?"

"I'd like that."

"Same time, same place?" he asked.

She checked her watch. "Tomorrow starts in exactly two hours and fifty minutes."

He didn't dare move a muscle. Had he heard it correctly? Was he invited to spend the night?

She lifted the coffee table lid and produced a comforter and pillow. "It's comfortable here, if you want. Or I can see you after school tomorrow."

"Are you sure it's okay?"

"I'm okay with it."

"Will you wake me up tomorrow?" he asked. "I don't want to miss it."

"I'll make sure you don't miss it," she said as she pushed the pillow and comforter into his chest. "Good night."

He was entranced watching her saunter to her bedroom door. Behind that door, she'd be naked. She'd beg for him, just like Renny said. He'd be waiting to show her how he could be gentle and how deep his passion grew for her.

"Good night, Martel."

CHAPTER 8

S HE'D PULLED ASIDE the curtains so moonlight could filter into her bedroom and wake her sometime during the dark of night. She showered and put on a sheer gown with embroidered flowers over her nipples. He would be able to see everything. The gown was only a shadow covering, something to stall him for a few seconds before he unleashed her.

With her heart pounding in her ears, she lay back on the bed, welcoming sleep because it would make the waiting disappear. Her hand brushed across the tiny flowers on her bodice then drifted down to the cavern between her legs.

She wasn't going to touch herself first. Like he had done over ten years ago, he would be the one to open her up again and set her on fire. The pain of knowing they'd lost all that time they could have been together was exquisite. She'd waited this long, she could wait a little longer.

HER CLOCK READ one-thirty when she awakened. The door to her bedroom creaked when she opened it, so by the time she made it over to the couch, he was already awake. He pulled his T-shirt over his head and shimmied his boxers down his hips as she drew closer.

He stood, completely naked, embracing her and letting her feel his hardness lodged between her thighs. He tipped her chin up with his right hand and then devoured her with a deep kiss. Her nipples knotted as she heard his hungry groan. His hands lifted the night-gown and then reached for her, massaging her wet sex, suddenly dropping to his knees and lapping her juices.

Crouching before her, he spread her thighs, running his canines along her soft bare lips, his tongue flicking her clit back and forth, making it stiff and throbbing.

She squealed as he pressed his thumbs against her nub and, with a slow downward stroke, lodged inside her opening where he massaged in circular strokes until she was quivering with pleasure.

"You are so sweet. Oh my God, so sweet!" he whispered.

Standing again, he pulled her body to his chest. His lips still wet with her stimulation, he kissed her. Their tongues played, stroking and darting until he suddenly hoisted her up, wrapping her legs around his hips, and brought her into the bedroom.

Damon laid her down, climbed over her, and peeled back the thin gown. His hands pressed over her nipples, down her waist, his forefinger finding the diamond stud lodged in her belly button.

"There it is. I've missed this little thing."

"I've missed this too, Damon," she said, stroking his shaft, squeezing his tip, and covering it with his precum.

He spread her knees to the sides, dove into her belly button, and sucked the diamond stud. His tongue painted a path down over the tiny stretch marks just below, and then further to enter her again. He looked up, watching her undulate under the gentle ministrations his fingers performed on her. She reached for his butt cheeks, sliding herself down and then rubbing her mound up and down his shaft.

Halfway in the seated position, she was desperate to have him deep inside her. She arched up, and he let her impale herself on him, let her slide slowly until he filled her, let her move up and down on him, squeezing him inside with her muscles.

She leaned back, bracing herself with one arm while she angled herself a quarter turn to feel his powerful thrusts as his cock pressed the insides of her delicate walls. She matched his long fluid hip movements with her own, opening to him deeper.

His urgency spiked her libido, making her heart race. As he pressed his groin into her faster, he clutched her thigh and pressed her buttocks up into him from behind, forcing himself inside deep, riding her hard all the way to his hilt. Just as she was about to release, he slowed, peppering her with kisses, tasting and sucking the softness beneath her breasts, twisting her nipples until they flamed. He covered her mouth with kisses as she arched to press her chest against his, holding tight to his hips with her thighs.

When at last she spilled, he gentled, letting her ride the wave of her own orgasm. All of a sudden, he groaned, matching her pulsations with his own. His sad moan broke her heart as he filled her, holding her still until he was spent.

She drew his hungry kisses from him. Softly, they climbed down together, sweat rolling off their bodies, breathing hard as they collapsed in a tangle of legs, arms, and sheets.

The exhaustion was thrilling. Just as they used to do, she lay with him still lodged inside her.

Before she closed her eyes for the final time, he covered her arms with his, extending to reach her fingers and mate one more time with them, and squeezed.

"Welcome home, Damon."

SHE DARTED AWAKE, worried that she'd miss her first class. She smelled coffee just before Damon appeared at her doorway with a steaming mug. His red, white, and blue boxers were deliciously tented, and he caught her checking him out before he bent over and handed her the mug.

She propped a pillow behind her and raised her knees, leaning on the padded headboard. With both hands, she sipped.

The sex was better now that they were older. And she was more of a participant than she remembered from before.

He turned on his side, placing his coffee on the bedside table and then slid down next to her, his hand fingering the slit between her thighs. "I have to ask you a question."

"Go ahead," she whispered and took another sip.

He stopped fondling her.

"But don't stop doing that, please."

"You like that?"

"You know I do. Is that your question?"

"No, it's not." He rimmed her opening, and she nearly dropped her coffee mug. She bit her lips and closed her eyes.

Damon rescued the mug and placed it next to his.

"The question I have is, did you get bare for me?"

She felt wicked when she recalled the little appointment Kaitlyn had insisted she had done. Smiling, she covered his fingers with her own. "Partly. I did it so we could enjoy it together."

He directed two of her fingers inside, making her arch in pleasure, pushing up. His hot tongue flicked her bud back and forth. She jumped. She felt him move against the back of her hand. She withdrew her fingers just as he entered her one more time.

It was impossible to get enough of him. She considered calling in sick but knew that she'd enjoy the waiting all day until they could explore again. She'd feel her swollen sex as she walked, sat, drove her car. She'd remember this, the way he played with her body and took her until she was ragged and desperate to be taken again. The way he tasted her.

Afterwards, she quickly showered and then dressed. He was waiting for her in the kitchen with a scrambled egg.

"You need to keep your energy up. I have plans for you tonight, Martel."

"I can hardly wait. I get off at four," she whispered as her fingers touched his cheek. She planted a kiss on his lips. "I can't wait."

His hand had lifted the hem of her skirt. His eyes got big as he slid his palm over her buttocks and discovered she wasn't wearing panties.

"Very nice, Martel. Are you sure you're not itching to stay home?"

"I'm itching for all kinds of things I'm hoping you'll do with me."

His forefinger penetrated her one more time, and she sucked in air between her teeth. She lifted her skirt to her waist, staring down at the sight of his fingers massaging and then losing themselves in the lips of her bare sex.

Kaitlyn was right. She wasn't going to be able to keep her own hands off her pantiless, violated, completely nude sex all day until she came home to him.

He withdrew, slid the skirt down her thighs and rubbed his forefinger over her lips. "Now that's the way everyone should go to work. Wet and full of desire."

"Thank you, Damon."

She extricated herself from his arms and walked to the front door. Remembering she'd forgotten her purse and her keys, she turned. He was holding them in front of him.

"Did you forget something?"

CHAPTER 9

"**H**ONEY, I'M HOME!" Damon shouted as he walked through the front door.

"Out here," came the response from Renny. He was reading a magazine in his swim trunks, catching some sun. Damon retrieved a beer from the refrigerator and joined him.

"Well, would you look at that? You're actually smiling, Damon."

"Yup."

"Come on. I want the deets."

"No can do. My lips are sealed, Renny."

"Now that's a crying shame. Figured the longer I went without seeing you, the longer the very graphic tale of wanton sex and foreplay I'd get. Just what the hell were you doing for the past twelve hours?"

Damon was proud to share what he could. "It worked. Your idea worked."

"Really?"

"It did. We had a nice dinner. We watched the sunset together, and we didn't have sex."

"So why are you just now returning? She throw you out?"

"No, I told you it worked pretty good. We decided to wait until the next day, which was this morning. I slept on the couch and was rewarded with the gift of her presence early in the morning, and we fooled around until she left for work." He took a drink from his bottle and grinned.

"Pretty happy camper, then, I guess."

"Very."

"So, what's the plan?"

"I go back over tonight."

"Have you eaten yet?"

"Just a scrambled egg. I'm starving."

Renny took them to a local burger bar, which sat on the beach at Treasure Island, two towns away. They took a table outside under the thatched overhang, near the railing, watching people as they strolled or biked by. The sky had remained clear and bright blue, nearly matching the color of the ocean.

Renny stuck his French fries in the paper nut cup of tomato ketchup. "So, what is it with Martel? How far back do you guys go, high school?"

"Almost. She was finishing up high school, and I'd just done my first year of Junior College. Neither of us was sure what we wanted to do, although I was thinking about the Navy. She wanted to teach, but her mom was pretty torn up when she found out her dad was chasing his secretary, and he got up and left."

"Hell of a guy."

"We dated that whole year and into the summer. It got pretty serious, hot and heavy. I won't lie to you, it was a lot of fun. But as the months went by, I felt like I was going to just get sucked into all the small-town drama. I wanted to do more than play house, but, dammit, I really loved her. I know that now."

"And?"

"I got this crazy idea about joining the Navy to become a SEAL. This is the part I don't feel great about."

"So, you decided to try out. No harm in that, Damon. What, she didn't want you to go?"

"Nah, man. I never gave her the chance. It scared the shit out of me. I was young, Renny. Real young. I wasn't ready, but I didn't know how to tell her. I did a really shitty thing. I just left, and I left without saying good-bye. I figured I'd come back and, you know, make it right, but I just never did."

"That's pretty cold."

"It was a horrible way to treat her." Damon squinted into the horizon. "She was a virgin when I met her. I told her things to…"

"To get what you wanted."

"At the time I told myself I wasn't doing that. I loved her like a twenty-year-old sex-craved kid trying to play papa, and in the end, I just had to leave it all behind. It scared me. It really, really scared me, Renny."

"Well, did you try to contact her?"

"I did. Right after Basic. I came home to help my parents move. Her friends said she'd moved to Oregon. I didn't have the guts to face her mom. I could have tried harder to reach out to her. But you know, it was half-hearted. Neither one of us tried, really. So, I just felt she was done with me. But I always felt bad about it, Renny."

"Yeah. I have this rule. No virgins. It gets complicated."

"I was thinking about this the other day. In a way, this relationship stuff, not like between the Team guys, you and me or anything, but with women—that's the real hard stuff. I don't give a shit about jumping out of an airplane at midnight or swimming to place an underwater charge. Everyone thinks that's the hard stuff. But that's way easier for me."

"I hear you. That's why I'm not going to get married until I get out."

"Yeah. My marriage to Charlene was, well, it was because she wanted it. None of it ever rubbed off on me. I don't know why I got talked into it."

"I tried to warn you. Remember?"

"You did that. And I was too stubborn to listen. I think I was just a little bit lonely. Remember when we found those girls who had been kidnapped and sold off? The world is a pretty fucked up place sometimes. I guess I was just looking for a little piece for myself. A part of that magic I felt with Martel, to be honest."

"I hope you find it again."

"I think I did, Renny. I'm going to try to do it the right way this time."

"Kinda soon, don't you think?"

Damon shook his head. "I've thought about that too." He stared into the eyes of his buddy. "Maybe I just don't want to lose her again. She's the real deal. I think I'm finally man enough to handle it. All of it."

"A word of caution?"

"Oh, here it comes, that advice I'll wish I had taken later on."

"Can't help it, my friend."

"So, what's your advice?"

"Finish your divorce first."

Damon threw his napkin at him. "You asshole."

"No wait, I'm not done. Sleep on it a bit. Go back to San Diego and really think about if she'd fit in."

"I think she should make that determination."

"Then schedule a meet and greet. Take it slow. Ease into it. Make sure you're doing the right thing."

Damon grinned and had more of his beer.

"What's so funny?"

"That's what *you* told me to do. That's what *she* said she wanted to do. That's what *I* told her I wanted to do. And what did we do?"

"You jumped in with both feet."

"Yup."

They sat silent for a few long minutes. Finally, Renny spoke up. "That's how we roll, Damon. We go all in all the time. That's what we're trained to do. It's a skillset, to be honest. Keeps us alive and makes us more valuable. We're men of action, and that's not just ego talking. We like it dangerous and unpredictable and take command of the situation. Figure it out. Work together for a common goal. Watch out for the other guy. But when it comes to affairs of the heart, well, sometimes it's much harder to hold back."

Damon agreed. "Fire, adjust, ready, aim, and fire again."

"Got that right. Trained to deal with whatever we get. But the ladies are a problem. Always a problem."

Damon finished his beer and stood. "Come on. I think I have to get back. Want to pick up some things for dinner, and then I'll run you home."

"Playing house again, are we?"

"You betcha. And loving every minute of it. For now."

On their way back to the rental, Renny got a call from their LPO, Kyle Lansdowne.

"Got you on speaker, Kyle. Damon's with me."

"Oh good. Hey, fellas, I'm afraid I have some bad news. I'm going to need you back here for the big game coming up. I'm making arrangements as we speak. You'll get the email in about an hour as soon as it's arranged."

Damon leaned over. "How soon?"

"Hoping for tomorrow. I'll try not to make it too early, in case you had plans. I'm sorry. We got too many on injured reserve, and I need you guys."

"Roger that," Renny said.

They both knew the rules. No names of places or specific dates would be given, if it could be helped.

"You guys run into Andy? One of the new guys? He's out there somewhere too."

"Nope, not yet. Is he going back as well?"

"He's staying a bit longer. We may do some quick substitutions, so he'll be coming back eventually, but I need you guys now, unless you've stepped on a jellyfish or fallen from the sky paragliding."

"We did swim with some sharks, but I nearly have all my toes, Kyle," Renny quipped.

"Glad to hear it. That will keep your run times decent at least."

Renny placed the phone back in his shirt pocket. "I knew I should have muted it for a couple more days, dammit."

Damon didn't say a word. He was recalculating his plan, trying to cover everything in his head he needed to tell her. Renny was right. Things were going pretty fast again. He hoped that didn't doom his mission.

DAMON HAD BURGERS, stuffed with Jalapeno cheese sauce for the grill, a green salad with fresh lemon herb dressing he made from scratch, and corn on the cob she had left over from their dinner last night.

At four-thirty, she walked through the door, surprised to see him.

"Found your key under the doormat. Don't ever leave it there," he said, greeting her with a kiss.

"I completely forgot. I have a housekeeper who comes occasionally." She walked to the kitchen, her eyebrows drawn up in her forehead. "Whatever have you been doing?"

"Just something simple. Are you hungry?"

"As a matter of fact," she wrapped her arms around his neck, "I'm starved."

"Good." He patted her behind and picked up the hamburgers. "I'll put these on, and it will be ready in about ten minutes."

"I'm going to jump into the shower if you don't mind."

"Do you need any help?" he said at the sliding glass door before he walked outside to the grill.

"Always." She blew him a kiss and disappeared.

HE HAD EVERYTHING spread out on the table when she returned, smelling of fresh lemon soap. She wore a silk robe tied at the waist and was rubbing her hands together to finish working in the lemon-scented hand cream.

"I hope you don't mind, finished up your corn I found in the refrigerator. And I warn you, that cheese is hotter than I expected," he said, pointing to the hamburgers. "It's inside there. The cheese mixture is inside."

"Oh. I was wondering. Smells fabulous."

She sat down, lighting the two candles on the table. Damon brought over a bottle of red wine he'd opened and poured a glass for each of them and then sat.

He knew he was going to have to get right down to details so it didn't infringe on some of their playtime.

"We got a call today, and it looks like my stay is going to be cut short, Martel."

She frowned. "No. That's not fair. When do you go back then?"

"Looks like tomorrow."

"Both of you?"

"Unfortunately, yes. I'm so sorry." He reached over the table to grab her hand. "This doesn't usually happen, or at least it's the first time in six years it's happened to me. Usually we go home, work up, and study for our next mission, and then deploy. And, give or take, we know when we're going, within a few days or so."

"So this means there is an emergency somewhere."

"That's probably what it means. And don't ask me where, because I can't tell you."

"Right. I remember that."

He'd inhaled his food, pushing his plate to the side, sipping his wine, and watching as she picked at hers.

"You don't like the cheese?"

"It's really good. I like hot." She blushed and covered her mouth with her hand.

"Yes, I know you do. I'm glad you do."

He took another sip of his wine. She pushed aside her unfinished plate, picked up her wine, and toasted him by candlelight. "Our last night together at Sunset Beach," she whispered, her voice trailing off.

After their glasses touched, he drank the rest of his glass, allowing the full-bodied red to wash over his tongue, wiping out some of the jalapeno. She swirled her wine in the glass and finished hers as well.

"More?"

"I'm fine."

"Tell me something I don't know, Martel." He finished off the bottle and set them both aside. He took her hand in his. "We need to talk."

"I agree."

She watched him rub and squeeze her fingers, turning her hand palm side up and then down. Eventually he held her hand from across the table and leaned forward.

"I don't want to go. We have so much more to say and do. But one thing is certain, I don't want this to end."

Her warm brown eyes were steady, wide open, and he saw that she trusted him.

"How long will you be gone?"

"Could be a week, or it could be months, although that's not likely. Probably something short, but anything can happen. And that's what I wanted to talk to you about."

"I'll be working until Christmas break. Then I get two weeks until after New Year's."

"Would you consider coming to San Diego at Christmas? Unless I'm not back, of course."

"I could consider it." She smiled.

"I asked you before if you thought perhaps we could start all over again, and I feel like we have. I'd like to keep moving in that direction. I'd like to see if we can make it a more permanent arrangement."

She examined their entwined fingers. "I think that's going a little too fast for me right now. Would you consider working out of an East Coast team to be closer to me here in Florida?"

"I've got four more years left on this enlistment. I was considering getting out then. It probably wouldn't work to start up with a new team before I left. But we can talk about it. I know you love Florida. Maybe I can make you love Coronado. The weather is nice, but I'll admit this is nicer."

"Do you have these?" She pointed to the bright orange sky.

"Did we miss it?"

"Not quite."

They both jumped to their feet. She grabbed the comforter from the couch and wrapped it around both of them. He slipped his arm around her waist, and together, they walked over the sand dunes and onto the sparkling sand where they joined people emerging from their houses or filing through the beach access trails for miles in each direction.

It felt like they were going on a pilgrimage with all the other sunset gazers, soaking up the magic and majesty of the dying sun, struggling to spread its light but ultimately overwhelmed by the size and tenacity of the ocean.

"It's the same sunset. Just different latitude. Bigger waves. Sometimes a little colder. This beach is bigger with less people.

"I like the sleepy little beach town feel. I feel like I belong here, Damon."

"But you have an open mind?" He studied the side of her face.

"I have an open mind. But I'm a different woman than I was ten years ago. I have this place that I love, that feels right for me. It isn't something I want to give up."

"Don't worry, Martel. I'm never going to ask you to do something you don't want to do. Just think about it, okay? Think about coming out to San Diego, and we'll have Christmas together on that beach. See if we can create a little magic there too. What do you say sweetheart?"

He could see she was thinking about lots of things she didn't want to discuss, and he knew he shouldn't push. He knew if it was ever going to work between them, he'd need to be patient until she made up her mind.

He let her forefinger rub across his lips, her eyes studying the travel intently. She angled her head, watching her movements back and forth until she stopped, inhaled, and kissed him. Her natural kiss was sweet, not urgent. She gave into him then went deeper, as her chest rose, pressing her breasts against him. With the comforter hiding them, he slipped his hand inside her robe and felt the weight of her warm, perfect breast in the palm of his hand. His hand reached down to between her legs, not violating her, but teasing about something to come later on. With her next kiss, she moaned and then whispered into his ear,

"Are we done with the talking, Damon, because I can't think straight."

"Will people be leaving soon? We could fool around here."

"No," she whispered. "I want you in my bed. I want to smell the sheets with your scent all over them so I won't miss you so much."

"I like to be missed."

She pulled away. He couldn't see her full face because it had turned dark. "Only on one condition," she said. "It's only fun to miss you when I know you're coming back."

He stopped. Hesitated, holding her face in his hands. Just so she knew he meant what he said. "Yes. I'm coming back. Nothing could ever keep me away. Will you wait?"

"I did then. Believe me when I say I did. And, I am still, Damon.

That's a promise."

They slowly strolled to the house. She blew out one of the candles from the table and picked the other one and walked to the bedroom as he followed.

He checked his cell and saw the text. He set his alarm and placed it by the candle on the nightstand. The golden glow flickered. In the hush that was the miracle of them finding each other again after so long, she unpinned her hair, slipped open her silk robe, and let it drop to the floor. Her body was an altar of everything that was good, everything that was pure or could be perfect. It gave him strength and passion. It gave him a sense of home.

And he'd worship at that altar all night long, carefully and patiently showing her just how much she was cherished.

And that he'd never let her go.

CHAPTER 10

MARTEL HADN'T HEARD him leave, and she had been sure she would. She tried to stay awake between their multiple sexual encounters. She remembered having him whisper in her ear things that made her blush, that made every cell in her body scream with pleasure. She remembered seeing a slight pinkish cast to the sky at one point and knew she was going to collapse with complete exhaustion. He even kissed away some tears that surfaced, for some reason.

He asked her if he'd hurt her.

"Yes. You went away."

"I'm right here. Can you feel me? I'm right here, baby."

"Yes."

She'd wrapped her legs around his hips. She'd climbed on top and put on a floor show for him, writhing and reveling in the angle of his hips as he carried her, filled her, but mostly loved her fully. Ardent one moment and urgent another, each time was like she'd never had him before. The more he dove into her, the more she wanted. Her desire for him was outside the human bounds of sleep deprivation, she told herself. She could be this woman he kissed, tasted, pinched, and filled forever. The pain of the loss ten years ago was deliciously adorned in the whispers and fire of this special night.

She was forever altered and would never be the same again. She loved him as a mature woman, not a young woman. With hopeful illusions of a Happily Ever After out there somewhere, not that of a young girl's fantasy.

The sun was demanding, even though the waves lapped on the shore, asking her to sleep on, to dream until her prince came back to her bed. Maybe it was her imagination. It was daylight. Maybe he hadn't really flown back to California. Maybe he was making coffee in the kitchen and had decided to stay behind.

She rolled on her back and felt the throbbing between her legs and how red and swollen she must be. It made her smile that she could feel and would feel for days the result of his lovemaking. It made her want him still.

Slowly, letting the sunlight invade her space in tiny spoonfuls, as if it was lethal doses of reality, she opened her eyes to her new day.

She rolled on her side, burying her head in his pillow, and then held it against her chest and squeezed. She splayed her palm against the cotton surface as if she was caressing his cheek. She remembered he'd begged her to come for him, and she'd done it, watching how her peaking turned him into a man-beast who would take her hard and then ask for more.

She delicately pulled back the sheets, full of the scent of him, and stood naked, ready to face the day.

She needed coffee before her shower. She had enough time to grab something to settle her growling stomach on the way to the school. That feeling of new love deep down in her belly and the heaviness of her eyelids from lack of sleep made her smile. She was still in a trance, drugged with the spell of his strong body calling her to come to him anywhere.

Anywhere?

No. That would be a negotiation. There was lots of time for that.

She started her coffee. Wanting to add some half and half, she dove into the refrigerator to look for it and stopped short, seeing a red can of whipped cream and a note beneath the can.

'Martel, this is for the next time we're together. I completely forgot I wanted to taste this sweet cream between your sweet thighs. Save it for me, and hold that thought I know is going on in your head. I miss you already.'

She put the note on her refrigerator door and secured it with a heart-shaped magnet.

While the coffee was brewing, she retrieved her silk robe and secured the tie around her waist. She checked the time, and she was okay if she only took five minutes to say good morning to the ocean.

The air was chilly, and a white mist swirled between the houses nestled on the beach and the surf. All the sunrise watchers were gone this morning, giving her the beach all to herself.

Miss you already, he'd written.

Only if you're coming back home, she'd whispered last night.

The warm coffee tasted delightful. She sighed and watched a young family walking on the hardened sand, searching for shells and objects of interest. She pretended that she'd had ten years to teach her daughter how to throw rocks at the ocean, how to stick her finger down a hole in the sand and pull out a sand crab, how to dance in her nightgown by the light of the moon.

What am I doing?

She emptied the mug, dashing into the house and under the spray of the shower after tearing off her robe. In five minutes, she was fully dressed. She put last night's dinner dishes in the sink and added water. She grabbed an apple and took off in search of a bagel and her school.

KAITLYN'S SUB CAME over to her during morning break. "Do you know if she is home yet?" the young teacher asked.

"I think they'll be gone for the full week. They're in the Caribbean."

"Do you have the name of the place they are staying or a phone number?" the student-teacher asked.

"No. She never gave it to me. I think her mother might know. The office would have her number. Why?"

"That's just it. The hospital called. They asked me to try to get a message to Kaitlyn that her mother was admitted. I got the impression it wasn't a very good sign."

Martel had expected this, but not so soon. She hoped Phyllis would last at least until Kaitlyn and Greg came back.

"Let me have it. I'll see what I can do. Did you try her cell number?"

"Several times. I've left three messages already."

Martel figured they were on some day trip or tour and Kaitlyn wouldn't or couldn't answer it. She took the message and walked to a school ground bench and dialed the number.

"Duncan Center," the pert voice on the other end of the phone said.

"Yes. I'm a friend of Kaitlyn Carrington, who is on her honeymoon. I understand her mother has been admitted. Phyllis Carrington?"

"She was brought in this morning. You say you are a best friend or cousin of Mrs. Carrington's?

"Yes, ma'am. I was her daughter's maid of honor. Is Phyllis going to be okay?"

"I'm afraid I'm not allowed to give non-family members much in the way of information without a doctor's order."

"Can I see her?"

"Everyone on her floor is hospice. You have to be suited up to see her, but we can arrange that by the time you get here. Can you come today?"

"I'm a teacher, and I can perhaps get off early, say three o'clock?"

"I'll ask her doctor. When will Kaitlyn be home?"

"She's gone for the week. As I said they're in the Caribbean, on their honeymoon."

"Oh dear. See if you can reach her, and I'll do the same. I'm going to need to locate Mrs. Carrington's Health Care Power of Attorney. Her doctor doesn't seem to have it."

"I don't understand."

"Health saving instructions. That sort of thing."

"So she's not expected to live long, then, I take it."

"Again, I wish I could help. We have the HIPAA rules..."

"I get it. We've been trying, but unless I hear, I'll be by the hospital around three. Phyllis knows me. I'm not asking to insert myself where I wouldn't be wanted."

"I'll try to make it happen. See you later this afternoon."

Martel informed the district office what was going on and asked to leave early, citing she had a film the class could watch for the last hour of school if someone from admin could monitor them. She'd already given out the assignments for the day.

They granted her request and asked to be kept informed.

SHE CONSIDERED CALLING Damon but wanted to see Phyllis first. She also hoped Renny might have Greg's cell phone number, since she didn't know anyone else from their circle of friends she could call.

Adrenaline kept her going. The excitement of her new relationship mixed with the feeling of loss while he was away on deployment and now Phyllis. Everything in her life was in flux. The huge emotional swings would take its toll when she finally had a minute to herself. The quiet, peaceful beach was calling her.

The medical center was a private clinic with lush grounds, resembling more of a country club than a hospital. But as she drove past the tall palm trees, the sparkling water and the bird sanctuary, she was struck with what a beautiful place it would be to just pass away into the sunset.

If there had to be a place, that is.

A large hearse was pulling around the back side of the single-story campus, and she shivered. All of a sudden, the idyllic setting began to feel more like a scary movie where awful things happened behind a backdrop used to disguise their real purpose. She was driving through the valley of the shadow of death, just like the Bible said.

She parked, yet something inside her wanted to run. Was she ready for this? Martel felt guilty, disgusted with herself. This was the least she could do for her best friend, to the kind and gentle woman she'd shared secrets with.

Be brave.

She was directed down the wide hall to the right. A nurse was waiting with a disposable gown, gloves, and a headpiece-type contraption with a clear plastic visor covering her face.

Dammit, another veil!

The attendant slipped blue gathered paper slippers over her shoes and opened the door, taking her arm and bringing her into the dark room.

The entire wall over Phyllis's bed was jammed with electronic devices that beeped, flashed colors of red, yellow, and green. There were tubes everywhere. One connected her to an oxygen mask with straps adhering over her ears. She had an I.V., as well as a much larger tube extending out the bottom of the bed from under her sheets.

Phyllis looked so tiny compared to all the equipment, like she was an eight-year-old who'd just had her tonsils out. Her wig was removed, showing her shiny bald head. But her color was good, and she seemed to be breathing comfortably. She wore bright red lipstick, which nearly made her laugh. It had been applied slightly askew.

The nurse nodded to her.

Martel took her hand and called out. "Phyllis? I'm afraid you probably think you don't know me, but it's Martel. I came to see you as soon as I heard."

Phyllis opened her eyes and started to laugh, then coughed. The nurse was right there, adjusting a machine and repositioning her facemask that had gotten dislodged.

Kaitlyn's mom smiled. Her eyes still had that will to live, that fire and fearless courage Martel wasn't sure she herself had.

"Look at us two, would you?" Phyllis growled. She tried to sit up, and the nurse stopped her. She motioned with her finger on her other hand for Martel to lean in closer. Phyllis' right hand clutched Martel's and wouldn't let go.

The nurse slid a chair to the back of Martel's knees, and she sat, leaning over.

With their faces not more than two feet apart, Phyllis still insisted on leaning forward when she said, "Let's just rip out all this stuff and go get an ice cream and run on the beach, okay? Would you please break me out, honey?"

The nurse was giggling.

Phyllis pointed a bony finger at her. "You think that's funny? You never know, it might be just the cure I need."

"Maybe an imaginary beach and imaginary ice cream," the kind nurse softly purred in return.

Phyllis dismissed her with the brush of her hand. "Not the same thing. Not the same thing at all!"

"How do you feel?" Martel asked her and then regretted it when she saw Phyllis' expression.

"Like the turkey at Thanksgiving. I've been stuffed with crap, stitched up, basted, and herbed, and I have a butt plug I didn't ask for," she said as she glared at the nurse. "I mean, when I was a much younger woman, I might have tried one, but it makes me itch."

Martel put her hand up to her mouth to stifle the laughter that was exploding her chest.

"I can't believe you. Your sense of humor is out of this world."

"Yes, ma'am. And that's right where I'm going, too."

"Phyllis, don't say that."

"Should I say, *'Have a nice day?'* perhaps?"

Martel shook her head at the nurse. No doubt they'd been seeing a lot of this behavior.

"Only one way to go, and that's fighting. It makes no sense to me to spend your last moments on earth being miserable, crying your eyes out. Besides, these people don't even know me. They see it every day."

Martel recalled the sight of the hearse driving around the backside of the hospital.

"Well, now that I'm here, what can I get you?"

"How about a young man, like your SEAL friend? I never got one of those. I didn't even know they existed, or else Kaitlyn might not have had the father she did have for all those years!"

Martel was laughing so hard she couldn't see out of the visor. Tiny teardrops obscured what her own eyes didn't.

"Maybe I could find you a retired admiral, Phyllis," she finally managed to get out.

"An admiral! Now wouldn't that raise eyebrows at the Club? Find me a bald one, and we could cross-dress."

"Now I know why Kaitlyn is so normal. You did a good job, Phyllis. She was lucky to have you. I can only imagine what growing up in your household would be like."

Phyllis swished in the air. "It was easy. She was a good kid."

"You were happy," Martel said through her tears.

Martel sighed. She was watching someone leave this earth she would have really liked to get to know. It was so unfair. She rubbed her fingers over the older woman's and then patted her hand.

Phyllis gripped her hand tightly, attempting to lean forward again, and whispered, "Go find your daughter. Tell her yourself what you did for her. She deserves to hear it from you."

CHAPTER 11

THE BASE AT Coronado was a beehive of activity. Renny and Damon arrived just in time to grab their pre-packed duffle bag, stored in the Team 3 building, jump on the transport plane, and takeoff not more than a half an hour after they landed.

"Shit, Renny. Looks like I'm destined to never be able to keep my word."

"She's gonna understand, Damon. You call her as soon as we hit the island."

Everything about the operation was ass-backwards. There was no preflight meeting. There was no explanation of duties. It was just hurry up and get your butt on the plane and the rest would be explained later.

Damon and Renny pointed out to each other the lack of newbies on this trip. There were only going to be fourteen this time, and most of them had been in for ten years or more. Not only that, nobody was injured or recently injured during the past twelve months.

Kyle was going to meet them over at Cape Verde. He was already there working out some evacuation plans with one of the carrier groups in the area. At least, that's what their state department liaison told them.

The rest of the story Damon suspected was just being made up. Nobody really knew what was going on.

They stopped over for a refuel in Maine before taking the final leg across the Atlantic to Cape Verde. A ship was going to bring them closer to the African coast, if that was required, and Damon suspected it would be a halo jump in the pitch black of night or a landing with their inflatables. Either way, it would involve a night landing... on the dark continent of Africa. He'd looked over some of the information about Cape Verde, sure that he had traveled here in the past. He discovered he'd been to one of the other islands.

Landing at the short strip was a harrowing experience. The local contractor brought in the big transport like he was piloting a dust cropper, except the behemoth didn't maneuver anything like a glider or smaller twin engine. They started their approach by clipping a palm tree, toppling it on top of a water truck that immediately exploded, sending water everywhere. He hoped that wasn't their drinking supply.

Crossing his fingers, Damon heard the squeal and saw the white smoke of the tires skidding nearly the whole distance of the strip. They almost took out an old naval barracks. The transport literally was within two feet of kissing the concrete bunker.

Damon was grateful they had any landing gear left.

After a quick tire change, the big green transport took off again, abandoning them on the dusty hot tarmac. There was no one else in sight.

Damon had read this was the airfield European and US Forces had used to support operations in Morocco and elsewhere, sometimes dropping off humanitarian aid or equipment when hotspots flared. More than one African leader, having lost a recent election, found this to be a point of no return, as he was jetting off to Paris, or London, or the Caribbean, never to be heard from again.

Other than a few rusted planes and piles of parts, nothing looked like it was fly-worthy. Certainly no sign of jet fuel. It was the perfect place to drop the Team and would not attract attention. In fact, this was the part of the island nobody wanted to live on. Rainfall was practically nonexistent. The population liked to live somewhere green or closer to the industrialized port city of Mindelo, where they were told all the jobs were.

A convoy of black suburbans scampered across the tarmac like spiders on parade. Of course, their LPO, Kyle Lansdowne, was driving the first vehicle. He hopped out, sweat having soaked under his arms and nearly reaching his waist. He barely greeted them, pointing to the other vehicles. The elite squad loaded their gear and crossed in the opposite direction from where they'd arrived, through a chain-link fence that had been partially torn down.

The road was nonexistent. For a time, they traveled down the gully of a winter stream, passing a dead cow on its parched banks. The cow's belly was bloated, and its legs reached for the sky. There were small houses nearby, put together with corrugated metal and rusty wire, but the area now appeared abandoned.

They turned around a former school, covered with graffiti Damon couldn't recognize. Parts of an old chapel still stood in the center of the complex, indicating perhaps it had been a mission school at one time. Its walls were blown up in places all the way to the foundation plates. Rubble littered the former schoolyard, making passage difficult and slow. Several large rocks bounced up and hit their undercarriage.

Kyle didn't take the time to stop and check for damage.

They started to climb, doing switchbacks up the steep terrain, and as they did so had a view of the harbor, filled with commercial fishing boats, small dinghies, and three or four military-style former gunboats. None of it looked familiar.

After another ten minutes, they had traveled halfway up the hillside to the Blue Marlin Hotel, a huge white square structure that reminded Damon of a concrete factory. Balconies had been attached to the *outside* of the building. Holes had been blasted in the walls, to accommodate windows. Around the edges, local craftsmen had wedged small rocks, cementing them to hold everything together.

The Blue Marlin was a poster child for building a huge eyesore out of completely recycled material. It had no redeeming qualities whatsoever.

As if reading his mind, Kyle turned off the engine and spoke for the first time. "Have no fear. It has a pool"

Inside, the lobby was cool. Deep royal blue neon light strips encircled the downstairs, also defining the front of a huge bar made out of black granite. Above the lighted glass shelves containing hundreds of bottles of liquor, hung a large mirror, the edges of which were painted in Parisian Metro-style letters, complete with colorful pre-Victorian pictures of well-endowed ladies in various degrees of undress.

The concrete floor had been polished to perfection. It looked like they were standing on a black glass lake.

Somebody whistled as the team huddled in the center of the room. Damon looked up to find railings and balconies installed on the inside as well, a series of metal cat walks crisscrossing back-and-forth between the floors. He guessed it had been some kind of factory converted to hotel or night club use. He also suspected it had something to do with the drug trade.

"Sit down and take a load off, gents." Kyle barked.

They dropped their bags at their feet. Some men sat on them. Damon and Renny stretched out on the deliciously cool floor.

"We don't have to worry about our footprint here, since anybody who has the technology to pick up a signal would be off the coast. That would be military or pirates. And, in this part of the world, we're talking the same thing, unless they are U.S. assets. We had a drug and human trafficking operation here that we have just discovered, and it's staggering how much money flows through this little shit hole."

He continued. "What you see here is an old brothel converted from a UNESCO water treatment plant facility."

Kyle paused to let that sink in.

A water treatment facility on the side of a hill?

"You will notice the one thing missing here, of course, is water. But the World Bank gave them a few billion, so this is what they got for their investment in the country's economic development."

"Some of you have been to the Canaries and you've been to Cape Verde before, perhaps. In case you didn't know it, they speak Portuguese and a kind of creole pigeon-English-Portuguese dialect, and when they don't wanna listen to you, they'll make it *real* obvious. Don't worry about it. You won't understand a word if they don't want you to."

The group chuckled. Damon always liked how colorful Kyle could be when he was describing a new location.

"And don't let this place fool you. It's the site of a lot of pain and misery, not to mention bloodshed. Most of the people who died here were young girls. This is going to shock you because it sure fucking shocked me when I heard it. Last year, before they shut this place down, it was estimated they were trafficking more than four thousand girls annually."

Comments from the team were muttered and frequent.

"Right now, this little square of real estate is costing Uncle Sam close to one billion a year. It's not for rent. It's for a payoff. We are given this place and access to and from this place for thirty days and thirty days only. After that, it's business as usual, unfortunately. It's a real Quid Pro Quo, and yes they do exist. Someone got their finance minister and his family out, and in exchange, we get to rent this. You know how it goes, we clean it up, take the bad guys out, and their competition comes in and fills in the gaps, right?"

Most of the Team shook their heads. A couple of the men said "right."

"We'll be talking to the US Carson City out of here when we're done. They'll take us to another airstrip, undetermined at this point, so we can fly home. If we get everything done in a week, then you get to be back before Thanksgiving. If it takes thirty days, then we probably fucked it up pretty good."

"I want you all to divide up in the rooms upstairs, and yes, there is an elevator. There is even a swimming pool on the roof level. Bear in mind, if you were swimming in that pool or laying out next to it, satellites, birds and drones will take pictures of your sorry asses. So, I suggest you swim at night, if we're not working. No, I don't wanna have to remind anybody about the rules. This is a big one."

He surveyed the circle of men. "We meet back down here in about four hours, okay?"

Renny and Damon ran up the flight of stairs to the third floor, having spotted a large conference room with double glass doors overlooking the largest balcony and catwalk. If a room was a room, then a large conference room like this would be perfect for the two of them.

What they found was an executive club level meeting room, complete with another stocked bar, and a see-through mirror between the bathroom and the large king size bed in the bedroom. They searched for a second bed, and Renny informed Damon that they'd have to be sharing the bed.

"Sorry, kid."

"Let's put something over that mirror, because I sure don't wanna watch you take a shit or even a shower," Damon told him.

Renny found a box of tarps left over from a painting crew. "You bring the duct tape?" he asked.

"I sure did. Always, man." As Renny started to hang the tarp, Damon jumped up to help by positioning it. Their divider was complete in less than two minutes.

"I'm gonna give Martel a call, okay?"

"Go for it. I'm taking a shower."

Damon sat on the enormous chocolate-colored leather couch located underneath the largest picture of a woman's boobs he'd ever seen. He outstretched himself, glancing up at the erotic shapes, looking like they were floating all around him, and dialed.

His call went right to voicemail.

"Hey, sweetheart, I'm thinking hard about you right now, and I sure do miss you. We got here, and we're safe. And it looks like it's not going to be a long one. Other than that, I don't know anything. But I can't wait to be back home."

He continued letting his eyes lazily wander over the long circular strokes in the picture and figured out that some of them had been made by a woman's breasts.

"I've been thinking when I get back it might be a good idea to plan that trip. Or maybe I can fly out there, pick you up and accompany you to my humble abode."

He hit the pound sign. It wasn't how he wanted to sound, so he erased the message and started over.

"Hey, sweetheart, we made it over here safe. Renny is fine and says hi too. I'm thinking of you a lot. I can't believe just twenty-four hours ago we were doing some pretty nice things. I hope you found the whipped cream. I hope you think of some good uses for it when I get home. I can't wait to see what you come up with, if you know what I mean. Call me when you can."

He hesitated then added, "I can't stop thinking about you, miss you, and, well, wanted to say… I love you, Martel. I can't believe I was so stupid not to tell you that before I left. But I do."

He signed off. "Talk soon, bye."

He made the sound of two kisses and then sent the message.

CHAPTER 12

S OMEWHERE, HER MOTHER had the adoption papers. She had reduced all of her mother's things to one bank box, much of it mementos she couldn't bear to read, like her parents' marriage certificate, her birth record, and pictures of a family long gone.

Shortly after Phyllis had grabbed her and given her the command, the machinery above her head started sounding alarms, and Martel was quickly whisked from the room. She waited for over two hours and then was told Phyllis was still alive, but sleeping.

And she might not wake up.

Had Kaitlyn's mom expended the last bit of her life to deliver that message? Martel wondered how she would be able to tell her best friend.

A light mist hit the windshield as she drove home.

Heaven is crying.

She didn't want to think about all the decisions she made so many years ago. She was grateful she had her mother's wise counsel to fall back on. But there was one day when she actually came close to contacting Damon's parents, in an effort to find him.

"What's got you so blue, Martel?" her mom asked.

"What if something's wrong? What if he's sick somewhere or had an accident or something?"

"Okay. Then call them."

Her mom was good at not pushing. She stood in front of her with her arms crossed until the weakness in her legs forced her to sit down.

"You have to make a decision, one way or the other, Martel. You lay out all possibilities, the reasons for and against, and then you decide. I know there's part of you that doesn't want to do this. But you know how this story goes. I mean, it's been sixty days, and you've not heard one word, you've not read anything in the paper, and none of your friends have said anything, except that he joined the Navy. What does that sound like?"

She'd been right. And while the relationship with Damon may have been a mistake, her baby wasn't. That little life deserved to grow up and be a shining light for any of the childless couples she'd been reading about. She held the decision to bestow on one of them a miracle.

So she never called. After she made her choice, and the introductions were over, they chose the home up in Oregon, because it was closer to the new parents. Her sole job was to bide her time, get ready to attend college in the fall, and stay healthy.

The day they called her to let her know her mother was struggling and at the edge of her own life, the kind hospice nurse told her that her mother took great pleasure looking at the pictures Martel was sending. She kept them in a leather folder in her purse.

"She wants you to do nothing but focus on the rest of your life, Martel. She doesn't want any shame to fall on you."

"Tell her I want to be there."

"I will, but she wants you to stay in Oregon. She understands and told me expressly to let you know this. I'm afraid there won't be any other messages, Martel."

The private shelter on the Oregon coast was a refuge. The small staff was experienced working with unmarried mothers coming from all sorts of situations. After her mother's passing, they helped her plan the service and supported her decision not to attend.

Martel continued sorting through the papers in the banker's box until she found the leather envelope containing her pictures. They'd been placed in plastic sleeves, organized by date. One by one, they chronicled her development, some ultrasounds, and the view of her body from the side. On the back of the last picture, when she was nearly seven months along, her own handwriting displayed a message for her mother. She'd just gotten the news she was having a girl. Years later, it was now a message to herself.

Very soon now, you'll get to see her.

She was sure her mother was delighted.

Behind the last picture in the box was a folded sheaf of papers. When she unfolded it, she found a copy of the adoption contract, first signed by her and then countersigned by the baby's future parents below.

Martel had never seen the paper after she'd signed it. But her mother somehow had. The couple had only been known to her as Mark and Lori, and she wasn't told exactly where they were from, but she guessed it was some place in Oregon. Lori was a teacher like Martel wanted to be some day. And Mark was the principal of the school Lori worked at.

They really had turned out to be the best choice, the perfect parents. The contract spelled it all out: Arrangements for the Oregon stay, her doctor visits and hospital paid for up front, and her own clause. Everything was there, including that it was her wish not to be part of the baby's life after the birth. The records had been sealed forever, she was told.

Except now Martel had their last name. Newberg. Mark and Lori Newberg.

Should she try to call them? Her mother had thought it best if she didn't. But Kaitlyn's mom clearly was in the other camp. Now, ten years later, her perspective had totally changed. She was warned that this might happen, but she signed the paperwork anyway.

How hard would it be to trace them down? Would she be in some legal jeopardy if she tried to reach out? She just wasn't sure.

A red dot blinked on her cell. She saw that Damon had left her a message.

'Hey sweetheart...'

Before she returned his call, she searched her heart. She was actually contemplating doing the unthinkable. But she wasn't doing it for him. This wasn't even something she was doing for herself. She wanted her daughter to know that she loved her, would always love her even though they'd barely met. The gift of her life was for her.

There was more research to do, making sure she wasn't doing anything illegal for one. She didn't want to interfere with her daughter's adoptive parents, insert herself where she didn't belong. When she sorted all that out, she'd consider telling Damon. If they continued their relationship the way it was planned, it wouldn't be right if she kept him from the truth.

But how and when? That was the real mystery that could threaten the balance of everything.

She dialed Damon's cell. Her heart was on high alert.

"There you are!"

"Here I am. Wish you were here too."

"I'd Roger that. Tell me you're looking out at the beach. Probably sunset now, right?"

"It's been a bit rainy, so it's a little on the gray side. But the clouds are beautiful. Lots of purple tonight."

"Nice."

"How about there?"

"Not so glamorous. It's been overrun with people who were just trying to survive and left in a hurry. The other side doesn't look like such a wasteland, I'm told."

"So, no beach time, I guess."

"Probably not. We're a few miles away. Hey, I found out we can do Facetime calls. We'll have to set that up. Can't do it tonight, but maybe tomorrow or the next day."

"That would be nice, Damon. Just let me know."

He must have detected something because he asked her if anything was wrong.

"Kaitlyn's mother I think is passing. I've tried to get hold of her. Renny doesn't have Greg's cell number, does he?"

"He's not here right now, but I'll ask him." He hesitated. "You knew she was sick, right?"

"Oh yes. It just surprised me. I'll feel better when I reach Kaitlyn."

"You sound tired. You should flip off your phone and turn in early. Doctor's orders."

"I think I'll have a bath and do just that. How about you?"

"Getting ready for a meeting downstairs. I rested on the plane, so I'm good to go. Sorry that this will have to be a short one, Martel. But I appreciate the update and the chance to hear your voice. I'll text you if I have Greg's number anywhere."

"Thank you. Please be safe."

"I made a promise, and I intend to keep it."

"I believe you. I'm still figuring out what I want to do with that whipped cream when you get home."

"There you go. And we're on for the visit to San Diego?"

She heard some voices in the background before she could answer.

"That's my cue. Gotta go. Are we still on?" Damon rushed.

"Yes. Let me give you the dates I can be there. Are you sure you'll be home?"

"Better be. Okay, they're screaming for me now. I'll try to call next chance I get. Love you, Martel."

"Coming back at you ten times over. Be safe."

But he had already disconnected the call.

CHAPTER 13

"WE HAVE A wrinkle in the plans," Kyle Lansdowne started. "Turns out we have a possible hostage situation going on. Senator Raymond's daughter, Samantha Raymond is possibly being held against her will. She was part of a missionary group and aid outreach in Nigeria, passing out Bibles and doing things State didn't realize was going on."

Damon knew this was bad news.

"She's gotten romantically entangled with one of the sons of a very powerful Nigerian businessman, Kwanda Freescott. He's a bad dude, responsible for running arms, embezzling funds meant for domestic help, and we think he's partly involved in the trafficking. We don't know about the boy."

Kyle went on to further elaborate how assessment was that the boy was somewhat naive, perhaps dazzled with the friendship with the Senator's daughter, and had experienced a recent evangelical conversion. But they had credible intel that found the group was going to use Samantha as leverage to get the U.S. to back off their enforcement efforts to shut the cartel down.

"Does she know about the trafficking?" Coop asked.

"We aren't sure, and we think not. The Senator certainly has no knowledge of it, or so he says. Seems that Samantha lives with his ex, who has had some major involvement with a group doing these things all over Northern and Central Africa. Part of their ilk was rescued in Afghanistan, many of you might know, about five years ago."

Damon knew it was sometimes difficult for State to control these groups, especially since the government relied on them occasionally for on the ground intel. The delicate balance was where people were killed and unpredicted outcomes happened.

It would be right where they were going.

"We were prepared to do an amphibious landing in Benin. Now that we understand she's here on Cape Verde, we'll be staying here. And our timeline has moved up a bit. We can't be here very long before we start attracting attention. We are not being hosted by any official government entity. We have a promise of some cooperation, but when the shit hits the fan, you know how much weight that means."

"Any friendlies on the island?" Fredo asked.

"Lots of Europeans live here. Historically, people here actually fought in our wars, including the Revolutionary and Civil Wars, even Vietnam and World War II. So we have some friends, especially amongst the older population. With the reduction in the slave trade during the 18th and 19th centuries, the country, as part of Portugal, fell on hard times. It's had to claw itself back and is still struggling with their new independence in 1975. Eradicating the drug trade necessitates an all-out purge about every ten years. But this human trafficking explosion caught everyone off guard. They walk a line between being friend to the U.S. and depending on support from Uncle Sam, as well as Portugal and Europe. They also have a sizable Chinese population, which is becoming interesting." Kyle paused. "We also think they wish the Senator's daughter wasn't involved, so maybe we'll have some help. We just don't know. What they do understand is that if anything happens to her, all Hell will break loose."

He gave instructions for everyone to get some rest, go for a swim, if necessary, and be ready in the morning for another updated briefing.

"Remember what I always say, don't trust anybody until you see they've taken up arms by your side to defend you. Until then, don't assume anything. If we can negotiate our way out of something heavier, trust me, we're working on it. And no mention of the Senator's daughter, either, got it?"

The cold fish sandwiches provided by their contractor provider were delicious, but Damon didn't appreciate the hot and spicy pickle relish that burned the roof of his mouth.

Someone finally asked about the bar.

"It's right there. It's open, but make sure you're ready to go with all your faculties at a moment's notice. That's a warning I don't want to have to repeat."

TWO SMALL TOUR busses arrived with their breakfast the next morning. They were issued local currency and shown maps of the town of Mindelo, marking the coast guard and police stations, as well as the one hospital on the island, in case of an emergency. Renny and Damon were grouped with Coop, Fredo, T.J. Talbot, and Tyler Gray. Kyle and the rest of the team were in the other van.

Their goal was to scope out each of the five sites suspected of housing what remained of the large operation that had been located at the Blue Marlin. To that end, their drivers posed as real tour operators, taking them to local bars and a couple of cathedrals for pictures. Each of the vans took a different route, and they agreed to meet up at a local tourist restaurant for lunch.

Damon's driver was from Ukraine, but he was a member of the U.S. Embassy staff. He had married a local girl he met on vacation and never left the island, except to travel to Washington for his citizenship and training. Overweight, in his fifties, and probably a heavy drinker, he showed them pictures of his young children, his "second life," as he called it.

Alexi had lots of stories, and he spoke a wicked Ukrainian-Cape Verde pigeon, or *Kreole*, as it was called.

Fredo, raised Catholic, asked about church attendance on the island. They had stopped at a quaint chapel with a stone-inlay parking lot overlooking the blue harbor. It was a favorite place to get married, he'd told them.

"Oh, we have ninety-five percent attendance here. Being from so many worlds, non-believers are considered the odd ones. We have generations of Muslim and Jewish settlers who came to escape the Inquisition. But I would say the Catholic church is the strongest."

Inside the chapel was a sacristy dedicated to war heroes, which surprised Damon.

"An honorable way to die," Alexi sighed. "And a completely wasted chance at happiness, too," he added. "Sorry, but that is my view."

"It might surprise you, but we got those too. Even some on the Teams," mumbled T.J.

"Your Kyle says all of you are lifers, yes?" Alexi asked.

That drew hearty laughter.

"We got no one and dones here," said Cooper. "As for lifers? That's not a term I'm very familiar with. At some point, the old bod begins to break down and other shiny objects start catching our eye."

"Most of us will have knee or hip replacements before we're forty," added Damon. "Renny here is going for a brain transplant next year."

"I highly recommend that, Renny," barked T.J. "What the hell's the matter with you two? No wedding bells?"

"Fuck sake, T.J." Renny started as they piled into the van. "I'm one and done on that. And this one's fresh out of the ocean and still flopping around on deck."

Damon didn't care for the laughter taken at his expense.

"I hear he has a hook in his mouth, though," Cooper added, punching Damon in the arm.

"Afraid so. We'll be doing Facetime non-stop here." Renny would not give up.

"Does your wife like to wear skimpy underwear, and those little thongs?" asked Fredo.

"Not for you, asshole," Damon barked.

Cooper was right on that one. "Oh, Fredo has his own collection. He has a thing for lingerie. He just likes to compare."

Alexi's expression went from jovial to concerned.

"Hey, no worries, Alexi. We're just joking," soothed T.J. As he began to loosen up again, T.J. delivered the kill shot. "Fredo harkens back to his roots. Before becoming a SEAL, he was a helluva pole dancer at one of those bars in East L.A."

"Compton," Fredo corrected.

They all laughed and for the next half hour, Alexi said nothing at all. It was kind of a relief to Damon.

They traveled, through an industrial zone packed with warehouses. Driving around the side streets was extremely slow and tedious, due to the number of lorries of varying sizes picking up and making deliveries to the harbor. Since most of the island's food had to be imported, Alexi explained, large warehouses were necessary for storage. Apparently when the island was first used for inhabitants and not just farm animals, even water had to be imported, he explained.

"I'm getting a good feeling about this place. They'd have an easy time with lookouts," said T.J., who pointed out several armed men on top of the flat roofs of some of the buildings. "And they can nearly walk from one to another. No one would ever see them from down below."

Just as he said that, they watched two men leap from one building to land on their feet on another.

Alexi pointed out several more as they snaked through the bustling streets.

"I'm wondering why they'd ever take a chance and run an operation way up the hill like the Blue Marlin," asked Damon. "That seems too risky, in my opinion. They have it all here. Up there, you got one way in and one way out."

Alexi had a quick answer for that.

"For the limos, the businessmen from London, Amsterdam, Washington, D.C., my friends. It's for the floor show. You get all those dolls lined up on the balconies over there, and it's like Disneyland for perverts."

"So, they used it for staging?"

"Exactly. We locals call it the tasting room, you know, like they have for the wineries?"

"Then they could store the rest here in warehouses," whispered Renny.

"Or hold them when they offload from the ships that bring them in." He went on to explain. "The local population can't provide enough women for the trade. Besides, they have to have local cooperation. You have an expression about not shitting where you eat? Why piss off the locals, steal their women when you need their protection?"

It was making perfect sense to Damon why the operation was so successful.

"Where do they come from?" asked Tyler.

"The orient, some from Africa. You have to realize this island was developed and paid for many times over by the slave trade. The sex trafficking business is very lucrative."

Silence descended on the van.

"I know your Kyle is interested in this Freescott boy. This is the warehouse for his winery on the other side of the island."

"Winery?" asked Cooper.

"Oh yes, the Portuguese have been making wine on this island for centuries. Other than grazing cattle, it was the first agricultural endeavor here. Old families, even some pirates settled here and became huge landowners and winemakers. And Cape Verde was discovered by the Venetians for the King of Portugal, so there you go. Even your Francis Drake sailed here as a privateer."

Coop dictated addresses to T.J. who was taking copious notes.

"I like that one, and that one over there. Notice the men on top," Fredo whispered.

"Got it," answered T.J.

THEY MET UP at the Dockside cafe and tourist stop, where their van blended in well with several others from a cruise ship that had docked in the bay that morning. They took a long table and fought off a group of Italian tourists from the ship, who were jabbering like magpies and unhappy being rejected. Kyle and the rest of the Team arrived shortly thereafter.

They all ordered lobster, and beer on Alexi's recommendation.

"Don't bother with the salad. Don't order anything else that can't be frozen or stored. Fruit is excellent, though!"

Damon and Renny each ordered a half-pineapple hollowed out with a variety of local fruits that was refreshing. The lobster reminded Damon of the gulf coast in Florida.

"You guys been to one of those gulf beaches in Florida?" he asked the group.

"Outstanding!" said Kyle. "I'd like to take the kids there some day. Christy's been dying to get me committed to a trip."

"You go to one of their crab places, and you walk away—no, wait, you slide your way back to your car, you're so covered in butter," Damon added.

"What the hell are you doing out there? You're from California, Damon," asked Fredo.

Renny interrupted Damon's response. "Long story, Fredo. Don't get him started. Trust me. You don't want to hear it."

They laughed.

"I'm sorry. You did say that you are in a new relationship, Damon? Fellas, I'm wanting to hear those stories about sex on the beach and all that stuff we don't get to do any longer, right?"

"He lives vicariously through you guys," Coop explained. "He even gets turned on with Mia's soap operas.

Alexi laughed. "You should watch Ukrainian soap opera." He summed it up with, "The best ever!"

"Said no one," added Kyle.

The conversation got serious and only lasted that way for a couple of minutes.

"You all have your nominations?" Kyle asked, making eye contact with each of the Team, as they nodded. "You got your addresses and description, and your case for why, all that stuff?"

Again, everyone nodded.

"Anyone got to stop by and pick anything up on the way back?

"T.J. and I would like to see if we can pick up some Tramadol and some alcohol swabs. They sell it cheap here."

"Okay, you make sure to do that. Anybody else?"

T.J. raised his hand like a schoolboy. "I saw an advertisement for Pirate beer. I'd like to try out a case of that if we can keep it cold."

Alexi agreed. "Good local beer. Two Ukrainian fellows started it."

"Of course," T.J. said.

CHAPTER 14

PHYLLIS CLUNG TO life until the day Kaitlyn returned, never regaining consciousness.

"Not exactly the welcome home party you were hoping for. I'm so sorry, sweetie."

"They were good about updating me. Only thing I regret is that I didn't get to talk to her. I'm glad you did, though. The staff said she enjoyed your visit. Thanks, Martel."

"She called me the first day and we had a really good talk. She was so helpful. I had no idea your mother had such a sense of humor."

"Oh, there are stories. She was quite the character." Kaitlyn's voice hitched. "I go from giggling at all the things she did growing up to being really sad." She sighed. "It's a big hole to fill. But we had some great years, and she got to see Greg and I get married. I'm grateful for all that."

"I visited her when your sub told me she'd been admitted. She was joking about getting me to rip out all the tubing and take her to the beach with an ice cream."

"Yup. That's Phyllis."

Martel's cheeks were streaked with tears. She knew Kaitlyn's probably looked the same.

"I felt a little guilty that perhaps I'd been partially responsible for getting her so worked up."

"Yeah, they told me. Don't feel that way. She probably did it on purpose. I know she couldn't have been very happy there. It all turned out the way it was supposed to."

"You're amazing, Kate."

"No, actually, I'm a little tired." She chuckled. "You probably think me a freak, but we don't do grieving in my family. She wouldn't want it that way."

"My mom was the same way when she passed."

Martel paused several minutes while a wave of sadness passed. Kaitlyn waited.

"You need help with anything? I presume you're going to take a few more days off?"

"No, I'm sticking to the schedule. I'll be missing the latter part of the school year anyway, and I need to save my sick leave."

"That's right. I forgot. And doing something you're so good at is probably the right way to spend your days now."

"That's exactly right."

"But what about her service? Can I help you with that?"

"Would you be surprised to learn she already had it all scripted and planned out? She even printed the announcements, leaving the date and times blank so all I have to do is fill them in. I would be crying, but I can hear her laughing behind me. I turn around, expecting to see her."

That part gave Martel a shiver.

SHE AND DAMON video phone conferenced nearly every day over the past week. He looked good. Being over there with his buddies seemed to buoy his mood, and some of the adventures they'd been having reminded her of how he'd been like in his early twenties. His language got filthy, however.

Renny inserted himself into their conversations often, and it annoyed her. She wanted alone time with her boyfriend, not this Boy

Scout who wanted to play pranks on him. She hoped Renny wasn't getting the two of them into trouble.

She firmed the dates for the visit to Coronado and informed her landlord in Sunset Beach when she was going to return. She bought some new clothes.

Martel also made an appointment with an adoption attorney to discuss trying to locate the adoptive parents she'd placed her daughter with.

PHYLLIS' MEMORIAL SERVICE was something she never was going to forget. She'd requested to have an open casket. She had it in her will that she be dressed in a red designer suit she'd recently purchased, with matching red elbow-length gloves. The funeral home had trouble fitting the enormous red hat adorned with colorful flowers inside the casket, but they made a good try of it. Even the look of it stuffed into the box was so Phyllis.

Kaitlyn wasn't the only one who heard her mother laughing. Martel began to imagine the same thing. Especially when she took a closer look and discovered Phyllis' red gloves clutched her favorite romance novel, an especially steamy one where the hero on the cover was shirtless and wore a kilt.

Martel couldn't look Kaitlyn in the eyes for fear of bursting out laughing as she walked back to the pew. They held hands all during the service, squirming, each struggling, but not for the reasons the audience thought. Ladies from Phyllis' bridge club sat in a row behind them, and every one of them wore a flowered hat as well, as though it had been planned out in advance.

It probably was.

There was a stirring gospel song performed by a handsome male Jamaican soloist she liked to go dancing with before she got sick. He was thirty years her junior. Several nurses from the care facility and one of her doctors attended. She even had flowers delivered by the florist she used to send to friends, and she had a big arrangement prepaid and delivered to her daughter, with tuberoses and light pink roses that had been in her wedding bouquet. She'd personalized the private note that was delivered with it.

Martel felt the strength and power of this magnificent woman reaching out to her, guiding her hand. Phyllis had never given up on life, how to live it and how to exit. Now more than ever, she wanted to take Phyllis' suggestion.

Martel knew Phyllis would be cheering her on.

Attorney Gran Karmody had a big office on the top floor of a bank building in Tampa. Dressed in a white suit, complete with a brocade vest and gold watch, his large moustache and snow-white hair created an imposing figure on billboards, but even more so in person. He reminded her of all the images she had of a typical shrewd country lawyer, and could have been a fabulously wealthy divorce attorney.

But he had a calling. When she'd asked around for the name of an attorney to handle an adoption situation, his was always the first one on everyone's lips. He lived to place children into childless couple's homes and he fought for the birth mother and child just as if he was defending someone before the Supreme Court. It was the only kind of law he practiced.

His firm handshake nearly left a welt on the back of Martel's hand.

After she explained her situation, he didn't say a word, but remained leaning onto his desk, his hands folded before him, studying her with eyes she was sure didn't miss a thing.

"First of all, I want to say that you are a very courageous woman." His southern drawl and demeanor was charming… and just as disarming. She guessed he was probably the most formidable attorney she'd ever met.

Martel was glad that she wasn't dressed down like she had feared.

"I'm relieved," she said, placing her palm against her upper chest, swallowing.

"Well, I mean it. Now, I wouldn't normally take on a case like this. But I am moved by your story. I'm going to tell you not many women would go about this in this fashion. As a society we operate on fuzzy logic. Out of sight. Out of mind. Sometimes unwanted pregnancies are seen as inconveniences. But in my opinion, most of the women who give their child up for adoption do it because they love them. And you, little lady, are certainly one of those."

Martel was surprised. All the rehearsing in front of her bathroom mirror had paid off. She didn't want to be misunderstood and didn't want her emotions to cloud the delivery.

"Here's the problem. You signed a piece of paper"—He held up her copy of the contract—"*This* piece of paper, and it says right on it you are giving up forever your rights to any kind of claim on this child. That means even a phone call. The law is very cut and dry on this subject. They paid your expenses, and they have the right to expect what they purchased. They didn't purchase your child, Miss Long—They paid for the opportunity to be able to raise this child without any interference from you."

"And I agree with that."

"So, you can see what's happening here. Your life has changed, but you still said you would honor this contract, and that's a problem. But..."

"*They* can change their mind if I ask them."

"And that's exactly right. I'm going to recommend that you let me talk to them first. Ordinarily, when lawyers get involved it makes everyone nervous, and they should be. But in this case, they might need the kind of assurances I might be able to give them. I can tell them just what you told me. You don't want to interfere. They will forever be her parents and the people who loved and raised her. But, Miss Long, if they say no, I'm afraid I'm going to have to decline to represent you any further, because I just don't believe in undoing something as loving and unselfish as your action to give her up."

Martel's heart was beating so hard, she thought perhaps she was shaking the floor.

"Do you understand me, Miss Long?"

"I do. I completely agree."

"One other thing that bothers me a bit. This deal only goes for you. Your new beau, the father of this child, has no part in this, even though he may want to. That's a whole other can of worms. I don't want to get him started down any path where he might feel he has some rights here, because that wouldn't be fair to the parents. Assuming your child is happy, they are reasonable people, AND you are respectful of their position, they may include him at some future date, but I'm not going to even bring it up. We don't need that kind of complication. Are you okay with that?"

"I am." She hesitated to ask him her next question. "What are my chances?"

"You met them back then. I'm guessing your meeting was amicable, and you've lived up to your part of the bargain. We'll just have to see what's in their hearts. I really can't predict, Miss Long. But I promise I'll argue your request with all the delicacy and respect I can muster. And if they say no, I'll make sure to leave the door open and let them know, if they change their mind, I'll always be here. Now, is all that acceptable?"

"Thank you, Mr. Karmody," she said as she stood.

"You got it, ma'am. My pleasure."

MARTEL WALKED OUT of the office arm-in-arm with the spirit of Phyllis Carrington. She even bought an ice cream on the way home.

CHAPTER 15

T HE TEAM MADE a schedule of the couriers, the deliveries and police that frequented the two buildings identified as most likely to be working the illegal network. After days of night surveillance, Kyle was confident several of the other targets could in fact be decoys, or places where things could be quickly stashed if an operation went against the cartel's interest.

During the day, those buildings were generally not guarded.

Damon, Renny, Coop and Fredo were assigned to break in, and verify this. And they had to do it in the middle of the day, without causing attention.

The team wasn't heavily armed. Fredo did carry his usual supply of flash bombs and explosive caps, but everyone else brought only their designated sidearm. In Damon's case, it was his SigSauer. Coop carried a medic bag, and Fredo was responsible for communicating with Kyle.

Armando and Danny had quietly broken into adjacent buildings to set up cover from the roof. One factory manufactured tee shirts, dresses, and other textiles for the tourist trade. The other was a packing and shipping operation. They'd been selected because of a series of external fire escapes, leading inside without detection. They signaled they were in place and Fredo gave the green light.

The four others split up, each attempting to break in from opposite sides of their targeted buildings. Damon and Renny made it inside and noticed Fredo, who managed to jimmy a sliding metal door that had come off its track. They peered through the furniture, boxes and household goods stored in clusters around the ground floor. There were catwalks and tiny offices upstairs, but no real second floor. Under a tarp in the corner, a brand-new police vehicle was stored.

Renny was in charge of taking pictures with the specialized phone, for uploading back home. Kyle gave the go-ahead to check out the offices upstairs. The team found them all completely vacant.

Damon verified all clear in the rear alleyway while Fredo and Coop attempted to leave the broken cargo bay in the same condition as they'd found it. The other door was left locked.

While Danny and Armando repositioned themselves, the four men loitered nearby, slowly working their way to the other building they needed to investigate.

Given the all-clear, Damon and Renny couldn't get the deadbolt open on the heavy metal door facing the narrow alleyway at the rear. They found an open window instead and crawled through. Fredo and Coop joined them. The four entered a small office, set up with a telephone, a copy machine, and a cot with pillow and folded blankets. The door leading to the warehouse portion locked from the inside. Fredo opened it a crack, and bright light shone through, nearly blinding them. Music played in the distance.

The warehouse was not vacant but very much in use. Bright hanging fluorescent lights illuminated the huge space, revealing shipping boxes and wooden crates stacked over one story tall. Tables were laid out in lines, end to end. Piles of books sat at various places at the tables. A variety of mismatched chairs were placed along the lines for seating. A big screen T.V. hung from the wall. Two leather couches sat facing each other with a small trunk being used as a coffee table between them.

But there wasn't any evidence of anyone working there.

Finally, a door opened. The sound of music got louder, and then they heard the remnants of a toilet flush as a male worker brought out his portable radio, set it on one of the tables, and sat with his back to them. He began boxing books in cardboard mailers.

Coop motioned for Renny to take pictures before they closed the door and checked in with Kyle.

"Check to see if the phone line is live," Damon could hear Kyle's squawk over Fredo's mic. He picked up the receiver and heard a dial tone, nodded, which was then relayed to Kyle.

Coop broke into a locked file cabinet and perused files inside, holding his flashlight in his mouth. He pulled out a letter and a couple other items, folded them, and tucked them into his vest.

Damon located an untaped box of books ready to ship out. Inside were illustrated children's bible stories, written in Portuguese. He held one up, and Coop directed him to tuck it in his medic backpack.

"We're done here," whispered Fredo. "Moving out.

ALL SIX OF them returned with their goods to the Blue Marlin.

"Wish we could have had a look upstairs in that building, so let's assume they sometimes have a crew sleeping over, just to be safe," Kyle said.

"So, are we good to go tonight then?" asked Coop.

"I think that's everything we need. I agree, the wine storage facility is where we'll likely find the girls and hopefully Samantha."

He gave instructions on who were on the two teams. Armando and Danny would first get into position to cover them from adjacent rooftops Armando had already picked out. The remaining ten would split into two teams and would break in, hopefully with the element of surprise.

No one had seen Samantha Raymond during their many surveillance forays, but several other women with armed male escorts were seen entering the building only at night. During the day, two shooters were camped out on top of both buildings, frequently changing locations. And, they were wired. But at night, for some reason, the rooflines were left unguarded.

"Get a power nap. No distractions or calling home. We got to be focused. Make sure you bring everything with you in case we don't come back here, as nice as it is. Check your weapons, your tools of the trade, gents. We roll at midnight. It's a new moon, so the odds are in our favor."

Kyle's instructions were simple, and easy to follow. It was the unknown that always fucked with them, Damon thought to himself. He crashed hard as soon as his head hit the pillow.

ON THE WAY to the site, Renny offered Damon some bubble gum. His mouth was parched, and he noted he hadn't been hydrating enough. Of course, the salty food they'd been eating, especially the locally prepared fish dishes, didn't help.

Alexi and the other driver waited nervously while the Team took what they needed and left the rest, heading to the two buildings.

Armando and Danny signaled they were in place and the roof was secure. Kyle gave the all clear for the rest of the team to get into position. It had been determined that no deliveries happened at night until early in the morning at 0600. That's when trucks would be arriving to start loading freight, occasionally with an armed guard contingent in a Jeep or Rover of some kind. Their goal was to strike before any of the increased manpower arrived. The two breaches had to be timed perfectly.

An abandoned chair sat outside the rear entrance, illuminated by a single bulb fixture.

"Danny, can you kill the light?" Damon heard Kyle ask.

A second later, they heard the ping of a rock and then the tinkle of glass as Danny's slingshot removed the problem. They waited to see if anyone took notice, and after five minutes, continued with the plan.

The other building was lit with a large high-pressure sodium vapor light mounted tall that would have to be shot out during the breach. They were ready. Kyle made the decision not to use their NV goggles because they expected someone would throw the lights on.

Fredo first checked the door, and found it locked. He applied the explosive charge, while Coop rigged up the other building. With Armando and Danny ready—and the charges placed, Kyle gave the go.

The blast tore the metal door off its hinges. Amongst the screams from what sounded like women, Fredo, Damon, Renny, and the others on their squad entered and quickly fanned out to the sides, their backs against the wall. It was pitch black until someone flipped the switch and the room lit up like Christmas. Fredo threw some smoke to help as the team looked for guards they expected would be present.

Women and children ran back and forth in their night clothes through the smoke, looking for a safe place to hide. Two shooters started firing down on the SEALs. Jameson and Tucker quickly took them out.

Damon tripped over a cot, which turned out to be lucky as he heard a round hit the concrete floor where he'd been standing. Before he could fully turn around, T.J. fired, hitting the shooter in the head. He tossed the MP5 over to Jameson, who would be their designated indoor sharpshooter, along with some clips.

As Jameson focused on picking off men pouring out from several upstairs rooms, Damon and Renny counted the women and children, looking for Samantha. He called for Cooper when he found one of the girls had gotten caught in the crossfire and had taken a round to the upper thigh that was bleeding out dangerously. The nimble medic quickly applied a tourniquet while Damon covered him and continued sorting the women.

Renny's scream pierced the air.

"Go. I'm good," yelled Coop. He pulled the young girl to the side and deposited her in the huddle of other prisoners.

Damon found Renny on the ground, but alive. He'd been stabbed in the chest and somehow the blade had sliced under his armor. It was still protruding, the pearl handle covered in bloody fingerprints.

T.J. nodded to another interior doorway, directing Damon to take out a man talking on a hand-held radio. Without any hesitation, he flew at the young guard, twisting his neck and sending him to the floor in a heap. When he opened the door, he spotted Samantha scampering to hide herself in the closet of a makeshift bedroom.

"Sam? That you?" Damon asked.

She slowly poked her head out between the clothes. Damon saw movement on his right and quickly disabled the young man holding a large machete over his head. The man's arm was clearly broken, but Damon went down on his knees to break the guy's neck when Samantha screamed, "No!"

That's when he realized the boy was Kwanda Freescott's son.

Tucker burst into the room and helped Damon remove Samantha and Mr. Freescott after securing his wrists in a zip tie. The painful process had the young man screaming as Samantha fought to be at his side.

Damon held her by her hair. "I'm going to tie you up just like him if you don't cooperate. We're here to rescue, not assassinate. We're taking you home."

"I don't want to go home!" she screamed.

Damon shoved her on the bed and zip tied her wrists, pushing her out of the room behind her lover. The building had become eerily calm, except for the moaning and crying of the huddled women and children.

Fredo rushed over, eyeing the two captives. "Kyle wants to know how many."

"I counted twenty-two, plus these two."

Fredo relayed the message and came back with instructions. "We take them with us. He's leading another seventeen over, and they'll be turned over to the locals. We take these two back with us."

The other driver agreed to wait for the police, while Alexi drove them to the harbor. He tossed the Freescott kid to the side and took up a seat next to Renny. T.J. gave him a wink and nod, indicating he was free to mess with his buddy to keep his mood light until they got some medical attention.

"Just another day in paradise, right?"

"Fuck you, Damon. I see you went for the girl while I took the blade."

"Yeah, I got the cushy job, didn't I?"

He saw Kyle smile and lean against a window as the van bounced around, eventually coming to a two-lane freeway with a sign showing a boat, water and an arrow.

"See that? We're going on a little fishing trip, Renny."

His friend's eyes got wide. "I'm not standing anywhere near you, Damon."

Now that would be funny, puking all over the Team.

With all the adrenaline coursing through his system, he figured it was the same as consuming a full bottle of Dramamine.

But it still would be funny.

CHAPTER 16

M ARTEL ANXIOUSLY WATCHED the ground rise up to meet the plane's landing gear. It had been three months since she'd seen Damon, though they talked frequently on video chat. When she learned about Renny, she didn't even mind that occasionally he'd pop up on the screen, his chest still wrapped in white bandages.

She'd had lots of time to think about what might or might not happen this trip. It needed to be more than just a good time. If they were going to take their relationship to the next level, which meant revealing her decision of ten years ago, it had to be something she was certain of. What Damon was asking was for her to see herself living with him in California. Taking her from the roots she'd planted in Florida, tearing her away from the beautiful sunsets and the white beach. Nothing in California could ever match that.

But she would give it an honest try. She guarded her expectations. She was looking for real this time.

Damon met her at the luggage turnstile. He'd let his stubble grow, and it roughed him up and gave him an even more masculine, older look she liked.

"Hey, babe. I've missed you so much," he whispered as they embraced. He carefully placed a long kiss on her lips in full view of the entire planeload of passengers. She could tell her cheeks had pinked up.

"Me too. Merry almost Christmas!"

"I'm not thinking Christmas at all. I'm so distracted with you being here, it could be Valentine's or Fourth of July."

She wrinkled her nose. "Valentine's is fun. I like that one."

"Oh, you do, do you?" he answered, his hand smoothing over her butt and making her jump.

"You're ruining my reputation," she whispered.

"Oh, they know. Look at them," he said as he caught several people watching them. "They know what you're all about."

He picked up her bag, and they walked through the lobby to the short-term parking lot. Damon opened the passenger door of his brand new bright blue Hummer, and helped her up the step to inside the cab.

"You went shopping."

"I didn't want to ferry you around in my Jasmine."

Jasmine had been the name of his old Ford pick-up he'd owned ten years ago. "You still had her? You mean you left her out to pasture?"

He smiled and closed the door. He tucked her suitcase into the second seat. Once behind the steering wheel, he explained.

"Jasmine was costing me a small fortune to keep her tuned up and working reliably. She was letting me down a bunch. So she's now happy, getting greasy with all those old crusty guys at the wrecking yard. She was a classic, but after we got back, I decided I'd reward myself with a new set of wheels. Meet Monica."

They drove down along the waterfront district, past several cruise ships in port, and several military floating museums, including the USS Midway. Tall silvery structures overlooked a packed marina filled with expensive yachts. They passed the Convention Center and continued South and then across the Coronado Bridge to the strand.

"Are you tired or are you up for a burger and a brew?"

"I want to see some place where you hang out. Some place, that

Scupper, is that it? Is that nearby?"

"Yes, ma'am."

She noticed the sun had set some time ago, but the orange glow didn't stain the sky as long as it did in Florida. But the weather was nice, even in the middle of December.

"You're looking for the sunset, aren't you?"

"I've gotten accustomed to it."

"They're nice here, but Florida's warmer, when it doesn't hurricane."

Walking through the doors at the Scupper, she studied the artwork covering the walls, pictures of Team guys and sailors, photos of various ships, flags from different campaigns, and copies of telegrams and letters from Presidents. One entire wall contained pictures of young men who had not been able to come home. It was very sobering. Damon watched her carefully.

They were seated outside on the patio, next to a fire pit.

Everything she saw was unfamiliar. It was busier and larger than her sleepy little Sunset Beach town. The cars were more expensive and the streets were teeming with groups of handsome muscled men and young women out having a good time. She could feel right away it was a faster pace, like how Sonoma County had felt when she returned there after living in Oregon for the year on the coast and for her college.

He kept watching her.

"What do you think?"

"It suits you, I can see. You're happy here, aren't you, Damon?"

He nodded and sipped on his beer. "Very."

She raised her glass and toasted him. "That's why I like it."

THE TOUCH OF his hands on her body was like heaven. She even felt slightly embarrassed standing naked against him in the shower. He soaped all the airport and Florida dust from her skin, massaged the back of her neck until she relaxed and became putty in his arms again. It didn't take long. He was patient.

Their fooling around in the shower spilled over to the bedroom, where at last they lay together, wet but warmed by the sensual shower. He pulled the comforter over them, making a tent. She felt the creases at the sides of his mouth, the way his ears felt like velvet, the smell of his chest even though she'd soaped him off and rinsed him with her bare hands. His whispers drew out all her animal spirits until at last he touched her like it was the first time.

As she peaked, her orgasm taking over her body, she held him as tightly as she was able. She needed to feel him deep and to experience how well they fit together and how she never wanted to let him go.

Her life was full, surrounded by strong women from her past, and a mission and fire in her soul. She was living the life, holding the man in her arms that few women had the good fortune to love. He was fearless, and through that, everything was possible.

For now, she tossed aside her worries as well as her plans and just enjoyed the way he coveted her and turned that night into magic.

HE TOOK HER to breakfast at a restaurant beside the Convention Center, where they meandered down the pier, eyeing expensive yachts from all over the world.

"I came here the morning after I went skydiving for the first time," he said. "I was scared shitless, and after doing that, I just wanted to stock up on carbs big time. I felt as strong as a Sherman tank, and as light as a feather!"

"If that is your way of asking if I'd like to jump out of a plane, I have to tell you that I'm an earth person. I do gardens, enjoy road-trips, and love beaches and beautiful blue water. But floating through the sky? I don't think I could ever do that."

"Would you trust me to go tandem?"

"Not sure what that means."

"I strap on behind you, I tell you what to do, and we fly together. You'd love it."

"Damon, you're crazy. I'd never do that."

"Sure you would. I know you have it in you. Don't you want to find out?" He held her hand. "I'd be right there with you the whole way, strapped to your back."

SHE KNEW THAT if he waited until tomorrow or the next day she'd chicken out. Before she knew it, they were at the glider center, watching one plane after another load up, take off and then allow their passengers to slowly float back down to the ground. Except for the idea of seeing houses that appeared one-half inch wide, the process didn't look scary at all.

They were fitted with tandem chutes. A short instruction class began, telling her how her chute would open, what she would see, how to land, and how to position her arms and angle her body for the maximum good experience.

And then they were off in the airplane that didn't have a door on the large opening she watched in front of her as they climbed to over thirteen thousand feet. The cars and trucks were the size of chocolate sprinkles on the doughnut she ate this morning. Panic was setting in. She considered asking Damon to take her back to the base.

"Stand up, sweetheart," he whispered and kissed the side of her cheek.

She did so, and he hooked himself to her harness, and they walked to the opening like one crab-like being. "When do we…"

Damon nudged her into the opening and over the edge. The freefall she experienced wasn't what she expected. Instead of falling, she was being pushed up by air coming from the earth.

He reminded her to keep her mouth closed because she'd been

screaming. He touched her arms and she assumed the "W" position she'd been shown.

"Lean forward, legs back. Now pull this."

All of a sudden, the chute unfurled into a beautiful red and yellow kite flying overhead. Objects on the ground were still very small, but the closer they got to earth, the warmer the air got. They could talk because the wind had stopped screaming all around her.

"See? Not so bad now, right?"

"It's beautiful."

"There's Mexico over there." He started pointing out ships and buildings they'd passed, including the harbor and the Convention Center. "There's my Hummer, see it?"

Now his truck looked the size of her little fingernail.

He showed her how to pull on the weighted steering, making them turn, first to the right, and then to the left, hitting thermals which sent them back up small distances. It was peaceful and kissed with glorious sunlight. And she was with him.

She held his hand as he steered the glider expertly, prolonging their descent. And as they got close to the ground, he asked her to shoot her feet out in front, while they landed on his, and then they tumbled in the grasses and stopped.

On her back, tethered in the straps of her chute, her arms out to the sides, she looked up at the sky, blue and overwhelming, and felt the magic and the power of being alive.

He was there, watching her, kissing her gently, and witnessing the miracle together. She trusted him. She trusted herself not to let fear hold her back.

She embraced her future, whatever that was to be.

THE NEXT MORNING, she received the call from Gran Karmody. The Newbergs wanted to meet with her and discuss her request.

Martel knew that her past had finally come back to greet her.

Would she be risking this beautiful love story for the chance to meet her daughter? She felt like she was stepping through another doorway to the freefall, except this time, she wasn't strapped into safety.

It would be completely uncharted waters.

And it would be worth it.

CHAPTER 17

D AMON WATCHED MARTEL chatting with several of the SEAL wives at the Team 3 Christmas party, held at the Brownlee home. As was usual, the Brownlee's tree filled the nearly two-story Spanish Renaissance home in one of the most exclusive areas of Coronado. Many of the SEAL children, if they were old enough to remember, were excited to find their little gifts the Brownlees placed under the tree. A crowd of nearly a dozen, including some toddlers who were shoved aside by the older children, had to be reminded to be careful not to disturb the tree or the ornaments.

Martel laughed at their antics, trying to follow the action while turning back to stay involved in the conversation with the wives and girlfriends.

Dr. and Mrs. Brownlee were Libby's parents, Coop's in-laws. A noted psychiatrist and frequent talk show guest as well as bestselling author, Dr. Brownlee had become the Team unofficial shrink, in all ways but legally. His own brother, Will, had been a Navy SEAL medic who perished in Grenada. As was tradition, his name was engraved on the ceremonial KA-BAR knife presented to Coop when he got his Trident. Kyle had ordered him to find out about the family of this fallen Bonefrog, since Coop had just lost all of his in a tornado in his home state of Nebraska.

And that's where he'd met his wife, Libby, who was Will Brownlee's niece.

The party was packed this year. Sometimes, the Team was deployed overseas, and only the wives and children were present. Or some of them would be on temporary assignments or extra training duties. But this year, it was nearly a full house. Luckily, the weather was nice enough that tables were spread outside around the huge Brownlee pool and patio area.

"That sure didn't take you long," whispered Cooper. He was joined by T.J. in admiring his choice.

Damon didn't mind the implied dig. His divorce had just been finalized since he hadn't contested anything and let Charlene keep the house.

"Funny how the right woman comes along at just the right time," he said as he smiled in her direction. Then he faced Coop and T.J. "We were sweethearts ten years ago, just before I got out of Dodge and signed up. I'm lucky she seems to like having me back," he said.

"I'll bet. Night and day between her and the other one," T.J. mumbled.

"She who will remain unnamed," added Coop.

"May she rot in Hell and choke on the house payments," said Damon.

"Glad that's all settled then." Coop sipped on his mineral water. "So, have you asked her yet?"

Damon squinted and sucked in air through his teeth. "We're not quite there. Close. But not quite there. Lots of implied consent, if you know what I mean."

"Oh, sweetheart, I love you. I never want to be without you!" T.J. mimicked, pumping his hips.

Damon still didn't take offense. "Not like that at all," he shook his head. "We're taking it slow and steady. We're exploring all sorts of options. Just getting to know each other again after such a long time apart."

"I myself like it slow and hard," mumbled T.J.

"The exploring part sounds kind of fun to me. You use handcuffs and strawberry gel and the titty cream?" asked Coop.

Damon did begin to get rattled at that comment. "How come you fellas never talked about this before with me?"

"Because you were a married man. Miserable, but married, Damon," answered T.J.

"We live vicariously through all of you divorced or single guys. We like hearing about new love and wicked sex. Sometimes being long-term married with a couple of kids running around begins to get a bit routine, if you know what I mean," added Coop.

"But that's what I want."

The two SEALs stared at Damon incredulously.

Damon couldn't hold it more than ten seconds. His smile cracked, and soon they all were laughing. As they wandered off in search of another victim, T.J. punched him in the arm. "Good one. You're all right. I was worried about you for a while."

ON THE WAY back to Damon's place, he asked her how she felt being at the party.

"Lovely ladies. And those kids, they're bright, mostly polite, but Danny's got a little hellion."

"Oh, that's Ali. He rescued him from Iraq and adopted him. I think he was about three or four and had been living in a war zone. All his family was killed. His father died trying to save him."

"That's an amazing story."

"He's deadly accurate with a slingshot. Danny taught him and usually, his little brother, Griffin, has a bruise on his forehead. Griffin is his favorite target."

"That's terrible."

"He's been sent home from school dozens of times. They've got their hands full."

"Luci is lovely. She's got the patience of Job with three boys."

"So you didn't really answer my question."

"I can see why you love working with these guys and their families. I understand now. I never did before. But you all are a big family."

"Something goes wrong, we're there for each other. The wives too. Only thing we aren't supposed to do is gossip, but it happens sometimes. Sometimes the wives don't get it, start moving out of the circle, and that just does not work here. We stick together."

"I can see that." Martel continued to stare through the windshield, and sighed.

Damon wondered if he'd come on too strong. But he needed to know there was no resistance on her part. His goal was to get her to commit, agree to move out to California as soon as she could arrange it. He was ready to lay down roots and make up for lost time.

But she was being a little elusive.

"What's wrong?"

She turned. "Nothing. Why would you think that?"

He shrugged. "I don't know. You just seem…preoccupied."

"Well, it's all new, Damon. I grew up in California, but I spent most of that up north, as you know. A world apart from Southern California. And nothing like Florida."

"I didn't have to spend much time getting adjusted there," he chuckled.

"It's really not the same thing, Damon. In Florida, things are slower. You take off your uniform, your big boots, put on your shorts and flip flops. You hang out on the patio and watch the sun set every night. You eat seafood and dance at moonlight."

She meant it. Life was harder for her in San Diego.

"Would you miss it?" He focused on his driving so she didn't feel pressured.

"I'm learning to adjust. I could probably learn to adjust anywhere if you were there, Damon. And I like the Damon I fool around with here. I like his shower, his bed, his aftershave. I even like the way he drives his new truck."

"Hummer."

"It's a truck."

"No, it's a Hummer. Big difference." He pulled over and turned off the engine. They weren't home, but near a little park overlooking the ocean. A large gray cruiser glided past them on its way back to the base. "Come on," he said as he pulled her over the gear shift and out through the driver's door.

Martel was laughing, pretending to try to get away. With her hair blowing in the gentle breeze and the water as a backdrop behind her, Damon fell to his knees.

"I'm crazy about you. I don't need any more time trying to figure it out. I want you here. I'm all done with my search. You're the one, Martel. Please tell me you'll marry me."

He could see a cloud form in her eyes. It wasn't the pure love and acceptance he'd expected. Was she going to say no?

She slowly knelt down in front of him and took his hands in hers. "Just give me a little time. I want the same thing, Damon. I move a little slower. Remember, I'm working on Florida time."

He tried not to show his disappointment. He'd been totally convinced she would be delighted, and they'd be making their rounds tonight, telling everyone they were engaged. What had happened?

"Damon," she started, "Think of it this way. A good couple who are going to spend the rest of their lives together is a blending of two people. They are not the same. You're the guy who loves doing things that are wild and active. I read, and yes, I enjoy learning about all the things you do, but my world is one of books—and teaching children to read. And maybe it takes longer for my brain and my heart to get in sync. It's not a bad thing that we approach life differently. We can't all be heroes and save the day. And you wouldn't want that, either."

He could see she'd spent a lot of time thinking about it, which bothered him further. He was torn between asking for explanation and considering that it would be best to let her figure it out on her own. He wouldn't be able to convince her. She had to get there on her own. And that's why she was here.

She wouldn't have come if she wasn't considering spending the rest of her life with me.

Their hands were still clutched together. She reached over and touched his cheek. "Damon, sweetheart, I want this to work. I really do. I'm sorting, processing, letting pieces fall into place. That's what works for me."

"You're right." He had to cut off the discussion. Perhaps he'd scared her or started out wrong.

They held hands back to the truck, and he helped her in again. Before he closed her door, he leaned in. "You just let me know if you have questions I need to answer. I'm going to let you do the sorting out, like you said. I trust you, Martel. We have no secrets, right? There isn't anything or anyone standing in the way? I just want to be sure."

Her eyes watered. She touched his cheek again. "No."

But she was still crying when he pulled up to his place. And she couldn't tell him what movie she wanted to go to tonight, since that had been the plan. He suggested they rent one, and she was agreeable, but didn't have any preferences.

He knew he could make love to her, perhaps brighten her mood, caress, and work out all the second thoughts or worry she must be harboring. But he sort of didn't want to do that tonight.

"It's a lot to take in here, I know. Why don't you take a shower and go to bed early? I'm going to stay up and watch a little T.V. Then I'll come and join you," he said, giving her a short kiss.

She didn't pull him to her. She didn't do anything at all except nod, look at her feet, and slip away into the bedroom, closing the door behind her.

He sat for several minutes in the dark and stared at that door. He didn't know what was on the other side, but it wasn't anything he could fight or manipulate. He had to wait. That was the most fucked up thing in the world right now.

PAST MIDNIGHT, DAMON awoke with a kink in his neck from falling asleep upright on the couch. He'd been tired. Kind of a nervous energy, he thought.

Opening the door slowly to stop any noise, he tiptoed inside the bedroom, removed his shoes and clothes, and slipped into the sheets in his boxers. Her warm body had heated up the bed, and he became aroused, in spite of his decision to pull back a bit on his expectation and emotions.

But he felt her hand travel over his chest and up his neck. He accepted the gift of her soft body as it touched his, her thigh over his, her breasts rubbing against him, and the moan she gave him as their lips touched. She pulled her hair back and continued to kiss his neck and down the center of his chest. Her right hand smoothed over his thigh, lacing her fingers up and then down as they traveled toward his package. She arched up and placed him between her breasts and squeezed their flesh together.

His hardness was instantaneous as she undulated over him, gently riding his thigh, letting him feel her mound pressed firmly against him. She spread her legs wide, held onto him with both hands, massaged him up and down, and then touched his tip with her tongue, rubbing and probing. She gently sucked as he breached her lips, her tongue wrapping around him.

She kissed him from stem to his tip—then squeezed and fondled his balls. Her breathing became deep, the pressure increased until he couldn't be still any longer. He sat up, partially, framing her face with his hands.

"That's so nice, sweetheart."

She drew him in deep, all the way to the back of her throat and held him.

He was about to burst. He needed to get inside her, but she was insistent, working up and down on his shaft, increasing his size, turning him into a Grecian column.

He slid up the bed and she followed. Leaning against the padded headboard, he watched as her long hair framed her face, as she climbed up first one thigh and then the other. She gently rubbed him back and forth against her pulsing sex. She braced herself, holding on to the headboard with both hands while she angled her hips and let him seat completely inside her.

Damon gasped when her muscles enclosed him, as he felt the warm friction of the insides of her channel. He brought his hands to her breasts. Moving his hips, he forced himself deep inside her. She leaned over, presenting her nipples to his mouth and he sucked them into peaks. He pushed up and inside, back and forth until the movement became faster and faster. His thighs slapped against hers, his cock gliding quickly through the gateway of her sex. Until she arched up and moaned. Her insides fluttered.

He grabbed her ass, gripped her hips, and quickly flipped her over to fuck her deep from behind as she came. The satisfying constriction of his balls, responding to the new position, sent him spurting inside her. He held her tight against him, pushing as she pressed back against him. She found his hands and added pressure, followed his fingers as they tweaked her bud.

And then they stopped, breathing, waiting for the pulsing to stop, prolonging the moment for as long as they could.

The next morning, she was back. She matched every advance he made. She walked around in her robe untied, teasing him with her nakedness. They spent the next two days in bed. All the things they needed to do were put onto the backburner as he explored how deep and long he could feel consumed by this woman. He was going to give her every ounce she demanded. He'd be relentless. The two of them together would not be like Coop and T.J. Their only routine was feeling more, getting deeper and making the addiction last forever.

This was the way he was supposed to live.

SHE WAS TO return home in three days. She told him she'd extended her stay by two because she'd run across an old friend from Oregon, who was now living in the Bay Area.

"Great. We'll take a road trip!" He was all for it.

She stood against him, touching his lips with her forefinger. "Damon, I need to meet with her alone."

"Sure. I'll drive. You have your meeting, and we'll do some fun stuff, and then return. It'll be a great trip."

Her eyes studied him. "This is important. This is something I need to do by myself."

"What do you mean?"

"I want to just fly up there on my own. They're living in Palo Alto now. I haven't seen them in ten years."

"Them?"

"She's married. We have some history. I needed to clear the air with her at first. Later, perhaps another visit, we can all be together, but not for this first meeting, Damon."

He broke away, sitting on the couch. He didn't like what he was hearing.

"You've never mentioned this friend. What sort of friend are we talking about, Martel? A lover?"

"No, please. I'll tell you all about it after the meeting. I promise. I just need you to trust me."

"But we decided not to have any secrets. And now you've got

one. I'm not part of that."

"It isn't like that. Believe me, this is different. I'm going to tell you the whole story, soon. I'll be safe. I've made a promise to myself, to her, to my mother. I'm promising you I have to do this initially by myself. I just can't talk about it further."

He stiffened.

"This is really strange, Martel. What the hell is this all about?"

"Something that happened when I was in school up in Oregon. It's not bad—"

"Then tell me!"

"I promise I will. I'm just not ready yet."

So that was it. She had some big fucking secret he wasn't included in. Was this some former colleague, a lover? Did she have an affair with a woman? Is that what she was afraid to tell him?

He wanted to ask but didn't want her to be offended in case he was wrong. He decided to go for it anyway. "Look, Martel, if this woman is someone you were romantically involved with, I don't care. As long as you're not asking me to share you with her husband, or share me with her, I'm fine with something from your past that meant something to you. I wasn't there. But now that I'm here, I really beg you to let me be a part of it."

"You will be, Damon. I promise. It isn't fair to ask you, but I must ask that you trust me."

SO, THERE IT was.

She took all her things, and he even dropped her off at the airport the next day. Her friend, she said, was going to meet her in San Francisco.

"I'll text you so you know I've gotten there safely," she'd said.

"Fine. Can I ask one more question before you go?"

"Of course."

"Are you coming back?"

The look on her face broke his heart. As he watched her cross the concourse toward the gates, he wondered if it would be the last time he'd ever see her.

He wanted to feel something, but he was in shock. Maybe he was dead and had just figured it out, like in the movie.

This was friendly fire. The worst kind.

CHAPTER 18

E VERY TIME MARTEL felt the cramp in her stomach and her shortness of breath, she put it out of her mind. Someone had told her that the Special Forces operators did a good job of masking pain, even being able to stop bleeding in a critical situation, if they were trained properly.

She was far from having that skill. But distraction was helping.

The bay wasn't anything like Tampa Bay, where the water was so delineated people could live along the edge. These edges curled around like some alien oil painting. Parts of the bay were purple, part dark brown. It reminded her of her trip to Yellowstone when she was a child and viewing all the little steamy mud pools of different colors.

When the wheels touched the ground, she was shaken to reality. Lori Newberg was going to meet her at the luggage carousel. Although she'd seen the woman years ago, she wasn't sure she'd recognize her.

As she descended down the escalator, the Newbergs stood together, arm in arm, a safe distance from the limo drivers who were picking up their charges. Lori's hair was shorter now, and had turned salt-and-pepper gray. She wore a red long-sleeved wool dress with a hooded rain parka in a light tan color. Mark wore a long black raincoat over his suit trousers. He'd worn a white shirt and red tie. His horn-rimmed glasses pegged him as a professor at Stanford or a school administrator. Neither of them smiled. In fact, Martel saw Lori tighten her grip on her husband's arm and seem to draw strength from him.

She'd rehearsed what she would say to the couple, and now everything she'd practiced went out the window. When she noticed Lori's eyes were watering, Martel knew what to do.

"First, let me say I'm grateful. Very grateful for what you've done and also for giving me the opportunity to speak with you both. I hesitated for so long—"

Mark pointed to the moving turnstile. "What color? I'll get your suitcase."

"It's big and brown with a turtle design on it. I bought it in Hawaii."

As Mark ran off to get the bag, Lori cleared her throat. She inhaled. "Well. Here we are again. I wasn't sure how I'd feel about all this."

"Me too." Martel smiled at her. She could see the woman was stressed, as she would be.

"God, did you bring sand from Florida?" he said struggling to get the handle pulled.

"Oh, I didn't tell you, I've been visiting friends in San Diego. I've been in California over a week now."

"Christmas break for you too, right?" Lori asked as they made their way out of the baggage area and into the parking lot. A light rain was falling.

"Yes." She was going to tell them about her new boyfriend but decided not to do so. "And in case you're worrying I brought such a big bag, I'm only staying until tomorrow and then I fly home—I mean I fly back to San Diego and then back to Florida in another four days."

"You said you got a room in Palo Alto?" Mark asked. "Where is your reservation?"

"The Stanford Court. Thought I might go do some last-minute Christmas shopping too." Her attempts at being light-hearted were not working. Not only wasn't she relaxing them, but she was making herself nervous as hell. She started noticing everything she didn't like about her wardrobe, starting with the new loafers she'd bought that were giving her blisters. She wasn't used to wearing long pants and wool, multi-layers and sweaters, even in the middle of December.

"Stanford Court is nice, and it's not far from our house, is it, Mark?" Lori asked.

"Yup."

As Mark opened the car doors for both her and Lori, she thanked them both for picking her up at the airport.

"No problem. We're glad to," Mark said.

No one said anything on the way to Palo Alto from the airport. Afternoon traffic was beginning to congest the freeway. She used the time to send a text to Damon, which wasn't read. She added another line, asking what he wanted her to get for his late Christmas present.

Martel checked in, giving the bellman ten dollars to bring the bag up to her room.

She'd already called ahead and knew that they had a bar area and coffee shop off the lobby that wouldn't be very crowded that time of day.

"Should we sit in here?" she motioned to the tables. Two big screen T.V.'s were playing sports, but the volume was mercifully turned low. She let them select the table. Mark ordered a Scotch, but Lori and Martel both had water.

Mark leaned into the table, his brow furled. "I have to air some-thing first, if you don't mind. Are we going to be sued?"

"Oh heck no! Why—oh you thought since Mr. Karmody con-tacted you that I had those intentions. I don't."

"Well, that's what he said too. I feel I should tell you that Lori and I are not rich, but we'll spend every penny we have trying to defend our right to keep Ainsley. We have several friends who are well-connected here in Silicon Valley who said they'd help. I'm not here to fight—"

"Nor am I," Martel interrupted him. "Honest. I'm not here to interfere with your rights as her parents, her *real* parents. I'm just here to make my request. Just once, I'd like to talk to her, to have her hear it from me that I didn't abandon her, that I arranged it so you could have her, and raise her the way I couldn't. But I didn't abandon her." Martel feared the last part. "I did it for love, because I love her."

Lori's eyes were spilling over her lower lids now. "Why do you have to do that? Whatever gives you the right?"

Martel looked between the two wonderful people who were lucky enough to have her little girl. It was strange sitting across the table from them and feeling grateful for what they'd done. She wished she could make them see that.

She took Lori's hand. "Because I wanted her to know that she was and is loved. That she wasn't discarded. She's always been loved."

Lori withdrew her hand and blotted her eyes with the napkin. "We've told her that many, many times."

"I know that. But I want her to hear it from me."

Mark was concerned for Lori, and it was obvious he was going to support her in any way she wanted. He waited until her composure came back.

"Why should I trust you?"

"Because I only held her for a few minutes. I just wanted her to know what was in my heart when I let her go."

Lori looked into her lap. She extracted a picture of a preteen girl, tall and lanky, blonde, wearing a basketball uniform, holding a ball in her hands. She was the spitting image of her father.

Martel didn't want to touch the photo but stared down at her daughter, seeing the shape of her face, the way her button nose flared out to the sides but had a flat spot, just like hers. When she held her in the hospital, she'd noticed all those things. She'd kissed her forehead, and handed her to the nurse.

Something distracted her on her blouse, and Martel noticed she'd been crying.

"She's beautiful, Lori. She's even prettier than I imagined."

Mark spoke up. "She's a helluva basketball player. She's good at every kind of sport we can find her. She plays soccer, baseball, basketball, and now she wants to play volleyball. If it has a ball, if it moves, if she has to shove aside three other players first, she'll be the first to the ball every time."

Of course, that made perfect sense.

"What did her father do? Is he athletic?" Lori asked.

Martel smiled. "Yes. You would say that."

LORI ASKED IF Martel was still teaching. They let her know that Mark had accepted the administrator's job at a large charter school in the area. Lori was now working toward her degree in counseling and administration, but teaching was still her first love.

"Where did you get the name Ainsley?" Martel asked.

"It was my mother's."

"It's beautiful."

They laid down ground rules for a meeting, giving them time to sit down with her and make sure her daughter was comfortable with it. It was decided that sometime in February when the school had a ski week break would be best, and Martel agreed.

"We talked between us about the possibility she might want to reach out to you someday." Mark frowned. "Are we still of the same opinion?" he asked his wife before he continued.

"Yes, I feel comfortable with that."

"We decided that it should be her choice, not yours and not

ours," he said.

"I can honor that. I think we have to be very transparent. I don't want any secrets." Martel nearly choked on that word.

"Exactly."

Before they parted, Martel reached into her purse for the leather folder with the pictures of her pregnancy, nearly month by month.

But the package wasn't there.

CHAPTER 19

D AMON JOINED RENNY and a couple of the single Team guys at the Scupper. It didn't feel like two days before Christmas. He'd brought Martel some expensive lingerie, but now he wasn't sure she'd be around to open them up. So he didn't bother buying a Christmas tree. Kyle, Cooper, T.J., Fredo, and several other married guys with kids were busy attending ballet recitals, quick trips to Disneyland or one of the Aquariums, or a Mexican cruise.

The banter was stupid. He felt like a loser, listening to stories about trying to bag girls, as if that was everything in the whole world. Several wanted to know about Florida, especially if there was good action there. He humored them. He lied. And he felt shitty about it, too.

Taking another drag on his long-necked beer, he caught a whiff of his own body odor. He hadn't shaved nor taken a shower since he'd taken Martel to the airport yesterday.

Renny slid closer to him, and Damon frowned and slid away. "Get off me."

"What's eaten your candy cane, asshole?"

Damon shrugged.

"So who is this friend she wants to visit?"

"Beats me. Some chick she met in Oregon."

Renny considered something before he spoke. "You know, lesbian girls can be pretty hot. Have you seen—"

Damon shoved him off the bench and walked out to the strand.

Like a fly on a piece of flypaper, Renny was that stray dog that would never leave him alone. He ran, catching up to him, and just matched Damon's long strides. Even assuming the position.

"See, if you're mad, Damon, you gotta walk like this." He slapped Damon's bicep and pointed to himself. "You kinda hunker down and slink down the sidewalk." He exaggerated leaning back, letting his legs kick out in front of him like the cartoons on the old R. Crumb comics.

Damon had loved those books. The beefy girls had perfectly round tits and thighs that could crush a man's head between them. Quirky and an acquired taste, but he liked them.

Charlene made him get rid of them when they got married. Renny had been right about her all along.

It was impossible to be mad at Renny for too long. He was an easy friend because he wasn't discerning. He'd taken that knife blade to the chest to defend the Senator's daughter and never complained about it once. Renny had expected at least a phone call from the Senator. They teased him no-end about it.

He was proud to be part of one of the most successful raids they'd done and it made up for the last two that didn't go so well. They'd rescued over forty women and six children. They were due to be shipped out to South America, headed eventually to the U.S. or Canada. From there, the women would be lost, the children used and abused or worse, snuffed out. It felt good to clean out their inventory of death and destruction.

But except for a very few, the general public would never know. The Senator was too busy running for re-election. At least that's what they told Renny. This type of operation could never be leaked.

So maybe that was weighing on his mind as well. Just a confluence of timing that wasn't working for him. Unfinished business, because the bad guys would always be out there. Some of the good guys would pay the price, have accidents. That was unfair, but what they signed on for.

He owed Renny an apology.

"Sorry, man. I'm in a lousy mood. I shouldn't have come."

"You did the right thing. You were alone and wondering what she was up to. I'd feel the same way, except I would have snuck up and had her followed. And then, if there was a woman, or another guy, I would have pounded the shit out of them, either way."

Damon knew Renny wouldn't do that.

"So what is it, really? Just spill it. I'll make it worse!" Renny said brightly.

"I don't know," he lied. He didn't tell anyone he'd asked her to marry him and she'd turned him down. *Nicely* turned him down someone would say. As if there was anything nice about it. He missed their connection, the intensity with which she gave herself to him. He wanted to inhabit every square inch of her body, her thoughts and her soul. He couldn't help it if he was selfish. He'd had a taste of that, and he got hooked forever.

'*I'm done looking*' he'd told her. Maybe he nixed it by not buying her a ring. But what they had was bare naked truth and that sense of belonging as if they were originally one body and somehow got separated and now found each other again. He didn't want anyone else. He didn't want to pretend to be happy. He wanted to feel like he did when they were skydiving. Watching the wonder in her face as she screamed, even if she did slime him. He held her arms out, felt her joy and mirth melting into him as he kept her in the air, opening up her world to the view from thirteen thousand feet.

Not every man could do that for his woman. Not every woman could be present for it. It took someone special to let him be in control, to understand that he loved teaching her about flying, about sex, about what this whole brotherhood thing was all about. He thought all that was important to her, because it was important to him.

Renny had been prattling on about something he hadn't been paying attention to.

"Ice cream?"

"Sure."

They hadn't really had dinner, but he didn't want any. Renny ordered a sundae for him because he didn't care. He checked his phone and didn't get a text from her saying she was back. That either meant that she'd stayed another night, or she didn't want him to pick her up, or worse yet, she'd flown all the way back to Florida.

"Fuck it."

"Fuck what?" Renny brought his waffle cone Sundae covered in chocolate sauce and whipped cream, placing it right in front of him.

He stared at the whipped cream, let his finger dive into it and brought a huge glob to his mouth.

"I got a spoon here, Damon." Renny passed the white plastic utensil over the table for him.

"I don't want to eat it with a spoon. I want to eat it with my finger."

Renny put it down and stared at him. "Something's not right here."

He thought about it then scooped up another fingerfull and stared down the street.

The sky was orange as the sun set. There were so many things like Florida, and so many things that were completely different.

"Do you know whipped cream tastes different here?" he said to Renny.

"You guys broke up. She's not coming back. That's what happened."

"I can always tell when I'm being lied to. It's one thing to have a woman lie to you about your performance. I don't mind that kind of lie because they just want to make you feel special and all. But when they say they want to be a part of your life and then hide something really big, that kind of a lie makes me feel like I've been stupid."

"Are you sure you're not overreacting? Maybe you should talk to Kyle, or Coop or one of the other guys. Just how do you know she's not leveling with you?

"I don't know, but I just know. I'll find out, eventually. Ten years from now, I'll be at some second or third wedding for you or one of the other guys, and she'll just walk into the room. We'll stand there, sniff the air, and test our ability to make each other miserable."

"Holy shit, Damon. This scares me. That's it. I'm staying over tonight. We're going to get some movies and we're going to get you so fuckin' drunk you'll think you were back in Florida."

"You know what, Renny? Maybe I am. Maybe I am."

THEY'D STOPPED BY to buy some snacks and beers. Damon bought just about every kind of chocolate bar he could find in the liquor store. The Indian clerk squinted at him, lowering his forehead in disapproval.

"What? I have a sweet tooth," Damon said. Renny was still cruising for the perfect bag of chips.

"No man, you have a death wish. That stuff'll kill you, my man," he said in his clipped Indian accent.

"It's chocolate!"

"Yes, and a whole lot of other things too. But it's your life, my man."

Yes, it is my life. The clerk had been exactly right. This was his way of dealing because he didn't want to think too hard on two things: what he was missing, and how to fix it.

BACK AT DAMON'S place, Renny started straightening up the dishes left with cereal and milk stuck to the sides of the bowl. He picked up a pair of jeans and a shirt, moved his shoes to the side where they wouldn't trip on them, and then walked into the bedroom.

"Come on, Damon, let's wash your sheets. That will help you sleep better. That's what you need."

"I thought we were going to watch movies tonight," Damon said as he began stripping off the blanket and the top sheet then the bottom sheet.

"We will. We put these into the wash, and then we settle down and watch some serious porn. This way, when you wake up with a headache, at least your sheets will smell nice. Unlike the rest of you."

Renny was right. Damon picked up the bundle and walked to the bathroom where his stacking washer-dryer was. He stuffed the sheets and blanket into the front loader. As he swung the door closed, a leather folder, like ones that hold pictures, fell to the ground. He picked it up and sat on the bed.

They were pictures of Martel when she was much younger. The photo was taken from the side, so that in each one, her belly got bigger and bigger.

These are pictures of Martel being pregnant.

He let the photos drop to the floor as he braced his forehead in his hand.

So that's where she's gone. She's had a baby with someone. She's gone to see her child and to be with the man who gave her that child. That's the secret she didn't want to tell him. It wasn't a woman she was visiting. It was a man.

Her lover.

Renny didn't ask anything when he saw Damon sitting on the bare mattress. Instead he knelt, picking up the photos and one by one examined them, and then put them into the leather pouch.

"I don't understand, Damon. What are these?"

"It's the reason she isn't coming back."

"But what does it mean?" Renny asked.

"What do you think it means? That's Martel, goddammit."

"But how—?"

Just then, they heard Damon's door open. Renny stood, but Damon remained seated. Martel appeared in the entrance, righting her suitcase. She saw the folder in Renny's hands, walked over and took the package from him.

Renny looked between Martel and Damon and back again. "Sh-Sh-should I leave?"

No one said a word, so Renny slipped on his jacket, stepped into his canvas slip-ons and did just that.

Damon couldn't look at her. Once again, he felt cold. He had no way to put all this together. He wanted information but he didn't want to ask.

She walked in front of him and sat down on the bed beside him. Her pretty pink nails opened the pouch, worn and scuffed, opening the flap enclosed with a Velcro tab. She pulled out the pictures, neatly tucked into plastic sleeves, and placed the stack on her knees.

Martel put her arm around Damon's shoulder. At first he wanted to pull away, but she held him, then pressed her forehead against his, with her right hand holding the pictures in her lap. She held up one, searching his eyes for any expression.

"This picture was taken about four months after you left Santa Rosa."

She wasn't smiling.

He looked at it again, and then took it in his fingers, squinting to see it more clearly.

"This picture," she said as she held a second one up, "was taken a month later."

Damon added it to the other one.

"And this one the month after that."

He took the picture from her hand again and stacked it with the other two.

"And this one, and this one, and finally this one. I took this one when I was living up in Oregon by the ocean. I stayed there while I had the baby, Damon. Your baby. Our baby. Our little girl. And I made sure she got a chance at life. I interviewed and found the perfect parents for her. That's what I did ten years ago while you were off being a Boy Scout."

Damon's finger rubbed the last photo, tracing the outline of Martel's belly over and over again.

She leaned into him and whispered in his ear, "I found her, Damon. She's beautiful."

He searched her eyes, streaming tears. He was a jumble of emotions. Part of him was angry, part was scared, and there was a huge part that loved this woman and what she had done. She'd taken care of his little girl when he wasn't capable of being there for either one of them. He didn't deserve her. He really didn't.

"Say something, Damon."

"I'm ashamed."

She adjusted his hand so he could look at the pictures again. "No, we made a mistake. But *she* wasn't one of them."

"So this is what you were doing?"

"Yes. I haven't spoken to her yet. I met with her parents. I asked, and they agreed to meet with me. I wanted to see her, Damon, and they've agreed."

"But why? I mean, why would they let you come in and upset everything?"

"Because I'm not. She belongs to them now, not to me, or us. They are her parents and always will be. I just wanted to see her happy and tell her that I love her, that she's always been loved. Not abandoned. Loved. Wouldn't you want to know that if it was you?"

"But what about us?"

"This changes nothing, Damon. This was the one thing I needed to do, to clear up on my own. It was that hole in my soul nothing or no one in this world could fill."

She reached down into her purse and brought out the picture.

"This is Ainsley, your daughter."

His eyes filled with tears as she held him. He swallowed hard, unable to speak, overcome with the miracle presented to him. Finally, he found his courage. "Do I get to meet her?" he asked.

"If you want to. If she wants to. If we get permission. But some day, Damon, I'm sure you will. Can you be patient?"

He dropped the pictures and pulled her close to him. It all came into focus now. He'd left. He went off, running from the only miracle in his life. But Martel never did. She never left. She kept the dream and the flame alive.

As long as she was beside him, he'd let her teach him that. As long as they were together, anything was possible.

EPILOGUE

O NE OF THE first things Martel did when she returned to Florida was to visit Phyllis at the cemetery. She sat on the cold stone bench nearby, contemplating the headstone engraved with the face of an angel and Phyllis' dates. She had been buried beside her late husband.

"You're going to have to give me a sign, tell me what he thought of your red dress and your choice of reading material. I hope you didn't get into too much trouble about your evenings dancing under the stars with that handsome Jamaican fellow. Did he sing to you, I wonder?"

She could see it all clearly. Phyllis, young and healthy, smiling and showing everyone around her how fearless she was.

She listened to sounds of an ordinary day. Phyllis didn't respond.

"I found her, Phyllis. Her name is Ainsley, and she's a doll. We're arranging a meet and greet right around Valentine's Day. Her mother says she's gifted in sports. Who knew, right?"

SHE DROVE BACK toward the coast and north, passing the ice cream shops and fish places along the two-lane highway, driving through towns so small that if she blinked, she'd miss them completely. Here it was January, and people waded around in their bathing suits and flip-flops, carrying beach chairs, dragging wheeled coolers behind them—stopping traffic—headed for the beach. There were no freeways, very few high-rises, and everyone was from someplace else.

Martel was coming full circle. She'd been drawn here by a friend on vacation. Her friend went back to California, and Martel stayed. She found her little beach bungalow, where she could wake up late at night and see the glistening waves in the moonlight. She loved the power of the orange and purple hues at Sunset—that time of day when the sky seemed to fall and cover everyone in gold.

Walking back inside her rented place, she knew she was going to miss how safe she'd felt here, how her discarded fears and new dreams adorned the walls, like a spell, keeping all the good inside and shedding off the bad.

Her journey had been rocky, but she'd managed to finish on her feet, fate having brought the man she'd always loved back into her life. In June, she'd be moving out of this little place. Someone else would call it home, and she hoped for them it would bring all the magic and happiness she felt while living here.

She and Damon compromised on the wedding. She had people in Florida who would want to attend. He had friends in San Diego who wanted the party. So, they planned a small early June wedding and reception at the gazebo at the beach and the audience would sit facing the ocean. Martel and Damon would take their vows at sunset and watch until the sun dropped into the water.

Then they'd leave for their honeymoon in San Diego, starting with a reception for all of Damon's Team buddies and family in California, on to her new life with her SEAL husband. There was an adventure there, for sure, but she'd miss this place.

Her landlady said she hoped Martel and Damon would return and gave them two free weeks of their choosing as a wedding present. It was their first one.

It was a tradition she wanted to keep, once a year coming back to this place that meant so much to her. A place she ran to when she needed it, the place that healed her and brought her the man she loved and much more.

There was a lot to look forward to between now and June. Top of her list was her Valentine's trip to California where she'd get to meet Ainsley for the first time. She had feelers out at several schools in the San Diego area, and she hoped to interview.

But mostly, she planned on enjoying the peace and calm, living alone, and preparing for the rest of her life. When she closed that door for the last time, she didn't want any regrets. After all, her adventure was only beginning.

And no matter where she was, her heart would always be here, on the white sugary sand and clear blue waters at Sunset Beach.

TREASURE ISLAND SEAL

Sunset SEALs Book 3

SHARON HAMILTON

CHAPTER 1

N AVY SEAL NED Silver fingered the pendant his father had left him. He should have been happy to receive such a gift—this "piece of eight" treasure mounted in a sterling silver setting adorned by a voluptuous mermaid. His dad wore it just about twenty-four seven. He'd whispered to Ned when he was little that the mermaid had been his secret love, number two to Ned's mother, of course. Something about that story pissed him off every time he recalled it.

"He wanted you to have it, Ned," his mother whispered, pressing the piece into his palm and then curling his fingers around it.

"I always pictured him taking it to his grave." He let the curves of the mermaid glisten in the sun, the tail slowly moving back and forth as he fluttered his fingers underneath her. He'd touched it only once over the years, when he'd found it on his dad's dresser. It called to him.

"No, he never wanted that for her," his mother said casually. "It would be like burying her alive all over again. At least, that's what I think your father would say."

She was referring to the fact that the coin pendant had been plucked from the warm waters of the Florida Keys by the "Pirate" Jake Silver himself more than thirty years ago, on a pleasure dive with his best friend. Back when his dad was healthy. A risk-taker. Just after Ned was conceived and during what his mother called a "rough patch".

He caressed the shapely form of the mermaid with his thumb, fondling her with respect. It was a symbol that the torch had been passed. Ned would be his own man now, regardless that he'd become one of America's elite warriors a decade ago, a member of Seal Team 3 out of Coronado.

She belongs in the ocean anyway, never to be buried on land, he heard his father say.

At least some of his dad's tall tales had taken hold. He remembered them more and more as the days passed since his father's hospital confinement and ultimate death. It was funny how that worked, he thought. The long good-bye brought back into focus all the stories and memories they'd shared over his lifetime. Bringing back that which was lost. Memories buried and now unearthed. Strangely, this gift symbolized the last handshake between father and son, a compass to point the way to Ned's future. A portent of what was to come.

His mother used to laugh a lot more before his dad got sick. Old Pirate Jake drank like a fish until the very end, often didn't come home and never called her, either. She loved the bastard and welcomed him back every time. She was the backbone of this family, and her love was strong enough to keep them all together when money was tight and Ned scented fear in the household.

Even from a young age, Ned could smell fear around him. It was a constant friend, even though a pesky one.

Today, after the funeral, his mother looked tired and cried-out, her lips forming a thin straight line as if they'd never shared a smile between them or had ever mated. She was stern but unflappable. Her worry lines were deeper despite the makeup she'd recently started to wear.

His father had taken a long time to die, and he took a piece of her with him to his grave.

"Thanks, Mom," he said as he felt her body melt into him when he hugged her. He vowed to spend more time with her because of the void left with his dad's passing. He sensed her vulnerability and fragility. The hero in him grew taller and his chest sprang out. He knew he couldn't right every wrong or save everyone on the planet, but it didn't stop him from trying.

She wiped her cheeks and plastered a brave grin to her face without changing the vacancy in her eyes.

It scared him when he realized that now more than ever before, it was important that he remain safe and always return home from deployments and dangerous trainings—*for her,* since there wasn't another woman in his life. She wouldn't be able to handle that on top of his father's passing. She loved him with everything she had. He loved the mermaid and the promise of adventure.

Ned slipped the mermaid around his neck like a tiny silver anchor.

"It suits you."

In truth, he'd always thought it was gaudy, that his dad had been showing off. But her face brightened, and that was worth everything. After all, it was just a trinket that lay buried for nearly four hundred years until the Pirate stole her away from Davy Jones himself, claiming her for his own. He could do that. He could watch over both his father's women.

His mother's half-sister, Aunt Flo, the one everyone worried about, approached and hugged them both.

"So good we could all be together, isn't it?"

She realized her words fell flat.

"Well, all except for—" She stopped herself and then redirected, something she'd learned to do in numerous therapy sessions and hospitalizations. "Well, we should all do something like go to a movie!"

That fell even flatter. Ned didn't have words, but his mother did, ever the gracious one in the family, regardless of how she was treated.

"Flo, I know what you meant," his mother said as she extricated herself from the bear-hug. She was covering for his poor aunt, just like she did when she paid for the items Flo had stolen from the dime store and insisted she'd bought with her own money. She had a full drawer of lipsticks she never wore and owned more socks, still in their wrappers, than she owned underwear. She was a compulsive gambler, too, with a terrible memory of what she'd spent. The wheels were beginning to fall off the cart more and more every day.

Ned needed a break. Growing up, he thought she was funny and couldn't understand why his father got so upset being around her. Now he understood. Now he could get away from her.

Ned gave his aunt a peck on the cheek and headed toward a small group of friends from high school who had come to the memorial. They were signing the guest book and placing a picture on the poster.

"Hey, Carson, thanks for coming, man."

Tanned and looking like a professional surfer, his best buddy on the swim and basketball teams in high school showed off his pearly whites. "No problem. I found this nice one here of you and me and your dad. Thought maybe your mom would like having it around."

Ned eyed the small photograph with him and Carson in their Cubs Little League uniforms, his dad playing coach. Coach Silver had insisted on grabbing the number one for himself, which Ned had forgotten, and it made him chuckle.

"What a couple of skinny kids we were then," Ned whispered. After some thought, he added, "What were we, ten?"

"Just about," said Carson, his arm around the shoulder of a pretty girl, also from their school. *Jackie*, he thought. Ned couldn't remember her last name and wasn't sure she was actually in their class or the one below.

"Jackie? That you?"

He'd always had a major crush on her, but Jackie hadn't given him the time of day. Now it was completely different, and the roles were reversed. She'd grown up nice, and it appeared to be her turn to want to make an impression.

"Ned. I'm so sorry," she said timidly.

He accepted her floral-scented embrace and noted Carson's worry line form at the top of his nose, so he kept their hug brief. He scrambled to fill the air with something else.

"So you guys seeing each other now or what?"

"Gawd, Ned, we're married five years now, have one kid and another one we're working on."

Although Carson was casual, Jackie blushed. Ned couldn't help but look at her belly and then cursed himself and glanced away.

"I'm sorry. I've not been around much, and I've lost track of time and all my friends." It was all he could think of, and it was a dumbass excuse at that.

"Oh, shut up. You were off being a hero while the rest of us went to college and started families. I can't believe you aren't married yet, you stud."

Ned had always been uneasy with the reputation he had as a great lover of women when, in fact, he had little experience. Most people would be surprised to learn he couldn't remember his last sexual encounter. He loved women, but he didn't like the drama he saw between the sexes, and he never liked hooking up with damaged goods. He stuck to what he was best at—*saving the day.* If women didn't come running after him, then he wasn't going to run after them, either. Time appeared to have slipped away while he was off being a hero.

He shrugged.

"A Navy SEAL. That's so impressive," Jackie gushed, batting her eyes. "Your dad must have been proud."

That one hurt. Good old Pirate Jake was long in the stories but short in the ways he showed his pride or affection. Growing up, Ned had taken it to mean his dad wanted him to be a man's man. Now, at thirty-one, he figured most men-women relationships caused more scars than bridges or healthy connections. He saw more anchors than golden magical bonds. Maybe he really was in love with mermaids, who floated around in the light blue waters of their own world, skimpily clad and elusive. Beautiful to watch but impossible to love.

So he decided to tell the truth because his dad wasn't there to smack him.

"To be honest, Carson, I think my dad would have preferred I go to college like you and become a tax attorney."

The couple gave him long looks, blinking slowly.

"Just kidding." He glanced down at the picture again and saw the gold and silver mermaid pendant around his dad's neck. Even as the team coach, he was still showing off. His life was bigger than his death, and there wasn't a chance he'd ever be forgotten.

CHAPTER 2

Madison Montgomery eyed the group of silver-haired bikers who had blasted their way into the Salty Dog. Iris picked up her order tray and rounded the bar until Madison grabbed her by the arm.

"Hold it there. These guys might mean trouble. I'm going to take them. Sorry."

Iris pouted. "I can handle them."

Madison towered over the part-time college kid by four inches. From a wealthy Northeastern family, Iris embodied an ingenue having her fling in Florida's gulf coast. Madison dropped the rag she'd been using to wipe the wooden plank bar and brushed her waist-length blonde hair, including one errant curl over her forehead, back behind her then looked down at the young woman in a death stare.

"That's exactly what I'm afraid of. You get the next one, but watch the bar for me."

It didn't matter what Iris was going to say. Madison was three feet away already.

She had a habit of not looking too closely at the rough crowd and never making eye contact until she'd spoken. She didn't care what they were thinking coming in as long as they were on her side by the time she finished her speech.

They were a collection of misfits, covered in tats and torn jeans, revealing oversized hairy legs. One was wearing the bottom half of a green leisure suit with a yellow stripe down the side. That's when she knew they weren't badasses at all but posers. They could wear all the bandanas, leather jackets and earrings they wanted, but she wasn't fooled and knew she could mess with them. They were probably accountants trying to play like the Sons of Anarchy. The one with the black eyepatch spoke to her first.

"Madison, dearie. How's it going, sweetheart?"

She recognized him immediately. He was the owner of the *Barry Bones* dive boat and sometimes treasure scavenger, except his name was Noonan. He was an occasional friend but mostly a past boyfriend of her mother's. Growing up, Madison even wondered if he was her father, until she was introduced to him years later. She knew it needled him that she'd thought that way about him so decided to pour it on a bit more than usual.

"Hey, Dad, you're looking pretty poor." She pointed to his lower thigh, indicating the whiteness she witnessed. "You need a little more beach time and less time on the gulf."

"Ahhh, don't ruin my reputation. If I'd have knocked up someone so fine as your mother, I would have tied her up and kidnapped her until she'd put a ring on it. Never happened. You know that. Not that I didn't try."

The statement was meant for his buddies, not really for Madison's ears.

That got a rousing series of shouts from the table and demands for three pitchers of beer, the cheapest way to go. Older, divorced men like this were, for the most part, penniless, and sharing apartments or sleeping on the beach. It was easier to forget to leave a tip if they ordered this way, always with the chance that someone *else* would pay the bill.

Iris was giving her the cold shoulder—even colder than usual. It was amazing how younger women were brought up these days, especially the ones who had been pampered by parents who were basically buying them off with expensive toys and vacations so they could get away from their own kids. Of course, many of the younger crowd had never had to fully provide for themselves. They didn't depend on being nice, so they weren't. It was a shame.

Madison placed the plastic pitchers under three of the taps, turning them on to load side by side. Iris interrupted one to fill three glasses and then returned the pitcher but left the tap off. She wasn't going to give the younger woman the satisfaction of seeing a ripple in her calm ocean demeanor.

The pitchers were delivered along with five glasses. "I'm going to see if the cook has some extras he can throw in. Be right back," she said and turned before the crew could respond. She headed to scrounge some freebies from the kitchen. Even that wouldn't generate a tip.

The Salty Dog's huge Louisiana Cajun cook was ordering young Latino boys around the kitchen like the place was on fire. It smelled like it, too, and there was more smoke than usual.

"You got anything I can give to some penniless seniors, Washington?"

"Oh, I gots oysters. Up until five minutes ago, they was barbecued perfect. But now they's smoked real good. They still look pretty, though," he said, pointing a large stainless steel spatula at a plated dozen oysters covered in red sauce, sitting under a heat lamp.

"I'm taking them, Mr. Jones."

"You do that missy. You do that," he said to her back. As she slipped through the doorway, she grabbed a bag of dinner rolls.

Madison could tell her ass was being checked out like she had eyes sewn into her rear jeans pockets. It came with the territory. If she'd wanted a "safe" job, she could have worked in a Real Estate office. But then, she'd have to contend with the possibility she'd die of boredom or fall asleep driving on the way home from the office. This worked fine and paid well, and her boss never came. It was just a temporary duty until the next underwater film or salvage dive job.

"Here you go, boys. Bread's on its way," she said as she downloaded the oysters onto her group's table without sliding them into their laps. The scramble to grab an oyster or two was messy and a little ugly. She added the rolls to a red plastic basket and dropped it off too. "That's to mop up the butter."

As the evening wore on the crowd got younger until all the "normal" people—the ones with jobs or ones who cared about their jobs—went home. In between was a smattering of older retirees. If they had money, they were in pairs. If not, they were men drinking by themselves, fantasizing on being able to bag a younger woman who might be drunk enough and wouldn't look too closely at his teeth, the grey he was covering up, or the gut he'd lovingly grown over the years.

She rarely saw a real silver fox, but those were the kind of experienced men who could satisfy her and turn her bones to butter. Men her own age were practically in diapers. She preferred the imperfect older men with tats, stories of ups and downs without regrets, and sexual experience. She liked making them feel loved. She was good at that.

Noonan himself had tried to fix her up with some of his friends, but she turned them all down before a coffee date. She was picky. She wanted a date to know exactly what to do and to be a real man, not some pretend postage stamp on a love letter. Settling down would be as difficult as bottling the ocean. It was unnatural, and except for various economic reasons, there was little reason to go there.

Being free was where it was at. At just under thirty, Madison didn't care about aging. She cared about losing her freedom.

She checked the time and discovered it was nearly midnight. Her mother would be stopping by to make her nightly visit.

Noonan LaFontaine's eye was bloodshot as he approached the bar, barely able to walk without tilting. His buddies had been long gone.

"Hold on there, Skipper. Tell your brain you're on land," she said to him and laughed at his delayed expression. Leaning into the countertop, she added, "Hope you'll let me call you a cab."

He nodded, but before she got out her cell, he grabbed her wrist. "I was lookin' for your mama, little one."

"Haven't seen her. Should be any time now."

Noonan craned his neck, checking out the outdoor restaurant, then scanned up and down the u-shaped bar and the clusters of tables along the walls. He shrugged. "The heart's willing but the body, it just won't cooperate."

She was touched Noonan wanted to see her mother. She'd been turning him down for the last twenty years, as Madison could recall. But their chemistry was something special and her mother looked younger and happier whenever the old salty captain was around.

Every woman wants to be some man's fantasy.

"I can give her a message, if you like," Madison said, placing her cell to her ear.

He waited until the cab was ordered before he answered her. "Tell her someone special has passed into the locker. I think she'll know who that is."

"Cryptic!" she said, wrinkling her brow.

"Secret!" His eyes got wide and he was a man of thirty again. Madison had asked about their relationship so many times just the mere mention of his name gave her the stop motion with the palm of her mother's hand before she could utter another syllable.

"Noonan, I'm sorry that I bug you about being my dad."

"It's okay. I guess I'm a little flattered. I still dream about what it would be like if she could ever get that heartache out of her system."

"My dad?"

"Not him. She never loved him. It was someone else."

Madison frowned, even though she knew it was true. Her mother had been fairly honest about the things she did tell her. It was all the things she didn't tell her that gave her worry.

"So this—"

Noonan cut her off by putting his forefinger to his mouth and whispering, "Shh."

She saw the soft underside of a very lonely man.

"You got any gigs I can join? Anything at all coming up?"

"We got a little contract to do a salvage, but they're looking for something specific, not looking to raze the ship. When I'm sober, I'll tell you about it. Maybe I could hire you for two, three days. We aren't quite sure the coordinates yet. Depending on the water depth, I might say no."

"How about an underwater porn film about a mermaid and a handsome seaman?"

"You okay with exposing yourself to millions of eyes?"

"Mermaids don't have anything down below that isn't naturally covered up, you know. And as for showing my tits, well, I practically do that every day wearing these tee-shirts." She held back the shoulders of her white Salty Dog shirt and showed how it stretched.

"Always a ham. You just like the attention, Madison. Always did. You're just like your mama. Just as pretty too. She broke men's hearts everywhere she went. Everywhere…"—he started, spreading his arms out wide to the sides—"everywhere she went, there was always lots of blood and bleeding. Near suicides. Your mother was an addiction, someone impossible to get out of anyone's system." He leaned closer to her. "Don't you do that with your life. Bestow your womanly wiles on some nice young man and make him the king of your kingdom and you'll live that fantasy your mother never found."

Madison straightened up. She was almost going to cry and that never happened.

Noonan put his finger to his lips. "Don't you tell her. Just tell her someone special is passed on and I wanted her to know about it."

Noonan made his way outside, got in the cab, and left safely. Madison spent the rest of the evening looking for her mother as every new face came through the entrance.

But her mother never showed.

CHAPTER 3

NED OFFERED TO help his mother sort and pack some of his father's things. Since he was their only child, his parents stayed near the base in a small house at Imperial Beach, California. The house was barely a thousand square feet, with just room enough for his mother's roses and the brightly-colored flowers she liked to grow year-round.

This year had taken a toll on her garden. She'd spent so much time at the Pirate's side in the hospital. The numerous close calls had gotten more frequent over the past two months before his passing, when she'd dropped everything and rushed to try to be there in time to send him off with a kiss.

Margaret Silver always said she had the greatest marriage in the whole world, although that same world knew it to be a complete fantasy.

"You know, Ned," she said as she began boxing books to take to the library sale, "in all the years we've been married, we never had a cross word. Not one."

Ned wasn't quite sure he'd heard her correctly. She had taken on some of Flo's air and penchant for coloring the truth to suit the moment. It was her way of spreading her brand of harmony over everything, just like those delicious peanut butter and jelly sandwiches she used to put in his Captain America lunch pail.

"You just never disagreed with him, Mom. You went along with anything he said."

"I was born to be married to Jake Silver. My job was to keep him operating within the lines he never wanted to look at," she said, fondly smiling at something out towards the distant ocean.

Ned had grown up riding the school bus that drove right past the obstacle course on Coronado, watching the men climb up those ropes like monkeys and wondering what it would feel like to ride in a little rubber raft while working with eight other souls to make sure it didn't capsize. He'd never considered doing anything else but join the Navy, like his dad.

But unlike his dad, Ned had become a SEAL. Old Jake had tried out twice and quit both times. When Ned got his Trident, his father didn't come to the ceremony and stayed drunk for a week.

Served the old bastard right.

He hadn't wanted to be there when his dad passed, so when he came back from his last deployment, he was disappointed his stubborn dad was still alive. Checking his conscience, he didn't feel bad about one bit of it, either.

But his mother told him later Jake Silver had wanted to be sure he got home safe. He passed away the next day. That one did get to him. He had still been sore from the twenty hour transport plane ride and had planned to sleep for a week. Instead, he'd had to get out a suit he never wore, that still fit him after ten years. Duty and honor. That was it.

He had never brought friends over to the house for fear they'd find his dad in some undressed drunken state. Ned kept the secret, just like his mother did. Coach Silver was the most popular parent-coach on the Little League schedule. All the dads loved him, since short travel games were sources of some of the great parties the parents had, made better by the fact that his dad didn't have to pay for any of it. He was the coach. Number One.

The boys his own age idolized the former Navy man who had

stories about slashing through jungles in Southeast Asia. Forbidden to read dirty magazines, the boys especially appreciated the tattoos of naked buxom ladies up and down his "Popeye" arms. His dad gave names for all of them and hinted he'd slept with each one. He was built like a bulldog and just staring down someone could stop a fight before it began.

Maybe it made him stronger. Ned didn't resent him. He just didn't want to be that kind of an imposition on anyone else. He loved working with his Team. And, as with many of the other guys he came to consider brothers on SEAL Team 3, being a SEAL was way more fulfilling than anything else he'd ever done. It gave him an outlet for his anger, being in such intense physical shape all the time, preparing for battle. Knowing he was responsible for each man on his right and his left, and that he would die to protect them gave him purpose. A strong, cohesive, unbreakable unit—he was part of something greater than he ever could be alone. They were a force for good. He could right some of the wrongs in the world and get paid and trained to do it too.

It was the perfect life. The bigger he got, the more muscle mass he put on, the faster and stronger he got, the less he resembled his father in anything they could be compared to. He was the exact opposite, determined to contribute more than his dad had ever done. It wasn't that he hated the man, he just left a big fucking hole. Old Jake left his mom damaged, but it was what she chose, and he'd agree with that, too. Yet that flaw was so great he couldn't even feel proud of his son.

So Ned's way of seeking his dad's approval was the opposite of his mother's. The more his dad didn't pay attention, the bigger and stronger he wanted to be.

Margaret Silver brushed the hair from her forehead and placed her hands at her hips. "Whew! That was a job. We did that in less than a quarter of the time I'd calculated."

"It helped that they were just old books neither of us wanted. Nothing to sort or ponder over, Mom."

"I don't even know why he had so many. I mean, this house is so tiny, and I never saw him read one of them. Did you?"

"I think he was going for the osmosis type of learning. Having them around him made him feel smarter. Maybe he learned without reading."

If ever a man could do that, his dad would be able to.

"I guess. It was always something I wanted to ask him, and I just forgot. Why he would want to hang on to books he never read will always be a mystery, then."

Ned stacked the last box near the front door. "Mom, should I load these up in the truck? I can drop them off at the library downtown tomorrow, if you like."

"Thank you, Ned." Then she noticed another small stack of books on the coffee table she'd set aside. "You know I thought perhaps you'd like these. The one on the top is a book of poetry about the sea. Maybe you should have it."

She held it out to him. He didn't want to take it but also couldn't turn it away.

"Okay, just this one. But all the rest of these are going to the library, no offense. I have less room in my condo than you do here."

"Fair enough." She smiled as he shoved the book into his back pocket. "I hope the library can take them. Lord knows I don't know what to do if they don't," she said as she opened the front door.

"They sell them, Mom. They make money for the library. So either way, it helps."

"That would be nice. See if you can get a slip of paper with the book count for our—my taxes this year."

"Will do," he said as he lifted the first box and headed toward his four-door pickup.

After they finished loading, he gently proposed they get started on his father's clothes. She hadn't touched a thing in their bedroom since the day he went to the hospital. His pills and water glass, still with water in it, sat beside the vanity sink in the bathroom. His slippers were tucked under the bed on his father's side. The bed on the other side was obviously slept in. His father's side had a fresh, ironed and unused pillowcase with eyelet trim, matching his mother's wrinkled one.

When Ned walked into the closet, he could smell the alcohol and the beer and cigars his dad liked to consume. Margaret sat on her side of the bed and watched him.

"Mom, where's your stuff?" Everything hanging up belonged to his father. His shirts were neatly pressed and starched, his pants hung on individual hangers, and even his bathrobe was hung with its cuffs tucked into the pockets as if it could walk on command.

"Over there," she said, pointing to the dresser.

Ned turned, his arm full of shirts, and examined the tall boy dresser with deep drawers. He had never realized all his mother's clothes were neatly folded inside, never hung up.

"Don't you have a coat? Any dresses?"

"They're in your bedroom closet, honey. I didn't like them smelling of cigars. It makes me sneeze."

Ned was struck by the fact that she still called it his bedroom. He'd visited them so infrequently over the past several years. Most of their get-togethers were done at a local restaurant, where his father's behavior was muted and under control.

He placed the stack of shirts on the bed behind her, while her fingers lovingly touched the buttons on the long-sleeved cuffs. "I'll drop these off at the Salvation Army too. I don't want to bag them, cause then they'll get wrinkled. But you kept these all ironed and starched, didn't you?"

"I love to iron. It soothes my mind."

That sounded just like Aunt Flo, and that scared him. He retreated to the closet again, removing another stack of shirts and some slacks. He brought a large packing box and placed each pair of shoes carefully inside as she watched.

He knew she wouldn't have been able to do it on her own. Just before he was to carry out the box of shoes, he stooped to pick up his father's blue and green plaid slippers.

"Don't! Don't take those. I can wear those," his mother said.

"But Mom, they'll be too big for you. You'll trip. Why don't you let me get you a nice pair of women's slippers?"

"Ned, I want these," she said, her backbone showing. "I like the feel of them on my feet. And I'll be careful."

Ned tucked the slippers under the bed but on her side this time.

THEY SAT IN the tiny kitchen eating peanut butter and jelly sandwiches and canned soup. Ned had a beer, and his mother had a cup of tea. He'd never realized how small the house was. Growing up, it was just the place to sit, and do homework at night, or sleep. Ned's whole world was outside the doors and windows of the tiny home. His focus was never inside.

He'd also forgotten how quiet it was. The neighborhood had stayed modest, unlike other neighborhoods in the San Diego area. There were a lot of original couples, like his parents, who had bought when the subdivision was new and raised their families there. Kids could play out in the street until past dark or ride their bikes to the beach to watch the sunset. Anywhere important, he could go on a bike. Now, sitting in the sparse kitchen with his mother, he enjoyed the satisfying calm. That pit in the bottom of his stomach wasn't there. He didn't smell fear, because the generator of all those things was absent.

All that was left was the quiet.

As he drove away near sunset, he recalled the discussion he had with his mother. He stopped to watch the sun melt into the horizon, reached up, and held the mermaid pendant between his thumb and first two fingers.

He had thought the little place would be perfect for her now and offered to have some of the minor repairs done to make it easier. She could read, garden, or do whatever she wanted to now that she no longer needed to tend to his dad.

Her answer was odd. "But whatever will I do with myself?"

Ned had never wondered about that. She'd lost her job. Indefinitely furloughed and not needed. Even though old Jake was gone, she wasn't ready to stop being a wife and caretaker. Of course she would need some time to get back on her feet. She'd never considered another life.

"You have money, Mom. You could travel. Go on a cruise. Maybe you and Flo could take a train ride up north and see Canada."

"By ourselves? The two of us?"

"You could hire someone to go with you. Maybe one of the helpers at Flo's clinic would be available, like a companion nurse. Would that make it easier?"

"I don't think Flo would like going to strange places. She'd be confused all the time. I think it would be hard on her."

"You could room together. She could take the second bedroom here."

"Oh, no. I think we've got to face facts. Flo is going to need some full-time nursing. I'm going to look for a memory care center for her. I think in another few months she's going to stop remembering who I am. She has no friends, or at least none that she remembers. Your dad left me a little life insurance. If that's not enough I could sell the house."

"And then where would you live? Don't you want to stay here?"

She'd thought about it for several seconds before she answered.

"What if I went on an adventure, Ned?"

And like a turtle peeking out from under its shell for the first time, Margaret Silver wanted to see the real world. She wanted an adventure. He tried to hold back the hope that was springing from his chest, making him feel warm and glad to be among the living.

He walked across the sand to his truck after all remnants of the sun were gone. Driving the few miles to his condo complex, he knew the world had changed. The passing of his father had altered both his and his mother's trajectories.

Like falling from an airplane, he suddenly felt untethered, unrestricted, swimming through the blue sky toward an uncertain but somehow exciting future.

He grabbed the book of poetry but left everything else inside his truck and went inside his tiny box of a home, alone, but oddly happy.

CHAPTER 4

MADISON RANG HER mother first thing in the morning and got no answer. She called the next-door neighbor, Mrs. Potter, whose cheerful voice annoyed her.

"Oh dear. I did see her yesterday morning. She was putting bird food out in the feeder. We have a terrible problem with the black crows and squirrels this year and they're scattering the seed everywhere, making a mess."

Madison cut her off or she'd get a description of the grime collecting on the insides of Mrs. Potter's washing machine.

"When was that?"

"I think it was about eleven. Maybe earlier. I didn't see her the rest of the day. She went for a walk afterwards, but came back an hour later."

"She was dressed, then, not looking ill?"

"Oh just like she always is. Wearing that bright-colored kimono over her black stretchies and that big red clip doing a piss-poor job of holding all that hair up. She had lipstick on, too, as I recall." Mrs. Potter began prattling on.

That relieved Madison a great deal. "I'll stop by to check on her later before I go to work. Thanks for the information."

"Should I stop by for a peek?"

"No, please don't."

Her mother had complained numerous times about her nosey

neighbor, which is why Mrs. Potter was the first person Madison thought to call. If her mother was about, and dressed, then it ruled out so many awful things.

She took her coffee outside, checking the beach, which was beginning to warm up. The sunrise was long gone. Birds were slowly being replaced with beachcombers and scavengers looking for pieces of sea glass and colorful pieces of shells.

Barefoot and still wearing her favorite pair of stretchy pajamas, she walked in a straight line to the gentle surf. The water was calm, looking crystalline and transparent. September and October were her favorite months here on the gulf. The crowds were small, and the winds were mild between possible storm developments. But the long, sunny, languid days were just the elixir she needed to stay sane and whole. The calm before the storms of life. She wondered if the storms she seemed to run into were just her way of fully embracing and enjoying the life-restoring calm of the ocean.

The beach heals everything, was still her favorite slogan, hanging in various forms in every room in her house, even the bedroom. Her mother had painted a huge one that still hung in her living room.

Madison sat, giving the cool surf a wide berth. She wasn't ready to get wet just yet. She watched an older couple walk hand-in-hand along the shore and mosey back to their address. It made her wonder about her mother and the mysterious someone special Noonan had mentioned last night. She knew studying her mother's face would tell her part of the story that would probably never be fully revealed.

Mother, what is this private world you live in and why do you leave me out?

She loved her as surely as she was sitting on the beach this morning. But she was a daughter to this magnificent woman, and that meant that her mother's embrace would only reach so far. And her mother's world of love would remain private no matter how much she tried to pry a little crack to sneak inside her womanly shell. She lived and taught Madison not with words, but by example. Unlike most women, her mother wore her flaws on the outside and saved her insides for the very best part of her.

Did you share yourself with this someone special?

Madison was convinced she did.

Noonan had said there might be salvage work coming up. That brought a smile to her face and a scurrying in her belly—that quest for the storm and excitement of an adventure. Diving around shipwrecks was always risky and never predictable. But the secrets they told of humanity long gone were fascinating. She loved delving into the mystery of loss and separation. It wasn't a morbid head-space. It celebrated the shadows of a life lived and now gone. Uncovering those secrets was like figuring out what had happened to her mother in the space of years that floated by before Madison was born.

Madison had had her little flings, mostly with older married men because it was safe. She could send them home to their wives transformed. She liked to think they were happier men and even their wives would benefit from the spark she brought to their lives.

Afterward, although she knew it wasn't common at all, her spirit was calm with the separation as she retreated to the land of her own making, alone and satisfied to be there. All the cliches aside, she was happy to be her own best friend, her own cheerleader, like all the books and gurus talked about. As long as she was free to swim in whatever blue ocean that lay before her. She knew she always would live by the sea, finding things discarded by the petulant being with an unpredictable energy. As long as she didn't fight, the ocean gave her everything she needed.

She twisted her bright blonde locks into a bun and walked through the cool ankle-depth waters, the waves washing away her footprints as if she'd never been there at all. She remembered the

James Bond actor she met on the set of his new movie two years ago. Ruggedly handsome and tall, he was even better looking than how he appeared on the screen and Madison had seen every one of his movies. She was hired to be the body double for the villainess in the movie, the dark mermaid who would first make love to him and then try to kill him on an underwater dive. An evil, black siren.

Madison had to wear a cap glued with bits of dark black hair to hide her sundrenched locks that glistened like gold, even when wet. He was a good enough swimmer to do the takes with her. Back and forth they frolicked in one embrace after another, constrained by equipment and wetsuits, until the scene called for the two of them to emerge from the surf to strip and make love on the beach at sunset. It wasn't hard to feel what it would be like to wake up with him in her bed. And for several mornings they did just that. Nicer still that it was private—no black wig that might get dislodged, no one giving direction. Just the sound of their lovemaking and the background of the breathing ocean.

Her heartbeat raced as she remembered the incredible feeling of being the object of his desire, even though she knew it would only be for a week, maybe two. He made promises but she never did, knowing full well he'd never keep them. He promised to write, promised to stay in touch, promised to never forget her. That part she did believe. But as to the writing and keeping in touch, unless he was feeling her quickening libido, well, their magic would not stretch between Florida and Hollywood. Like a tender child growing up without the love of a parent, the magic would fade away into a beautiful memory like the clouds in the sky at sunset on Treasure Island.

She never looked him up on social media either. It didn't matter if she missed his encrypted message left so that only she would understand it. If she didn't look, she would never know. And she'd never be disappointed.

But a new film would be fun. Her heart could take one more big, epic romance before—what? She was speaking like a crazy woman. She was not thirty yet. Maybe for her birthday Poseidon himself would come to rescue her and take her below, shower her with jewels and gold, and keep her all for himself. Everyone would wonder. But she might like feeling she belonged to him, even if the world didn't know.

A true, private love would be something she could live for.

MADISON LIKED THE little artist community by the beach where her mother lived, mostly made up of old hippies and even beatniks from the Upper East Side in New York. Some of them were poets and had made and lost fortunes on their art, had it stolen or had managers abscond with all their loot. Living at the beach community of Treasure Island was a leveling out process where it didn't matter whether they were rich or poor. They had to have that inner spark, like her mother did. They had to have talent of some kind, some creative talent, or they were really good at making martinis or cooking a wild seafood pasta.

Madison had grown up with these people and had ridden on the shoulders of some who had graced the covers of Playbill, Vanity Fair, and Cosmo. They laughed reading the articles speculating where they'd disappeared to. Nobody came there looking for the rich and famous. Some were. Some weren't. And no one in the group cared.

Her mother had been in love with one or more of them, sometimes at the same time, which made for a confusing childhood. There were songs written about her. She'd taken in her share of broken, tarnished stars, polished them up, and sent them back out to shine again, hopefully living an inspired life.

Her dad would drift in every other year or so. He and her mom would do the tango, baiting each other to be the first one to fall in love again. Always one of them would, dragging the other one back into memories too sweet to ever forget. Then it would be all bedroom time and shouts and screams throughout the night followed by fights within three days and another separation. Then quiet.

"Ah, he's like the ocean. He comes in bearing gifts. Refreshed and ready to try the impossible again. He deposits his shells, takes a piece of me back with him, and disappears back out into the ocean to chase something else. It's his life, not the life I want. But he's hard to resist."

Madison had asked her if she loved him and why he didn't love her growing up.

"I'm his little girl, mama. Doesn't he care?"

"He's not capable. He wants to, but he can't get away from himself. But he made you and for that I'm eternally grateful."

Another time, she'd put it this way, "I love you, Madison. That's all you need to know. You don't want a man who doesn't know where he stands or isn't sure which wave he'll ride. You take the lighthouses in life. Sometimes they're boring as hell, but they'll always be there."

Except her mother never followed her own advice. Being hard to resist was always the most prominent feature of her love affairs, and often, the quality of her new love was held in highest regard. It was like the pull of the moon on the ocean. Only releasing to grab hold again. Dangerous and unpredictable. But yes, oh so irresistible.

Her mother would brush her long hair every night before bed. Just the two of them with the sight of the moon twinkling on the water beyond. The sound of her mother's brush and the warm feel of the boar bristles on her scalp were just as soothing as listening to the surf lapping on the sand all night long.

As she started puberty, she worried perhaps she had too much of a fixation for her mother, even going so far as to wonder if she perhaps loved her too much or was falling in love with women and not boys. But what Madison came back to time and time again was that one quality in her mother she found so special in a man.

Her mother was irresistible.

At her mother's cottage door, she knocked. Wind chimes started up as if recognizing the daughter coming home one more time. The alleyway leading down between modest and brightly colored shacks was covered in white rock and crushed shells. It was early for the beach, and only a stray dog wandered along the path.

Her mom had painted her house a deep rose color, trimmed in vanilla. A large vine with bright purple-pink flowers was holding up the overhang above the front door. Madison noticed that someone had tried to paint in between the crisscrossing vines that wrap themselves around the wood bracing like Sleeping Beauty's castle, but had given up. She wondered how long that had been there, but it was the first time she'd noticed it.

Madison knocked again.

She heard music, which grew louder as her mother graced the doorway with a bright, warm smile. "What a nice surprise!"

That's what she always said. But she knew her mother meant it every time. It would take her several minutes before she could untangle herself from her mother's arms. Her big grey hair was tied up with a bandana ending in a floppy bow at the upper right side of her forehead.

"I'm painting again, Madison. Come! Let me show you."

The one thing Madison had loved about this house was the great room off the kitchen that faced the ocean. They'd had large dinners where they'd moved all the furniture out and brought in folding chairs and served over thirty on occasion. But everything about the back of the house was focused on the ocean, facing west.

In past years, Madison's old room had also been the craft room. Often, she'd wake up and work on sewing or painting projects, sometimes working until dawn. After Madison moved out, her mother returned it to the library it had been before she was born. With two high-backed chairs facing each other, the room was so filled with books that it totally insulated the sounds of anything else, even the traffic outside and calls from the ocean. Many nights she'd stop by late for a visit and find her mom curled up in one of those chairs asleep with a book in her lap and a fuzzy afghan around her shoulders.

But now the living room was packed with brightly colored canvases depicting beach scenes peppered with colorful shacks and crushed shell trails. She was working on several at once, just like the history of her love life.

"You're going big, Mom. How long have you been doing these?"

"I just started yesterday morning. I stayed up all night long painting. Remember when we used to have those marathons, honey? I've got my mojo back!"

Madison didn't cheer because she wasn't sure where this was all going.

"What brought all this on?"

"I smell Fall in the air. I was feeling just a bit down, frumpy. Very low energy. It was like all the fun had been taken out of life. I got fed up and decided to do something I hadn't done. So, I walked the neighborhood until I found inspiration. I went to the art store and bought all the large canvases they carried. Bought some new brushes and acrylic paints I'd never tried before. I was seeing flowers, pretty houses all in a row. This place I love." She smirked at her daughter. "You don't believe me, do you?"

"No, it sounds exactly like you, Mom."

"This house holds the soul of my life. I've forgotten to celebrate it lately. That's what I'm doing now."

Madison was heartened with the news. Her mother wasn't old, barely sixty, and was very attractive still, though her attractiveness was—yes, there it was again—in her irresistibility! She did have some of the sparkle back. As she thought about it, Madison had noticed some kind of glum smoke bomb hanging over her head lately.

"I'm glad. I worried. You didn't answer your phone this morning."

"I turned it off so I didn't ruin the inspiration."

"Yes, well, your usual appearance last night at the Dog was missing. You were missed. Noonan missed you too."

"Noonan? Gosh, I haven't talked to him in months. What's he up to?"

"He says he might have work for me. A special dive. I wish it was a film."

"Oh that was a once in a lifetime event, Maddie. Those are like glass ornaments on your Christmas Tree of life." She picked up a brush and pointed to her. "Something to be celebrated!"

Then Madison remembered Noonan's words.

"He had a message for you."

"Who? Noonan? I hope he's not considering trying to court again. This shop is closed while I explore my new full throttle mojo experience!"

Madison stepped closer to her mother and whispered, "He says someone special has passed. He said you'd know what that meant."

CHAPTER 5

NED GATHERED WITH several other members of their team at the Rusty Scupper, their local Team hangout. Kyle, his LPO, was present, along with Cooper and T.J., but all the other guys were single or divorced, so it was mostly an unofficial pre-bachelor party. One of the newbies had gotten engaged. The divorced SEALs gave him advice, since this was his first rodeo.

One of the first things any newbie did when they came to the Scupper was check out the Wall of the Fallen, originally over the bar but now nearly covering the back wall—a private "meeting" room with pictures of campaigns and team flags and mementos. Ned always swung through there if it had been awhile, just to check out if something new had been added. Sometimes the pictures were hard to find, like the time he discovered the photograph of a warlord they'd captured that the military had tried and executed. His disheveled face, with his hands tied in front of him in a dirty, wrinkled shirt and his hair all askew looked completely different than the military man they'd seen on TV with his chest covered in medals he earned while slaughtering, not protecting his people.

The room was a shrine to who they were and what they stood for. To the average person, it might seem like some kind of sick reverence, but for every one of these bad guys they'd captured or killed—which wasn't the goal like it had been years ago—thousands of American and Allied soldiers would be safer, as well as scores more of their own citizens. It was for the little people they fought. Not for the big wigs. Not even the big wigs in the military. After all, they were a force for good. There were bad guys lurking in the halls everywhere.

He took a seat at the table, which was already knee-deep in advice to the new groom-to-be.

"Make sure she shows up at the bonfires, man. She needs to make friends amongst the wives, not outside, or you'll have trouble," someone said.

Kurt, the newbie medic-in-training, looked no more than eighteen years old. His eyes were big, and his ears stuck out as if shaving had made them more prominent. Ned could tell he was nervous as hell about the wedding but even more apprehensive of the bachelor party these guys were going to throw.

It was legend, but rarely occurred, that sometimes grooms were sent away the night before the wedding, drunk, with a one-way ticket to someplace in Alaska or Greenland. But just the fact that it had occurred once or twice, causing brides and her parents to have a reception without the groom, later to be followed up with a civil ceremony, made many of the young, newly-engaged SEALs worry. And the stories were embellished and expanded to such a degree that no one could remember exactly who these fiascos had befallen. They became things of urban legend, a weapon the older guys used to mess with the heads of the tadpoles.

Coop decided to intervene. "Nah, kid, don't listen to those guys. As a matter of fact, don't listen to anybody who's divorced or not happily married after a divorce. You'll ruin your career and your love life if you spend too much time hanging with them." He pointed to the other end of the table with his mineral water and lime.

That caused a ruckus as the hardcore group objected.

Ned sat still, not having much of an opinion, which Kyle noticed.

"I'm sorry about your dad, Ned. Christy called you?"

"Yes, she did. Thanks, Kyle."

"I was real sorry. I try to get to all my guys things like that, but the briefing in D.C. took longer. I'd have rather been at your side."

"No problem. I totally understand. I was there mostly for my mom anyway. My dad and I weren't that close."

Kyle nodded, tracing the bubbles scurrying up the side of his beer glass. "A common reflection, Ned."

The two of them listened to more of the banter before Kyle added, "You did good over there this time, Ned. You're turning into a lifer."

Ned shrugged. "Never thought I'd spend so much time in Africa. When I signed on, it was all Middle East stuff. Now, things have changed."

"The world is changing. We're changing our focus as a country too. Personally, I think we'll see more things in the Caribbean and South America coming up. I think the training missions are a complete waste of time, teaching the bad guys how to kill us best."

"I don't miss those. Although, sometimes they were fun. I guess some people were just not meant to carry telephone poles and wade around in little boats." He was referencing a group of young recruits from Greece who had gotten shipped into a BUD/S class and refused to do any of the hard labor, especially the twelve-man teams carrying telephone poles down the beach. They didn't earn a Trident, just a certificate, but none of the men thought they even deserved that.

"Wish I had some videos to show the head shed," Kyle mumbled. Then he asked, "You plan on taking any time to do something special?"

"Nothing planned as yet. I'm helping my mom get her place cleaned up. You know, get all my dad's stuff out. It's hard for her."

"I'll bet. How long were they married?"

"I think they were pregnant when they did, so I guess thirty-one or thirty-two years. At least thirty."

"Well, your mom will get on her feet. You'll see. If they were happily married, she'll get married again. Just you wait."

Ned chuckled.

"What's so funny?"

"It's a matter of perspective. Honestly, Kyle, my dad was an ass-hole. My mom loved him anyway. Through her perspective, they had the greatest love story in the world."

"Yeah. I sure hope Christy doesn't have to fantasize like that with me." Kyle took another drink. "How about you, Ned? I never see you bring anyone to our gatherings."

He shrugged again. He was doing a lot of that lately. "I'm think-ing I'll be more like Tierney. Heck, he was older than me when he got married. Worked out okay for him. I think I might have to retire before I settle down. It would be complicated trying to have a family and do what we do. But that's just me."

Kyle nodded again and then slapped him on the back. "Well, then you stay single, hear? We need men like you. And while you're at it, keep an eye on Kurt here and make sure he doesn't wind up on a detour flight with a couple of hookers. He doesn't deserve that."

Ned chuckled again. "No one deserves that."

ALTHOUGH HE'D PROMISED otherwise, right after Kyle and Cooper left, he abandoned the bachelor group and headed for his condo. He was tired. But he knew it wasn't from any physical workout or regimen. It was from a whole lot of emotional energy he'd expended taking care of his mom. She was going to need some assistance before he would stop worrying about her.

Tomorrow, she was going to visit a new memory center that had been built just north of San Diego where patients participated in advanced clinical trials, the stay partially being underwritten by a couple of large drug companies looking for cures for dementia and Alzheimer's. He was proud she was taking such a measured approach, and although she'd invited him to come along, he knew he would be more needed when it was time to actually take Aunt Flo there. He promised her that. This was something she had to do on her own, he said, and she agreed.

All the boxes had been dropped off today at the thrift store and library. He washed his truck, went for a short workout before heading to the Scupper, and then decided to retire early.

His condo was very sparsely furnished. He just couldn't decide what to buy and the down payment on the place had eaten up all his enlistment bonus, which left him with just a thin margin of savings. Like his old place living at home, his focus was never inside his small space, but outside. The reason he'd bought the condo was because it had a view of the water. A tiny sliver, but a view anyhow. He'd paid a twenty thousand dollar premium for that view. And he loved the bright orange and pink sunsets.

He grabbed the book he'd brought from his mom's house, slunk back into his couch, and propped his feet up on the coffee table.

The small paperback was dog-eared. It looked like some do-it-yourself publication without a lot of fancy embellishments or anything on the back cover but another picture of a long, white sand beach.

'Gifts From The Sea'

He read farther, 'A compilation of short stories and poetry from the Gulf Coast.'

Ned knew his dad had a friend who lived there still. He was the buddy who had partnered with him that day when his dad found the pendant. Ned had been to several trainings on the east coast of Florida, probably near the old Spanish Galleon wreck they'd explored. He remembered seeing a map of the coastline littered with wrecks, some of them with undiscovered treasure. His dad told him he loved it there. Ned wondered why the family hadn't moved to Florida, since it would have been so much less expensive.

But for some reason, Pirate Jake stayed away and let himself go.

Inside the back cover flap was a picture of a group of young people standing in a cluster with parrot drinks in their hands, toasting the camera. On the photo credit, Ned saw his father's name.

'Photo courtesy of Pirate Jake Silver.'

Suddenly, Ned was interested. He flipped through the pages, letting his fingers smooth over the paper, scanning the short stories and poems written by different people with names he didn't recognize. He came to a page that had been folded over.

'Amberly'

It was written by a man named Darrell and was a glowing, gushing description of a woman named Amberly who had captured his heart. He described her swimming through the water and lying in the sand. Without being overtly sexual, it was a passionate piece and hinted of deep intimate knowledge. He likened her to a beautiful mermaid he could never capture.

Ned knew his dad liked this piece. He wondered if this was his dad's mermaid as well, the secret love he'd whispered about so long ago, embodied and captured in the silver pendant that was the only thing his dad had given him unselfishly.

He glanced at other poems and saw one written by Amberly Drake.

I am following so close I fear you'll see me,

And the secret love I hold will be revealed,

Before I can even bring the words to my lips.

Is it true that you can fall in love,

The first time you look into someone else's eyes,

And feel their soul meld with yours?

As one who is used to seeing the door close behind those I've loved,

This time it will hurt.

Forever.

CHAPTER 6

MADISON HADN'T WANTED to leave her mother, but she was due to be at work, and they'd had several no-shows lately with the wait staff.

Her mother's face had gone from a look of pure delight to that split-second expression of horror, followed by her quick adjustment as she donned her mask and covered up all feeling, which wasn't her usual style. Madison knew it was self-preservation. No amount of inquiry would bring out what her mother wouldn't tell her. It was hard to do, but she had to be good with it. Her mother promised she might stop by later on and asked if she could tell Noonan to look for her.

It was past the lunch crowd, a lull before the early diners, usually older patrons, came for the seafood specials. Washington Jones was meting out his private brand of fear on the younger Latino kitchen help, working his way through the usual turnover statistics. With the clanging of pots and pans and shouts, it was murder and mayhem in that hot little kitchen—barely big enough for Jones' girth, let alone other man-boys trying to avoid crashing into him with their platters of food prep.

The sounds were oddly calming. Normal life.

She stocked the bar, and wiped down the countertop and all the stools again, even though it had been done by the previous crew. She cleaned all the tables and cleared someone's salad lunch that had been forgotten. All of this felt like gardening, painting, or walking along the beach, these simple routines that gave her time to think. Funny how cleaning up someone else's mess was soothing to her, but it was.

There was a new musician playing tonight, and he came in early to make sure everything was set up properly so he could start at five. He'd come highly recommended by a friend when they watched him perform at another crabby joint along the peninsula.

He was tall and extremely handsome, slightly older with grey hair at his temples. His quiet demeanor and wonderful manly scent didn't overpower her. It did make her long for the arms of someone who could cherish her, even if it was for one night.

His sly smile and dimpled chin were disarming, not that she was putting up any resistance.

Garrison Cramer was a born horse trainer, if there ever was one. Her heart raced, and she tried not to let their eye contact linger or he'd get the message she wasn't ready to deliver.

"You get a big crowd on Fridays?" he asked as he set his guitar against the stand.

Madison had been re-wiping the tables out on the patio near his "stage" right in front of the dartboard and several other children's games.

"Yes, it's one of our busiest. But this time of year, the snowbirds haven't returned, so it's mostly locals getting their fill of the nice beach vibe after the craziness of the summer, and before the craziness of the holidays."

"That mean you're local?"

She held out her hands, one clutching her wet rag, the other with her spray bottle of cleaner, "That's me. Born and raised." She wanted to ask where he was from but pegged him for some place in the South. He didn't have a Florida accent, and he definitely wasn't Texas.

"Good to know."

Okay, dammit. She had to ask. "You're from Tennessee, North Carolina or—"

"All over. I've lived in Nashville, Memphis, Mobile, Atlanta—you name it. I've played there."

She decided to give him slight encouragement and just play it out. "One of the original rolling stones, then, is that right?"

"Yes, ma'am," he said softly.

His words hit her chest like the gentle gulf wind. Then he raised the stakes.

"At your service."

He probably noticed she'd grabbed a plastic menu and fanned herself. She couldn't look him in the eyes any longer because it was going too fast. But that had never been a problem before. This quiet man was taking full control.

"More of that where it came from, darlin'."

Her little smile was pathetic. "I'll bet. Well, you make a helluva introduction. Don't you give a lady time to adjust herself?"

He slowly perused up and down her body and whispered, "No adjustment needed. But I would like your phone number, if you don't mind."

That was a little over the top, and she needed the breather. "How about we settle for a crab salad, as promised and on the house, and then we can take care of that business later?"

"Suits me fine. Am I allowed a beer? Just one?"

"Monty has a policy he allows one an hour, but if you fall off that stool, you're done."

"No problem. I'll be in full control."

I'll bet.

She turned to go when he called after her. "By the way, I'm Garrison Cramer. And you are?"

"I'm Madison." She turned quickly before her cheeks flamed further and heard his soft whisper behind her back.

"Of course you are."

MADISON'S EARS BUZZED every time she looked at the handsome singer perched on the stool on the patio, who had the ear of everyone in the room, including just about all the ladies, both young and old. If there ever was a troubadour, who could wiggle women out from behind their wedding vows, he was the right kind of sweet-sounding, buttery-tongued devil well practiced at it. It was such a welcome change.

She counted her lucky stars. She was about to take on a new adventure and perhaps a new adventure with her heart as well. Things were beginning to feel exciting. Instead of regretting her threshold of thirty—when the doorway between youth and the beginnings of aging begins to sound alarms—she was headed right into a storm, willing to tether herself to the mast of a handsome, perhaps dangerous, stranger.

Their eye contact was smoldering but infrequent. He was good at giving the same look to several other ladies in the audience, too, and that became less attractive as the second and third hour passed. It didn't preclude some experimentation. However, she wasn't going to chase.

Noonan sauntered in, wearing a fresh pair of jeans and a long-sleeved, even ironed shirt with snap buttons on the cuff and cowboy boots. It was not the beach vibe she was used to seeing him in and it made Madison convinced her mother must have called him. He was definitely dressed up.

Even his patch was clean.

"Hey there, dearie. Your mom been by yet?"

"So she called you?"

"She left a message. I was indisposed." He wiggled his eyebrows. "Can I have a beer? My usual."

"Sure, Noonan. Shall I put it on your regular tab too?"

"Nah, I brought money tonight. I'm going to try to talk your mother into having dinner with me."

Madison checked her cell. "At eleven o'clock? She doesn't eat that late."

"Says who?" Madison heard her mother's voice from behind. "When I was your age I ate all the time, it seems."

She looked gorgeous. Reds and oranges were her best colors. Her grey hair, streaked with light and dark patches, was confined to a neat, French roll at the back of her head. She wore turquoise jewelry she'd bought once in Arizona, the squash blossom pieces looking opulent and over the top as they contrasted against the rose reds and oranges of her oversized silk scarf, covering a black top over black jeans. Neither one of them looked like beach people. They looked like tourists.

Or people on their first date.

Her mother flashed the one-eyed pirate a wide smile Madison hadn't seen since this morning. Whatever had happened with the news about the "special person," she was over it and moving on with gusto.

"Hello, Noonan."

"Amberly. Looking mighty fine." He watched to see if she liked his comment before he followed it up with a sexy smile.

"As do you," she said as she looked away quickly. "Maddie dear, can I have a beer?"

Madison gave her the same Red Flamingo beer Noonan preferred. The two aging, former lovers clinked glasses and moved to a table out of earshot of Madison. It didn't take more than thirty seconds before her mother reached out across the table and gripped Noonan's hand. Their bodies leaned across too for a private chat. She had never seen Noonan so attentive or sober.

As the evening drew to a close, her mother and Noonan were

still talking. Neither one of them had eaten much of their dinners and finally directed them to be removed. The rowdy crowd had started to arrive. The music was coming to a close, soon to be replaced with some canned country greatest hits that the crowd could dance to under the warm Florida night.

And, probably because she'd been distracted with the steady stream of drinks she was pouring for the thirsty crowd and straining to hear whatever was being discussed between her mother and the Pirate, Garrison Cramer was chatting up two very young lovelies. Their eye contact had ceased, and it was clear her vision for a night of awesome sex was completely out the window.

He did give her another one of those sexy smiles as he rounded the bar, his arm over both their shoulders on his way out. "You workin' tomorrow?"

"Maybe," she said, making a fake attempt at stubbornness.

"Then maybe I'll see you. Until then, be good."

She watched the three of them exit the bar area with envy. After their car left the parking lot, she noticed she'd been grinding her teeth.

Noonan appeared at the bar with his arm around her mother's waist. "Hey, kid. I just wanted you to know that I paid my bill this time." He winked. His nose had turned bright red, and she hoped, wherever they were going, although she had a pretty good idea they might be headed to her mom's cottage at the beach, that her mother was driving.

"You even left a tip. Iris told me," she answered.

"And he didn't use my credit card, either," added her mother.

"Maddie, I got the official word about the dive. We start Wednesday, so get two, maybe three days off if you can. I'm putting together a crew now." He smiled down on her mother's face and then added, "I think you'll like who I'm going to invite to come along."

"James Bond?"

"Nope. It's a secret."

"Great. I'll let Monty know tonight. Where is it?"

"It's a barge. Went down about two hundred years ago, delivering molasses and staples en route to Tampa Bay from Cuba."

"A barge? No passengers?"

Noonan winked. "We're not looking for passengers. We're looking for the cook's dog."

"After two hundred years?"

He smiled. "Well, not exactly the dog. The dog's collar. That's the prize."

CHAPTER 7

NED'S MOTHER CALLED him the next morning letting him know that the memory care facility had an immediate opening for Aunt Flo and wondered if he could help move her.

"Normally, the wait time is over six months. But they just had someone leave, and it's ours if I can get her over there by five."

"Will she cooperate?" he asked.

"It depends on how it's done. That's why I want you there. She still remembers you rather vividly. For me, sometimes, there can be a tug of war. She knows I control most of her finances and her life. When she's conscious to understand that, the bits and pieces that come through are sometimes scrambled."

"Okay, I'll be there as soon as I can."

"I have the board and care home collecting her things, boxing them up discreetly."

"I'm on my way."

When he arrived, all Hell had broken loose. When Flo came back from lunch and scoped the boxes and all the packing, she left the facility, heading out a rear exit door that had remained unlocked. The staffers had searched everywhere, hoping to find her nearby.

Ned looked for some trace of where she'd gone, assuming she'd left by the exit.

"Isn't this close to your house, Mom?" he asked.

"It is. But it's still about twenty blocks away. That's a half mile."

"I'm wondering if she's trying to make it back to your place."

"I'm not thinking she could ever figure that out. Not sure I could either," his mom said.

"What exactly happened?"

"It was the packing, all the boxes and stuff," one of the staffers said.

"That must've totally freaked her out. How could you have let that happen?" he asked.

"You know how it goes. They were supposed to hold her in the dining hall then take her to her mailbox and the library for a short film. Instead, she got loose, walked in here, grabbed her coat and gloves, and was out the door before we could catch her."

"That's why she needs a facility more for her memory than anything else," said his mother, worry laced in her voice. "She's very mobile and strong. And she looks very normal. If somebody didn't know better, they might even let her drive, you know?"

Ned's alarm bells went off like a fire station. "Yeah, that would be a danger to her and everyone else."

"The problem for me, of course, is that I've always sort of been the one to look over her, and I've had to come to the conclusion that there's a limit to what I can do. I have to face the fact that she needs expert help, something way beyond what I'm trained for."

"You've got no argument from me." Ned turned to the two male attendants. "You got any ideas?"

"If she went out the back, I'm thinking she'd stay off the road. But all the yards are fenced on this side."

"What about beyond the yards?"

"Nothing?"

"As in what?"

"No houses. Just a thick brush. Weeds. Deer and raccoons, that kind of stuff."

Ned and the male nurses wandered up and down the back of the large property. Then he remembered that there had been a small creek running by his mother's house and wondered if it also ran behind the board and care. He directed the two staffers to follow behind.

They scaled a chain-link fence, walked through dense brush, and came upon a homeless encampment set up under the trees, tucked away so that it was invisible to any neighbor or street nearby. The encampment had tents, bicycles, and even a patio umbrella. He heard a radio playing in the background.

In the middle of a semi-circle of several transient males was Aunt Flo. She was decked out to the nines, wearing her Sunday best, including white gloves. It was a scene he never thought he'd see. He walked up behind Flo, put his finger to his lips so that the other men seated at the circle wouldn't reveal his approach.

"Hey, Aunt Flo, it's great to see you!"

Just when she turned, he put his hand gently on her shoulder and gave her a big grin.

"Oh, Ned!" she said as she rose. "We were looking for you everywhere! Your mother was worried sick!" She extended her hand toward the group of males in an attempt to begin introductions. "My memory sometimes fails me fellows, so could you tell me your names again, please?"

The group stared at each other and, one by one, began to rise slowly. One of them was on crutches, and another had an artificial leg from the mid-calf down.

"Kennie."

"I'm Regis."

"I'm Army Daniels. From San Diego."

"My name is Boris, and I am from Russia. Nice to meet you." He gave a quick bow, then added, "We weren't quite sure what to do, but we figured someone would come along looking for her. We were prepared to take her to the police."

Ned reassured them. "No problem, gents. You guys did the right thing. I'm glad you didn't get her scared." He put his hand on Flo's shoulder again "Sometimes she gets scared, doesn't remember where she is. Isn't that right, Aunt Flo?"

Flo rolled her eyes, swatted the air in front of her face and addressed her group of comrades still standing in the circle. "Isn't it just like a man? You look all over for them, and when they finally pop up, they act like *you're* the one who was lost!"

Several of the men chuckled. One spat a black gob of phlegm. Boris didn't say anything.

The peg-leg homeless man said, "You go with your nephew now, Flo. I'll let the two of you work things out, okay?"

His reaction seemed to please her. "This has been a lovely visit, gentlemen. Next time I will bring you all some of my very best lemonade and chocolate chip cookies. Will you guys be here tomorrow?"

They looked between themselves, and all five of them nodded their heads.

NED RACED WITH the two women north to Flo's new home, hoping to reach it by five o'clock. They had brought as much as he could carry in the back of the truck, covered by a tarp. The rest of her things, he would pick up later and have delivered.

Flo went without incident. She loved road trips and excitedly talked about her new friends and what a nice garden they tended. Ned was never surer that his mother was doing the right thing, even that perhaps it was long overdue.

About five miles outside San Diego, his aunt fell asleep against the window, on the driver's side behind Ned. He thought about bringing up the poetry book he'd studied last night and decided against it. The air was already thick with things unsaid.

His mother broke her silence first.

"Ned, you're going to get a call from a friend of your father's. His name is Noonan LaFontaine, the former Navy diver your dad served with and spent some time with in the Florida Keys before you were born."

"The guy who was with him when he found this," he said as he held out the pendant.

"The very same. He wasn't able to attend the funeral, but he wanted to express his condolences, and he's invited you to come out and spend a week or two with him in Florida."

"Not sure I can get the leave, Mom."

"Well, you think about it. I gave him your cell." Before he could protest, she'd already given him the palm of her hand. "I know. But in a way, he's family. Not by blood, but he and your dad had a bond."

Ned wasn't sure he wanted to spend any time around someone who was close to his father. But he was more than curious if this fellow was one of the little groups in the picture from that poetry book. He also considered the possibility that his dad was someone different in Florida than he was in San Diego.

"Don't do that anymore, Mom. You know you're not to give out my phone, my picture, or anything about me."

"Yes, yes, I know. This is different." She continued. "I think you should go, that's all. Flo will hopefully be settled. You've helped me. You've just gotten back from overseas. Take a little time, a little beach time. Your dad always drew a great deal of strength from the beach."

"Are you talkin' about *my* dad? The pirate bastard?"

"He wasn't always that way. We were so happy when you came along. Everything was perfect. We laughed at your antics. He was a different man then." She watched the countryside stream by, the gentle rolling hills, still brown and unrecovered from the hot summer. Between expanses of dead were bright green rows of tended gardens. It was a huge flower-growing region with peaceful, uncluttered farmland, looking the way it probably did a hundred years ago.

"This isn't going to be one of those surprises like, 'Hey, he's your dad' or anything is it?"

His mother in profile smiled, shaking her head. Then she turned to face him. "I've only ever slept with one man, and that man was your father."

"The Pirate bastard, not this Noonan guy, right?"

"Right."

"Okay, I'll talk to him. Just trying to get my bearings here."

She chuckled. "He used to say that all the time. I used to laugh every time he'd say it, because for all his planning and calculating, when he was sailing in those days, he always managed to get lost. It was sort of our joke. He planned so hard only to get lost, whereas everyone else on the planet just got lost."

He could feel the lid on her personality curling at the edges as if she was gradually releasing something she'd kept bottled up. In another place, in another lifetime, she might have been a completely different person.

LATER THAT NIGHT, Ned got the call he'd been expecting.

"I'm a friend of your father's," said the crusty voice of someone who could have been his father's twin.

"I've heard some of the stories, Mr. LaFontaine. I'm just—"

"Oh, this is far more than about your dad, Son. I've been contracted to do a special dive for a private individual to look for an artifact that was sunk some two hundred years ago off the *gulf* side of Florida. I'm hiring a team, and as a former SEAL, I know you've got some great experience. That's what I need."

"I'm still active, Mr. LaFontaine, but I've never done anything like that. The equipment is all different."

"No, it's not. Mine just has more stickers and stuff. It's more beat-up because I don't have a rich Uncle Sam. And of course, you wouldn't be bringing yours. You'd use mine, Son."

"When are you going out?"

"We start Wednesday."

"You have full permission?"

"Yup. Florida's signed off. We're below the monetary limit anyway. We're looking to get something more sentimental than valuable."

"How deep?"

"It's shallow. Way less than a hundred feet. Probably sixty to eighty. Lots of people have gone after things there, but the storms this year really pushed things around, scrambled the wrecks, so it could be deeper, but not by much that close to the coastline. It will be warm, so we'll wear our shorties. I'm not bringing anyone on who doesn't have a lot of experience. And, in case you're wondering, I don't dive any longer. I'm the captain."

"Have you calculated the weather for next week?"

"Are you kidding? It's gorgeous this time of year. Not a hurricane in sight, not yet. We'd have lots of warning. And this isn't the Caribbean, you know. Not that unexpected stuff. You've been there, of course."

"I have."

"Well, this will be like diving in a nice, warm swimming pool. Crystal clear water and not mucked up with overpopulation. Just all the things you like about the ocean. We're keeping to all the rules. This isn't a pirate mission, despite what you may have heard about me."

"Yeah, I heard so many stories I stopped believing in them long ago."

"That's a shame. Your dad was a helluva guy and an even better storyteller."

"Said no one ever in California."

Noonan chuckled, which led him into a coughing fit. "Sinuses," he said by way of explanation. It sounded like full-on bronchitis to Ned.

"So you and Mom kept in touch, then?"

"No, not really. I never met her. I kept in touch with your dad, but the last time I talked to him was from the hospital. He'd borrowed someone's cell. He told me all kind of nice things about you. But come out here, and I'll tell you all about it, if you're interested."

Ned had to admit he was. Although he had no burning desire to know more about his dad's past, he was interested in the area. He too had loved the Florida weather, the coast, and the vibe of the little beach towns he'd visited on the Atlantic side, where they'd done most of their training. He decided to test for Noonan's sense of humor.

"So you sure you're not my dad? If secrets are being revealed, I just wanted a little forewarning."

Noonan nearly coughed himself to death. "Shit no. Your dad would have killed me if I'd ever laid a hand on that woman." After Ned didn't respond, Noonan added, "But knowing your dad as I do, I don't blame you for asking. I'll be able to tell the first time I see you if your mama messed around with anybody else. You'd be old Jake's boy. Like it or not, you'd look just like him. I know you would."

Ned was sold but didn't want to let the old captain know. "I'll think about it."

"Nope. If you say no, then I've got someone else to call. That's the way we roll here. I'm not here to drag you to the beautiful Florida coast. You gotta feel like coming, like you're being led on a strange new adventure. Quit the stuff in your head, and just come on over. We'll sort out the rest of the world another day, hear me?"

"Yessir, I do."

"So you'll fly into Tampa, and I'll pick you up when you text me your flight."

"Where will I stay?"

"Well, that's up to you, but you're welcome to reside on the boat, or you can room in town, Treasure Island. There are a bunch of little vacation rentals available. I can see if I can fix you up. Can you spend like $50 a day on a place?"

"That's doable."

"Then no problem."

"Alright then. I'll text you when I get it arranged. When do you want me?"

"As soon as you can get here. Doesn't matter to me, as long as you're flexible with the accommodations."

"Sounds good. Gotta check in with the Team and then I'll let you know when."

"Glad to have you aboard. Oh, and one last thing, you'll get paid three hundred dollars a day, but not until we find what we're looking for. That's the deal. But I'll provide all the gear and chow when we're out. Okay?"

Ned called Kyle next and got the okay to leave for ten days. He checked online for flights out of San Diego and found a direct one to Tampa. He got out his black duffel bag, leaving his heavy equipment tucked inside the safe bolted to the floor of his condo. He began packing trunks and a couple of nicer shirts just in case some nice seafood dinners were in the offing.

He could finish tomorrow. But just in case he forgot, he placed the little book of poetry on top of the clothes already in the bag.

It was his ticket on his new ride, the roadmap to help get him lost, just like his father had done so many years ago.

CHAPTER 8

MADISON'S MOM ASKED her to join her for lunch before she went to work. She found her mother out on the beach, seated in the sand, throwing rocks and pieces of shells into the surf. The day had turned out slightly overcast, so it wasn't overly hot.

Madison sat right next to her. "I'm guessing you had a fairly nice evening last night. When you guys are getting along, you make the finest looking couple." She threw her arm around her mother's shoulder and drew their bodies close then released her.

"Noonan's an acquired taste. He can be charming, or he can be just downright irritating. I like him both ways, but only when he's irresistible."

There was that word again!

"Well, I'm happy for you."

Her mother continued tossing rocks and shells into the surf. Madison could tell she was trying to figure something out, and once she did, there was going to be a proclamation.

"So what did you want to talk about?"

"Can't I have lunch with my daughter?"

"Yes, but twice in two days?"

"Just humor me. These are strange times."

Madison decided she'd take the more direct approach. "Can I ask you who the 'someone special' was? The one you and Noonan were talking about?"

"He was special." She squinted at the horizon. The combination of escaping sun from behind a silver cloud and the gentle breeze off the ocean made her eyes water. Madison didn't think for a minute she was crying.

"He was one of those men you meet probably once-in-a-lifetime. I think I knew these last few days that he was leaving this world. There was just heaviness in the air. I was feeling tired, like something inside me was dying too. I actually think it's like that with some special people, don't you?"

Madison knew that the only person she could ever feel this way about would be when the time came for her mother to pass on. But she didn't want to utter it, for fear of making it so. She was well aware that the universe was a fragile place.

"You've got me there, Mom. I've never met anyone like that in my life. So I'm going to have to defer to your experience."

"I'm going to be spending a lot of time here looking at the ocean. It's all I can do."

"Are you okay? I mean, should you be alone?"

"I'm not alone. I've got the Crabby Crew—my friends. Heck, even if I did want to be alone, they'd never let me. There's always time for celebration, song, and good wine with that crew. You've met them."

"Yes, I know them very well. You're blessed, Mom." Madison hesitated to say it. "And you've got Noonan too. He doesn't mind hanging around, I'm sure."

"Noonan!" She threw a larger smoothed rock into the surf after barking his name. "Last night was about sharing grief, healing. Having someone close who is going through the same thing, someone familiar around you to take away the vacantness. He did his job well, God love him."

Madison thought that was a beautiful way to describe her friendship with the old sea captain. "So not just for the sex," she whispered.

"Not hardly. We'd have needed more alcohol for that. Maybe some dancing. No, this was communion. Healing each other because we could."

Madison could see the two of them were on the same wavelength.

"That's enough!" her mother finished. She stood, leaned over, and gave Madison her hand. "Come on. Let's go inside and have a bite."

She'd set a table with fresh Gloriosa Daisies in the middle, the bright yellow sunshine cheering the whole place up. She'd made a salad, chilled, and added fresh crabmeat to the top just before serving. She knew it was Madison's favorite.

"Do you want some white wine?"

"I'm good." Madison waited for her mother to sit down and then continued her questions. "So when Noonan said he was gone, that means he passed away?"

Her mother picked at her salad, and nodded, yes.

"How serious was it? Or were you just friends?"

"It was complicated. In all my years meeting and having men friends, it always got confusing once sex became part of the package. Rarely did it enhance. In fact, it usually ended things. I was hesitant to spoil such a perfect friendship. I don't think I laughed so much in my entire life before or since. But as for the sex, well, it was pretty much consuming. The closer we got, the closer we needed it to be. We both knew it couldn't last, except in here."

She placed her palm over her heart and gave Maddie one of those "I-am-Buddha-and-you're-a-devotee" stares.

"This was before you met my dad, right?"

"It was. Nearly two years."

"So what happened? Why didn't it last?"

"Because his heart wasn't his to give. I felt like a thief. But I couldn't help myself. I nearly packed up and followed him all the way across the country. And I'm so glad I didn't."

"So he was a friend of Noonan's too?"

"That's how I met him. They had served together in the Navy, and he came out to help him with a salvage. They were lucky enough to score some pretty incredible things, back before there were so many rules about what you could take and what you had to leave behind or register with the state. He was out for the summer visiting his old friend. Noonan had gotten out nearly six months before."

"You said across the country, where?"

"California. Moved back to California. Back to his wife."

"Mother!"

She shrugged, her large hoop earrings flashing in the afternoon sunlight. "Back in the day, I didn't worry too much about that. I figured if you threw your net out there and caught a fish, it was fair game. I didn't think about things so much like I do now. That's what age and making lots of mistakes will bring you. The trick is trying to stay *fresh* while you're getting *old*."

"Did you ever see him again?"

"I never did. I expected that one day he'd come walking right back through that door." She was pointing to the entrance. "And now I know that will never happen."

"He's gone on to fight battles elsewhere. Maybe someday you'll meet."

"I suppose I will. In time. I hope he was happy. I hope he had a good life. The world's a little sadder now, knowing that we won't meet again here at the beach at Treasure Island."

"So this was your house then? You stayed here together?"

"No, it was always my house. But I let him stay. He could've stayed here the rest of his life. He made a good choice."

"He'd already chosen, Mother."

"Exactly. And in a strange twist of fate, he honored me by keeping his promise—to someone else. He made the right choice."

HER MOTHER'S WORDS haunted Madison on her way to the Salty Dog. As soon as she stepped inside the door, the familiar smells of cook Washington Jones' barbeque and creole sauces, the general noise from the emergencies going on in the kitchen as if they battled demons escaping the gates of Hell, and the gentle country music playing in the background greeted her. It was going to be another big night. The liquor would be flowing and the plates would be flying, while the guests would consume obscene amounts of shellfish and fixings. There would be one or two major crises in the kitchen. Someone would be fired. Someone would quit. Several of the wait staff wouldn't show up and hoped to keep their jobs by showing up the next night.

It never changed. That was what was so special about this place. Everything happened at random, yet, they were all in the same pattern. Predictable in their unpredictability.

She even found herself whistling before the guitar man snuck up on her and scrambled her brain with a, "Good evening, sweetheart," whispered so close to her left ear that she could feel his hot breath on her cheek.

There he was again and she was still as breathless as the first time she saw him. Maybe it was her female alarm clock going off, her need growing so huge she didn't care about the fact that he probably slept his way up and down the Florida coast and wouldn't remember her name in the morning.

But that didn't matter. Not right now.

"Garrison Cramer, if you aren't the original Salty Dog. Just look what the sea breeze blew in tonight."

"Am I forgiven?"

"Were you bad?"

His eyes twinkled when he smiled. "I was. I was very bad. You would have been proud of me."

She felt her cheeks flush, even though threesomes had never been anything she'd ever been interested in. But her mind was overloaded with the images, and she felt her panties go wet.

"You must lead a charmed life, Garrison."

"I am. I am blessed." He stepped closer. "So am I forgiven?"

"Let's just wait and see, shall we? What happens when your groupies show up again?"

"Oh, I don't think that will happen. They've probably moved on."

She found the opportunity to stick it to him good, at last. "Then, Garrison Cramer, you weren't bad enough. I'm going to guess they'll want a three-pete."

"Most the time, I prefer the company of just one good woman." He winked and left her soaked with sweat and gasping hard to catch her breath. It was hot enough to rival anything cook Jones could stir up.

During one of his breaks, the handsome singer asked her for a dance, and she dutifully accepted. Their foreplay—rocking back and forth to a tune not quite a slow dance, facing each other, then him spooning behind her as their hips swung in tandem—gave a healthy boost to her libido, not to mention respect from every other woman in the bar. He was a smooth dancer, he led well, and, just like Mr. James Bond, she could tell what it would feel like to wake up in his arms in the morning.

If it all went right tonight.

But it didn't. Just before midnight, a married couple got into a fight. She slapped her husband across the face, and he was preparing to retaliate when several men at the bar jumped him. The guitar man jumped in too.

In the tussle of bodies, Garrison Cramer got a belt to the nose and left with blood streaming down the front of his shirt, racing out the door on his way to the Urgent Care center.

CHAPTER 9

N ED SILVER WATCHED the blue waters beneath him as his plane
cruised in to land at Tampa Airport. It was a cloudless day, one
of those clear ones he still loved about San Diego and Southern
California. But the turquoise waters of the Florida coast were spectacular. He'd already flown over so much white beach his eyes
almost hurt from the brightness.

He was excited about the new adventure coming up, the chance
to do a pleasure dive and not something ordered by the military. Not
that he minded that, either, but this was a different kind of excitement.

It was like how he felt going across the Pacific Ocean on an air-
craft carrier once, standing with hundreds of other men looking out
to the horizon in search of land. He understood how some of the
early sea captains must have felt racing out into the middle of the big
blue waters of the world, in search of adventure, whatever was out
there. It was an urge as old as mankind itself, something he shared
with every other person who felt the power of the ocean in comparison to the relative little power of his own body. The meeting
between air and sea satisfied something deep inside him.

He exited the plane, walking through the lobby filled with families greeting their loved ones. The aloha shirts and different
languages than he was used to in San Diego, reminded him of some
of the Caribbean places he'd been to.

On his way to baggage claim, one crusty character stood out. It had to have been his dad's former Navy buddy, Noonan LaFontaine. The guy had wiry salt-and-pepper hair that sprouted every which way like dead grey straw, as if the wind was blowing through the airport. He sported a black patch over one eye, and he had a three-day stubble. He could've been a character actor in a pirate movie. He had everything but the parrot and the peg leg.

"You got to be Jake's kid. There's no doubt about it," Noonan said as he embraced him in a bear hug. With his hands gripping the tops of his arms, clearly five inches shorter than Ned, the pirate shook him and said, "You're just like how I pictured. The spitting image of your dad. I think he didn't die at all. I think you're just some kind of a trans-portal guy, you know? Like in those science-fiction films?"

Ned wanted him to release his hands but there was something about Noonan that he tolerated over any other man who would try to touch him.

"I've been told that a time or two, mostly by my mom." He stepped back. "You do know most of my dad's friends are dead?"

"So are mine. That's why I hang with the younger crowd." Noonan shrugged.

Ned adjusted his weight, pulling his laptop case over his right shoulder, and left the pirate to walk toward the baggage carousel. Noonan ran after him, laughing up a storm, waving to people he saw and thought he knew, and generally making a small spectacle of himself. Ned held his breath and wasn't sure this was the kind of vibe he was looking for in a boat captain. Although this was going to be a pleasure dive, there were always risks involved.

Ned's duffel bag was one of the first to come off the carousel. Noonan tried to grab it, but Ned shoved the computer case in his chest instead. "I'll take it, Gramps."

Noonan howled and slapped his knee over that one. It was only barely after one o'clock, but the pirate already smelled of alcohol. It was, as would have been his father's scent, the unmistakable Eau De Beer.

On the way out through the revolving doors, Noonan directed him to the short-term parking lot. "I'm so happy you decided to come, Neddie."

Ned stopped, squared him up, and drilled a look that didn't require words, but he spoke anyway. "For the record, Gramps or Noonan or whatever you want me to call you, the name is Ned. I haven't been Neddie since I was six years old. I hated it then, and I hate it worse now. So if you don't want me to turn around and catch a plane back to California, you better not call me that again. Agreed?"

"I don't have a problem with that. I was just being…"

"You were being an asshole, like my dad. If you stop being an asshole, we'll get along just fine. You have to know that my dad and I were never close, so if you're thinking you're going to take his spot or be just like him, and that's gonna make me feel real comfortable or good, you've got shit for brains. So let's just get that straight out and on the table right now okay?"

"You don't have to say it twice, Son. I know all about your dad." His bloodshot eye nearly teared up when he finished his thought. "I know your dad better than you do."

The man turned and made a beeline for the parking lot. Ned's long legs kept pace with the pirate, but he had to work at it to do so.

They jumped into a light turquoise pickup truck with the Barry Bones logo on the side, depicting a patched pirate face missing several prominent teeth, grinning wide, sporting an earring and wearing a red bandanna. Noonan could've posed for the picture except for the teeth.

Ned strapped in after loading his duffel in the back. He held his laptop on his knees. Noonan jumped in and avoided his seatbelt.

Ned watched the blue waters on either side of a large arched bridge leading from the highway system outside of Tampa over to the gulf beaches. He'd never seen so many boats in one place before. Houses along the shore all had docks, and many also had swimming pools, something he didn't see in San Diego much. The weather was perfect, similar to San Diego but warmer. In the distance, he could see the ocean.

"I was thinking I'd bring you by that little place I found, get your gear dropped off, and we could go grab something to eat if you're up to it.

"I could do something to eat."

"If you don't like what I got for you, just stay put for a couple of days, see if it wears on you. I managed to get it for free, so you won't have to pay me or anybody else back, okay?"

"Geez, thank you. How'd you arrange that?"

Noonan grinned. "I don't have a lot of money, but I do have friends. At my age, kid, friends are everything."

"I haven't been to this side of Florida before. It's nice," Ned muttered.

"I've spent most of my time on the other coast, to be honest. But I love the gulf side much better. Warmer, I think, more temperate. And it's slower. I mean, we got lots of tourism here, no question about it. But it's happier. You know what I mean?"

Ned stared straight ahead as the bridge dead-ended into a small two-lane boulevard, heading north and south along the beach.

"This here is Gulf Boulevard, for obvious reasons. You have your beachside properties, and then you have your inland properties, which sometimes are on a waterway. In any direction, you're no more than five or six blocks from some body of water. I think that's why I like it"

Noonan turned right and headed north. Ned saw glimpses of turquoise water and white beaches in between two-story rental units and occasionally a large condo complex. Along the way, it was dotted with beach shops and rental agencies, renting everything from vacation cabins to surfboards, golf carts, and beach bicycles. He passed a lot of ice cream stores. There were shops on both sides of the road selling fishing and beach gear, flip-flops, bathing suits, tanning lotion, and a couple of *taquerias* with open air *palapas* just like Ned had seen in Mexico. There were lots of fish and chips places and a smattering of outdoor bars with brightly-colored umbrellas. Occasionally, they had to stop between lights to allow couples or families to cross the road, usually towing a canvas wagon filled with towels and equipment.

They also passed several groups of walkers and occasionally a tandem bicycle. Ned felt himself starting to relax, even though Noonan was quick to hit on the gas and slow to hit the brakes.

"See? Nothing fancy, but not too shabby, either."

They turned left down a paved road that ended at the edge of a wooden bridge over the sand dunes. It was the Treasure Island beach access trail. Off to the side was an alleyway, unpaved, just wide enough to accommodate two cars passing. On both sides of the path were smaller shacks, some of them well-painted and others left to the sea's devices. Vacation rental signs hung in most of the yards or attached to the upper eaves of the houses, colorfully lettered in bright Caribbean paint, with names like Pete's Paradise and Laura's Lair. Pictures of fish, starfish, and mermaids adorned fences and sides of buildings. Noonan pulled into the driveway of a tiny pink house that sat right on the beach.

"It isn't much, I warn you. This place is going to get torn down, and the owner has plans to build a McMansion sort of triplex building. He wants to live upstairs and rent out down below. But for now, this place is vacant, and it has a little bit of furniture. I hope you like it. And the price is right," he reminded as he exited the truck.

Ned ran right behind the pirate, his canvas slip-ons crunching on the white mixture of crushed shells and stones. Noonan produced a set of keys and unlocked the front door, which was slightly warped, causing Noonan to have to lean into it hard with his shoulder. At the second try, it gave way and let them enter, but part of the door trim had cracked.

Inside, the house smelled of mildew, but Ned thought it was nothing that a few open windows wouldn't take care of. It hadn't been updated in many years. That surprised him, because Ned thought all these beach properties saw themselves underwater every few years due to the storms. But this one looked like it had survived many seasons of Winters and lots of Fall hurricanes.

"Home sweet home, kid."

"It's funky. I like it." Ned walked through the doorway into a small bedroom, which barely had room for the king-sized bed. He'd been dreading to discover a lumpy full-sized mattress so was thrilled with the king.

He threw his duffel bag on the bed, unzipped it, and hung up a jacket and two shirts he brought. Noonan was watching him, leaning into the doorway.

"Don't know if you smoke, but they'll allow it, too."

"I'm not a smoker."

"Good to see you're prepared," Noonan nodded at the shirts Ned was hanging up.

"I thought I should bring something for at least one night out. Do you have any plans for that?"

"Let's see what kind of luck we have first. Good idea though. You never know what the sea is going to bring you. It could be cause for celebration."

"I don't care about what the sea brings me, as long as the restaurant doesn't refuse to serve me."

"You're a very astute traveler. I'm not gonna take you anywhere a pair of khakis and a T-shirt wouldn't do. But it's good to be prepared."

Noonan returned to the living room. "This is always how I judge the bones of a house. I like to be just outside the sand bar like this one is. I like to be able to see the water, have my coffee out on my private beach, or sit out at night under the stars. This one has a fire pit too. Nobody will bother you here. Everybody who lives on the street is from somewhere else. Some people live here, some people are running away, and some people just don't know what the fuck they're doing."

Ned found himself chuckling. The pirate was easy to like. Maybe it was the smell of the ocean or just the fact that the damned view was stunningly beautiful, but Ned knew he was going to be okay. And Noonan understood Ned needed some alone time. There would be no father-son play acting here, and the old captain would be a good resource so Ned could explore this area more.

"If you want to get a car, you'd have to go into Largo or someplace. I should've asked you at the airport. The cars are a little expensive. You can get along just fine here in a golf cart. And where we're going to be is just down the road a bit. I got the Bones all fueled up and ready to go."

Ned shook his head. "I don't think I want to rent a vehicle but will play it by ear. Only thing I want is to get some groceries. Do you have time to run me down to someplace I can fill up my fridge?"

"Of course. Let's go do that now, and then we can head over for a late lunch/early dinner. I've got some people I want to introduce you to."

Ned purchased staples he was going to need, going off the list he made before he left. They stowed everything away, chilled the beers, and were ready to go.

He discovered his stomach had been doing flip-flops. The small breakfast he'd been served on the plane wasn't quite enough to keep him going. He was itching to have some fresh seafood.

Noonan hit Gulf Boulevard one more time, and was pointing out various bars, restaurants, and places of interest. He showed him where the best place to buy wine was, and where not to buy a rubbery pizza. He recommended a little Mexican place within walking distance of Ned's new cottage and told him to avoid the tandoori restaurant next-door.

They pulled up to another bar restaurant combination with an outdoor patio sprinkled under colorful beach umbrellas. Even at three o'clock in the afternoon, there were a good number of cars in the parking lot.

Ned waited for his eyes to adjust to the darkness. The food smelled great. Noonan was dragging him over to sit on a stool at a huge U-shaped bar. The shapely female bartender was leaning over to stock beer bottles in a refrigerator, and it was hard to miss how perfect her ass was. Not that he was looking.

But when she stood, her shoulders and back were covered in bright white-blonde ringlets of spun gold, reaching down all the way past her waist. She was tall, her arms well-tanned, but when she turned to face him, her blue eyes flashed, and then she looked away. He couldn't take his eyes off of her. She was some kind of angel, her face beautiful without the aid of any makeup that he could detect.

She chanced another look at him, and he felt a warm ripple wash all over him again. Whoever she was, he was sure he'd never met anyone like her before.

"Madison!" Noonan was calling to her.

She approached almost timidly, except he sensed she was far from timid. Her gentle scent wafted towards him, and he felt completely enthralled, enchanted. He was laid out bare and could not stop staring.

"This here's my buddy's son, Ned Silver." He leaned over the counter. "He's a Navy SEAL, but shhh! We don't tell anyone."

Ned was irritated. "Come on, Noonan. You know that's not cool."

The girl's eyes were all over him. He felt he might blush. "Your secret's safe with me," she whispered, holding out her hand. "I'm Madison."

She gave a firm handshake. Her palm was warm and as sweaty as his was. "Nice to meet you, Madison. I'm Ned."

"He told me that already," she said as they continued shaking hands. She smirked and withdrew her paw because he wasn't going to let it go.

"She's part of the crew, Ned. She's done lots of underwater film work." Ned glanced up at her. "Tell him about that James Bond film you were in."

"Thunder Dive," she said. The dimple at the side of her mouth formed and then disappeared. "I did the body double for the bad girl." She watched his reaction like it was important to her.

"I saw that movie. I liked it. I thought they filmed that in the Caribbean."

"Nope, right out here." She angled her head back to point to the beach.

"How'd you get that job?"

Noonan inserted himself. "Are you crazy, Ned? Look at her!"

I am, dammit. I'm just trying to talk for Chrissakes!

"I did some water skiing shows at SeaWorld a few years ago, and some underwater film photography, and, well, I don't know if they even auditioned anyone else. I just got the job."

She had a nice shrug too. He was going to have to stop staring or he'd be drooling soon.

"So you like to dive then?" He didn't like how it sounded.

"I do. I even go deep. Mostly for pleasure. There's not a lot of work out here now, unless you want to help raise an oil platform." Her big blue eyes rolled, and she twisted her upper lip.

The air was thick between them. Noonan was chuckling under his breath. Ned licked his lips. His mouth was parched.

Someone called Madison's name, and she excused herself.

In her wake, Ned's insides were all jumbled up, yet he didn't have the desire to get everything straight. His heart raced. Expectation zoomed and made fun of his ordered life with everything put in its proper place. Logic was disappearing. Teetering out of control, he felt like he'd been hit by a tsunami.

And he loved it.

CHAPTER 10

MADISON COULD FEEL his eyes on her behind. Although she didn't mind the attention, she'd already written Ned off as a lost cause. He was too young, too clean-cut, didn't display enough flawed behavior or personality. And he certainly didn't need her brand of healing.

As she waited on tables, she scratched her head several times and asked for customers to repeat the order. She was distracted by her thoughts, not really thinking about him as a potential partner—she just couldn't stop thinking about him period.

Besides, soon Garrison was going to be sauntering in, no doubt needing an evening of commiseration. She had visions of being extremely careful as she kissed him, avoiding his poor nose. That's what she had in mind. She had no appetite for picking up a youngster.

But every time she turned, every time she looked over her shoulder to make sure someone was tending the bar, every time she heard old Noonan laughing or hit the wooden countertop with his fist, attention always drifted off toward the newcomer. The most irritating thing about it was that he didn't seem to mind the attention, either.

When Garrison Cramer finally darkened the doorway, swinging his guitar case over his shoulder, he gave her a wink and a puppy dog smile. One of his eyes had a deep purple ring beneath it. His nose was red, and there was a surgical strip covering a tiny cut above the bridge of his nose. He was a tall, dark, and dangerous piece of maleness in need of all the things Madison loved to dish out.

"Am I forgiven?" He stepped so close she could feel the heat of his thigh against her without them touching.

"THAT DEPENDS ON how bad you were." She stared back up to him, unafraid, enjoying the scent of his being. He was a land lover, no question about it, and she was queen of the ocean. There were lots of interesting contrasts and other things they could explore together.

"Now as for being bad, that's where you come in, Madison."

Her spine tingled in such a good way. She looked down at her feet, inhaled, and smiled to herself. If they were alone, he would've brought those big arms around her waist and plastered her with a kiss so deep she knew she would be hooked. But in public, all she could do was feel the tension in his chest. His breathing sounded like the roar of the ocean.

And all the better, college kid, clean-cut Navy seal Ned fucking Silver was watching the whole thing. She hoped he took it as a warning that she would not be easy to charm.

"So is that a yes?"

"Right now,"—she looked deep into his eyes—"I'm having the time of my life just having you wonder about that. But I would say, the odds are definitely in your favor."

"Then I better get set up, right? And would you do me the honor of accepting a dance with me sometime tonight?"

"I'd like that, Garrison. I'd like that a lot."

She watched him walk away, enter the patio area, greet several people casually, remove his guitar and set up his stool and equipment.

Madison made the mistake of noticing the perch next to Noonan was vacant. Half a beer was left on the counter, as well as an unfinished crab salad. She approached the pirate.

"You get stood up already?"

"No, he saw some people he knew from San Diego or Norfolk." Noonan pointed to an area across the patio where Ned was seated with his back to her, talking to two other clean-cut, muscled, and overly tattooed guys. He rubbed the bridge of his nose. "You and the crooner an item? Isn't he a little old, worn off parts around the edges a bit?" Noonan quizzed.

Madison slapped him with the end of her bar rag. "I like his voice, and I like it that the only strings that come with him are the ones on his guitar."

"You are so much like your mother. Does she know you do this, pick up guys at work?"

She gawked back at Noonan. "This is work?"

Iris was making drinks behind the bar. Madison asked her to go wait on Ned and his friends.

"I can't. I got my hands full here. I've got an order of ten."

Madison took her tray, pulled her order chits from the back pocket of her jeans, and crossed the patio to serve them.

Ned gave her a warm smile. "Madison, these are some of my friends." To the group, he explained, "Madison's gonna work on the dive I've been hired for."

"Nice to meet you," said one of the SEALs. "I'm Andy." He extended his hand.

Madison jammed the tray into her chest, put the notebook in her left, and shook his hand as well as the young sailor's across the table from him, who said his name was Reed.

"So I'm going to guess you guys also fish together?"

They all chuckled. "Yes, ma'am," came the answer in unison.

"Madison here's some movie star. Got to be a Bond Girl, isn't that right?" Ned informed them.

She was thinking about all the fun things she had done on that shoot, which made her blush but kept her lips sealed.

"Really?" asked one of the gentlemen.

"I've done a few things. Most of them I'm proud of." She gave them a winning smile. It was her job to keep the customers happy, after all. Besides, Boy Scouts like these were good for business. "Now, what can I get you?"

Before they began ordering, Madison heard the syrupy sweet voice of Garrison Cramer. "Ladies and gentlemen, I just wanted to dedicate my first song to the most beautiful woman in this whole place. Miss Madison? Would you take a bow please?"

Her cheeks flamed instantly as all eyes quickly turned in her direction. She gave a delicate bow then blew Cramer a kiss and got a standing ovation.

She focused her attention back on her three SEAL customers. Brushing the hair from her forehead, she used her little notebook to fan herself. "Well, that was unexpected." In the background, she heard Garrison Cramer singing a beautiful love song.

That raised Ned's eyebrows. "Well, I was going to ask you for a ride home later on, but I can see you're otherwise occupied."

"Really? You think?"

"Yes, I think he has plans for you tonight, and God knows I wouldn't want to impose. I am looking to make friends since we're gonna be working together. I don't know this area at all, and I don't have a car. I'm sure I'll work it out, somehow."

One of the SEALs offered, and Madison couldn't miss Ned's stern response, shutting the man down.

"You always have Noonan," Madison pointed out. She observed the pirate sitting alone, waiting. She felt a little sorry for him.

"Yup. And speaking of the man, I should get back over to him. I'll catch you guys tomorrow night?"

"Sure thing. We don't go back till next weekend. Shoot, I like the scenery here so much I might never go back to Little Creek," said

Andy.

Ned stood, brushing past her, emanating a little grumble as he did so. Removing a twenty from his wallet, he placed it on Madison's tray. "I've got their first round, okay?"

"Got it." She stared up at him and caught a wink.

"I hope you don't mind, I was messin' with you a little bit. Just a little good, clean fun."

That's when she realized he wasn't going to be easy to get rid of. And he was a whole lot smarter and probably more experienced than she thought he was.

About an hour later, Madison nearly ran into Ned rounding the corner from the kitchen.

"I'm about to take off. Can I ask you for a dance, sort of give the singing cowboy some competition?"

"I'm kind of busy. I'll take a raincheck." It was what she had to say to stay in control.

"It might increase his ardor, could be real good for you," he suggested, giving her a wink.

"Like he needed it," she teased in return.

Ned shrugged. "If you say so. I would have thought you'd have gone for someone who wasn't so long in the tooth and didn't lust after anyone in a skirt. He's kind of obvious, don't you think? But you know what they say, whatever *floats your boat.*"

He had just made fun of her in the most gentlemanly manner, catching her off guard.

"And how would you know what sort of man I like to play with?"

"Oh, it's play, is it? Well then, darlin', I'm out."

"I meant that in rhetorical terms," she protested. "I meant—"

"Sure. It is a big game for you, isn't it? You like to be in control, because that makes the man need to be stronger, right? Have you ever just let a nice, smooth man take his time, and rock your world, and you didn't have to do a thing?"

That was unexpected. Madison thought she should be offended. "Supposed to be fifty-fifty, doesn't it?"

"Only if you don't trust the one in control. How nice would that be to anticipate, but not know, except to recognize that you don't have to lift a finger and you let him do all the lovin' and you get to do all the enjoyin'? Think about it."

He turned on his heel. She had turned down the dance, after all, so there wasn't anything left to be said. But it pissed her off to see him clear the doorway and disappear into the night air. Noonan wasn't anywhere to be found, either.

The singing cowboy acted like he never saw a thing. Except he suddenly looked like second place to Madison.

CHAPTER 11

NED WENT FOR a barefoot run on the beach just before the sun rose. He did thirty pushups and a couple dozen sit ups. With his ankles caressed by the surf, he stretched, rotating his arms and doing neck curls in both directions. Satisfied he'd continued his routine on the first morning in a new location, just like he'd been trained, he surveyed his surroundings.

Take care of your body and your mind, and everything else works out.

By the time the grey pink sky turned into a full-blown rose orange, several other runners and bicyclists had joined him. A group of older women walked briskly past him, several of them waving.

Today, they'd start the dive.

Ned thought he would sleep well last night, but he wound up tossing about. He finally changed the sheets, putting the others in the wash. The lull of the machine whir was the last thing he heard before crashing. He couldn't remember the dream he had, but they had been vivid and filled with bright color.

He made coffee and had a bowl of granola with a banana. He checked his computer for news from base. On his cell, the informal group chat he had with several of the Team guys had deteriorated last night into nonsense. Someone posted a picture he shouldn't and asked that everyone erase it, which Ned did. He was glad he missed the drama of the night with a bunch of horny single guys trying to...do what? Live a normal life? It was far from normal. Waiting wasn't normal. Recovering after a deployment wasn't normal. There was still all the shit going on at home with their community, family, and their uncertain future. As much as they tried to be a force for good, there was still the realization after they came home that nothing really ever changed.

The news was the same. Someone got hurt in a training accident. One of their old instructors was retiring, and a party was planned. Someone else was getting married and another party was planned at the Brownlees, their official Team party after the deployment and the debriefing. He was sorry to miss that one. He liked Coop's in-laws. Coop was a regular stand-up guy too. Both he and Kyle had always treated Ned with respect.

He finished his breakfast then made a peanut butter and jelly sandwich and wrapped it in plastic. He brought two bottles of water and two apples, placing everything in a gallon plastic bag, sticking it in his slender dive backpack along with an extra pair of trunks and T-shirt and some heavy-duty sunscreen and bug repellant. Under his khakis he wore trunks. Hoisting the backpack over his shoulder, he stepped into his canvas slip-ons and walked out to the alleyway and then to Gulf Boulevard. He'd driven past the dock last night and knew it would be just a short walk.

Noonan kept the Barry Bones at a sport fishing club berth, although he wasn't a paying member. Ned was told the private clubhouse was a popular meeting place for boats taking tourists fishing out on the bay, and the Bones was one of the most requested dive boats. Although not as many shipwrecks as on the Atlantic side, there were still a fair number of good sites for novice divers to check out. Noonan told him he was known to bring back everyone safely, albeit a little drunk.

He wasn't like any of the big party boats with scores of partygo-ers who practically had to be lifted off when they came back to dock.

Those black pirate ships blasted music and poured booze to excess, feigning to terrorize the quiet beachgoers on the shore. Their Hollywood-style swashbuckling was ridiculous but entertaining for many of the college and younger honeymooners who knew nothing about pirates, boats, or diving. Ned had seen real pirates, and those guys were definitely not funny.

Noonan had piles of wet suits and equipment laid out for his three divers. He pointed to Ned's pile. "Check them out for me, will you? That suit's about your size. Might be a little big."

Ned held up the shortie, the preferred choice for warm water dives, cutting off just above the elbows and above the knees. It was intact but had definitely seen better days. He checked the gauges and connections on the tanks and tried on the one-piece headgear with the built-in com.

"Do we each have a spare?" Ned asked.

Noonan gave him the thumbs-up, pointing to four tanks secured in a stand on board. Ned took his equipment and stepped off the pier and onto the boat. Below deck, were two bedrooms—one was probably Noonan's with an oversized bed no larger than a single on land. The other room had four bunks, no wider than a double ironing board, but otherwise spacious and adequate. He knew that's where the three of them would sleep, if the dive required they stay overnight on the gulf.

The galley kitchen had a big stainless steel sink, a microwave and built-in coffee maker, and a one-burner propane cooktop. A small stainless fridge was secured underneath the countertop. Beyond was the head with shower. He stowed his pack, setting it on a lower bunk, and poured himself a mug of coffee, climbing back up to see if he could help Noonan with anything.

"No, I think I got everything. I got a fridge down there if you need to keep anything cold, and sorry, I was going to get donuts but never left the ship."

"No worries, Noonan. I'm good. Hope you got beer for the return trip."

"That I do," Noonan said as he organized ties, buoys and ropes, placing them in several plastic containers smelling of fish and probably used for storing fresh catch. Ned figured the empty large blue container with a drain in it at the stern near one of the outboards was for placing things they found on the dive.

"What time are the others coming?"

"Madison's usually early. But I said eight o'clock." Noonan checked his watch, "Anytime now."

Ned saw Madison's shapely form in her dark turquoise suit, carrying a pair of bright pink flippers. She'd also brought snorkel gear which Ned found amusing. She gave him a big smile and waved.

"Hey, Noonan, how deep are we going?" Ned thought perhaps he'd misunderstood.

"Less than a hundred, maybe eighty, how I pegged it. I was out there two days ago and located it with sonar, marked it with a buoy."

"Morning," Madison said to him. Her fresh face was more exposed now that all that blonde hair was tied back in two long braids she lashed together with hot pink bands. She could have made a beautiful Viking princess in a movie shoot, if they wore wetsuits.

"You have a nice night?"

She wrinkled up her nose.

"I warned you about the cowboy."

It was nice to see her laugh. "He's not a cowboy."

"And?"

"He's a good dancer."

"And?" He was enjoying the tease. He also noted she wasn't as frosty as she'd been last night, which meant one of two things, and both of them were sending visions to his head that were damned distracting.

She shrugged. "I'm not used to waiting in line. And that's all I'm going to tell you!"

Well, good for you. He'd been right about her.

She filed past him, greeted Noonan, and examined the equipment he'd left out for her. She'd brought her own secondary tank, brightly colored in psychedelic patterns. Ned continued to sip his coffee. Noonan showed her the headpiece they would wear and demonstrated the wire for the com.

At last, the third diver, Travis Hicks, arrived, running down the dock in red flip-flops, an open palm trees shirt exposing a white hairy chest, matching red trunks, and a Yankee baseball cap worn backwards. He also wore thick glasses and would need a mask enhancement.

Shortly before nine o'clock, they took off in the forty-one foot Barry Bones, headed due West. Ned deposited his mug in the galley downstairs and then took a seat up front next to Madison, avoiding the loud twin diesels at the rear. Travis sat next to Noonan on the bridge, watching the scanners logging the depth of the Bay. It took nearly five miles out before the floor dropped below thirty feet, and quickly, they were in much deeper waters.

Nearly an hour after leaving shore, they came upon a red buoy bobbing in the relatively calm blue waters of the Gulf. Noonan dropped anchor and turned off the engines well in advance of the marker. He had been showing Travis the debris field ahead that led to the barge they were going to explore.

"You're going to have to swim in a ways to get to the main hull. I didn't want to disturb it when we dropped anchor."

The four of them congregated in the galley table so Noonan could share the pictures he'd brought.

"Here's what the barge looked like new. The *Regina Cubana*. It slept nearly twenty-five men, and had a regular run all over the Cuban and Florida coastline. But who we're looking for is Otis. He was the cook's dog. That mutt had traveled all over the Caribbean, but they lived in Cuba, and that's where the cook signed on. Never traveled without the dog."

"You said it was the dog's collar we're after?" asked Ned.

"Yes, and I have a picture of it." Noonan scrambled through a folder of maps and pictures, magazine clippings. He pulled out a drawing of a necklace around the neck of a pretty island girl. It appeared to have jewels encrusted around the choker with a cross dangling in the center.

"That's no dog collar," gasped Madison.

"No, it's not. And apparently, the gems are nearly worthless, except that they are old and have history. It was a piece of costume jewelry created for the governor's wife to wear when she was out in the countryside. It was a replica of the real thing that is in a British maritime museum in Antigua. Story has it that this was the mistress' slave girl, and when the woman died, she left her the fake. The family, of course, inherited the real one. She was our cook's wife, but not for very long. When she passed, our man took to the sea with his favorite mutt, Otis, who didn't mind wearing this thing around his neck on all the voyages he went on. This dog and the collar were considered to be good luck to the men who worked the barge."

"How will we find something like that?"

"It's platinum and probably glass, if any of it remains. Our metal detector will pick up whatever's left. Of course, it will look like a pile of rocks," said Noonan. "It won't resemble anything in this picture. You'll have to use your imagination. Two hundred years under water does things. It will be full encased in hardened rock and coral."

"Were they hauling anything valuable?" asked Travis.

"Probably not, at least not what was listed on the manifest. There were three survivors who managed to escape in a small rowboat, who told the stories."

"Who hired you?" asked Ned.

"A family in North Carolina traced their ancestry to this woman, the former slave girl, and got permission to petition the estate for our dive. They want the collar. It's worthless other than the sentimental value of it. And we're given some rights to items we find worth less than five hundred dollars, but everything has to be catalogued first. And no human remains, no bones or anything that would destroy their graves. Understood?"

"After all these years, you won't find any remains," said Ned.

Noonan chuckled. "Depends on what fell on top of them. I've seen some things that would scare the liver out of you. Bodies floating to the surface after several hundred years under water, if the conditions of the wreck are right. They just melt into the sea by the time they get close to the surface. Really weird stuff."

Madison had a disgusted look on her face.

"Most of what was being transported when the freak hurricane hit was perishable: Grain, molasses, honey, and some lumber from Cuba on its way to up near the panhandle. It was a little too far offshore for most those who survived the sinking to be able to swim to safety, unfortunately."

"Did they carry passengers?" asked Travis.

"Not listed. But back then, there were always stowaways. This was fifty years before the Civil War, the slave trade was still going strong, but there were runaways. Who knows who could have been on board? The accommodations would not be very deluxe, even for the captain."

Travis and Ned suited up as Noonan helped Madison with her equipment. She strapped her extra tank to a belt around her waist. Noonan asked Travis to man the metal detector. All three of them tested the battery-operated com system and would do so again once in the water. They would be going with a long dive line so Noonan could signal them if he needed them to surface. The Bones didn't have anything more sophisticated than that. There wouldn't be any small submersibles sending pictures up top.

Ned followed Madison and Travis into the water. They adjusted their face masks and tested the com, gave the thumbs-up to Noonan, and, one by one, descended into the warm water of the Gulf and into the deep.

Madison's bright pink fins were easy to spot, her long legs slowly pedaling her forward and down into the darker water. Lack of silt made everything clear, sending down shards of light from the surface. Varieties of colorful small fish curiously hung around them. He could see several sparkling particles floating, catching the sun's rays before they descended further. The temperature of the water was much cooler, but still not as cold as he expected.

The image of Madison's shapely form was something Ned liked watching as they continued their descent. He was hopeful for what lay below and the promise of recovering objects long lost. He savored the recreational aspect of their adventure. No bad guys coming after them. No worries about being detected or having a malfunction with their rebreathers. It was just a pleasurable journey into the unknown with someone who was also an unknown factor in his life.

Of all the things he thought he would be doing, this wasn't one of them. He was following a mermaid in a turquoise wetsuit with pink fins. But, unlike his father, he was going on a treasure dive.

For a dog collar.

CHAPTER 12

T RAVIS REACHED THE floor first and began swishing the lighted detector over the debris field as Madison and Ned caught up to him. She knew from prior salvage dives that often the more experienced divers were the first to get down to a site, looking for the easy finds. This was different. It was going to have to be a meticulous combing of the area, identifying the spots they'd come back to and inspect further. Sort of like an archeological survey. She'd brought her waterproof camera and started taking pictures of areas Travis lingered on.

He found some tracings and pointed down to several mounds of reddish-brown rocks less than a foot tall. Madison shot several photos of the area and moved on.

Ned's flashlight was wider and threw out more light than the ones Travis and Madison had. She gave him a thumbs-up when he located what appeared to be a hole several feet deep and about twenty feet wide. It looked like a crater of some kind.

She dove in after Ned and took pictures. The sides of the crater looked like the frayed edges of a basket. Pieces of metal and crusted timbers long gone lay strewn around the floor. Madison catalogued everywhere Ned illuminated. She stayed close by his side.

"What do you think made this?" she asked into the com.

"Looks like a blast to me. Not sure if it was something dropped from the surface or internal, but it looks more recent than the wreck itself, if that's what we've found."

She nodded her head.

"Hey, guys, we definitely need to get back here," they heard Travis call out.

Travis was hovering over a debris field that mounted up nearly twenty feet. At the ocean floor, they found the remnants of a ship's anchor that was protruding from the sand nearly three feet, with a point fashioned at the end of the curved tip. Next to it was a concreted tube, appearing to be part of a cannon, also buried in the sand floor.

"That definitely didn't come from a barge," said Ned.

"Neither of them did. That's the shape of some of the galleon's anchors I've seen," said Travis.

The two objects were firmly planted in the seabed and did not budge.

"Noonan's going to have kittens over these. Make sure you get some great shots, Maddie," said Travis.

"Go check out that crater behind us, Travis. Tell me what you think," asked Ned.

On his way past them, Madison heard Travis say, "Make sure you take pictures of that wall of debris, Madison. See if you can find an inscription on either piece. Noonan is going to blow his mind when he sees this."

"I'm on it." She dove closer. Ned's light made a wide arc as her hands smoothed over the pitted surface of the cannon. She spotted a reddish pile knee-high to one side. She asked for light, then took pictures of all of it.

"You see anything?" Ned asked.

"No, but Noonan will look these up. I don't think he expected our barge to be anywhere close to another ship. Maybe it crashed on top of it."

"And that pile looks like cannonballs."

"I was thinking the same thing. Red means iron, right?" she asked.

"Yup. Noonan said a year later someone came in to recover what they could from the barge. They would have seen this stuff too. It must have moved during storm seasons."

"It does look like something had been dragged through this area. See the shape?"

She pointed out to him.

Ned nodded, giving her another thumbs-up.

"Let's look at the cannon," Madison said as they heard Travis behind them.

"Hey, guys, you got pictures of the insides of that thing?" he asked, meaning the crater.

Madison nodded.

"That's not a blast. That's a salvage suck. Somebody's been working on this site, or tried to. Some of these commercial salvage operations use those power vacuums. I think that's what was started there."

"You see anything small enough we can bring to the surface?" asked Ned.

"I wanna come back down with the nets," said Travis. "Over there, I picked up metal. You could bring up one or two of those smaller stones, and we can have a look."

Madison tried to pry loose a couple of the tiny mounds no larger than the size of an orange, choosing the darker colored ones, but couldn't dislodge it. Ned assisted with his knife until they broke one free. He pointed to the surface, and everyone nodded agreement. They tugged on the dive line three times, indicating they were ascending. Noonan tugged back his acknowledgement.

Slowly, the three of them ascended, taking turns to examine the small rock. Madison carefully peeled off soft debris then handed it back to Travis.

"You want to be careful, Maddie. Some of these attached sea skeletons can be sharp," Ned informed her.

In their hand-over hand maneuvers up the line, her arm got hooked inside Ned's left. One of his hands accidentally brushed her backside. One pink fin swished the side of his thigh. She felt his hand on the back of her waist when they neared the surface. The gesture was more than telling her she could go up first.

As she reached the ladder, Ned began removing her fins, one by one, his gentle fingers gliding around and under her heel to release her foot from the plastic form. He was careful, measured, and very, very slow, much slower than he needed to be, going out of his way not to cause her any pain or discomfort at all. With her heart racing, she watched his dedication to her safety and noted his huge hands tenderly gripping her ankle. When he was done, he looked up at her and gave her feet a squeeze. He tucked the fins beneath his arm and then removed his own and climbed the ladder behind her.

Up top, Travis was describing to Noonan what they'd seen. Madison was barely paying attention. She felt her backside warmed by the heat of a very powerful man standing behind her, barely touching, but pressing a towel to her neck and shoulders. She unzipped the front of her suit several inches, as if needing to breathe. Ned's hand grazed her hip as he turned over control of the towel to her, squeezing her shoulder through the cotton. He set down the fins and pulled off his facemask.

Still with her back turned to him, she had difficulty removing her mask. Part of her braid on one side had gotten entangled in the rubberized collar. Ned's fingers slid up her neck, pulling the material away from her skin, stretching it and pulling it off her skull smoothly until she was free.

She turned to say thank you, but he'd already started hosing off both their masks and fins with fresh water. His suit was unzipped nearly to his waist. His rippled abs were difficult not to notice. When he peeled down the upper layer of the suit, his huge bare shoulders dwarfed her. His sculpted and tanned torso took her breath away as she followed the lines of his magnificent body to where the suit remained just below his waist.

She put the towel to her face, inhaling deeply, and then squeeze-dryed her braids one by one.

Noonan was ecstatic. "Madison! Show me the pictures, girl!"

Ned leaned across her, his arm touching her frontside, picked up the camera and tossed it to the captain.

"You good?" he said as he smiled down at her. "Everything okay now?"

"Yes, thank you. I get that sometimes. So anxious to get that mask off my face, I sometimes get my hair caught."

"We wouldn't want that now, would we?" he said, his palm brushing down the braid behind her right ear.

She was putty in his hands and tried desperately not to show it.

"I think it's a panic thing." She shrugged and tried to be casual, but she knew he saw right through it.

Noonan was having kittens. "I can't believe it. Oh my God! Oh my God!" he said over and over again.

"So what do you think about the suck hole?" Travis asked him.

"That hole's at least a year old. You'd see some sharp lines in the sand if it was this season. This whole place has been rocked by the weather, most of it for decades. But I'm going to have to do a little research to make sure no one's made a claim. I don't want to get myself or the estate into trouble."

"What does that mean?" asked Ned.

"Means I have to inquire about the claims in this area. I didn't look for a salvage claim. I was mainly worried about some of this being a registered historical site, since the barge was well known and had already been salvaged and left with no value declared. But no one filed anything for it since way back in the 1880s. I'm going to have to dig around for a day and see what I can find back in Tampa."

"Can we go back down?" Travis asked.

"Let's not draw attention to it. I'm pulling the buoy, too. We don't want to say anything until I get my research done."

"Damn it," said Travis.

"And you make sure to keep your mouth shut, too, son. No barking off your mouth to any of your friends I tried to hire. Understood?"

"I got it! You can trust me!" Travis said, holding his hand over his heart.

"So now what?" Madison wanted to know. She was standing perpendicular to Ned and could still feel the warmth from his body. He could have distanced himself, sat down, or started to put away the equipment, but he remained there.

"We can grab a bite. I got some breakfast burritos I'll microwave up and let's talk. Then I'm going to head back in. You guys can stay, if you want!" Noonan said with a grin.

Everyone chuckled.

"Ned, would you wind up the dive line and Travis, will you kill that buoy?"

"Yessir," they both said.

"Madison, help me in the kitchen, would you?"

She followed Noonan down the ladder, at the last minute looking up to watch Ned winding the plastic dive line around from his elbow to up over his wrist and into his hand with the other one leading the way. He was staring right back down on her without a smile, and again, her heart raced.

The small space made it impossible not to rub up against everyone. Madison was used to this on many of the dives she'd been on, but this time, with the presence of this one big guy who she guessed was about six-five, the space seemed half the size.

As directed, she sliced fresh fruit and lay down a platter in front of Travis and Ned, who were waiting. Noonan asked her to slip in across from Ned, and he brought beers and a couple sodas, sliding in next to her. When the microwave went off, he added half a dozen breakfast burritos and a tamale, which he chose. He returned with plastic forks and paper towels.

The food was good. But distracting was the fact that her knees touched the front of Ned's, and he wasn't moving. Neither made eye contact, but from the side, she knew he was having a hard time containing a grin. The frown creasing the bridge of his nose was artificial, self-made. When he spread his knees to the sides, it allowed her more room, until he closed his legs against hers, trapping her gently. He was messing with her again. She had not picked up any of this in the brief time she'd gotten to know him.

Noonan was scanning through the pictures she'd taken. "See that?"

Travis spoke up. "We did. We're thinking iron? Like cannon balls?"

"Looks like it to me." He enlarged the picture of the anchor and then the cannon. "No forge marks?"

"I didn't find any weld marks either. Just a couple feet of it sticking out of the floor. That would give some indication of age, right?"

"A mark would be best, but based on what I've seen, the shape of this tip could have come from a smaller anchor. Sometimes the galleons had several, depending on the depth and the weather."

"This is way more exciting than a dog collar," said Travis, his mouth full of beans and eggs.

"You be sure to watch your mouth, kid. I mean it." Noonan pointed directly at the young man's nose. "I'll kick your butt if you breathe a word."

"Hey, I got it. No problem here. How long before you know?"

"That depends on what I find," Noonan blurted out.

THE RIDE BACK was longer. Noonan didn't want to retrace his exact same course in case he was being tracked. They stopped several times for a quick swim in the warm water. Madison stripped down to the tank suit she had on under her wetsuit. It wasn't brand new, but it was a lovely shade of rose-red and knew it showed off every curve of her body. She did water wheels in the warm water, swam several long strokes back and forth, and enjoyed the sun. Ned swam along next to her and back, never far away. Noonan and Travis watched from the boat, in a private conversation.

At last, Noonan made a hard turn east and back to the boatyard.

The awkward moment finally came upon them as Noonan slowed the Bones and turned over the bumpers while Travis and Ned allowed the graceful insertion, tying her off.

Noonan placed Madison's camera in his duffel added the object, which was staining everything red and muddy despite being wrapped in a towel. He wiped down the bridge and then connected the electronics from the pier.

Ned walked alongside her as she held her wet suit over one arm, swinging her pink flippers back and forth as they traversed the gardens of the club in silence. Noonan had told them not to expect to go out tomorrow, so that left the calendar wide open. She had three glorious days off where no one expected her. Ned was here on vacation, at Noonan's beck and call. It was all lining up to be something more than a treasure dive.

At the edge of the parking lot, Ned placed his palm at the side of her face.

"I had a good time. I'd like to take this a little farther if you're willing, Madison."

That was a good line. Not cheesy. Not practiced. Could Ned be one of the last really good guys? Could she ever live with herself if she didn't give whatever it was he was offering a try?

The answer to that was no.

She dropped her fins and pack the same time his other hand came up to her face. She held her breath while he slowly arched down, touched her lips gently with his and then pulled back. She didn't discourage him, instead wrapping one arm around his waist and letting her fingers search up his back to pull him down to her. He exhaled and pressed against her mouth in a deep, exploratory kiss.

She was glad she'd taken hold of his waist or else she would have been washed out to sea.

CHAPTER 13

I T HAD BEEN years since Ned had felt the kind of urgency he had this afternoon. It just wasn't his style. He was good at going slow, taking his time, showing respect for the lady if he had designs on her. But the truth was, he'd never met that many women he urgently wanted to be with. Not like Madison. Not the way he felt today. Something pulled at him in ways he'd never felt before. Sex was never just sex for Ned, and that's why it hadn't come up that often during his first years in the Navy, even when everyone else was going out getting laid just to be doing it. Intimacy was about sharing something special with someone else, not blindly slapping thighs and getting it on like an animal.

But today, he wanted all of it—the sex, the talking with his fingers, exploring with his body in non-verbal ways he'd never done before.

The attraction he felt for Madison came clear out of the blue, taking over. He watched her drive, watched as the wind blew her blonde hair off her face. He couldn't focus on anything else.

He toyed with her hair, interfering with her driving and making her laugh. With that bit of encouragement, he separated her long braids and combed her long locks with his fingers. He slid as close to her as he could, then kissed her ear, pressing her hair behind, then delicately kissed her neck. Her soft moan urged him on. He felt her pulse quicken where he kissed her. She gripped the steering wheel tightly.

By the time they arrived at her cottage, her shorts were unzipped and hanging off one hip. His pants were sliding so much he was practically bunny hopping the few steps to her front door. He kicked off his canvas slip-ons and tore off his shirt, watching her slide those shorts down slowly in a tease. She slipped her shirt over her head and walked slowly, one foot in front of the other, to where he was pinned on the couch, desperately trying to get his khakis off without showing her his red, white and blue shorts.

She kneeled over him, her breasts ripe and tasting sweet, all puckered and full as he played with her. His hands gripped her ass and squeezed, causing her to moan and lean into him as he buried his face in her chest.

"Do we have anything?" he asked. "I didn't—"

She slowly shook her head. "Sorry, but I'm on the pill."

"Should we wait?"

She slowly shook her head again.

His fingers slipped under her lap, rimming her opening. She raised one hip, stared at him with her azure blue eyes, balanced herself on his tip, and then pulled herself down on him.

The feeling of joining with her was exquisite. With her hands braced on his shoulders, she bounced up and down on him, sometimes looking down and touching his shaft where he entered her. Her breathing grew heavy as he stretched and slid along the sides of her sex, pushing in places, rubbing in others. Between each thrust, they watched each other, registering how right and beautiful it felt, their bodies mated as one.

He adjusted his hips to soar up and into her, sending her higher on his lap, deepening his penetration of her channel, driving her into little ripples of pleasure. She answered his thrusts by squeezing her internal muscles, and each time, he grew bigger, wanted her harder and faster.

She clutched her breasts, arched back, and begged for him to take her again. She lifted her right knee, and he helped her rise up, only for her to come crashing down on him. Up and down she used her leg to give traction, riding him, sheathing him in her warm juices, all the while asking for more. Her pink lips sucked his. Her little mewling sounds whispered into his ear nearly drove him over the edge. His hands explored the soft moistness beneath her breasts, squeezing her nipples and then hungrily plunged his tongue into her mouth.

He felt her heart beating frantically as their undulations continued, and then she started to shatter. He removed his hands from her backside and held her face watching the ecstasy fall like a wave across her cheeks and lips. Her eyes fluttered. She inhaled, her body burning with her desire. He stilled so she could feel the full force and power of her beautiful orgasm and kissed her neck until her breathing slowed and she opened her eyes.

Those blue eyes hooked everything he had inside. He was far from done with her. The edges of her lips curled. Her pink lips pouted again as she kissed him.

"Nice," he whispered. "This is so nice. I could do this all night."

Her smile got crooked as she continued her undulations. Her fingers ringed his shaft and they both looked down at their joining. She leaned into him, and then leaned back as he held on, squeezing her buttocks.

He was frustrated he couldn't get deep enough. She rode his groin as he thrust, pumping furiously, then holding her hips tight against him as he rammed himself deep with quick motions.

Her arms wrapped around his neck, her legs wide at the sides, so he picked her up and carried her into the bedroom, still fully seated inside her.

Her bed was covered with pillows like a field of flowers. With one sweep of his arm he sent the pillows flying except one pink heart. He lay her down tenderly and tucked it under that beautiful ass of hers, propping her pelvis up until fully available to him. The pink lips of her sex opened before him like petals as he played with her bud and got her writhing on the bed. He bit the inside of her thigh, traced her opening with his thumb, and then pressed her nub before slipping two fingers inside her. She moaned, arching backward. He moved her knee over in front of her, spread her cheeks and entered her from the side, holding her belly with his palm and pressing her against him. He thrust deep, pressing hard.

Her breathing became ragged. Her hands flew up, covering her face as her sweet lips called to him.

"Yes. Oh please."

He felt her loss of control as she began to shudder. He quickened his movements, expanding the crescendo overtaking her body. He added to the fire of her climax by pulling out and lapping her juices. Her fingers gripped his shoulders as he drank from her, flicked her bud with his tongue back and forth, and lazily inserted two fingers. She went wild, gripping the sheets at her sides and rocking up and down into his face.

He was getting close to orgasm himself. She spread her lips, massaging her own nub, then brought his face down on her, before drawing him up to her and locking him in a deep kiss. She angled her pelvis until his shaft was snagged on her opening again, and with one more thrust, he was inside again furiously pumping.

He was getting harder, his girth expanding. He moved back and forth against her as she moaned, shook and squeezed him inside.

He flipped her over and entered her from behind, hoisting her hips up into him as he pressed, pushing all the way to his hilt and holding her there until he could feel her insides fluttering again, milking his shaft.

He slid the pillow under her belly, kissed her shoulder, and fondled her bud with his right hand until she started to moan again. His hip movements were fast, getting faster.

"Is this how you like it, Maddie?" he whispered in her ear.

"God yes! Don't stop." She reached back and squeezed his left butt cheek.

"I have no intention of stopping."

He altered the pace, slowing, kneeling back and letting her change positions again so that they were facing one another. His fingers lazily snaked through her scalp as he explored the beauty of her face. He placed her legs up over his shoulders and began the long rhythmic way home, the slow penetrations gradually getting faster and faster until at last he felt her muscles clamp down on him and he reflexively burst inside her, plunging and spilling, filling her with everything he had as her head tossed from side to side. She gasped, pressing his buttocks against her and then held him there.

Her arms flapped to the sides like a rag doll. Ned covered them with his own, clutching her fingers between his and resting his head against her chest as he caught his breath. Her soft body, tanned and lithe, drew out of him all the monsters of loneliness and his thirst for relevance.

He knew he wasn't done fucking her. It would be food for his soul, watching her come, seeing the way her breasts shook in the late afternoon sun, exploring all the places where the delicate fine hairs on her body lay like gold against her flesh. He craved to bring her to the edge again and again, and then set her free, feeling the power of his desire for this beautiful woman who had opened up all the parts of himself he'd closed down years ago.

There wasn't any logic to it. He had a need of her that would never be satisfied.

Finally, the sunset was upon them, sending orange fire onto the walls of the bedroom as they watched it set in each other's eyes. He had never found such peace in a woman's arms before. She was quite simply, perfect in every way he could imagine, the answer to all the questions he'd had about the world. He was all in and completely captured.

"Do you like to swim naked in the ocean, Ned?" she whispered.

"Don't think I've ever done it," he answered, tracing her lower lip with his forefinger.

"Would you like to try it? With me?"

"I'll do anything with you, Madison."

"Anything? Isn't that dangerous?"

"No. It used to be, but not any longer. This is right, Madison. You feel it, too, I know."

"I do."

"So if you want to swim in the gulf naked, I'll be right there beside you."

She got up slowly, combing her hair with her fingers. Her long torso, her nude sex, and her perfect-shaped breasts with her pert upturned nipples were a wonder. He held her hand and allowed her to pull him off the bed.

"Hop on," he said, bending over. She climbed his back, holding onto his shoulders and wrapping her legs around his waist. "Blanket, please," he whispered, taking her over to the bed and lowering one knee, so she could pull one of the sheets. "I'm not wanting to get arrested and have to spend a night in jail," he laughed.

"Only if I could be there with you."

With the sheet around her shoulders, he ran through the back door, over the sand dunes and onto the beach. He knew his ass was in full view of the sunset watchers as he ran, the sheet streaming behind them like a cape. She was giggling, laughing and celebrating his run until they hit the water. He let her slide down, picked up the sheet and tossed it onto the sand. Her naked body frolicked in the surf until he caught her and pulled her down and they tumbled in the tiny waves, rolling over and over on the wet sand. He picked her up and threw her over the next wave, then dove in beneath her and brought her up to the top again. He rolled over on his back and kicked, while she worked to keep up with him until they got out to the deeper water.

He held her with one arm around her waist while they both tread water, facing the sunset.

She watched the dying sun, and he watched it in her eyes and face. He'd never been happier. She threw her arms around his shoulders again, pulling her knees up and wrapping them around his torso. Leaning back, he floated with her body on top. One hand stroked her backside from her neck to the top of her thigh.

"Are you sure you weren't born in the ocean? Maybe you're descended from a God."

He liked that thought. "And you are my mermaid, my muse."

"What have we started, Ned?"

"Something better than treasure. Whatever it is, I never want it to end."

"Me neither. Me neither."

It wasn't the water but tears she shed as he kissed her again.

"I like it deep and dangerous," she whispered into his ear.

He felt the space between her thighs, running along the lips of her sex with his forefinger but not penetrating. "Right up to the edge, Maddie, and then I'll save you. I'll get you in the middle of danger. Then I'll go in deep and save you every time."

She clung to him as he paddled back toward the shore and quickly retrieved the sheet to protect their nakedness. Together, they walked back to the cottage. He heard a couple of people clapping. Someone else shouted something he couldn't quite hear.

He looked down at her. "Did we make a stir?"

"I think so," she whispered back. "But I think they liked it."

As they got to the back door, he picked her up and carried her into the bathroom. "Time for a hot shower and shampoo. All I can say, Maddie, is your neighbors better get ready, because I'm just getting started."

CHAPTER 14

THEY STAYED IN bed the entire next day. Only thing that was part of her normal routine was the coffee in the morning, which she brought to him. He barely let her drink hers.

They ate fruit when they were hungry, sipped some white wine she had opened in the refrigerator, and munched on some cheese and almonds, but mostly the day was about sex. The natural way their bodies worked together was thrilling.

Ned kissed her. "That's what I love about you. It's fresh, honest. You don't hide anything."

"Well, I wouldn't go that far!"

"I know it's true because I'm the same way. I've never met anyone like you, Madison. Never."

"Kiss me, Ned."

He kissed her lips, her eyelids, her neck under both ears, the palms of her hands, and then back to her lips.

"I want us to stay like this, always," he whispered as his hand smoothed over her hip and thigh, back and forth. He dipped his head and kissed her breast. "Connected, feasting on each other," he said as he angled his head, pulling her hair back behind her ear. "Touching the treasure of your golden body."

His tenderness moved her. She let the backs of her fingers sweep across his cheek. She'd always fallen for the bad boys. The strays in life. What was that all about? Always trying to heal someone broken.

There wasn't a single thing about Ned that was broken.

She'd been thinking about her conversation with her mother and decided to bring it up.

"I figured out something, Ned."

"What?"

She propped herself up on her elbow, the sheet wrapped around her body. Ned pulled it back with his forefinger because it was blocking his view.

"Go on," he said after he kissed and nuzzled her nipples thoroughly.

"I think my mother was in love with your father."

He stopped.

"Your father is the *someone special* who perhaps broke her heart."

"You think so?" He was still kissing her chest.

"The pieces all fit. He comes out here to do a salvage with Noonan and meets her. They fall in love, but then he tells her he's married. He went back to California to be with your mother. Did you know that?"

Ned sat up, frowning. "He cheated on my mother?"

"I'm thinking so. My mother said this special person was a friend of Noonan's, and he went back to California to be with his wife. She told me he honored her by keeping his promise to his wife."

"Meaning if he'd have met your mother first and not second, you'd have been my sister, not my lover?"

She hit him with a pillow. "That's not funny."

"I think it's hilarious. Now the old bastard is somehow responsible for me finding you too. I can't get away from this jerk."

She hugged his back. "Ned, consider that he was a different person then. Don't you remember anything good about him? Anything at all?"

"He kept to himself. My biggest problem was that he wasn't very affectionate to my mom. I don't remember when that happened. But she loved something about him."

"Everyone deserves that," she said, rubbing his upper arm with her hand, back and forth. "Consider what my mother told me. He honored *her* with the right decision. He did the right thing. He was married. He never came back."

"But why, Madison? If he loved her?"

"Because he could put it aside to do the right thing. Maybe he did it for you. Have you ever thought about that?"

She considered perhaps she'd burdened him with too much talk about the past. Maybe Ned's father always expected to come right back into her mother's house one day if and when his wife was taken first. But it happened the other way around. Fate made him an honorable man.

At the cost of his soul.

It was just a theory, though. Madison had never met the man nor Ned's mother. But there was something in Ned's DNA that brought him back to Florida, and yes, perhaps his father had paved the way.

"Have I upset you?" she asked, rubbing the tops of his shoulders and squeezing the nape of his neck.

"I don't want to be mothered. I don't want your help, if that's what you're asking."

She was surprised at his tone.

"Explain."

He turned on the bed, crossed his legs, and faced her. "Madison, this is my life. This is your life. It has nothing to do with the past. This is about the here and now, about us, and what we make of it. I don't need to think about the past. I don't need to know or even suppose all this is connected like some cosmic mystery. My mind doesn't work that way. I don't worry about the choices I made or what my dad did. It has nothing to do with me. That was his life."

He couldn't see the blind spot that was the size of the Titanic, the flaw in his thinking. But she saw it, and to herself she heard the truth.

Everything is always connected. It's one big circle.

There was the cook who took his little dog, Otis, on a voyage. The cook's wife wore the necklace that was a gift of the governor's wife. The family of that woman wanted to find that necklace, lost at the bottom of the Gulf at Treasure Island, where her mother and his father were once lovers. It *was* all connected.

It would be hard to prove this to him, and perhaps he didn't need that. But just like love, she couldn't prove it existed, but she knew it was real.

CHAPTER 15

NOONAN CALLED A meeting of the crew. Madison took Ned back to his place so he could put on some fresh clothes.

"Just move out," she said. "Stay with me. It's only for a few more days. Maybe you'd decide to stay here."

Looking up at her while he rummaged through his duffel, he was tempted to tell her what she obviously wanted to hear. Heck, he wanted to say it, too. But something was clouding the back of his mind, and until he figured it out, he wasn't going to commit.

There's that logic creeping back in.

It was almost like he was two separate men. One made careful, slow decisions, and now he had spawned this other Ned—the impulsive one who would throw away anything to be with her. And he barely knew her.

His logic side won out, convinced that if they were meant to be, she'd be patient to wait just a little bit longer until he could settle what was going on inside him.

He held his arms out to the sides, still seated on the bed. "Come here, Madison."

She sat in his lap, her legs stretching over his thighs with her right arm wrapped around his shoulder.

"Time for a little talk."

He could feel her tense.

"No, not *that* kind of a talk. There's no question you and I have made this connection and that we were destined to find each other. It makes no sense at all, but it's true. But it's like we're setting out on this journey in a dinghy. We're talking about the ocean here. Unless you were talking about some beach or vacation romance, and for the record," he leaned over and planted a soft kiss on her lips, "I'm not."

She sighed, pressing the side of her face against his. "I ache so bad for you, Ned. Don't scare me like that."

"Hey!" He turned her head by tipping her chin. "I need this. I want this, Madison. I've just arrived here, and my whole life has changed. I can forget about it when we're in bed together. I want it to last forever. But I can't wish away what my past is. What my job is. And you wouldn't want me to anyway."

It broke his heart that he could feel hers pumping so fiercely, and not because of her feelings for him, but because she was afraid. He realized he was too. And there it was again, that past. Just like his father, he was caught in two worlds, two realities. Ned didn't want to make the choice his father did, not only because it was his father's way, but because he wanted to have it all. And that's what he hadn't figured out yet.

She began to stand, and he knew she was frustrated again. He grabbed her arm and brought her back to his lap. "Trust me, Madison. I'm slow. I don't do things like this. God help me, but I think about things maybe too much, but it's also who I am and how I've been trained. But I always figure it out eventually. What I want to give you is more than a couple of fun days in bed and some sexy time at the beach. I want to give you so much more."

She hugged him, kissed his ear, and whispered, "Don't take too long, Ned. Don't break my heart."

"Never," he whispered back as he held her tight. "If I come walking through your door with all my stuff, I'm never leaving."

Her blue eyes teared up.

"I'm like that guy in the movie who found a mermaid and tried to take her home. In the end, he had to let her go to save her life."

"Her name was Madison."

"Really? I didn't know that. You are my mermaid. But ours is a different story."

Their kiss was deep. The feel of her tears brushing against his cheek, he took as her honest gift. She trusted that he wouldn't break her heart, and he'd keep that promise. But he didn't want to live one life and wish he'd lived another. He couldn't do that to her.

"I have something for you," he said as he stood, holding her with his arm around her waist. "Close your eyes." His impulsive side had completely taken over, and Ned let him rip.

She did as was told. Digging around in his bag, he found the book of poetry, which he'd go over with her later, then found the velvet bag with the pendant in it. He unclasped it and placed it around her neck. He was fully aware of the valuable gift he was bestowing on a near-stranger. Except she wasn't really a stranger. And maybe the mermaid his father had fallen in love with was gone, but Ned's mermaid was here, in front of him.

She held her fingers to the pendant and opened her eyes without being told. Turning to see herself in the dresser mirror, he placed his hands on her shoulders. With his face next to hers, he whispered, "He found this here. I'm returning it to where it belongs. I think it was really meant for you."

Her shocked expression and the floodgate of tears warmed him.

"I can hardly see it through my tears, Ned. Oh, it's priceless!"

"He was with Noonan when they found this. He used to wear it all the time, and I resented him for not giving it to my mother."

He turned her to face him, cupping her face between his hands. "He used to say all the time that he'd had a secret love with a mermaid. I think he intended that I give it to mine."

"But your mother—"

"Never claimed ownership. She wouldn't have worn it, ever. My mother had all the rest of him."

She turned back to look at herself again. "It's the most precious thing I've ever owned, Ned. But with all your family history, are you sure? I don't want to take a family heirloom."

He chuckled. "Oh, but I've been thinking about what you'd look like with it on for the past day. It's just a pendant. I already gave you my heart."

Noonan's phone call interrupted their kisses.

"Yes, Boss?"

"Where the hell are you guys? I've been waiting here for a half hour, dammit. We have things we need to go over, and right away."

"Got it. We'll be right there."

"I'm assuming you're with Madison 'cause she didn't pick up, either."

"You'd be right," he said, smiling at her fingers covering her lips.

"Well, dammit, get your clothes on and get down right away."

"You got it."

He shrugged. Her eyes were still sparkling, remnants of her tears collecting in the sides of her eyes.

"Duty calls." He pulled her against him. "But I can't wait to fulfill all those dreams I had about you wearing only this as I watched you call my name." He brushed the hair back from her face, kissed her forehead, and did a quick change while she looked on.

On their way out, Ned noticed a skinny dog sleeping on the deck outside the back door. If he'd had more time, he'd have fed the poor animal. But before he could make it out of the doorway, he reconsidered.

"Just a sec. I saw something I just have to take care of."

"What?" she asked.

Ned pulled down a can of beef stew he'd bought, emptied it into a dish, then filled a small plastic bowl with water, and gave it to Madison.

At the door, the dog lifted up his head and began to skitter off toward the beach.

"Here you go, boy. I've got some food for you," he said, extending the bowl toward the scrawny animal. He laid it down and took Madison's bowl, setting the water beside it before backing away. He stepped inside the living room, closing the door.

The two of them watched as the dog sniffed the food and then started gulping it down. Ned could see the ribs on the side of the mutt and wondered if a previous owner living here had left him behind. He was heartened that the dog ate.

"Aww. Poor thing. I'm so glad you fed him. I can't imagine how some people treat their pets," she said.

"I'll get some regular food maybe tonight. See if he comes back. But that should do him some good now."

Ned was happy he'd solved his conscience. The brownish mutt looked up at him with warm brown eyes and licked his nose. The bowl was empty.

It made him proud to be that kind of a man.

"JESUS FUCKIN' CHRIST," Noonan said, checking his watch. "Don't they teach you to be on time? You start all your missions like forty minutes late?" he barked at Ned.

They had agreed to meet at Flamingo Pete's, a crusty bar up the road in Indian Shores. Ned understood Noonan was trying to be stealth about his new find.

Travis had a stupid expression on his face and had devoured a plate of French fries. Noonan didn't even ask if anyone wanted to eat.

"What did you find out?" Ned asked, not addressing Noonan's dig.

They were seated at a high table off in the corner near the parking lot. Traffic noise made listening difficult, but Ned knew it was chosen for that reason.

"I got a friend who does these subcontracts out to bigger dive companies. They hire him when they get a good lead. Otherwise, he goes out on his own. He said there was a buzz about ten years ago about something, but he looked into it and can't find a claim. I don't want to show my face around the office. I tried Googling the area and can't find a damned thing. But ten years ago? I mean there wasn't that much out there. At least not on this coast.

"He checked archeological sites, not just pleasure dives?"

"He did. Looked up all the bigs and couldn't find anything. He was going to go back to the office on Monday to do some additional digging around, but we have a couple of choices."

They waited.

"We can file a claim, like the family did for the salvage. I mean, we have a right to be there. But we're supposed to let the State of Florida know what we suspect we've found. On the other hand, we could also tell the estate what we found on their dime, so to speak. I mean, it's a grey area."

"Who are they?" Madison asked.

"From North Carolina. Some businessman there owns furniture stores or something. I dealt with their attorney."

"So you're diving for people you don't really know?" asked Ned.

"Hey! May I remind you that you're in the same boat!"

"But I assumed—" Ned began to protest.

"You know what they say about that word. Look, we have to make a decision."

"What if we go back down there this weekend, look around, and then wait until your friend gets more information on Monday?" suggested Madison.

"We could. I mean, we are legally allowed to be there," Noonan answered.

"Let me get this straight. What you're saying is that there's the proper way, and then there's a smart way," added Ned.

"Yes. And either way could be dangerous. Not for finding a fuckin' dog collar. That was a no-brainer. No problem. But now, if we've found something big, well, people have disappeared over that. And if we report it to the State, there's no guarantee that someone doesn't get tipped off, you know. I mean, I want to trust everyone in government, but Ned, do I have to tell you there are dirty players out there, especially if we're talking about—"

Their waitress appeared, asking for their drink order. Before Ned could decline, Travis ordered a beer. Ned knew Noonan wasn't happy with that. When the waitress went away, he scolded the young diver.

"Shit, Travis. We're trying to be left alone. Just where is your head at?"

Ned's growing concern over Travis as a dive partner was tarnished further. They all searched around them for signs anyone was interested in the foursome, waiting until the beer arrived, and then Ned continued.

"I like Madison's idea. We go look for something concrete first, something we can have verified before we make a claim."

Travis asked, "And what about the red rocks, Noonan? Anything come of them?"

"Mush. It might have been an iron tool of some kind. But it was like red pudding, just fell apart in my hands," said Noonan.

"That's too bad," whispered Madison. "I was hoping for something there."

Ned continued with his question. "What *are* the rules about this sort of thing? I mean, does the fact that you got the permission for the one dive mean that anything as a result of that dive is also theirs?"

"It could. One could argue either way. We were given the authority to keep some artifacts for ourselves, limited to a value of five hundred dollars. So we find a chest, something special, well, you couldn't argue that it was worth less than five hundred, could you?"

Travis suddenly pushed his arm across the table at Madison.

"Where'd you get that?" he said as he pulled the mermaid pendant with the eight coin up from her chest.

Noonan slapped his hand. "You don't touch a lady like that, you dumbass. That's her person and her stuff." He sat back and winked at Ned. There was a reason he didn't want to acknowledge the pendant to Travis, so Ned played along.

Madison was just as smart. "A friend of my mother's gave it to me." She tucked it into her shirt and added, "It's a replica. If it were the real thing, well, would I be wearing it around?"

Travis grinned, "Still a pretty nice piece. It suits you, Madison. I like it."

Ned's concern over their situation grew. He locked eyes with Noonan. He wished the old pirate hadn't included Travis in his findings. Maybe it would be a good idea to surgically remove him from the group, make up something to send him away thinking their find was not really the valuable wreck of a Spanish Galleon. It was all getting sticky.

But Noonan was being honorable to the young diver. "So I agree. We go down one more time, see if we can find anything we can research. And then we'll reassess on Monday after I hear from my buddy."

"I'm cool with that," said Travis.

Madison nodded. She looked at Ned. "Are we in?"

"Hell yeah," Ned answered.

"Okay, it's oh-eight-hundred, same place?" Noonan asked the group, and everyone agreed.

NED AND MADISON stopped at a local pet store and bought a small bag of kibble and some canned food to moisten it up.

"You mind slumming at my place tonight?" he asked her on the way back to his cottage.

"As long as I'm slumming with you, I don't. It does smell a little bit. Do you have any candles?"

"We'll get some."

They stopped at a beach shop where he let Madison pick out three pillars. He also bought some shampoo and shower gel and sweet-smelling hand soap. He knew ladies liked that sort of thing. This pad had never been intended to be a place to entertain her in.

They also bought some ice cream and stopped and ordered Mexican food to go.

The dog wasn't there when they returned. He left the water, but started another dish with the new food he bought, substituting it for the dirty one, before going inside to have their dinner.

Madison set one of the candles on the table between them. She placed another one in the bathroom with the shower gel and soap, and she placed the third one by his bed on the tiny bedside table. He liked watching her work her magic, setting up a stage for the evening, not being shy about what she wanted to do.

They ate without speaking. He was hungrier than he'd thought.

She leaned back, sipping on her beer. "Are you nervous about this?"

"No, not at all. I've made love to a woman before," Ned said with a completely straight face.

She rapid-blinked at the joke. "You know what I mean."

He pulled her hand to him and kissed her palm. "I do. I get your meaning. I'm on your wavelength. Totally." He followed it up with a smile as she put her hand back in her lap.

He picked up the two empty containers, taking them to the trash in the kitchen. "Ice cream?"

"Maybe later?"

"I think you're gonna be busy later. No time for ice cream."

"Depends on how you use it."

He'd opened the gallon lid and was just about to scoop himself a large bite. He stopped mid-air and pointed the spoon at her. "You have a point there. I might need further instruction. Should I bring it into the bedroom then?" He raised his eyebrows like he was waiting for her command.

"No. I have something else in mind, first."

"Okay. She's being all mysterious tonight." He put the lid back on the ice cream and placed the spoon in the sink.

"I'm not being mysterious at all. I just find there are things more important than ice cream. First things first. And then dessert. That's just the way I look at it."

He quickly arrived at her side, pulled her up, and started to remove her blouse.

Behind him, he heard a bark. The dog had finished the plate of food Ned brought him and walked away.

"He says he likes it," said Madison.

"Oh, so mermaids talk to dogs, do they?" he said while he removed her bra and gasped at the look of her breasts with the pendant hanging between them.

"They do."

"What else do they do?

"They have very sensitive fingers," she said as she slipped her hand inside his waistband and grabbed him.

"Oh, sweetheart, you are so right."

"They like deep diving too."

"I can just bet they do." He knelt before her, unzipped her jeans, and pulled her pants down to her knees. He placed his hand on the juncture between her thighs. He rubbed her panties back and forth, curling two fingers to fondle the ridge between her lips. "They love to dive for buried treasure," he said as he exhaled and slipped her panties down over her jeans.

As his fingers breached her swollen lips, he felt her hands on his shoulders. She leaned over, spread her knees, and gave him access. His tongue slid inside her opening. He leaned back and looked up at her.

"Nice. You are so sweet." With one arm under her knees and the other under the small of her back, he picked her up, her jeans still flapping behind. Until he could remove everything.

While he undressed, he watched her position herself back on his bed, prop her little butt under one of his pillows, and fondle the necklace glistening between her nipples.

She squeezed her little rosy pink areolas until they got stiff. She licked her lips. His cock was rock hard and ready. He wasn't going to think about anything else tonight except how many times he could make her come.

There would be time tomorrow for his logical side. But in the meantime, there was a lot of her golden flesh to kiss, to explore.

And there was a whole gallon of ice cream to eat.

CHAPTER 16

TRAVIS AND NOONAN were waiting for them when she and Ned arrived. They were a whole ten minutes early. They'd even had time to take a morning run on the beach. Their stray followed them part of the way then greeted them when they returned. He was left with some food. Neither one of them were able to touch him yet.

Madison's wetsuit and flippers were loaded. Ned grabbed his equipment from the pile Noonan had once again assembled on the pier and checked it.

The morning was a little cooler with fingers of light grey fog stretching out into the gulf like those of a skeleton. No one was out yet, but Sundays were light days, especially for the drinking crowd, Noonan told them.

He let Travis pilot the boat for a bit while he grabbed the two of them, directing them down into the galley for coffee.

"What's up?" Ned asked as he was handed his coffee.

"My guy called me last night and asked if we'd said anything to anybody."

"Uh oh," said Madison. She knew there was the only one place such a leak would come from.

"I knew it, dammit." Ned started grinding his teeth.

"I'm gonna tell my friend to just file a damned claim for us to-morrow. Try to make a mistake on the coordinates and correct them later."

Madison didn't know that was an option. "Aren't you going to confront him?"

"Trouble with all these treasure seekers, they all try to stay secretive. Like pulling teeth to get anything out of my buddy. He just left it at that; it was a rumor."

"Could be the old rumor," Ned added.

"The coincidence is uncanny," Noonan said. "I don't trust him. But then, who would Travis know? He doesn't know anybody. He's not plugged in at all."

Madison disagreed. She knew if there was one rumor it had the potential to get out of control. "You have to find out who he talked to about our dive. Maybe someone knew he was going and got it out of him. Someone could have just been smarter."

"I'm with Madison. I think someone's just fishing."

"Well, I'm going to have a little talk with him when I go up top. Just keep your eyes and ears open. Let me know if you see anything about him that sets you funny," sighed Noonan.

"I wanna search his pack." Ned wasn't kidding.

Madison thought it was an excellent idea.

"Go ahead, but I don't want to know about it, okay?"

"Agreed. Unless I find something."

"I'm going up. Make it quick. I'll make sure he's tied up for ten or so."

After Noonan climbed the ladder, Ned grabbed the diver's backpack and unzipped the large side first. He found a hash pipe and a small tin foil wad in a baggie.

"Fuckin' drugs," he muttered.

"That's not bad, Ned. You should see what people do here," she added.

Ned continued with his search and found a cell phone, a change of shorts, some candy, a soda can, and a small wad of dollars.

"Doesn't look like anything here is out of the ordinary."

Madison unzipped the small bottom pocket and found a sketch-book and black felt tipped pen. She flipped through the pages. Travis was actually a fairly good artist, which surprised her. The last page drawn on was a sketch of the anchor. She held it up to Ned.

"Sonofabitch."

"Might not mean anything. He might not have shown it to anyone," she said.

"It depends where he drew it. I don't like it."

"He doesn't say where it came from. It could have been an illustration from a book, for all anyone knows."

"Why are you defending him?"

"I'm not. I'm just thinking you're getting a little paranoid, that's all."

"You haven't seen the kinds of things out there I have. There are people who will sell their children to get their hands on something that has the potential to make them some money. The world is a very wicked place."

"I know, but don't make things up that don't exist, Ned. This isn't proof he showed anybody."

"But—"

Noonan's booming voice told them to get topside.

A rubber pontoon boat with several divers lay off to their left. The fog had partially obscured them. Madison wondered if they'd followed the group.

"Who are they?" asked Ned.

"I think they're just weekend divers," said Travis.

"How do you know that?" Noonan drilled him. "You know any of the guys over there?"

"I can't tell. But no, I don't think so. I don't know anyone that has an inflatable like that. They're all in black. Look like research grunts to me," answered Travis.

"We're changing course," Noonan said and took over the wheel.

He passed a map to Travis. "Find me something over here," he said pointing to a deep portion of the gulf. "I'm going to pretend we're on our way over there. I don't want them following us."

Travis pointed out the notation of a fishing vessel that sank ten years previous. "We could be doing a recovery dive there."

As Noonan veered left, the boat next to them continued straight ahead, right toward the spot they intended to explore, disappearing into the mist.

"Shit," he muttered under his breath.

But they stuck to their plan, even went so far as to prepare for a dive. Noonan shut the motor down and was preparing to drop the anchor. Travis slipped off his khakis and tee shirt then put the wetsuit on over his underwear. He folded his clothes, leaving them in a plastic cubby, placing his red cell phone on top.

Madison noted that the other phone Ned found in the galley was brown. She held the phone up so Ned would see it. Noonan was perplexed.

Ned picked Travis up under his arms and threw him overboard before he had any of his gear on. The metal detector crashed in behind him.

Travis scrambled to retrieve it. "Hey! What the hell was that for? You asshole. Keep your hands off me."

"Who'd you tell, Travis?" asked Ned, leaning over the boat.

"What do you mean? Tell what?"

"Crank her over, Noonan. Let's see how bad he wants to talk."

Before Noonan could turn the key, Travis was sputtering, screaming, "No!" He swam to climb up the ladder, the metal detector in his left hand. Ned grabbed the machine and then kicked Travis in the chest, sending him backward into the water again.

"Who was it? You're not getting back on this boat until you tell me."

"How the fuck? Oh, come on, Noonan. This guy's wacko."

"Tell him what he wants to know," shouted Noonan.

Travis hit the water with his fist, "Fuck!"

Madison could see no one was going to budge. Noonan edged closer to Ned. "You wanna explain this to me?"

"He's got two cell phones. Either one of them could track us. He has a sketch in his backpack of the anchor."

"All right. Let me explain. Can I come up now?" Travis pleaded.

Noonan helped him up the ladder and threw a towel at him. Ned ran below decks and came up with the other phone, which he held in front of Travis' face.

"They told me to call them when we got to the site. Look, you're gonna file a claim anyway, and you have the right to be there, like you said."

"Who are they, Travis?" asked Noonan.

"They're just kids. Went to high school with them. Look, they don't dive. They don't know what the fuck they're doing."

"So why do they care about the coordinates?" Ned asked.

"I don't know. They just gave me a hundred bucks to do it. That's all. Honest, I didn't tell them anything."

"How did they know then?" he asked again.

"I scored some weed from one of them. I owe him a little bit for it, and I told him I was going to be paid for this dive, and he agreed to wait. When I got back, he was waiting for me, and I told him we were going back, but I didn't have anything for him yet. But I promised I would. When he asked about it, I told him I couldn't talk about it."

Both Ned and Noonan swore at the same time.

"You are a fuckin' idiot, Travis," barked Noonan.

"They aren't connected to any of this stuff. I don't even know if they swim. I do a little bit of drugs with them, nothing bad, a little stuff here and there to take the edge off."

"You don't have anything you need to take the edge off except the occasional thought running through that pea-sized brain about getting a job. You just have to get high until that little 'feeling' goes away. You're off this dive, Travis," yelled Noonan.

Madison didn't know what they would do. If they went back to the dock, tossed Travis, and then went back out, it might attract too much attention.

"We can't risk it. We have to go back." Noonan looked like he could throw everyone overboard; he was so angry.

"I say we go out, but he stays in the boat. Maddie and I can take the gear," said Ned.

"You could come with us, Noonan," Maddie suggested. "Travis can watch the bridge."

"Nope. Not putting my boat in the hands of a kid who did this."

Madison knew he was thinking about it, seriously. Finally, he made a decision.

"Okay, you two go. Travis and I stay up top," Noonan finally mumbled.

"Then let's crank her up. First, we get rid of this." Ned pitched the brown phone as far as he could, where it made a tiny splash and disappeared.

Noonan grabbed Travis' other phone and pitched it as well.

"Hey!" Travis protested.

"So you get a new phone out of me. You get to be the dumbass, and I have to buy you a new fuckin' phone. But I don't trust you with either. Ned, Madison, I want your phones."

"Hold up, I'm not throwing my phone overboard," objected Ned.

"No, I just want to hold on to them to make sure he doesn't give out a signal. That's all."

Travis sulked with his arms crossed over his chest. Noonan started the motor, and Madison watched Ned slip on his wetsuit, sliding the zipper up his front slowly, giving her a wink. He helped her zip up hers and then planted a kiss on her lips.

"Here's to another adventure."

She'd been sure she didn't want to fall for dangerous guys, but what they were going to do was dangerous. She sat next to Ned as the boat turned, heading North East, holding his hand and enjoying the feel of his warmth as their thighs touched.

CHAPTER 17

IF THIS HAD been a mission for work, he'd have a boatload of guys who could probably overtake an oil tanker, subdue the crew, and drive the thing back to port. They even used to joke about it. He had backup and backup for his backup. He'd be properly armed. They'd have some of the best equipment made and all the experience and training necessary to use it.

But this was different. He didn't even have his sidearm. He had his KA-BAR, but a lot of good that would do except punch a hole in that big grey bubble of a speedboat. Noonan's electronic equipment was easily twenty years old, and what had been upgraded had been a patch job. He had wires held together with duct tape. He had cracks in the hull of the boat repaired with some kind of super glue. One of the outboards was smoking, and that worried him, too.

Noonan, while he might have been fit at one time, was not the man he was as a Navy diver. Like his dad, he'd aged. Ned had seen those pictures of the two of them standing together. They had both been rugged and built and could handle long swims, planting explosive devices and helping the Coasties before the drug problem got as bad as it did. They rescued distressed families that had been victimized by pirates and sailors unlucky to be abandoned at sea.

But Noonan wasn't in that shape any longer. He only had one eye, which meant, even if he had a weapon, he wouldn't be reliable. Their third was Travis, who had created the problem in the first place and whose loyalties were questionable.

And then of course there was Madison. She was the fittest person on the team besides him. She had the drive and the smarts. But she'd not been trained, and if anything happened to her, he would never be able to live with himself.

In addition, she was a beautiful woman, eye candy. He had no right getting her into this vulnerable spot.

It was a risk. If the bad guys were anywhere near where they were heading, he'd make sure they turned back and gave up on the search. So his logical side calculated that it was a risk, but perhaps one worth taking. As long as everything looked doable.

Noonan's boat would still outrun the other one. He was used to these waters and the weather was good, except for the mist that was now dissipating. Soon it would be hot. No bad weather in sight, and no clouds even.

He knew how people got hooked on treasure. He'd heard the stories. Like the gold fever was in California during the rush. Kings ransomed their kingdoms for a tulip bulb at one time. There was a chance that they could secure something that could set him up for life. Noonan deserved it too. Even Travis could come away with something. If they did this properly, they might be able to claim their treasure. There were a lot hurdles to climb, but he allowed himself to enjoy the fantasy.

He and Maddie could get a fine house by the beach and just sleep and make love for the first year then figure out the rest of their lives after that. That's what he was going for. That brass ring.

The necklace his dad brought back was proof that fortunes were made out here in the waters off the Florida coast. People had blind luck all the time and went home rich. What were the odds they could start out looking for a dog collar and find the motherlode? They all deserved that shot.

He used Noonan's binoculars to scan the horizon constantly as they traveled. He searched every inch of water, every ocean swell. Much easier to spot another boat when it was calm too. Lots of things made this find a possibility. It was as if the ocean was laying low for them, calling them to come take her, plunder her wealth and then spend the rest of his life worshiping her.

Noonan raised his eyebrows, and Ned shook his head.

Travis looked bored, leaning on one arm and then sulking and finally falling asleep.

Noonan checked with him one more time. Ned stood this time, scanned the whole gulf in a three-sixty as the boat slowed. Noonan was paying attention to his coordinates, watching the underwater topography dancing in green outline.

He joined Noonan at the bridge. "I don't see a thing. We have a perfect day for this too," he told his father's friend.

"Thanks, Son." He killed the motor and glanced over at Travis who threw over his light anchor while the winch released the other one, which hit bottom at seventy-five feet.

"You see anybody, you let us know. Don't try to be a hero," he cautioned Noonan. "Are you sure you're going to be okay?"

"I'm fine. I feel kind of bad about the kid," Noonan shrugged. Travis was still giving him death stares. "He's harmless. Stupid as hell," Noonan let his voice carry so Travis could hear it. "But he's just a dumb kid. I did stuff when I was young, too, that I now regret."

"Anything else we should look for?"

"Just get some good pictures. Don't spend too much time on the anchor and the cannon. Go farther in, maybe check on that debris wall. Oh, and I brought this." He pulled out a long canvas bag that looked like it held a pool cue. Inside was a wicked crowbar about two feet long, with a two-pronged edge on one end that could saw through wood, and a hook to use while climbing. The other end was fashioned in a smooth square tip, arched slightly like a regular crowbar, with a slot in the middle for removing nails or other pieces of metal.

"Where'd you get this?"

"One of my friends, God rest his soul, left it to me in his will."

"This thing looks like an ancient Viking grappling tool." Ned had never seen anything like it.

"Maybe it was fashioned after one. But it was made in the USA. Got that stamp right there."

Ned fingered over the flag and the words. "Son of a bitch."

They brought a plastic-coated wire basket that was sometimes used to catch lobster during their pleasure dives. Ned wound the crowbar through the mesh holes, securing two sides with plastic Velcro straps.

He adjusted his tool belt containing his KA-BAR and pulled on his one piece facemask. Madison was already at the back, sitting on the deck, dangling her flippers in the water. She was wearing the gloves Noonan provided them both, holding on to the metal detector.

"Can you hear me, sweetheart?"

"Yessir, I do."

"I'll follow you." He adjusted his feet into his own fins, slipped into his gloves, and shoved off the deck into the water.

Madison was first to check their coms under water. "I like that you and I can talk dirty now and no one will know."

"I never knew mermaids had such dirty minds."

"We've been holding out on all of you guys. We're more than a pretty face, you know."

"Tell me about it, Madison."

"Here, I turned it on for you." She handed him the metal detector. "Just pass it back if you want to trade off."

"Thank you, ma'am." The green screen was blank. He slipped the strap around his forearm, held it by the bicycle grip on the aluminum shaft, and angled the wire end in front of him as he followed her pink flippers down into the deeper water.

The turquoise water got darker, so he turned on his spotlight, which only made it worse, so he switched it off. Though the water was calm, a golden shower of sediment surrounded them, probably pieces of shells and rocks that picked up sunlight from above. A small school of yellow and black striped fish scurried around them, curiously interested in Madison's pink fins. She was descending slowly and then stopped to let the fish encircle her. "Look at these guys. My entourage!" she laughed.

"They love you, Madison. You're a mermaid. They like your fins and wish they had pink ones too."

She laughed as several of the larger ones allowed her to touch them carefully.

He followed her graceful legs deeper until they descended to the floor. They'd kicked up some silt, so waited for all the dust to settle before assessing their bearings.

The anchor and cannon were nowhere to be found. The debris field wasn't as richly laden with rocks and pieces of metal as before. He did a sweep with the detector, and it didn't register any metal. He thought perhaps there was a dark shadow several yards off to the right so he pointed.

"I'm looking for that wall of debris. I'm seeing a shadow over there. How about you?"

"Good eye. Put your light on."

He felt like an idiot forgetting the lamp. As soon as he switched it on, he found a row of timbers tied together with iron straps lying on the sand. Ends of the wood had been eaten away, and Madison could actually pull small chunks apart with her hands. Fragments of the old timbers dissolved into a cloud of silt, rising toward the surface.

He swung the detector over the platform, and it registered as he followed the bands of iron and the bolts, now concreted with ocean debris. He located a tiny hatch not more than two feet square. Inside, he flashed his light.

There were mounds of rocks scattered all over the floor inside the hatch.

"What do you see?" she asked him.

"Come take a look. Looks to me like remnants of soft cargo."

She floated near his face, and he illuminated the small hatch space. It was difficult to see anything that stood out to them as being metal until he saw what appeared to be a circular pile of red rocks.

"I'm going to guess a coil of chain, maybe?" she asked.

They followed along the top of the platform until it became buried in a debris field. More timbers laid across the space, and beyond, when he added light, he came to what looked like another wall of debris.

"This might be the backside of what we saw before. Doesn't look the same."

"No, it doesn't." She examined the pile of rotted timbers, covered in starfish and sea flowers. "Run the wand over here," she asked.

He traveled from the base of the wall up nearly fifteen feet. All along the way, the detector registered iron or nickel. Madison took pictures as they traveled the wall.

At the top, he crested what he was certain was remnants of a large wooden-hulled ship on its side. It appeared as if it had floated or been dragged over the timber platform, with pieces of lumber scattered all over where it inserted in the sand beyond, as if these pieces fell back onto the ship after the landing.

"Whoa!" Madison said. "I gotta get some pictures of this!"

They slowly examined the slightly curved structure, which was riddled with huge gaps where fish swam in and out. He noted part of a wooden railing. Madison documented the curve of an arched doorway.

There didn't appear to be anything left of the ship, really, except this piece. If there had been interior spaces, they were crushed during travel or when it landed. They cleared the hull remnants, coming to an eerily bare and pristine patch of white sand. Something lay on the floor, and at first glance, it appeared to be a body. He held up, showing Madison with his lamp.

"What is it?" she asked.

"You tell me. It can't be a body."

She was first to swim toward it. Then she stopped, floating above it. "You won't believe this, Ned."

The net and metal detector were slowing him down, but as he approached and showed the light on the object, he stared back into the face of a woman. The statue of a female body was encrusted in sea scales and coral. Part of the colorful detail had been recently exposed, scraped off by some force of nature. Only the head and shoulders of the statue were visible. While Madison was photographing her, he removed a small shovel from his tool belt and tried to scrape the sand away. It hadn't been buried by centuries of debris. This was something that was recent or was recently unearthed.

He moved the metal detector over her body, and the machine lit up. Something was buried beneath her.

"Help me with this, Madison. Can you remove some of the sand holding her down?"

"This can't be wood, Ned. It looks like carved stone. Is it marble?"

He smoothed his fingers over her shoulder. Then he scraped it with the tip of his knife and then tapped it lightly.

"I think it is marble. It isn't painted, Madison. It's inlay."

It occurred to him that perhaps the object was newer than the age of a Spanish galleon.

They finished digging around the statue, revealing her form had been broken just below her waist. The roughly four-foot section of her body was lifted carefully. They lay her back down on the white sand and set their attention to the dark stones beneath where she lay. It looked like she was lying in death over a pyre of coal.

The metal detector lit up and vibrated in his hand, registering eighty-eight.

Silver!

Rounded pieces, like charcoal, were scattered just as if someone built a fire beneath her. He was able to dislodge one of the pieces, handing it to Madison to document. She placed it in the basket. He removed several others, all of them slightly larger than a walnut. Madison took pictures of all of them and the area from which he'd pried them loose.

As he worked to dislodge another, a chunk with several clusters of what looked like black seeds the size of grapes came off. The detector also registered silver.

Madison looked up at him. "Do you want to go to another site to search?"

"I'm going to mark it, first." He tied a piece of red Velcro to a rod of crusted metal sticking out from the hull behind him.

"What about her?"

Ned considered whether it was wise to try to move her. If they dropped her, she might shatter as she fell back down into the wreck.

"Let's try it. Now I'm wishing we had Travis."

"I'll tell you right away," she said as she started to lift, "if I can't handle the weight."

He'd thought it would be lighter in water, but since it was a solid piece of stone, it wasn't. He tied the detector to his belt and tied his basket to Madison's, and they slowly ascended after pulling on the dive line three times and receiving the all clear in return.

As they neared the surface, Madison's grip was failing. Ned quickly untied the basket and let it float back down to the floor, encircling the lady of the sea's torso with the basket tie line. He knotted it and began to pull it toward the surface. He wasn't going to make it.

"Let's lash it to the dive line. Maybe if we get Noonan's help, we can get it up the rest of the way."

"Good idea." Madison swam around the body of the statue, entangling the dive line around her arms and her torso, being careful to avoid her neck area, which was the narrowest part.

Noonan must have sensed something was wrong and began pulling up as they pushed. Ned wished he could see the pirate's face when the body of a goddess popped up out of the water at him.

A net was thrown into the water, and he and Madison wrapped the lovely lady in it. They both watched as she was hauled up and out of the water with Noonan's winch.

"I'm going back to get the basket," he said.

"I'm coming with you."

"No—"

"Nonsense. It's the rules. Pairs. Never dive alone, Ned, you know that. Even for a quick dive to the bottom."

The dive line was thrown back into the water. He encircled Madison's waist as her arms held him around the shoulders and they pulled themselves down hand-over-hand using the line to descend.

"You are a mermaid. You belong under water, Madison."

"But I'm much better on land."

"I like you both ways." He pressed his faceplate against hers. "Kissing you."

"Right back," she said.

She pulled the basket up. He used an oversized toggle clip to attach it to his belt. "You go first."

She scrambled and gripped the line, using her shapely legs in those ridiculous pink flippers to propel herself up slowly, with the line as her guide. He was right beneath her.

Enjoying the view.

Noonan was babbling. He was dancing around the boat, stepping on things he was so excited. "Tell me what else you saw!"

Travis was drying off the lady of the ocean. "She's made of stone. Not wood. Stone."

"I know," said Noonan. "Listen, let's get her ashore. Travis, pull up the anchor, please."

Noonan began retracting the heavy anchor with the winch then checked with everyone. Ned was sorting through the rounded pieces of debris in the basket. He'd forgotten to remove his mask.

Madison tapped on the glass and then helped him remove it. "Now who's the fish, huh?"

"I remember once when I got a snorkel for my birthday. I slept with it on for a week," he said. "Funny, I'd forgotten that."

"Are we good to go?" Noonan shouted.

Ned gave him the thumbs-up. Then he pushed Travis back as he bent to examine the basket.

"No, son. You've already got a lot more to answer for first. We'll be fair, if there's anything. But you stay away now. You've breached the trust of the group."

Travis fell back into the seat and wrapped his arms around his torso again, without saying a word. Ned knew he was going to be a problem. He hoped that Noonan's friend had figured out a way they could go back and mine that wreck, but it wouldn't be with Travis.

The engines kicked in. Madison shared the pictures with Noonan as he piloted the boat down the coastline before he doubled back and headed North to Treasure Island.

It was still early afternoon, and Ned had searched the waters the whole way, not seeing another vessel until close to the pier. At the dock, Noonan ran to get a wagon they used to haul in catch on their fishing trips.

They loaded the lady, who was now wrapped in a blue tarp, onto the wagon. Ned carried the blackened pieces in his dive bag which he slung over his shoulders, leaving the basket behind on the boat.

They greeted several older gentlemen sitting at the bar watching a baseball game. They passed through the outside of the club restaurant and into the parking lot. It took all four of them to load her into the back of Noonan's truck and closed the tailgate.

"No quick stops, Noonan, or she'll come flying out and take your tailgate with her." Ned laughed at how much it did look like he was hauling a dead body around.

"Okay, I'm off. I'll call you tomorrow as soon as I hear from my friend. Can you take Travis back?"

"Sure," said Madison. "You've earned a nice dinner, Travis. Thanks for your help."

"Nah, just drop me off on Gulf Boulevard. I've got plans."

Ned and Madison watched the young man walk sullenly down the road.

"Something doesn't feel right about that boy," Ned whispered.

"It's going to be a problem. But hey, you've got the pieces?"

"Oh fuck yes. I forgot all about them."

"Well, I'd say Noonan has all he can handle tonight. We'll return them to him tomorrow. I'm up for a nice dinner and a margarita. How about you?"

"Me too."

As she was pulling back onto Gulf Boulevard, he was thinking about that gallon of ice cream. It was going to taste very sweet tonight.

CHAPTER 18

M ADISON ORDERED THE house *especial* margarita that was nearly as wide at the top as her fingers could spread. The frozen mixture gave her a brain freeze. She held her nose while Ned sat back in his seat, sipping his beer, laughing at her.

"For being a bartender, you don't seem to be able to deal with your liquor," he said playfully.

"I'm used to pouring drinks, not drinking them. Besides, it's an occupational hazard, and I tend to give alcohol a wide berth. Otherwise, I'd fall overboard like so many other bartenders who get hooked by the demon. And then they get fired. They're worthless."

"I've known one or two of those," he nodded.

She leaned into the table, knowing that the top of her tank gaped open for his benefit. It only took seconds before he noticed.

"You know, one thing is a mystery to me," she started.

"Mystery? What mystery?" His steady eyes bored into hers between their slow scanning.

The several sips of margarita began making her head fuzzy and hoped their food arrived soon. "You hung out with some pretty crusty dudes. You have seen so much in the world—more than I ever will."

"That's a fact, and I hope it will always stay that way, Madison."

"But how come it didn't taint you?"

He shook his head and then shrugged. "No idea. I haven't a

fuckin' clue."

"When I first met you, I thought you were too much of a Boy Scout," she added.

He leaned into her, his lips inches from hers. "I am a Boy Scout. Through and through. I'm a force for good. I save the day. But I'm completely smitten by a mermaid." He kissed her.

She explored his face, the crease at the side of his full, sexy lips and the way his hair curled a little too long over his ears. His long lashes and warm brown eyes made her heart race.

"You're quite a package, I'll admit." After another kiss, she said, "I always liked the bad boys, the ones that were rough around the edges, maybe a little unfair, or didn't always do the right things. I liked finding their good parts, their soft parts. That was always the fun of it, because I feel deep inside everyone wants to be good and whole and to be honorable."

"You've found my soft parts, Maddie."

"Yes." She felt her cheeks turn pink.

He picked up her hand and kissed her palm. She loved that he did this often. It wasn't the back of her hand or her fingers. It was her palm, the warm underside of her heart that he kissed. "I was in hiding until you came along. Getting too close was something I always feared, in the romantic sense, that is. I loved my mother, and I guess I loved my dad, and they loved me back, or did the best they could. But I don't think I ever saw this."

"What?"

"What we have. I never saw my parents look at each other the way you and I do. I guess I thought it was all fake, something you'd see in the movies. My *Operator Brain*, as they call it on the Teams, was dominant. It would survive even though I would see unspeakable horror and disappointment. Like I was floating above it. Waiting. For you."

"So I did recover something inside you."

"Oh you definitely did that, Madison."

She laid her palms against his cheeks. "Damn you, Ned Silver, now I'll never be able to kiss another man again. You better not break my heart, because then I'd have to kill you!" she said between her tears.

He slipped off his chair and came to a kneel, holding her with his big arms wrapped around her waist and back, letting her head rest on the concrete that was his right shoulder.

When he released her, he said, "I don't want you to ever kiss another man, to ever look at another man for the rest of your life." He lowered his forehead, pointed two fingers in her direction, and then aimed at his own eyes. "You and me, together. You'll never be safer, Maddie. You let me fight the wars, and you keep stoking the fires when I come home. That's the way it's supposed to work."

"Is that fifty-fifty?"

He sat back in his chair. "You do remember that little thing I told you the other night. The part about lying back and letting a slow quiet man rock your world? I am that man, Maddie. That's all I want to do. It's dumb. There are lots of logical reasons why I shouldn't feel this way, but I do."

"I thought you were being overbearing."

"Because you knew I was right, didn't you?"

She glanced down at her toes. "No." But she started to smile anyway.

He laughed. "I watched your expression, and do you know what I saw?"

"I couldn't possibly imagine. Humor me." She put her chin in her palm, elbow on the table.

"I saw fear at first, because I figured you'd never had that. And that's when I knew I could be that man for you. I just knew I'd have to bide my time, but you would belong to me one day."

He was right.

He slid his chair over. "Here, let me help you finish your drink, and then let's get the hell out of here."

"No dinner?"

"We have ice cream, remember?"

Her ears buzzed as he helped her into her car and prepared to take over the driving. Their waitress ran after them with their dinner order wrapped in a white plastic bag. Ned took the order, passing it over to her to hold, and handed the waitress some cash.

"Gracias, senor. Have a good evening," she said in her clipped English.

AT NED'S DOOR sat the stray dog, who barked at them when they drove up.

"Hey there, buddy," he said, as he knelt down and extended his hand. The dog was hesitant at first but finally got close enough to make a lunge, quickly licked his hand, and then sit back down.

"Speaking of being claimed, I think you've made a lifelong friend," she said. It touched her how tender Ned had been to this stray. "You should give him a bath when he's ready for it, and let him sleep inside. I don't mind dogs at all."

"He's not quite ready, I don't think. But let's see if he'll come inside. I'll get his food."

Once he opened the door and stepped back, the dog slipped past him and then sat by the outside door across the living room.

Madison put the food on the small table, lighting the candle there. Ned fixed some mixture of kibbles and wet food, opened the door, letting the dog out, and placed it down on the patio for him. The animal gulped it down like he had done before.

"That's amazing," Ned said to the glass, watching him eat.

Madison came up behind him, covering his backside with her front side. "They say strays always pick the best humans. I think he's a very smart dog. What are you going to call him?"

Ned inhaled sharply. He turned, holding his arm around her waist. "Otis. I think I'll call him Otis."

THE FOOD WENT largely untouched. They took turns feeding each other until the passion of their bodies took over, making concentrating on anything else an impossibility. As was his custom, he picked her up and brought her into the bedroom. He shed her clothes, peeling them off carefully, until she was left naked on the bed.

"I'll be right back!" he said as he removed his clothes and left the room.

Maddie quickly got the pendant from the tiny pouch she kept in her purse and put it around her neck. She lay back down on the pillow, waiting for him.

Light showed from the kitchen and then got closer as she saw him at the doorway with the lit candle in one hand and the ice cream in the other. Out of the top of the carton was one large spoon.

Placing the candle on the bedside table, he lit the second candle. His eyes flashed in the warm light of the flame. Her breathing was hitched as she mused what he was up to.

"I want to see all of you," he whispered.

She sat up, leaning against his pillows as he climbed on the bed with the ice cream.

"Look what she put on for me," he said, fingering the pendant and then squeezing one breast.

"I thought you'd like it."

"I do, sweetheart. I surely do."

She followed his deliberate scoop, the muscles in his arm flexing deliciously. He held the spoon to her mouth, and she licked the tasty cream. He rubbed the back of the spoon over her lips as he licked his. She watched his eyes intently as he followed the rise and fall of her belly. She felt her body begin to flutter away, nearly on the edge of orgasm, without him doing anything but feed her ice cream.

The cool back of the spoon smoothed over her nipples, first the right one and then the left.

She closed her eyes and moaned. She felt the spoon travel down her abdomen, linger on her bellybutton, and then travel farther, leaving a trail of melted ice cream. She kept her eyes closed as he journeyed to the lips of her sex and rubbed the spoon against her, drenching them in the cold cream.

Next she felt his warm lips and tongue drinking the juices, sucking and lapping the ice cream off her tender parts, kissing her bellybutton, laving over both nipples. And then, slowly, she heard the spoon and the carton drop to the side on the floor as he mounted her, rubbed his cock up and down her dripping sex, and then thrust deep inside.

Her eyes flashed open. His face showed exactly what she was feeling, the ecstasy of their joining. The gentle rocking motion of his hips back and forth began a slow ride she never would tire of. The more he gave her, the more she wanted of him.

He'd talked about a quiet, slow man who could take control and rock her world. His sweet lovemaking melted whatever resistance and doubt she had. She had found her lifeline—her dive line. The way to Heaven itself.

CHAPTER 19

I N THE MORNING, Ned cleaned up the spilled ice cream quietly, letting Madison sleep. He slipped on his American flag boxers and made coffee then went outside to watch the sunrise. Starting his day by staring out at the ocean over a deserted white sand beach definitely changed his whole focus. Even in San Diego, where the beaches and blue sky and weather were all beautiful, there was traffic. It was a city. In Coronado, where they'd worked out, tourists watched as they phased through parts of BUD/S. His condo was above the skyline, but it took a half hour before he'd see any real big patch of blue water or beach.

This really was like paradise. He understood how it had changed his father. He understood why, when his dad went back to California that he could never quite get back here, and Ned understood more than ever why his father was so angry and sullen. He hadn't belonged there. He'd belonged here.

Ned wondered if he'd never met Madison if he would feel the same way, and he guessed he would. It was that one slice of Heaven he'd never allowed himself to taste. Everything about being alive was sweeter. He was tired of the gritty, dusty, and dirty parts of the world.

He was thinking about Madison's offer to have him move in with her. Caressing her nude body all night long, not being able to keep his hands off her, and waking up so damned sleep-deprived and ragged were exactly how he wanted to feel all the time. It was the kind of excess that was natural and right. It was truth and beauty. Once this whole thing with Noonan was put to bed, he'd sit down and talk with Madison, and if he didn't get so damned distracted with how her lips moved, how she ate ice cream, how she drank her coffee, and how she felt in the warm shower beneath his fingers, he could design a life the two of them could share.

It's a fuckin' good problem to have.

Within minutes, Otis found his way from wherever he'd been sleeping and curled up at his feet. Ned leaned over and was able to pet the dog.

"You want some breakfast, Otis?"

The dog cracked his head, one ear arching up, indicating he knew what the word food meant.

Ned made him another mixture, leaving the door ajar. Otis sat quietly on the other side, waiting. He grabbed the bowl and was headed outside when his cell buzzed, nearly bouncing off the kitchen counter. It was his mom. He picked it up, cupped it between his ear and shoulder, poured himself another cup of coffee, and took the food out to Otis, closing the door behind him.

"Hello, Mom. How is everything? How'd it go with Flo?"

"Better than I expected. She seems to have calmed down. It's less upsetting to have her in one place, for her, as well as everyone else. I think she'll like it there."

"That's good news. I've been thinking about you and hoping it was going okay. And you? You holding up?" Ned knew she would still hold a bit of guilt about sending her sister to the home.

"I'm adjusting to being alone now. Didn't realize how much of my time it took to take care of your dad and to shuttle Flo around everywhere. Haven't gotten used to it yet."

The slight negativity in her voice worried him.

"Nobody expects this to be easy. Such big changes. I think you're doing a way better job than you give yourself credit for." He hesitated but then added, "And I know how you loved dad. I can see that now."

"Thank you, Ned." He could tell she was beginning to cry.

"I shouldn't have said it. I made you sad."

"No, it's just nice to hear it. I never wanted the two of you to be so distant. You weren't when you were young."

"Funny you should say that. I was just telling Mad—I was just talking yesterday about him. Remember when you bought that snorkel mask and I wouldn't sleep without it for a week?"

She laughed. "I do. Your dad thought that was so funny. He bought that for you for your birthday. It touched him that you wanted to snorkel like he did."

"I've been recalling some of those times, Mom. Some of them have come back to me. I don't know why it changed."

"He never could stop drinking. I used to call him the King of Good Times. The party animal that he was, he could never find solace without the alcohol. It was a shame to watch it destroy everything he loved. You know, he used to talk about taking me to Florida, but after he got so bad, he didn't want to go any longer."

Ned felt his mother's heartache. Felt for the life they could have had. "I love you, Mom."

"And you were the joy of my life, Ned. The real love of my life. Honest."

He watched the gentle waves undulate while he waited for her to continue. He wasn't sure where he should go with this honest reveal.

"How about you?" she asked, finally.

He leaned back against the chair and checked out the sky. That was a big, long question. How could he tell his mom that his whole life had changed, that there was something else bigger out there for him now?

"I'm on an adventure, for sure. I love this place and everything about it. Old Noonan is a character, and I've met some other salty characters." He felt his voice lower and get husky. "And some lovely girls."

"Ah, well, that's good for you."

"Yes, it is."

"Is he anything like your father?"

"Who? Noonan? No way. I mean in some things, yes. I could see how they liked to do things together, especially drink, you know. But Noonan has a pretty good gig here, out on the water, taking people diving. It's a nice lifestyle. Pretty colors, white sand beach, and turquoise water that's crystal clear to swim in. I can see why Dad liked it."

"Now I wish I'd gone."

"You've never been? You might have stayed out here if you'd come."

"I made another choice. I had to be the one he came back to. That was important to me. Later, well, maybe I waited too long and should have encouraged it. Maybe it would have been better for us. But back then, it wasn't right for me to follow him around. He had to want to come home. I never begrudged him his trip. I guess it was his last taste of freedom."

"You were pregnant, weren't you? Don't answer that if you don't want to."

"I think you knew all along it was that way. But we were married. It all happened so fast."

There was another pause. Ned watched a pelican dive into the ocean and come up with a wiggling fish it inhaled as it floated in the glassy blue water.

"Maybe you should come out here some day and look around. I'm beginning to feel like I was meant to be here, Mom. I really was."

"That sounds like you've met someone. Does Noonan know?"

"That's how I met her."

His mother was quiet. Then she sighed. "Old Noonan. Your dad idolized him, wanted to be just like him. Always looking for that one big deal to make him rich."

Ned laughed. "He's still doing that."

"He never had any money, your dad said. We bought a house, had a car, and went on trips. Noonan, he said, just lived like a beach bum. He gave up everything. Never had a family. It's funny how two friends can both envy the life of the other."

Ned had never thought about that before. Noonan had remained a rolling stone. His dad got the good jobs, until he became too unreliable to hold down one, and had the wife and child. He got to be the Coach and live through the eyes of his son, be part of a community. Noonan had his freedom. And he had a dream. Pirate Jake had buried his.

"Well, just give it a thought. I'd be happy to show you around here. Give yourself permission to heal, Mom. You deserve it."

"Thank you, Ned. I will. Does this mean you're not returning?"

Had he said that? Is that what he meant?

"No, I'm not there yet. But trust me, you need to see this place. It is paradise. I think it would change your whole life."

He signed off with his mom without telling her specifically about Madison, deciding to do that later.

Otis had finished his food and disappeared around the corner.

Ned wondered if his mother had ever read that little book of poetry. He guessed that she hadn't, that she'd given him the space to have his secret. And, if she didn't know, she wouldn't have to wonder. At the right time and place, he wanted to let Madison read that beautiful piece someone had written, the one his dad liked. And see the picture of the vagabond group of hippies and beatniks who had found themselves at Treasure Island.

One thing at a time. A few pieces had to drop into place, first.

The next call Ned got was from Noonan.

"What's up?"

"Trouble."

Ned sat up. "What happened?"

"I need to come over. Can I?"

"Sure. When?"

"Now."

"Okay. I've got Madison still sleeping, but I can fix you breakfast if you're hungry."

"I'll be right over." Noonan disconnected before Ned could ask anything more.

He opened the door to the bedroom quietly and saw her lying on her back, her long hair strewn over his pillow, her arms up over her head and her legs entangled in the sheets they'd completely rearranged last night. Between her breasts she still wore the mermaid pendant. From the waist up, her form was one of a statue like the one they'd found. Her breasts were full and perfectly round, larger than his hand could manage no matter how hard he tried. Her nipples were soft and inviting.

Her eyes opened slowly.

"You were awake already?"

She arched, stretching her long arms, and gave him a crooked smile. "Not telling."

He sat on the edge of the bed. She wrapped her arms around his waist and begged him to join her.

"I can't. Noonan is coming over. Something's wrong. You're going to need to get dressed quickly, okay?"

She sat up, keeping the sheet across her chest. "That sounds bad."

"I hope not," he said as he pulled the sheet down. "I had all kind of plans for today."

"Ice cream?"

He shook his head. "Sorry, the ice cream is all gone. But trust me, we'll get more."

"You better."

She got up and slipped into the bra and panties that lay on the floor where Ned had left them last night. She threw the tank top over her head and pulled up her jeans. She stopped.

"Ned? You're standing in your shorts. Aren't you going to get dressed too?"

It jolted him back to the reality of what their morning would be like. "Yup, so sorry. I was overcome with your beauty."

Madison helped him crack eggs. Ned put spinach and cheese into the mixture, cooked toast, and made more coffee. They heard a knock at the front door.

Noonan came barging in. The front side of his shirt was covered in blood, and on his knees were two dark red stains. His eyes were wild. Ned looked outside and saw the tarp still in the back of his pickup truck and then closed the door. Madison brought him a towel.

"Is this you?" she asked as she pulled off his shirt, examining his chest and back.

"No. My buddy, Gary. I found him at home this morning. His throat had been cut. Like a dumbass, I thought I could help him. But he was already dead several hours."

"Did you call the police?"

"Not yet."

"Shit, Noonan, you should have done that right away. Got your phone?"

Noonan pulled it out of his pocket and held it above his head. "Wait a minute. Hear me out first."

Madison pulled on Noonan's jeans, causing his cell phone to fall to the floor, which Ned grabbed and returned to him. "I'm washing these too." She started to take them away. "Ned, do you have a washer?"

"It's in the garage."

Noonan was standing in a navy blue pair of mid-thigh free rangers. He crossed his arms as if giving his tits privacy and looked ridiculous.

Madison returned from the garage. Noonan handed her the bloody towel. "Better put this in there too."

"Come on. Let's get you cleaned up before I have you sitting down on anything."

As he passed by the door to the beach, he spotted the dog. "You got a dog?" he asked.

"No, the dog got *me*. Now get in here, Noonan." He dragged the man into the bathroom and turned on the shower. He shoved lemon shower gel into his belly. "Strip and wash."

The pirate took off his undies and tossed them behind Ned.

"There's a towel on the toilet seat for you."

Madison took the underwear with her nose upturned, holding it by her thumb and forefinger. When she came back, she poured the egg mixture into the frying pan and started to make the scramble. Then she buttered the now-cold toast.

"Did he say anything?" she asked as Ned made orange juice.

"Not yet. I'm going to strangle that little shit Travis if he's involved in this."

Noonan waddled out with the towel around his waist and collapsed into the couch. He looked in shock.

Ned handed him a glass of orange juice.

"Better start spilling or I'm calling the cops myself."

"Gary, that's my buddy, and I had a conversation last night. When I told him what I'd found, he told me to hang onto it and not to talk to anyone. He said he had some feelers out to a couple crews, you know, people he could trust. They were interested and wanted to see pictures. So he planned to go down to the survey office this morning and poke around. We were to meet at T.J.'s about five last night so I could show him the statue and the pictures. He never showed. I called him a dozen times."

Noonan laced his fingers through his hair and leaned over his towel-clad knees.

"You should have called me, Noonan."

"Well, Gary does get smashed now and then. I just thought he holed up somewhere. But when I couldn't get him this morning, I started to worry."

"Drink some juice, Noonan. You want coffee?"

"No. No coffee. My nerves are shot already. Look at this." He held his hand up, and Ned could see how badly he shook.

"Take the juice. So where was he? How did you find him?"

"He has a little place over on West Eighth, has a girlfriend there. He's been staying with her sometimes and now is watching her fish while she's on a cruise." Noonan rolled his eyes and drank down his orange juice.

"I found him just inside the front door, which had been kicked open. They ransacked the house too, pulled everything out of the shelves, drawers in the bedroom, kitchen."

"Was he tortured?" Ned asked calmly.

"What?"

"Cigarette burns on his chest, cuts? Little finger clipped?"

Madison reacted, putting her hands over her ears.

Noonan was thinking, turning his head from side to side, trying to recall.

"Come on, Noonan. It's important."

"His mouth. He had blood coming from his mouth. Oh, and I remember now, they'd knocked one of his teeth out and it was lying beside his head."

"No, they *pulled* it out, Noonan. That's what they do."

"Shit."

Ned knew that all of them were now known to whoever wanted

to get Noonan's buddy. "Did you go back to your place?"

"No. Last night I went to my sister's in Sarasota. I got spooked when he didn't show up."

"Did Travis know about this guy?"

"Sure. We had dinner together a couple of times. Travis loves the stories."

"Then don't go back to your place. Do you think they know where I'm staying?"

"You don't think—"

"Shut up, Noonan. They were looking for information. What did you tell Gary? I need to know everything."

Madison brought him a plate of eggs. Ned waived his off. Noonan ate nervously.

Before Noonan began, Ned had another idea. "Give me your keys."

"Oh fuck, I left them in my pants."

"Not to worry," said Madison, who went to the garage and retrieved them.

"I'm parking your truck in my garage so no one can see it. Hard to mistake that turquoise truck with a pirate painted on the door."

"They'd go to the boat. Oh God! You don't think they'd mess with my boat?"

As he left the house, he called back. "At this point, we're trying to protect your life. You can always get another boat."

He opened the garage door then pulled Noonan's truck inside. He poked his head out onto the alleyway, didn't see anyone watching, and hit the remote. Judging from the angle to Gulf Boulevard, he doubted anyone would have seen it passing by there, either.

He dropped the keys on the counter.

"Now, you tell me what information you gave Gary, because whatever he knows, they know too."

"I told him we found the lady. I figured it would do no harm. I asked him not to tell the crews about it, because the statue was distinctive. I told him I had pictures I could show whomever. He wanted to see them, so he could verify that he had. They'd ask him this."

"Does he know we were diving at the barge?"

"Yes, of course. I told him that's how we discovered it."

"Then they know where to look."

"So no one has checked the survey office, then?" asked Madison.

"I don't think Gary ever made it. He'd been dead awhile."

"They'd look for Noonan at the Salty Dog," gasped Madison. "Should I call in?"

"Not yet." Ned hated to do it, but he had to be honest with Noonan. "I think we have to face the fact that we're outmatched. We have proof of the find. We might be able to confirm we were out there. But the biggest problem is someone's trying to get information, and maybe they have it now if they checked the tax office. They'd see you got a permit, right?"

"Yes, they would."

"We have to involve the police. For your safety."

"But, Ned, that means we have to give up the find."

"I hope not. But, Noonan, they're going to kill you if they don't get what they want. I'm sure they know about you from Travis. That means they know about me and Madison. I can't fight all that by myself."

"Should I call Travis?" asked Madison.

Ned didn't want to tell them, but it was best. "I don't think Travis cares any longer. I'm pretty sure no one will find him now."

CHAPTER 20

MADISON WONDERED ABOUT her mother and whether or not she was safe. Ned was going to take Noonan down to the Treasure Island Police Department, now that his clothes were clean and dry. They moved the wrapped statue to Ned's garage until they could sort everything out.

She'd met several of the local police and fire regulars at the Salty Dog over the years, and they were a decent bunch of guys. She told Ned. But one thing still bothered her.

"Ned, I need to check in with Monty. He's called like three times this morning. I think he expects me to come in."

"I'd prefer you didn't."

Noonan piped up. "Ned, I think she'd be a helluva lot safer there than at her place alone. Just until we get finished."

"I could come with you, but what would be the point? At the Dog, at least I'm doing something. There would be lots of eyes on me."

She could tell he was reluctant, but in the end, he agreed.

"You have an extra tee shirt I could borrow?" she asked.

"Of course I do."

She pulled off her tank top and donned his SEAL Team 3 grey shirt with the navy blue and gold Team logo. He touched the mermaid pendant.

"You wear that thing inside. Don't show it to anyone, understood?"

"I got it."

"Hey, Ned, did you take the rocks, the ones you said pinged for possible silver?"

"They're in my dive pack."

"Let's bring them. We can show those, I just don't want to say anything about the lady of the ocean."

"I should call Mom and give her a heads-up."

"She'd kick your butt if she found out later you didn't," barked Noonan. "Your funeral."

Ned laughed. "Now I know where you get all that fire, Madison."

"Got that right," said Noonan.

He smiled again, his hands placed at her shoulders. "Get straight to work, honey. We'll follow you down as far as the police station, but you go straight to work. You can call her there, okay?"

"Okay. Let me know how it goes."

"Will do."

She followed Noonan's truck down Gulf Boulevard. Occasionally she let another car slip in between them, but no one appeared especially interested in the two men in the turquoise vehicle.

When they pulled into the parking lot of the City complex, she remained heading North and in less than ten minutes was at the Salty Dog.

Stepping through the doorway, she felt like she was coming back home after a long vacation, instead of only three days away. But so much had changed. Behind the bar, she found the beer had been left unstocked. Dirty dishes were piled in the sink so she set them aside and hand-washed nearly two dozen glasses, leaving them to air dry on a towel on the counter. She had never seen it left in such a disorganized and dirty condition before.

Iris arrived an hour late, frosty as ever. "Well, look at what the cat dragged in. Old Garrison was heart-sick, missing you. He'll be glad you're back."

"It's nice to be missed," she said with a cool stare to Iris' back.

Without offering explanation or helping to clean up, Iris greeted the next couple who came in and took her first order.

Cook Jones exited his kingdom, presenting Madison with his specialty—jambalaya, which he knew to be her favorite. "Don't go kissing anybody for a few hours, or their lips will swell up and look like mine!" He grinned, proud of his concoction.

"Oh, bless your soul, Washington Jones. Just what I needed!"

The warm soup was just the right kind of spicy, and after a few sips Madison went back to her cleaning. She wiped down the counters and all the tables, which had also been ignored.

She told Iris she had to make a phone call, brought her jambalaya to one of the tables in the corner and dialed Monty first.

"Where the hell have you been?"

"I told you three days, Monty. I was gone for three days. I'm here now. Got here before Iris."

"Thank God. It was a mess last night. I had to bring in one of Jones' boys severance, and stayed until closing, and even then we didn't finish everything."

"I noticed. I've taken care of the tables and the glasses. Anything else?"

"The beer bottles—"

"Are already done."

"You have a nice vacation?"

She smiled to herself. "You could say that."

"You had some visitors in here last night asking about you and Noonan."

"Oh?" Madison's pulse quickened.

"Yeah, a couple. She said she went to school with you."

"Who were they? What did they look like?"

"To be honest, it was dark and we were kind of busy. She acted like she was a friend. Your mother was here, so I told them to go speak to her."

"You did what?"

"Just a friendly chat."

"What happened to my mom?"

"Nothing. They just chatted. Your mom finished her dinner and left. She was in a fine mood. I think she was looking for Noonan."

"Where did the couple go?"

"They'd already gone by the time your mom left. I think they're coming over tonight, or so she said."

Madison could hardly breathe. The next person she called was her mother, but she didn't get an answer.

She dialed Ned.

"We're in the interview room. I'll have to call you back."

"No, hear me out. Some people came in here last night looking for us, and Monty had them talk to my mother. Now she doesn't answer, Ned. I'm worried."

"You stay there."

"Not on your life. I'm going to check on her."

"Not alone, Madison." She heard him excuse himself and then he continued, "We're going to be here for an hour or more. Then I'll come get you."

"I need to make sure she's okay."

"You stay safe. Don't go anywhere."

"But—"

"I'll break away and come get you soon. Madison, I have to know you're safe."

She didn't want to promise Ned, but in the end, she did. During the next half hour, she tried to call her mother six times, never getting an answer. Madison wondered if she was going through one of her inspirational moods where she switched off everything electronic except her coffee maker.

Then her mother called.

"Oh my God, Mom. I tried calling you like twenty times."

"Maddie, can you come over?"

She sounded like she'd been crying.

"Mom? Are you okay?"

"Just come over."

The call disconnected.

Madison tried to call back but her mother didn't pick up. Then she dialed Ned, but his phone went right to voicemail. She also tried Noonan, with the same result.

She called the Treasure Island Police Department and got a recorded line with a promise of a returned call within thirty minutes. The recording went into, "If this is an emergency, hang up and dial 9-1-1."

She knew she shouldn't do it, but her mother needed her. Maddie had promised. Her mother wouldn't ask unless it was important.

She threw down her towel, grabbed her purse and headed to her car.

CHAPTER 21

"WE'VE ALREADY TOLD you several times. Look, we have a few items we brought up from the dive. Gary was supposed to contact a couple of reputable crews to see about going forward," Noonan boomed.

The interview room was hot. Ned knew they'd be separated soon if they really suspected Noonan being complicit in the murder of his friend. He'd get his hour or two, and Noonan would probably wind up being here the whole day. He checked his phone and saw several calls from Madison, and that worried him.

"You wanna tell us why you're checking your phone so much?" asked one of the detectives. "As a matter of fact, can I please look at your phone for a minute?"

Ned had nothing at all to hide. But he hadn't played the Navy SEAL card yet, either.

"Sorry, but I got classified numbers on here. I'm an active duty Navy SEAL, and I can give you my credentials, if you like, since you didn't ask for them."

He reached into his back pocket and provided his California Driver's license and his military I.D. It seemed to give him some space. The detective's eyebrows rose.

"What brings you out to Florida? You do treasure hunting too in your spare time?"

"As he's told you, Noonan got a contract to do this dive. My dad and Noonan served in the Navy together. And he's just passed. I came out here to see Dad's old friend here, and visit some of my dad's haunts."

The detective checked with his partner, who nodded. He returned his cards. "Thank you for your service, son."

"I'm lucky to do it, sir." Ned added, "And as to your question about my phone calls, my girlfriend is worried about her mother, who apparently had a conversation with individuals last night asking for Noonan. She's not been able to speak to her since."

"Oh shit," Noonan whispered, covering his face.

"When did you find out about this?" the larger detective asked him.

"Just now. She called me. Now she's calling me back and I gotta take these calls."

"Mr. Silver, you can step outside and make your calls. Noonan, I'm going to ask you to stay behind just for a few more minutes."

Ned was shown to the lobby by one of the detectives, who identified himself as Wade Corrigan. "Listen, I've known Noonan since I was a kid, and I don't suspect him of anything. And everyone knows around here that he's just a good old guy. We have a new police chief, hired from outside our state, and I just need to make sure there are no holes or I'll get my ass chewed. Make your calls, and then I need to talk to you about something."

"Sure thing."

Ned rang Madison. It rang and then went to voicemail. "Shit."

"Well, keep trying. I'm sorry about all this. You want me to run you over to her mom's?"

"That's just it, I don't have the address. Never been there."

"And Noonan?"

"Oh yeah, he knows. He'd have to come with us. Can we make this happen?"

"Let's go do it, son."

Even though the big detective was only about ten years older than Ned, he placed his hand on his shoulder and showed him the way back to the hallway and knocked on the door.

"Hey there, we're gonna let him go, aren't we?" he asked the other detective.

"I'm thinking yes. I've got to go over to the crime scene again."

"Listen, I'm gonna give Mr. Silver an escort to the mother's house. I need Noonan to give me the address."

"No, I want to come," yelled Noonan. "I need to be there."

Ned had to say something. "Fellas, time's wasting. Send him over in a patrol car if you have to, but let's get some speed on this mission."

"Very well. We can do that. You ride with Corrigan. I'll get a patrol unit out front. He can get us there faster."

"I'll call you," Corrigan motioned to his partner.

"Thanks, fellas," said Noonan, shaking hands.

Seconds later, Ned was seated next to Detective Corrigan, speeding behind the flashing patrol car headed North. At this rate, it wouldn't take more than a few minutes for them to arrive.

"You know this Travis Hicks kid very well?" Corrigan asked him.

"Noonan used to use him on dives. I didn't know him at all. But we think he's the one who had the connection to the folks who were involved with the murder. And now that someone's come to the Salty Dog, I'm sure of it."

"He's been in and out of juvie since he was ten. Not supposed to tell you that. We found him out at the dock. Apparently he slept on the Bones."

"Is he okay?"

"Not exactly. He also had an encounter with a knife while shaving."

Ned felt bad about the kid, even though he had put everyone in danger. "That's too bad. I think Noonan was way too trusting. Lived in kind of a fantasy."

"That's the thing out here. We're supposed to make it look like paradise all the time, but bad things happen. We're supposed to keep the bad guys away from the senior citizens, who sometimes haven't a clue what kind of danger they're in."

Ned felt the same way about his job.

"I get it. We do the same thing on the Teams. We go out there doing things so everyone can go crazy batshit over-spending, going to coffee, playing on the beach, and living it up. We both make it safe for their families. Neither one of us can talk about what we see, either."

"Absolutely. Wish I could stop the dreams, though."

"Me too, brother. Me too."

The patrol car took the turn toward the beach a little too quickly and sent up a huge dust cloud, but he managed to keep the car on the road. He left his lights on but turned off the siren.

The tiny house with bright flowered vines all along the front porch looked innocuous enough. But since Madison's car was there and she wasn't answering her cell, Ned's operator brain kicked in, and he was looking for options. One dark SUV was parked around the corner in the alleyway the police cars had just blocked off. It appeared to be vacant.

"I'm going to make my way around the side and see if I can look inside any of the windows."

"Look, we gotta do this the right way. I can't have you involved."

"But I'm trained—"

"No can do. You know the rules. We have to attempt to contact the occupants first."

"Who's going to do that?"

"He is," detective Corrigan said, nodding toward the red-headed patrolman, who was leading outside his patrol car, his weapon raised. Noonan was instructed to stay in the car when he tried to open his door. "He's the one with the bullet-proof vest."

Ned heard the scratchy instructions coming from the young policeman's shoulder microphone.

"You stay here," Corrigan whispered and drew his weapon holding it with both hands, aimed at the ground, following well behind the young officer.

Ned heard the young policeman yell, "This is the Treasure Island Police. Please exit the domicile with your hands up."

There was no answer. Ned's blood pressure soared.

"Anyone home?" the young policemen shouted. When he got no answer, he knocked on the front door with his fist. "We need you to come out with your hands up. This is Treasure Island Police. We need your cooperation."

His demand was met with a blast coming from inside the home, piercing the wooden front door and hitting the young officer in the chest.

CHAPTER 22

M ADISON ARRIVED AT her mother's place, opening the front door without knocking. She walked into a living room full of people. Her mother was one of the five, the only one with her hands tied in front of her. Her clip had come out of her hair, and her large house dress was slung over one shoulder, like she'd been shoved down onto the couch and made to sit.

She was startled at first, but seeing her mother's eyes and the tears streaming down her face broke her heart.

"I'm so sorry, Maddie. They made me call you," she said as she shook her head.

Madison scanned the four strangers and didn't recognize any of them. They were young, hard-looking kids, the kind she wouldn't have wanted to serve at the Dog. The woman motioned to the young man next to her and he grabbed Madison by the forearm and plunked her down onto the couch next to her mother. He pulled a thick zip tie from his back pocket and secured her hands together.

"We were hoping that would work out this way," said the woman, who sat across from them in an overstuffed chair. "So far so good."

"What do you want?" demanded Madison. "We don't have any money. Take whatever you like, but you can see, my house looks just like this one. We don't own anything of value. Why are you doing this?"

"Oh, don't play dumb with me. We're here for cooperation. We understand you're quite the looker. Oliver and Carlos here might want a little more private cooperation, nothing harmful, of course. We understand you've seen some treasure, and we want our fair share."

"What's your fair share?" Madison sneered.

"All of it."

When Madison scoffed, the woman continued. "You'd better consider this. Isn't it worth less than your lives? How about the life of your mother?"

One of the men tugged on her mother's hair, pulling her head back and placing a knife below her chin. Her mother cried out and Madison attempted to lunge for the woman but was yanked back by one of the other men. Both women were pushed back together onto the couch.

A tall, pockmarked youth who appeared not to be older than a teen ducked his head and examined the action on the beach outside. He paced the room holding a rifle, sneering down at her.

"Oh God, Maddie, forgive me," her mother whispered.

"Shh!" said the woman. "What I want to know is where Mr. Noonan LaFontaine is. And I understand he has your boyfriend with him?"

Madison had to think quickly. She wasn't sure what to say. Her mother arched back at the word boyfriend.

"They went to the survey office, I think. Then they were going out today to do more exploring."

"Yes, that's what we're interested in. So where is the stuff you already brought up?" she asked.

That confirmed Travis had been the one who had given out the information. He was the only one, other than the dead man, who would know.

"He has them."

"Who?"

"Noonan. He has them in his dive pack."

"And what else did you find?"

"N-nothing. There were several rocks, about seven, eight rocks we brought up to have tested. Nothing conclusive."

"Then why go to the survey office?"

"To expand their claim. They have a permit to dive."

"Travis said you found a statue. Where is that statue?"

Madison was stumped at first. "In the back of Noonan's truck, last time I saw."

"So you were going to meet up with them later on today?"

"Y-yes." She was delighted that apparently the woman didn't know the police had gotten involved.

"And what about the mermaid?"

"The what?" Madison asked.

"The necklace."

Madison exchanged a look with her mother and saw recognition in her eyes that her mother knew about the necklace.

"It's a copy. A fake. But it looks real."

"Give me a look at it."

Madison lowered her head, reached behind her neck, and unclasped the pendant. She was about to hand it over to the woman when her mother tried to touch it with her bound hands. "It's just an old trinket, something we got in St. Pete at one of the dive shops. Looks real, though." She could tell her mother was in shock.

"Here. If this is what you're looking for, knock yourself out. Go buy ice cream for your crew with the proceeds."

The woman grabbed the necklace and, with her other hand, slapped Madison across her cheek. Her mother reacted in protest.

Both women watched as the team ogled over the naked mermaid as if she'd been violated by unclean hands. Madison knew it meant something to her mother, but whatever it was, it wasn't worth her life to try to get it back. Time was on her side. She decided to get into conversation.

"I'm not sure what you think is going on, but this dive is not a treasure dive. They're actually looking for a dog collar. I'm not sure what Travis told you, but we found the barge. Just a big box of a thing. Sunk over two hundred years ago. The dog collar was a necklace the barge's cook owned. It was a fake. The setting was platinum, but the stones were glass. There's a family in North Carolina who want it for sentimental reasons. Travis knew all that."

Madison could see she'd gotten the attention of one of the men, who frowned. "That little shit."

"She's lying, Oliver."

"Well, you can see for yourself. The permit says we're looking for a dog collar. It was just a funded three-day dive for wages. Not for loot."

"What about the old ship?" the woman asked.

Madison was getting into it now. Lying was getting easier. She was mimicking all the things she'd seen Noonan and his friends exaggerating about while they drank in the Dog. She'd heard the tales for years.

She wrinkled her nose. "There was no ship. Come on. Travis knows the difference between a barge and an old ship. The thing was square. It was carrying things from Cuba to some place along the Florida coast. Mostly molasses and stuff. We found broken pots and piles of old tools that had turned to red pudding. The statue was probably someone sending a sculpture for a garden. Who knows? But as far as treasure, I hope you didn't spend too much money on Travis. He took you for a ride."

"Yes, well, we took care of that."

Madison wanted to not show fear, but Ned had informed them already that Travis probably wasn't among the living. She tried one more tactic.

"Look, if you let my mom go, I'll stay with you guys, and I'll take you there myself."

"You know how to find it?"

"Yes, I do."

The woman stood. "We don't need her then," she said, pointing at Madison's mother.

Just then, they heard a siren close and then silence. A second later, someone shouted from outside, "Treasure Island Police. Open Up."

In slow motion, Madison grabbed for the knife above her mother's head and watched the shooter raise his rifle and blast through the front door.

CHAPTER 23

NED NEARLY TRIPPED on Noonan as he ran around the side of both cars to where the fallen officer lay. He was trying to get up, but the wind had been knocked out of him.

Ned quickly dragged him away into the bushes at the side of the house, not wanting to be the object of a second blast.

Screaming erupted inside the house, the unmistakable sound of Madison's pitch, but unlike anything he'd ever heard from her before. Things were crashing, and he also heard broken glass as someone either broke in or out of a window on the beach side.

He scanned the area. Both Noonan and the detective were gone.

Out from the splinters of the front door came the shooter, looking like a scared kid.

Ned yelled at him.

"You don't want to do that, Son!"

But the kid was panicking and slowly raising his rifle to take direct aim at Ned.

His operator brain kicked in. Like it was a part of his body, he pulled his KA-BAR out of its sheath and in one well-practiced move, threw it as hard as he could before the kid could take proper aim. It caught him near the clavicle, sinking into soft tissue there. The force of the blade knocked the boy back, and he dropped his rifle.

Ned bolted, kicking the weapon to the side, but his target was completely overtaken by the shock of that huge knife handle sticking outside his chest. Blood was spurting over his chin, spilling down his torso and onto the ground.

Ned burst inside, where it had gotten quiet all of a sudden.

He was trained to look for a weapon first and then for blood. He found both immediately. Madison was holding a bloody boning knife, her arm also covered in crimson streaks. A man had fallen against the wall, leaving bloody smudge marks behind him, immobilized and dazed. Noonan had tackled a woman and had dislocated her shoulder. Her white face showed the agony she was in as she moaned. Detective Corrigan was placing a zip tie on one man, sitting on another who appeared unconscious.

But then he looked back at Madison. Her shocked expression wasn't nearly as profound as the expression from the woman in front of her, an attractive grey-haired lady who must have been Madison's mother. She stared at Ned like she'd seen a ghost.

"Jake?" she called out.

Ned thought she was crazy, driven mad by the circumstances they were in.

"Jake! You came back!" she said again.

Ned looked around, hoping to find someone else standing there, but she was addressing him.

"No, Jake's my dad. I'm Ned."

The woman fainted.

A flurry of police cars arrived and neighbors began piling out from their beach bungalows, wearing bathing suits, flip flops, and straw sun hats. A couple of the onlookers were drinking cocktails.

Ned approached Madison, and she collapsed into him.

"Hey, Madison, let me take this, okay?" he said as he carefully unpeeled the knife from her fingers. He was thinking she looked like the day he'd gone hunting with his father and killed his first rabbit. It was too late to regret not taking the animal's life. Madison was still processing what she'd just done. Glancing over at the man leaning against the wall with a stab wound in his chest, Ned noticed he was still moving, and was grateful.

"You did real good, Madison. You didn't kill him."

She frowned as if seeing him for the first time and didn't know who he was. "But I wanted to. He was going to kill my mother."

At the sound of her daughter's voice, her mother sat up, dazed, but apparently unhurt.

Police were filing in. The detective brought Ned his KA-BAR, wiping it on the jacket of the woman Noonan had tackled and subdued. "You dropped this."

"Thanks, man."

He sat Madison down, worried she would be going into shock at any second. He sheathed his knife and noticed the pendant in the fingers of the groaning woman on the floor. He picked it up, rubbed the silver mermaid clean, and placed it in Madison's hands, curling her fingers over it just like his mother had done when she presented it to Ned.

"This is yours now."

Her mother blinked several times, having watched him hand her daughter the pendant.

"Maddie? Explain this to me."

Madison uncoiled her fingers and touched the curves of the silver mermaid. Ned saw that she began to piece together what had just occurred. "This is mine, Mom. Ned gave it to me. He got it from his father, Jake. Mom, this is the man I love, Ned Silver."

"THE MAN YOU love? You said the man you love?"

"I did say that?" Maddie smiled up to him in the shower. Her slippery body gliding past his filled him with joy. He wasn't sure it would come back so fast.

"I liked hearing it. Of course, I never expected to hear it from some crazy woman, covered in blood and holding an eight inch serrated blade. That's a lethal weapon."

Madison nodded her head and looked down at her toes. Water sluiced over them both. The shower smelled of lemons. All the blood was gone. Ned had inspected every part of her and found nothing scratched, bleeding or bruised. He'd tickled her while he was doing it, too. Her warm psyche came back, which was what he'd been most worried about.

The police had detained them just for a few minutes and then let them slip away in Maddie's car. Noonan took charge of her mother, since both of them were going to the hospital to be checked. The ordeal had left her mother short of breath, and Noonan thought he might have cracked a couple of ribs.

The young red-haired officer showed Ned the three-inch bruise that was forming in the middle of his chest, just before he put Maddie in the car and drove her home. To his place.

All the remnants of the danger had been washed away. He'd massaged her neck and shoulders, working her into putty. He said he wanted her to sleep, told her she should go to bed and just rest until tomorrow so everything could settle down inside her.

She nodded agreement as he dried her off. Yet she leaned into him while he dried himself off. He picked her up and brought her into the bedroom. At the back door, Otis sat. He stopped.

"You're going to have to be patient. You'll get fed later," he said to the dog, who turned his head and flipped one ear up over the other.

"That's not fair. You should feed him. I'll be fine."

He kissed her then lay her on the bed. She immediately passed out.

He prepared kibble and meat for Otis and brought him a fresh bowl of water as well. He sat down on the patio chair and watched as the late afternoon sun hung in the sky. The sounds of the ocean and normal life soothed him. Even the sounds of Otis chowing down was a welcomed noise.

He pulled the pendant from his jeans and brushed over the curves in the mermaid. Madison had taken it off for the shower, but he knew the only place for her to be was around her neck.

He thought about coming out at sunset to watch like all the others did on Treasure Island, like people did in little towns all up and down the peninsula along the Gulf. It was a ritual, a healing ritual, he thought.

He watched Otis scamper around the corner again and disappear. Ned walked back inside, went to the bedroom, and studied Madison sleeping, her arms out to the sides, her long blonde hair streaking across the bed.

She's the real mermaid. She's the one my father hoped I'd find.

Gently, he put the chain around her neck and clasped it, marveling how it looked balanced between her two beautiful breasts.

The necklace belonged to Madison.

And Madison was his.

CHAPTER 24

MADISON GOT A week off after the rescue. Her boss was just grateful that, when Ned went back to California, she'd agreed to work behind the bar at the Salty Dog.

Noonan was able to partner with a large salvage operation, who had a team of attorneys all over the survey filing, and had the tax office issue a new warrant for additional finds. They were estimating the find to be significant. Noonan was finally able to embrace the possibility he could wind up a rich man. But not even that could tempt Madison or Ned to go back out into the water and hunt for treasure.

They spent lazy days and nights in bed—going to bed late, walking the beach at sunset, and waking up early to catch the sunrise. Otis began walking with them during these beach forays, or sat beside them on the blanket while they basked in the sunset. Eventually they were able to bathe him and bought him a fluffy pillow so he could spend his nights inside.

They'd skirted around the subject of what their forever looked like. Madison knew Ned would have to go back to Coronado soon, and that was going to be a real test of their relationship. He wanted her to move back with him. She wanted to stay in Florida. The issue remained unresolved. They still had a few days before he'd be returning to sort it out. She also knew he was wrapping his head around decisions he might have to make, since it wasn't his plan to remain in the Navy as a career.

Madison's mother got her little place put back together, had it completely repainted and went on an entertainment spree with her old friends. She explained that her mother often went through these swings. One moment reclusive, painting, reading, or gardening, and the next minute, she was having parties. Up until tonight, her mother had kept her distance.

One such party was planned for this evening, and her mother wanted them to come. It was a special invitation. Madison knew Ned was a little nervous about it.

She bought him a new shirt, a beautiful turquoise blue with pictures of starfish, seafoam and sand. His tanned skin and dark features made him look stunning in it.

"I'm still going to wear khakis and flip flops."

"As will most of the rest of the crowd."

Madison wore a light yellow dress with a low neckline, perfect for displaying the mermaid pendant. She was going to braid her hair, but Ned insisted she wear it down and free. As was their custom, he placed the pendant around her neck and kissed her shoulders.

"She's not going to pepper me with questions, is she?"

Madison looked back at him through the mirror they were standing in front of. "Shouldn't she?"

"What kinds of questions?"

"The usual kinds of questions a mother will want to ask someone involved with her daughter."

He frowned.

She turned, wrapping her arms around him. "Just be yourself, Ned."

When they arrived, they could hear the party going in full force. Her mother had strung party lights around the backyard. There were five golf carts crammed into her driveway, plus a couple of bicycles. Ned parked in the alleyway, and as they walked to the front door, another golf cart arrived with four more partygoers, all grey-haired friends of her mothers, who greeted them warmly and then danced into the house.

"Honestly, Madison, these guys act like they're on college break," he said, following behind.

"Some of them came here on Spring Break and never left!" She laughed at his puzzled expression.

"Will Noonan be here?"

"I'm guessing he will, but I didn't see his truck out front."

Inside, the place was festively decorated. The sliding glass door to the beach was wide open and half the partygoers were outside dancing to saxophone music.

"I'll introduce you to him later. He used to play with some really big bands in New Orleans and toured the world. Fascinating man," she told Ned.

"One of your mother's boyfriends?" he asked.

"Oh, I'm sure. Most of them are."

"How did you handle that growing up? I could never see my parents—"

"What's wrong?"

Ned pointed across the patio at several people drinking cocktails and laughing.

"I'm sorry. What are you looking at, Ned?"

"That's my mother!"

"No way. Which one?"

"Can't you tell?" he said exasperated. "The only one wearing a dark color. The lady in the navy dress wearing pearls."

The woman he described was standing right next to her mother, and the two were chatting, which surprised her most of all. Her mother was gracious, vivacious, and was wearing one of her brightest kaftans adorned with a shell necklace. She was telling some kind of story, her arms flying about her head. She made Ned's mother laugh. The two of them were having the same light pink cocktail drink.

"Ned, I didn't know anything about this," she whispered.

"Hello, kiddos!" A familiar voice came behind them. Noonan was clean shaven, had gotten a haircut, and once again had washed his patch.

Ned grabbed him by the collar. "Did you have a hand in this? You invited my mother to come talk to my father's ex-girlfriend?"

Madison was concerned he'd start making a scene. "Ned, stop it. You're going to embarrass me."

"Madison, this is not okay. You can't go playing with people's pasts like that, their deep-seated feelings. Just invite everyone to a party and ask them to mingle. This isn't a petri dish, you know."

"I invited her," said Noonan, recovering from the manhandling.

"And I accepted. I wanted to come," said his mother.

Ned turned to face her. "Are you okay with this? Do you know who she is?" he said pointing at Madison's mother standing at her side. People began to stare and even the music stopped.

Madison's eyes filled with tears. Ned looked like a cornered bull. She felt so sorry for him. She brushed the tears from her cheeks and scolded Noonan.

"You should have told me. I could have prepared him."

"Why?" said her mother, her forehead furled, one hand on her hip. "He's a big boy. She's a grown woman. Why does she have to get permission from him to do anything? Noonan was just being nice, Ned. He paid her way."

"Mother?"

"I didn't realize it would upset you so, or I wouldn't have come." She was close to tears.

Noonan had to remind him, "Hug your mother, Ned."

"Oh, God," he muttered, holding her tight. "I'm sorry you got put in this position."

She looked confused, her arms flapping around his back before she finally hugged him back.

"Wait a minute." Madison's mother spoke up.

Ned dropped his arms and stepped away.

"You take a lot of liberty, Ned. This is *my* party. Noonan asked me, and I told him he could invite her. We both thought it was about time she was included. She has a family here, friends if she wants it, and the rest of her life to spend however she pleases. Are you even a part of the human race?"

Madison tried to pull her mother off, but she wasn't having any of it.

"Let me finish, Maddie. He's made the scene, not me. He gets to live with it."

"He's trying to protect me," Mrs. Silver said. "That's all. He's just trying to protect me."

Ned stormed out of the house.

Madison looked between her mother and his mother, unsure what to do. "I'm sorry, sweetheart," his mother said to her. "I didn't realize he'd be so angry." She touched the pendant. "Look, Amberly, she's wearing Jake's pendant."

"As she should," said her mother.

The crowd started talking again, and someone put on music. Noonan stood still, looking like a fifth wheel. He finally shrugged and said, "All I wanted to do was surprise him. I never intended this to happen."

"It's okay, Noonan. We know. It's not you." Madison addressed Mrs. Silver. "Well, I'm glad you're here. We're all so happy you came to see our little piece of paradise. I've wanted to meet you." They clasped hands.

Her mother barked at Noonan. "Go get this girl a drink, please."

"Yes, ma'am." He departed on his mission.

Her mother began slowly. "So I have a theory, maybe a confession to make. My theory is that Madison is the real mermaid. Margaret, you might think me crazy, but Jake never should have been wearing that thing. It belongs on a woman's body. He never offered it to me, either. It never was for me or for you. It was for her."

Mrs. Silver's face was streaked in tears.

Her mom put her arm around Margaret Silver. "Come on, he was the sonofabitch we both loved for a time," she started. "You more than me. But let's be totally transparent here. He was a major handful. I loved him. But he knew I wouldn't put up with him. He knew it wouldn't last and I didn't have to say a thing. He knew you were the only one who could love him that much. He made the right decision. And I think, in that man's heart, he wanted us all to be here, together. This necklace brought Ned here. He brought back a little piece of Jake too."

Madison watched the two women walk away, holding hands, talking like two long-lost friends. Noonan handed her the drink that was ordered, but Madison had a hole in her heart the size of the State of California. Now she had to face one more challenge. What she'd do with the rest of her life if Ned left her behind, just like his dad left.

Except Madison was sure she had enough love for him. But she wasn't going to beg.

She didn't want to follow Ned, either, so set her drink down and walked through the patio and out toward the shore. The sky was orange. The surf was light greenish blue. Large puffy clouds caught purples and yellows as the sun met the horizon. She'd always told herself the beach could heal anything. It was the balm that would soothe anybody's soul, no matter what.

She inhaled, hoping that she could bring it all in and wash away all her sadness. She did it again, waited, and then let her breath out. Then she heard his voice behind her.

"Maddie, I'm a complete fool."

She didn't turn, in case her mind was playing tricks on her.

"Sweetheart, can you forgive me?"

It was Ned. She turned, letting him see her tears, not being afraid to let him see that she didn't want to lose him.

"You have to make up your mind, Ned, which way you want to go. You once told me I had to let a quiet man come in and rock my world, and I did. I tried it, and you were right. It's what I'd always wanted. But—"

She sniffled. It was a really ugly sniffle she had to wipe on her dress, but she didn't care.

She looked back at him and saw his tears.

"You're a good man. Probably the best man I've ever met. But you've got to stop saving people who don't want to be saved."

He blinked, not sure what he'd heard.

"You have to trust too. Like you asked me to trust. You have to let me love you back. I don't need saving, Ned. As long as I've got you, everything is perfect. Your mother made her choices. Now you've got to make yours. Ours, Ned. Are we going to live for this, today, or are we going to live in the past?"

He stepped to her, slipping his arm around her waist. She pressed her cheek against his, stepping up on tiptoes. Then he held her face in his hands, bent down, and kissed her.

"Today. It's all about today, Madison. No more ghosts or regrets. From now on. I'm not going anywhere."

She laughed. "You better not, or I'll have to kill you."

They heard the patio break out in cheers and clapping. They both turned their backs to their audience.

"Oh God, we have to go back and face them?" he mumbled, his arm around her shoulder.

She laughed, "I am. Are you?"

"Abso-fuckin'-lutely!"

ESCAPE TO SUNSET

Sunset SEALs Book 4

SHARON HAMILTON

CHAPTER 1

J ASON KEALOHA STEPPED out of his Hummer. The sunset was
bright orange with purple and grey streaks across the early
evening sky. The blue waters of the Gulf of Mexico were chummed,
darker than he'd seen in pictures, worried and angry, like his own
insides. He could hear the chants of his ancestors, especially the
white-hairs, older women who pounded drums and beat their palms
on their thighs.

He'd felt this way in full battle gear, stepping out of a Hummer
into some hellhole as death and trouble lurked. Those voices kept
him connected to his ancestors from long ago, giving him encouragement and reminding him that they held a spot for him if things
should not turn out. Sometimes that made all the difference. Sometimes it made him settle so he could hear the voices of the other men
on his SEAL team, follow instructions quickly and clearly, and be
that missing piece of their puzzle, their force for good when they
worked so seamlessly together.

Today, that calling, that rumble left him nervous. He had a mission. He held it between the fingers of his hands, those same fingers
that wiped dirt from the face of his dying brother after several of
their Team had been taken down in that red clay earth in Nigeria.
He whispered things to his buddy that were untrue, that he'd be
okay, that he'd make it back to the base and the evacs were on their
way. His buddy knew he was speaking the lies you tell a dying man

when there is no hope. You don't ask if they're in pain because you want them to focus on your eyes and the lies so you can walk with them home.

The blue urn was fashioned with a Trident, compliments of the Navy, as if a family member wanted this on their fireplace mantle. But his buddy Thomas had no family. There were no parents, no women or children to mourn over his passing. That's why Jason had adopted him as his brother. The bond never stronger than that day Thomas passed into the hands of his ancestors, who would take the Haole boy and love him to eternity, until Jason joined again, and they fished the waters of Heaven together. The kahuna would pray over him and bless his journey, so his uhane, or spirit, could travel into the afterlife and to a time of great joy and celebration. Jason asked them to take care of this peaceful warrior, abandoned at birth, but never in battle.

Jason's spine was straight, his footsteps sure. He held the urn as the valuable treasure it was, as if presenting it to the hungry mouth of the ocean. If Thomas' uhane absorbed into a stray shark or large barracuda or even a dolphin or great whale, so be it. Far better than to rot in the ground somewhere and be eaten by worms, to smell, putrefy, decay, and become something unholy and unclean. Thomas was a warrior. His warrior spirit would live on in the unlimited ocean or inhabit the body of a great animal.

The setting sun stung his eyes, dry from the tears he'd shed in silence and in the privacy of several darkened rooms and spaces. On the plane from California, he had held the urn. He tendered it carefully upon touchdown and set it at the desk of the rental car agency when he picked up his Hummer. The clerk eyed it suspiciously but didn't ask.

That made Jason smile. It was the first time he'd smiled in three days.

The chants got louder the closer he came to the ocean. He'd

walked the archway of the wooden bridge leading across the dunes to the beach from the street, the one that had brightly painted arrows labeled Paris, New York, Barbados, Texas, and even San Francisco, pointing right, left, and straight up. He traveled on sure footing through the soft white sand to the harder white-grey sand then the wet sand that was slightly tan in color, the path bathed in the light blue and white gentle surf.

Sister ocean was a gentle lover, covering his toes with the lacy foam of her underskirts without revealing her modest parts.

With a wash, his sandaled feet were bathed in sea water up to his ankles. The women started hitting the drums louder, their voices arching up an octave. Watchers on the right and left stood still as he carried out his mission. Nobody stopped him. Everybody kept still.

The butterflies in his gut began to flutter. He took in a deep breath and released the metal canister top, allowing the salty air of the Florida Gulf to mate with the ashes of his buddy just before he heard the kahuna chant the story of how he would travel to the place of eternal sunshine and love. That was Jason's Christian grandmother's doing. She told him it was a place of eternal sunshine and love because her God was the God of Love.

That was good enough for Jason too.

He raised the urn as a sacrifice to the God of the Sun, reached back, then tossed the grey contents into the ocean. Thomas' cloud of bones and flesh hung in the sky, arched and then dissipated into the air before dropping into the bay.

"Safe travels, Thomas," he mumbled. "I look forward to the fishing, the laughter, and yes, the beautiful women with big breasts that will suckle us both and feed us roast pig!"

He laughed. The villagers in Nigeria where Thomas had been killed would be horrified with the knowledge they'd feast on pig.

All the more reason to do so, Thomas, my friend. My one true friend. My brother. Life was unkind to you, but I promise to make up for it.

He wanted to send him off with laughter because his grandmother had taught Jason that death was a celebration.

Now that you're gone, I can sing the truth. It's no fuckin' celebration. It's the end of one thing and the beginning of another. I am so sorry we did not do the Haka for you. Make them show you in Heaven. And think of me down below.

The waters completely absorbed the particles.

"I will miss you Haole boy. Now you won't have to wear so much fuckin' bugspray and sunscreen. And the angels in Heaven don't wear panties, I'm told, so pick the prettiest and have at it, please, for me."

Jason put the lid on the metal container, brushed off the ash clinging to it, then set it back out of reach of the surf. He washed his hands in the water, drying them on his khakis. He didn't have to examine the beach to know there were eyes on him that might not have approved of him dumping Thomas into their bay.

So be it.

He didn't want to spoil the serenity of the moment, so he saved the urn without tossing it too, because that would make the tongues wag and might bring the authorities. He held the container to his chest and watched as the sun melted into the horizon. The orange turned into dark purple then grey. The wind kicked up. A few gulls flew past, and a pelican dove into the water right near where part of Thomas had landed. It caught a fish.

"Okay, so maybe you won't be a mighty fish. Maybe you'll be a pelican. Or a baby pelican when she brings this to her nest."

That gave him the second smile of the day.

The old kahuna his father, now dead some twenty years, used to consult, cackled in the distance. Jason could see the old man dance around the room like a bird, making fun of the brave warrior who had died so others could live.

It didn't matter that the whole world didn't know about Thomas' sacrifice. He did. So did the rest of the team on SEAL Team 3.

Jason's heart clinched, squeezing one bloody tear as if it made a fist.

It's delicious to miss someone, he thought. *It enhances the feeling of being alive.*

WHETHER IT WAS the pain of loss or the joy of celebration and communion, the tug, that dull ache in his heart felt exactly the same. If he were a zombie, he used to watch in those old horror films when he was a boy, he would have no heart, no expression, and would feel no pain. But because his pain was big, his heart was big. And that made him happy.

Jason scanned both directions, the orange remnants creeping back out to the dark blue water. He knew why Thomas had enjoyed this beach of his boyhood. He could see him frolic in the waves as a young man, throwing shells, playing with other boys, making sandcastles, like Jason liked to do.

But this wasn't Hawaii. This was the land of Thomas' ancestors. These men and women were perhaps like ones who had invaded the islands, altered the local Polynesian population culture forever, and mated with women, leaving mixed raced keikis behind. In Jason's land, it didn't matter, because Hawaii was stronger and more beautiful than any of the devastation she experienced by any of those who tried to conquer her. She would remain beautiful as the old Hawaiian women were. Their hips would rumble under their bright muumuus. Their full lips would be painted bright fuchsia or red.

Thomas' relatives were sailors—perhaps pirates, misfits or young men looking for adventure in the Florida Everglades—blown off course from the Caribbean or Cuba. They could have been couples fleeing the big cities of the north or the children and grandchildren of spring breakers, snowbirds, vagabonds, or people just wanting to get as far south in the United States as they could go.

Jason always heard the chanting when he watched the sunsets on Kauai. He didn't hear the ukulele music or the slide electric guitars commonly piped in many of the hotel lobbies, airports, and shopping centers.

He heard the drums and the chanting. His family roots ran deep.

His grandfather said they could trace their ancestors back over four hundred years. When asked, his mother wouldn't tell him if this was true. "They were legendary fisherman, canoe-builders, and engineers who liked to use the powers of the ocean to harness speed and balance."

His grandfather found employment after the Second World War, being unable to serve himself. He liked to show off to the American GIs who were stationed there by climbing coconut trees in his bare feet without any equipment.

Thomas had told him about how everyone came out at sunset. He called it sacred time, and Jason agreed. It was a time to reflect on the day, the dying day, and let the fantasy of the future run wild in the waves and travel between stars at night. It was the celebration of the unknown, as one day collapsed into the arms of the night and then the night fell into the arms of the next morning. It was the cycle and circle of life repeated over and over again, like the lapping of the ocean in its most liquid form, eroding the hardness of the rock and sand on the shore.

He inhaled. The early evening mist on his face felt good. The older couples strolled north and south along the water's edge. The children squeezed out that last bit of play before they had to come inside, running east and west before slipping into well-lit homes for dinner.

Three older gentlemen in flip-flops and swim trunks with pot bellies and well-tanned skin, one sporting a white ponytail, blasted passed him on their balloon tire motorized bicycles. They were easily in their retirement years and yet looked extremely healthy and happy.

Life as it should be.

He came upon a young woman seated on the sand, a blanket pulled around her body. She wore a large floppy straw hat that covered her almost to her shoulders. Most of her face was obscured in the shadow of the wide brim, and her oversized *Jackie Onassis* sunglasses covered up whatever was left of her face. He knew she was young, because she wore pink frosted lipstick.

As he walked past, he looked down on her. She immediately turned her head to face the other direction. Jason continued his walk.

A few yards later, he felt like running, so placed the canister beneath his arm and assumed a gentle jog. He traveled about twenty minutes, and although he wasn't winded, it was awkward running with a big blue jar in his armpit, so he slowed to a walk.

He examined the row of little bungalows and beach shacks that lined up beyond sand dunes rising up to the right. The windows were no longer bathed in orange, and warm yellow-glowing lights brightly twinkled within the walls. Some houses had fire pits in the yard, where family and friends gathered.

He did an about-face and turned back in the opposite direction, jogging again. When he encountered the young woman with the hat, he slowed and then walked several paces past her. Maybe it was his superstition, the way he'd been trained, or was really a skill he had, but he could feel her eyes on his back.

He sat to fully appreciate the darkness descending all around him. One by one, everyone had disappeared from the beach.

Except the girl in the floppy hat.

Headlights from a beach park vehicle downwind shone on her briefly—just enough so he could see the hat shaking. Even her upper torso, in that one flash of a second or two, was vibrating. Her hands moved to her face under the hat. As the light was redirected elsewhere, in the darkness, he heard her sniffle.

She'd been crying.

He stood, working his way over to see if she needed assistance. Before he could reach her, she scrambled to her feet, nearly tripping on the blanket she'd thrown aside, and ran straight for the wooden arched bridge and beach access path leading to the parking lot and the main street beyond, leaving the blanket behind.

And then she disappeared.

CHAPTER 2

KILEY RAN AS fast as her legs would keep her upright. She clutched the oversized hat with her right hand and in her left, she carried her beach bag, which now felt like it weighed fifty pounds. She nearly stumbled several times in the soft sand, her balance thrown off by the dark night. Ripping off the hat, she stuffed it into the bag and tried to stay on her feet, keeping her forward momentum. She felt bound by heavy chains pulling on her body, yanking her down into the abyss of the ocean. Her feet felt encased in concrete.

They found me!

She didn't dare turn around to see if the hulking man continued to follow her. That wouldn't be their style anyway. They would've sent two or three goons together. A single guy like this could be the lookout and then they'd come for her later, so she ran until she hit the wooden bridge, stubbing her big toe on a nail that popped out. But she kept going, knowing that her foot was bleeding. At any minute, the floor would collapse and she'd be swallowed up by the earth underneath.

The house she rented was located on the left side, so she abruptly turned right and ran until she came to another access road dead ending at the beach. Just after she rounded the corner, she hid, looking down the narrow alleyway to see if she could discern any movement. There was not much of a moon tonight so her eyesight failed. Movement here and there turned out to be palm fronds or other bushes blowing in the gentle breeze.

Her heart thundered, almost to the point of making her choke with each inhale and exhale. She could hear her breathing inside her head as she stumbled in the dark. Her throat was red hot, starved for moisture, her lips parched and raw from her gasping run.

She was going to have to find some way to defend herself when she ventured out again. The steak knife in her bag wasn't nearly good enough as a weapon.

What was I thinking? Of course they would find me!

Desperate for something safe, a place without fear of being discovered, she had just wanted to get her life back. She was tired of the months of dangerous investigations, the police interviews which went nowhere, and the phone hang ups—all due to the articles she'd written for several Northwest newspapers, including the Columbia Passage. She'd run away to the land of her childhood. It wasn't safe back in Portland any longer. Probably never would be safe there again.

She'd revealed information she obtained from an anonymous source about the sex and drug trafficking trade, which had made her persona non grata in the town she loved. She had a target on her back—prey for the monsters who ran the child exploitation and sex trafficking ring in the Portland area. What started out being something she was deeply committed to, saving young innocent lives, had now turned into something that could very well cost her own life.

Alone, even disconnected from her fellow reporters, she didn't know who she could trust. She wasn't sure she could trust her own editor, who promised to guard all her secrets and her sources. But somehow these had been inadvertently leaked. One of the college interns helping her was killed in an auto accident, and one of the victims she used as a source had disappeared. Could it have been someone on the paper staff or a worker at the coffee houses she frequented? Everyone around her was a suspect.

Her parents had sold their Beach House in Florida five years before. After their failed attempt to relocate to Northern California to be closer to Kiley's brother, they moved to Portland to be part of their daughter's life. She knew her mother was hoping that she'd find a nice young man, settle down, and raise a family. It felt like they moved to Portland just to witness such a happy event.

But that was not to be. A year after their move, both her parents passed.

Her work was taking so much of her time that she even lost touch with her brother, Sam. Now, asking for Sam's help, would only land him in the same kind of trouble Kiley was in. Even though they weren't close, she wouldn't dream or wish this on anyone. She'd decided not to let him in on what she'd uncovered.

Kiley checked her bearings then slipped across the alleyway that separated the first row of beachside cottages with the thicker row of larger homes that bordered Gulf Boulevard. These places occasionally were two and three stories, unlike the bungalows on the gulf side. Smaller shacks were torn down so that huge homes could replace them, all built so they would also have ocean views.

Every dog bark made her jump. Every door that slammed sent her reeling for cover under a tree or beside a fence or hedge.

Gulf Boulevard was busy this time of night, people going to and from dinners or beginning the evening bar hop scene. She could only risk being seen for short periods of time, so she crossed the busy street and entered the subdivision of houses on the canal side of the peninsula. These homes were larger still and away from beach traffic, huge mansions with well-manicured garden areas that would rival a botanical garden. Some of these homes had names affixed the iron gates that kept the occupants safe inside, as if they were huge ocean-going vessels.

She followed the roadway, walking around parked cars and staying in the shadows away from the bright streetlamps occasionally illuminating the area. Sometimes, a car would come from behind, and she would dip inside a gated area as if returning home. Gradually the street veered to the left and ended in a cul-de-sac.

She could see the shivering waters of the canal outstretched behind the large homes. Beyond the canal were lights from a neighboring island, including a strip of beach shops and outdoor restaurants. Music wafted through the night air. She could even smell freshly barbecued seafood.

The cul-de-sac was a dead end for her, so she crossed the street and returned one block then meandered through the subdivision to the first intersection, where she turned. She wandered back-and-forth until she found herself at Gulf Boulevard again but several blocks north of the beach access.

She pushed the button for the pedestrian crossing and quickly traversed Gulf Boulevard, slipping into the first beach access alleyway that appeared. She heard the sounds of people having dinner or gathering outside their houses, enjoying fire pits or having cocktails on the patio.

She kept her eyes peeled for anything that resembled the huge hulking form of the strange man. She'd developed a sixth sense about being followed over the past few months, and tonight was no different, even though she saw no evidence. Her senses were still on high alert and her heart continued racing due to the close encounter.

After winding her way through the driveways and small alleyways connecting various properties to the beach access, she was at last at her front door. Rummaging through her beach bag, she searched for her keys despite the straw hat stuffed tightly there scratching her fingers. She quickly unlocked the front door, closed it quietly so as not to attract attention, and turned the deadbolt, feeling some semblance of safety.

Tossing her beach bag to the side, she heard all the contents scoot over the tiled floor: her cell phone, her lipstick and sunscreen, her book and the serrated kitchen knife she'd put in there for self-defense. She quickly crossed the room and checked the sliding glass door to the sand dunes and ocean beyond, locking it.

At last she began to feel safe. She slumped into her living room couch, propped her feet up, and tried to relax, inhaling long deep breaths through her mouth then exhaling slowly through her nose. She'd been taught this to avoid panic attacks dogging her recently. After several minutes of growing calm, she poured herself a tall glass of ice water, pulled a kitchen chair up to the sliding glass door, and watched for evidence of anyone coming toward her or looking at her from the outside.

She found none.

Kiley thought about what had happened. She'd been watching the sunset when the big man tossed dust and ashes to the ocean. At first she didn't understand what he was doing, taking him for a homeless crazy tossing sand. But then she realized he had poured—no, thrown—someone's remains into the surf. It was fascinating to watch his muscled shoulder and huge arm pull back and then toss the fragments from the jar he held. Someone nearby had gasped. People stopped talking. Out of the corner of her eye, she saw some-one point while others softly chattered like birds on a wire.

Growing up on Sunset Beach, she had never seen this happen before. She thought it was against the law.

But then, he began to run North. Her eyes followed him until he was lost in the crowd of sunset watchers. Several minutes later her reverie was disturbed when he came back, and this time, he slowed down, taking a seat a few yards away from her. Her pulse had raced again as she watched for any further advancement.

She drank her ice water as she continued scanning the beach, still searching for any signs of danger.

Had he sat near her *on purpose*? Had he watched her the same way she watched him, out of the corner of her eye?

After several minutes, her breathing slowed, and her heartbeat returned to near normal. She'd drained her glass of water. It left her chilled.

My blanket!

Her senses, still not returned to normal, began to perk up a tick or two as she squinted, trying to see where she'd left it. She also wondered if the strange man was still there. If he was homeless, he'd most likely be wrapped up in it. Perhaps infesting it with fleas or using it as a place to cover up peeing on himself. She'd brought that blanket all the way from Portland. It was the fuzzy go-to thing she'd always drawn comfort from, nearly as precious as a child's blanket. She couldn't let it become fouled by some berserk behemoth who didn't respect the laws of the beach.

Kiley unlocked the sliding door and stepped out onto her patio. Breathing in the ocean air several times, she felt her soul fill with courage and hope. She was wrapped in her imaginary safety blanket of happy memories from long ago.

The beach heals everything.

The saying had been painted on a plaque on her apartment wall in Portland. It had been in her bedroom growing up, and it followed her to Europe when she did her semester abroad in Paris. It journeyed with her to London and Scotland and throughout Italy as she made her way traveling all summer before the fall semester.

It was the first thing she unpacked when she came back to Sunset.

Carefully, she traversed the soft sand, noticing what appeared to be the discarded blanket off to the left. As she approached, she sniffed but didn't detect an odor. But she discovered that someone had folded the blanket and left it there for her. As she bent to pick it up, a male voice behind her whispered, "I'm glad you came back for it."

She whirled around, clutching the blanket to her chest. She wished she had a knife or a pair of scissors or something to defend herself. But she was going to face this person no matter who he was. She was tired of being so frightened that she could hardly think. She couldn't sleep. She was exhausted from running, hiding.

Before she could get the words out of her mouth or scream for help, he approached her. His huge shoulders and upper torso blocked what little light came from the stars and the crescent moon rising above him. His size and girth registered quickly. She would not be able to fight him off or outrun him.

"Leave me alone!" she yelled.

"Hey, I mean you no harm."

"*I said* leave me alone, "Kiley reiterated, holding her palm out in front.

"I scared you. I'm sorry I didn't mean to. I apologize. Please, it upsets me to know that I scared you. That's not me."

"Did you not hear me? I want you to leave me alone." She turned to go.

"Wait. Please. Don't be frightened."

She hesitated and then rotated halfway in his direction, still ready to run if she needed to.

"What—what were you doing out here with that…" She pointed to the metal canister barely visible tucked under his arm.

"I came to carry out my best friend's wishes. My buddy lost his life overseas, and I returned him to the sea, to the gulf. This is where he grew up."

She noticed his English had a slight accent she couldn't make out. She corrected her focus.

"I'm sorry. But this isn't a good time for me."

"Nor for me. But please accept my heartfelt apologies for scaring you. It would bother me if you walked away thinking I meant you any ill will or harm."

He didn't sound like a monster or like someone who wanted to take her life. He began to sound like someone she might be able to trust.

That's a ridiculous thought! But before she could fully adjust, she was speaking again to the stranger.

"I've just moved back here. It's been a very difficult few months for me. I…"

What am I saying?

In spite of everything else, her chest tightened. Her breathing became staccato and dangerous. She knew what it was. It was a full-on five-alarm panic attack. At a very inconvenient time.

"I don't feel…"

Just before she lost consciousness, she had expected to hit the hard scratchy sand as her body collapsed, but powerful arms cradled her gently, breaking the fall.

And then everything went black.

CHAPTER 3

JASON HAD NO problem catching the young woman, being especially careful to make sure her head and shoulders didn't come close to hitting the sand. Completely unconscious, her body rolled into his upper torso, which made it easier for him to scoop her up, his right arm placed beneath the backs of her knees. She was light and supple. He judged she was about twenty-five years old.

The blanket he had so carefully folded for her was discarded, lying in a heap at his feet. He didn't want to risk losing his balance and hold her too tight so he didn't retrieve it. He swung her back and forth as if holding a child, rocking and whispering reassurances that she was going to be fine. He caught himself speaking to her in his grandfather's native tongue.

Just as he suspected, within seconds, she began to gain consciousness.

Of course she was confused. It was a lot to take in. She'd been afraid of him after all, had been fleeing for her life, and now he was holding her, trying to be as tender as he could. He kept his arms out in front, so that as she came to, she wouldn't know how close to his upper body she had been.

"You're going to be okay, miss. You'll be just fine."

"What? Where am I?" she mumbled, stirring in his arms.

"Just take a deep breath in. Keep breathing. That's it. You're gonna feel fine in just a couple of minutes."

At last she realized that he'd been holding her, which caused her to clamor to get to her feet, nearly pushing him aside.

"I told you to leave me alone!" she said as she straightened her clothes.

He couldn't see her face but he was sure she was glaring at him from the sharpness in her voice.

"Okay, okay, take it easy." He stooped, picking up the blanket and shoving it in her direction until her hands could locate it. "Here you go. Take your blanket. Wrap it around yourself so you don't get cold. Are you sure you're okay?"

"Of course I am!" she retorted in a huff.

In the blackness between them, he shook his head and allowed a grin to separate his lips, since she probably couldn't see him anyhow. She was one stubborn and bitter woman, who, unfortunately, still thought he was the enemy. If she only knew.

"What's so funny?" she demanded.

Okay, so much for not being seen.

He allowed himself a chuckle and really didn't care whether she believed him or not. The whole situation was beginning to annoy him. "I've tried just about every way I know how to convince you I mean you absolutely no harm. But if you want to be that way, fine. I don't know what fox got in your hen house but, lady, there's no problem on this end. Now if you don't mind I'm going to get as far away from you, your hat, your blanket, and this beach as possible."

"You have no idea what I've been through," she spat. It stopped his intention to run away.

"How could I? You won't listen to a damn thing I have to say." He let his shoulders fall as he sighed, trying to relax the muscles at the base of his neck. "Look. Let's just call a truce and go our separate ways. Does that meet with your approval, or is there something you don't like about *that* comment?"

His night vision must have kicked in, because he saw her hand flash through the air a millisecond before her open palm slapped him across the cheek. Memories flooded his brain of growing up on the island. Two nasty Samoan sisters in his school who outweighed him by at least three times had bullied him all through grammar school and into Junior High. Until that fateful day he hit one of them back and got expelled.

Reflex made him grab her forearms and yank her into him.

"Stop it, you Haole tart. I won't hurt you but I'll defend myself."

She was wiggling in front of him, trying to keep air space between them. Then she was kicking his shins with her bare feet, hooking herself around his thick legs and trying to get him off balance. Her fingers reached for his face to scratch him, but he could hold both her wrists in one of his hands, the other arm around her waist, immobilizing her the more she tried to struggle.

He stood like granite, gripping her tighter. He gave her absolutely no room to move as he pressed her up against his chest.

"Stop it. You're being a child. I'm not hurting you so just quit."

"I don't quit. I will never quit. I won't quit until you let go of me. I'm going to scream rape if you don't let me go!"

That really pissed him off. He squeezed her wrists together, holding them with just one hand. It made her cry out so he placed his other hand over her mouth. Pressing his nose to her face, he whispered, "Stop it. Dammit. Quit this."

For several long seconds with their noses pressed against each other, he matched her deep breathing with his own. He assessed her willingness to be reasonable, felt her weakness, and was thankful as she finally stopped fighting him. Her flowery scent made his ears buzz as he allowed her hot breath to wash over his face.

She was strong and determined. Angry and not afraid to fight against an impossible opponent, no matter the danger. She was right. She was not a quitter.

It took another few seconds before she must have determined that there was no real danger present, because just as soon as her fear left, she was shuddering in a series of sobs racking her body. He relaxed his grip on her forearms and folded her into his chest and let her cry against him.

He felt like his hands were too big and clumsy for her delicate neck and shoulders as he brushed up and down her spine, squeezing the top vertebrae until she relaxed further, her shaking now subsiding.

He shielded her from the wind coming from the South, brushed her hair from her face and placed a soft kiss to her forehead. "Don't be afraid. I'm not going to hurt you. I only want to help. Please do not be afraid. I'm here now. Nothing is going to harm you."

Her arm wrapped around his waist, not reaching very far, as she snuggled in the safe space he'd created for her. Jason felt a twinge of regret that he'd been so harsh with her. Her head rested on his chest just below his chin. He ran his fingers through her hair, sifting, whispering things he'd heard as a child when he'd jump into bed at night with his mother after he had nightmares.

Whatever horror movie that had been playing in her head must have been something frightening. He knew what fear smelled like. He'd seen women panic and faint in the path of danger, unable to defend themselves or their loved ones. He'd seen it all too often, and all too often he'd not been able to save them either.

She leaned back, trying to see his face. "What language is that?"

Language?

He must have been chanting, or speaking the circular rhymes they'd sing as kids. It came as second nature, and he couldn't even remember what he'd said.

"Hawaiian. Something my grandmother taught me."

His right palm brushed tentatively against the side of her face, and then he released her all at once and stepped back. His arms fell to his sides.

"I'm sorry. It was a panic attack," she mumbled.

"No, not exactly. The attack was when you passed out. You are scared of something, little one. That was pure, cold fear." He sighed again, wanting to hold her once more, but resisted.

She wrapped the blanket around her.

"Are you in danger?" he asked, suddenly wishing he'd not been so forward.

"A little. But I'm far enough away from all that. Thank you, and I apologize how ridiculous I was."

"No apology necessary. Fear does strange things to people sometimes. But you were brave. You fought well."

"No I didn't. I was pathetic."

"You were difficult to stop. That speaks to your courage, not your skill."

"Did I hurt you?"

Jason let her fingers reach for his cheek which had now turned warm and was probably swollen. She'd packed a good swing and the sting surprised him. He did not back away, allowing the touch. His heart was pounding, beating like the drums of his ancestors as she gracefully twisted her wrist and brushed the backsides of her fingers across the side of his face all the way to his ear.

He could have easily taken her in his arms, and he knew perhaps she'd let him kiss her, but he stood like a statue, feet planted in the sand, like the surfboards standing guard at Hanalei Bay. The wash of waves lapping on the shore stilled his restless and troubled soul, while the distance between their bodies remained. She had the touch of his grandmother and some of the older women of his community—the way she used to bless his cuts and bruises, especially the ones left by the two Samoan sisters.

This stranger was a healer, and yet Jason knew she didn't understand yet what her true capacity was.

As HE DROVE to his motel room, he knew that, if the Gods of his ancestors wanted him to meet her again, they'd create the opportunity. The empty urn sat next to him on the front seat of his rental Hummer, as if Thomas was witness to this magical connection he felt to her. Maybe Thomas was laughing at him.

He glanced down at the seat.

"We won't speak of it."

The urn obeyed.

But all the way back, he couldn't forget the feel of her shaking body against him, the scent of her hair, the tiny beads of sweat at the sides of her cool forehead, and her probing but gentle fingers.

He thought about her while he showered and then watched moonlight glisten on the water of the Gulf. He thought about her as he lay naked in his bed, his head propped against his forearm.

Jason had left the sliding glass door open a few inches so he could inhale the ocean air all night long, which was always his custom wherever in the world he traveled, if it was safe. He dreamt of the beaches back home, lush and full of the scent of flowers floating all around him. He thought about the tanned Polynesian girls he'd dated and made love to on the beach, their modest nakedness a thing of beauty and grace. He felt their full lips, and the smooth flat of their noses as they cuddled, giggled, and whispered things to him. In those days, drunk on the discovery of sex, he didn't realize how the ocean, the beach and a woman's body could heal all those broken parts he could not.

He thought about the girls he met in Coronado who were a bit too fast for his tastes. They wanted everything now, hard and deep, leaving him aching for a simple touch of kindness or a word of wonder.

Like a metronome, the constant rhythm of the ocean sang him to sleep in stanzas stitched together by the calling of sea birds.

The last thought he had before he drifted off was that Thomas had brought him here to Sunset Beach. It was a bigger purpose than the final goodbyes to his friend. Thomas wanted him to see the place where he'd grown up, to see the beauty and treasure buried here. In time, he'd find out just what that treasure was.

As one door closed, another one was waiting to be discovered. Whatever was on the other side of that door was his destiny.

Tomorrow would be a new adventure.

CHAPTER 4

KILEY'S NUMBNESS CONTINUED all night long.

She couldn't get warm, even when she put on flannel pajamas—a rarity in Florida. She believed her heart had slowed down so much, all the blood had rushed into her lower body. She shivered in bed, getting up in the middle of the night to take a hot shower. Her body temperature held long enough so she could fall asleep for a few hours. But then she woke up again in the blue light after midnight.

Her dreams were smoky, bright orange and powerful like the campfires they'd made during college. In Oregon, you could make a beach bonfire if you wanted to. It was considered a form of eco-cleanup, since there were so many pieces of driftwood washing up from the tall trees that had been harvested over centuries all along the coast. She could feel the spirits of the indigenous peoples, the First Nation, dwelling in the tall trees, looking down on them, waiting.

She hoped it was still the same today, because those trips with friends were the highlight of her college days. They'd sit in circles, gathered like Native Americans, telling stories by campfire, playing music, and drinking beer while the fire crackled and sent sparks up to the sky. Oregon was always damp. Even on bright summer days and early fall afternoons, there was moisture in the air.

Unlike today, she didn't worry then about who might be lurking in the forest or around the barn. Not that it had been safer. Her perception of life had totally changed. She recognized it as a form of PTSD, something her editor teased her about.

She rolled on her side and watched the waves in the moonlight, grateful whomever had designed this little bungalow had thought to put a small window at sleeping-eye level in the bedroom.

She pulled the blanket up to her ears and detected the stranger's manly scent. Kiley remembered the heat of his enormous chest and how his shoulders rose up like mountains of muscle. Nobody looked like that in Oregon, she thought. Not even the football players in college.

She had no idea there were so many evil men and women who preyed on the weak and vulnerable for their own advantage, who had no conscience and would hurt others until someone stopped them. That awareness had taken a long time to fester and grow. It came later, after her parents were both gone, when she experienced what it was like to be truly alone. She was free to go about her life and explore what she wanted to. It was a fair trade to the other darker feelings of loneliness as she pursued her quest for relevance.

It all started one day when Corbin Newman III, her editor, had given a lecture in her English class about writing for the *Columbia Passage*, Oregon's largest paper. He told the story of its long history of righting wrongs, speaking the truth, and searching out knowledge that lay buried, either intentionally or unintentionally. His salt and pepper hair, worn a little too long, curled up at the ends. He also wore round, silver glasses like John Lennon. She never saw him in anything but faded blue jeans and a long-sleeved, button-down shirt, usually rolled up to mid forearms. He had delicate, expressive fingers and hands he liked to use when he spoke. But his eyes were as blue as the water in the Gulf. That was the most shocking thing about him.

He mesmerized the entire class with his stories. He wore suede Birqs with striped socks and wore his wristwatch backwards with the clasp on top of his arm, the dial close to his body. Although married, he never wore a wedding ring, which had been the topic of conversation for several days after he spoke.

Like a moth to the flame, it was rumored that he usually picked two or three young Lewis & Clark girls to do his bidding, calling them interns, but they were much more. Everyone knew he cheated on his wife, and everyone wanted to be one of those girls anyway.

That had been off-putting to Kiley. Maybe that's why Newman fawned so much over her, agreeing to start her out at the paper before she graduated. She talked her way out of impromptu dinners and tried not to be alone with him in the car. Her roommate thought she was completely nuts.

But there was no denying that Corbin Newman III could tell a good story with the reverence and skill of a world-class yarn-teller. He taught them that, if they were going to report the news, they had to make the reader care about the people in the story. Not telling a lie. He wanted them to throw a heavy dose of imagination and fiction, supposition, and mystery into their pieces so someone would look for their byline.

And it worked. Kiley's byline was elevated to the editorial page. Her research on child abuse and women's shelters drew lots of comments on the digital version of the *Passage*. She had a social media following and presence, and she'd been asked to speak at women's conferences and for graduate studies courses.

Kiley wondered why she was even thinking about her editor this evening as she adjusted her body, lying on her back and staring up at the ceiling. She was as far away from that culture and climate as she could be, except for the fact that she was beside a large body of water, the Gulf. In the Pacific Northwest the ocean was angry and churning all the time. So strange that it was called *Pacific,* meaning peaceful. There was nothing peaceful about that ocean or the rugged people who haunted the forests and tolerated the mist and the cold.

She shuddered again, pulled up her covers, and, after battling her racing mind, she finally fell asleep again.

IN THE MORNING, her phone rang, waking her up. The room was bright. With no job to get to, she'd actually slept in until nine o'clock.

Amazing!

"Kiley. You were supposed to call me yesterday. I start wondering when I don't hear from you." Newman sounded slightly annoyed, maybe a little urgency to his voice.

"It got to be late, and—"

"Fuck sake, Kiley. It's three hours earlier there. If it was midnight, and I know you go to bed early, it would only be nine o'clock here. That's acceptable for a phone call."

So she'd gotten caught. "Sorry, Corbin. I was exhausted and nearly passed out."

That part of the excuse was correct.

"You going to get me that story for next Friday? I'm saving a big spot for it, and I have nothing to fill that hole if you don't come through."

"I'll make it. I always do."

"You make me nervous. All this sneaking around."

"We live in a digital age. I can write from anywhere," she informed him. That wasn't the real reason, of course, but it was logical.

"Well, I still think you should check in with the police there, and have them touch base with Portland's finest. You're alone, unprotected."

"What makes you think I'm all alone? I do have certain social skills."

"Oh, that's right. You were a serial dater in Portland. Forgot about that."

The comment hurt. He used to tease her about never getting out of the house, chiding her that there was more life than in the romance books she read every waking second she could. It was of no use trying to explain it to him. She'd rather crawl into a book and live there and would do it in a heartbeat if given the opportunity.

"You worry too much."

"Well, when my lead investigative reporter runs clear across the country because she thinks someone is after her, I do worry. I've got a paper to run. Everything you do in Florida you could do here."

"Except I don't think it's safe."

"Don't you think your imagination is getting the better of you? I mean, we did that story last year about the chief of police in Vancouver. He was related to half the town, and nothing happened when he got fired and then went to prison. Then you write about a women's shelter and supposedly get all sorts of calls…"

"They were real calls, not supposed calls, Corbin."

"Honey, ex-husbands are a dangerous lot, I'll grant you, especially when their wives take off in the middle of the night with their kids. I'm not condoning any of that, but just consider you are overreacting, won't you? And if not, why don't you get the authorities involved?"

"Because then they'd want my sources, Corbin. You taught me that."

"They might even help your story, give you information about some of these Joes. They could do drive-bys and keep you safe. You know they do that."

"I'm safer here."

"In Florida?" Corbin sighed. "You sure you're not just running off with some beach bum, taking a little vacay in the sun?"

"No, the threats were real. My dead cat was real. My slashed tire was real."

"But you've never been physically accosted. That's what I'm saying."

"I won't dignify that comment. Corbin, you know a woman has the right to protect herself, and I'm feeling I need protection. Not in Portland. I need some distance for a while."

Whether or not there was anyone after her, she didn't want to tell him she'd had a meltdown at the hands of a stranger, on whose enormous chest she'd unloaded her tears. Finally, she added, "Besides, a couple of goons in leisure suits would stick out like a sore thumb."

"You're blowing smoke up my ass, Kiley. Haven't you ever been to Miami?"

"So what's gotten you so irritable, Svengali?" It was the name all the girls in the dorm had given him. Kiley knew he liked having women throw themselves at him every day. She imagined he would feel virtuous if he didn't partake, and got off on it occasionally.

"We have another missing girl. I would have put you on that case. It could just be an immigration issue or mix up. But this time, she's not fifteen. She's twenty-five."

That did concern her. "What's the story?"

"She's from Ecuador, very small for her age, not even five foot. We're guessing that if she was abducted, like the other victims you discovered, the kidnapper mistook her for a fourteen-year-old girl."

"When did this happen?"

"See, I knew you'd be interested in covering this. But you can't do it from Florida."

"Humor me, Corbin. Just a few of the details."

"It happened the day before yesterday. She was living with a local attorney in town…"

"Who?"

"Miles Benson. Do you know anything about him?"

"Nope. What kind of law does he practice?"

"Well, that's why we think it could be an immigration issue. He is an immigration attorney. Maybe she didn't want any hassle from authorities. Maybe she was unhappy in the household and had no one to turn to. She worked as an *au pair* for the children. But she cooked, cleaned and drove them to all their school things."

"And the attorney called it in?"

"His wife did, yes. According to her, the lady just disappeared."

"Just like the other ones. You know this is connected, Corbin."

"Well, then you're going to love this. She also has long black hair and typically wore it in a ponytail, like many of the other girls."

She thought about it before she replied. "Corbin, I'm still not coming back there."

He sighed over the phone. "I was afraid you'd say that. I can't say as I blame you. You still have files here. Can I assign them?"

"Go ahead."

"And you'll get me my story in time for Friday, right?"

"Yes, I will." She paused. "Who are you going to put on the story about the missing girl?"

"Martin."

"No, you need a woman on it. The mother has to be interviewed and separately. Are the police involved?"

"Of course they are! This story made headlines this morning."

"Because it's number four."

"According to you, at least number four."

"Yes, probably more like ten." She considered the staff at the paper. "Why don't you put Carmen on it? She speaks Spanish. She can talk to the family of the girl back home."

"Family? According to Mrs. Benson, this girl had no relatives. She was brought up by an agency."

"But she had friends, people Carmen could interview. Nobody's going to trust Martin."

"But he's ten times the reporter, Kiley. Carmen's more interested in the political stuff, the demonstrations, social justice causes."

"Which would be perfect for Martin. He can get in people's faces. This needs to be handled with delicacy. She'd be talking to people who don't want to tell their story for fear they'll be sent back home. And I like the idea of a woman asking all those personal questions, not a man, Corbin."

"Bingo. Okay, I agree. It's probably an immigration issue. But I'll put Carmen on it for a few days and see if she digs anything up."

"Tell her we can talk via Skype if she wants."

"I'll tell her. Not sure she'll be very thrilled."

"Just because we don't hear about all the suffering that goes on with these women, with children smuggled into the U.S. against their will, doesn't mean it isn't a huge story. Not as juicy as a strike or demonstration. This stuff is more underground, hidden. And it's just plain evil. If my story does what I think it will do, and I have to stay here for a few more weeks, Carmen's going to have all the follow-up. It's a great opportunity for her. With her help, all the little loose ends will be tied up, and we'd have developed a huge case for the police."

"And not something you want?"

"It won't bring back my cat. It won't bring back my peace of mind when I walk out into the dark parking lot downtown. I'm not doing it for recognition. I'm doing it for the women. And right now, with all those stories, I'm too radioactive. Carmen will do a much better job finishing it."

"What about your apartment?"

"Megan's boyfriend is moving in. That was already in the works. I was going to have to move out anyway. I'm just giving her all the furniture and household stuff. She can hold everything else for me until I return."

"So what do I tell people, Kiley?"

"Tell them I'm on a writing retreat. That part is even true."

"And when they ask me where?"

"Tell them Chicago or Cincinnati. Don't mention Florida, please."

"Alright. Now, if you don't get that story in, I'm going to cut back your salary, Kiley. Don't play games with me, okay?"

"This is not a game, Corbin."

"Are you going to give me a forwarding address?"

"Nope. Anything you need to send, you can email to me. My check is on automatic deposit."

"Well, are you having a good time, at least? On the beach some-where?"

"Don't assume anything. And why would you care?"

"Come on, Kiley, why don't you trust me? Don't you think someone should know where you are?"

"There are people who know where I am."

"Really, who?"

"Look, Corbin, we agreed I was going to disappear for a while. That way when anybody asks you where I am, you don't have to lie."

She checked the time and realized she'd been on the line too long. Somewhere she'd read that anything over three minutes could be traceable, even with a burner cell.

"I'm going to sign off now. I'll call you in a couple of days. You can email me the pictures, and I'll take a look to see if I recognize her, okay? And have Carmen call me if she wants some background information, some of the things I've been working on. There's a new shelter I ran across that I want her to check out"

He gave no objection.

KILEY SHOWERED, MAKING the conscious decision not to open her laptop until she was ready to write. She fixed a light breakfast, made coffee, and walked outside on the sugary white sand beach in front of her bungalow.

This place is worth every penny!

She'd paid double the rental amount to be right on the beach. It wasn't just the view she liked, it was the fact that the constant sound of the water lapping on sand drowned out all the other neighborhood noise and some traffic on Gulf Boulevard. She took the lease for three months and had to pay it up front. It cost nearly what it cost her to live for a whole year in their converted artist's flat in the trendy warehouse district of Portland. Though she had to share, that space was huge, nearly three times the size of this cottage.

She intended to stay the entire three months, since the agency made it clear there would be no refund.

With her coffee mug, she walked out amongst the early morning crowd. She'd noticed already that the people gathering for sunrise were considerably different from the sunset crowd. Kiley loved both times but was probably partial to sunsets. Nothing in Portland, even before or after a big rainstorm, looked even vaguely similar.

She began scanning for interesting shells and soon came upon the place where she'd sat last night, recognizing the divots her feet had made in the now-warm sand. As if retracing her steps while investigating for clues, she sat in the exact same location, even placing her feet into the craters of sand.

There were several pelicans soaring over the calm waters this morning. After becoming more interested in a particular area, they would fly up twenty or thirty feet and then dive into the water, smashing their foreheads against the water's surface. Her mother told her they had extra bone in their skulls for this very reason. The awkward snow-white bird floated along the surface for a few seconds, securing and probably eating part of the fish he'd caught. Then he took off toward land, bringing breakfast to his young and his mate.

She studied the beach people, devoid of children at the present time. Groups of colorful joggers drifted past her as she sat and enjoyed the morning. Sipping her coffee, she prepared to go inside and work on her deadline, her spirits brightened. Kiley could almost envision a day when she could finally relax and enjoy the beach community of her childhood.

She thought about the plaque she'd brought with her.

The beach heals everything. The message hit her right in the middle of her chest. She could feel the sheer terror this poor young woman was going through. If she was still alive, and that was a big if, she'd be locked up, confined to a cage somewhere. She'd be defenseless, probably naked, the end of her suffering beginning to be the one thing she'd most desire. The girl was a long way from the home of her childhood and probably convinced no one was even interested in looking for her.

Kiley allowed only a sliver of that fear to slip in, and then she shut off those thoughts. Given the choice of living in a cage or being killed, she wasn't sure which option she could face.

Maybe I should just stay here forever.

CHAPTER 5

"**H**EY, JASON, KYLE told me you were out here. How's it hangin'?" barked the voice of Andy Carr, one of his Brothers from SEAL Team 3 in Coronado.

"I'm good. I'm good. That's right. You're detached now. Are you here?"

"Almost detached. Waiting for the paperwork. Hell yes, I'm here."

"You bought a little place here," Jason said into his cell. "How close are you to Sunset Beach?"

"Fuck you, Jason. That's where I'm living, man."

"I apologize then. I could have had you join me when I freed Thomas."

Andy cleared his throat. "I was partly calling about that. So you did the deed, then?"

"Last night, at dusk."

Neither man said anything for a few minutes. Jason watched a young, sunburned red-headed boy of about ten skim the flat surf on a boogie board strapped to his ankle.

"I'm sorry I missed it. But I'm glad you gave him a proper send-off. Thanks for doing that."

"Yup. It's what we do." He was surprised to experience a tear slipping down his cheek. He flicked it away with his thumb and forefinger.

"So where at Sunset are you staying? If I'd have had half a brain, I would have insisted you stay with us."

"I'm slightly south. St. Pete's."

"Ah, man. You're paying nosebleed rates. How long are you staying?"

"I was thinking about five, six days."

"Well, that settles it. Bring all your gear and come on over. Don't argue, 'cause Aimee will kick your butt. Just check out and come on. You're like five, ten minutes away at high traffic."

"I don't want to impose."

"God, Jason. I feel totally like a stoned teenager to have missed what you were doing. I probably even saw you walking down the beach, and it just never registered, man."

"No worries. I knew you had a place nearby. It was cool the way it worked out. It was just him and me. Like it always was." Jason decided to leave out his conversations with Thomas from inside the urn or the words of his ancestors. Andy would never understand things like this.

"You lie well, Jason. Now get your stuff, and Aimee and I will give you the grand tour. You probably got sick of hearing me talk about it."

Jason chuckled.

"It's right on the beach. Probably not as nice as Hawaii, but she and I make a pretty good team, and we're thinking of making the arrangement permanent."

"Thought you were going up to Little Creek."

"I am. Team 4 is deployed right now, so I have a little time before we re-hook up."

"Where is their theater?"

"Oh, it's all over the place. They've been doing some stuff in South America and the Caribbean. Mexico. I'm hoping it will be a good fit. They lost their senior medic a year ago evacuating some embassy staff and friendlies in Venezuela. Everyone on that squad is new, so Kyle wants me to push it and grab that job. He's tight with their LPO, Peterson."

"Good. Well, it sounds like you've got a plan. I liked Aimee that one time I met her at the party."

"Quit talking and get over here, Jason. I'll start fixing lunch."

The clerk at the front desk grilled him about his desire to check out early. "Did you find another place discounting their rooms? There's a lot of that going on. I have authorization to match any deal they offered you."

"No, sir. I ran into a buddy, and he won't take no for an answer. I knew he was in the area, but he called me just now, and he's insisting. Sorry, man."

"Well, that I can't match. But I will do this for you. I won't charge you an early cancellation fee if you promise to give us a try next time you're out here. How's that?"

"More than fair. Done deal."

Jason held the slip of paper he'd written the address on in his right hand, steering the Hummer with his left. In less than five minutes, he was slowly driving down a narrow alleyway over white sand and crushed shells. He saw Andy standing outside a garage door with a couple of beers in his hands.

The house had recently been painted a coral-red color with off-white trim. New windows had been installed on the second and third floors. A concrete mixer and some tools were propped against the other garage door. Bags of concrete were stacked several high.

Andy insisted on handing Jason a beer first, and then they hugged. He peered into the truck. "Where's your stuff?"

"Just a duffel in the back. No firepower."

"Really?"

"Oh, I'm packin', just didn't bring any of my long guns." Jason was quick to correct Andy's misconception. He didn't know anyone who didn't travel armed. Most of the SEAL wives and girlfriends did as well. Where it was illegal to carry, they were more careful. But it didn't change their behavior one bit.

Jason hooked the duffel over his shoulder and presented Andy with a bottle of wine he'd bought at the bar at the hotel.

"I know jack about wine, but they told me it was good," Jason said.

Andy tucked it under his arm and showed the way to a new glass front door. Once inside, the faint smell of paint and other odors stubbornly clung to the air.

"So, we knocked out the ceiling here and made this catwalk with landings going up to the second and third floor rooms."

Jason admired the woodwork. Bleached and tumbled by the ocean, lightly sanded and varnished with a clear coat, the finish taking on the color of driftwood. He smoothed his fingers over the handrail and spindles made from pieces of wood in varying sizes.

"I like the way this feels. This almost looks like driftwood," he said.

"Well, it kinda is. Everything in here is recycled, except for the windows and the roof and some of the hardware. Even some of that came from a salvage yard. They find all sorts of shit after those hurricanes. People go along and collect all this stuff, throw away the garbage, and clean up and re-sell some of the metal, tile, and wood. Lots of wood."

The pattern on the handrails was totally random, some pieces laying at an angle, some vertical, and others horizontal, which reminded Jason of the old Hawaiian plantation designs he'd seen at museums growing up. Interspersed here and there were rusted pieces from the insides of machinery. They'd used gears, car parts, pieces from the backs of wooden chairs, and metal railings, all making an eclectic patchwork design. One panel even held an old rusty hand saw. On the second floor was a cozy platform with an overstuffed couch placed to take advantage of the ocean view. There appeared to be two bedrooms on that floor, and following the stairs up to the third floor, Jason guessed it was a master suite that covered the entire space.

One side of the living room had a recycled glass and metal garage door opening to the beach and ocean beyond. With chains on either side, the door would roll up and could be secured there, exposing the living room directly to the outside.

"Where did you guys find this place?" Jason asked.

"Actually, Aimee found it. I'll let her tell you the story. We just put a little down, and did a lease option. We're using the cash to do the work, and then we'll get a loan to cash the former owner out."

"So I guess you're staying, then." Jason noted that he'd never seen Andy so happy.

"Fuckin' A. Nothing could tear me away from this place. I'll fly up to Little Creek, but I'll be back here every chance I can. I'll be one of those *one and dones.*

"You impress me, brother." Jason said, taking a long drag on his beer. "Going all domestic and only after one deployment."

"I have over three years left. But, when you meet the right woman, it changes you. So it's not my fault!" Andy was grinning, wiggling his eyebrows up and down. "You remember Cory Phillips?"

"Yeah I've met him a couple of times." Word had spread quickly about all of Cory's problems, and Jason thought he'd been booted out.

"Cory grew up here. I think he knew Thomas."

"No kidding? Where is Cory now? He's on Team 8, right?" He was trying to be polite and show some respect.

"Four. He was four. I'll be joining up with his old team. Kyle helped set it up and said they were a good group. Anyway, Cory's coming here for a couple of days. You'll get to see him. He's been in San Antonio at the burn center."

"Oh, I'm so sorry. I didn't hear about that. How bad is it?" Cory's battle with drugs, alcohol, and gambling, as well as other vices were legendary, but he didn't want to add credence to the rumors. Jason hoped his injuries weren't major.

"Not a patient. He's taking the burn course rotation. It's a one-year billet like the long medic course. Then he'll probably re-engage with Team 4. It came at the right time. Cory pulled things out at the last minute. He sounds great on the phone."

Andy looked up and spotted Aimee coming through the front door.

"Who sounds great?" she asked. She gave him a big smile.

She was carrying groceries, so Jason scurried toward her, took the two brown bags from her arms and set them on the kitchen counter. Aimee thanked him and approached Andy.

"Who were you talking about, sweetheart?" she asked again.

"Cory. He's stopping by later. He just called." Andy embraced her. "And look who else I dug up!"

"I see," she said. "Looks like my plans to finish painting the guest room are flying out the window."

Jason began to chuckle. "Good job, Andy. Invite me over to keep from having to get your hands dirty."

"Not true. I cry foul!" Andy protested.

Aimee tilted her forehead in Jason's direction. "We're delighted you stopped by. This sort of thing happens every day, so no worries. I'm more than used to it."

"You've done a beautiful job, Aimee. It's going to be magnificent."

Jason could see she appreciated hearing that. She studied the beams above her head and the filtering light coming from clearstory windows placed around the perimeter of the upper ridge. The area reminded him of a crow's nest.

"Some days, it almost feels like a church," she answered. "So you're still at Coronado, right?" Her lavender eyes sparkled in the late morning sun.

"Yes, ma'am."

"Jason came out to do Thomas' honor flight. They were very close," Andy added.

"Oh yes. That was awful. All the locals remember him. They've plastered pictures of him over several of the hangouts." She examined her feet, and then flashed those lavender eyes at him again. "I'm so glad you could be there for him."

The conversation came to an awkward close. Jason quickly added, "He'd have done the same for me. He didn't have family."

"We were his family," added Andy.

"Indeed." Jason held his beer up, toasting it in the air, an action Andy mirrored, just before they finished off their bottles.

CORY ARRIVED JUST after they'd finished lunch. Jason hadn't remembered him being such a clown. He teased and danced around Aimee, making her laugh. On several occasions she blushed. He was respectful, but Jason could tell Cory had stopped by to see Aimee, more than Andy.

His former team buddy pulled him aside.

"I should explain that Cory and Aimee have some history." Jason could see pain in Andy's eyes. "In fact, they were together when I met her."

Jason shoved his eyebrows nearly to his hairline. "Whoa. That's a bit awkward."

"It's cool. But I'm just explaining why I give him some liberties. He's done a good job so far. If he crosses the line, I'll put him in his place. But Aimee will always be a friend, and I wouldn't want it any other way."

"You're a better man than me, Andy."

"Nah, I just love her. That's all."

"So when's the wedding?"

"Listen to you! We've been so busy getting this place ready. But I wouldn't have put in for the transfer if we hadn't talked about it and agreed. Probably next year."

Jason knew why Andy didn't have a date. Aimee hadn't fully decided to marry him yet. But he was going to hold back on telling Andy and let him figure it out for himself.

"You're a smart man, Andy. The woman always decides," he said.

Andy sighed, watching the two friends laughing in the kitchen while Aimee was cleaning up. "Ain't that the truth?" Then he asked, "What about you? Anyone you've got tucked away somewhere?"

"You know me. I'm a little slow when it comes to all that. But I have my eye out for something special."

"As in here, in Florida or California?"

"None of your fuckin' business, asshole," Jason whispered.

They both laughed.

"You know, Damon's out here. He and Martel are coming over Wednesday night for a little party. It will be a nice little reunion. If you dare bring that *Something Special* around, I'd like to meet her."

"We'll see. Way too premature at this point. But I'll work on it."

"You do that. You work on that hard." He gave Jason a crazy grin. I'm counting on you. One by one we're all dropping like flies. I think you're next."

"Don't count your chickens. But, if I don't come back tonight, don't wait up for me, okay, sweetie?"

Andy punched him in the arm.

"Oh, so she lives at the beach."

"I don't know where she lives, but I'm going to find out."

Jason didn't want to answer any more questions, so he asked if Andy wanted to join him for a walk on the beach. He needed to get away from what was beginning to feel slightly restrictive.

"Go for it. I'm going to stay behind this time. It's going to get beautiful out there in about an hour."

"Yesterday was breathtaking." Jason could still see the bright orange glow in the back of his mind. He was anxious to replay, if not relive some of that encounter.

Aimee broke away from the kitchen to lead him upstairs, giving him one of the two rooms on the Gulf side. "Cory will either sleep on the couch downstairs or up here in the other guest room. But I'm warning you. He snores, although maybe now not so much. He's stopped drinking."

"So I've heard. Good for him. That's not an easy thing to do. You and Andy must have helped with that."

"Timing. Everything is timing," she said before she left the room.

Jason hung up a shirt he'd brought, laid out his shaving gear, then put on a light-weight windbreaker, and headed to the surf.

He thought about Aimee's comment.

Everything is timing, isn't it, Thomas?

Instantly, he was transported to Africa, the Nigerian village that caused all the carnage. The mission suddenly became doomed in failure when an elder objected to the SEALs evacuating young girls who had essentially been brought to the village as slaves and were to be married off to some of the older, more wealthy members. The "brides" were a gift from a local warlord, in exchange for their cooperation.

State didn't have all their facts in order. He'd been told it wouldn't be the last time they'd sacrifice their lives for faulty intel. But, at best, what had been a very tricky op, now ratcheted up ten clicks, with no one to help the little squad who had been sent out to pick up the girls. They'd learned, in a life or death situation not to rely on the local Afrika Corps. And since it was thought that too much of a show of force would draw out the bad guys, they had a skeleton crew. That meant shooters and medics.

But in fact, the opposite turned out to be true that day. In the shootout that occurred, two girls were re-captured, two others were killed, half of Kwanda Freescott's men were incapacitated, while the leader and the two girls retreated back into the brush and disappeared.

Afterwards, Thomas was helping one of the girls into the back of the van they were using when a sniper picked him off with a glancing shot to the head that did enough damage to end his life. Jason was there within seconds, regardless of his own safety. He held Thomas, told him the evac team was on its way, described the land where he was going and how there would be greeters to welcome him, and urged him not to be afraid.

As his best friend's life drifted away, Jason wept. Even in the community of brothers so tightly woven together into the tapestry of that force for good, he felt all alone for the first time.

HE'D BEEN SITTING just past the surf, watching the oranges swirl and outline the billowy clouds. Jason could see how Thomas would love it here. It wouldn't bring his friend back, but he decided to explore the community, just as if his friend was doing it himself. He owed that to him. The two of them had talked about spending some time on Kauai, but Jason never got the chance to share his ancestral home.

Another lifetime, brother.

He sensed someone was behind him and turned, finding the woman he was hoping to see at the beach tonight.

He scrambled to stand, but she stopped him.

"No! Don't get up," she said. Her nerves were still on edge. But, without the floppy hat and the huge sunglasses, the woman he saw in front of him was a vibrant, natural beauty. His body immediately warmed to her presence, as it had done last night.

"Then come, join me," he said in a whisper.

She halted and, thinking better of it, slowly took a seat where he'd been sitting. He gave her space right next to him.

"I'm Kiley," she said as she extended her hand.

He placed one palm beneath hers and then the other on top. "I'm Jason." After giving her a slight squeeze, he withdrew, placing his hands in his lap. He was going to move very slowly, since he didn't want to raise her fears again.

"I came down here when I saw you, because I still feel I need to apologize for my behavior last night."

"Don't worry. You don't owe me anything. I probably came on too strong, but I wanted to convince you that I had no ill intentions."

She nodded. "No, I was the idiot." She let out a huge sigh. "My life has been a basket of snakes, lately."

Jason hated snakes.

"You don't have to tell me anything, Kiley. I just want you to be safe. I don't really need all the details."

"Of course you don't. Why would you?"

Her comment was a bit on the snarky side and Jason didn't like the tone. He squinted, looking down on her, wrinkling his brow. She was damned hard to figure out. He decided he better stop trying. He sensed something might be wrong with her or her situation. She was damaged, somehow.

"I'm sorry. I can't seem to help lashing out at you. It isn't you; it's my situation. But that's all I'm going to say."

He didn't believe her. "You sure?" He grinned at her shocked expression. "For someone who doesn't want to talk about it, you seem to bring it up a lot."

She attempted to get to her feet. He'd just pushed her over the edge.

Dammit!

He held onto her forearm, but only with enough firmness to let her know he wasn't going to let go. If she insisted, of course he would do so. He wanted to make it clear she still had the control.

"Stay. Don't go."

It was too awkward for her to continue to rise, so she collapsed back down onto the sand, and withdrew her arm from his grip.

"Can we start all over?" he asked.

Looking into her warm eyes, he saw intelligence, honor, strength and something else he couldn't quite figure out.

She nodded, not looking at him.

"Where would you like to restart this from?" he asked.

Her glance at his lips gave him a most delicious signal. He slowly moved his face closer to hers until he was about two inches from her. He licked his lips and then pressed them against hers. He felt her jolt, and then soften to him.

He separated and angled his chin in the opposite direction. She matched his movement and met him halfway again, where their lips touched. She opened to him but he didn't take advantage.

Instead, he cupped her cheek with his hand, stroking down the side of her face, his fingers sifting through her hair.

Should I stop?

He was fairly certain she'd agree to anything he asked of her. The idea thrilled him. And he understood what a gift that was.

She held his hand in both of hers and kissed his palm. "Come inside. With me," she whispered. "Please?"

Her shyness moved him. He was falling off a cliff like one of those deep dives off the rocks back home. His body was soaring through the sky as if he was a bird.

They held hands as she led them to a bungalow three houses to the left of the beach access path. She pressed her back against her sliding glass window, and before letting him inside, she drew her arms up around his neck and pulled him down to her in a full-blown passionate kiss that lasted several minutes. His hands roamed down her backside, and over her arms, while his kisses were placed under her chin and beneath her ear. He loved her faint flowery scent and the way her delicate breathing grew strong and robust, as the woman came alive in his arms.

He pressed her lower torso to his hardened groin, and she moaned into his ear.

She broke off their embrace, opened the door, and stepped backward into her living room. He followed her every movement and closed the door behind him.

The interior of the little home smelled like her. She had a candle burning on the kitchen counter, which gave off a golden angel-light. But his eyes were focused on the movement of her body as she continued to walk backwards, drawing him into the bedroom, where she dropped his hand and began to remove her top.

He stopped her.

"Let me," he whispered, kissing her ear. "I want to do it all."

"Oh my God," she sighed before she wrapped her arms around his neck and shoulder and drew her knees up around his waist.

He chuckled. "Clothes are awkward. If you'll just have a little patience, I'll have you naked and wet in two minutes. And that's being slow."

His fingers probed the waistband of her jeans, sliding over her smooth buttocks. Once, again, he drew her in, and showed her what a good fit they were, and once again, she moaned.

He pulled her oversized tee shirt over her head, as she undid his fly. Her fingers found him just as he removed her bra. She slipped his pants down over his hips just before he knelt in front of her, slowly sliding her jeans over her well-developed hips. The scent of her arousal caused a deep pounding in his chest. He placed one hand between her legs, and lazily let his forefinger travel the length of her opening, spreading her moisture.

With her hands pressed into the tops of his shoulders she leaned forward and widened her knees, allowing him access to slowly insert two fingers. He kissed her breasts and then let his tongue leave a trail down to her belly button as her breathing became ragged. She gripped his shoulders nearly to the point of causing him pain.

On his haunches, he leaned back to observe her arousal as his fingers slid in and around her opening. Her eyes were shut, her lips flushed out into a plump O, driving the need to taste her. She widened her stance farther, mewling soft squeals as his tongue probed and drank from her elixir. His tiny lapping movements made her shudder. She squeezed her right breast, keeping her grip tightly onto his left shoulder. She seemed starved for what he fully intended on giving her.

Abruptly, he picked her naked body up, and walked her on his knees onto the bed. His fingers splayed out and touched her perfect body. His knee nudged between her legs and she raised one thigh, arching to meet him. He crawled up over her, placing his hand under her neck and then holding her head while he devoured those lips, giving back the same intensity he was dishing out.

He angled his hips, his growing erection persistently working against the lips of her sex, probing and testing for an opening. When at last he found her, he moved his arm to the arch in her lower back, elevating her pelvis so he could thrust deep, holding her tight against him.

Jason had not thought to ask her about protection, so he stopped. Her body began to move beneath him, her hands gripping his butt cheeks, begging him to go deeper. He leaned over and whispered, "Should I—?"

But she put her hand over his mouth. She stared into his eyes.

"Fuck me."

"Yes ma'am."

CHAPTER 6

WAKING UP IN the pink glow of early morning, with his huge, muscled, and fully sleeved arm still holding her body against his hip was awkward. The level of feasting on each other's passions was so intense she wasn't sure she could look him in the eyes. He had demanded she show him how to please her. He guided her to what he wanted her to do. Though her pheromones were raging wildly, it was the most intentional lovemaking she'd ever had. His body was a love-making machine.

She felt his tongue touch the side of her neck before she felt his enormous hands capture and claim her left breast. He squeezed her nipple, which made her arch up and feel the dull ache for him again, spiking her body back to life.

Because he was so massively strong, he had no trouble moving her body up and over him, planting her on his cock, maneuvering her up and down just the way he needed it. With her eyes closed, she focused on the feel of his girth, on the sweat forming inside her thighs as they moved together.

"Open your eyes, Kiley," he whispered, still moving her slowly up and down on him.

She timidly obeyed. She'd never found it so hard to make eye contact with a sexual partner. Jason demanded it.

As if he knew what she was thinking, he murmured, "I like to watch it on your face when you come."

The wave of pleasure flooded over her like the ocean, tickling and sparking every cell in her body. She moved her knees, bringing her legs in front, sinking in deeper to his thrusting motion beneath her.

Her eyes began to flutter as if she was going to faint, but it was her body's warning. She was about to experience an orgasm unlike she'd ever felt before.

Jason sat up, bringing her with him, and then pressed her back into the bed. Moving her legs to his shoulders, he undulated his hips in a circular back and forth that coated and touched everywhere inside her channel.

She threw her head from side to side, and then rose her chin to the ceiling as he picked up the pace. He stopped long enough to caress her neck with his probing fingers, following up with soft kisses. He gently bit her earlobe. She grabbed his ass with her right hand and squeezed as hard as she could. He drilled her deep, relentlessly, and at last slowed so she could feel her own orgasm punching into motion, milking him. Her moans spurred him on, pressing her limits and making her explode. Her body shuddered with full release.

In between thrusts his sweet kisses continued the slow burn as her body completely gave him all the power.

Finally, his heart-breaking moan claimed whatever holdback she had felt, when he released into her. His fingers clutched at her scalp as if needing to attach. His other hand rose her pelvis up to receive every drop he had to give.

The healing, sensuous dance didn't satisfy her. She was hungry for more. It was the perfect way to begin a day.

After their breathing slowed, he carefully extricated himself from the tangle of sheets and her limbs, returning with a cool towel. The damp cloth felt heavenly as he began to dab her forehead. She felt delirious with the levels of abandon he'd brought her to. His warm smile as he worked to soothe her burn was something she couldn't take her eyes off of. He gently spread her legs and held the cool towel against her swollen lips, and then gently kissed her.

Who was this man? Where on the planet had he come from? The right side of his body was completely covered in tats, designs with parallel lines and swirls she was certain meant something. Everything about him was sculpted and toned as if he was a bodybuilder. His thighs were larger than the diameter of her waist. When he walked, she could see muscles in his butt cheeks flex and release. She held the towel between her legs, mesmerized by the sight of him.

"You okay, Kiley? I didn't hurt you, did I?"

"No." It was all she could say.

"You want some help with that?" he nodded to the towel he'd given over to her.

She didn't know how to answer. She finally burst out laughing. "You've taken all my words away, Jason." It really was funny, this effect he'd had on her. "I'm a newspaper reporter and I don't have a thing to say."

He lay on his side next to her, propping his head up with his elbow, and lazily ran his fingers up and down her midsection. There were no sexual parts there, but the movement itself was so stimulating, she had the urge to kiss him again.

She touched his cheek. Her forehead leaned against his. Their legs were still entangled.

"Tell me something," he whispered.

She pressed her forefinger over his mouth, rubbing back and forth.

"Tell you what?" she whispered as she watched her finger travel over the fullness of those lips that could drive her wild.

"Tell me how you feel."

She palmed his cheek, drew her face to his, and whispered. "Like you've charmed me with a spell I will not recover from."

His fingers stopped sifting through her hair, and for a few seconds, she thought perhaps she'd said something wrong. Then his face broke out into a wicked grin.

"What?" she softly demanded. She studied the designs that covered his shoulder and upper arms, the pads of her fingers traveling over the exquisite artwork as if it was a relief.

"I'm a medic. So I will bring you to the edge and then a little further. And then I'll catch you when you fall. I'll work my magic on you, revive you, and make you need my healing ways."

She blinked. It was a strange answer. But it completely fit.

"So you are addicted then? Is that what you're saying?" She continued touching his lips.

"I hope so. As I think you are to me, Kiley. I like the way you taste, the way you move. I like what you show me in your eyes and in your heart."

She nodded, even though she was incapable of any serious concentration. "What are all these designs?"

"They're warrior designs. Some of these patterns have covered the men of my family for generations."

"Are you a warrior, Jason?"

"I am."

"For real?"

"I am."

"Like a cage fighter or something?"

He rolled over on his back, laughing so hard he began to cry. With his arm over his forehead, she noted that they were the size of her thighs. The lines almost appeared to come alive as the muscles moved underneath. Even his belly laugh was sexy.

"You obviously work out," she posed.

"Yes, I do. I do every day."

"Like you pull trucks by rope with your bare hands or something? You do—what?—a hundred sit-ups without getting winded?

Could you pick up this bed and hold it over your head?"

"I've never tried those things." He rose up just enough to kiss her again. "I get to do cool stuff. I'm a man of action. That's what we call it."

"We? You part of some alien space force or something?"

"Hardly, Kiley. I'm just a man."

"Just a man you say. *Just* a man. You made love like five times last night. Now I suppose you'll tell me the bad news. You're part of some ancient brotherhood cult and you run naked and throw telephone poles."

"Now, that I've actually done. Well, with some help from my friends."

"Do your friends look like you?"

"No. We're all different. We come from all over the world."

"You all have these markings?" she asked.

"Well, some of us do. Not like these, though. And I don't run naked down the beach, but some probably have. But these types of tats are special. These are a chronicle of my heritage, my Polynesian ancestral heritage, Kiley. So, someone else's would be different."

"So, what are you, a big soccer team?" She knew that was wrong. "Maybe not soccer. Soccer players are skinny. But how about Rugby then?"

"I love Rugby. We have a Hawaiian form of Rugby that's even more challenging. And there's a famous Rugby team who do Maori chanting before their games. Ever heard of the All Blacks Haka?"

"The what?"

"It's a Maori All Blacks Haka. I've watched them several times. They do this chant that scares the liver out of the opposition."

Kiley had never known a Rugby player.

"So are you a sports figure of some kind?"

"No."

He knew she was pressing for answers and wasn't going to give her any until he was good and ready to. She hoped that he wasn't going to keep secrets, but she'd play along for a bit.

"I know," she giggled. "You're a personal trainer!"

His eyes roamed down her frontside. He angled his head to take a different view. "Would you like that?"

"I think I'd find it distracting," she said, avoiding his eyes. "I'd probably drop the weights on my foot, something like that."

"Why do you say that?" He gently brushed the hair from her face.

"I'm just a klutz, that's all. Not very coordinated."

"It's just a matter of training. With focus and discipline, you can make your body do anything you want it to do."

"Can you heal the dead?"

She realized right away the mistake she'd made. He sat up and turned his back to her.

"Jason, I'm sorry about that comment. That was stupid of me. I wasn't thinking."

"It's okay," he said to his lap.

But she could tell something was eating a hole in his heart. She waited. Finally, he turned, flipping onto his stomach and peered into her eyes.

"I'd give anything to be able to do that. Life is random. We do the best we can, but sometimes, that's not good enough. He didn't have to die. He shouldn't have died. But he did, and I was spared. There have been times when I've beat myself up about that. But it is what it is."

"And you're going to honor him by living well," she said, stroking his forearm. She let her fingers mate with his, examining the roughness, the cuts and divots made in his flesh. He used his hands for something, and he obviously worked hard. She drew his palm to her cheek and held it there, returning his gaze.

Then she drew his hand down her frontside, guiding him to the juncture between her legs. She felt shy all of a sudden.

"Sorry."

"You sure apologize a lot, Kiley. Don't ever apologize for things you don't mean to. It's the way you are. And…" he said as he placed his hand under her thigh and bent her knee, "I find you perfect just the way you are. This is magic," he said before he kissed her belly button. "And I'm in the mood for a whole lot more."

KILEY'S CELL PHONE rang, waking them up. It was Carmen. She took the call in the living room.

"Hey there," she whispered. "So Newman put you on the story."

"Was that your doing? Because I'm not happy." Carmen was smart, but Kiley had always felt their communications started way too adversarial. "He should have finished your work instead of taking me off my desk."

"Between you and me, Carmen, he'd have fucked it up, and you know this."

"I don't dig seeing naked women horribly brutalized and left for dead, Kiley. I cannot understand how you get off on that shit."

She could tell changing her mind was going to be a waste of time, so she didn't argue with her. "Just give it a few days, and if you can't, you can't." She sighed. "And for the record, I don't get off on it. I'm trying to see to it that it stops happening."

"Well, there you go again. Saving the world, Kiley. That's not my gig. I don't want to dig into the crap, seedy underbelly of society. I want to experience the excitement of life, not muck around in detritus. Look, it's not that I can't. I don't want to."

"But you've always been in favor of defending the little guy. That's what you're all about, Carmen. This is a wrong that has to be exposed."

"Yeah, is that what you're doing? Run off to lie on the beach in Florida?"

Panic began to seep into her veins with a cold fear that someone, probably her editor, had not kept her secret safe. The betrayal hurt.

"Who told you that?"

"Everyone knows, Kiley."

"In just a couple of days, I'll be sending in the end of the series. Then I'm going to turn in all my notes to the police and let them do the rest. After that, I'll be coming back. You just do your investigation and feed me some of the facts, and I'll help steer you where I think your investigation has promise. I've spent a lot of time studying this whole ring of bad boys. I've even met many of the players."

"Is it true someone killed your cat?" Carmen asked.

"Yes. And slashed my tire."

"And you don't think I'd be in any danger, Kiley?"

"Not after I publish my story. But you'll have all the background to do a killer follow-up. That's something I'm just handing you, Carmen. If we expose this ring and get the light of justice shining down on them, you'd be helping the community. Heck, you might even get a medal for it. There could be a Pulitzer in it for you."

Carmen agreed to scan and send pictures and a copy of the reports on file. Kiley gave her a couple of women's shelters she could go interview, including the name of one of her sources who had been nearly killed in a botched trafficking event.

"I'll call you back in two days, and if you have questions, put them in an email. No messaging. I won't have this phone when I call back, so don't try, okay?"

"Geez, this is all very cloak and dagger-like."

A dark cloud of worry fell over Kiley when she considered that perhaps Carmen hadn't taken her cautions seriously enough.

"Be smart. Don't talk about it to anybody but Corbin, and even then, don't tell him everything. Don't leave your notes around your apartment or at your desk at the paper. If we're careful, we could be doing a really great thing for the Portland community. But it also extends way beyond our city."

"I'm on it. Look for that email in an hour or so, Kiley."

"Thanks. You're going to be great. Oh, and Carmen, no more talk about Florida. I'm not there. That was just a ruse."

"Okay, if you say so." Carmen hung up.

When Kiley turned around, Jason was standing against the wall, his arms crossed over his chest. He didn't look happy.

She wondered how much of her conversation Jason heard. Before she could try to give an explanation, he straightened up, his fists clenched at his sides.

"What the hell are you into, Kiley?"

"I can explain, Jason. I can explain it all—well, most of it, anyway."

"You fuckin' better. Just answer this question first, are you doing anything illegal here, because if you are, I cannot be involved. And I can't know anything about it."

"No. Come. Sit down, and I'll tell you what I can."

He sat across the coffee table from her, again crossing his chest with his arms, waiting.

"I'm working on a story for the *Columbia Passage*. That's the big newspaper in Portland, where I live. I've uncovered some facts about a human smuggling ring operating out of several shelters in the area. I've been working on this story now for nearly two years. And I've so far published three installments. I'm about to publish the last one, but before I could get it done, I started getting death threats by phone. I got some letters at the office too. Someone broke into my apartment and trashed the place. Luckily, neither I nor my roommate were home at the time."

"Who did this?"

"The police said kids."

"And why don't you believe them?"

"Because, Jason, they cut up my cat. They gutted him and left him on the couch. It was horrible. And then the next day, someone slashed one of my tires at the paper.

"But you don't know specifically who."

"We have problems with street gangs in Portland like every big city in the U.S. I think some of the City staff are somehow connected. There are some city-sponsored women's shelters created by the Mayor and his task force. But they may not be so innocent as far as how they handle teen runaways and battered women. They have a lot of young immigrant girls. And my research has led me to believe there are organized crime figures involved. They might have compromised certain city officials, too. My editor says the Mayor has asked that I stop publishing the stories, that it sheds a negative light on their good works. He also said it might be dangerous—to me."

"He actually said that?"

"He told my editor he got an anonymous call. It was a warning."

"That's an understatement. You have police involved, right?"

"Only for the burglary. They filed it primarily as an animal cruelty case since nothing was taken. That's all. I didn't offer anything about the investigation I was doing. I guess they didn't put it together, so not really. Not yet at least."

"Kiley, this is absurd. You can't take this on all by yourself."

"I've got the backing of the paper on this. The power of the press and public opinion will definitely be on my side after I'm finished. I just want to lay out the evidence so the public sees everything. If I go to the officials, they'll find some way to bury it. I know they will. But if I get the public on their cases, we have a much better shot at exposing them and hopefully getting them rooted out."

"This is your plan?"

"Well yes, that's my plan."

"Fuck."

"Hey, that's not nice."

"Somebody's gotta tell you the truth. How the heck did you get involved in this story?"

She sucked in air, proud that she'd been trusted with this very important assignment. "My editor gave it to me for a series on runaway girls in the Portland area, except that the more I looked into things, the wider my search became. The story started out about a young illegal immigrant disappearing. But now we're looking at ten missing girls. Only four of them have been found. I've got to wrap this up, finish my story, and then lie low for a while."

"You think? Like forever."

"I hope not."

"So that's what you do. You're an investigative journalist?"

"Yes."

"And you thought, when I met you at the beach, what? I was one of the bad guys, like a hit man?"

She avoided his stare.

"Look at me, Kiley. Is that what you thought? I mean you were *that* scared?"

"Well, yes. Jason, I'm probably blowing it out of proportion. But my mind just isn't letting me relax, so I've been seeing bad guys everywhere. I finally had to leave Portland and go somewhere I felt safe."

He shook his head.

"Unbelievable," he mumbled. "You're wrong, Kiley. There are no safe places. I've seen firsthand what these cabals do. I've seen what lengths they'll go to keep anyone from interrupting their operation. You do not want to be messing with them. Trust me on that."

Kiley sat back. A whole new set of questions started flashing in her mind.

She began slowly, needing to unpack her concerns, one question at a time. It was rather backwards, she realized. Here she'd slept with the man, and now she wanted to know who he was. Her *Aunt*

Itoldyouso was having a temper tantrum inside her brain.

Kiley, what have you done?

"I know you're not a Rugby player. What exactly is it you do, then?"

"I'm a Navy SEAL."

CHAPTER 7

B Y EARLY AFTERNOON, and they'd basically stayed in bed nearly the whole time, even while she was peppering him with questions about his SEAL training. He was careful to reveal just enough to satisfy her and not lead to more questions. Jason knew he was overdue with the check-in and Andy's house would be wondering where he was. They didn't realize he was a mere six or seven houses down from them.

His concern for Kiley's safety bothered him so much that he needed to make a call to his LPO, Kyle Lansdowne, but out of earshot of Kiley. Although it frustrated Team guys from time to time, they all knew they were prohibited from interfering with any domestic criminal behavior. Recently, the Navy had made examples of SEALs trying to blur that line. He didn't want to be one of the casualties, just because he was trying to help someone do something for the good of society.

Convincing Kiley would be another story, though. She'd already asked for his help, suggesting he be her bodyguard.

"You don't get it. I'm supposed to be working up to our next mission overseas. I can't just take off and play policeman."

She'd agreed with him, but he could see she wasn't happy about it. He needed some guidance. He considered talking to Andy, but since he was on his way to Team 4 and wasn't in a leadership position either, he decided against it. Cory would be a loose cannon.

Damon, if he stopped by, would probably be no better.

The other thing that bothered him was that perhaps he'd involved them all too much already. He was certain Kiley had no clue what she was getting into. She had a fantasy about making the world a safer place. That was *his* job, and it involved a hell of a lot more sacrifice than most people would even want to know about. He certainly wasn't going to be the one to tell her. She already had some TV notion of what a SEAL was. And that wasn't her fault. Everyone underestimated and misunderstood them all, but that was how the Teams wanted it to be. The less the general public knew about them the better. If they did their job well, everyone would be safe at home and they'd know nothing about what really lurked outside the borders of the U.S.

He also wasn't suffering under the delusion of complete safety at home, either. He could defend himself and her. He just couldn't go policing society and interfere with his brothers in blue. It was a delicate balance. He had to be careful what he said, and he had to make sure he didn't get involved in anything he could lose his Trident over.

And, as much as he loved their physical relationship, he'd sort of put the cart before the horse. It wasn't wise what he'd done. He had no right staking a claim on her when he didn't really know anything about her.

But over half the guys on the team had violated that one dozens of times. It still was no excuse, though.

She kept looking over at her computer, and he knew she was itching to get back online and file her story.

"Listen, why don't I leave you alone for a few hours?" he asked. "My friends down the beach haven't heard from me since yesterday afternoon. I should check in, and then you can join us down there, or I can return later. How does that sound?"

"You're right. I should get the article written."

"How long do you think you'll be?" he asked.

"Two, three hours. I'll send it off, and then perhaps we can grab some dinner?"

"Sounds like a plan, Kiley."

She began sorting through notes and turned on her laptop. "Once it's out of my hair, then I will take your suggestion and turn over all my notes and assist the police, if they'll let me."

"Why wouldn't they, Kiley?"

"I don't know. Call it a reporter's instinct. The one thing I've learned about all of this is that things are never what they seem."

"And you don't really know who you can trust."

"Exactly. But my editor thought they'd stop once the stories got published."

Jason knew that was complete folly. But until he had more information on where he stood, professionally, he wasn't going to say anything to her.

He wrote down the address of Aimee and Andy's house and handed it to her. "You can't miss it. Think deep pink and red mixed. There isn't anything remotely similar in color or intensity."

She took the piece of paper and laid it next to her laptop.

"And you should text me when you head over there so I can watch for you," he added.

She placed her fingers over his mouth. "I will follow your instructions to the letter," she said, her arms wrapped around his neck. "Thank you for caring, Jason. I mean that."

"I should be driving you down to the police station, not sitting here listening to your stories. That's the right thing to do, so don't thank me, Kiley."

"It will work out. You'll see. Now that you're here, I'm safe."

Jason bristled at that. "You need anything, anything at all, you let me know. That's my cell." He pointed to the number under the address.

She held his face between her hands. "Didn't you hear me? I'll be fine. You don't have to worry about me."

"I'm going to worry about you plenty. But I like the idea of you being over at the big house. Where I can watch you."

"Thank you. I'll be there before you've had your sixth beer."

Their kiss bordered on some further fooling around, but in the end, they separated. Jason slipped out the sliding glass door and onto the beach.

About halfway to Andy's he dialed Kyle Lansdowne.

"Hey there, Jason. Everything go smoothly?"

"Yessir." He wasn't sure how to begin.

After a minute of air silence, Kyle began, "You know, for a not very talkative guy, you're sure not doing a lot of talking."

Kyle's sixth sense about these things was legendary.

"I met this girl."

"Oh boy. What is it with you guys and Florida? If anything happens to Christy, I'm giving up everything and heading out there. They must put something in the water. And to make matters worse, Christy has been working nearly twenty-four seven. Hell, I'm about to call up Collins and ask him if we could just take a temporary duty to Iraq to go vaccinate some kids or something. At least it would get me out of having kid-duty for the sixth day in a row."

Jason chuckled, "I feel your pain, sir."

"No, you don't. You've got no idea what it's like to be past your prime, hearing about all your guys getting laid and having girl issues. Is that what this call is going to be about? You need more time off so you can cement your relationship? Do you want to know how many times I've gotten that call, son?"

Jason knew he'd calm down, but he just let him rant on. Kyle abruptly laid the phone down to straighten something out. One of his three was crying after he was done.

"Honestly, I don't know how they do this. Tomorrow, I have to take the three of them to a birthday party, one of Maggie's friends. I'm going to strap Brandon to the nearest tree. That means all I'll have to do is watch out for Luke, and at his current age, he still likes girls and thinks they smell nice."

"Well, you give Brandon my best, then. Tell him he should soak in the bathtub, and that will take care of his sore behind."

"Was I that obvious?"

"He's always the one you're talking about getting into trouble, sir."

"Okay. Well, now that we got all that out of the way, what's the emergency?"

Jason took a deep breath and sat on the bench, donated by the good people of Sunset Beach, about ten steps from the beach access. He watched the constant parade of old and new bodies in various stages of undress and inebriation.

"So this girl is an investigative reporter?"

"Uh-oh. You better run. You didn't say anything you regret, did you?"

"No. Not really."

"Well, which is it—no or not really?"

Jason felt Kyle's mysterious powers of getting anything out of anyone working extremely well.

"The problem is on her end. She's researching a story about the sex trade, and more particularly, she thinks she's identified some key players in a big human smuggling ring up in the Portland area where she lives."

"Okay. I'm holding my breath here."

"She's written some high-profile articles for the Columbian something-or-other."

"Yea. I know it. And?"

"She thinks she's being harassed. Well, she knows she's been harassed. They tossed her place, she's gotten some death threats and the worst part is, they sliced up her cat."

"Holy shit."

"Yeah. Cut up one of her tires too. So, I think she was pretty smart. She hopped on a plane and came to Florida, where she spent some time as a child."

"Where are her folks? What kind of a father lets his little girl do that stuff?"

"Gone. She's all alone."

"And no ex gunning for her? Jilted or jealous boyfriend?"

"Not that she's mentioned."

"But of course you didn't ask her because you thought it would interfere with your chances of getting laid, right?"

That was a funny line, but Jason held it in. "Actually, we didn't have any problem in that department."

"You've only been there what, two days? God forbid you'd have to wait a week to get in bed with her. So do you want my quick answer or my long answer, Jason?"

"Well, wait. You don't even know the question I'm going to ask you."

"I think I do. I'm a lot smarter than anyone thinks I am. I even let Christy think she's way smarter than me because, well, when a woman feels like she's worshiped, she puts it out like nobody's business."

"Well, you would know, Kyle."

"Watch it. Okay, just humor me. My short answer is run, after you pick your clothes up, that is."

Jason chuckled again. He waited for the long answer.

"My quicker answer is run."

Jason felt cheated. "But…"

"The complicated answer requires a question from me. Is this Miss Have-A-Good-Time or Miss Permanent sort of thing? I mean you guys are all about instalove, so forget that."

"She's in danger, Kyle. And that's what we do. We ride in and save the day."

"In Portland. You're gonna do this in Portland."

"I was thinking if…"

"Are you kidding me? You seriously think that is a good idea?"

"They're gonna kill her, Kyle. I can just sense it."

"And I'm saying I'm going to kill you if you don't stop thinking about it."

Jason had never felt this way. For once, the Navy, his career, his LPO didn't have the answers he wanted them to have.

"Look. What you don't yet know is there's talk of another quick mission, like two weeks max. Back to Benin or Nigeria. And don't go telling the other men. It might happen this week. I can't have you missing your obligation because you're playing private dick in Portland. The timeline's been tentatively moved up. So even if I did give you the green light, you'd have to turn around and fly back here if it was a go. That could happen tomorrow the next day. I'm just staying by the phone. Our ten-day window has shriveled like my grandfather."

"I'd be okay with that."

"And then who would protect her?"

"At that point, I get the police involved."

"Um hum. The same police she doesn't trust now. You think you can pull that off? Seriously, Jason?"

"If it was our only option, and for her safety."

"Personally, I think she better stay there in Florida. I'll grant you a few more days, since you're with the other guys there. Do not breathe a word to anyone."

"I won't. Thanks, Kyle. I have one more question."

"Go ahead." Kyle's voice held exhaustion.

"What if she's working the other end of the same group we've been working with? You remember that guy Colin Riley? He lives in

Portland, doesn't he?"

Kyle exhaled. "Because we're not that lucky, Jason."

Saying good-bye, they disconnected. Jason checked his cell, thinking he might have gotten a call while he was talking to Kyle, and discovered it was a text from Andy.

'I'm guessing we're counting chickens, then?'

He texted back. *'I'm right outside your door.'*

'Um. No, you're not. We're on the patio.'

Before him was a familiar circle of friends sitting around a back-yard fire pit. Like the parties on the beach at Coronado, they hadn't scrimped on the fire, which sent fingers of flame several feet above the grate.

Damon rose and shook his hand. "Hey, Jason. Thanks for taking good care of old Thomas."

"You bet."

"You remember Martel?"

"I sure do. Didn't come to the wedding, but that party was hard to forget. Didn't remember too much of it, though."

"No one did," barked Andy.

Jason waved to Aimee and Cory then waited for Martel to take a seat before he sat next to Andy. He addressed Damon first. "Are you hooking up with Team 4 like Andy here?"

"Martel's a teacher. And she's got a dream job neither one of us wants her to give up. But after my billet is done, I'm not re-upping."

Andy sat up straight. "How does that work? You're on one side of the country, and she's on the other?"

"You forget, Andy, I get summers off. It's better to be in San Diego at that time, anyway. Cooler." Martel told him.

"We do rack up the miles some. It's not forever," Damon added.

"Where the hell did you slink off to last night?" Cory barked.

The guy might have his drinking under control, but his mouth was still a problem. Jason wasn't sure he could spend too much time around the man.

Aimee frowned. "Cory, you're being obnoxious."

"Did they work on that elbow in San Antonio?" Andy asked, changing the subject.

"I'm having to get surgery in a couple of months. Doing some PT which is supposed to help. But they're not happy with some of the muscle attachment. Of course, those take longer to heal." Cory looked glum, staring down at his beer.

With one major injury and recovery Cory'd already used up his free bite. He would get rolled, and if he wanted to stay in the Navy, they'd have to give him a desk job. He noticed Andy frowning, probably thinking the same thing.

"How long are you out here?" Damon asked Jason.

"Originally five or six days. But, if I asked for it, I could stay longer."

"Shoot. Rumor has it we might have to go back before the weekend. But Martel's staying, of course. If your friend doesn't work out, I'm sure she can set you up with someone from her school."

It wasn't on Jason's radar. He was distracted by thinking about how Damon knew the trip was going to be cut short.

The rhythm of their banter cascaded all over Jason and it wasn't long before his edginess about being around Cory deflated. He was working on trying to extract Damon's good intel when the ping on his cell phone diverted his attention.

He held his cell up and addressed the crowd. "Looks like she's on her way. You'll get to meet her shortly. I'm going to head down the beach to make sure she doesn't get lost."

Jason jogged barefoot on the warm sand until he saw her small frame coming towards him. When she spotted him, she ran straight into his arms. She hugged him, coming up on tiptoes. Her joyful smile made him happy too.

"You did it, right?" he asked her.

"I did. Waited just long enough to see that my editor got it. Friday, it goes out in the paper and the whole world will know."

"Did you talk to him?"

"No. I'll get the scoop when I call Carmen in a couple of days."

"Good deal."

She turned, pointing. "Look at that sky. You know, I never tire seeing it. I used to miss these colors." Facing him, she continued. "Portland has all those big clouds, the sweeping vistas from the hills surrounding the river, but it rarely has something so absolutely thrilling as that sky."

He wrapped his arms around her, spooning behind. He considered everything Kyle said to him on the phone and brushed it aside.

He decided they'd had enough drama today. It was time for him to show her off to his friends, and then he had plans to create magic all night long. He knew just what he needed to do to chase those fears away.

He heard the chanting again, and that rumble in his belly that told him something spectacular was about to happen.

CHAPTER 8

KILEY WOKE UP in a panic. She'd been in a dream—caught in a box-like container at the bottom of the ocean, the force of the water pressing on her chest. She began beating against the walls of her confinement and tried to scream, but no air was coming out. She felt caught, bound by invisible ties that kept her from breaking free of the confined space.

She awoke, gasping for air. She was still fighting until she heard the soft, reassuring voice of Jason beside her, kissing her, speaking to her in hushed tones. She still felt like she had to get away. Her heart felt that he was trying to help her, but her brain would not loosen the grip of panic. Back and forth she went, torn between two powerful scenarios, until her fear took dominance.

She struggled but managed to scramble to her feet, where she looked down on his shocked expression. Her arms wrapped around her upper torso as if to protect her from the man she was sharing a bed with.

He was making his way quickly in her direction, untangling his legs from their sheets, but she warned him.

"Don't! Please, just let me get my bearings." The words didn't even sound like her own. He crouched in front of her. Even that motion made her feel like he was a giant panther, ready to strike without warning.

"Kiley, it was a dream. You're safe."

She couldn't speak.

"It's a panic attack. Brought on by stress, all the things you worry about when you shut down. Happens to all of us in some circumstances. There is no danger here, Kiley."

But she still didn't want him to touch her, to come anywhere near her. She remembered to breathe. He was asking her to breathe, and then she saw him taking in slow, deep breaths and blowing them out, in tandem with her.

As the air refreshed her lungs, new oxygen cleared her brain. Her heartbeat slowed. Looking down on him, she was filled with regret, and began to cry.

His arms were wide. He urged her, "Come to me, Kiley. Let me hold you."

She closed her eyes as black spots began to form in her eyes.

"No!" she shouted at the sickening feeling she was out of control.

"Just come here, sweetheart."

Tears rolled down her cheeks. Her shoulders slumped, and she collapsed on the bed. Within seconds Jason's warm arms took hold of her as he pulled her up into his chest, rocking her back and forth.

She was mumbling something about having to get out of a box.

"You're safe. I got you, Kiley. There's no box. You're free."

Free!

She lost herself in his warmth, his massive hands rubbing her back to life as he held her and sang to her, his voice lilting. The vibration from his chest seeped into her own until she melted. Melding into his powerful arms, she needed his strength, and felt soothed by his rhythmic whisper-song.

She jerked back to life, her arms seeking him as he continued his chant and the rocking motion forward and back, like she was a tiny ship on a very big ocean. Her fingers touched the smoothness of his skin, pressing into him. Her arms slipped up and around his neck. She floated up into the direction of his voice, her lips desperate to feel the taste of his song.

"Jason!" she gasped.

"Shhh. Shhh. You're safe. Can you hear me, Kiley? You're here right now with me, and you're safe."

"Yes. Love me, Jason. Please make it go away."

"I'm right here, sweetheart."

Their lips collided with need. His fingers worked up the back of her spine, into her hair. His lips caressed her neck, her ear. The more he kissed her the more she felt his fire, his passion.

"You're okay, Kiley. Everything's fine."

"Love me, Jason. Please, love me."

He moaned, holding her so tight she thought perhaps she wouldn't be able to breathe again. Those soft words brought her back to life as his flesh made her body tingle with desire. She was beneath his massive form, her arms at the sides, fingers entangled in fingers, her inner thigh rubbing against his hip, needing him with a burning she'd not felt before.

He inhaled, crouching above her, not pressing into her body, but angling over her. His face down, he leaned closer until he covered her mouth. His tongue sought refuge inside her while his cock pressed, finding the glory trail that led inside her. Inch by slow inch, she felt the power of his pulsing cock, rooting out all doubt and cancelling all her worries.

There was freedom in the way he played her like an instrument, letting her body soar. She grew wings. She drew light from him, her hands touching his patterns and loving the stories there without even knowing what they were. His deep guttural moans sang of welcome satisfaction when he began their descent. He held her shaking body, whispering things she didn't understand until her breathing settled, and she glowed from the feel of his flesh pressing into hers.

He covered them with the bedsheet, still inside her, and commanded her to go back to sleep.

LIGHT FROM THE morning covered her face and chest. She was alone in the bed. She smelled coffee. Opening her eyes, she saw a dark form sitting in the corner of the room, not making a sound. Afraid at first, before she saw him raise a mug to his lips and drink.

She wondered what he was thinking. Was there a dark cloud hanging over his head? Had she ruined her welcome?

"Ready for coffee?" he asked softly.

She sat up, rubbing her eyes and repositioning her hair. "Yes. That would be wonderful."

His naked form, a combination of oversized muscle mass and tiny waist, was just as beautiful to watch from behind as it was to see him come back. His careful hands cupped hers and placed the mug there so it wouldn't tip. He took up a seat next to her. His face stayed close while she drank her first sips. He brushed the hair from her face and studied her, concern creasing his forehead.

"Do you wake up like that a lot?" he asked.

"Just started happening again. I don't remember where I was but it felt so real. No idea what triggered it. I've always been afraid of getting trapped under water or buried alive. It's a dream I used to have when I was a child."

"Can you remember when it started?"

She smiled, remembering playing all afternoon in the lush back-yard of her family home. Her mother would let her play there for hours all alone.

"What's the smile for?" he asked.

"I used to have this playhouse, it was an old abandoned green-house covered in vines at our old house. We'd moved into a new neighborhood, and I didn't know any of the kids, so my dad repaired it, converting it into my special playhouse and I loved being there." She looked up at Jason. "I felt safe there."

He nodded. "That sounds like a happy memory, not the stuff of nightmares."

"It is." She shook her head. "I mean, it was. It was my sanctuary, and I'd hide there all day. What about you?"

"I used to have a pretend house, a fort, really. I made this special place in the foliage, cutting branches and making room for a private space only I knew how to get into. It had a winding path, completely obscured from the outside so I could sneak in there and watch people walk by, listening to them without being detected. I used to pretend I was on a secret mission."

"Like you do now?"

"No, it's completely different. But I guess the sneaking in and out is the same. I liked knowing I could be very quiet. Learned to hold my breath and avert my eyes so they wouldn't know someone was there. I'd surprise little ground squirrels when they discovered my hiding place."

Kiley took another sip and smiled. She wondered whatever had happened to that little house they left behind when they moved again. Her dad had strengthened it so well it was probably still there, she thought.

"I loved that garden. I had a bedroom that overlooked the yard and the greenhouse. The house had two upstairs bedrooms and two big attics, and while my parents and my brother slept downstairs, I had the whole upper floor to myself. One night, I locked myself in the attic and couldn't get out."

"What did you do?"

"I cried myself to sleep. I spent the night there. I woke up in the morning hearing my mother screaming, thinking I'd been kidnapped. I used to wake up remembering that when I was a kid. Hearing her scream was worse than being alone."

He pressed his palm against her cheek. "I think under stress, perhaps part of that fear gets launched, like some kind of pattern.

Don't run away from it. Embrace it until it no longer makes you afraid."

"Jason, I'm so sorry about this morning. I haven't had that dream for years until this week. Not sure why it's coming up now."

"Well, look at the situation you're in. I think it's perfectly understandable, considering." He examined his fingers curled in his lap. "It's a form of stress. We've seen it on the Teams. As medics, we're always on the lookout for someone who doesn't get enough sleep or can't sleep. Perhaps that experience held more trauma than you realized at the time."

"Maybe."

"That's why I want you to consider carefully what you're doing."

"I have."

"I know it's what you're telling yourself what you want to do, but is it really something you can handle, something that is healthy to be involved with?"

She was unclear about his intentions. Did he not understand how important it was for her to do something to save those victims? That she had the power to stop some of it. Surely he didn't expect she could just walk away? Anger began to spread as her heartbeat kicked up.

"Are you telling me I should abandon my cause? Do you know what I've seen, uncovered? If I told you—"

"I don't want to know, because I'm not supposed to be involved. But I can imagine. I've seen some pretty awful stuff too. We're trained for that, or at least try to be. You're a civilian. Don't underestimate the effects of fear on the human body. Sometimes long-time criminals who get away get tired of looking over their shoulders and commit a crime just to be caught so they don't have to live with the uncertainty of it. It takes lots of training to not allow your fears to make choices that might not be in your best interest. Think about that, Kiley."

"I can handle it."

But she could see he wasn't convinced, and that bothered her. Maybe he didn't believe in her abilities to finish her mission.

"Don't you think I'm strong enough to deal with it?" she asked.

"How can you prepare for something you don't completely understand? Did it occur to you that what you've stumbled upon is bigger than it appears on the surface? What if you've hit a hornet's nest? Make sure you're not spinning a fairy tale, Kiley. Very dangerous to underestimate the enemy. And it comes at you when you least expect it."

"Now you sound like my editor. Although at first, he didn't believe a word I was saying."

"I believe you, Kiley. But I'm not sure you're seeing the big picture. You didn't sign on as a detective, and you have no training in that. These guys do this sort of thing all the time, and even they miss stuff. They get blindsided by things out of their control. And they're trained to look in all the right places. You could have stumbled onto something like that."

"You're scaring me, Jason."

"Good. I think you should take on a heavy dose of reality. Not fear, but the reality of the situation."

She winced. The more they talked about it, the worse she felt.

"Kiley, let's just wait to see what happens with the story. Maybe you're right. Maybe shining the light on their activities will cause other wheels to grind into motion and the authorities can do the rest, like you hoped. But it takes more than hope and determination to come up against these guys."

She finished her coffee, frowned and handed him the mug.

"I think you worry too much, Jason. I must have just forgotten where I was. That must have caused the dream. You're acting like I have some form of latent trauma, which is ridiculous. I'm going to take a shower."

The warm water completed the job of bringing her back to life. She thought about the other SEALs she met last night and the women who were with them. She had expected to hear war stories, but all they talked about were the practical jokes they played on each other all the time and the things they did while they were waiting. Lots of waiting. It was a surprise to learn that was their biggest complaint, to be all geared up and ready only to have to wait and hope that their timing wasn't off.

She told them a little about what she'd been doing, trying to expose abuses going on in women's shelters and how young women and children were being smuggled into the city and used for sex. She'd uncovered a network of City-sponsored women's shelters that were fronts for what looked to her like organized crime enterprises. That's when the team guys got silent. The questions stopped and she hesitated to go into much more detail. She saw their eyes travel from her face to Jason's. Some kind of signal was given.

"You're naming names in this article of yours?" finally asked Cory.

"Some, yes."

Corey returned her comment with a whistle. Jason's former teammate, Andy, made a point of telling her he hoped she was taking precautions and that she should be very careful.

"Hell, I'd just stay here," Cory answered.

The conversation ended. After they'd consumed all the beer, Andy handed Jason a guitar and asked him to sing.

As the water continued sluicing down her body, she remembered Jason holding the guitar with reverence. She remembered how his magic fingers toyed and tuned the strings just like he'd played her body. He closed his eyes and began singing old favorite Hawaiian songs, his voice lilting and full of passion. Into the firelight, he sang his gift that soared to the heavens with the fingerlings of fire.

As she dried off, she remembered the hush that came over the group and his peaceful smile as he dedicated a Hawaiian love song to Kiley he refused to translate.

When she walked into the bedroom to gather her clothes, Jason was on his phone. He hung up, a somber expression taking over his face.

"Bad news?" she asked.

"I'm afraid so. I've got orders to report back to Coronado."

"Just you?"

"No, Damon and another guy here from our Team. We're to catch a flight tomorrow around noon. So this is our last night here."

She was crestfallen. There was so little time. So much had not been said.

"So what does that mean?"

"Well, it means we're going to get together tonight, like we planned. But it will have to be an early night. Then I've got to leave you, Kiley."

"How long will you be gone?"

"Can't say, and we really never know." He shook his right shoulder. "They'll have all the details worked out by the time we get to California tomorrow. We could fly out right away, or it could be hurry up and wait."

"Is this how it always is?"

"More and more, yes. We're called as needed. Stuff happens. It never happens on schedule."

He watched her get dressed. She could tell he wanted to say something but was holding back. Then he whispered, "I'm so sorry, Kiley. I truly am."

It sounded more like a final good-bye than a good-bye for now. Her stomach began to burn. She was fighting inside—fighting something she would have to accept later. This untimely mission might mean that the relationship which had begun between them would forever be dashed, never given a chance to grow and develop into something she was sure would be beautiful and everlasting. But was this her imagination running wild again? Was he right? Was she chasing windmills and trying to do things that were impossible? Was any of this real?

His face was without emotion. A mask had covered what was once there.

Unsure whether or not it was her right to ask, she decided to pose her question.

"Will I see you again?"

"Of course. Sort of depends on you, though," he said.

"How do you mean?"

Jason's face was hard to read. "We've had a nice time together. Kind of took me by surprise, to be honest. I normally don't do this sort of thing," he said.

"What sort of thing?"

"Jump in fast. Play house on the first date, that sort of thing. Maybe I've been unfair to you. I'd like to stay in touch, but I have no expectations, nor do I have any claim on you, Kiley. You're here, in Florida, but your real life's in Portland. My life's in Coronado, and it has to remain that way. I expected we'd have some time to talk, you know. Get to know each other more, but—"

"We've talked," she joked, trying to keep it lighthearted, but her insides were shredded. She hoped her mask was holding up as well as his was.

"Yeah, we did." He looked down at her with a grin that sent sizzles down her spine.

She knew he was right. They'd jumped in so deep without knowing anything about each other, and now separating so soon felt like the end of a beautiful dream. It was going to be hard to concentrate, thinking about what a wonderful time they'd had. It was more than sex for her. She was going to miss him for reasons she couldn't work out yet. She just knew it was going to be the case.

"You didn't get to see the best part of Florida," she finally said.

He studied her body slowly, the grin deepening. "I think I saw all the best parts of Florida. Those are places I'd like to return to, some day, when the time is right."

"So would I, Jason. Is it wrong for me to want to see you again? After I get home, can you visit me up there?" A tiny slip of fear cooled her veins. She didn't want to hold on too tightly. She could scare him away.

"You're still thinking about going back to Portland?"

"I can't stay here forever."

Jason looked through the window to the beach and waves beyond. "There are worse places to be. It's kinda grown on me. But I understand. Hawaii will always be my true home, too."

She walked to the sliding glass door, looking out at the ocean. She didn't want this to end, but she was a grown up. The best thing she could do right now was to show him that. Besides, there had never been any promises made, like Jason said. Their worlds were so far apart it was hard to imagine they could stay connected, as nice as it felt to think about it that way.

"Come on. Let's take a walk," he urged.

He took her hand, and they made their way down to the surf. Kids were digging in the sand, creating forts and collecting shells. Couples of various ages walked slowly by. The bicycle crowd was missing today, but a group of women runners greeted them. It was almost painful for her to see normal life breezing by, seemingly carefree, while she was carrying such a heavy burden, knowing that she was going to have to let go of something she wasn't ready to release. She was going to miss him.

Barefoot, they let the water lap at their feet. The full noonday sun wasn't out yet. He pulled her hand and they walked along the shore.

"Tell me about Hawaii?" she asked, thinking it might be the last time they could talk about it.

"Hard to describe how I feel about her. Whenever I think of home, I smell flowers, I see dancing, family get-togethers, the little kids running around, barbequed pig and fresh fruit. Hawaii is like a beautiful woman with a perfect body, who will never grow old. The sunsets are like here."

"Sounds beautiful."

"People come from all over the world. We used to say in high school that Hawaii always breaks everyone's hearts. They want to come back, but most never do. I guess that's like here," he said.

Kiley didn't agree. "No, you're wrong. People come here to heal. I have this plaque at my place—"

"I've seen it. The beach heals everything."

"Yes. That's the way it is. There's a part of me that never wants to leave. Yes, I've carved out a place in Portland, but when I'm done saving the world, maybe I'll come back here and just heal."

"That's when you'll fall in love, Kiley."

The comment disturbed her. He was slipping away right in front of her and there wasn't anything she could do about it. And then his final thought drove the final wedge into her heart.

"When your work is done, you'll find someone on a beach just like this. And you'll set down roots. I'll go home to Hawaii and pick myself a nice island girl and make lots of *keiki*, kids."

She turned so he wouldn't see her tears. Mustering all the strength she could find, she bravely continued, trying not to let her voice waver.

"After you're done saving the world."

He nodded, "Yes, after I'm done."

The timing of all this sucked. Why couldn't they have met in a different time. Maybe same place, but different time.

"So why did you say it was up to me?"

He led her to sit on the sand several feet from the surf.

He kissed her hand. "When you're done battling those demons

in Portland, if you come back here, maybe I'll join you. But only after you're done. And only after I'm done."

What was he saying? Was there hope, still? Taking a deep breath, she stopped short. She didn't have words to answer him.

"Don't make promises you can't keep, Kiley." He faced the ocean, but his hand still held hers. He rubbed his thumb over her knuckles.

Was he asking that she give up her dream? Did he mean she should stop defending the helpless victims of these predators and creeps?

"But you would give up being a SEAL? You would consider getting out?"

"I didn't say that. Not yet. The work isn't done. I have a contract to fulfill. I made a vow and I'll not go back on that word. But there's always life after. And I won't fight someone else's war. I do what I'm signed up to do. I don't make the fights."

She wasn't sure she fully understood him. So she asked.

His answer surprised her.

"It's hard enough being with someone. Impossible if their battle and inspiration is elsewhere. If I put my Trident away, I want only one thing to focus on, one project left to accomplish. And for that, I'd give the rest of my life."

SHE WATCHED JASON all evening as he laughed, drank beer and savored the buttery crab they'd all been looking forward to. They told more silly stories. He demonstrated part of a Haka, a fierce Maorian dance he'd learned growing up. The patterns on his chest and arms seemed to come to life as he danced. Andy and Damon even joined him, playing the comic relief, unable to even partially imitate all Jason's moves. He stretched his neck, stuck out his tongue and puffed up his chest, his enormous hands balled into fists he'd slap against his thighs. He was twice the size of anyone else in the restaurant.

With twice the heart.

She met Madison, introduced as Ned's girl. Her mother was right in the middle of the conversation, along with her salty pirate boyfriend with a patch.

If they'd had more time, she would have participated more. But tonight she wanted to watch him, absorb everything about him so she wouldn't forget a single smile, laugh, or glance back in her direction.

And the more she watched, the greater her heartache.

Later, when they returned to her place, she found it difficult not to cry as he softly worshiped her body for the last time. He chuckled, trying to console her, pretending that she was being silly. But he knew. He just covered up that part of him better. She was certain he would miss her too. She'd touched his heart and he had fed hers.

She was going to crave him forever.

Kiley had told herself she'd get up and kiss him good-bye, but when she awoke, he was already gone. On the kitchen table, he left a note with a bright fuchsia flower on top of it. He just signed his name and wrote his cell number.

CHAPTER 9

J ASON LET ANDY and Damon imitate his dancing from last night while they waited for their plane in Tampa. He didn't mind the joking around, because it took his mind off of things he had no right to think about. Unwelcome thoughts and anxiety over flying left him grateful for their antics. They'd waited in line to turn their cars in, waited in line to board the plane. Sat in crowded seats until they were upgraded to First Class. He drank a beer, hoping it would help him sleep, but fussed, napping off and on all the way back to San Diego.

He tried not to think about Kiley, but it was impossible. He'd done the right thing to not encourage her too much, but he still felt bad about it. It felt dishonest. Was he doing it for her, or for himself? If she'd have asked him, perhaps he would have just junked his whole career and disappeared with her. But that wasn't really who he was. And she was woman enough not to ask that of him. But it still hurt.

Everything else around him was just noise. He hitched a ride to where he'd left his truck, grabbed clean clothes and his gear after a quick trip to his apartment, and headed back to the SEAL Team 3 building where they'd discover the details of their mission.

He could always tell the importance of the mission by the number of cars in the lot. Today, it was packed.

His team didn't always go out together, often divided up into squads, depending on the action and the talent they required. Sometimes they'd employ other Special Forces talent on loan from other branches or specialists from the CIA or State. The group who stood up front with Kyle had some new faces.

But two of the faces he recognized were Kelly Fielding and Sven Tolar. He'd not been on the op when Team 3 had rescued Kelly's sister in the Canaries, but Sven had been a regular at the Team building, working out with the guys. Jason had sat in while he talked about his FSK days as part of the Norwegian Special Forces group. Jason knew him to be a fierce warrior.

Jason received thanks from several brothers for carrying Thomas home. A couple of training buddies were there, as well as several men he'd gone through BUD/S with who had been medically rolled and graduated in later classes. Several asked about Andy, and Jason relayed the good news of his transfer and remarks about the new house they were working on at Sunset Beach.

He sat down with Ned and Damon. T.J. Talbot joined them, as well as several others from the previous missions.

Kyle Lansdowne began his address to the group of approximately sixty SEALs from Team 3.

"Welcome, gentlemen. We've assembled a rather large group here today, as I'm sure you've noticed. Most of you know everyone on board, but we have a few froglets here, so let me introduce you to the team."

"We have Lt. Commander Andrew Gibson, who led one of the previous forays this mission is a follow-up to."

Gibson stepped forward and waved. "Glad to be with you, fellas."

"He is joined by Lt. Jack Gridley, who has not only recovered from his honeymoon the last time, but now has a bouncing baby boy at home. That means she forgave him enough to have sex with him at least once."

The men laughed. Gridley turned bright red from the attention.

Although an officer and former cop, the Lt. looked barely old enough to be out of high school. He was a by-the-book officer, not quite sure of himself. That's why the team liked to needle him so much. Gridley had learned one thing that would lead to a successful Naval career: let them do it, as long as they didn't push too far.

"So his wife wants you guys to be really careful with his person, if you know what I mean," Lansdowne continued. "Apparently, she's not done with him yet."

The group chuckled again. Trace and Tucker riddled him more than others.

"Are you sleeping in separate beds yet?" Tucker asked.

Trace added, "I'm more interested in the naked penance you had to do as you begged for forgiveness to keep your marriage intact."

Gridley appeared to be a good sport. "Only for you, Trace. We're hoping not to have to make a do-over. If we do, we'll re-do our vows, unlike others I know here."

Jason knew the two older SEALs on the Team were much revered. Both had been involved in messy first marriages and were happily married the second time around. Trace married Tyler's wife's older sister, Gretchen, and was fathering her three girls from her first marriage to the former NBA star Tony Sanders.

Gibson was a good Commander, mostly because he trusted his enlisted men and rarely overruled them. He didn't brag and rarely showed off. He liked to joke but kept his opinions about anything controversial to himself. Jason felt lucky to be under his command.

Lt. Gridley was also well liked, his confidence growing with each successful mission he was part of. In the field, he stuck to Kyle Lansdowne like glue.

Kyle introduced Sven Tolar and Kelly Fielding, who were on special assignment from the State Department.

"We're going back to the Canaries." The lights dimmed and pictures flicked on from the last mission there, including pictures of two associates of the now-deceased gun-running billionaire Lars VanValle—Nigerian warlord General Two Fingers, and Jens Vandershoot, both captured on the previous trip but subsequently released.

"We don't yet have all the details, but have reason to believe they are back in operation, being funded by their benefactor's heirs, who now run the cartel from Europe. They have a fleet of cruise ships they've recently purchased on the open market from a now-defunct Italian cruise line, and are operating them as floating brothels."

Kelly Fielding stepped next to Kyle and interrupted, "If I may?"

Lansdowne nodded.

"They are learning. We have intel that says they have sold shares in these ships, "condominiumized" them, so to speak, using some Dutch loopholes in maritime law. That makes this a legal enterprise. In short, they've gotten quite blatant, giving partial title to these floating palaces, even registering them such that wealthy business-men can claim a tax deduction and write off the expenses as legitimate costs. What is illegal, however, is the trafficking of young men and women, who are conscripted for sex and the chance of a better life amongst the rich and powerful."

The room was deadly silent. Jason knew this sort of crime, the selling of human flesh, was on the top of their team's most hated list. Variations of the same themes had been operating for centuries and had touched just about every country in the world.

His grandmother told him stories of how early slaves had first made it to the Hawaiian Islands from the Orient, and that some of his ancestors had borne some of that guilt.

His LPO continued the logistics, how the team would be flown over and what the squad breakdown would be. They were to leave at 0800 for the flight to New York and then on to Gran Canaria via a stopover and plane change in Madrid. Jason calculated the flight times and discovered it would take them over thirty hours to reach their destination.

He hated long flights almost as much as he hated long airport waits. He'd be exposed to both this time around.

He made plans to have an early dinner with Ned and Damon, plus a couple others on the team before returning home to re-pack and get to bed at a decent time. He knew better than to be able to count on getting any sleep on the planes, since flying made him nervous.

On their way over to the Rusty Scupper, Jason dialed Kiley and was pleased she picked up right away.

"Africa? I didn't know we had troops in Africa," she said.

"Well, not exactly a deployment of troops. Just a mission. And that's an approximate. I can tell you more when I return. But I thought you'd worry less if you knew it wasn't somewhere in the Middle East," Jason said, even knowing there really was no completely safe place to be. The places that looked quiet and normal were some of the deadliest. Africa was in some ways more dangerous. But she wouldn't suspect that.

"You've got that right. So when do you leave?"

"Tomorrow. Early. So this will have to be good-bye for now."

"For now. That's how you say it."

"That's how we say it. I didn't get to mention some things you need to know. You can't just call me, Kiley. I mean, I won't pick up. I will call you. My phone's shut off as soon as we take off. It might take me days to see a message from you. But it doesn't mean I don't care, okay?"

"I got it."

"I'm going to send you my LPO's wife's contact information, so if there's anything that comes up and it's like an emergency, you can call Christy."

"LPO?"

"Leading Petty Officer. He's sort of my direct boss, Kyle. You can ask Aimee about it. She's met them both. If you have any questions, talk to her, okay?"

"I will. I was going to see Aimee tomorrow. She and Andy wanted to take me shopping, distract me, or so they said."

"I think it's a good idea. Stay close to them, at least until Andy's gone. And just as an aside, stay away from Cory."

"Why?"

"Just do it, okay? If you're going to hear any horror stories, I want to be the one to tell you."

"Fair enough."

Jason knew she wanted to ask more questions so he offered help. "What else do you want to know?"

"How long will you be gone?"

"Depends. We really don't know."

"Will you stay in San Diego long after you get back, or will you come back out to Florida? Or maybe stopover in Virginia, maybe you could come down for a visit? Is that in the cards?"

"Kiley, I wish I could say. Everything's up in the air. Best not plan on anything. But I'll do what I can to be in contact. Sometimes we can facetime, but no guarantees."

"Can I write?"

"I'll read it when I get back. Writing's good."

"What if—?"

He knew what she wanted to know. "If anything happens to me, you'll be contacted. That's not going to happen, though. The best thing you can do is just go about your life. Focus on what's happening in Portland. And I still think you should contact the Pinellas County Sheriff. I would feel much relieved if you did that, Kiley. Don't try to do this alone."

Jason pulled up to the restaurant next to Damon's truck. He waved, showing he was still on the phone. Damon went inside.

Kiley whispered, "You forget, they don't know how to find me.

I'm small potatoes, Jason. All I did was knock the hornet's nest around a bit. Besides, Carmen doesn't even know for sure where I am. I'll get a good feel for what's going on when I call her today. Perhaps it will spur an investigation, maybe even a grand jury probe. That's what we're hoping for."

"I still think it's foolish not to involve the local law enforcement guys. But, hey, I don't want to use up our time talking about it. Just be careful and know that I'll be thinking about you nearly twenty-four seven. That's a promise."

"I can make the same promise, Jason. And I'm going to say the same thing you told me. Don't worry, okay?"

He chuckled. "Fair enough." He didn't know how to end the call. He decided to give advice he'd once heard someone else give. "Stay busy and stay with other people in our community. That way, the time goes by faster. Don't find yourself alone. Stay with friends, people we know. Be social, connected. Don't try to do this on your own."

"Thank you. But I still am going to miss you."

"You better. I'm counting on you being able to show me when I get back. Be safe, Kiley."

He wanted to say more, but the timing wasn't right. And he'd not practiced that part enough. This was all new territory. He'd never left for a mission with someone like Kiley behind.

"Jason, I know you're doing something good for the world. I'm proud of you. So, go save the day, or something like that."

"That was perfect. Be safe, Kiley. I'll call you when I can. Miss you."

"Miss you more. And about the calling, I'll be getting a new number, so I'll leave you a message when I do. And I still miss you more."

"Impossible. Sweet dreams."

He hung up because they easily could have spent an hour saying good-bye. He knew something new was brewing. It was like the panther his grandmother had talked about, lurking in the jungle. He'd been so afraid when she'd told him the stories he couldn't sleep for two days. Even though she told him panthers didn't live in Hawaii, he didn't believe her.

He now knew what she'd been trying to tell him. She wanted him to keep an eye out for danger, lurking where it was least visible. Hiding somewhere ready to pounce.

Jason knew he couldn't control the circumstance, but he could stand ready. He could call on the chanting of his ancestors to ward off the evil panthers lurking in the jungle, while he transformed like the ancient warriors centuries ago.

He knew exactly what this new transformation was. The goddess of love had captured his heart and was holding him hostage. Like a tricky panther, he'd use it to spur him on to pay attention.

There was now more to live for.

CHAPTER 10

AIMEE AND MARTEL took Kiley shopping where she bought two more cheap prepaid cell phones and some groceries. They visited a bookstore Martel wanted to check out. Aimee stopped by a local hardware store and picked up paint she'd ordered, along with some painter's tape and extra rollers. Afterward, they had lunch together at a tiny brewhouse down by the beach.

Breathing in the fresh gulf air was the best medicine in the world for Kiley. Today was windy, and several large dragon kites were flying high, soaring and diving in the fall wind.

"Are your guys nervous?" Aimee asked.

Martel shrugged. "I can never tell anymore. It's like they train them how to talk to us. You couldn't get a thing out of them they don't want to tell us. But he did tell me Africa."

"That's what Jason said too." Kiley was enjoying the camaraderie with the two SEAL wives. "Are you going out to San Diego at Christmas break, Martel?" she asked.

"Yup. I'm taking an extra week, so I'll be there almost a month. I'm hoping to spend enough time there to get pregnant. That's the plan, anyway."

"Oh! That's exciting!" said Aimee. "But aren't you going to stay teaching here?"

Martel smiled. "I think so. But if the timing works, I might be able to take maternity leave and have the baby in San Diego, which would be way better. We'll only have a year left on his enlistment after that, so we'll see."

Kiley asked, "Why doesn't he transfer to an East Coast team?"

"He might," Martel returned. "If he stays in, he could join Andy maybe on Team 4. Maybe if Jason transfers, too, well, they'd all be together. But we have to wait to see. A lot can happen in the next year plus. First, we gotta get pregnant. I can teach anywhere but I love my school, and this is now more my home than San Diego. But we'll see."

"I guess you have to stay flexible," Kiley added, watching the two kites nearly collide.

Aimee nodded. "Way better than regular Navy where they're stationed all over the world or gone for huge blocks of time. I can't complain, really. As long as Andy is happy. So far, he's gotten along well with the Team 4 guys he's met."

"When does he start?" Kiley asked.

"Twenty-one days. We've been doing a big push to get the house finished before he has to leave again."

Both the wives looked at Kiley. Martel spoke up first.

"You can ask us anything you want to know, Kiley. Lots of times, the ladies have questions."

Kiley appreciated their kindness but had found herself distracted by the screams from a child who had fallen in the surf and was brought up sputtering by one arm, his mother wrapping him safely in a huge beach towel to quell his sobbing. That also reminded her of the phone call she was going to make to Carmen this afternoon, and her stomach lurched. "I'm not sure we're there yet. What a sweet guy. If only we had more time before he left." She knew it probably wasn't a very good lie, but wasn't going to make all her feeling public. Not yet.

"He's so wonderful, Kiley. Not a big partygoer and just a solid guy. All the Team guys like him," said Aimee.

Martel agreed.

"Well, we've really just met." Kiley hoped they would drop the subject. "Like you, Martel, we'll have to just see how it goes. It's going to be hard to maintain a relationship with someone when we're both so dug into our jobs."

"I enjoyed being up there." Martel reached for another French fry and dipped it in catsup. "Portland is a great city. But I can't see a Hawaiian boy living in the dreary rainy winters in Oregon," she added. "Florida would be a much better fit."

"San Diego," said Kiley. "I think that's where he wants to be. He has to be near the beach."

Martel agreed.

Aimee's eyes sparkled. "I think the two of you make a cute couple. I can see you living here. I'm keeping my fingers crossed for both of you," she continued. "I'm hoping Team 4 is in your future! Yours too, Martel."

"Amen to that," Martel said as they toasted their white wine.

Kiley liked the idea more than she wanted to let on.

AIMEE DROVE THEM back to her house where Kiley said her good-byes and walked along the beach until she came to the access path that led to her place. With a persistent wind blowing off the gulf, the beach was sparsely populated. The fat tire motorized bicycle brigade had swollen to four, all of them men and all but one silver-haired, riding their bikes in flip-flops and swimming trunks.

Kiley tried the sliding glass door onto the patio and was reassured to find she'd remembered to lock it before she left. She went around and entered through the front door.

Inside the house, she put away her things and unboxed one of the cell phones, turning it on. Then she removed the sim card from her old phone, cutting it with scissors and flushing the pieces down the toilet.

She dialed Carmen.

When the reporter's voicemail came on, Kiley left a short message.

"Hey there, it's me. I'll try you at the office. This is my new phone number."

She left a brief message for Jason before she called the paper asking for Carmen.

The receptionist didn't recognize Kiley's voice, which was a lucky break. She was transferred to the features desk, and again, she heard Carmen's voicemail. "Okay, quit playing hard to get, Carmen. I'm here. Waiting for your call."

When she didn't hear from the beat reporter after an hour, she called her editor.

"Kiley, I'm glad you called...just a minute while I close the door."

Corbin Newman's voice was heavily laced with stress. He'd never taken the time to close his door on their prior calls.

"Is everything okay? I was actually calling for Carmen—"

"There's been a development, I'm afraid," he interrupted. His breath sounded constricted and the pitch of his voice was a little higher than normal. She heard fumbling as he'd put the phone to his ear while walking from the office doorway. The familiar squeak of his rolling desk chair told her he was now ensconced behind his desk.

"Tell me, Corbin. What's happened?"

"Carmen's missing."

It took a couple of seconds before Kiley could fully comprehend her editor's words. Something at the back of her brain screamed a denial. Her Aunt Itoldyouso was standing in the distance with her hands on her hips, shaking her head.

"Since when?"

"Since yesterday. I didn't want to call you to worry you further, after our last conversation, but was just going to call you this morning when we still hadn't heard from her. I have Fred and Doris headed over to her place now."

Fred was their head of security. So Newman suspected foul play.

Kiley instinctively scanned the patio and the beach beyond in both directions through the still-locked and closed sliding glass door. Nothing caught her eye. She ran to the front door and double locked the deadbolt and door handle. Her fingers felt clammy, and sweat poured from her armpits. The familiar thump, thump-thump of her elevated heartbeat made her teeth rattle.

"Talk to me, Corbin."

"We're stumped, Kiley."

"So how do you know she's missing, then?"

"She was to do an interview with KRVR. The article hit the papers yesterday—"

"I thought it was coming out Friday."

"We upped it. There was interest, you know, rumors of the article coming out. I can smell a request to cover up news a mile away. KRVR left me a message late yesterday afternoon when she didn't show up for the taping. It was going to be their lead story on the evening news, and the old lady was furious with me, like it was my fault."

The public radio station was owned by the ex-wife of a wealthy Oregon state representative. She ran the station like her own private fiefdom. Kiley could only imagine how Rosalie Conden had boxed his ears. He was probably still sore.

"So what did they say then, on the newscast?"

"Oh, they announced they were doing some investigative reporting on your article, didn't mention anything about Carmen, thank God, and just indicated there would be more coming. Rosalie had her toy-boy do it, the anchor, what's-his-name."

"Charley Gleason."

"That's the one. It made me nervous to look at him deliver his script. It's got me spooked, Kiley. Are you sure you've not heard from her?"

"Positive." Kiley had forgotten to check for messages before she destroyed the sim card, and she swore at her aunt, mentally. "What's the feedback on the article?" She inhaled deep and waited for an answer.

"Oh geez, like a bomb went off. We've been doing nothing but fielding phone tips all morning. I had to hire an extra receptionist to handle the volume. And then there's the mayor. Haven't returned his call yet. I spoke to the chief, briefly, and promised we'd cooperate fully when I located either you or Carmen. He wants a call back from you, especially. They're all talking about it in the bullpen."

"And Martin? I'll bet he's chomping at the bit."

"I haven't seen him."

That gave Kiley an idea. "Go check Carmen's desk. Make sure she didn't leave her story files behind." It had always annoyed Kiley that Newman didn't allow them to lock their files, not that a zero-skilled person couldn't pry open a desk drawer. But there had been accusations of some "lifting of the jewels" as Corbin had phrased it during one office meeting when it came up. His answer was, "Take everything home with you unless you need it locked up in my safe."

He always considered it sheer stupidity if a staffer lost out on a scoop because they'd been careless to leave things so easily accessible.

Newman gave Kiley the cell phone number of Chief Rayburn. Just before they signed off, he barked, "Oh shit. I'm getting a visit from the mayor as we speak. Call me back after you call the chief, okay?"

"But—"

"Just do it, Agnes." His tone changed as Kiley could hear sounds that the door to Corbin's office had opened. In a syrupy-sweet voice he continued, "I'm sure he'll come home by tomorrow. I'll help anyway I can. Um, I have to go now, Agnes. Don't worry. Your cat will come home. You'll see. Bye."

The line disconnected.

Kiley stared into the phone like it was the end of a lifeline that had been cut from her arms. Carmen was missing. Jason was clear across the country or halfway around the world by now. Aimee and Martel were probably still at Aimee's house, making plans to paint one of the bedrooms upstairs. People passed by in the distance, but their images were blurry. Then the outline of the glass door became wavy as she realized tears were streaming down her cheeks and dropping onto her chest.

Her fingers were stiff and cold as if the wind was blowing through the glass. She touched the warm wetness of her tears on her shirt. How she wished they were tears of joy, how she wished those huge arms of his could grab her, hold her until she stopped shaking.

She'd been grinding her teeth while she was thinking. She'd felt so safe being all the way on the east coast, far away from the dark danger lurking in the streets and alleyways of Portland. She had allies, but none of them were truly available. She considered her options, and as she thought about it, she began to feel better.

I told him I could handle it. That's what I promised. That's exactly what I'll do.

Kiley knew she needed to reach out to Jason. But she didn't want him to worry, because once again, she told herself, *You've got this. You can handle it, Kiley.*

She grabbed her cell and dialed Jason's number again, hopeful he'd pick up, even though he'd told her he wouldn't. After three rings, it went to his voicemail, just like before. The sound of his voice, though canned, still ran her libido around the track and left a deep cavern inside her that hurt as she experienced the reality of the distance between them.

The beep on the message made her jump.

"Jason, this is—" What was she doing? Of course he'd know who it was. "Kiley here. Say, I forgot to tell you I've got some news, and it's not good. But I'm taking charge of the situation. Nothing for you to worry about. If you get a chance, please call me back. I need a little advice. But don't worry."

She hung up, afraid she'd begin to sound emotional. That was the last thing she wanted to show him. But in her haste, she didn't say anything about hoping he landed safely or to stay safe himself. It was all about her.

"Argh!" she screamed as she pulled on her hair.

She toyed with the idea of calling him back and correcting the last message. But that would sound pathetic. She searched her options and came to the conclusion she only had a limited few, and most of them were dangerous.

Then she remembered the phone number to Jason's LPO's wife, Christy. But she hadn't saved the contact information before cutting up the sim card.

Some investigative journalist you are. Losing important information!

The unexpected news about Carmen and everything else had rattled her. She stopped chastising herself and vowed to ask Aimee and Martel later on.

Calm down. All will be well. Keep it together, Kiley. You can do this. You can do this!

Her last remaining piece of hope she spent on one last call to Carmen.

"Please call me back, Carmen. I'm worried about you. I just need to know where you went and who you talked to. If you can hear this—"

"Hello?" a male voice answered, interrupting the message she was leaving.

"Who is this?" she asked. Her heart leapt to her throat.

"Who is this?" he asked. The voice sounded familiar.

"Martin? Is that you?"

"Kiley. So you're back from vacation then? You sure left a shit-storm here. When are you coming back to the office?"

The coldness returned, freezing her tongue to the roof of her mouth. Her stomach lurched again, this time nearly making her heave. She didn't have any answers for him. She. Had. Questions.

Sucking it up, she forged ahead, "How did you get Carmen's cell phone? And does Newman know about this?"

"I'm at her place now. I'm with Fred and Doris. Well, I was here already, but they've just arrived. Say, we're real worried about—"

"You broke into Carmen's house?"

"She left the back door open. It wasn't hard. Kiley, are you back from Florida? There are so many people who want to talk to you."

"No. But I'm coming."

"That's good. I think that's really good. Fred's calling the police. He's found something—"

The line went dead.

Again, she stared at the keypad, once again cut off from—from a friend. An ally? Or did Martin have something to do with Carmen's disappearance since he hadn't reported in? Maybe he'd taken Carmen's notes.

She was running out of people to trust. Martin knew about her being in Florida, like Carmen said. Everyone knew.

Kiley remembered what Jason had told her, "Stay busy. Stay with people in our community." Maybe it was time to include Aimee, Martel, and Andy in what was going on in Portland, fully brief them before she returned there. Her editor had been right. *Someone* needed to know where she was and what she was doing. Someone who could do something about it. By default, that would be Andy and the girls.

But first, she dialed the number Newman had given her for Chief of Police Rayburn and left her message.

"This is Kiley Worthington, investigative reporter for the *Columbia Passage*. My editor has told me you want to speak to me. I will be flying back to Portland tomorrow, and I'd be happy to answer any of your questions when I get there. I'll check in with you when I land. Thank you, and I hope we can work together to help clean up a couple of things I've uncovered in the course of my investigation. I'll explain everything when I see you tomorrow or whenever. Thanks. Bye."

She quickly made online reservations for a direct flight from Tampa to Portland, paying an enormous amount for the ticket. She'd call her landlady tonight and see if she could get an extension on her stay or some sort of early cancellation discount. If that didn't work out, she figured she could always stay with either Martel or Aimee when, and not if, she returned to the gulf. She'd ask them later on this afternoon.

By tomorrow, she'd be in Portland, and she'd start facing her fears head-on. She'd share her notes with the police, hopefully retaining the anonymity of her sources, and help them find those ten girls and wherever Carmen was holed up. She knew those notes held the answers they needed to complete the mission. Maybe Carmen was just in hiding, keeping herself safely stowed away from harm. She hoped that was the case, though unlikely.

Part of her was excited for this new adventure. The rest of her was filled with the physical pain of missing Jason, almost like an addiction. But it didn't stem from fear. It came from somewhere else. He'd instilled in her the confidence to quit running and start crashing through the waves like one of those rubber boats he talked about. With Jason on her side, the odds were in her favor.

You got this, remember?

She knew he'd be proud of how she was handling things.

CHAPTER 11

THE ENTIRE TEAM took the State Department passenger plane to JFK Airport, but from there they were split into three groups of roughly twenty men. Jason was glad he was traveling with Damon, T.J., Coop, and Kyle. Sven was also to be on their hop to Gran Canaria. Each airline took a slightly different route, but they all had only one stopover. Flight times ranged from seventeen to nineteen hours in length. This was the grueling part for Jason.

As luck would have it, they barely had enough time to grab a quick bite to eat before their plane began boarding. The others would be close behind, within a few hours. Several First-Class tickets were available, and the Team opted to give Jason one of them, due to his size. Tucker Hudson scored the other, for the same reason.

The "old man," as they called Tucker, was easy to get along with. Nearly as big as Jason, he was firmly packed and could have done professional wrestling, he was so fit. His run times beat almost everyone on the squad. Jason respected his quiet demeanor, especially under fire.

"How's the little one, Tucker?" The older SEAL was starting all over again, at over forty years of age.

The plane had leveled off, and they'd just been served their drinks.

"Kimberly's getting huge. Almost walking now."

"No shit?"

"I know. Time has just flown by. Seems just last week she was born. She's a strong kid. Got tree stumps for legs and, man, can those little legs kick."

"I'll bet," chuckled Jason. "I'd expect nothing less."

"Some of Brandy's friends have boys that are dwarfed compared to her. We're always trying to be so careful she won't fall on one of the kids in her playgroup. I think she's twice their size."

"I'll bet Brandy's happy being a mom."

"Oh yes. She's already got her waitlisted on two preschools and has signed up for baby swim and baby gymnastics. Personally, I think it's a bit much, but Brandy was always a big gal, you know, and she doesn't want Kimberly to not know how to move her body. She wants her to be graceful, if you catch my drift."

Jason knew if he had a daughter some of the same issues would come up. "Daikon legs, they say in the Islands."

Tucker squinted at him a bit and then decided not to explore the term further.

"Whatever. But I doubt she'll be a ballet star," Tucker said, finishing off his drink.

The thought of having a daughter born with huge calves and "cankles" had never entered his mind before. "She's just probably self-conscious. See, in my culture, being big was actually something that was highly prized. The girls were beautiful when they were young, but our women get bulky fast."

"Yea, but they could beat the shit out of anyone who messed with their kids, I'll bet."

Jason nodded. "Very true."

They were served another scotch.

Tucker leaned over and whispered, "Frankly, they should just leave us the tray of little bottles. Everyone else is having wine or beer."

"I'll see what I can do. It is a shame to waste all that booze, isn't it?"

"Damn straight," Tucker grumbled.

"Funny how some people worry about body image so much. In my family, the men got skinny and small and the women got huge. Kind of a role reversal thing," Jason told his buddy.

"Women are more highly prized in your culture, then?"

"It depends. I think it's more about size than gender. I had two Samoan sisters who used to beat the crap out of me every chance they could get. My dad and grandfather thought it was funny, and it wasn't, really. Grandpa would whisper to me, 'Hit her back,' and I never could for fear my grandmother would cast a spell on me. They did it because they outweighed me by double."

"That can't have been very good for your ego," Tucker barked. "So, what did you do, or did you live continuously in fear?"

"One day, I hit her back. She, the older one, had a black eye that nearly extended from her unibrow down to her jaw. Big and purple. Looked like a birthmark. And with her bloodshot eye, she looked like a witch in a Disney movie. My dad was worried we'd have to leave the island."

Tucker found that funny and belly-laughed for several minutes. "There's something so pure about that, Jason. A bully is just a bully when it comes down to it. That was justice. You're a force for good."

"I spent half the year mowing the family's lawn, too with one of those push mowers as my penance. They'd sprinkle the grass with dog poop from the neighbors."

Tucker was losing it, but Jason had never considered it a funny story.

"Did they ever outgrow their obsession to torture you?"

"When I outgrew them. They were still tilting some three hundred pounds at barely sixteen, but I got to be six foot my Freshman year in high school and that kind of ended their fun. Plus, I could way outrun them."

Tucker shook his head, still guffawing from time to time, until the urge left him.

"So were you not closer to your mom than your dad? For some reason, I thought you would be."

"I think I was. Dad was not comfortable around kids. He loved us, but he was more westernized. Worked in a big hotel and had ridiculous hours. Mom and her sisters were the keepers of the stories. I seemed to cleave to that side of things. I was always fascinated with the pageantry of the feasts, the dancing. I started getting my tats at about eleven."

"Whoa! That's not something I could have done. My mom would have shredded my skin with sandpaper if I'd done that."

"Only thing important to my mom was that it looked good. We were starting to experiment on ourselves, and, well, you know, we didn't know what the hell we were doing. And, it's permanent, you know."

"Fuck yeah. I could see how it would be kind of important. I had my ex's name altered, and I can tell you it's not an easy thing to do."

"You shed blood for Brandy. That's a good man!"

Tucker roared at that one, and they clinked their plastic glasses and demanded more. The skinny male attendant did leave them the rest of the tray this time.

"I'm going to sleep through dinner, I think," said Tucker.

"Breakfast. We got breakfast coming, not dinner. And not for another four hours, Tucker."

"Well, if I pass out, wake me, okay?"

"Roger that, buddy."

Jason knew he was going to have to pee, so decided to do it now before Tucker got too comfortable.

"That's a good idea, son," Tucker said as he followed him to the restroom compartment ahead of them.

Jason could hardly fit inside the doorway of the little room. He wasn't sure Tucker would be able to.

He washed his hands and waved to the rest of the squad sitting in the back of the plane then took his seat. He checked his phone and saw the message from Kiley, but was unable to play it. He saved the number to her contact and hoped he'd had enough alcohol in his system for the long nap he desperately needed. But that depended on whether his bladder would let him.

JASON WOKE UP as the plane lurched forward on their ascent. The force of his body against the strength of the seat belt popped the device open and he hit his forehead on the seat in front of him. If Tucker hadn't been seated next to him, he'd have been sprawled on the floor in the aisle.

Tucker's quick hands yanked his shoulders back so his body didn't rise en route to a short flight into the attendant cabin.

"You all right?" he shouted over the noise of the engines.

Jason checked his shoulder, then his chest and held up the broken seat belt with his left hand. "That's never happened to me before."

"Me neither."

Jason had gotten drunk and sober on the plane, the flight was so long. They had each been served double helpings of breakfast, which helped. They'd passed on the mimosas. So when they deplaned in Madrid, both Tucker and Jason went on a quest for some strong coffee and located a small espresso stand. The rest of the squad hung together in the waiting area for the Iberia prop jet to Gran Canaria.

He excused himself to try calling Kiley, but the phone never picked up, since no answering message had been created. He swore to himself internally when he saw the second voicemail, she'd left him and wished he'd tried to listen to that first.

Her first few words sent him immediately into a runaway elevator.

'...but I'm taking charge of the situation. Don't worry.'

It had the opposite effect on Jason. He hoped he could make contact before they boarded. He paced in front of Tucker and a handful of the guys seated in the waiting area until their flight was called.

This time the plane was packed with tourists. The seats didn't incline, and there was no first class. Both he and Tucker were seated in a middle row seat with college-age kids on either side of them. At first, sleep was impossible due to the banter between the aisle seat and the window inhabitant. Tucker stopped it on his side by growling with his eyes closed. Shortly afterwards, Jason could detect some of Tucker's world class farts, and that seemed to quiet the whole back end of the plane for nearly an hour.

Finally, nearly twenty-four hours after landing in New York, they arrived at Gran Canaria and the port city of Las Palmas. They were shuttled by van to a small resort right on a stretch of pristine beach with a view of the blue waters of the Atlantic in severe contrast to a line of stark white cruise ships.

Kyle and Jack Gridley were to take Kelly Fielding and Sven Tolar and check in with their Spanish liaisons downtown, as well as secure reserved transportation, while the rest of Jason's flight was left to explore the picturesque town nearby with its numerous watering holes and restaurants. The brick streets and bright-colored plaster storefronts looked like a patchwork quilt of different cultures: Portuguese, Spanish, and old Morocco. They were to return before nightfall to connect with the other members arriving on later flights and to go over the plans for the subsequent days.

He walked with a group including Coop, Fredo, Jake, Damon, and the brothers-in-law Tyler and Trace. Several other groups went ahead separately.

Damon left a message for Martel while Jason did the same for Kiley. "They're shopping. I think that's what she said they were going to do. Martel turns her phone off."

"I got a message from Kiley that there's a little wrinkle in her plans. I'm kind of worried about her. I would think she'd want to be available after that, but who knows?"

"I'm sure they're fine. She'll call. We're what? Five hours ahead here?"

"Yup."

"Might be late, but she'll call," reassured Damon.

Jason walked with his hand in his jacket pocket, gripping the cell he hoped would vibrate soon, connecting him to Kiley's world. He wished she'd gone into detail about the concern he heard in her voice, but there wasn't anything he could do but wait.

Worry over Kiley's phone call made it difficult to play the part of a casual tourist. The fact that all the guys were excessively built and inked didn't help either. Their sunglasses matched, being Navy-issue, which was a dumb mistake someone should have caught.

Though they were on an island with miles of beautiful beach rimming the perimeter, it didn't feel anything like Jason's homeland. For one, the foliage was scarce, not because it wouldn't grow but because every stick of wood was harvested and made into fence posts, used to patch a wall, or turned into some small trinket at the tourist stalls. It was cleaner than he remembered Cape Verde had been, and it had more of a European population of visitors, mostly young twenty-somethings in beach attire. Jason's teammates wore too much clothing and didn't smile.

Well, not until they were eating fresh fruit from a street vendor and a local burro peed on Damon's shoe. That started a series of pranks until they found a pork barbeque stand that served ribs, of all things. The dinner was simple. It consisted of ribs, red rice, beans, and pitchers of some local drink made from coconut milk. In fact, Jason couldn't recall seeing a green vegetable anywhere.

The pork was divine, dripping in hot barbeque sauce with

chunks of pineapple in it. They ate steamed yams seasoned with cinnamon, brown sugar, and butter for dessert.

The sun was hanging low in the horizon, so the group comman-deered two donkey carts and had a race back to their hotel. Dusty and smelling of alcohol, they entered the lobby to a room filled with newly arrived team guys who were tired, cranky, and lacked any sense of humor.

A list of room assignments were given out. Jason and Damon had been placed together, so they headed to the second floor to unpack their minimal load.

"Have you heard anything from Martel?" Jason asked on the way up the stairs. He was taking them two-by-two, the alcohol in his system giving him an extra spring in his step.

"Not yet. I'm sure she'll call tonight. Might be late." Damon un-locked their door and stepped into a huge room with a balcony overlooking the blue Atlantic. "Wow. This is hella better than last trip."

"Well, you forget, this isn't Africa. It's part of Spain," reminded Jason.

"Would you look at that?" Damon said, opening up the sliding glass door to the balcony.

Jason looked out. A gentle warm breeze blew from the ocean. The surf was flaccid but rolled in nearly a half mile. "Damn, if the surf was any bigger, this would be perfect. I'll bet it is during storm season."

"You're probably right. Just look at all the blue water and beach. Does this remind you of Hawaii?"

Jason listened for a minute and then shook his head. "Not a bit. You can barely hear the ocean. There are no palm trees to sit in the shade. No sounds of the women singing, no smell of flowers. In fact, I don't see any green at all."

"You're kidding. You've got the sun, the beach."

Jason sniffed the air. "Actually, it smells of burro pee."

"Shut the fuck up," Damon said as he looked down at his stained pants and leather sandals. I'll wash everything out tonight. Will that suit you, your Highness?"

"As long as you get that sick puppy smell out, I'm good."

Damon leaned against the railing. "You sure this doesn't remind you of Hawaii? It's an island."

"Nope. That hot, dry sun? Hawaii is gentle. This is harsh. You turn into a prune here. Even too hot for swimming."

"Sort of like Florida, then?"

"A lot like Florida but different." Jason picked one of the beds and then unpacked his shaving gear. He leaned against the doorway of the bathroom just as someone whistled from downstairs.

"Showtime!" said Damon, jumping to his feet.

"Listen, if she calls and I'm asleep, I don't care how late it is. Wake me up, okay?"

"Will do, Jason."

They ran downstairs to join the rest of their teammates who were gathering, waiting for instructions.

CHAPTER 12

K ILEY CALLED AHEAD to make sure Aimee and Martel were still home and then walked the short distance to the Carr residence. Andy was puttering in the kitchen, and he directed her to go upstairs to see the girls.

"Martel talked to Damon. They arrived safely," Andy shouted up the stairs after her.

Kiley leaned over the railing. "When was that?"

"They just hung up. About five minutes ago."

"I wonder why Jason hasn't called me?"

Andy shrugged. He held a glass of wine in his right hand. "Are you staying for dinner?"

"Do you have enough?"

"We've got plenty."

"Okay then. Let me go check in with Aimee."

"Roger that," Andy said and went back to his food prep.

She found the two girls painting the smaller bedroom a light shade of blue. "Wow! Looks nice, Aimee."

"You think so? I debated. I thought maybe this room would make a nice nursery, if that should happen. But I liked this blue, and it goes with the color of the sky, so I went with it."

Kiley smiled at Martel. "Andy says you got a call from Damon?"

"Yes, he told me they landed safely. He said Jason has been try-ing to reach you."

Kiley checked her phone. No messages registered there. "I gave him this number to call. I'll give him a try right now. Just a minute."

She ran to the master bedroom, sat on a chair on the deck overlooking the ocean, and dialed Jason's number again. He picked it up on the first ring.

"Hey there. I've been worried—"

Kiley was relieved to hear his voice. "Nothing to be concerned about. I told you that."

"You need to tell me what's going on, Kiley."

"Corbin published my article early, and they've been getting tips pouring into the paper. He's got the police chief calling me, so it looks like we're getting some action."

"That's good news. So what was the complication you talked about? And, honey, don't ever leave a message like that again, okay?"

"Fine. I won't."

"And? The complication?"

"Now Carmen's gone missing."

"What?"

"I'm going to fly back there tomorrow and do some digging. Find out who she talked to. And now since the police are interested, I'll have someone to give my information to. I'm going to help them, Jason."

"Hold it, Kiley. They said you could help them?"

"Well, Corbin said—"

"Did the police say they wanted your help?"

"The chief called my editor; said he had some questions for me. So, I've left him a message and told him I'd answer all his questions tomorrow when I arrive."

"No way, Kiley. You didn't promise to go back to Portland?"

"I think it will be fine now. I have allies. Michael is on the story, so is my editor, and I have the ear of the chief."

"This is the chief you didn't trust to give the information to before?"

"Yes, but that was—"

"The one hired by the mayor you said told your editor to bury the story?"

"Yes, but that was—"

"And you haven't received any reassurances from anyone. You were not even sure you could trust your editor, last I heard."

"But with Carmen out of the picture, who's going to go interview the houses, and the—?"

"What houses, Kiley?"

"The group homes several of these women were staying at. I've got notes, and interview tapes from the staff. If I have to, I'll share these with the chief so he can do his investigation."

"Have any of the girls been found yet?"

Kiley hesitated. "Just the four."

"It's a very bad idea to go back to Portland," he whispered. "Promise me you won't do that, not until I get back home."

"But you said—"

"I said I couldn't interfere. And I can't. But I can keep you safe. Don't you see the problem?"

"Yes, you're halfway around the world."

"Exactly."

"But I gave my word, and besides, everyone's pulling in the same direction. The police are on board. All the research has been done. Now I just have to give them what they need to launch their investigation."

"You're still in danger."

"But that was only until the report was filed. Now that it's out, the public knows. It's like shining a light on it. I think all the pressure was to stop the publication of my report. That's been done. The cat's out of the bag."

"Except you said you needed to help them with their investigation. You honestly think you'll be able to be involved in that? The police don't work that way, Kiley."

"But I have the notes, the interviews."

"Correct. And that puts you in danger."

"Well, I'd just be helping them. All I would do is show them my findings."

"Which was not in the paper. Not all of it, right?"

"Right."

"So it sounds to me that if Carmen were somehow interfered with, someone didn't want that research to go forward."

"But she never had all the information."

"And don't you suppose they know that by now?"

It hadn't occurred to her that Carmen's status, if she was in harm's way, was altered by the fact that the paper published Kiley's article. A wave of ice water filled her veins and caused that familiar shiver down her spine.

"Who has that information, Kiley?"

"I do." She didn't want to admit it, but Jason was right. And then she thought about her phone. "I should at least talk to the police in Portland, though."

"Probably. They'll find you, if you don't."

"Through my cell. I have to get rid of the cell. I gave that number to the chief."

"Look, Kiley. Wait until I get back. Hopefully, it will be just a couple of weeks. We're not expecting to be here long. I'll ask Kyle tomorrow if I can have leave after we return stateside. Then I'll accompany you. But wait until I get that permission, okay?"

"What are you going to tell him?"

"The truth, or what I believe you told me was the truth. The missing girls, especially the new one. We can look the articles up online. I can't break any laws, and I can't interfere with local law enforcement. But I can protect you. We do that all the time. We protect State Department officials, embassies, traveling heads of state."

"Okay. I'll do it. I'll wait here. And I'll get rid of the cell."

"I think that's wise."

Jason's silence made her nervous. "What are you not telling me, Jason?"

"As much as I hate to say it, I think you should tell Andy. I'd like to hear what he has to say about it. Have him call me if he needs to. But let me ask you one question first."

"Okay."

"Were you absolutely certain you were being followed or that the thing with your cat wasn't just some random act of violence? Were you convinced someone was out to scare you off the story or, worse, silence you permanently?"

It was an easy answer. "Yes, Jason, I was. The letters and the phone calls I got at the paper. And I still am, now because of Carmen. There are too many women missing."

"It has to be someone you exposed or partially exposed in your articles. As long as you can still hurt them, you're in danger. If it ever was real, it still is real. Understand?"

"Yes, I do." She was completely deflated.

"When you set up your new voicemail on the new number, don't use your voice for the message. You have to be careful, Kiley. You know this. Let's be smart."

These were going to be the longest two weeks of her life. Things were spinning out of control, just like Jason said. Just when she thought she had a plan, the goalposts changed the game. He was right. Maybe she shouldn't have assumed her plan would work. She started to doubt herself and feel the burden of what she was putting others through.

Aimee opened the slider, poking her head out. "Everything okay?"

Kiley had been staring off to the horizon. She wanted to go home, have a couple glasses of wine in the bathtub, and go to bed early. But there was a job that needed to be done.

Aimee sat down on a wicker chair next to her, propping her feet up on the crosspiece in the railing. The sun was just setting.

"I thought when I was living in Oregon, with all that rain, that perhaps I'd embellished the golden sunset a bit. I figured it couldn't possibly be as bright and beautiful as I remembered as a child. But I was wrong. It's even more stunning than my memories and the colors are even brighter."

"I know. Once you get some of that gulf sun in your hair, on your skin, in your eyes, I think it travels to your soul. You take a little piece of it with you forever. Almost haunts you, doesn't it?" Aimee answered.

She remained quiet until Kiley developed the thoughts and words she wanted to use.

"That was Jason."

"I figured as much."

They were joined by Martel, who announced, "I think we need some wine right about now."

Aimee called after her, "Tell Andy to hold off on dinner a bit. But we'll be down shortly."

"Sure thing." Martel closed the glass behind her and the two women were alone again.

"Is it good news or…?"

"What I came over here for was to tell you guys I decided to go back to Portland. I'll explain more when Andy's here, because Jason actually told me to make sure I included him."

"You figure it's safer now?"

"Actually, it's not. But I just promised I wouldn't fly back there until Jason could go with me."

"Makes sense."

Martel was back with a bottle of red wine and three glasses. "Your man is not a happy camper and he said if we weren't down there in thirty minutes, he'd eat by himself and we could go out for a burger."

"Oh, Lord." Aimee shook her head. "He's a creature of habit. Likes everything spelled out. He has rules for everything. Stews about most things and stubborn as they come."

"Oh, that's Damon to a T," said Martel as she poured their glasses. "To the magic of Sunset Beach!" They touched glasses after repeating the toast.

"Mmm. That's good," said Kiley. "I could use a little magic right now."

"So you were telling us you wanted to go back to Portland?"

"I called the reporter who was doing work for a followup article, working with my editor, and now she's gone missing. We have officially four missing girls, and now this reporter. But I've uncovered evidence there are many more. Maybe as many as ten."

"A serial killer?" Martel asked.

"No, it's a human trafficking ring. Very organized, in fact, probably professionally managed, and it has important ties to local government. The piece was to hit the paper on Friday, but my editor printed it early. He felt pressure and was afraid he'd be asked to bury the story. But that put Carmen, the staffer we added to the team, in danger, I think. I was having her follow up on some of the interviews I'd done, to see if we could get some quotes and perhaps their cooperation. It's one thing to talk to a reporter anonymously. Quite another to get involved in a corruption scandal. That's where this is all headed."

"Just what did you expect to achieve going back? Didn't you say you lost your cat, and they vandalized your car?"

"Yes. I think those were attempts to warn me. I thought maybe the article would take some of the pressure off, but it looks like

Carman may have walked right into it. I'm worried. I wanted to go do some digging in person, see if I could help find her. I know right where to go too."

Martel was puzzled. "I'm not understanding this, Kiley. Like you told us at the bonfire, once everything came out in the paper, wouldn't that begin to shed light on what was going on? You were thinking the public would demand that investigation."

"I did. And I think that will happen. But I can't just sit here while I've put Carmen in danger."

"Perhaps," Aimee said, her finger pointing to the sky. "You don't know for sure you did."

"Well, yes. I thought we had a couple of days to do a little more research before the final piece was published. And then we could turn over the complete package to the authorities. Now that won't happen. If something's happened to Carmen, it will be my fault."

"Man, you're awfully hard on yourself," said Aimee. "I thought your editor was the one who made the assignments."

"I overruled him. I made him take Carmen. She didn't want it, either. But I got her involved because I thought she'd do a better job interviewing some of the victims I'd located."

"Wait a minute. You found some of the missing girls?"

"I found other girls. Not the missing ones. But I think some of them knew the missing ones."

"How many girls are we talking about, Kiley?" asked Martel.

"I've got tapes on six. Some written material from three more. With very little verification, I could make a case for at least ten girls who have disappeared that we know of. If this criminal enterprise has been operating for many years, then there could be many more. Hundreds, perhaps."

Kiley noted Aimee's pensive stare at the ball of light now melting into the horizon. Within seconds gray streaks formed, the orange and golden yellow clouds were outlined in light purple, and then everything began to fade, going purple and deeper gray. The water on the gulf went from bright azure blue to navy within ten minutes. The pilgrimage to the surf was over and now was reversing, as people made their way back to their homes or cars parked nearby.

The magic was dissipating, and Kiley actually felt sad.

Aimee continued staring at the water as she whispered, "Do you think we're in danger here?"

Before she could answer, Andy slid the glass door wide and jolted them all. "Hey! I got beautiful steaks downstairs, corn on the cob and a killer salad. I'd like some company for all my troubles."

AFTER DINNER, AIMEE began clearing plates. Kiley rose to help her.

"No, you stay put and tell Andy what you started to tell us upstairs. I've got this."

"Thanks, babe," Andy winked.

Martel opened and then began to pour their second bottle of wine of the evening.

"So, Andy, I talked to Jason earlier and he asked that I explain the pickle I'm in. He said you'd have some good advice."

"Okay, shoot," said Andy.

"Darn, I didn't bring my computer. I shouldn't have left it at the house, either. That was totally dumb of me."

"I've got a laptop. Can you log in on mine?"

"I can try."

"No, Andy, you have all that encrypted stuff. You don't want to mix this stuff with your SEAL things." Aimee pointed to the ceiling. "Martel, go get my laptop on the side table upstairs on my side of the bed."

Martel took the stairs two at a time, her long graceful legs digging into the polished wood with her toes. She returned not more than a couple of minutes later.

Aimee dried her hands and opened the computer to a guest icon.

"Here you go. Log in with Safari, or do you use Chrome?"

"Chrome."

"There. Now put your passwords in and we'll delete everything when you're done."

Kiley found her portal at the paper and called up the four articles on human trafficking, dragging them to the four corners of the screen so Andy could read them all. She proofread her last article and was mortified to find a couple of typos.

Andy was able to read and summarize at the same time. "So you were looking into the case of an immigrant girl from Central America smuggled across the border by Coyotes. She traveled with a group of three other young girls, all ranging in ages from ten to fourteen."

Andy read further. "You found they came from the same village, and—their parents wanted them to have a better life in the United States. So, they allowed the four friends to come to the U.S. to work as domestics."

He sat up, frowning. "That's a little young, isn't it? Ten?"

"I was able to contact their parish priest, an American who had been in the Peace Corps and stayed to continue his work there. He said the girls in that village often married before they were fifteen. He told me a man and woman, recruiters, came into the village and looked for girls they could find from poor families, where the parents would appreciate not having to feed one more mouth. And they were compensated." Kiley watched as this sunk into her friend's faces.

"They sold their own children?" Aimee said, covering her mouth.

"Yup."

"Isn't that against the law?" asked Martel.

"It is," started Andy. "But you wouldn't believe the plight of children all over the world, Martel. It's not a safe place for a child. They are bartered for pennies in many areas of Africa, the Orient, even South America. There are groomers too. People who train them for the slavery they'll be doomed for. Mostly the sex trade. And they get them hooked on drugs, so they won't go far. If they don't know the language and have no papers, once they get to their destination, they owe their entire existence to the people who brought them over. And many don't survive the trip, sadly."

"That's what Jason said. You guys were finding these people in Africa. Is that why he's gone, to look for smugglers?"

"Last two trips have been all about the smugglers. Very dangerous people, Kiley. When you were here, I thought you were talking about some guys who liked to get their jollies having sex with young girls and were kidnapping girls for that purpose. But you're talking about a whole organization. Is that right?"

"I'm afraid so, Andy. If you read on, you can see that there are a number of shelters in the Portland area, funded by some church groups and private businesses, formed to help stem the homeless growth in the area. Originally, they were for unwed mothers, runaways, and girls leaving abusive homes. These houses took care of them until they could successfully get a job and be on their own."

"I don't see anything wrong with that," whispered Martel.

"The city began to give tax breaks to organizations who ran these. And my guess is that the introduction of the money, brought the crime. All the houses were full all the time, more shelters were needed, and the program expanded. This happened under the radar until people started noticing the girls didn't stay in the area but were shipped all over the United States."

Kiley waited while Andy read on, Aimee looking over his shoulder.

"You did a good job documenting everything, Kiley," Aimee told her.

"I didn't give names. Those I kept confidential, but I have all of them in my files. I interviewed a couple of social workers from Texas who came out to Portland to check on two girls who came through their area and were transferred to one of the shelters. They were unable to locate their girls. I have their pictures. Both of them were twelve, best friends. And it happened the same way. They told us that they came from the same village, and immigration picked them up abandoned by their Coyote in the middle of the desert. They had the address of one shelter with them as their final destination."

"Wow, so someone in Mexico or Central America knew about the place in Portland," said Martel.

"I think so. When the social workers inquired, the house was registered with the State of Oregon under a special license. They were told there were regular inspections, medical and dental services provided, as well as English instruction and skills training. But when they came to check, there wasn't any record of the girls ever having gone through the system."

"How did you get their information, Kiley?" asked Andy.

"They saw my first article in the paper and called me. That led to an interview with the head administrator at the place. I talked to several girls who lived there. It was orderly, clean, just how the social workers had found it earlier in the year. But no one ever remembered seeing the two girls from Guatemala. It was like they disappeared into thin air."

"So you know who's doing this?" asked Andy.

"It goes all the way to the mayor's office. Someone in that office, maybe the mayor himself is either running it, or just making sure it continues to operate. But that's what I put in my article that came out yesterday."

"Way to make friends in high places," Andy whispered. "So you left before this fourth article came out?"

"Yes. I listed the names of the ten girls I knew had been at one of the houses, even recently. And I mentioned the mayor's office. That came out yesterday. I had Carmen following up with another reported missing girl, a domestic helper, and she was reported missing by the wife of a very prominent attorney. An immigration attorney. I checked my records and his name was listed as one of the owners."

"That's an awful lot of coincidences," said Martel.

"My research found that the numbers were increasing, too."

"I agree with Jason. You shouldn't be poking around Portland on your own. I'm off to Team 4 in a couple of weeks. I think you should continue to lie low in Florida. But maybe you should move in with us and let the house go, Kiley."

"I live alone now that Damon's gone," said Martel. "I don't mind the company."

"And there's a couple other things, too, Kiley. We got two guys on the team with Jason who are married to girls from Portland and their families still live there," said Andy.

Kiley was beginning to spring hopeful.

"I'm going to read all this. Why don't you stay the night here, and in the morning, I'll try to put in a call to Kyle and Jason. No promises. But maybe we can plan something out."

"I want to go back to my own bed, Andy. And my computer and other things are there. I shouldn't have left them alone."

Andy stood up. "That settles it. I'm walking you back to your place then. From what you've told us, we can't be too cautious."

CHAPTER 13

T HE PICTURE IN the newspaper didn't at all resemble the woman they brought into Natalia's shelter yesterday. Battered about the head with one eye swollen shut and a cut lip, this woman was nearly unconscious, which might have been a blessing. Natalia requested she be seen at an emergency room, but was flatly overruled. Dr. Nash was going to stop by this afternoon sometime, and he was late.

Natalia helped the woman out of her bloody clothes and into her own personal shower because she had installed grab bars. She was no problem to help, since she was very slight, tiny, like a child, almost like all the other ones she'd tended to before. Except this woman, unlike the others, had an education and a job at the same newspaper that published her smiling face. And she wasn't young. It concerned her that there might be a husband or family missing her. Natalia didn't like changes in the routine, because that made her have to think too much.

She laid a clean nightie and a pair of fuzzy socks on the closed toilet lid, with a dark green towel. She knew the drill. Everything the woman touched, even the sheets she slept on, would be burned in the incinerator at the back of the building after she was gone.

She was well paid to not take chances, to clean up the messes and ask no questions. It was the price of what little freedom and auton-omy she had. It allowed her to save money, buy things for herself, go to the store to purchase food and pretty clothes, and have the big bedroom with the view of the river. But caring for these orphan women was getting old and Natalia was growing weary of it. Especially with this one so badly beaten up. Natalia wondered if this signaled a change in where they got the girls.

But something else was different about this woman. She spoke English. None of the others she'd tended to had. They came from all over the world, walking into her shelter frightened preteens and walking out into their new lives—lives they'd never dreamed of before—happy. At least, that's what she told herself.

As she checked on the sleeping form of the reporter, she feared the woman's fate might be dangling in Natalia's hands. This woman had been beaten, unlike the others. And that also made her think. She didn't like thinking.

She'd gone to church in Ukraine with her grandmother when she was little. Her babushka taught her how to cross herself, which she now did, reciting the prayer she'd learned. It was one of the only things she remembered about her religion, about her family, about the country she would never see again after she was taken.

From the living room, Natalia heard her two yellow canaries singing in the morning sun. They'd both had a bath and had fresh paper and food in their cages. She sat at the kitchen table, drinking her now-cold tea, and looked down at the newspaper with the smiling picture of the woman whose name was Carmen.

She began to remember her grandmother's house.

Her grandmother's friends told her he was a savior and would take Natalia out of the poverty and hell that was their home. But when she recalled the washed and starched white lace curtains and little yellow birds her grandmother raised and then sold in exchange for extra food or socks for her or some soap or milk, Natalia hadn't thought of that home as living in poverty at all. Sometimes the house was cold and there would be little food, but she didn't starve, and blankets always would warm her.

Her grandmother's loving arms were what she missed most the day the man took her away. Her grandmother was inconsolable, but her friends smiled and told Natalia that it was all for the best.

She would have liked that one last hug. As best she could remember, she was about four years old the day she left.

She'd held the man's hand as he walked her to his warm automobile, a car that drove smooth with music, and a driver with a hat sitting in front. She held his hand all the way to the airport, where fresh clothes were put on her, her hair was braided, and a young lady named Lucy even put pink lipstick on her lips, and then smiled at her handiwork. Natalia didn't like the taste of the bitter substance and wiped it off on her sleeve when the woman looked away.

She climbed metal stairs to a small plane with wide butter-colored leather seats. Lucy strapped her seatbelt on for her and sat across from Natalia while the man smiled and bowed his head and then ignored them both.

She stayed in the man's big house in New York for the first few years, while she learned how to do chores as she grew and was able to assume more and more duties. She was instructed never to play with the other children in the house, who used to make faces at her. She sometimes snuck food off their plates when she cleared the dishes, such delicacies she'd never tasted before.

She asked about her grandmother many times but never heard anything more about her. In time, she settled into a routine. She became friends with the family dog, Jigs, and would take him for walks around the property, which was gated with armed guards stationed at every entrance she'd ventured to look at. One day, the woman of the house bought a yellow bird, and that became Natalia's fascination and mission in life. She devoted herself to tending to it, changing the paper in its cage. She changed the water twice a day and made sure he never ran out of food. In exchange, he sang the most beautiful songs, just like the birds her grandmother raised.

After the first few months, she would have agreed, if anyone had asked her, that her life was infinitely better than where she'd come from. All her physical needs were met. The young woman who slept in the same room with her wasn't unkind, but she didn't have the same kind of relationship she'd had with her grandmother. Natalia knew she was no longer loved. She was cared for but not loved. And she became satisfied with that.

She felt looked after, useful. She had plenty to eat and warm clothes to wear and a warm bed to sleep in at night. Lucy taught her how to read, since she didn't attend school like the house children did. She took to it voraciously. Her whole world expanded when she could read about fantasy stories from different lands. She learned about the land of her birth. She learned about America from reading the newspaper every day. Compared to other people's lives, she had to admit she was very, very lucky.

Sometimes the man came into their room at night and would sleep with Lucy. She put her hands over her ears and hid her head under the covers so as not to see or hear anything, because she sensed the man was hurting her roommate. Afterwards, Lucy would cry. Natalia tried to ask her if she was okay, and she was scolded and told to shut up.

And then one night, she chanced a glance over at Lucy's bed and found the man having sex with her from behind, but he was staring straight at Natalia. She froze in place, disturbed with his expression, and then rolled over and tried to sleep. When he left, he whispered something to her, but she didn't listen.

Natalia asked Lucy about the man the next morning when they were doing the laundry, but Lucy slapped her and told her never to bring it up again. Weeks went by without any more visits. Lucy seemed to relax and even started to smile more.

And then one night, he came into the room and visited with Natalia. Nothing was ever the same after that.

Lucy left one spring day, and when she returned with the man, there was another little girl like she'd been once, a brown-skinned girl from Africa who was now about the age Natalia was when she came to the house. Lucy coldly told her that she was going away and that it was now Natalia's job to teach Adoara how to read and write, and do the chores of the house. Doing this and showing her how to take care of the canary for the lady became the two bright spots of the day. The nights were painful and much dreaded. She began wondering if she could run away, perhaps take Adoara with her, since she knew that the cycle would be repeated, and someone else would be brought to the home when she was replaced. And then Adoara would have to bear the man's attentions.

She began to plan, and then a miracle happened. The man was shot by his business partner, or so the newspaper said. She was given a ticket to report to Portland to visit a woman who cared for young orphans, all like her, all without papers. She was told Adoara was placed with another family on the east coast.

Natalia was good at nursing scared children back to health. Many of them came with infections and colds, dirty clothes. She became the big sister to scores of girls who came into the house and then left as they were adopted out.

Except she eventually learned the truth about the adoptions. The girls were sold. Natalia herself knew that no one would ever want her, so when the opportunity came up to start another home, Natalia was put in charge. She now had a house of her own to run. She didn't have to worry about money, food, or her safety. She had no desire to leave because she was not a legal resident unless she married someone. The thought of letting a man touch her ever again was so abhorrent that marriage was not an option. She didn't feel pretty. In fact, she felt scared. But the scars were really on the inside where no one could see. She bore her shame quietly and the people who came and went, bringing her the young girls she took care of, all seemed to understand her circumstances. No one ever reached out nor was interested.

She felt invisible.

Natalia had followed the stories in the newspaper about human trafficking and now knew that she, at a mere twenty-five years old or so, was part of a criminal enterprise. That could mean deportation if she were caught. How would she ever survive, or worse, would she go to jail? So although she knew it was wrong, she continued working for the men who paid the mortgage and the expenses, gave her spending money, and most importantly, left her alone. She didn't drive and had no bank account so kept everything in cash in a jar in her snow boots. She had to buy another pair to hold the next two jars of money she saved. It became a game, something she did for fun because she had nothing to really spend her money on, but she liked seeing it grow.

She prepared oatmeal for Carmen and went into the bedroom to wake her up.

Carmen could barely sit up. Her eye looked even more inflamed than the day before.

"Where am I?" she asked.

"You're safe. No one's going to hurt you here. I have a doctor coming to give you some medicine. And I brought you oatmeal."

"I don't eat breakfast and I hate oatmeal. I have to get out of here," Carmen said.

"No, that's not possible."

"What do you mean, it's not possible? You can't hold me here." She attempted to get up and then saw the handcuff attaching her ankle to the bed frame.

"It's for your own protection, Carmen." Natalia said. "Here, just try it." She held the bowl of oatmeal out, and Carmen swiped it away, the bowl shattering and sending milk and cereal all over the bed and the carpet.

"You know who I am and you're still keeping me here? That's against the law."

"I don't have the key. Even if I wanted to help you, I can't. They gave me the device here but didn't give me a way to take it off. But these people are not monsters, Carmen. They take—"

"What the hell are you talking about? I'm a free woman! They have no right to do this. And look at my eye, my face." She touched her cheek and winced. "Look what they've done."

Natalia was disturbed by the violence forced upon the reporter. It was never discussed before. She knew with the articles appearing in the paper that something dangerous was brewing. But she kept her calm and didn't let on that she was concerned.

"You have to help me. Call my editor, my friends, please! You are the only person who can help me. I think they're going to kill me."

Natalia thought that was ridiculous. She scowled. "I have worked for these people for several years now. They don't hurt people. They help people."

"They *steal* women. They steal boys too. They kill people. I've learned so much about them. They're dangerous. Trust me, when they are done with you, they'll dispose of you too. They're a bunch of thugs, mobsters. It's a huge ring, and you're helping them."

Natalia wished that she hadn't heard those words. It was so much easier when they didn't speak English.

"I have to clean this up. Your doctor will be here shortly."

"My doctor? You mean the executioner. Please—what's your name?"

"Natalia."

"Listen to me. You're in danger. I don't understand what planet you're from, but when you're no longer young and pretty, they'll have no more use for you."

"I resent that!" Natalia was actually offended. "They've never laid a hand on me, and they don't abuse the girls I've taken care of here at the shelter."

"The shelter. That's a sham. It's a grooming house for foreign prostitutes. They train girls to perform sex for men who like young girls. Boys too. Have you had boys here?"

"Never. No one ever has sex here."

"No, they sell them. They do the bad things somewhere else. But, Natalia, you have to understand, just because you don't see it, surely you understand what's happening. You can't be that stupid!"

She fell back onto the bed and began to cry. Natalia did feel sorry for her. Unlike the other girls, if she somehow had managed to free her, Carmen would be able to fend for herself, get help, and go back to her old life. But of course, that was impossible. She thought perhaps she'd question Dr. Nash when he arrived.

"Give me a phone. I need to call the police. We have to hurry. I have to get out of here."

Natalia looked at Carmen's ankle, now red and slightly bloody from her pulling on it. She didn't have anything strong enough to cut through the chain on the cuffs. She could go to the hardware store and buy some bolt cutters, but if Dr. Nash came by and found Carmen unattended, Natalia knew she'd get in trouble.

And she didn't have a phone. She'd never wanted one before.

"I don't have a phone, Carmen. I don't have anything I can use to remove that device."

"Do you have a neighbor? Someone you could borrow a phone from? Is there a phone booth outside?"

"I don't know." She shrugged.

"Well, look, dammit!"

She went to the window overlooking the street with the river beyond. Since her living space was on the second floor, over a parking structure below, she had a clear view of the block. There was a phone booth outside the convenience store she sometimes shopped at about a block away. But just then she saw a large black Mercedes pull up in front, and two men got out. One of them looked up at her through the window and nodded, giving a little wave.

Her blood pressure spiked as she stood at the crossroads, suddenly wanting to help the woman and not knowing what to do.

She waved back.

And then there were the sounds of footsteps coming upstairs to her front door.

"Natalia!" yelled Carmen. "Help me!"

She remembered the look on her grandmother's face when she was taken away that day. All of a sudden, it occurred to her that the woman she'd loved so much did nothing to stop her from leaving with that man who later abused her.

Sold? Was I sold like one of her canaries?

Rage boiled her blood as she recalled being raped repeatedly, her private parts bloodied and torn, her future stolen, the future of all the other women she'd been reading about stolen at her very own hands. The scars from the rapes weren't what made her ugly. It was what she had done that made her despicable. Unworthy of being loved. She was a non-person.

As she greeted the two men who wore black gloves, men she'd never met before who smiled and respectfully greeted her by her name, who'd been told perhaps the most intimate details of her life, how she'd been compromised into this position, she found it quite easy to lie to them.

"Gentlemen, she's in the bedroom. She just woke up. I'm afraid she doesn't like oatmeal."

The younger, shorter one gave her a smirk. "That's okay. We'll make sure she gets something good to eat. We'll take good care of her. You don't need to worry."

He reached into the breast pocket of his suit jacket and took out a thick envelope. Natalia saw the gun strapped to his side. He was about to present her with a lot of money, but the money didn't mean anything anymore. As her hand went forward to accept his gift, she lunged, grabbed the gun from his holster and shot him right above the bridge of his nose.

As the first man fell backward, Carmen let out a blood-curdling scream, which distracted the second one, who had begun unholstering his weapon. Natalia did as she'd read in her detective novels. She held the revolver with both hands and shot, hitting the man in the throat. He stumbled forward, trying to reach out to grab Natalia, and would have, if she hadn't backed up just enough so he fell to his knees, clutched his throat, tried to stop the blood spurting from his neck and fell on his belly. She aimed the barrel at the tiny bald spot centered at the back of his head and pulled the trigger.

CHAPTER 14

"**W**HAT THE HELL'S the matter with you, Kiley?" Corbin Newman III screamed into the phone. "We expected you back in Portland today. That's what you told Chief Rayburn, which I relied on, since you didn't have the courtesy to return my call as you promised! You promised, God dammit! And since your number was disconnected, we had no way to check in."

"That's why I'm calling, to let you know."

"You've left me in a pickle, little lady. I'm not happy about all of this. There's a very real chance the paper's going to get sued over your allegations—unsubstantiated allegations now since you couldn't be bothered with completing your investigation."

"That's not fair. You published it early." Kiley had never heard him so angry.

"Oh, fuck You! You're the one who dug up all this dirt. Problem is, I trusted you with the details. I promised the chief you'd be bringing all that in. I got the mayor all over my ass and more attorneys and other media outlets interested in me, personally, dragging Rosalie and her radio station through the mud as well, than if I'd cured Herpes or something."

"Corbin, listen to me. The facts are true. All the facts stand," she insisted.

"Really? Well, where are all those sources? You better have them all wrapped up, checked, and double checked. You better have fingerprints and blood samples because you're going to have to help defend all of us in court. These guys don't mess around. I think you're about to be arrested."

"What? That's ridiculous."

"Really? Have you talked to the chief?"

"He's going to be my next call."

"I don't know this for sure, but I think they're sending someone out to interview you, someone from the F.B.I."

"But they don't know where I am."

Kiley heard papers rustling in the background. "How does 917 Beach Access Road do for you? Is that close enough?"

That was the address of her rental bungalow. Now she saw how Jason had been right. She should have contacted the Pinellas County Sheriff's office days ago, when she first came out to Florida.

"I don't understand why all this is centered on me, Corbin. Everything I said in my articles is true. I have the tapes and the interview notes. And I can't be made to produce them, to protect my sources. But I can voluntarily turn them over to law enforcement. I want to cooperate. We're all on the same side."

"You would think so, wouldn't you? This is worse than a hornet's nest. People are going to die."

"Pardon? I don't understand."

"This morning. There's been a shooting. Two property owners were shot in their own building. One of those centers."

"Which one?"

"On Canal road, warehouse district, close to the river."

Kiley knew about the shelter but hadn't interviewed the staff yet. It was one of the places she asked Carmen to check out.

"How could I be involved in that? I'm not in Portland, Corbin."

"There were no girls there. Looks like there had been, but everyone's disappeared. If what you suspected is true, someone could be cleaning up loose ends. All those girls you thought you wanted to help are disappearing faster than my first marriage. They're scattering. We're not going to have any witnesses."

"Where did you get this information from?"

"Well, not from the mayor. He's not talking to me anymore. He told me personally he was going to see to it I paid for creating this stain on the good city of Portland and, indirectly, on him."

"So who told you the girls are disappearing?"

"Martin. He found Carmen's phone, some of her notes she'd left behind. He's been doing what he can, but honestly, Kiley, you need to be here to help direct him. You need to give us something as a cover. No one will talk to him. He got a tip from his friend at the police."

"I told you that was going to happen. So does anyone know where Carmen is?"

"That would help a lot. But no. Nobody's talking, if they know."

Newman was calming down, and with that, Kiley could finally think. At least Carmen hadn't turned up dead, although that was still a likely scenario. Kiley knew things would be unraveling quickly, and in the broad brush of sweeping everything into the trash, people's lives were at stake and their livelihoods messed with. An old reporter she met at a press dinner told her that, when a scandal brewed, the guy or gal in the white hat who came in to save the day was usually the real guilty party.

"They'll make sure everyone else pays. They'll make deals and clean up the whole thing and walk out a hero. That's the one you have to go after. Eventually, you'll get him, but you have to be patient and persistent," he had told her. She'd never forgotten those words, which now haunted her.

That was going to be her new focus.

As PROMISED, AND using her last burner, she called the chief. This time, he answered the call before the second ring.

"Well, well, well. Look who we got here? I'm guessing this is Kiley Worthington?"

"Yes, sir. I apologize for the change of plans. I was advised not to return to Portland, sir."

"I see. Well, I hope you have a good lawyer. He could tell you I can demand your presence here. And if you don't comply, I can have you arrested and escort you back. Whichever you prefer."

"I plan to come willingly. I am making arrangements now."

"I'm assuming you know that this is now a murder investigation?"

"My editor said two homeowners were—"

"I wouldn't exactly call them homeowners. They were on title, along with a whole group of investors. What they have here is the equivalent of a modern-day covered hopper car scheme. They launder some of their losses, and get a tax break doing it. The big difference is, they didn't lose money. They were making money. Lots of money."

"Why are you telling me all this? I thought you said I was a suspect or something."

"I know you aren't. But that doesn't mean you won't get charged with something. I'm trying to press you into service. I need your notes, your audio recordings of all your research, which I understand from your editor you have on your person."

Kiley admitted she did. There wasn't any point in not doing so.

"Why don't you go after the other owners? Maybe they were involved," she suggested.

"I'm not as quick and smart as some, but I know a who's who in the local crime scene, and these guys don't play nice. I'm the last person in the world they'd voluntarily speak with. They have a whole building of lawyers shielding them. No. I need to get the little people. The people you talked to. I want the victims in their own words. And we're in a race against time, because every one of those people you mentioned have a target on their backs, thanks to you."

"But I didn't give any names."

"Oh, they got the names, Miss Worthington. I'm the one who doesn't have the names. I need you back here ASAP before you wind up disappeared as well."

"Then I should go to the local sheriff here."

"I've already called them. You'll be hearing from them very soon. And I wouldn't try to run or hide."

Her body was drenched with sweat. Her stomach yawned. She could feel the bile collecting there, could smell fear seeping through every pore in her body. She felt just like the first day she arrived in Sunset Beach, where everywhere, every shadow, was a hiding place for someone out to get her. Now the police were out to get her too. And the one person who could protect her, or had any possibility of protecting her, was clear across the globe. But he'd also told her he couldn't get involved, or he'd lose his Trident. In a way, it was lucky he wasn't here. She was going to have to figure it out on her own.

And then just let things fall where they may.

She saw the folly in her earlier assumptions about how she could control this, could help orchestrate an investigation. Jason was right. It didn't work that way at all. She should have listened to him in the first place.

Now, it was too late.

CHAPTER 15

T HE MORNING HAD been spent down by the pier. The men were broken up into four groups, monitoring the coming and going of passengers and the ship traffic. Jason's group consisted of eight men, while several others of the squad looked for places to hole up for the night under cover of darkness. Lt. Gridley and a handful of men stayed behind at the complex to monitor calls between Washington and the Stennis Carrier Group patrolling offshore several miles. Sven Tolar, former Norwegian Special Forces officer, or FSK, and now a freelance SEALs resource team member, was explaining how the port was operated, and what the SEALs should be on the lookout for.

"The harbor can take up to seven large cruise ships before they have to use the older pier a short distance away." Sven pointed to his left, where a military gunboat ominously sat.

"That's a little unusual, isn't it, Sven?" Kyle asked.

"I've seen it. They don't have their own Navy, so they have to rely on the Spanish for their defense. Generally, Madrid doesn't want to part with their hardware this far away from home, but perhaps, there's a good reason," Sven said, shrugging his shoulders. "Or, maybe they're also looking for the contraband, since we have their permission to be here."

"So it's not exactly a secret we're here?" asked T.J. Talbot.

Kelly Fielding spoke up. "Only approved through diplomatic

channels. The local military police and civil guard aren't supposed to know. But I wouldn't worry about it."

She sat back and smiled, wiggling her eyebrows.

Sven leaned over and planted a kiss on her cheek. "You're scaring the Indians, Kelly."

"Watch it," murmured Danny Begay.

"My apologies, Native Americans," Sven corrected. The crowd, including Danny, chuckled.

It had been rumored that Sven and Kelly had hooked up after one of their earlier missions, a relationship that was off and on. Jason had been told it was mostly due to Kelly living in Portland with her former father-in-law, yet still going back and forth doing State Department work on a contract basis. Sven was in a similar stage in his career. It was a matter of timing, Kyle had told him.

Sven continued, "In cases of weather or other issues, like a problem they had several years ago where a cruise ship was towed into port, having run into a fishing trawler several miles off the island, they digress. Before the transport arrived to deliver the ship back to English shipbuilders, it had to wait, tying up two berths because of how they had to secure it. All the passengers had to be disembarked for another ship, so space had to be made for that."

"I'm going to guess some captain lost their job over that one," said Jason.

"Oh, but there's more! When a huge storm arrived, the ships in port had to stay a couple of extra days until the weather cleared, and the whole area was backed up. During the storm, several cruise ships anchored a mile out to sea because there wasn't any more room and they were low on fuel. One of the passengers was thought to be having a heart attack. Unable to arouse the interest of any pilot during the storm, the captain took it upon himself to run his beautiful ship, the size of a football field, aground at the largest tourist beach on the island. They sent the passenger to the hospital, where it was determined he had heartburn."

Their group groaned.

Kyle turned to Cooper. "We heard that story, didn't we? Weren't we on that ship?"

"I think so, a year or so later," Coop agreed.

Sven continued, "The captain was tried and sent to prison in Italy, even though he did what he thought best to save the life of the man who was ill."

"So, don't have a heart attack on a cruise ship if it's not convenient to dock," someone murmured.

"Probably good advice," answered Kyle. "Although, those of you who were with us on that cruise from Italy to Brazil, when we got attacked by terrorists in these waters, know how generally lacking in real security training the crew on board these ships are."

Jason had heard the stories of how Kyle, Fredo, Cooper and others saved the ship and enlisted the passengers to help them during the takeover and eliminated most of the terrorists in the process.

"We have a full house, then, and with that Spanish cruiser, there's no more room," observed T.J. Talbot.

"You would be correct. But take a look on the horizon and tell me what you see, son," Sven said, handing T.J. his scopes.

"I'll be Goddamned. I count two, no, three ships out there," T.J. answered. "Did we know this?" He looked squarely at Kyle, who was also checking out the horizon.

Without removing his binoculars, Kyle answered him, "Nope. Sven's just demonstrating how we need to be looking all the time. All of you do." He handed his glasses to Cooper, who then passed them around so everyone could look at the white ships at sea.

"We don't know who they are yet," Sven added. "They could be all legit."

"Would they try to sneak in at night?" asked Damon.

Cooper, Kyle and T.J. laughed at that comment.

"They don't even come in on their own in broad daylight. Always use pilots, trained captains familiar with the harbor. But at night? That would be suicide," answered Sven.

Damon turned bright red and shrugged. "Just thought they'd have enough equipment to do it," he mumbled. Jason slapped him on the back.

"These puppies are not like subs. They don't maneuver very well. Think Titanic," said T.J.

"The most dangerous place for a big cruise ship is arriving in port. That's where there's wreckage, recent changes in the ocean floor due to storms or earthquakes or acts of intentional sabotage. So it's not really a dumb question at all, son."

Kyle went on to explain they were expecting a ship to arrive sometime within the next two to three days, and it was said to be carrying up to fifty women and possible other contraband, eventually destined for the U.S.

"All we know is that it will have Dutch registry, Vanderdam Shipping, which is solely owned by the Vandershoot family."

"Dutch registry but Italian crew, right, Kyle?" Sven Tolar winked.

Kyle cracked a smile. "That's right, Sven. As usual, you have good intel."

"That slippery bastard escaped by bribing his way out before they could bring him back to Spain to face trial the last time we caught him," said Tolar.

"Yeah, and this time, he gets to be escorted by the Carrier Group and personally delivered to stand trial either in the U.S. or Spain. We've got them on standby to take the girls, too, if we need them," Kyle informed them.

Cooper shook his head and chuckled. "Did anyone think that one through? You got, what, two hundred sailors on board one of those cruisers, and they're taking on fifty young girls?"

"We're using smaller ones, Freedom-class littoral combat ships, about a hundred, give or take. We've got a couple on standby. They're faster and maneuver better close to land, should we need it," said Kyle. "They're practically brand new and have training facilities on board, so they're set up like a college dorm, if needed."

"Well, all right, then," Coop fist-bumped Kyle. "It's back-to-school night!"

"And you'll be on land, Coop, sorry to say," Kyle barked.

Kelly spoke next. "We're reaching out to the port officials, who are supposed to cooperate with some intel as to the schedule over the next few days. We have our eye on a couple ships, but so far, not certain. We've got to be ready to go when we get the call."

The team parked their vans at various points along the waterfront. Inside, they stored scuba gear, underwater explosive charges, and some light arms. But Kyle stressed the use of arms was only in an emergency. Like most of their missions of late, they were doing surgical strikes with hand-to-hand combat, using the element of surprise. This allowed them to extract safely without drawing attention to themselves.

Jason guessed they'd brought a bigger team because of the number of hostages.

Kyle's small group retired upstairs over the restaurant they'd been stationed at all afternoon. It was to be their temporary staging compound. Taking shifts, Jason offered to be first on watch.

"You got things under control back in Florida?" Kyle asked him.

"For now, yes. I hate not being in touch, though. But Kiley was going to fly back to Portland today and I talked her out of it last night."

Kyle grabbed Jason's shoulder and shook him. "You stay focused on what we got going on here. There'll be time enough when we're done. I'm hoping this one won't take too long, so you're in luck."

"Yeah, but you know how that goes."

"I do. I do indeed." Kyle kicked out his sleep gear and passed out bottles of water. "Stay hydrated, everyone."

The air was hot and muggy. Sven had told him of the beautiful beaches on some of the other islands he'd vacationed on, but Jason knew it was never their luck to get to see the good parts of a country or people. He'd heard about guys being stationed in a concrete bunker for several weeks, spending their whole deployment playing personal video games on their cell phones and being completely out of touch back home. It was more like how decades of previous military operations had been conducted in Panama, Vietnam, and of course all those during World War II. It was only within the last twenty years that communication technology had changed so drastically. Zoom hadn't even been around ten years yet, so all the guys who served during Desert Storm didn't have any of that.

He hoped that didn't make them a bunch of yuppy warriors as he scanned the horizon and remarked at the movement of the stars now beginning to appear. The nature of his job was still the same. It was brutal, because rooting out evil was always one of the toughest things to accomplish, and always only a few could do it.

I am that man, he whispered from the Navy SEAL prayer. Kyle was right. He'd better keep his mind on the job and what he could control, not what he couldn't.

He heard Thomas whisper to him, like he was calling from inside that fucking blue urn.

You got this.

Jason sent him back a message, *Yup, I do. Remember how we loved this?*

Loved, as in used to?

I'm good with it, Thomas. You've got bigger problems. Are you a pelican or a sea turtle?

Jason heard the sound of laughter all around him. He quickly glanced up to make sure it wasn't real. And that brought on another wave of belly-laughing from Thomas. Jason mentally put the top back on the urn, and the laughter stopped immediately.

He whispered a prayer to the ocean to deliver up the soul of darkness, to make his movements swift and purposeful. To anticipate every move and be the lethal dose to send that evil soul back to the underworld. He heard the women chanting in the background, felt the firelight against his face and his tiny heart beating inside his chest as he watched the dancing and the magic displayed. His ancestors sang and danced with their gods because they spent so much time with them all alone, at sea, crossing miles and miles of uncharted waters, seeking land.

When all you had to observe was just water, the sky, and the stars at night, it was healthy to believe in the songs and dancing.

Kyle was suddenly next to him. "You okay?"

Jason didn't know what he was talking about. "Pardon?"

"You're singing."

"Oh, sorry." Jason scanned the room. Damon was nodding his head, yes. But no one else was paying attention. "I do these chants to keep myself alert."

"Well, stay with us in the here and now, Jason. No imaginary worlds."

That pissed him off. Kyle must have seen it in his face because he turned back.

"If I hear anything, I'll let you know. Christy knows how to reach me if need be. You did tell her to call Christy if something comes up, didn't you?"

"I did." The problem for Jason was that Kiley was so darned head-strong and overly confident he worried she didn't plan very well. He was going to keep that to himself.

SEVERAL HOURS WENT by. Jason was fast asleep, having been relieved by the second watch. He was awakened by the squawk of Kelly's com. She bolted upright and turned the device down, not to wake anyone else up, but it was too late.

"Come again?" she whispered.

They all listened while her eyes flashed recognition, and she gave them all the thumbs-up.

"Roger that. We'll be ready," she signed off.

She took a deep breath and flashed a smile as the other men began to repack and straighten their gear. Damon handed Jason an energy bar, which tasted marvelous.

"We've gotten confirmation from the Harbor authorities a Dutch registry cruise ship has requested a pilot at sunrise."

Jason didn't see a speck of early morning sun, but Kyle checked his watch. "We've got about one hour forty. Did they say it was only one ship?"

Kelly nodded.

Sven talked into his mic while Kyle informed the other groups. He called the carrier group from his sat phone to be on standby. He was told the mission was still a go from Washington.

The sky started turning a muddy pink color with streaks of gray here and there. There was no wind. Jason figured it was already nearly eighty degrees and the sun wasn't even showing yet.

"I got visual," Coop said.

Jason borrowed the scope and saw the white hull of a ship slicing through calm navy blue waters, leaving little wake that suddenly disappeared as the ship slowed. The pilot boat was speeding out from the harbor master's house, headed straight for it. He was surprised the ship wasn't any larger than she was.

Three blasts from one of the cruise ships jolted the morning calm, indicating she was going to leave port.

The Spanish gunboat wasn't there any longer, and a Magnum Class cruise ship was powering up, preparing to depart, it's pilot boat heading slowly toward the open sea, waiting. Very slowly the ship backed up and then turned, it's ballast tanks sending out their contents, helping it maneuver the bow until it was pointed in the opposite direction from where it started. Once the behemoth was fully engaged, it began the process of heading toward the horizon, picking up speed and swiftly passing markers until it was several lengths from the pier and approaching unobstructed open sea.

The waiting ship accepted the pilot as his pilot captain pulled away and made a wide half circle, coming back to port. Within minutes, the Dutchie began to move forward. It's sleek lines and quiet engines hardly disturbed the early morning air. Not long after, it was docked, powered down, and tied off. Jason saw a line of people along the railing, heard some announcements over a loudspeaker on the ship, and watched the two gangways move into position just before a procession of white uniforms traveled up the ramp and into the belly of the beast.

"It's the Vanderdam Orca," Kelly confirmed, her finger pressing the com in her ear.

"Okay, so listen up. We have an advanced team heading over to board her now. They're posing as an engineering crew doing quality checks in the engine room. The ship's Chief Engineer is a friendly."

"So far, so good," mumbled Coop as he adjusted the Velcro pockets in his vest, stuffed with gadgets. "I'm going to be roasting alive in this get-up."

Jason thought he looked ridiculous. With a red bandana around his neck, his mid-shin length khakis, canvas slip-ons, a long-sleeved shirt with a string of palm trees painted across his chest, and the vest, he didn't fit the picture of a tourist, a fisherman, a dock worker, or a beach bum. And he certainly didn't look like a soldier. The long-sleeved T-shirt took care of covering up all his tats.

Jason was only armed with his KA-BAR, but he suspected a couple of others would have light arms. It had been discouraged, so being one of the newer SEALs on the squad, he didn't want to push his luck.

They piled out of the building in groups of two or three and scattered, as they'd been instructed. Kelly walked with Kyle, who wore a yellow baseball cap backwards, and made an introduction to a security guard manning the gate before any of the passengers or other crew could board. They stopped approximately twenty feet from the gangway and waited.

A handful of orange-suited workmen walked past Kelly and Kyle and made their way on board. Jason stepped closer to Coop and asked, "What are they waiting for?"

"The ship has to clear customs, I'm guessing," Coop answered, focused on the activity before him.

Jason observed several Team Guys scattered all around the dock, some pressing against the fencing and a couple others sharing a cigarette. No one made eye contact with each other. A flurry of dockworkers were lining up electric carts to begin bringing provisions on board. Covered carts and refrigerated compartments waited. Two forklifts stood idly by, their operators waiting. Porters with baggage handcarts and six-passenger golf carts waited to transport passengers to shore for their excursion groups. Buses were lined up in a row in the parking lot, their drivers waiting.

At last, a blast from the ship started everyone in motion like a swarm of ants. Something was announced over the ship's loudspeaker. The white-uniformed port officials returned to the pier, briefly stopped to talk to Kelly, and then returned to their offices.

Streams of passengers began exiting the ship. Jason, Damon, T.J. and Coop were hailed by one of the golf carts and hopped aboard, where they were allowed to enter the security area, joining Kyle and Kelly. Several others of their team were allowed through on foot.

Kyle called the four of them into a huddle, passing out badges on lanyards. "I want you guys to find someone in customer service.

Locate Amber Lynd. She's supposed to let us know where all the girls are. We don't want any of them leaving, just yet. Not until we can get the ship secured."

"Secured?" asked Jason.

"You remember, the advanced team?" Coop reminded him.

"I don't want you to do anything but locate them. They will probably be together, but might be on a couple of floors, in groups."

Kelly added, "Be aware they might have customers still in their rooms. And some of them will be scared to death and ready to bolt given the opportunity."

"Do you think Vandershoot is on board?" Asked T.J.

"Oh, he is. He most definitely is," said Kelly.

"Now, let's go quickly. Your passes will get you through the metal detector."

Jason panicked. "I brought my KA-BAR."

"Yeah, and I'm thinking a couple of you brought sidearms too. Kelly's going to lead you through. If her people are not guarding the machines, we wait, understood? This is either going to go very quick, very smoothly, or it will be long and drawn out. I don't want a firefight, is that clear?"

The group nodded.

"Okay, here goes. God, I hope this works. Just follow Kelly."

The group followed behind the State Department operative, who showed her Special Agent badge and was allowed to bring her group through without going through the metal detector. Their action didn't seem to raise any suspicion from the crew.

But Jason was concerned about Kyle's comment.

Once inside, the crush of passengers lined up, cascading down the stairwell and awaiting their debarkation, was difficult to maneuver through. In places, Jason had to nearly shove people aside to get past them.

"Coop and Jason, go do me proud. The rest of you, follow me.

Coop, I'm going to be at the theater entrance. That's deck five."

"Roger that. So you want one of us to stay behind when we find them?"

"Yes."

"Then I need another volunteer," said Coop.

Kyle grabbed Damon and shoved him toward Jason. "And now there were three."

As Kelly and the other three SEALs headed toward the elevators, Coop, Jason and Damon took to the stairs, avoiding passengers who weren't paying attention to where they were going. A maze of handcarts and elderly people with luggage made their path more like an obstacle course. Coop checked the ship's map, mounted on a side wall.

"We have to go up two more. See here, customer service?" he pointed.

"Got it."

A cluster of confused and clamoring passengers had congregated at the long line of customer service counters, manned by uniformed hospitality crew who were trying to smile and attend to complaints and questions. Jason read the name badges and didn't find Amber anywhere. Finally, he heard Coop whistle. He was standing next to a white-blonde representative who pulled them into one of the booking offices.

"Okay, here's where they are. On the eleventh floor, at the back, that's stern." She handed them a paper sheet with the floor maps similar to the one posted. "I haven't been up there today, but yesterday, they had an armed guard posted on both sides. But there is a utility stairway where the guard can be bypassed. You enter that series of passages through the galley, the kitchen."

"All we're doing is confirming where they are. So they're all together?" Coop asked.

"I think so. I saw a couple of Vandershoot's men escorting two girls last night. I can't be certain where they are right now, but his men have suites all over the ship. It would be impossible to check all of them."

"Okay, thanks. If we have a question, how do we contact you?" Coop asked.

She passed out cards. "That's my direct extension, but do not leave a message. You can access our phone system from any floor, the white house phones. But be careful. You don't look like passengers and it could raise suspicions."

"Okay, thanks," Coop said.

"We appreciate what you're doing," Jason added.

"I hope you succeed. I have my own reasons," Amber whispered.

The trio chanced using the elevators and found them to be packed with passengers going down. When they finally caught one going up, it stopped at every floor until they came upon Deck 11.

The lights and sparkling pale peach and silver interior of the ship were beginning to annoy Jason. He felt like he was climbing around in an ice palace.

"Let's stick together until we find out if there are guards," Coop instructed.

They turned left, walked single file down the narrow hallway, past several service doors, which Coop pointed out, and then to another lobby which accessed a couple of restaurant entrances. Beyond this lobby was another long hallway, which curved slightly, revealing two uniformed crew members standing next to each other, blocking the entrance to the rooms on the other side of them.

Coop pretended to check the room numbers when the crew noticed them.

"Dammit, it's on the other side." He shrugged. "Sorry fellas," he said. Neither of them smiled in return.

Coop crossed the lobby area to the opposite side and found the same situation. This time, they managed to turn around before being spotted.

"Damon, you stay here and monitor. We'll come get you in a bit after we report to Kyle," whispered Coop.

"No problem."

To avoid the crowds again, the two of them ran down the seven floors and found the theater entrance, which also happened to be stern. The doors were unlocked. Jason slipped inside the darkened theater behind Coop, where they found Kyle.

"Deck 11. Rooms 11204 and 11205 are probably where they start. Two guards posted on each side, and I didn't see a firearm, but I think they were packing. Looks like they have about twenty rooms total, including the insides," Coop told him.

"Good. Did Amber say anything else?"

"She said she saw a couple of the girls with Vandershoot's guys last night," Jason answered.

"And his men are all over the ship," added Coop.

"Okay, so we have them pretty much all in one location, which is great news." Kyle shook their hands. "Gents? How about a little cruising today?"

CHAPTER 16

KILEY REMEMBERED A discussion of Christy Lansdowne from Martel and Aimee. She knew it was the only thing she could do that she was one hundred percent certain was right. Everything else was just going to be by chance, dumb luck, a little magic, and hoping and praying she could pull off a return to Portland without getting herself or anyone else killed.

She'd tried calling Jason several times but knew he was probably in the middle of their operation. She decided to give up trying, to not interfere with his life any more than she already had, and just do what he'd suggested, to call Christy.

She'd made her airport reservations then called her landlady and left a message about vacating early. That left her cold. She didn't allow herself any space to grieve or feel any disappointment. She was making the motion, taking the steps she was required to make, trudging forward on the only path left open to her.

She was hoping this lockdown of her emotions would keep her from erupting and completely falling apart. It was one of the hardest things she had to do. She was convinced this was the right way to go about it, but wasn't sure she had all the skills she'd need. But she was just going to press on and not think about the consequences if things didn't turn out satisfactorily. A happy ending was too high to shoot for. She wanted an ending resulting in freedom for some, with minimal numbers of people hurt, including herself.

She told Aimee she was coming over to spend the night if the invitation still existed, and was welcomed enthusiastically. She hadn't told them yet about her return to Portland, but regardless of their opinion on the subject, her resolve was strong and nothing would break it. She'd already mentally kissed good-bye to this little cottage, the scene of so much possibility and love shared. If she could do that, walk away from all of that, she could do whatever else was required of her.

She packed enough for a couple of days, just enough to get her back home, and included the Beach Heals Everything sign that always traveled with her. She also made sure all her notes were tucked into her computer case. All the rest of her clothes, candles, and trinkets she'd purchased she left in a big box and was hoping to impose on Aimee and Andy to get them mailed to her later.

Before she picked up the phone, she walked outside on the patio and smelled the salt air and listened to the sounds of the surf pounding against the firm sand. The breeze was warm on her face. The moist air kissed her cheeks, implanting the memory she'd have forever of walking the shoreline, being a tiny speck of sand amongst the billions of other specs of sand. She'd found hope and healing here. That was going to be important to remember. She doubted she'd ever be able to bring herself to return here. But who really knew?

Kiley brought a baggie outside with her and filled it with bits of sandy shells without even selecting anything special. When she looked up at the moonlight on the ocean's undulating surface, she remembered Jason throwing the ashes of his best friend into the wind. Part of her would be left behind as well. All those wishes and fantasies scattered randomly, released forever.

Back inside, she zipped the top of the baggie closed, rolled it carefully, placed it in a paper bag, and added it to her carryon bag. She sat, took out her cell phone, and dialed.

"Hello?"

"Christy, we haven't met. I'm Kiley, a friend of Jason's. I met him here in Florida."

"Oh Jason. I love that kid," Christy said. "Kyle's told me Jason's quite fond of you. What can I do for you?"

"I'm not sure if he's told you, but I've gotten myself into a jam, and I have to return to Portland to help straighten out the mess I made of things."

"Oh, what kind of a jam?"

"Just stuff. It's way too much for me to explain right now." Kiley felt hot tears collect at the edges of her eyes. "I've hurt a lot of people. I didn't realize the consequences of my actions, and it's not right. I've exposed a lot of people to danger."

"I'm so sorry for what you're going through, but how can I help?"

"I just wanted you to tell Jason that—oh gosh, this is so hard to say."

"You sound like a sweetheart, Kiley. Wouldn't you rather tell him yourself?"

"I'm not sure I'll be given the chance to do that. Just tell Jason something I never told him myself, and I should have." The tears were really coming down now. She sniffled and wiped her cheeks.

"Are you all alone? I wish I could come over there and give you a big hug."

"I'm going over to see Aimee and Andy. They live just a few houses down from me on the beach, Sunset Beach."

"We've heard so much about it, Kiley. Such a beautiful place. Kyle's wanted to take me there, take the whole family there for a vacation some time. We all wish the two of them well and wish they hadn't decided to stay in Florida. But that's a good idea. You don't want to be alone, Kiley, not tonight."

"In the morning, I'm going back to Portland. I want you to tell

Jason that I'm going to try to fix everything, take responsibility for all the damage I've caused. Just tell him that, in case—"

"In case what? Are you in some kind of danger?" Christy asked.

"He knows all about it. He won't be surprised. Tell him I wish we'd had more time."

"Listen, Kiley, you need to get over to Andy's right away. Promise me you'll do that."

"Oh, don't worry. After I hang up, that's where I'm going." She faltered. "I want you to tell him that I think I've fallen in love with him. He made it so easy for me. I mean, not at first. I thought he was a stalker or worse. But, Christy, I've never felt so loved before."

"That's the way these guys are. It isn't always easy, you know, but I've told that to many women over the years, that they will never meet anyone who will love them so thoroughly ever again. It takes a special man to do the things they do. They're the real deal, Kiley."

"Well, I'm going back to right some wrongs. Who knows, if I succeed, then maybe I'll get to tell him all these things myself."

"I hope so, Kiley. What else can I do for you?"

"You can pray."

"I will do that. And I'll pray for Jason too. I hope you guys will be able to finish all those unfinished conversations, Kiley. It's hard when they leave, but so special when they return. You'll see."

"Thank you. That means a lot."

"Why don't you go get some rest, and when I can, I'll deliver a message to Kyle for Jason on your behalf. I'll make sure he knows all about our conversation. So take good care of yourself and call back if you need anything else, okay?"

"Yes, ma'am. I will. Thank you again."

"Good night."

As she took one last look at the cottage, she wondered if she'd ever find such a special place again. She turned off all the lights, locked the front door and left the key under the mat, as was done when she arrived. She found her way back to the access road, headed toward the water, and walked alone to the glowing house Andy and Aimee were working on, her computer case and overnight bag slung over her shoulder. Even at this late hour the house looked warm and inviting.

Aimee met her at the back door, worry lines on her forehead.

"Did she call you?" Kiley asked.

"Of course she did. She was worried. What's going on, Kiley? She told me you're going back to Oregon? When did you decide this?"

"Tonight. If I stay, they're going to maybe have me arrested anyway. They have my address. The police were going to have me escorted home. It's now a murder investigation, Aimee. I've put a lot of people in danger, people I was hoping to protect. I have to go back to make it alright, if I can."

"But you promised Jason you'd stay—"

"That was before I learned people are in danger, Aimee. Two people, perhaps more, are already dead. I've got to find my colleague. I'm the reason she went missing."

"You don't know that for sure. Please, don't do this."

"I'm so tired, Aimee. I just want to crash."

"Okay, I've made a bed up for you downstairs. What time is your flight?"

"One o'clock."

"Well, I'll get you up for breakfast, but I'd like you to discuss this with Andy first. And we can get you to the airport if you still want to go."

"Thanks. I appreciate that."

Kiley let the computer bag and the canvas overnight satchel fall to the ground. Without even changing her clothes, she removed her shoes, and crawled into bed, completely exhausted. Then she remembered she still had the burner on her possession. Pulling herself out of bed, she slid the case open, removed the SIM card, and flushed it down the toilet.

Crawling back to bed, she fell asleep with the sounds of the ocean transporting her back to happier days bursting with unlimited potential and endless golden sunsets.

CHAPTER 17

Damon and Jason stared at each other, tasked with monitoring any traffic coming from or going to the rooms down the hall. Kyle sent Coop to join several other guys at the bridge. Jason worked hard to keep up with Kyle as he scurried up the carpeted grand stairway to the eleventh floor where Damon stood waiting. He was about to turn left, toward the bow of the ship, but Jason corrected him and sent him right.

"They're on both sides, here and here," he told Kyle.

"Stay here for a second," Kyle said and disappeared.

"What the fuck's going on?" asked Damon.

Jason had no idea. Their LPO returned and was on his sat phone.

"Yes, I can confirm four." He walked past them through the lobby area and disappeared around the corner for a private conversation. When he returned, his eyes were smiling but his lips were slammed shut in a straight line.

"You're not gonna tell us, are you?" Jason said, his voice barely audible. Damon's puzzled expression only deepened.

They followed Kyle down the other side hallway.

Kyle turned halfway to address him. "That's right. You'll see. I wasn't sure it was going to work, but we're gonna give it a go. You guys find something in there you can use, hang out in the lobby, and keep an eye on whomever comes and goes, okay?"

"Roger that," Damon whispered, shaking his head.

The service closet he'd pointed to was easy to jimmy open with Damon's handy multitool, which didn't even leave a dent or mark to let on someone had tampered with it. Best of all, Damon didn't make a sound doing it.

Inside, the small space had metal storage shelves containing cleaning supplies, soap and paper products on top, with a row of buckets and rags on the bottom shelf. Smack in the middle of the area was a rubber two-tier wheeled cart stacked with trays of dirty dishes.

Jason could see that there was a pulley system that apparently brought supplies from the kitchen and took dirty dishes, utensils, and trays back down to be cleaned. A large red button to the right of the plexiglass chute cover appeared to operate the system with an easy up or down arrow. He noted the opening was large enough to accept a child or small man, perhaps a woman inside. If the down arrow was pushed, it could give someone an escape hatch to the fourth floor and the kitchen area below.

But it would never accommodate Jason's large frame. Probably was too small for Damon even.

"I saw waiters riding one of these down from the dining room when a bunch of us took a San Diego to Mexico cruise last year."

"Seriously?" Damon whispered; his forehead wrinkled.

"Yup. He even balanced a tray over his head, held on with the other hand. But these are little guys."

"No wasted space."

"I'll bet there's a maze all over this ship the passengers never see."

Damon whistled.

"Come on, let's quickly transfer the dishes and get this cart out to the lobby like Kyle asked." As Damon began the transfer, Jason checked the hallway in both directions to make sure no one was coming. He could hear the guards just around the bend, their voices bouncing off the slick metal-paneled surfaces of the narrow hallway. He guessed their accent was either Dutch or German.

With a bucket and several rags, along with some rolls of toilet paper, they wheeled the cart to the marble-floored lobby area and began to wipe down handrails, spraying cleaner while they worked. Jason covered the stairway to the half floor while Damon worked the lobby elevator doors and beyond where a glass railing overlooked the interior lobby cathedral.

Uniformed staff passed by and didn't say a word. Several young waitresses took the elevators down, speaking in some Oriental tongue. There were no passengers coming through, so Jason guessed they were all housed in the bow where he noted the larger suites were located adjacent to the pool and private access to the gym and spa areas.

He joined Damon, looking over the glass balcony at an empty interior. Only the sounds of bottles being stacked, and glasses being stored interrupted the happy music piped in from everywhere that was giving him a headache.

Several floors down, they watched Kyle talking to a ship's officer, along with three other uniformed personnel. One of them appeared to be the captain. The two smiled warmly and shook hands then separated. Fredo and Cooper headed off with the handsome officer, while Kyle disappeared in the opposite direction, his phone to his ear.

They continued their mock cleaning until Jason felt the rumble of the ship's engines cranking up. There were sounds of shouting as something was developing at one of the lower levels. Jason ran to the side, the sliding glass doors opening to the outside deck. As they glanced down, they saw the ship actually pushing away from the pier, without the gangway and umbrella covering being removed first. Several armed guards appeared, running down the pier, until they ran into a group of Civil Guards, who had taken a reddish-haired, pink-skinned gentleman in a white suit prisoner and were leading him to a waiting police vehicle just beyond the gates.

The security detail stood down immediately and watched as the man was escorted by them in handcuffs.

"Holy shit, he's right," said Jason.

"Is that who I think it is?" asked Damon.

"Fuckin' Jens Vandershoot."

"We better get back to the hallways," barked Damon as they turned to go back to their positions. Just before they left the deck, Jason saw the gangway twisted like soft aluminum and fall into the sea.

"Did you know about this?" asked Damon.

"Fuck no. But he said something about going for a cruise today. Do you suppose everyone got on board? Now what do we do?"

"We each take a hall and don't let anyone pass," said Damon.

The two guards on Jason's side were still there, but they were rapidly speaking into a device that crackled and gave back no instructions. Doors were opening on the floor. Jason could see young women poking their heads out and being ordered to return their rooms. But panic was beginning to take over, and a small crowd had developed behind them.

Jason knew the guards were about to abandon their post and got ready to detain them. He hoped the women stayed out of his way. He surprised the first guard and quickly held his knife to the man's throat. He saw movement out of the corner of his eye as Fredo, T.J., and several others came barreling down the hallway, giving the assist, tossing the man to his knees and securing his hands with zip ties next to his encumbered teammate. Danny and Trace reassured the girls that they were safe and escorted them back to their rooms.

Jason's pulse was racing as he leaned against the wall, fumbling for the pocket to stow his knife. T.J. walked up to him and placed his hand on his shoulder, and squeezed until it hurt.

"Are we having fun yet?" T.J. said, his eyes sparkling.

Jason licked his parched lips and discovered he'd been holding his breath, so let it out and took in another. "Mother of God. Did we just steal a cruise ship, T.J.? Is that what we did?"

"Nah, we just borrowed it for a bit. We got a little rendezvous all scheduled with the U.S.S. St. Louis in about three hours. All is well. You did good, kid."

CHAPTER 18

ANDY WAS NOT happy with Kiley's decision to return to Oregon without Jason.

"You're being short-sighted, Kiley. I'd go to the sheriff here."

"And get arrested? Sent back there in handcuffs?"

"But, Kiley, the more you try to do on your own, the worse it's going to look for you," he added.

She was getting angry. "Andy, I don't think you understand. I have no options. I have to go back."

"You're relying on a couple of phone calls. These are not people I know or would put any trust or faith in. They may be good people, but, Kiley, we're talking about a murder investigation, and the possibility that you may be a huge target. It's like just walking in and saying, 'Here, take me.' That isn't smart. You're giving up."

"I am not giving up!" She stood, pushing back from the table laid out with her breakfast Aimee so lovingly arranged. A breakfast her stomach wouldn't let her touch. "Are you saying you won't take me to the airport? Because I'm going. I'll take an Uber if I have to."

"I'd rather take you to the sheriff's department, Kiley. That's where you need to be right now. You have nothing to hide. What could be the harm?"

"Because after they're done with me, maybe they won't let me leave—"

"Yeah, for good reason," Aimee inserted.

"It's for your own good," pleaded Andy.

"But what about the women I exposed? I won't get there in time to help find them. Carmen? Should I just turn my back on everyone? The paper?"

"You're not thinking straight, Kiley," whispered Aimee. She came around the table to give her a hug.

"Don't!"

Aimee backed up, her palms stretched outward. "Okay, do it your way, Kiley. We just want to make sure you stay safe. Jason would want that too. You know he would," she continued. "Christy said—"

"So my conversation's been bantered all about then. The *personal* things I said to her were revealed to you."

Andy stood, yelling, "Stop it. You're only thinking about yourself and your own guilt. What about us, Kiley? Have you even thought about what all this could do to us? You staying here has involved us, and I'm not allowed to get involved. I'd like to pass this off to the proper authorities, but you won't let me. And just like your friends back in Portland, you're going to go streaking out on your own with no consideration for anyone but yourself. You lied to them. You lied to us. Worst of all, you lied to Jason. He believed you when you told him you'd wait for him to return. Doesn't that count for anything?"

"I don't want him risking his career to help me. I got myself into this mess; I'll get myself out of it." Then she addressed Aimee. "And, my feelings don't have anything to do with it. I'm sorry I ever embroiled any of you in this."

Aimee hung her head, silver tears coursing down her cheeks. Andy placed his arm around her, sat beside her, and gave her a hug. Finally, he looked up, and asked, "At least can I make some phone calls? We've got contacts in Portland. Maybe they can help you."

"What do you mean?" Kiley asked, returning to her chair.

"One of my buddies, Tyler, he's over there with Jason right now, is from Portland. We have another Team guy, Trace, his brother-in-law, who married Tyler's wife's sister. She still lives in Portland. Tyler's parents are still there. And…"

Andy waited until Aimee looked up at him. "Should I get him involved?" he asked her.

"Better him than putting this on the Grays or Gretchen's family."

"Through another one of our guys, there is a man there who might be of some help. He's a billionaire whose daughter we rescued last year, from pirates doing the same thing you've run into. Who knows, maybe they're all connected. Jason spoke to me about this even. I'm assuming he's talked to Kyle. But I think if it's protection you need, this Colin Riley could be of help. He'd like nothing better than to help you get these people. But at least he'd know how to keep you safe."

"What makes you think I can trust him? Some of these organized crime guys have money too. And they're connected."

Andy leaned forward on the table, reaching for Kiley's hands. He squeezed them. "He's been trying to recruit several of us from the Team to form a kind of *Posse Comitatus*."

"Now who's talking illegal, Andy?"

"I'm not doing it. Some are considering it. That's probably not the right term, but what I mean to say is he wants to create a force for good. If it can be done, he'll do it the right way." He sat back, removing his hands. "You know what they say…the enemy of my enemy is my friend? He hates those guys with a passion. He'd like nothing more than to help others now that he's got his daughter back."

Finally, Aimee agreed.

Andy placed the call to Brandy, Tucker's wife. She gave him Riley's contact information and the number for a former San Diego policeman who was starting to train to work for Riley, Bryce Tanner.

Andy said that Brandy was very reluctant to give out this information.

"But she trusts me. I said it was a matter of life or death, and that you were in love with one of our guys. That was what she cared about the most, just for your information."

"Sounds like someone I should meet, if I get the chance," said Kiley.

Aimee stepped into the conversation. "You put any of this in a newspaper when all this blows over, I'll be coming for you as well." The stare she gave Kiley scorched her toes.

THE THREE OF them headed for Tampa airport in plenty of time to catch the plane. It had been arranged that Colin Riley would send a driver and a car to pick her up at the airport. She said her good-byes and promised to pick up a burner phone in one of the airport shops and give them an update when she landed.

At last, seated by herself in the only open seat she could get, a first-class ticket that cost as much as most people's mortgage payments, she relaxed and fell asleep.

IT WAS RAINING when she touched down, which she'd totally expected. It matched the way her insides were feeling. She turned on her cell and left a voice message that she had landed and was headed to the exit outside baggage claim, which was the arranged pickup location. She asked that they forward her new number to Jason and to Mr. Riley and his team.

She decided not to call her editor until she'd had a chance to discuss her situation with Riley. She was one of the first passengers to exit. She traveled down the gangway, approaching the concourse, her computer bag and case strapped over her shoulder. It gave her no joy to be home. It really didn't feel like home.

A crowd was waiting to board the next flight. There was an airplane representative waiting just outside the entrance.

"Miss Worthington?" the attendant said. Her accent was Russian.

"Yes."

"Hi, I'm Amanda," she said, extending her hand. As they shook, the woman continued. "We've made some special arrangements for you to exit the terminal with private security for your own safety. Do you have other luggage?"

"No, this is it."

"Great. Now, if you will follow me."

Kiley started to walk behind the young woman, and then asked, "This was arranged by Mr. Riley, is that correct?"

Amanda turned and gave a nod. "Yes, ma'am. He wanted to be sure you were kept safe. It's all been arranged."

"But what happened to the driver I was to meet down by baggage claim?"

"Oh, we're working on the approach. The drivers and pickup areas have had to be moved due to the construction. We didn't want you to have to walk to the other terminal, so he'll meet you downstairs instead. Much safer." She wrinkled her nose.

Kiley was surprised Mr. Riley had agreed to come himself.

They walked through a security door and down a stairwell to a private parking lot designated for personal jet travel. Several expensive vehicles were waiting, some attended to by uniformed drivers. She appreciated not having to walk in the rain.

"Can I carry any of your luggage?" Amanda asked.

"No. Thanks. I'm fine." Kiley clutched her computer bag tight against her body and continued.

"Here we are."

A black Bentley with blackened windows sat with its motor running. Waiting to open the passenger door was the driver in uniform, including a hat and black leather gloves. He tipped his hat and reached down to take her bags.

"No thanks, I'm good."

The door was opened. She ducked to step inside the darkened interior. Before her eyes could adjust to the darkness someone had a hand over her mouth, and she smelled some sort of pine tar substance, which made her dizzy. Her legs and arms stiffened, and she collapsed on her knees inside the cab, falling on her computer bag.

No one helped her up. The door was closed behind her.

And then she passed out as the car motor revved up.

CHAPTER 19

THE U.S.S. St. Louis was a fast ship, especially for its size, span-
ning over the length of a football field. It was outfitted with new
equipment being used by the Navy for the first time, enabling them
to track and monitor shipping lanes increasingly at risk in the
Mediterranean and the north coast of Africa. The Team Guys were
fascinated with the grand tour they received. But one of the things
the St. Louis could not do was show up at the harbor in Las Palmas,
since there was no agreement between the Navy and the local
autonomous government on Gran Canaria.

The incident with the Dutch ship had already created a stir. Kyle
was told all would be arrested if it returned to port, so the Vanderdam Orca was already headed back to a friendly port at Gibraltar.
This meant the SEAL Team was to be transported by a small fleet of
fishing boats conscripted for the mission, where they could be
dropped off at various locations on the island, regrouping later.

Jason couldn't wait to let Kiley know he would be home sooner
than originally thought. He was still shaking his head how quickly
the mission came to a conclusion. They'd rescued thirty-seven
women, most of them from Eastern Europe and Africa. They'd
seized a cruise ship worth more than the entire GDP of the Canary
Islands. It would be converted to conservation and humanitarian
aid, possibly returned as a desperately needed hospital ship. But the
whole incident would be years in the paperwork filing alone, not to

mention the diplomatic issues it raised.

But Vandershoot would serve time, either in Spain or the United States, because of the flagrant nature of his offenses and government agreements to cooperate in ending human trafficking. At least, it was a start. All the men on the team were pleased, nearly celebratory.

Kyle, Coop, Tucker, Trace and several others were eating dinner with Jason and Damon, when Kyle got a call from Washington, relaying a message from Christy. He was given permission to speak with her privately.

When he returned to the group, he was silent. He didn't even laugh when Damon and Fredo imitated one of Jason's Maori chants. He'd promised to add some of his routine to their exercise program.

But when their eyes met, Jason knew something was wrong.

"You have news?" Jason started softly, fear curling up from his belly.

"I do. You want to do this here, or you want to do it private, Jason?" was Kyle's response.

It wasn't a hard decision. These were his brothers, as dear to him as Thomas had been. He also trusted Kyle wouldn't offer him the choice if it was really bad, so he agreed.

"Kiley's been kidnapped, Jason."

This was not expected. "This happened in Florida? How are Aimee and Andy?"

"What about Martel?" asked Damon.

"Everyone in Florida is fine at the moment," said Kyle. "She went back to Portland, and they took her from the airport."

"But how could that be? She told me she was waiting to go back. I'm practically back home now. What happened?"

"There have been some murders in Portland, related to the stories she was following for the paper. I guess she got threatened by the police, and they were preparing to arrest her and bring her back anyway." Kyle leaned forward. "I'm not real happy about this, but apparently our friend Andy got in touch with someone you know very well, Kelly. Your father-in-law."

"Oh shit. He didn't," she said.

"He'd sent a car over to pick her up, but someone got to her beforehand and she never showed."

Jason had never felt so helpless. He couldn't believe she would actually be so careless with her personal safety. "I don't even know where to start, Kyle. Are the police on it? Does anyone really know anything or are we guessing here?"

"Riley's on it. He's got a former cop working on it too, to be a liaison."

"That would be Bryce," mumbled Tucker. "Wow, this is a real shitstorm. It keeps getting bigger and bigger. Now they've gotten my household involved. This is dangerous stuff."

"We need to get to her," said Jason. "Can I get released on an emergency basis?"

"And do what?" asked Kyle. "Get involved with a shootout with the local mob? A shootout with police? Take your pick, Jason. Your Trident could be at risk here. I'm not sure there's any arrows in your quiver, if you catch my drift."

"But I have to do something. You can't just make me wait here, processing paperwork, sitting on my ass wondering if—"

"Kyle, you should let Tucker, Damon, and Jason go. Get them released," Coop said.

"That your professional opinion, Coop? You gonna risk my career, too?"

"I'd do it for you, Kyle. You know I would. We'd all do it for each other."

"But for what? If I thought it would do any good, I could justify it."

Tucker pounded the table. "Fuck this. Riley's been after me to join his little venture. Maybe it's time to go do it." He turned to

Kelly. "You know what he's capable of. Does he have the network, the resources to do a hostage rescue?"

"I would never underestimate Mr. Colin Riley. Those who dare do so at their own peril. He has more allies than I'll bet the police up there have. And it's what he lives for. He could do it. I don't know what he's got planned, but I think he could."

"Thanks, Kelly." Tucker stared back at Kyle. "My mind's made up. I'm all in. Those are good enough odds for me. I'm taking them, if you'll let us. Get the three of us released, and I'll do what I can to keep the youngsters from getting snagged by something awful. I saw firsthand from the look in Bryce's daughter's face what those guys can do. This has got to stop and I won't be able to live with myself unless I try."

"I'm in too. No matter what. I've gotta try," said Jason. "I don't care what it costs me. We have to stand up to this evil challenge." Jason felt the whole room was with him as well. He was grateful for the moral support.

"And you, Damon?"

"Shit, Kyle, Martel would never forgive me if I didn't try. Besides, there's no risk. She wants me to go teach school or something. There's no way she's gonna go live in San Diego. That was a pipe dream. My priorities are all changed."

"They must be putting something in the water there," Kyle said, shaking his head. "What is it?"

"It's the sunsets. And while you're at it, release me too," said Ned. "If I can't defend one of our own, what's the point? The war's come to our soil. Time to do something about it."

Kyle studied all four of them, one by one. Jason knew he was trying to sort out all the screaming going on inside his head. And if he didn't do it quickly, he was about to lose his whole squad.

"God damn it! Give me a minute." He whipped out his sat phone, got up, and headed outside the dining hall.

"What if they say no, Tucker?" Jason was worried.

"Well, we could start a mutiny here, but somehow, I don't think that will turn out as well as our cruise ship caper," answered Tucker. "It's out of our hands, kid. Sucks, but they own us. If they say no, then we stay."

They didn't have to wait long. Kyle barked at the doorway. "Come on, you four. We're cutting you loose. There's a Seahawk getting ready, with your names all over it."

In less than ten minutes from start to finish, the four SEALs boarded the brand new forty-two-million-dollar bird and were dropped off on the far side of the harbor. Lt. Gridley and two men were on their way to pick them up and escort them to the airport. They wouldn't get there for at least another twenty-four hours. But they were on their way.

CHAPTER 20

KILEY WOKE UP lying on a dirty mattress that smelled of things she didn't want to think about. Her neck was stiff, and she had a throbbing headache. Her whole left side was painful, like she'd been thrown on the mattress roughly like a piece of meat while she was unconscious.

She heard coughing and realized she wasn't alone. Opening her eyes, daylight seeped into the structure somehow. She sat up and discovered she was in a cage. Immediately, her chest began to constrict and she became woozy.

Breathe! Breathe!

Scanning the warehouse-type building, she saw more than a dozen other cages, all containing young girls. Some were sleeping on dirty mattresses like hers, but others were sitting up, their backs propped against the metal sides of the compartments. Most of their expressions held sad contemplation.

"Hello, does anyone know where we are?" she called to the room. Her words echoed ominously.

Most of the girls looked up, and a couple of them stood. One of them put her fingers to her lips and motioned for her to be quiet. Then she pointed to a roll-up doorway and a desk manned with a guard, who was hunched over, snoring.

Kiley searched the cage and discovered her purse was missing.

And so is my computer!

She felt the pocket of her jeans and was gratified to learn that the thumb drive she'd made of her computer's contents was still there.

Thank God!

She tried to get her bearings, listening to anything from outside that might give her an indication where the warehouse was located while several of the girls watched her. She heard freeway traffic, which wasn't much of a help. But then she heard the sound of a train streaking by and then quickly disappearing. It wasn't one of the long trains hauling freight but probably a passenger run.

She heard a police or ambulance siren off in the distance and then heard the sudden blast of a large vessel traveling nearby, just like the cargo ships that went in and out of the harbor along the warehouse district of Portland. There was a commuter run she'd taken many times, so she was fairly certain she knew what general area she was housed. She was within a dozen blocks of her old flat and probably had jogged past this building.

She stood and studied every cage, wondering if she'd recognize anyone. All the girls had long brown or black hair, all were very slight, young, and terrified. Most of them appeared to be either Latino or Asian. Carmen was not among them.

The sounds of a diesel vehicle of some kind came very close to the roll-up doors and then shut off. She heard several car doors slam shut.

Quickly, she looked for something she could use to protect herself. There were bottles and some shipping crates next to the wall, but nothing she would be able to reach. She did notice a crowbar someone had used to open those wooden crates. Wood shavings had spilled over the table where the box had been unpacked and had partially obscured the crowbar.

Sitting down, she examined the mattress. It was made of old ticking material and had buttons sewn into it, holding the layers together like they did in the old hotel rooms she'd seen. As the sound of men's voices became louder, she wiggled several of the buttons back and forth until she found one that was slightly loose, enough to get her fingers under it as she pulled, and it broke off in her hand. Kiley examined it closely and discovered it was made of metal. Portions of the little disc had been clipped and folded back on itself, and that's where she focused. She carefully pried several teeth of the metal back until she had a very small sharp edge no wider than a half inch across, but it was better than nothing. She tucked the disc inside her shoe, down by her toes, making sure nothing sharp would cut her own flesh if she had to walk.

The door opened, and four men stepped inside, all wearing suits and black gloves. One of them swiped across the face of the young boy who had been guarding the cages. The young man fell backwards, his metal chair scraping on the concrete floor and then skidding several feet before stopping. He scrambled to his feet, holding his nose and trying to stop the profusion of blood cascading down over his lips and onto his shirt.

Another car arrived, and a fifth man entered, dressed in a police uniform.

Kiley studied the tall lanky cop, considering whether she might have met him somewhere before. Then she recognized him as one of the men from the mayor's task force on human trafficking, a man she'd interviewed for her story. At the time, she'd thought him very helpful, but when all the leads he gave her dried up, she had wondered.

Well, the answer was right in front of her, heading across the floor between the other cages and walking deliberately in her direction. He hadn't tried to cover his face, which gave Kiley the sinking feeling he wasn't worried about her recognizing him for a very specific reason.

She'd come to the end of her tether. This was where the story was going to end. She'd be written up under Michael or Corbin's heading,

Local Investigative Reporter found Murdered in Warehouse Sting Operation.

She remembered what the old reporter had told her. It verified his story. It was always the ones who were in charge of the clean-up that were the guilty ones. Those were the ones to watch, be patient, and go back and keep drilling for more information after the scandal was sanitized.

That probably also meant her other hunch had been right. The mayor was involved up to his eyebrows. Or, at best, he was somehow compromised.

"Hello, Kiley," Officer Damien Woodhouse said, standing with his hands on his hips in front of her door. "Are they making you comfortable?"

She didn't look at him.

"You get a little rest?"

He kept digging.

"Hmmm? You always had so much to say, so many opinions, so many theories and ideas. I enjoyed your articles in the paper, although you were a pain in the ass."

She glared up at him. "Good."

Reflexively, he lunged for her through the bars, but Kiley was quick to back up out of his reach.

"I tried to warn you several times, Kiley. You just wouldn't give up. Now see what you've brought on yourself? On the reputation of the paper? Did you know that there's going to be a full retraction printed tomorrow? Too bad you won't be seeing it, though. I wrote the piece myself."

One of the suits walked over to Woodhouse. "Can you hang for a bit? We've got to pick up a package. I'll be back and we can load them up." He glanced down at Kiley. "Finish things."

"Sure, I'm fine. You leaving the kid?"

"You're his ride. I guess so."

"Okay with me. You count the inventory?"

"Sixteen."

Kiley knew that didn't include her, but she didn't dwell on that. The odds had just swung in her favor slightly. She had to find a way out of the cage first. But she had a plan.

Once the door slammed shut, she put her plan into motion.

"I guess you're too scared to let me out to go pee. Did I get that right? I should just pee all over the mattress?"

Woodhouse's eyes flared. "I'm not afraid of you," he sneered.

Kiley shrugged. "Suit yourself." She began to wet herself.

"Hey! Julio!" he called to the injured guard. "I need the keys. Quick!"

Julio came running. They both fumbled with the keys, which released the door. Officer Woodhouse pulled Kiley's hair, yanking her from the cage and sending her toward the restroom in the corner. As they neared the packing table, Kiley struggled, attempted to give him a knee to the groin, but he was quick enough to step away. Just for an instant, he lost his grip. It gave Kiley just enough time to grab the crowbar from under the shavings and swing at Woodhouse. The sharp end of the curved tip struck the officer across his cheekbones, nearly severing his nose from his face.

As he screamed, crashing to the ground, Kiley took his gun. A large pool of blood seeped from underneath his skull as his body went limp.

She had no idea how to shoot. But it was good enough to scare Julio into thinking she could.

"Unlock them all, right now, or I'll drill you."

The girls became agitated, whining and begging to be let out first. Julio danced around each of the cages until all but two were opened. They heard the sound of a vehicle outside, and all the freed girls ran in the opposite direction, toward a dark corner near the restroom. Kiley hoped she didn't have to do something to make the gun operable, like slip off a safety or cock it. She vowed that if she survived this ordeal, she'd learn how to handle a gun properly.

The door opened a crack. A woman's face peered in—someone she didn't recognize. Kiley aimed the pistol at her, and she shouted back, "No! Don't shoot!" in Eastern European accent, perhaps Russian.

But what happened next surprised her even more. From behind the woman stepped Carmen. The whole left side of her face was swollen and bright purple, but she was very much alive.

"Carmen!"

They ran to each other and hugged. Then Kiley turned on Julio, demanding, "Finish, until they all are released."

"Kiley, this is Natalia. She saved my life. She used to be one of them," Carmen said, pointing at the small crowd huddling together at the rear.

"Thank you, Natalia. I—" She remembered what the men had told Officer Woodhouse. "Oh my God, we don't have much time. They're coming back. There are four of them."

"We can take the bus," Natalia said.

"What bus?" asked Kiley.

"There's a detention bus outside," said Carmen.

"Do you know how to—"

"Yes, Kiley, I used to drive a school bus before I became a reporter. Let me check for keys. Be right back."

"Help me," she said to Natalia, who then ran for the girls and motioned for them to follow her back outside.

Julio was trying to quietly slip through the doorway, and she yelled at him, pointing the gun at his face again. "No way, Jose." She directed him over to one of the cages, grabbed his keys, and locked him inside.

She heard the diesel bus start. Natalia led the girls out through the door and up the steps into the white Department of Corrections bus.

Kiley was the last one to climb aboard.

Carmen ground the gears and the engine nearly flooded out, then lurched forward. Several of the girls screamed. Carmen swore, but then adjusted the clutch and smoothly drove them across the parking lot and out onto the street.

Kiley sat back and only then did she loosen her grip on the gun. She wondered if it was even loaded.

CHAPTER 21

WHEN JASON AND his three teammates landed in New York, all of them had messages delivered during their direct flight. The WIFI was out on the plane, so none of them were able to play the messages until they landed.

Jason's was cryptic. Kyle gave him little details, but left him Colin Riley's number so he could be filled in. Damon was on the phone with Martel. Ned was speaking to Madison, who was working at the Salty Dog, while Tucker spoke to Brandy. It was clear Brandy was getting an earful from her husband. But nothing was going to dampen Jason's mood.

He dialed Riley's number, and after a greeting, he put Kiley on the phone with him.

"Are you okay? God, Kiley, I thought we'd lost you."

"I'm fine. And better still, Carmen's fine. And did you hear?"

"Honey, I'm hearing all sorts of things. Everyone is getting clued in, trust me. I got Tucker, Ned, and Damon with me. We're about to board a plane for Portland in about a half hour."

"I'm so glad you're on U.S. soil, Jason."

He heard her struggle to breathe. He knew she was crying. He felt his own eyes begin to water as well. "I never would have forgiven myself if something had happened to you. Promise me you won't do this anymore. Please—"

"We saved sixteen girls. The mayor is going to jail, along with several from his task force. The F.B.I. is chasing bad guys from here to whatever crevice or crack they crawled out from. This time, the good guys won, Jason. I can finally say, I'm a force for good. Jason, I did it!"

"Kiley, but not again. Do you promise me?"

"I'm not going to promise you anything until you get your butt over here. Then we'll talk. And Mr. Riley here wants to have a sit down with all of you, too. I think you'd better hear what the man has to say. He wants me there as well."

Jason smacked his forehead with his palm but bit his tongue. Now that Kiley had had a taste of adventure, he could see she was hooked. The scared woman he met on the beach that day had turned into a monster.

Did they have a chance?

He heard Thomas cackling in the distance. If he were here in person, Jason knew he'd be rolling around on the sand, throwing shells or rocks or pieces of his sandwich at him.

THE BLACK LIMO picked up the four SEALs at the airport and shuttled them to a large gated estate overlooking the city of Portland. They carried their Navy-issue duffel bags over their shoulders, walking through a lush garden of blooming roses and rhododendrons. A light mist covered everything. The leaves sparkled with silver in the moonlight.

Riley's ornate front door opened, and Kiley ran to Jason's arms. The force with which she hit him nearly toppled them both. He'd planned to be stern with her, to talk some sense into her, but he found himself laughing instead.

Tucker was the first to enter the house, shaking Colin Riley's shriveled hand as he sat in his specialized wheelchair. Behind him stood Tucker's friend, Bryce. He made all the other introductions.

Jenna Riley appeared and timidly greeted the men, again thanking them for her rescue.

Riley bent to the side to look for Jason and then motioned for him to come over. With Kiley wrapped around his waist, he stepped into the foyer with all the others, and shook the man's hand. Although bound in a wheelchair, Colin Riley's bright blue eyes were those of a serious warrior.

"Thank you, sir," Jason said.

"Oh, that didn't turn out because of me. It's all her. Do you know what a special lady Kiley is?"

"Yes, sir, I think I do."

"I tried, but I nearly lost her. She pulled the whole thing off. This time, we won without any loss of life for any of the victims. I wish we could do them all that way, but—"

Kiley interrupted, "When the odds are in your favor, you win."

Colin Riley chuckled. "That's one way to put it."

They were served a platter of sandwiches and some soup, which was Riley's steady diet. The chitchat was light until Jenna excused herself.

"You've all got rooms upstairs we'll show you to. In the morning, after you've gotten some good rest, I want to have a serious discussion about what your future could look like," began Riley.

Tucker squirmed in his seat. Ned and Damon glanced at each other but didn't reveal any emotion. Finally, Tucker spoke up.

"I think I know what you're going to say, Mr. Riley. And these guys know I turned you down last year, and I'm glad I did. But I'm going to keep an open mind. And I'm sure these guys will too." He squirmed again. "I just want you to understand Brandy and I are a team. I don't do anything unless she okays it. So you're going to have to be patient with me, with all of us."

Damon and Ned nodded. Jason also agreed.

Riley flashed them a big smile. "I would expect nothing less. But for you guys, it's worth the wait. Take as long as you want. Now get some rest, and let's talk about what is possible, for all of us."

Colin Riley turned in his chair and zoomed across the marble floor like he was racing to be first.

"I don't think that guy will sleep a wink tonight," Tucker whispered.

Bryce nodded. "He's a very special man. Been good to me and my family. I'd do anything for my girls." He faced the four Team Guys. "He's the real deal, like you are. All of you."

JASON AND KILEY were led to a huge suite with a four-poster bed and tall windows overlooking the lights of Portland. Rain was slicing against the glass. Behind them, a fireplace roared. He never thought he'd ever spend the night in such luxury. Ideas buzzed around his brain. It just wasn't anything he was familiar with, so it was hard to stay grounded.

Until he touched Kiley.

"Sing to me," she said, running her finger over his lips.

"Now?"

"Yes, now. I want to see it."

"The thing, with the jumping and faces and all?"

"Yup. That thing. I want to watch you."

"Okay." He backed up, opened his eyes wide, stuck his tongue out and jumped high in the air, coming down without a sound. His elbows stuck out to the sides, palms resting on his hips. He began the Maori moves everyone teased him for.

Kiley giggled and fell back on the bed, watching him.

He cut it short to just watch her. How close he'd come to losing her forever. And here she was, waiting for him.

He climbed on the bed, taking her in his arms, feeling the heat of her body releasing to him. It was risky, but Jason decided to tell her the secret he'd learned about her.

"You know what I thought when I met you?"

"That I was crazy."

"There was a little bit of that, yes. You remind me of the women in my family. They were healers." He took her hand, brought it up to his mouth, and kissed her palm. "Your hands, they're healing hands. Did you know that? It's a form of magic in my culture. Healers are special. They keep the flame of life alive. They sing and dance."

"That's the most beautiful thing anyone has ever told me, Jason. Does that mean that I can heal you?"

"You did already. You healed me that night I took Thomas back to my ancestors. You were scared. But you healed me."

She was watching his eyes. A tiny smile erupted on her pretty face. "I think you heal all the broken parts of me as well."

"We'll have to work on that," he said as he kissed her. His hand slid up her tummy and over her breast.

"I think I'd like that. The hard part."

He grinned. "Will you make me a promise, Kiley?"

He saw she was holding her breath, expecting some kind of a soft reprimand. He had no such intention. "Will you come with me, to Hawaii? Will you marry me in the traditional way?"

Her eyes filled with tears. He kissed them away, gently, ending at her lips, while she spoke those beautiful words, "Yes, Jason. I will be your island girl, your forever girl."

He started to remove her clothes, slow and deliberate like she liked.

"Would you promise me something as well?" She traced the bands of his ancestors, as if she could read the stories he intended to tell her.

"Anything."

She arched her eyebrows. Raising her head, she whispered in his ear, "Would you teach me how to shoot a gun?"

Did you love Escape To Sunset

Stay tuned to the rest of the Sunset SEALs series, as all four couples get to tell their stories about Sunset Beach.

Do you know Sharon has other SEALs series? Here is the list of her other popular and award-winning series:

SEAL Brotherhood

SEAL Brotherhood: Legacy

(SEAL Brotherhood couples, 10 years later)

Bad Boys of SEAL Team 3

Band of Bachelors

Bone Frog Brotherhood

Bone Frog Bachelor Series

Bone Frog Love (Love Vixen Series)

All of the above books are on ACX/Audible/iTunes, narrated by the masterful and sexy voice of Mr. J.D. Hart, who has narrated all my books from beginning to now.

ABOUT THE AUTHOR

NYT and USA/Today Bestselling Author Sharon Hamilton's SEAL Brotherhood series have earned her author rankings of #1 in Romantic Suspense, Military Romance and Contemporary Romance. Her other *Brotherhood* stand-alone series are: Bad Boys of SEAL Team 3, Band of Bachelors, True Blue SEALs, Nashville SEALs, Bone Frog Brotherhood, Sunset SEALs, Bone Frog Bachelor Series and SEAL Brotherhood Legacy Series. She is a contributing author to the very popular Shadow SEALs multi-author series.

Her SEALs and former SEALs have invested in two wineries, a lavender farm and a brewery in Sonoma County, which have become part of the new stories. They also have expanded to include Veteran-benefit projects on the Florida Gulf Coast, as well as projects in Africa and the Maldives. One of the SEAL wives has even launched her own women's fiction series. But old characters, as well as children of these SEAL heroes keep returning to all the newer books.

Sharon also writes sexy paranormals in two series: Golden Vampires of Tuscany and The Guardians.

A lifelong organic vegetable and flower gardener, Sharon and her husband lived for fifty years in the Wine Country of Northern California, where many of her stories take place. Recently, they have moved to the beautiful Gulf Coast of Florida, with stories of shipwrecks, the white sugar-sand beaches of Sunset, Treasure Island and Indian Rocks Beaches.

She loves hearing from fans through her website: authorsharonhamilton.com

Find out more about Sharon, her upcoming releases, appearances and news when you sign up for Sharon's newsletter.

Facebook:
facebook.com/SharonHamiltonAuthor

Twitter:
twitter.com/sharonlhamilton

Pinterest:
pinterest.com/AuthorSharonH

Amazon:
amazon.com/Sharon-Hamilton/e/B004FQQMAC

BookBub:
bookbub.com/authors/sharon-hamilton

Youtube:
youtube.com/channel/UCDInkxXFpXp_4Vnq08ZxMBQ

Soundcloud:
soundcloud.com/sharon-hamilton-1

Sharon Hamilton's Rockin' Romance Readers:
facebook.com/groups/sealteamromance

Sharon Hamilton's Goodreads Group:
goodreads.com/group/show/199125-sharon-hamilton-readers-group

Visit Sharon's Online Store:
sharon-hamilton-author.myshopify.com

Join Sharon's Review Teams:

eBook Reviews:
sharonhamiltonassistant@gmail.com

Audio Reviews:
sharonhamiltonassistant@gmail.com

Life is one fool thing after another.
Love is two fool things after each other.

REVIEWS

PRAISE FOR THE
GOLDEN VAMPIRES OF TUSCANY SERIES

"Well to say the least I was thoroughly surprise. I have read many Vampire books, from Ann Rice to Kym Grosso and few other Authors, so yes I do like Vampires, not the super scary ones from the old days, but the new ones are far more interesting far more human than one can remember. I found Honeymoon Bite a totally engrossing book, I was not able to put it down, page after page I found delight, love, understanding, well that is until the bad bad Vamp started being really bad. But seeing someone love another person so much that they would do anything to protect them, well that had me going, then well there was more and for a while I thought it was the end of a beautiful love story that spanned not only time but, spanned Italy and California. Won't divulge how it ended, but I did shed a few tears after screaming but Sharon Hamilton did not let me down, she took me on amazing trip that I loved, look forward to reading another Vampire book of hers."

"An excellent paranormal romance that was exciting, romantic, entertaining and very satisfying to read. It had me anticipating what would happen next many times over, so much so I could not put it down and even finished it up in a day. The vampires in this book were different from your average vampire, but I enjoy different variations and changes to the same old stuff. It made for a more unpredictable read and more adventurous to explore! Vampire lovers, any paranormal readers and even those who love the romance genre will enjoy Honeymoon Bite."

"This is the first non-Seal book of this author's I have read and I loved it. There is a cast-like hierarchy in this vampire community with humans at the very bottom and Golden vampires at the top. Lionel is a dark vampire who are servants of the Goldens. Phoebe is a Golden who has not decided if she will remain human or accept the turning to become a vampire. Either way she and Lionel can never be together since it is forbidden.

I enjoyed this story and I am looking forward to the next installment."

"A hauntingly romantic read. Old love lost and new love found. Family, heart, intrigue and vampires. Grabbed my attention and couldn't put down. Would definitely recommend."

PRAISE FOR THE
SEAL BROTHERHOOD SERIES

"Fans of Navy SEAL romance, I found a new author to feed your addiction. Finely written and loaded delicious with moments, Sharon Hamilton's storytelling satisfies like a thick bar of chocolate." —Marliss Melton, bestselling author of the *Team Twelve* Navy SEALs series

"Sharon Hamilton does an EXCELLENT job of fitting all the characters into a brotherhood of SEALS that may not be real but sure makes you feel that you have entered the circle and security of their world. The stories intertwine with each book before…and each book after and THAT is what makes Sharon Hamilton's SEAL Brotherhood Series so very interesting. You won't want to put down ANY of her books and they will keep you reading into the night when you should be sleeping. Start with this book…and you will not want to stop until you've read the whole series and then…you will be waiting for Sharon to write the next one." (5 Star Review)

"Kyle and Christy explode all over the pages in this first book, *[Accidental SEAL]*, in a whole new series of SEALs. If the twist and turns don't get your heart jumping, then maybe the suspense will. This is a must read for those that are looking for love and adventure with a little sloppy love thrown in for good measure." (5 Star Review)

PRAISE FOR THE
BAD BOYS OF SEAL TEAM 3 SERIES

"I love reading this series! Once you start these books, you can hardly put them down. The mix of romance and suspense keeps you turning the pages one right after another! Can't wait until the next book!" (5 Star Review)

"I love all of Sharon's Seal books, but *[SEAL's Code]* may just be her best to date. Danny and Luci's journey is filled with a wonderful insight into the Native American life. It is a love story that will fill you with warmth and contentment. You will enjoy Danny's journey to become a SEAL and his reasons for it. Good job Sharon!" (5 Star Review)

PRAISE FOR THE
BAND OF BACHELORS SERIES

"*[Lucas]* was the first book in the Band of Bachelors series and it was a phenomenal start. I loved how we got to see the other SEALs we all love and we got a look at Lucas and Marcy. They had an instant attraction, and their love was very intense. This book had it all, suspense, steamy romance, humor, everything you want in a riveting, outstanding read. I can't wait to read the next book in this series." (5 Star Review)

PRAISE FOR THE
TRUE BLUE SEALS SERIES

"Keep the tissues box nearby as you read *True Blue SEALs: Zak* by Sharon Hamilton. I imagine more than I wish to that the circumstances surrounding Zak and Amy are all too real for returning military personnel and their families. Ms. Hamilton has put us right in the middle of struggles and successes that these two high school sweethearts endure. I have read several of Sharon Hamilton's military romances but will say this is the most emotionally intense of the ones that I have read. This is a well-written, realistic story with authentic characters that will have you rooting for them and proud of those who serve to keep us safe. This is an author who writes amazing stories that you love and cry with the characters. Fans of Jessica Scott and Marliss Melton will want to add Sharon Hamilton to their list of realistic military romance writers." (5 Star Review)

"Dear FATHER IN HEAVEN,

If I may respectfully say so sometimes you are a strange God. Though you love all mankind,

It seems you have special predilections too.

You seem to love those men who can stand up alone who face impossible odds, Who challenge every bully and every tyrant ~

Those men who know the heat and loneliness of Calvary. Possibly you cherish men of this stamp because you recognize the mark of your only son in them.

Since this unique group of men known as the SEALs know Calvary and suffering, teach them now the mystery of the resurrection ~ that they are indestructible, that they will live forever because of their deep faith in you.

And when they do come to heaven, may I respectfully warn you, Dear Father, they also know how to celebrate. So please be ready for them when they insert under your pearly gates.

Bless them, their devoted Families and their Country on this glorious occasion.

We ask this through the merits of your Son, Christ Jesus the Lord, Amen."

By Reverend E.J. McMalhon S.J. LCDR, CHC, USN
Awards Ceremony SEAL Team One
1975 At NAB, Coronado

www.ingramcontent.com/pod-product-compliance
Lightning Source LLC
Chambersburg PA
CBHW050117030726
47505CB00007B/1916